crush

TRACY WOLFF

HODDER &
STOUGHTON

First published in Great Britain in 2020 by Hodder & Stoughton
An Hachette UK company

2

Copyright © Tracy Wolff 2020

This edition published by arrangement with Entangled Publishing LLC through
RightsMix LLC. All rights reserved.

This edition edited by Liz Pelletier.

The right of Tracy Wolff to be identified as the Author of the Work has been
asserted by her in accordance with the Copyright, Designs and Patents Act 1988.

A CIP catalogue record for this title is available from the British Library

Paperback ISBN 978 1 529 35558 1
eBook ISBN 978 1 529 35557 4

Printed and bound in Great Britain by Clays Ltd, Elcograf S.p.A.

Hodder & Stoughton policy is to use papers that are natural, renewable and
recyclable products and made from wood grown in sustainable forests. The
logging and manufacturing processes are expected to conform to the
environmental regulations of the country of origin.

Hodder & Stoughton Ltd
Carmelite House
50 Victoria Embankment
London EC4Y 0DZ

www.hodder.co.uk

To Elizabeth Pelletier and Emily Sylvan Kim
The two most kick-ass women in the business
There's no one I want to take this journey with more than you

Woke Up Like This

Being the lone human in a school for paranormals is precarious at the best of times.

At the worst of times, it's a little like being the last chew toy in a room full of rabid dogs.

And at average times…well, at average times, it's honestly pretty cool.

Too bad today is most definitely *not* an average day.

I don't know why, but everything feels a little off as I walk down the hall toward my Brit Lit class, the strap of my backpack clutched in my hand like a lifeline.

Maybe it's the fact that I'm freezing, my whole body trembling with a cold that has seeped all the way to my bones.

Maybe it's the fact that the hand clutching my backpack is bruised and sore, like I got into a fight with a wall—and most definitely lost.

Or maybe it's the fact that everyone, and I mean *everyone*, is staring at me—and it's *not* in that "best of times" kind of way.

Then again, when is it ever?

You'd think I'd have gotten used to the staring by now, since it kind of comes with the territory when you're a vampire prince's girlfriend. But nope. And *definitely* not okay when every vampire, witch, dragon, and werewolf in the place is stopping to stare at you with their eyes wide and their mouths gaping even wider—like today.

Which, to be honest, really isn't a very good look for any of them. I mean, come on. Aren't I supposed to be the one weirded out in this equation? They've known all along that humans exist. It's only been about a week since I found out the monster in my closet is real. As are the ones in my dorm room, my classes...and sometimes in my arms. So shouldn't I be the one walking around with my mouth wide open as *I* stare at *them*?

"Grace?" I recognize the voice and turn with a smile, only to find Mekhi gawking at me, his normally warm brown complexion more waxy than I've ever seen it.

"Hey, there you are." I shoot him a grin. "I thought I was going to have to read *Hamlet* all by myself today."

"*Hamlet*?" His voice is hoarse, and the hands that fumble the phone out of his front pocket are anything but steady.

"Yeah, *Hamlet*. The play we've been reading for Brit Lit since I got here?" I shuffle my feet a little, suddenly uncomfortable as he continues to stare at me like he's seen a ghost...or worse. This definitely isn't typical Mekhi behavior. "We're performing a scene today, remember?"

"We're not rea—" He breaks off mid-word, thumbs flying over his phone as he sends what his face says is the most important text of his life.

"Are you okay?" I ask, stepping closer. "You don't look so good."

"*I* don't look so good?" He barks out a laugh, shoves a trembling hand through his long, dark locks. "Grace, you're—"

"Miss Foster?"

Mekhi breaks off as a voice I don't recognize all but booms through the hallway.

"Are you all right?"

I shoot Mekhi a "what the fuck?" look as we both turn to find Mr. Badar, the Lunar Astronomy teacher, striding down the hall.

"I'm fine," I answer, taking a startled step back. "I'm just trying to get to class before the bell rings." I blink up at him when he stops directly in front of us. He's looking a lot more freaked out than an early-morning hallway exchange warrants. Especially since all I'm doing is talking to a friend.

"We need to find your uncle," he tells me as he places a hand under my elbow in an effort to turn me around and guide me back in the direction I just came from.

There's something in his voice, less than a warning but more than a request, that gets me walking through the long, lancet-arched hallway without complaint. Well, that and because the normally unfazed Mekhi scrambles to get out of our way.

But with each step I take, the feeling that something isn't right intensifies. Especially when people literally stop in their tracks to watch us go by, a reaction that only seems to make Mr. Badar more nervous.

"Can you please tell me what's going on?" I ask as the crowd parts right in front of us. It's not the first time I've seen the phenomenon—once again, I *do* date Jaxon Vega—but it is the first time I've seen it happen when my boyfriend is nowhere around. It's beyond weird.

Mr. Badar looks at me like I've grown a second head, then asks, "You don't know?" The fact that he sounds a little frantic, his deep voice taking on an incredulous edge, ratchets up my anxiety. Especially since it reminds me of the look on Mekhi's face when he reached for his phone a couple of minutes ago.

It's the same look I see on Cam's face as we sweep by him standing in the doorway of one of the Chem classrooms. And Gwen's. And Flint's.

"Grace!" Flint calls to me, bounding out of the classroom so he can walk alongside Mr. Badar and me. "Oh my God, Grace! You're back!"

"Not now, Mr. Montgomery," the teacher snaps, his teeth clicking together sharply with each word.

So definitely a werewolf, then...at least judging by the size of that canine I see peeking from beneath his lip. Then again, I guess I should have figured it out by the subject he teaches—who's more interested in the astronomy of the moon than the creatures who occasionally like to howl at it?

For the first time, I wonder if something happened this morning that I don't know about. Did Jaxon and Cole, the alpha werewolf, get into it again? Or Jaxon and another wolf this time—maybe Quinn or Marc? It doesn't seem likely, since everyone has been giving us a wide berth lately, but why else would a werewolf teacher I've never met before be so panicked and single-minded in his determination to get me to my uncle?

"Wait, Grace—" Flint reaches out for me, but Mr. Badar blocks his hand from connecting.

"I said not now, Flint! Go to class!" The words, little more than a snarl, come from low in his throat.

Flint looks like he wants to argue, his own teeth suddenly gleaming sharply in the soft chandelier lighting of the hallway. He must decide it's not worth it—despite his clenched fists—because in the end, he doesn't say anything. He just kind of stops in his tracks and watches us walk by instead…just like everyone else in the corridor.

Several people look like they want to approach—Macy's friend Gwen, for example—but a low, warning growl from the teacher, who's pretty much marching me down the hallway now, and the whole group of them decides to keep their distance.

"Hold on, Grace. We're almost there."

"Almost where?" I want to demand an answer, but my voice comes out sounding raspy.

"Your uncle's office, of course. He's been waiting on you for a long time."

That makes no sense. I just saw Uncle Finn yesterday.

Unease slides across the back of my neck and down my spine, sharp as a razor, causing the hairs on my arms to tingle.

None of this feels okay.

None of this feels *right*.

As we turn another corner, this time into the tapestry-lined hallway that runs in front of Uncle Finn's office, it's my turn to reach into my pocket for my phone. I want to talk to Jaxon. *He'll* tell me what's going on.

I mean, this can't all be about Cole, right? Or about Lia. Or about—I yelp as my thoughts crash into what feels like a giant wall. One that has huge metal barbs sticking out of it that poke directly into my head.

Even though the wall isn't tangible, mentally running into it hurts an astonishing amount. For a moment, I just freeze, a little shell-shocked. Once I get over the surprise—and the pain—of it, I try even harder to move past the obstruction, straining my mind in an effort to get my thoughts together. To force them to go down this mental path that is suddenly completely closed off to me.

That's when I realize—I can't remember waking up this morning. I can't remember breakfast. Or getting dressed. Or talking to Macy. I can't remember anything that's happened today at all.

"What the hell is going on?"

I don't realize I've said the words out loud until the teacher answers, rather grimly, "I'm pretty sure Foster was hoping you could fill him in on that."

It's not the answer I'm looking for, and I reach into my pocket for my phone again, determined not to get distracted this time. I want Jaxon.

Except my phone isn't in the pocket where I always keep it, and it isn't in any of my other pockets, either. How is that possible? I never forget my phone.

Uneasiness moves into fear and fear into an insidious panic that has question after question bombarding me. I try to stay calm, try not to show the two dozen or so people watching me at this very instant just how rattled I really am. It's hard to keep cool, though, when I don't have a clue what's going on.

Mr. Badar nudges my elbow to get moving again, and I follow

him on autopilot.

We make one more turn and end up at the door leading into the front office of Katmere's headmaster, also known as my uncle Finn. I expect Mr. Badar to knock, but he just throws the door open and propels us into the office's antechamber, where Uncle Finn's assistant is at her desk, typing away on her laptop.

"I'll be right with you," Mrs. Haversham says. "I just need one—"

She glances up at us—over the top of her computer screen and her purple half-moon glasses—and breaks off mid-sentence the second her gaze meets mine. All of a sudden, she's jumping up from her desk, her chair clattering back against the wall behind her as she shouts for my uncle.

"Finn, come quick!" She circles out from behind her desk and throws her arms around me. "Grace, it's so good to see you! I'm so glad you're here!"

I have no idea what she means, just like I have no idea why she's hugging me. I mean, Mrs. Haversham is a nice-enough lady, but I had no idea our relationship had progressed from formal greetings to spontaneous and apparently ecstatic embraces.

Still, I return the hug. I even pat her on her back—a little gingerly, but I figure it's the thought that counts. On the plus side, her soft white curls smell like honey.

"It's good to see you, too," I respond as I start to ease back a little, hoping a five-second hug is all that's necessary in this already bizarre situation.

But Mrs. Haversham is hanging on for the long haul, her arms wrapped around me so tightly that it's growing a little hard to breathe. Not to mention awkward.

"Finn!" she shouts again, paying no attention to the fact that, thanks to the hug, her red-lipsticked mouth is right next to my ear. "Finn! It's—"

The door to Uncle Finn's office flies open. "Gladys, we *have* an intercom—" He, too, breaks off mid-sentence, his eyes going wide as they find my face.

"Hey, Uncle Finn." I smile at him as Mrs. Haversham finally releases me from her honeysuckle-scented death grip. "I'm sorry to bother you."

My uncle doesn't answer. Instead, he just keeps staring at me, mouth working but absolutely no sound coming out.

And my stomach suddenly feels like it's full of broken glass.

I may not know what I had for breakfast, but I know one thing for sure... Something is very, very wrong.

2

So...What Did I Miss?

I'm about to work up the courage to ask Uncle Finn what's going on—he has a history of not lying to me (at least not when directly confronted)—but before I can force the words out of my absurdly dry throat, he yelps, "Grace!"

And then he's bounding across the office, straight at me.

"Grace, oh my God! Grace! You're back."

Back? Why do people keep saying that to me? Where exactly did I go? And why wouldn't they expect me to come back?

Again I search my memory, and *again* I slam right into that giant wall. It doesn't hurt as much this time as it did the first—maybe because the shock has worn off—but it's still uncomfortable.

Like Mrs. Haversham, Uncle Finn grabs on to me the second he reaches me, his arms going around my back in a huge bear hug, even as his familiar woodsy scent winds its way around me. It's more comforting than I expect it to be, and I find myself sagging against him a little as I try to figure out what on earth is happening. And why I can't remember anything that might cause this kind of reaction in my uncle...or anyone else I've run into, for that matter.

I was just walking down the hall to class, the same as every other student in the place.

Eventually Uncle Finn pulls back, but only far enough to look at my face. "Grace. I can't believe you've really come back to us. We've missed you so much."

"Missed me?" I repeat, determined to get answers as I take a couple of steps back. "What does that mean? And why is everyone acting like they've seen a ghost?"

For a second, just a second, I see a flash of my own panic in the look Uncle Finn shoots the teacher who brought me here. But then his face smooths out and his eyes go blank (which totally isn't scary at all), and he wraps an arm around my shoulders and says, "Let's go into my office and talk about this, shall we, Grace?"

He glances back at Mr. Badar. "Thanks, Raj. I appreciate your bringing Grace to me."

Mr. Badar nods in silent acknowledgment, his gaze narrowing on me briefly before he heads back into the hallway.

Uncle Finn urges me gently toward his office door—what is it with everyone moving me around today, anyway?—all the while talking to Mrs. Haversham. "Can you message Jaxon Vega and ask him to meet me here as soon as possible? And look up what time my daughter's"—he glances at me, then back at his assistant—"*tests* are over as well, please."

Mrs. Haversham starts to nod, but the door Mr. Badar walked out of swings open so hard and fast that the doorknob actually slams into the stone wall behind it.

My nerve endings go on red alert, and every hair I have suddenly stands straight up. Because, even without turning around, every cell in my body knows exactly who just walked into my uncle's office.

Jaxon.

One quick glance at his face over my shoulder tells me everything I need to know. Including that he's about to raise all kinds of hell. And we're definitely not talking about the good kind here.

"Grace." His voice is hushed, but the ground beneath my feet rumbles as our gazes collide.

"It's okay, Jaxon. I'm okay," I reassure him, but my reassurances don't seem to matter. Not when he's across the room in little more than a second, pulling me from Uncle Finn's unresisting grip and into his own muscular arms.

It's the last thing I expect—PDA in front of my uncle—but the minute our bodies meet, I can't bring myself to care. Not when all the tension inside me melts at the first brush of his skin against my own. And not when it finally feels like I can breathe for the first time since Mekhi called my name in the hallway. And maybe even a lot longer than that.

This is what I've been missing, I realize as I snuggle deeper into his embrace. This is what I didn't even know I was looking for until the moment his arms went around me.

Jaxon must feel the same way, because he crushes me closer still, even as he blows out a long, slow breath. He's shaking, shuddering, and though the ground has stopped actively rolling, I can still feel it trembling just a little.

I squeeze Jaxon more tightly. "I'm all right," I assure him again, though I don't understand why he's so upset. Or why Uncle Finn is so shocked to see me. But confusion is giving way to my barely contained panic in a giant way.

"I don't understand," I mumble as I lean back to look into Jaxon's eyes. "What's wrong?"

"Everything is going to be okay." The words are crisp, and his gaze—dark, intense, devastating—never wavers from mine.

It's a lot, especially combined with everything else that's happened this morning, and suddenly it's too much. I look away from him, just until I can catch my breath, but that doesn't feel right, either, so in the end, I bury my face against the hardness of his chest again and just breathe him in.

His heart is beating hard and fast—too fast, really—under my cheek, but he still feels like home. Still *smells* like home, like oranges and fresh water and warm, spicy cinnamon. Familiar. Sexy.

Mine.

I sigh again, burrow closer. I've missed this, and I don't even know why. We've been practically inseparable since I got out of the infirmary two days ago.

Since he told me he loves me.

"Grace." He breathes my name like it's a prayer, unconsciously echoing my own thoughts. "My Grace."

"Yours," I agree in a whisper I really hope Uncle Finn can't hear, even as I tighten my arms around Jaxon's waist.

And just like that, something comes to life inside me—bold and powerful and all-consuming. It slams through me like an explosion, shaking me to the depths of my soul.

Stop!

Don't!

Not with him.

3

Sleeping Beauty's Got Nothing on Me

Without thinking, I push Jaxon away and stumble back a few steps.

He makes a noise low in his throat, but he doesn't try to stop me. Instead, he just looks at me with his gaze as shocked and shaky as I feel inside.

"What was that?" I whisper.

"What was what?" he answers, watching me carefully. That's when I realize he didn't hear it, didn't *feel* it.

"I don't know. I'm sorry." The words come instinctively. "I didn't mean…"

He shakes his head, even as he, too, takes a definite step back. "Don't worry about it, Grace. It's okay. You've been through a lot."

He means what happened with Lia, I tell myself. But he went through a lot with that, too. And it shows, I realize as I look him over. He's skinnier than I've ever seen him, so that his ridiculous cheekbones and cut-glass jaw look even more defined than usual. His dark hair is a little longer, a little shaggier than I'm used to, so his scar is barely visible, and the purple circles under his eyes are so dark, they look like bruises.

He's still beautiful, but now that beauty is an open wound. One that makes me ache.

The longer I look at him, the deeper the panic takes hold of me. Because these aren't overnight changes. People's hair doesn't grow in a day or two, and they don't usually lose weight that fast, either. Something happened, something big, and for some reason, I can't remember what it is.

"What's going on, Jaxon?" When he doesn't answer fast enough, I turn to my uncle, a sudden anger burning just under my skin. I'm sick and tired of always being kept in the dark.

"Tell me, Uncle Finn. I know something's wrong. I can feel it. Plus my memory's all wonky and—"

"Your memory is wonky?" Uncle Finn repeats, coming close to me for the first time since Jaxon walked into the room. "What does that mean, exactly?"

"It means I can't remember what I had for breakfast this morning. Or what Macy and I talked about before bed last night."

Again, Jaxon and Uncle Finn exchange a long look.

"Don't do that," I tell them. "Don't cut me out."

"We're not cutting you out," Uncle Finn assures me as he holds up a placating hand. "We're just trying to figure things out, too. Why don't you guys come into my office, and we'll talk for a few minutes?" He turns to Mrs. Haversham. "Can you please call Marise for me? Tell her Grace is here and ask her to come by as soon as possible."

She nods. "Of course. I'll let her know it's urgent."

"Why do we need Marise?" My stomach tightens at the thought of once again being checked over by Katmere's nurse practitioner—who also happens to be a vampire. The last two times she's done that, I've had to lay on my butt in bed for way longer than I wanted to. "I don't feel sick."

Except I make the mistake of glancing down at my hands for the second time today, and it finally registers just how bruised and bloody they are.

"You look a little worse for wear," my uncle says in a deliberately soothing voice as we enter his office and he closes the door behind us.

"I just want to get you checked out, make sure everything's all right."

I have a million questions, and I'm determined to get answers to them all. But once I'm seated at one of the chairs in front of Uncle Finn's heavy cherrywood desk, and he's perched on the corner of that same desk, he starts asking questions of his own.

"I know this probably sounds strange, but can you tell me what month it is, Grace?"

"The *month*?" My stomach sinks like a stone. I barely get the next word out as my throat closes up. "November."

When Jaxon's and Uncle Finn's gazes collide, I know there's something really wrong with my answer.

Anxiety skitters down my spine and I try to take a deep breath, but it feels like there's a weight pressing on my chest, making that impossible. The pounding in my temples makes the feeling worse, but I refuse to give in to the beginnings of what I recognize could easily turn into a full-blown panic attack.

Instead, I wrap my hands around the edges of my seat to ground myself. Then I take a minute to list several things in the room in my head, just like Heather's mom taught me after my parents died.

Desk. Clock. Plant. Wand. Laptop. Book. Pen. Folders. Another book. Ruler.

By the time I get to the end of the list, my heart rate is almost back to normal and so is my breathing. As well as the absolute certainty something very wrong has happened.

"What month *is* it?" I ask quietly, turning to Jaxon. He's given it to me as straight as he could from the very first day I got to Katmere Academy, and that's what I need right now. "I can handle whatever's going on. I just need to know the truth." I reach for his hand, hold it in both of mine. "Please, Jaxon, just tell me what I'm missing."

Jaxon nods reluctantly. Then whispers, "You've been gone for almost four months."

"Four months?" Shock ricochets through me all over again. "*Four months?* That's impossible!"

"I know it feels that way," Uncle Finn tries to soothe. "But it's March, Grace."

"March," I repeat, because apparently repetition is pretty much all I'm capable of right now. "March what?"

"March fifth." Jaxon's voice is grim.

"March fifth." Forget panic, full-blown terror whips through me now, flaying my insides. Making me feel raw and exposed and empty in a way I can't describe. Four months of my life—of my senior year—have disappeared, and I can't remember any of them. "I don't understand. How could I—"

"It's okay, Grace." Jaxon's gaze is steady on mine, his grip on my hands as firm and supportive as I could ever ask for. "We'll figure this out."

"How can it be okay? I lost four months, Jaxon!" My voice cracks on his name, and I take a shuddering breath and try again. "What happened?"

My uncle reaches over and squeezes my shoulder. "Take another deep breath, Grace. Good." He smiles encouragingly. "Okay, now take one more and let it out slowly."

I do as he says, noticing that his lips move the whole time I'm exhaling. *A calming spell?* I wonder as, once more, I inhale and exhale to the count of ten.

If so, doesn't feel like it's working all that well.

"Now, when you're ready, tell me the last thing you remember." His warm eyes hold mine.

The last thing I remember.

The last thing I remember.

It should be an easy question, but it's not. Partly because of the yawning blackness in my mind and partly because so much of what I remember feels murky, untouchable. Like my memories are floating deep underwater and I can see only the shadow of what's there. The shadow of what used to be.

"I remember everything that happened with Lia," I finally say,

because it's true. "I remember being in the infirmary. I remember…
building a snowman."

The memory warms me, and I smile at Jaxon, who smiles back—
at least with his mouth. His eyes look as gravely concerned as ever.

"I remember Flint apologizing to me about trying to kill me. I
remember—" I break off, press a hand to my suddenly hot cheek as
I recall the sensation of fangs skating along the sensitive skin of my
neck and shoulder before sinking home. "Jaxon. I remember Jaxon."

My uncle clears his throat, looking more than a little embarrassed
himself. But all he says is, "Anything else?"

"I don't know. It's so—" I break off as one crystal-clear memory
sweeps through my brain. I turn to Jaxon for confirmation. "We were
walking down the hall. You were telling me a joke. The one about…"
The clarity is fading, being replaced by the fuzziness that envelops
so many of my memories right now. I fight through it, determined to
hold on to this one clear thought. "No, that's not right. I was asking
you the punch line. To the pirate joke."

I freeze as another, much more chilling part of the memory
becomes clear.

"Oh my God. Hudson! Lia did it. She brought him back. He was
here. He was right here."

I look between Jaxon and Uncle Finn, searching for confirmation
even as the memory swamps me. Drags me under. "Is he alive?" I ask,
voice shaking under the weight of everything Jaxon has told me about
his brother. "Is he at Katmere?"

Uncle Finn looks grim as he answers, "That's exactly what we
wanted to ask you."

4

Turns out the Sixth Sense Is Actually Human Sacrifice

"Me? Why would I be able to answer that?" Except, even as I ask the question, another memory hits me. I look at Jaxon, who is full-on horror-struck by this point. "I got between you."

"You did." His throat works convulsively and his eyes, usually the color of a starless night, are somehow even blacker and more shadowed than I have ever seen them.

"He had a knife."

"A sword, actually," my uncle interjects.

"That's right." I close my eyes, and it all comes back to me.

Walking down the crowded hallway.

Catching sight of Hudson, sword raised, out of the corner of my eye.

Stepping between him and Jaxon because Jaxon is mine—mine to love and mine to protect.

The sword coming down.

And then...nothing. That's it. That's all I remember.

"Oh my God." Horror swamps me as something new, and terrible, occurs to me. "Oh my God. "

"It's okay, Grace." My uncle moves to pat my shoulder again, but I'm already moving.

"Oh my GOD!" I shove the chair back, jump to my feet. "Am

I dead? Is that why I can't remember anything else? Is that why everyone was staring at me in the hallway? That's it, isn't it? I'm dead."

I start to pace as my brain wigs out in about twenty different directions. "But I'm still here with you. And people can see me. Does that mean I'm a ghost?"

I'm struggling to get my mind around that idea when something else—something worse—occurs to me.

I whirl on Jaxon. "Tell me I'm a ghost. Tell me you didn't do what Lia did. Tell me you didn't trap some poor person down in that awful, disgusting dungeon and use them to bring me back. Tell me you didn't do that, Jaxon. Tell me I'm not walking around because of some human-sacrifice ritual that—"

"Whoa, whoa, whoa!" Jaxon bounds around my chair and takes hold of my shoulders. "Grace—"

"I'm serious. You better not have pulled any Dr. Frankenstein stuff to bring me back." I'm spiraling and I know it, but I can't seem to stop as terror and horror and disgust roil around inside me, combining into a dark and noxious mess I have no control over. "There better not have been blood. Or chanting. Or—"

He shakes his head, his longish hair brushing the tops of his shoulders. "I didn't do anything!"

"So I *am* a ghost, then?" I hold up my hands, stare at the fresh blood on my fingertips. "But how can I be bleeding if I'm dead? How can I—"

Jaxon grabs my shoulders gently, turns me to face him.

He takes a deep breath. "You're not a ghost, Grace. You weren't dead. And I definitely didn't perform a sacrifice—human or otherwise—to bring you back."

It takes a second, but his words, and the earnest tone he says them in, finally get through. "You didn't?"

"No, I didn't." He chuckles a little. "I'm not saying I wouldn't. These last four months have given me a shit ton more sympathy for Lia. But I didn't have to."

I weigh his words carefully, looking for loopholes as I hold them up against the suddenly crystal-clear memory of that sword connecting with my neck. "Didn't have to because there's another way to bring someone back from the dead? Or didn't have to because…?"

"Because you weren't dead, Grace. You didn't die when Hudson hit you with that sword."

"Oh." Out of everything I'd braced myself to hear, that one didn't even make the top ten. Maybe not even the top twenty. But now that I'm faced with that very logical although unlikely answer, I have no idea what to say next. Except: "So…coma?"

"No, Grace." My uncle answers this time. "No coma."

"Then what is going on? Because I may have giant holes in my memory, but the last thing I remember is your psychopathic brother trying to kill you and—"

"You stepping in to take the blow." Jaxon growls, and not for the first time I realize how close his emotions are to the surface. I just hadn't figured out, until right now, that one of those emotions is anger. Which I get, but…

"You would have done the same thing," I tell him quietly. "Don't deny it."

"I'm not denying it. But it's okay if *I* do it. I'm the—"

"Guy?" I cut him off in a voice that warns him to tread carefully here.

But he just rolls his eyes. "Vampire. I'm the *vampire*."

"So, what? Are you trying to say that sword couldn't have actually killed you? Because from where I stood, it looked to me like Hudson *really* wanted you dead."

"It could've killed me." It's a begrudging admission.

"That's what I thought. So what's your argument, then? Oh, right. You're the *guy*." I make sure my voice is dripping with disdain when I say the last word. But it doesn't last long as the adrenaline rush of the last several minutes finally passes. "So where *have* I been for four months?"

"Three months, twenty-one days, and about three hours, if you want to get specific," Jaxon tells me, and though his voice is steady and his face blank, I can hear the torment in the words. I can hear everything he isn't saying, and it makes me ache. For him. For me. For us.

Fists clenched, jaw hard, the scar on his cheek pulled tight—he looks like he's spoiling for a fight, if only he could figure out who or what to blame.

I run a comforting hand back and forth across his shoulders, then turn to my uncle. Because if I've just lost close to four months of my life, I want to know why. And how.

And if it's going to happen again.

5

Gargoyles Are the New Black

"The last thing I remember is bracing for a blow from Hudson's sword." I glance from my uncle to Jaxon, both with their jaws clenched tight like they don't want to be the one to tell me something. "What happened then? Did he cut me?"

"Not exactly," my uncle tells me. "I mean, the sword connected, so yes. But it didn't hurt you because you had already turned to stone."

I play his words over and over in my head, but no matter how many times or ways I repeat them, they still make absolutely no sense. "I'm sorry. Did you say I turned to..."

"Stone. You turned to stone, Grace, right the fuck in front of me," Jaxon says. "And you've been stone every single one of the last one hundred and twenty-one days."

"What do you mean by 'stone' exactly?" I ask again, still trying to get my head around something that sounds impossible.

"I mean, your entire body was made completely of stone," my uncle answers.

"Like I turned into a *statue*? That kind of stone?"

"Not a statue," my uncle quickly reassures me, even as he eyes me warily, like he's trying to decide how much more information I can take. Which a part of me can understand, even as it annoys the hell out of me.

"Please just tell me," I finally say. "Believe me, it's worse to be trapped in my head trying to figure this out than to just know. So if I wasn't a statue, I was…what?" I cast my mind around for some ideas, any ideas, but nothing comes.

And still my uncle hesitates, which makes me think that whatever the answer is, it's really, really bad.

"A gargoyle, Grace." Jaxon is the one who finally tells me the truth, just like always. "You're a gargoyle."

"A gargoyle?" I can't keep the incredulity from my voice.

My uncle shoots Jaxon a frustrated look but finally nods reluctantly. "A gargoyle."

"A gargoyle?" They can't be serious. They absolutely, positively, can*not* be serious. "Like the things on the sides of churches?"

"Yes." Jaxon grins now, just a little, like he realizes how ridiculous all this is. "You're a gar—"

I hold up a hand. "Please don't say it again. The first two times were hard enough to hear. Just shhhh for a second."

I turn and walk toward the back wall of Uncle Finn's office. "I need a minute," I tell the two of them. "Just a minute to…" Absorb it? Deny it? Cry about it? *Scream?*

Screaming sounds really good about now, but I'm pretty sure it'll just freak out Jaxon and Uncle Finn more, so…

I breathe. I just need to breathe. Because I don't have a clue what to say or do next.

I mean, there's a side of me that wants to call them on the joke— so funny, ha-ha—but another, bigger part knows they aren't lying. Not about this. Partly because neither my uncle nor Jaxon would do that to me and partly because there's something deep inside me, something small and scared and tightly furled that just…let go the minute they said the word. Like it had known all along and was just waiting for me to notice.

For me to understand.

For me to *believe.*

So. Gargoyle. Okay. That's not too bad, right? I mean, it could be worse. I shudder. The sword could have chopped off my head.

I take a deep breath, rest my forehead against the cool gray paint of my uncle's office wall, and turn the word "gargoyle" over and over again in my head as I try to figure out how I feel about it.

Gargoyle. As in huge stone creature with wings and snarling fangs and…horns? Surreptitiously, I run a hand over my head, just to see if I've somehow grown horns and don't know about it.

Turns out I haven't. All I feel is my usual curly brown hair. Just as long, just as unruly, just as annoying as ever, but definitely no horns. Or fangs, I realize as I run my tongue over my front teeth. In fact, everything about me feels completely the same as it always has. Thank God.

"Hey." Jaxon comes up behind me, and it's his turn to rest a gentle hand on my back. "You know it's going to be okay, right?"

Sure. Of course. Totally no big deal. I mean, gargoyles are all the rage, right? Somehow, I don't think he'll appreciate my sarcasm, so in the end I bite it back and simply nod.

"I'm serious," he continues. "We'll figure this out. And on the plus side, gargoyles are totally kick-ass."

Absolutely. Giant, hulking pieces of stone. Totally kick-ass. *Not.*

I whisper, "I know."

"You sure about that?" He scoots closer, ducking a little so that his face is really close to the side of mine. "Because you don't look like you know. And you definitely don't sound like it."

He's so close, I can feel his breath against my cheek, and for a few precious seconds I close my eyes and pretend it's four months ago, when Jaxon and I were alone in his room, making plans and making out, thinking we finally had everything under control.

What a joke that was. I've never felt more out of control in my life, even compared to those first days after my parents died. At least then, I was still human…or at least I thought I was. Now, I'm a gargoyle, and I don't have a clue what that even means, let alone how it happened. Or how I managed to lose nearly four months of my life encased in rock.

Why would I do that, anyway? I mean, I get why I changed to stone—I'm assuming some latent impulse deep inside me came forward in an effort to stop me from dying. Is it really so far-fetched, considering I recently learned my dad was a warlock? But why did I stay stone for so long? Why didn't I come back to Jaxon the first chance I got?

I rack my brain, trying to come up with the answer, but there's still nothing there but a blank and empty chasm where my memories should be.

It's my turn to clench my fists, and as I do, my battered fingers start to throb. I glance down at them and wonder how I made such a mess of myself. It looks like I clawed my way through stone to get here. Then again, maybe I did. Or maybe I did something even worse. I don't know. That's the problem: I just don't know. Anything.

I don't know what I did for the last four months.

I don't know how it was possible for me to change into a gargoyle— or how it was possible for me to change back into a human.

And, I realize with a dawning horror that chills my very soul, I don't know the answer to the most important question of all.

I swing around to stare at my uncle. "What happened to Hudson?"

6

Vampire Roulette Isn't the Same Without the Blood

U ncle Finn seems to age right in front of me, eyes going dim and shoulders slumping in what looks an awful lot like defeat. "We really don't know," he says. "One second, Hudson was trying to kill Jaxon, and the next—"

"He was gone. And so were you." Jaxon's hand tightens reflexively on mine.

"She wasn't gone," Uncle Finn corrects. "She was just out of reach for a while."

Once again, Jaxon looks unimpressed with his summation of events, but he doesn't argue. Instead, he just looks at me and asks, "Do you really not remember any of it?"

I shrug. "I really don't."

"That's so strange." My uncle shakes his head. "We brought in every expert we could find on gargoyles. Every single one of them had conflicting stories and advice, but none of them even hinted that when you finally made it back, you wouldn't remember where you'd been. Or what you'd become." My uncle's voice is low and, I'm sure, meant to be soothing, but every word he says just makes me more nervous.

"Do you think something's wrong with me?" I ask nervously, looking between him and Jaxon.

"*Nothing* is wrong with you," Jaxon snarls, and it's as much a warning to Uncle Finn as it is a reassurance to me.

"Of course there isn't," Uncle Finn agrees. "Don't even think that way. I'm just sorry we're not more prepared to help you. We didn't anticipate…this."

"It's not your fault. I just wish—" I break off as I run into that damn wall again. I push against it, but I can't seem to get it to break.

"Don't force it," Jaxon tells me, and this time he gently wraps an arm around my shoulders.

It feels good—*he* feels good—and I let myself sink in to him even as fear and frustration continue to circle inside me. "I *have* to push," I tell him, cuddling closer. "How else do we figure out where Hudson is?"

The heat is on, but I'm still freezing—I guess spending four months as stone will do that to a girl—and I run my hands up and down my arms in an effort to warm them.

Uncle Finn watches me for a few seconds, then mutters something under his breath as he waves a hand in the air. Moments later, a warm blanket settles around Jaxon and me.

"Better?" he asks.

"So much better. Thank you." I clutch it close.

He settles back against the corner of his desk. "To be honest, Grace, we were both terrified he was with you. And just as terrified he wasn't."

His last words hang in the air like a heavy weight for several minutes.

"Maybe he *was* with me." Just thinking about being trapped with Hudson has a huge lump taking up residence in the middle of my throat. I pause, force myself to swallow it down, before asking, "If he was with me, do you think… Did I bring him back with me? Is he here now?"

I glance between my uncle and Jaxon, and they both stare at me with what has to be intentionally blank faces. The sight turns my veins, my heart, *my very soul* to ice. Because as long as Hudson is running around, Jaxon isn't safe. And neither is anyone else.

My stomach churns sickly as I rack my brain. *This isn't happening. Please tell me this isn't happening.* I can't be responsible for letting Hudson loose again, can't be responsible for bringing him back where he can terrorize everyone and raise an army made of born vampires and their sympathizers.

"You wouldn't do that," Jaxon finally tells me. "I know you, Grace. You would never have come back if you thought Hudson was still a threat."

"I agree," my uncle eventually says. As he continues, I try to hold on to his words and not the silence that preceded them. "So let's operate under that assumption for now. That you only came back because it was safe to do so. That means Hudson is most likely gone, and we don't have to be worried."

And yet he still looks worried. Of course he does. Because no matter how much we all want to believe that Hudson is gone, there's one major flaw with their logic—mainly that they're both talking about me being here like I *decided* to come back.

But what if I didn't? If I didn't make a conscious choice to become a gargoyle all those months ago, maybe I didn't make a conscious choice to become human again now. And if that's the case, where exactly is Hudson?

Dead?

Frozen in stone in some alternate reality?

Or hiding out somewhere here at Katmere, just waiting for his chance to exact revenge on Jaxon?

I don't like the sound of any of the alternatives, but the last one is definitely the worst. In the end, I put it aside because freaking out won't do me any good.

But we have to start somewhere, so I decide to go along with Uncle Finn's assumption—mostly because I like it better than all the alternatives put together. "Okay. Let's assume that, if I had control of Hudson, I wouldn't have just let him go. Now what?"

"Now we chill out a little bit. We stop worrying about Hudson and start worrying about *you*." My uncle smiles encouragingly. "Marise should be here any minute and if, after she checks you out, she decides you're healthy, then I think we should let things ride for a while. See what you remember in a few days, after you've eaten and had some rest and gotten back to a normal routine."

"Let things ride?" Jaxon asks, his voice dripping with the same incredulity I'm feeling inside.

"Yes." For the first time, there's a hint of steel in my uncle's voice. "What Grace needs right now is for things to go back to normal."

I think he's forgetting that having a psychopathic vampire on my ass has pretty much been the norm for me since I *got* to this school. The fact that we have apparently switched Lia out for Hudson just feels like par for the course at this point. Which is depressing, to say the least, but also true.

I swear, if I were reading this story, I'd say the plot twists were getting ridiculous. But I'm not reading it. I'm living it, and that is *so much worse*.

"What Grace needs," Jaxon corrects, "is to feel safe. Which she won't be able to do until we make sure Hudson isn't a threat."

"No, what Grace needs," my uncle continues, "is routine. There's safety in knowing what's going to happen and when it's going to happen. She'll be better off—"

"Grace will be *better off*," I interrupt as annoyance bubbles to the surface, "if her uncle and her boyfriend start talking *to* her instead of *about* her. Since I have a semi-functioning brain and, you know, agency in my own life."

To their credit, they both look shamefaced at the verbal slap down. As they should. I may not be a vampire or a warlock, but that doesn't mean I'm just going to lie down and let "the menfolk" make decisions about my life for me. Especially not when both of them seem to be of the "wrap Grace in cotton and protect her" opinion. Which also really isn't going to fly with me.

"You're right," my uncle agrees in a much more subdued tone.

"What do *you* want to do, Grace?"

I think for a minute. "I want things to be normal—or at least as normal as they can get for a girl who lives with a witch and is dating a vampire. But I *also* want to figure out what happened with Hudson. I feel like we've got to find him if we have any chance at all of keeping *everyone* safe."

"I'm not worried about keeping everyone safe," Jaxon growls. "I'm just worried about keeping *you* safe."

It's a good line and, not going to lie, it melts me a little on the inside. But on the outside, I stay tough, because someone has to figure out this mess, and since I'm the only one with a front-row seat—even if I don't remember what I saw from that seat—that someone is going to have to be me.

I clench my fists in frustration, ignoring the pain that shoots through my already abused fingertips as I do. This is important, really important. I have to remember what happened to Hudson.

Did I leave him chained up somewhere, a threat to no one?

Did he escape and that's why my hands are so beaten up—because I tried to stop him?

Or—and I hate this idea the most—did he use his gift of persuasion on me and get me to just let him go? And if so, is that why my memory is shot to hell?

The not knowing is killing me, as is the fear that I've let everyone down.

Jaxon fought so hard to get rid of Hudson the first time. He sacrificed everything, including whatever love his mother had for him, in order to destroy his brother—and to keep Hudson from destroying the whole world.

How can I live with myself if we find out that I just let him walk away? That I gave him a chance to continue wreaking havoc on Katmere and the world?

That I gave him another chance to hurt the boy I love?

That thought more than any other feeds the fear inside me and has me croaking out, "We need to find him," in a voice hoarse with concern. "We need to figure out where he went and make sure he can't hurt anyone else."

And we need to figure out why I'm certain I'm forgetting something very important that happened during those four months.

Before it's too late.

7

What I Don't Know *Will* Hurt Me... and Everyone Else

After Marise checks me over for what feels like hours, Uncle Finn finally lets Jaxon take me away. It's obvious from the way both men and Marise fretted over me that no one was taking my health for granted, which was comforting. Marise even checked me for a brain injury because, well, hello, amnesia.

But I am unbelievably healthy, minus some scrapes and bruises on my hands, and deemed fit to reenter Katmere Academy. Apparently, being stone for four months could be the next big health craze.

As Jaxon and I walk casually back to my room, though, my mind can't stop replaying a part of my conversation with Marise, when she was apologizing for not knowing more about gargoyle physiology.

"You're the first gargoyle to exist in a thousand years."

Fantastic. Because who doesn't want to be a trendsetter when it comes to their basic physiology? Oh, right. *Everyone.*

Not going to lie, I have absolutely no idea how to process the information that I'm the first modern-day one of my kind, so I file it away in a folder marked: "Shit I Don't Need to Deal with Today." And another one titled "Thanks for the Heads-Up, Mom and Dad."

Just then, I notice that Jaxon's not leading me to *my* room but to his tower rooms. I tug on his hand to get his attention. "Hey, we can't head to your rooms. I need to stop by mine for a few minutes;

then I want to take a quick shower and grab a granola bar before heading to class."

"Class?" He looks shocked. "Wouldn't you rather rest today?"

"I'm pretty sure I've been 'resting' for the last four months. What I really want to do is get back to class and catch up on what I missed. I'm supposed to graduate in two and a half months, and I don't even want to think about how many missing assignments I have."

"We always knew you'd come back, Grace." He smiles down at me and squeezes my hand. "So your uncle and teachers already have a plan in place. You just need to set up appointments to talk to them about it."

"Oh, wow. That's awesome." I give him a tight hug. "Thank you for your help with everything."

He hugs me back. "You don't need to thank me. That's what I'm here for." He pivots, and we switch directions and head to my room. "Mrs. Haversham should have emailed your new schedule by now. It changed at the semester, even though..." His voice trails off.

"Even though I wasn't here to change with it," I finish, because I've just decided that I'm not going to spend the rest of the school year tiptoeing around my new reality. It is what it is, and the sooner we all learn to live with it, the sooner things will get back to normal. Myself included.

I've got a long list of questions to ask Jaxon and Macy about gargoyles. And once I get the answers, I'm going to start trying to figure out how to live with it gracefully. Tomorrow. On the plus side, the fact that I don't have horns should make the graceful part a lot easier to bear.

Jaxon stares down at me, and I expect him to kiss me—I've been dying to kiss him from the moment he walked into my uncle's office— but when I lean in to him, he subtly shakes his head. The rejection stings a little, at least until I remember just how many people were staring at me when I was walking through the halls earlier.

That was more than an hour ago. Now that word has probably gotten around that the resident gargoyle is human again, I can't imagine how many people will be watching us—even though class is supposed to be in session.

Sure enough, when we turn the corner into one of the side hallways, people are everywhere—and every single one of them is looking at us. I can feel myself tensing up before we've taken more than a step or two. They drop their eyes when Jaxon walks by, though.

Jaxon wraps an arm around my shoulders, then ducks his head until his mouth is almost pressed against my ear. "Don't worry about them," he murmurs. "Once everyone gets a look at you, things will settle down."

I know he's right—after my first couple of days here, no one paid any attention to me at all, unless I was walking beside Jaxon. There's no reason to think that will change now. Thankfully. Notoriety isn't exactly my speed.

We book it to my room, turning what's usually a ten-minute walk into one that's closer to five or six. And still it isn't fast enough. Not with Jaxon beside me, his arm around my shoulders. His long, lean body pressed against my side.

I need him to be closer, need to feel his arms around me and his soft lips on mine.

Jaxon must feel the same way, because once we hit the top of the stairs, his quick walk turns into something closer to a jog. And by the time we get to my room, my hands are trembling and my heart is beating way too fast.

Thank God Macy left the door unlocked, because I'm not sure Jaxon wouldn't have torn the thing off the hinges otherwise. Instead, he pushes open the door and ushers me through it, hissing only a little as Macy's enchanted curtain brushes against his bare forearm.

"Is your arm okay?" I ask as the door closes behind us. Jaxon is too busy pushing me up against it to answer.

"I missed you," he growls, lips barely an inch from my own.

"I missed y—" It's all I manage to get out before his mouth comes crashing down on mine.

8

Put a Little Love on Me

I didn't know.

I didn't know how much I missed this, didn't know how much I missed Jaxon, until this moment.

His body pressed against mine.

His hands cupping my face, fingers tangled in my hair.

His mouth devouring mine—lips and teeth and tongue lighting me up from the inside. Making me want. Making me *need*.

Jaxon. Always Jaxon.

I shift against him, desperate to get even closer, and he growls low in his throat. I can feel the tension in his body, can feel the same need in him that is burning deep inside me. But through it all, his hold remains gentle, his fingers stroking my hair instead of pulling, his body cradling mine instead of trying to invade my space.

"Mine." I whisper the word against his lips and he shudders, wrenching his mouth from my lips.

I whimper, try to pull him back, but he shudders again, buries his face in the bend where my shoulder and neck meet. And then he just breathes—long, slow, deep breaths—like he's trying to pull my very essence deep inside himself.

I know the feeling.

I slide my hands down to his waist, and as my hands skim over him, I realize he really did lose weight while I was…gone.

"I'm sorry," I whisper against his ear, but he just shakes his head as he pulls me closer.

"Don't." He presses soft kisses along the length of my neck. "Don't ever apologize to me for what you went through. It's my fault that I didn't protect you."

"It's nobody's fault," I tell him, even as I tilt my head back to give him better access. "It just is what it is."

Tears suddenly burn my eyes. I blink them away, but Jaxon knows. His hands, already gentle, become downright tender as they stroke my arm, my shoulder, my cheek. "It's going to be okay, Grace. I promise."

"It's already okay." I swallow down the lump in my throat. "We're here, aren't we?"

"Yes." He presses a kiss to the sensitive spot behind my ear. "Finally."

My legs go liquid. Heat races through me. My heart trembles in my chest. Jaxon holds me up—of course he does—and murmurs, "I love you," as he gently scrapes his teeth over my collarbone.

And just like that, everything inside me freezes. My breath, my blood, even the need that's been burning inside me since he walked into my uncle's office. All of it…*gone*. Just like that.

Jaxon must feel it, because he stops immediately. And when he lifts his head, there's a wary, watchful look in his eyes that makes me feel like I did something wrong. "Grace?" he asks, shifting back a little so that he's no longer crowding me. "You okay?"

"Yeah, yeah. I'm fine. I just…" I trail off because I don't know how to answer him, don't know what to say. Because I want him. I do. I just don't know how to deal with this weird, uncomfortable feeling that's building inside me all of a sudden.

"You just…?" Jaxon waits for an answer. Not in an aggressive way but in a concerned way, like he really does just want to make sure I'm all right.

But knowing that only makes the feeling inside me worse, the pressure building until I feel like a rocket about to go off. "I don't... I want... It feels..." I sound like a jerk fumbling around for an explanation, but then my stomach growls—loudly—and understanding replaces Jaxon's concern.

"I should have kept my hands to myself until you had something to eat," he says, taking another couple of steps back. "I'm sorry."

"Don't be. I needed to kiss you." I squeeze his hand, glad to have an explanation for the weird feeling inside me. My mom always said that low blood sugar does strange things, and I can only imagine how low mine is right now, considering I haven't eaten in nearly four months. "I'll just grab one of Macy's granola bars and then go to class. You probably have to head out soon, too, right?"

"Sure," he says, but I can tell the light has dimmed in his eyes.

I know it's my fault. I know he's just being Jaxon and I'm the one who is suddenly acting all weird. But...I don't know. Everything just feels off with me, and I don't have a clue how to fix it.

I should probably lean forward so my hair brushes against Jaxon's hand and he knows everything's okay. Or at least lean into him for one more hug. But I don't actually want to do either of those things, so I don't. Instead, I smile up at him and say, "See you later?"

"Yeah." He smiles back. "Definitely."

"Oh, and for some reason, I've lost my phone. Meet back here?"

He nods, then gives me another little wave and heads out of my room and down the hallway toward the stairs.

I watch him go, admiring the way he walks, full of purpose and confidence and a come-at-me-at-your-own-risk insouciance that shouldn't do it for me but somehow totally does. Also, I am completely admiring the hell out of what his very nice ass does for those boring black uniform pants.

Once Jaxon starts to go around the corner, I step back into my room, then kind of pause as he turns to look down the hall at me. He's got a huge grin on his face now, and it looks good on him. As do the crinkles by the corners of his eyes and the lightness that seems to cover his whole face.

The grin fades just a little as our eyes meet—almost like he's embarrassed to be caught looking so happy—but it's too late. I've gotten a glimpse at what Jaxon Vega looks like when he's beaming, and it turns out I like it. I really, really like it.

The anxiety in the pit of my stomach dissolves as easily as it came, and suddenly it's the easiest thing in the world to blow him the kiss I couldn't give him earlier. His eyes widen at the gesture and, while he doesn't do anything as corny as reaching out to grab it, he does wink at me.

I'm laughing as I close my door and head for the shower. How can I not when the Jaxon Vega I get to see is a million times sweeter and more charming than the one the world knows?

But as I turn on the water, a chill works its way through me. Because if it turns out I let Hudson escape, if it turns out I really did bring him back with me, then I'll be the one responsible for hurting Jaxon and taking away his happiness.

No way am I going to let that happen to him. Not now. Not ever again.

9

Livin' on a Hope-Induced Hallucination

Three shampoos and two full-body scrubs later, I finally feel like a new woman. One who might not turn into a hulking stone monster at the least provocation. I wrap myself and my hair up in towels (hot pink, of course—thank you, Macy) and reach for my phone to check the time.

Which I can't do because *I don't have a phone*. Ugh.

Also, since there is no clock in the room and I don't have a phone, I'm feeling pretty grumpy as I slap moisturizer on my face and start to dry my hair.

The sad fact is, I'm going to have to get on this no-phone thing sooner rather than later. Partly because my entire life is on my phone and partly because I really, really need to text Heather. I can't even imagine what my best friend is thinking right now—except, of course, that I ghosted her for absolutely no reason.

Thankfully, my electronics are the only things missing. My backpack was apparently with me the entire time, and my school uniforms are right where I left them—in my closet. I take a minute to re-bandage my hurt fingers, then grab a black skirt and purple polo from my closet. I add a pair of black tights and my school boots, pause to slick a little lip gloss on my lips and mascara on my lashes, then grab my backpack and head for the door.

I don't know what time it is exactly, but Jaxon left here around noon. Which means I should have plenty of time to make my one o'clock class: Mystical Architecture.

I have no idea what kind of class this is, but the truth is I'm excited about it. Even though there's a part of me that wonders if I am now enrolled in it because I'm apparently a living, breathing example of mystical architecture.

Deciding not to dwell on the fact that I might be part of the props, I throw open my door and book it down the long dorm hallway, with its decorated doors and black sconces in the shape of different dragons. As always, I giggle a little as I pass the door decorated with bats.

The first day I got to Katmere, I assumed the room belonged to a Batman aficionado and thought it was the coolest. Now I know it's a vampire joke à la Jaxon's best friend, Mekhi, and I love it even more. Especially when I see that he's added a couple of new bat stickers.

I take the back stairs two at a time, my hand coasting along the elaborately carved banister as I do. I'm in such a rush to get to class, I don't notice a chunk of the banister is missing—and stairs—until it's too late and almost tumble through the hole.

I manage to catch myself, but as I do, I get an up-close look at the edges on either side of the gap. They're charred and blackened and look to be the victims of some kind of high-intensity fire. Someone obviously lost their temper...or at least lost control of their powers.

Dragon or witch? I wonder as I turn the corner into the north hallway where my architecture class is located. They're the only ones who can wield that kind of firepower. Which is cool but definitely a little scary, too.

Maybe I'm looking at this whole gargoyle thing all wrong. At least I don't have to worry about burning the school down when I'm a giant stone statue.

Warning chimes playing the Rolling Stones's "Sympathy for the Devil"—Katmere's version of a bell and Uncle Finn's own private indulgence—go off just as I slip through the doorway of my architecture class. I try to get the lay of the land and to find an empty desk, but I barely have the chance to inhale a breath before I jump a little as I realize Flint is crowding in behind me.

He puts a steadying hand on my shoulder even as a huge grin splits his face. "New Girl! You're back!"

"You already knew that." I roll my eyes at the greeting. "You saw me earlier."

"Yeah, well, I wasn't sure you weren't some hope-induced hallucination earlier." He wraps me in a huge hug and lifts me off my feet. "Now I know you're real."

"Why is that exactly?" I ask as he finally lets me down. He's so warm, and I'm still so cold that I think about burrowing against him for a second hug. But this is the guy who tried to kill me not that long ago. Sure, he's had the last four months to move on, but for me it feels like everything happened just a few days ago. Including him choking me out in the tunnels below the school.

But Flint just winks at me and says, "Because no one who doesn't have to be here would ever come to this class."

10

One Giant Pain
in my Ass

"F antastic." I give him my very best fake smile. "Because that doesn't sound ominous at all."

"Hey, I'm just keeping it real." He leans in close. "You want another tip?"

"I didn't realize there was a first tip," I answer with a roll of my eyes.

This time when he smiles, his teeth gleam white and just a little sharp against his rich umber complexion, and I can't help wondering how I missed it for so many days.

Everything about the boy screams "dragon," from the way he moves to the way his eyes track my every movement. And that's not even including the large ring on his right ring finger that I've never seen him take off—at least not in human form. It's literally a bright-green stone with a dragon etched into it set in an elaborate silver base.

"I'm going to ignore your lack of enthusiasm, New Girl, and tell you anyway. Because that's just the kind of guy I am."

"So magnanimous," I agree with a click of my tongue, although I can't keep the humor from leaking into my gaze. Staying mad at Flint is starting to feel impossible. "Or, wait. I think I mean murderous. Sorry." I deliberately widen my eyes. "I always confuse those two words."

Flint's cheeks flush just a little, and his expression shifts to a combination of embarrassed and impressed as he leans over and whispers, "Me too."

I meet his eyes. "I remember."

"Yeah, I know." He looks sad, but he doesn't try to argue with me. Doesn't try to pretend I don't have the right to be wary around him. Instead, he just nods toward the desks and says, "You might want to grab a seat in the back."

"Why is that exactly?" I ask.

Flint just shakes his head, and his signature big grin stretches across his face again. He holds his hands out in a half-conciliatory, half-do-what-you-want kind of motion. "Sit in the front for a day if you must. You'll figure it out."

I want to ask more, but the final bell rings, and everyone is rushing for a seat—as far back from the front as they can get.

So it was a real tip, then, and not just Flint's way of messing with me. Too bad I'm a little slow on the uptake, because now nearly all the seats in the back are taken.

Figuring the front can't be *that* bad, I start to make my way over to the row against the wall—the second seat is open, and it seems like as good a bet as any.

I'm almost there when a slender arm, bedecked in crystal enhancing bracelets, shoots out to stop me. "Oh my God, Grace!" Macy's friend Gwen beckons me over to sit next to her.

"Welcome back," she practically shouts at me as I slide into the desk in front of her. "Have you seen Macy yet? She's going to flip!"

She shoves a lock of her long, shiny black hair behind her ear as she talks, and when it falls right back into her face again, she makes an exasperated noise and leans forward to pull an antique hair clip— also crystal enhanced—out of her bag.

"I haven't seen her yet. My uncle said she's been taking a midterm since I…" I trail off awkwardly, as I have no idea how to finish that sentence.

Since I got back?

Since I became human again?

Since I stopped being a gargoyle?

Ugh. What a mess.

Gwen smiles sympathetically, then whispers something in Chinese to me. The look on her face tells me it's something special, but I don't have a clue if it's a spell or a blessing or something in between.

"What does that mean?" I whisper back as the architecture teacher, a Mr. Damasen, according to my schedule, lumbers into the room. He's a huge man—seven feet at least—with long red hair tied back at the nape of his neck and ancient gold eyes that seem to see everything.

Instinctively, I sit a little taller and notice everyone else in the class does the same—except for Flint, who currently has his long legs kicked up on his desk like he's on a lounger in the middle of the Bahamas.

Mr. Damasen zeroes in on him, his eyes doing this weird swirling thing that totally freaks me out. But Flint just keeps grinning that lazy, dragon grin of his and even raises his hand in a little half wave, half salute.

At first, I think the teacher is going to bite his head off—maybe even literally—but in the end, he doesn't say a word. He just kind of shakes his head before giving the rest of the students in the classroom a quick once-over.

"It's a Chinese proverb my mother used to tell me all the time when I was growing up and struggling to figure out my powers and my place in the witchcraft world. 'If heaven made someone, earth can find some use for them.'" Her bracelets clink together in a surprisingly soothing rhythm as she leans forward slightly and pats my forearm. "Don't be so hard on yourself. You'll figure it out. Just give yourself some time."

Her words are right on. So right on, in fact, that they freak me out a little bit. I really don't like the idea of the entire school knowing how I'm feeling. I thought I'd done a good job of keeping my emotions under wraps, but now I'm really doubting that belief, considering this is only the second time Gwen and I have ever talked.

"How did you know?"

She smiles. "I'm an empath and a healer. It's kind of what I do. And you've got every right to be freaked out right now. Just try to breathe through it until you get your feet under you."

"Fake it till I make it?" I joke, because that's pretty much been my mantra since I got to Katmere Academy.

"Something like that, yeah," she answers with a quiet laugh.

"Miss Zhou." Mr. Damasen's voice booms across the classroom like a lightning strike, rattling everything in its path—including his students' nerves. "Care to join the rest of the class in turning in your review packet for the midterm? Or are you not interested in obtaining those points?"

"Of course, Mr. Damasen." She holds up a bright-orange folder. "I have it right here."

"Sorry," I whisper, but she just winks at me as she gets up to add her file to the stack at the front of the room.

"As for you, Miss Foster, it's nice to have you back." I jump as Mr. Damasen's voice thunders so loudly, it practically rattles my eyes back in my head. He's made his way down my aisle and is now standing right in front of me, a textbook in his hand. "Here's the book you'll need for my class."

I reach for it gingerly, trying to keep my ears as far away from his voice as I can, just in case he decides he has something else to say. I now understand exactly what Flint was warning me about. Too bad I can't run down to the nearest drugstore and pick up a pair of earplugs before next class.

Turns out keeping my ears as far out of range as possible was a good move on my part, because I've barely got the textbook in my hands before he continues. "But you've chosen to return on the day we're taking the class midterm—something you are obviously ill-equipped for. So after I get everyone started on the test, come up to my desk with Mr. Montgomery. I've got a job for the two of you."

"Flint?" His name pops out before I even know I'm going to say it. "Doesn't he have to take the test?"

"Nope." Flint pretends to buff his nails on his shirt before blowing on them in the universal gesture for *I've got this*. "The person with the highest grade in the class is exempt from the midterm. So I am free to help with whatever you may need." The grin he shoots me as he says the last word is absolutely wicked.

I'm not about to argue with my teacher on my first day of class, so I wait while Mr. Damasen hands out thick test packets to everyone else in the room. Only after he's answered the numerous questions that go along with the test do I make my way up to his desk at the front of the class, Flint hot on my heels. I can feel everyone staring at us—staring at me—and my cheeks burn in response. But I'm determined not to let anyone know that they're getting to me, so I just look straight ahead and pretend Flint isn't standing so close that I can feel his breath on my neck.

Mr. Damasen grunts when he sees us and reaches into the top drawer of his desk to pull out a yellow envelope. Then, in a voice that I'm pretty sure he thinks is a whisper but is really more like a near-shout, he tells us, "What I need you to do is go around the school and take pictures of everything on this list and return the photos to me within two weeks. I need to use them as references on an article I'm writing for May's edition of *Giant Adventures*." He looks back and forth between us. "Your uncle said it wouldn't be a problem."

Trust Uncle Finn to try to fix everything—typical. "No, no problem, Mr. Damasen," I say, mostly because I don't know what else *to* say.

He hands it to me, then waits a little impatiently for me to open it. "Any questions?" he asks in a thundering timbre the second I set eyes on the list.

About a hundred, but most of them have nothing to do with what I'm supposed to photograph. No, my questions are all about how I'm supposed to spend the next hour and a half with the boy who, not very long ago, wanted me dead.

11

Just Call Me
Stone-Coldhearted

"Are you okay with this?" Flint asks after we've gotten to the hallway. For once, he's not joking around as he asks. In fact, he looks deadly serious.

The truth is, I'm not sure if I'm okay or not. I mean, I know Flint isn't going to hurt me again—with Lia dead and Hudson who knows where, there's absolutely no reason for Flint to try to kill me to keep me from being used in Hudson's bizarre resurrection. At the same time, I'm not super excited about rushing off to some of the (very) isolated places on that list with him, either. Fool me once and all that…

Still, an assignment is an assignment. Plus, if my doing this means I don't have to eventually take the midterm, I'm all for finding a way to make it work.

"It's fine," I tell him after a few awkward seconds go by. "Let's just get it done."

"Yeah, sure." He nods at the list in my hand. "Where do you want to start?"

I hand the stack of papers over to him. "You know the school better than I do. Why don't you choose?"

"Happy to." He doesn't say anything else as he starts perusing the list. Which should be a good thing—I mean, the last thing I want is for Flint to think we're good friends again. But at the same time, I don't like the way this feels, either.

I don't like the distance between us. I don't like this serious Flint who isn't joking around and teasing me. And I really, really don't like that every minute we spend in this hallway seems to make things more awkward and not less.

I miss the friend who roasted marshmallows for me in the library. Who made a flower for me out of thin air. Who offered to give me a piggyback ride up the stairs.

But then I remember that that friend never really existed, that even when he was doing all those things, he was also plotting to hurt me, and I feel even worse.

Flint keeps glancing at me over the top of Mr. Damasen's list, but he doesn't say anything. And that only makes everything feel even more off, until the silence stretches between us, taut and fragile as an acrobat's wire. The longer it goes on, the worse it gets, until, by the time Flint finally finishes reading the list, I'm about to jump out of my skin.

I know he feels it, too, though, because this boy in front of me isn't the same one who teased me when he first walked into the classroom today. His voice is more subdued, his attitude more hesitant. Even his posture is different. He looks smaller and less confident than I've ever seen him when he says, "The tunnels are on this list."

His words hang in the air, haunting the space between us. "I know."

"I can do them myself if you want." He clears his throat, shuffles his feet, looks anywhere but at me. "You can photograph something else on the list, and I can run down to the tunnels and take the pics Mr. Damasen needs really quick."

"I can't take any pics on my own. I lost my phone in the whole…" Instead of saying the word out loud, I wave my hand in what I hope he understands to mean *gargoyle debacle*.

"Oh, right." He clears his throat for what feels like the fourth time in a minute. "I mean, I can still go down to the tunnels alone. You can just wait here, and then we can do the rest of the castle together."

I shake my head. "I'm not going to make you do that."

"You're not *making* me do anything, Grace. I offered."

"Yeah, well, I didn't ask you to offer. I'm the one getting a grade on it, after all."

"True, but I'm the one who was a complete asshole, so if you aren't fine going down to those damn tunnels with me, then I totally get it, okay?"

I rear back at his words, a little shocked by his sudden mea culpa but also a little pissed off about how flippant he sounds, like there's something wrong with me for wanting to protect myself. Even knowing he felt like he didn't have a choice—even knowing that he probably couldn't have killed Lia without setting off a war between dragons and vampires—doesn't absolve him of what he did.

"You know what? You *were* a total asshole. Beyond an asshole, actually. I'm the one still sporting scars on my body from your talons, so why the hell are *you* suddenly the one standing here looking all sad and wounded? You're the one who was a terrible friend to me, not the other way around."

His eyebrows slash down. "You think I don't know that? You think I haven't spent every day of the last four months thinking about all the ways I fucked you over?"

"Honestly, I don't know what you've been doing for the last four months. I've been stuck as a damn statue, in case you've forgotten."

And just like that, all the fire seems to leave him, and his shoulders slump. "I haven't forgotten. And it really fucking sucks."

"It does suck. This whole mess sucks. I thought you were my friend. I thought—"

"I was your friend. I *am* your friend, if you'll let me be one. I know I already apologized to you, and I know there's nothing I can say or do to make up for what I did—no matter how many punishments Foster gave me. But I swear, Grace, I'll never do anything like that again. I swear I'll never hurt you again."

It's not the words themselves that convince me to give him another chance, though they are pretty persuasive. It's the way he says them, like our friendship really matters to him. Like he misses me as much as I'm finding out that I miss him.

It's because I do miss him, because I don't want to believe that all those moments that meant something to me didn't also mean something to him, that I make what may be my worst mistake yet. Instead of telling him to go to hell, instead of telling him it's too late and I'll never give him another chance, I say, "You better not, because if you ever pull anything like that again, you won't have to worry about killing me. Because I promise, I'll get to you first."

His whole face breaks out into that ridiculous grin I've never been able to resist. "Deal. If I try to kill you again, you can totally try to kill me back."

"There won't be any *try* about it," I tell him with my best pretend glare. "Only death. *Your* death."

He places a hand over his heart in mock horror. "You know what? You say that with a lot of conviction. I actually think you mean it." Contrarily, his grin only gets bigger.

"I do mean it. Want to test me out?"

"No way. I was in the hallway the day you turned to stone. I saw what happened to Hudson," Flint says. "You've become a total badass, Grace."

"Excuse me, but I have always *been* a badass. You were just too busy trying to kill me to notice." It's pretty hard to look down your nose at someone taller than you, but here, in this moment with Flint, I'm proud to say I manage it.

"I'm noticing now." He waggles his brows. "And I definitely like it."

I sigh. "Yeah, well, don't like it too much. This"—I gesture back and forth between the two of us—"is still a probationary thing. So don't mess it up."

He puts his hands on his hips, his stance wide like he's bracing for a blow he's totally willing to take. "I won't," he says. And he sounds surprisingly serious.

I hold his gaze for a minute and then nod, the smile I've been fighting since I saw him again finally crinkling my eyes. "Good. Now, can we please get back to the project? Or are we going to stand out here talking about our feelings all day?"

"Wow." He gives me a fake wide-eyed look. "Turn a girl into a gargoyle and suddenly she's all kinds of stone-coldhearted."

"Wow." I return his look with one of my own. "Turn a boy into a dragon and suddenly he's all kinds of ridiculous."

"That's not my dragon, baby. That's all me."

I roll my eyes but can't stop myself from grinning at his goofiness. It's really good to be able to joke with him again. "I hate to break it to you, *baby*, but I'm pretty sure it's the both of you."

Flint pretends to swoon, and I take the opportunity to yank the list of photography subjects out of his hands. I'm smart enough to know if I don't get the boy on task soon, there's no way we're going to finish this. And since I can use all the points I can get, we really, really should start moving.

Except, as I peruse the list again—this time with a much clearer head—I realize that we've got a giant problem. "Some of the things he wants us to take pictures of are way up high. There's no way we'll be able to get a picture of them good enough to use for research."

But Flint just winks at me, that wicked grin of his on full display. "You *do* remember dragons can fly, right?"

Oh, hell no. I shake my head. "I'm sorry, but our tree of trust is still just a twig. No way am I letting you take me up into the sky."

He laughs. "Fine, spoilsport. We'll focus on the easy ones today. But one of these days soon, I'm totally taking you flying."

I shiver and almost remind him he *has* taken me flying before—in his talons—but I don't want to break our newfound truce. "That'll take some convincing."

"I live to serve, my lady," he says as he drops into an elaborate bow, and I can't help but laugh. He is so ridiculous that it's hard to take him seriously.

I jokingly try to shove his shoulder, but damn, maybe he's the gargoyle here. He's definitely hard enough to be made of stone. "Come on, give me your phone and let's get started, you big dork," I joke, and Flint quickly hands me his cell. But as I turn around, I find Jaxon watching us with eyes that have turned to flat black ice.

12

"Finished with class already?" Jaxon asks, looking at me with a vague hint of what-the-fuck.

"Oh, no." I take a sizable step away from Flint—not because Jaxon has said or done anything to make me uncomfortable but because I can only imagine how I'd feel if I were just walking around the school and found him cuddled up with a super-hot, super-charming dragon. No matter how innocent it was. "It's just the class is taking a midterm, and Flint is exempt, so the teacher volunteered him to help me with an outside project I can do for the same points."

Flint casually leans a massive shoulder against the stone wall, crossing his arms and ankles as though he hasn't a care in the world. Jaxon's gaze stays steady on me.

"That's awesome. Less of that makeup work you were worried about, right?" Jaxon asks with a smile that doesn't quite reach his eyes. Then again, I'm probably being paranoid.

"Exactly. I just hope all the teachers are as cool as Mr. Damasen."

"Damasen?" Jaxon repeats with a startled bark of laughter. "I think that's the first time I've ever heard anyone refer to him as cool."

"Right?" Flint interjects. "I told her the same thing. The man's a monster."

Jaxon doesn't answer him. In fact, he doesn't even *look* at him.

Which isn't awkward at all.

"Well, I liked him. I mean, sure, he talks really loudly, but I don't see what the big deal is."

"He's a giant."

"I know, right?" My eyes widen as I picture the architecture teacher. "I think he's the largest person I've ever seen."

"Because he's a *giant*," Jaxon reiterates, and this time it's impossible to miss the emphasis he puts on the last word.

"Wait a minute." I can feel my mind stretching in an effort to internalize what he's saying. "When you say 'giant'...you don't mean 'big human.' You mean..."

"Giant." The remaining coldness melts from his eyes and is replaced by an amused warmth that finally has the tension leaking from my shoulders.

"Like the whole 'Fee-fi-fo-fum, I smell the blood of an Englishman' thing... That kind of giant?"

"More like the I-eat-babies kind of giant, but yeah. I guess the *Jack and the Beanstalk* reference works."

"Really?" I shake my head as I try to wrap my mind around this new revelation.

"Seriously, Grace," Flint reiterates. "Damasen's a giant. Has a whole stack of bones from problem students in his apartment to prove it."

My head whips around to Flint. *"What?"*

"But don't worry," he continues. "Foster doesn't let him eat any of the good students, so you should be fine."

Flint puts a valiant effort into keeping a straight face as I stare at him in horror, but in the end, he can't do it. He starts to grin, but the moment I narrow my eyes at him, the grin turns into a full-blown belly laugh.

"Oh my God. You should have seen your face." He glances at Jaxon like he wants to share the joke, but Jaxon still won't even look at him. What seems like sadness creeps into Flint's gaze, but he hides it with a big, goofy grin so quickly that I can't help wondering if I saw it at all.

"You're so mean!" I tell Flint and elbow him in the side. "How could you do that to me?" I turn to Jaxon. "Is Damasen even really a giant?"

"Yes, he's a giant. But no, he doesn't eat people." He pauses, then finally glances at Flint. "Anymore."

"Anymore?" I recoil in horror, at least until I see a tiny gleam in the corner of Jaxon's eye. "Oh my God! *That* was totally uncool. Why are you two messing with me like that?"

"I thought that was my job as your boyfriend," Jaxon tells me, but he's smiling when he says it.

"To freak me out?"

"To tease you." He reaches up, wraps one of my curls around his finger.

"Pretty sure he's just looking to make a point, Grace." Flint drapes a nonchalant arm around my shoulders and gives Jaxon a look that even I know is provoking as hell. "He wasn't happy to find out you might let me take you for a ride."

"Flint!" My mouth drops open for the second time in as many minutes. "Why would you say it like that?" I whirl to Jaxon. "He means dragon. I might ride his dragon!"

Flint waggles his brows. "Exactly."

I'm so embarrassed by my unintentional double entendre that I'm sure my face is beet red. "Flint! Stop!"

I don't have a chance to get him to clarify, though, because quick as a lightning strike, Jaxon lashes out...and punches Flint right in the mouth.

13

Sucker Punch Me
One More Time

For several long seconds, the whole world seems to go in slow motion.

Flint's head slams back on his neck, so hard that he stumbles away several steps.

In the meantime, Jaxon lowers his arm and tilts his head just a little, eyes narrowed on Flint while he waits to see what his former best friend decides to do.

And I just stand there in the middle of the two of them, head swiveling back and forth as I try to figure out what I'm supposed to do next. Yell at Jaxon? Yell at Flint? Walk away and let the two of them kill each other because, seriously? Testosterone, ugh.

Before I can make a decision one way or the other, Flint rights himself. I hold my breath, expecting him to launch at Jaxon right here in the middle of the hallway. But, as usual, he surprises me. Instead of lashing out with hands or fists or fire, he just reaches up and rubs the blood off his lower lip as he stares Jaxon down, a wicked gleam in his eyes that I can't quite identify.

And when he does finally speak, his words are as unexpected as the rest of his reaction. "You surprise me, Vega. You never used to be one to go for the sucker punch."

Jaxon just raises an eyebrow. "Perhaps you should look up that definition, Montgomery. It's not a sucker punch when you know it's coming. And deliberately provoke it."

Flint laughs, but he doesn't look away. Neither does Jaxon, who matches him look for look. There are so many undercurrents between these two big guys, I feel like I might get sucked under, too. I stand here, trying to understand what's really going on, what I missed. Because I definitely missed something. And then I decide that I don't actually care. If the two of them want to go around beating their chests and each other, I'm not going to stop them. But I'm sure as hell not going to watch, either.

"You know what? While you two figure out whatever this is"—I wave an arm back and forth between them—"I'm going to go finish my assignment. I'll find you later to return your phone, Flint."

I turn to walk away without saying anything specific to Jaxon, which apparently is what finally gets his attention. He catches up with me and stops my indignant march by wrapping his arm around my waist and pulling me in to his side. "You don't need to borrow his phone anymore," he tells me, lips against my ear.

It's the wrong thing to say to me right now, and the look I give him says exactly that. "I'm borrowing his phone, Jaxon, not 'riding his dragon.'" I use exaggerated air quotes to highlight just how ridiculous this whole thing is. "It's no big deal."

Jaxon sighs. "I don't care if you use Flint's phone or not. I just thought you might want to use your own instead." He uses his free hand to pull a phone from the front pocket of his backpack, then holds it out to me.

I look from him to the phone and back again. "That's not my phone. Mine is in a beach case, and it…" I stop talking as the truth hits me. "Wait a minute. Are you saying you bought me a new phone?"

He gives me an "obviously" kind of look.

"When? I've been trying to figure out how to find one when we live in the middle of nowhere, and you not only managed to get me one in an hour, you did it while you were taking a midterm? How is that even possible?"

He shrugs. "I don't know. I've been here longer? I know all the tricks?"

"Obviously. But you could have just taught me your trick. Then I could have gotten my own phone."

"I don't mind buying you a phone, Grace. Consider it a welcome-home present."

"You already got me a welcome-home present. You." I rest my head on his shoulder, bury my nose against his strong, warm throat as I try to figure out what I want to say. He still smells like oranges and fresh water, and as I breathe him in, it calms the anxiety in my stomach that I didn't even know was there.

"I guess I don't want you to feel like you've got to buy me things. Because you don't." I pull away just enough to look into his eyes. "You know that, right?"

He shakes his head, gives me a confused look. "O-kay."

Flint is still within earshot—and probably watching us walk away—so Jaxon pulls me into an alcove a few feet ahead. "What brought this on?"

I search for the right words as it strikes me again how little we actually know each other. "I wasn't raised to spend money like you. The pendant and now—" I glance down at the phone still in his hand. "A brand-new, latest-edition iPhone. It's a lot, and I just don't want you to think I'm with you because of what you can buy me."

"There's a lot to unpack in that sentence, so I'm going to need a couple of minutes to unravel it all. But first—" He slips the new phone into my jacket pocket, then takes Flint's out of my unresisting hand and leans out of the alcove into the hallway again.

"Hey, Montgomery!" He waits until Flint turns to look at Jaxon with an expectant expression on his face and yells, "Think fast," as he tosses the phone to him in a perfect, curving arc. Flint flips him off even as he catches it, which makes Jaxon laugh.

I swear, I'm never going to understand these two.

He's still laughing when he turns back to me, and for a moment, I can't help thinking about the boy I met four months ago. He never laughed, he never smiled, and he definitely didn't joke around. He hid his heart behind a scowl and his scar behind his too-long hair, and now look at him.

I'm not vain enough to think I'm responsible for all of it, but I'm grateful that I got to play a part in pulling him out of the darkness. In saving Jaxon as much as he's saved me.

"Okay, now, back to what you were saying," Jaxon tells me as we continue walking and make the turn that will take us to the entryway. "First of all, this probably sounds incredibly douchey, but it is what it is. Money isn't something I spend a lot of time thinking about. I've lived a long time and I've got a lot of it and that's just the way it is. And honestly, you may not think so, but I've been really restrained so far."

I reach into my pocket and pull out the thousand-dollar-plus phone he just gave me. "This is restrained?"

"You have no idea." The little half shrug he gives me is all kinds of sexy. "I'd buy you the world if you'd let me."

I start to make a joke that he already has, but the look on his face is too serious for that. As is the way he reaches down and clutches my hand like it's a lifeline. Then again, I hold on to him the exact same way, this boy who makes me feel all the things, all the time.

"Jaxon…"

"Yeah?"

"Nothing." I shake my head. "Just Jaxon."

He smiles, and as our eyes meet, I swear I forget how to breathe. I don't actually pull it together until he says, "Come on, let's finish taking some of those pictures before the bell rings."

"Oh, right. The pictures."

"You sound so enthusiastic." He shoots me the side-eye as we walk around a corner, and both his brows are raised. "They are important, right? I mean, you weren't going to ride Flint for some other reason, were you?"

"What?" I whip my head around, ready to tell him off, only to find him silently laughing at me. "Ugh. You did that on purpose."

"Did what?" he asks, all innocent except for the wicked glint in his eyes that he doesn't even try to hide.

"You're a—" I try to pull away, but he wraps an arm around my shoulder and holds me tight against him. Which leaves me with only one course of action: I elbow him right in the stomach.

Of course, he doesn't even flinch. He just laughs harder and answers, "I'm a…?"

"I don't even know anymore. I just…" I shake my head, throw up my hands. "I don't even know what I'm supposed to do with you."

"Sure you do."

He leans in for a kiss, and it should feel like the most natural thing in the world. I'm in love with this boy, he's in love with me, and I positively adore kissing him. But the second his mouth gets within range, my entire body stiffens of its own accord. My heart starts beating fast—but not in a good way—and my stomach starts to churn.

I try to hide it, but this is Jaxon, and he's always seen more than I want him to. So instead of kissing me the way I know he wants to, he shifts a little and presses a soft, sweet kiss to my cheek.

"I'm sorry," I tell him. I hate what's going on inside me, hate that we can't just pick up where we left off four months ago.

I hate even more that I'm the one driving this wedge between us when Jaxon has been nothing but wonderful.

"Don't be. You've been through a lot. I can wait."

"That's the thing. You shouldn't have to."

"Grace." He brings a hand up to cup my cheek. "You spent one hundred and twenty-one days frozen in stone to keep all of us safe. If you think I can't wait as long as it takes for you to feel comfortable being back with me again, then you really don't have a clue how much I love you."

My breath catches in my throat, along with my heart and, quite possibly, my soul. "Jaxon." I can barely get his name past the huge lump right above my vocal cords.

But he just shakes his head. "I've waited an eternity for you, Grace. I can wait a little longer."

I lean in to kiss him, and just like that, the sweetness between us turns to something else. Something that has my palms sweating and fear coating my throat.

14

She-Nanigans

My stomach bottoms out, tears well up in my eyes, and I forget how to breathe.

Because it's not how long Jaxon will wait that I'm worried about. It's whether or not I'll ever be ready for him again. Whether I'll ever find my way back to this beautiful boy who stole my heart so easily. So completely.

And I can't help but wonder exactly what it is inside me that's making me feel this way. Sure, there've been times before when I heard a voice, warning me of danger, telling me what to do in situations where I was completely out of my depth. Situations that I'd never before imagined being in.

Back then, I'd been so sure that the voice was just random thoughts, things picked up on subconsciously that my conscious mind hadn't quite registered until that moment. But now I wonder, could it be my gargoyle voice? Flint mentioned once that his dragon was sentient, that it had thoughts separate from his human form. Is it the same with gargoyles?

Out of nowhere, an irrational anger wells up inside me. At the gargoyle inside me. At Lia and Hudson. At fate itself for orchestrating everything that's brought us to this point.

I open my mouth to say I don't know what—something, anything that might explain to him the weird feelings rioting inside me—but he shakes his head before I can get so much as a word out.

"It's okay."

"It's not—"

"It is," he answers firmly. "You've been back all of four hours. Why don't you cut yourself some slack?"

Before I can say anything else, the chimes go off again.

Seconds later, students in purple-and-black uniforms flood the common areas. They give us a wide berth—Jaxon's with me, so of course they do—but that doesn't mean they aren't staring at us. Aren't whispering behind their hands as they pass by, gawking at the two of us like we're mannequins on display.

Jaxon reluctantly pulls away. "What's your next class?" he asks as he drops my hand.

"Art. I was going to run up to my room and change so I could take the trail outside."

"Good." He steps back, his dark eyes filled with understanding. "Let me know when you do plan on taking the shortcut. You shouldn't have to do that alone. At least not the first time."

I start to tell him it's no big deal but stop myself. Because it *is* a big deal.

And because I don't want to go down there alone right now, don't want to walk by the doorway that leads to the place where I almost became an actual human sacrifice, courtesy of the murderous Lia and her even more murderous boyfriend, Hudson.

So instead of protesting, I just say, "Thank you," and stretch up on my tippy-toes to give Jaxon a kiss on the cheek.

A huge screech sounds from several feet away that startles us apart.

"AHHHHHH! GRAAAAAAAAAAAAAACE!"

Because I'd know that screech anywhere, I shoot Jaxon a rueful smile and take a couple of steps back, right before my cousin, Macy, slams straight into my side.

She wraps her arms around me like a limpet and practically jumps up and down as she squeals, "You're really here! I wouldn't let myself believe it until I saw you! I've been looking for you *everywhere*!"

Jaxon winks at me and mouths, *Text me later*, before moving back into the passing horde.

I nod as I turn to embrace Macy, even going so far as to do the up-and-down tippy-toe/jump thing with her. And as she wraps me in a giant hug, I can't help but be grateful for her. Can't help but think just how much I've missed her, even though I didn't know it until right this second.

"How are you? Are you okay? How are you feeling? You look good. What class do you have right now? Can you skip it? I've got about a gallon of Cherry Garcia ice cream squirreled away in my dad's freezer—I've been stockpiling it for weeks, just waiting for you to come back!"

She pulls away and grins at me, then leans back in and hugs me again even more enthusiastically. "I'm so glad you're back, Grace. I've missed you so much!"

"I've missed you, too, Mace," I say as she finally lets me go. And because I have no idea which of her eight million questions/comments to start with, I say the first thing that pops into my head. "You changed your hair."

"What? Oh yeah." She grins at me as she runs a hand through her short pink pixie cut. "I did it a few weeks ago when I was missing you. Kind of an homage, you know?"

Of course it's an homage, because she still thinks hot pink is my favorite color... "It looks fabulous," I tell her. Because it does. And because she's pretty much the greatest cousin and friend a girl could ever wish for.

"So what class do you have next?" she asks, tugging me across the foyer toward the staircase. "Because I think you should blow it off and come hang in the room with me."

"Don't you have a class now, too?"

"Yes, but it's just a review for the midterm on Friday." She waves a hand in the air. "I can skip it to hang with my favorite cousin."

"Yeah, but your favorite cousin has art right now, and I don't think I should skip it. I need to find out if there's something I can do to make up for everything I missed." I eye her ruefully. "I am not prepared to repeat my senior year."

"If you ask me, you shouldn't have to make up anything. I mean, hello. Saving the world should get you straight A's, like, forever."

I laugh, because it's impossible not to when Macy is on a roll. And she is very definitely on a roll right now. "I wouldn't exactly call it saving the world."

"You got rid of Hudson, didn't you? It's close enough."

My stomach tightens. That's the thing. I don't know if I got rid of Hudson or not. I don't know if he's dead or off plotting his next act of world domination or trapped somewhere in between the two. And until I do know, I feel really shady letting anyone think I did something that might have helped "save the world."

For all I know, I made everything worse.

"I have no idea where Hudson is right now," I confess eventually.

Her gaze widens, but she catches herself and plasters a smile back on her face. "He's not here, and that's good enough for me." She hugs me again, a little less enthusiastically this time. "So what do you say? Cherry Garcia in the room?"

I glance at the new phone Jaxon gave me, note that I only have about fifteen minutes to make it to art at this point. And I do want to go, despite how tempting it is to crash in our room and have Macy fill me in on everything that's happened.

"How about we compromise?" I say, shoving my phone back into my pocket. "I go to art, you go to your last class, and we meet back in the room at five for ice cream?"

She quirks one brow at me. "You're going to show up, right? You're not going to blow me off for the resident vampire in chief?"

I burst out laughing all over again, because of course I do. How can I not when Macy is at her ridiculous best? "I'm going to tell Jaxon you called him that."

"Go ahead." She rolls her eyes. "Just make sure you do it *after* Cherry Garcia. I have so much to catch you up on! Plus, I want to hear all about what it's like to be a gargoyle!"

I sigh. "Yeah, me too."

"Oh, right. Dad told me you were having memory issues." Her face falls, but her frown lasts only a few seconds before she shrugs it off. "Fine, you can tell me all about what it was like to be reunited with your mate." Her eyes take on a dreamy cast. "You're so lucky to have found Jaxon so young. Most of us have to wait much longer."

Mate. The word goes off like a gong inside me, reverberating into every corner of my being. I haven't actually thought about it since I've been back. But now that Macy has brought it up, I have about a million questions surrounding it. I mean, I know Jaxon is my mate, but it's always been a really abstract thing. I'd just learned the term before I became a gargoyle and hadn't really had time to think about it before I ended up frozen in stone.

Because the idea of being so far behind the curve makes me uncomfortable, I decide to ignore the word—and my feelings about it—until I actually have time to talk to Macy and Jaxon. Or at least time to run to the library and look it up myself.

"I've got to go," I tell Macy, and this time, I'm the one to hug her. "I'm going to be late for art as it is."

"Okay, fine." Her answering hug is as enthusiastic as always. "But I will be in the room—with ice cream—at exactly four fifty-nine. I expect you to be there."

"Scout's honor." I hold my hand up in what I think is a close facsimile of the three-fingered pledge.

Macy isn't impressed, though. She just shakes her head and laughs. "Don't let Jaxon talk you into any shenanigans between now and then."

"Shenanigans?" I repeat, because just when I think Macy can't get more ridiculous—and fabulous—she does something to change my mind.

"You know exactly what I mean." She lifts her brows up and down suggestively. "But if you want, I can spell it out for you in the middle of the foyer here. You shouldn't let Jaxon take you up to his tower to have his—"

"Okay, I got it!" I tell her as my cheeks burn.

But she said the last loud enough to be heard halfway to Jaxon's tower, and as a result, there are a whole lot of snickers going on around us. "Art. I'm going to art. Now."

But as I make my way to my room to change and then hustle out the side door into the frigid March air, I can't help but wonder if Jaxon's even going to try to "shenanigan" me again. And what about my gargoyle is so against it.

15

Let's All Play Find the Homicidal Maniac

Art goes really well—Dr. MacCleary waives the first two assignments of the semester and gets me right to work on my third—a painting that reflects who I am inside. And since art has always been the thing that helps me figure out the world, it's definitely an assignment I can get behind.

Normally, I'd spend a bunch of time planning out the composition and light source, but after an hour of sketching a bunch of nonsensical nothingness, I decide, *Screw it.* I pick up a brush and spend the last half an hour of class giving my subconscious free reign on the canvas. What it comes up with—for now—is a swirling dark-blue background that looks a lot like if Van Gogh and Kandinsky had a baby.

Not my usual style, but then neither is dating a vampire and turning into a gargoyle, so...I'm just going to go with it.

At one point, I need to wait and let some of the colors dry a bit, so I grab my laptop from my backpack and log in to my wireless-provider account and activate my new phone. Minutes later, *dozens* of texts flood my screen.

I frantically begin scrolling through the texts from Heather that start with "How're you doing?" then move on to more concerned texts to a final, sad, "I hope you haven't texted back cuz you're so busy loving your new school. Just know I'm here if you ever need a friend. And I'd love a ping just to know you're alive."

I am officially the worst friend ever. My hands are shaking a little as I finally send a much-needed text to Heather.

Me: OMG I am soooooooo sorry.

Me: Long story. Lost my phone and Alaska shuts down in the winter

Me: Jut got a new one and I'm so sorry. FaceTime this week?

I don't know what more I can say other than, *The shitty friend award clearly goes to me*. I hate that I can't tell her the truth, but I hate the idea of losing her even more. I just hope she texts back when she sees my message.

I put my phone in my backpack and return to my painting, which I think is the beginning of a room or something.

Other than that, art is completely uneventful—and so is the walk back to my dorm room. Thankfully. I mean, yeah, people are still staring at me, but sometime in the last hour and a half, I've decided to take the screw-it approach to more than just my art. So when I pass a group of witches who don't even bother to lower their voices as they talk about me—proof that mean girls really do exist everywhere—I just smile and blow them a kiss.

What do I have to be embarrassed about anyway?

I make it back to my dorm room by 4:31 and figure I'll have ten minutes to start my "Find the Homicidal Maniac" to-do list before Macy gets back, but the second I open the door to our room, I get showered with a spray of confetti.

I shake off the colorful pieces of paper as I close the door behind me, but I'm smart enough to know I'm going to be pulling it out of my curls for the rest of the night—maybe even longer. And still, I can't help grinning at Macy, who is already dressed in a purple tank top and her favorite pair of pajama pants—tie-dyed rainbow, of course. She's cleared off her desk and covered it with a spare sheet (also rainbow), before setting up a smorgasbord of ice cream, Skittles, and Dr Peppers with licorice straws.

"I figured, if we were going to celebrate your return, we were going to do it in style," she tells me with a wink, right before she hits play on her phone and Harry Styles's "Watermelon Sugar" fills the room.

"Dance!" she shouts, and I do, because Macy can get me to do all kinds of things I would never do for anyone else. Plus, the song reminds me so much of my first night at Katmere that I can't resist. It's wild to think that was almost four months ago. Wilder still that it somehow feels so much longer and also way shorter than that.

When the song finally finishes, I kick off my shoes and collapse on my bed.

"Um, I don't think so. It's facial time—I have these new masks I'm dying to try out," Macy says as she grabs my hand and tries to drag me off the bed. When I refuse to budge, she sighs and walks over to the bathroom sink. Then adds over her shoulder, "Come on. One of us *was* solid stone for nearly four months."

"What does that mean?" I ask as a horrible thought occurs to me. "Does being a gargoyle do something to your skin?"

Macy lowers the array of sheet masks she's been studying like they're a map to the Holy Grail. "What makes you think that?"

"I mean, I've seen a lot of Gothic cathedrals in my time. Gargoyles aren't exactly the prettiest creatures."

"Yeah, but you don't look like a monster." If possible, she seems even more confused.

"How would you know? I probably have horns and claws and who knows what else." I shudder at the thought—and at the knowledge that Jaxon saw me like that.

"You do have horns, but they're adorable."

I sit straight up. "Wait. You saw me?"

I don't know why, but I'm a little appalled at that revelation. I mean, did they just leave me on display in the middle of the hallway or something? My breath catches as another horrible thought comes to mind. Does every mean girl in the school have a picture of me on their phone?

"Of course I saw you. You've been in a back room of the library for months, and before that you were in my dad's office."

My shoulders sag in relief. Oh, right. That makes a lot more sense.

I tell myself not to ask, that it doesn't matter. But in the end, curiosity gets the best of me and I can't help myself. "What did I look like?"

"What do you mean? You looked like a gar—" She stops, her eyes narrowing in indignation. "Wait a minute. Are you telling me neither Jaxon nor my dad showed you what you look like as a gargoyle?"

"Of course they didn't show me. How could they when I'm…" I hold up my hands and swivel them around in a demonstration that I'm human and not stone.

"Seriously?" She rolls her eyes. "Do you think I didn't take at least a dozen pics of you? My badass gargoyle cousin? Give me a break."

"Hold on. You actually took *pictures* of me?"

"Of course I did. You're, like, the coolest creature in existence. Why wouldn't I?" She reaches for her phone. "Want to see?"

My stomach flutters a little, butterflies waking up for a reason that has nothing to do with Jaxon or Katmere Academy and everything to do with what might possibly be in that picture. I know I shouldn't get upset about what I look like when it's so not important in the grand scheme of things. But I can't help it. I apparently have *horns*.

"Yeah. Yeah, I really do."

I close my eyes and reach for the phone.

As I do, I take a deep breath, hold it for the count of five, and blow it out slowly.

Then I take another breath and do the same thing.

When I'm finally ready for whatever monstrosity is going to be waiting for me—or as ready as I can be—I open my eyes and stare at my picture.

16

Nothing Wrong with Being a Little Horny

My heart explodes the second I see the picture Macy selected because—holy shit—I really am a gargoyle. I think, up until right now, there was a tiny part of me that didn't believe it.

But there I am, in all my gargoyle glory.

And while I am still totally freaked out by this revelation, even I have to admit, I'm nowhere near as hideous as I was afraid I would be. Thank God.

In fact, as it turns out, me as a gargoyle doesn't look like much of a monster at all. In fact, I look an awful lot like...me. Same long curly hair. Same pointy little chin. Even the same big boobs and ridiculously short stature. It's me...just made of light-gray stone.

I mean, yeah, there are a few additions. Like the short horns at the top of my head that curl back just a little. The giant kick-ass wings that are almost as big as I am. The relatively short claws at the ends of my fingers.

But—and believe me, I look closely—there is *not* a tail. Thank you, universe.

I can deal with the horns. Not happily, but I can deal with them, as long as I don't also have to deal with a tail.

Macy gives me a minute, several minutes actually, before she finally says, "See, you look amazing. Total badass."

"I look like a statue." I raise one brow. "Although I guess I could wait out a fight and win that way. Eventually. Boredom be thy sword."

Macy shrugs as she picks up a can of Dr Pepper and drinks it through a strawberry Twizzler straw. "I'm sure gargoyles have all sorts of cool powers." She waves a hand, and a second Dr Pepper floats across the room to me.

"See?" I pluck my drink out of thin air and take a long sip—also through the Twizzler straw because, while I might be a gargoyle, I'm not a total animal. "You can do cool things like wiggle your fingers and get a full face of makeup. All I can do is—"

"Save the world?"

I roll my eyes. "I'm pretty sure that's a bit of an exaggeration."

"And I'm pretty sure you don't know enough about who and what you are to decide if it's an exaggeration or not. Grace, being a gargoyle—" She breaks off, blows out a long breath, even as she runs a hand through her bizarre pink hair. "Being a gargoyle is, like, the coolest thing ever."

"How would you know? Marise told me there hasn't even been one for a thousand years."

"Exactly! That's what I'm saying. You're one of a kind! Isn't that awesome?"

Not really, no. Being the center of that kind of attention has never exactly been my vibe. But I've come to know Macy—and the current look on her face—well enough to know that there's no use arguing with her about this.

Still, I can't stop myself from saying, "'Awesome' might be a little bit of an exaggeration."

"No, it's not. Everyone thinks so."

"And by everyone, you mean you and your dad?" I joke.

"No, I mean *everyone*! They've all seen you and—" She breaks off, suddenly becoming incredibly interested in her soda.

Which seems like it bodes badly for me. Very, very badly. "Exactly how many people have seen me, Macy? You said I was in your dad's office and then tucked away in the library."

"You were! But you've got to understand: you were frozen in stone for almost *four months*. Dad and Jaxon nearly lost their minds with worry."

"I thought you said being a gargoyle is cool."

"Being a gargoyle *is* cool. Being stuck as a gargoyle…not so much. They tried everything to get you to turn back—and 'everything' meant consulting as many different experts around the world as they could find. And the experts all wanted to see you, because they didn't believe you were a gargoyle. They thought you'd been cursed by a witch or a siren or something. And then, when word got out that you really were a gargoyle…well, they all demanded to see you before they would consult."

I get up and start to pace the room. "So, what? They all just flew to Alaska to get an in-person chance to examine me?"

"Of course they did!" She shoots me an exasperated look. "I feel like you're not fully comprehending the whole only-one-in-existence thing. The experts would have flown to the moon, if that's where they had to go to see you. Not to mention, Jaxon and my dad would have flown them to the moon *themselves* if they thought it would help you."

I get that. It even makes a twisted kind of sense to me. And yet I still can't get over feeling squicked out at people I don't know examining me when I was totally out of it. And Jaxon and my uncle allowing it.

It's not even that I don't understand why they did it. I think about if my parents had survived that car accident and were in comas or something. If they needed medical care, I would have done anything I could to make sure they got it.

Not going to lie, though. It just feels like one more thing I've lost. And one more thing I couldn't afford to lose.

I stop pacing and sink back onto my bed in defeat.

"Grace?" Macy comes over to sit next to me, and for the first time since we ran into each other in the foyer, she looks concerned. "Are you okay? I know this is a lot, but I swear, it's a good thing. You've just got to give it a chance."

"What about my memory?" I swallow the lump in my throat, because I don't cry in front of people, even my best friends. "What if it never comes back? I know I was turned to stone, and maybe the reason I don't remember anything is because there's nothing to remember."

She shakes her head. "I don't believe that."

"That's just it. Neither do I." I start to speak half a dozen times, then stop myself just as many because nothing I'm going to say feels right.

Macy's quiet for a moment before she reaches over to squeeze my hand. "Let's just take it one day at a time for a couple of days. See what shakes loose as you settle into a routine. I promise, it's going to be all right." She smiles encouragingly. "Okay?"

I nod, the knot that's been in my stomach for hours finally beginning to dissolve. "Okay."

"Good." She gives me a wicked little grin. "Now, let's put on some of these face masks. I'll fill you in on the gossip you missed, and you can tell me all about what it's like to be mated."

17

Tunnel Vision

I can't sleep.

I don't know if it's because I've spent the last four months sleeping or if it's because of everything that's happened today. Maybe it's a combination of both.

Probably it's a combination of both.

Losing your memory will do that to a girl. So will finding out that the boy you're in love with, your *mate*, is the boy—the man—you're going to spend the rest of your life with.

Macy was all excited about it, going on and on about how lucky I am to have found Jaxon when I'm seventeen years old. I don't have to go through jerks like Cam (apparently, she and Cam broke up, badly, while I was busy being a statue) while I wait, and I don't have to worry about never finding my mate (apparently, this happens more frequently than it should). I have a mate and, according to Macy, that's pretty much the best thing I could ask for, better certainly than being human again. Better even than getting my memory back.

Mates are forever, after all, while almost nothing else is—or so she told me over and over and over again last night.

And I get it. I do. I love Jaxon. I have pretty much from the beginning. But is that because I love him or because of the mating bond, which supposedly has been in place from the moment we first touched?

Which means, what? That first day, near the chess table, when he was being so awful to me and I rested my hand against his scarred cheek, that's when we mated? Before either of us had a clue about the other? Before either of us even *liked* each other?

I swallow a lump in my throat. Before either of us even had a choice?

For now, I refuse to focus on the fact that he knew from that first touch but never told me. Once again, I file that tidbit in my "Shit I Don't Have Time for Today" folder—which I'm beginning to think might need its own filing cabinet before this mess is done.

Instead, I try to wrap my head around having a mate in the first place. I mean, I get it in concept. I've read enough urban fantasy and YA novels to understand the mating bond is the best thing that can happen to two people. But to go from that to understanding it as a real thing that has happened between Jaxon and me... It feels like a lot.

Then again, all of this feels like a lot.

Too much for me to sleep, anyway. Maybe too much for me to handle at all. I don't know.

I grab my phone and notice Heather texted me back earlier. I let out a slow breath as I read her message. She wants to FaceTime later next week, and I quickly shoot off a reply that it's a date. Next, I spend a few minutes thumbing through a news site, catching up on everything I missed in the world the last four months. Turns out I missed a lot. Eventually, though, I grow bored with the news and set my phone on my chest and stare at the ceiling.

But I can't just lie here all night letting the gargoyle thing, the memory thing, and the mating thing all run through my head on a continuous loop.

I'd watch TV, but I don't want to disturb Macy. It's late, close to two in the morning, and she has a midterm tomorrow. Which means I need to get out of here.

I roll off the bed, trying to make as little noise as possible, then grab a hoodie from my closet—the castle can be cold and drafty at night. Next, I slip on my favorite pair of daisy-patterned Vans and tiptoe to the door as quietly as I possibly can.

I have a moment's hesitation when I go to pull open the door—the last time I wandered the castle alone in the middle of the night, I nearly got tossed outside in the snow. I definitely do *not* want that to happen again. Mate or no mate, I can't go around expecting Jaxon to rescue me whenever I get into trouble.

Not that I imagine he'll be all that thrilled to rescue me anyway tonight. Especially since I canceled my plans to meet up with him, claiming exhaustion.

But things are different now than they were four months ago. No one's got any reason to try to kill me, for one. And for another, even if they wanted to, no one would ever deliberately go after Jaxon Vega's mate. Especially not after Jaxon nearly drained Cole for trying to drop a chandelier on me.

Plus, I'm a gargoyle now. If someone tries to hurt me, I can always just turn to stone. As exciting as that sounds. Of course, I have absolutely no idea how to do that. But that's a problem for another day, already filed away.

Before I can reconsider, I'm out of my dorm room and down the hall to…I'm not sure where yet. Except my feet seem to know what my brain doesn't, because it isn't long before I'm standing at the opening to the narrow hallway that leads to the tunnel entrance.

Part of me thinks I'm ridiculous for going in here alone—or at all, for that matter. Just this afternoon, I avoided heading this way with Flint because of all the bad shit that happened the last time I was down here.

But I'm not dressed to go outside, and suddenly the only thing I really want to be doing is working on my art piece. The only way to get to the art room right now is to go through the tunnels, so…it looks like I'm about to get up close and personal with the site of my almost demise.

Figuring the best way to get through the tunnels is just to get through them—no side trips, no detours—I make my way down the ever-narrowing, ever-darkening hallway as fast as I possibly can. My heart is pounding in my chest, but I don't let it slow me down.

I finally make it to the dungeon-like cells, with their creaking hinges and ancient chains. Since I'm alone and there's no one around to rush me, I let myself stop and look them over for a minute. At night, alone, they're even creepier than they are during the day. And they're plenty creepy then.

There are five cells in a row, each one equipped with an iron-barred door. Each door has an ancient padlock threaded through its latch bar, but each of the padlocks is closed (with no keys in sight) so there's no chance of anyone getting locked in the cells by accident... or, for that matter, not by accident.

The cells themselves are made of giant stones, each one about the width of a dragon's foot (or at least the width of Flint's foot, since he's the only dragon I've ever seen), and I wonder if there's a reason for that or if my imagination is just running wild. Either way, the stones are black and craggy and more than a little ominous-looking.

Then again, everything about the cells is ominous-looking—especially the three sets of shackles driven deep into the wall. Judging by the age of this place and the condition of the padlocks themselves, I would expect the shackles to be in pretty rough shape, too.

But they're not. Instead, they're a blindingly bright silver, free of any rust or sign of age. Which, not going to lie, makes me wonder how old they are. And why on earth Katmere Academy—which is run by my uncle, for God's sake—might have need of shackles thick enough to hold a rampaging dinosaur. Or, you know, a dragon, werewolf, or vampire...

Because thinking about it takes me along a disturbing path, one I'm not ready to go down tonight, I tell myself there must be a reasonable explanation—one that *doesn't* involve locking students up in a freezing dungeon for who knows how long.

Figuring I'm going to lose my nerve if I stay here any longer debating this, I take a deep breath and step into the fifth cell, which is the only one with the extra door that leads to the tunnels.

As I do, I brush a hand over the padlock on the door, just to make sure it's securely locked and no werewolf can come along and trap me in the tunnels.

Except, the moment my fingers brush against the lock, it clicks open…and falls out of the door latch straight into my hands.

Not quite the confidence builder I was looking for, especially considering I know it was locked. I know it.

Totally creeped out now, I slip the lock into the pocket of my hoodie—there's no way I'm putting it on the door until I'm safely back from the art cottage and heading to bed. Then I bend over and plug in the code Flint taught me for the tunnel door all those months ago.

I enter the last digit and the door swings open, just like it has every other time I've gone down here. But every other time I've been with someone else, and somehow that's made it less creepy.

Unless I concentrate on the fact that two of the four people I've been in the tunnels with literally tried to kill me here. Then it seems like pretty good odds that I'm by myself.

Deciding I either need to stop freaking myself out or go back to bed, I walk through the door. And try to ignore that all the candles in the sconces and chandeliers are still lit.

Then again, it's a good thing they are. Because it's not like I can just flip a switch and flood the place with light. Even though I want to. The bone chandeliers look a million times creepier now that I know they're actually real bones and not some cool student-made art project.

For a second, I think about forgetting the whole thing. About heading back to my room and to hell with the tunnels. Staring at the ceiling above my bed has to be better than making my way through Katmere's very own version of the Paris Catacombs on my own.

But the need to paint has been growing exponentially in me since I left my room a little while ago, until I can practically feel the paint brush in my hand. Until I can practically smell the pungent oil of the paints on my canvas.

Besides, if I let these tunnels—and the memories they hold—run me out of here now, I don't know if I'll ever again work up the nerve to come back.

With that thought in mind, I pull out my phone and swipe open the music app I downloaded earlier. I choose one of my happy playlists—Summertime (Un)Sadness—and "I'm Born to Run" fills up the silence around me. It's hard to be scared when American Authors are singing about how they want to live their life like it's never enough. Talk about an anthem tailor-made for this situation.

So in the end, I do what they suggest. I run. And not some little jog, either. I run my ass off, ignoring how the altitude makes my lungs feel like they want to explode.

Ignoring everything except the need to get through this damn creep-fest as fast as I possibly can.

I don't slow down until I'm running at a slant up the tunnel that leads to the art cottage. Once I finally make it to the unlocked door, I shove it and practically trip over my feet in my haste to get inside.

The first thing I do is reach for the light switch just to the left of the door. The second thing I do is slam the door shut as hard as I can and flip the lock. I know Dr. MacCleary says she always keeps the door open in case one of her students is inspired, but as far as I know, she didn't just narrowly escape being a human sacrifice. I figure that gives me at least a little bit of leeway.

Besides, if someone else is actually ridiculous enough to want in here tonight, they can knock. As long as I know for sure they aren't trying to kill me, I'll be happy to let them in.

Sure, maybe I'm being paranoid. But I wasn't paranoid *enough* four months ago, and all that got me was a vacation I can't remember and my very own set of horns.

That's not a mistake I'm going to make a second time.

After spending a minute just catching my breath, I grab the paints

I need and head into the classroom. I've already got a really clear idea of what I want the finished background to look like—and what I need to do to get it there.

With any luck, the monsters of Katmere Academy will hold off trying to kill me long enough for me to get something done. Then again, the night is young.

18

I Think I Had
Amnesia Once...
or Twice

"Come on, Grace, wake up. You're going to miss breakfast if you don't get up soon."

"Sleepy," I mumble as I roll onto my stomach and away from Macy's annoyingly cheerful voice.

"I know you're sleepy, but you have to get up. Class starts in forty minutes and you haven't even had a shower yet."

"No shower." I grab my comforter and pull it over my head, making sure to keep my eyes closed so I won't be blinded by the hot-pink fabric. Or give Macy the idea that I'm actually awake. Because I very definitely am *not*.

"Graaaaaace," she whines, tugging on the comforter as hard as she can. But I've got a death grip on the thing, and I'm not about to let it go anytime soon. "You promised Jaxon we'd meet him in the dining hall in five minutes. You *have* to get up."

It's the mention of Jaxon that eventually breaks through my dazed stupor and allows Macy to pull my comforter down. Cold air rushes against my face, and I make a half-hearted grab for the covers, still without opening my eyes.

Macy laughs. "I feel like our roles are suddenly reversed here. I'm the one who's supposed to be hard to get out of bed."

I make another lunge for the comforter and this time end up

grabbing onto a corner of it. "Give me," I plead, so tired I can't imagine actually getting out of bed. "Gimme, gimme, gimme."

"No way. The History of Witchcraft waits for no woman. Now, move it." She gives one more mighty yank, and the covers go flying off my bed completely.

I jackknife into a sitting position in response, prepared to beg if I have to. But before I can even get a sad-sounding *pleeeeeeease* out, Macy is grabbing on to my shoulders.

"Oh my God, Grace! Are you all right?" She sounds near tears as she frantically runs her hands over my shoulders and back and down my arms.

Her obvious panic clears the last of the fogginess from my brain. My eyes fly open, and I focus on her face, which looks even more terrified than she sounds.

"What's wrong?" I ask, glancing down at myself to see what's got her so worked up, then freeze the second I see the blood drenching the front of my purple hoodie. My heart is suddenly pounding in my throat as panic seizes my breath.

"Oh my God!" I jump out of bed. "Oh my God!"

"Stop moving! I need to see!" she tells me, grabbing on to the bottom of my hoodie and pulling it over my head in one fell swoop, leaving my tank underneath. "Where does it hurt?"

"I don't know." I pause, try to take stock of what's going on in my body, but nothing hurts. At least nothing that should warrant this kind of blood loss.

Another quick glance down shows me that my tank is solid white— no blood. Which means… "It's not mine."

"It's not yours," Macy says at the exact same time.

"Then whose is it?" I whisper as we stare at each other in horror.

She blinks up at me. "Shouldn't *you* know that?"

"I should," I agree as I still pat my arms and stomach for soreness. "But I don't."

"You don't know how you're covered in *blood*?" she asks

incredulously.

I swallow. Hard. "I have absolutely, positively no idea how it happened."

I rack my brain, trying to remember walking back from the art cottage last night, but I just draw a blank. There's not even a giant wall, like what happens with the rest of the memories I can't access. It's just…empty. There's absolutely nothing there.

Which isn't terrifying at all.

"So what do we do now?" Macy asks in a voice smaller than I've ever heard from her.

I shake my head. "You mean you don't know?"

She looks at me like my head just spun around three times and I'm one second away from spitting pea soup. "Why would I know?"

"I don't know. I guess… I mean—" I bring my hands up to shove hair out of my face, then freeze as I realize they're streaked with blood, too. And so are my forearms. I'm not going to panic. I'm not going to panic. "What do you normally do when things like this happen here?"

Now she's looking at me like I actually *did* spit pea soup. "Um, I hate to break it to you, Grace, but things like this don't happen here—at least not when you aren't around."

I narrow my eyes at her. "Fantastic. That makes me feel so much better, thanks."

She lifts her hand in a "what do you want me to say?" gesture.

Before I can answer her, my phone dings with a long series of text messages. We both turn to stare at it as one.

"You should get that," Macy whispers after a second.

"I know." Yet I make no move toward my desk, where it's currently charging.

"Do you want me to get it for you?" she asks when it dings three more times.

"I don't know."

Macy sighs, but she doesn't argue with me. Probably because she is at least as afraid as I am to find out who's texting me. And why.

But we can't hide forever, and when a third string of messages comes in, I bite the bullet and say, "Fine, get it, please. I don't want to…" This time I'm the one who holds my hands up—my bloody hands.

I want to wash off, am dying to wash off, but every police procedural I've ever seen is running through my head right now. If I do wash up, is that destroying evidence? Will it make me look more guilty?

I mean, it sounds awful, but I am currently covered in someone else's blood and have no idea how it happened. Call me pessimistic, but it sounds like a road map to prison to me.

And I know I should be concerned about who I might have hurt but, well, sue me that I don't feel bad if someone attacked me in the tunnels and I fought back. I have rights.

I groan. Why did that sound like I was practicing for my defense already?

"Oh no," Macy says after swiping onto my messaging app. "They're from Jaxon. Oh *no*…"

"What's wrong?" I demand, forgetting about evidence as I all but leap across the room. "Did I hurt him? Is this his blood?"

"No, you didn't hurt him."

Relief whips through me so fast that I go a little light-headed. Still, it's obvious from her face that Jaxon had something awful to tell me. "What?" I finally whisper when the silence between us gets to be too much to bear. "What happened?"

She doesn't look at me, instead scrolling up and down as though she wants to be certain she read the messages correctly. "He texted to apologize for missing breakfast. He's in my father's office."

"Why is he there?" I ask, dread pooling in my stomach even before Macy looks up from the phone with haunted eyes.

"Because Cole was attacked last night. It looks like he'll be okay after a day or two in the infirmary, but…" She takes a deep breath. "Someone drained him of a whole lot of blood, Grace."

19

Caught Red-Handed

"Cole?" I whisper, my hand going to my throat at the mention of the alpha werewolf.

Macy answers grimly, "Cole."

"I couldn't have." I glance down at my blood-streaked hands with a new kind of horror. "I wouldn't have."

I think, until this very moment, I was holding out for this being some kind of horrible feeding accident with Jaxon. Like, maybe this actually *was* my blood because I'd gone to his room last night and he'd bitten into an artery or something and then sealed it up like he did last time, after the flying-glass incident.

I mean, of course, if I'm being reasonable, I know Jaxon would *never* be careless enough to bite into an artery of mine to begin with. He definitely wouldn't leave me lying in bed, drenched in my own blood. And he sure as hell wouldn't drop me into a sleep so deep that trying to get out of it felt like what I imagine surfacing from a coma would. But still, I think I would rather have all those things be true than to find out that this is another person's blood I'm covered in. And that I might have been the one spilling it.

"I know you wouldn't do anything to Cole," Macy soothes, but the look in her eyes says otherwise.

Then again, the look in my eyes probably does, too. Because while

I can't imagine under what circumstances I would decide to attack an alpha werewolf—and then actually win the fight—I also can't deny that it is a hell of a coincidence that I woke up covered in blood the morning after Cole lost a lot of blood in an attack. Oh, and since it happened my first night back, that only ups the coincidence factor.

For me to try to believe that I had nothing to do with what happened to Cole—when even Macy says things like this don't happen at Katmere Academy—involves telling myself a lie of massive proportions.

And I'm a terrible liar.

"We need to call your dad," I whisper. "We need to tell him everything."

Macy hesitates, then says on a breath, "I know." She makes no move to call her dad or anyone else, though. "But what are we going to say to him? This is serious, Grace."

"I know it is! That's why we have to tell him." My mind is racing from one possible scenario to another as I pace the room.

"You can't beat an alpha werewolf," Macy says. "That's why this doesn't make any sense."

"I know it doesn't. Why would I hurt Cole in the first place? And if I did, why can't I remember anything?" I walk to the sink. Evidence or no evidence, now that I know for sure that this isn't my blood, I can't stand having it on me for one more second.

"Okay, so let's be logical about this," Macy says, coming up behind me cautiously. "What *do* you remember about last night? Do you even remember leaving the room?"

"Yeah, of course," I answer as I douse myself in soap and water. "I couldn't sleep, so I left the room around two."

I glance in the mirror and realize that there are a couple of drops of blood on my cheek as well. And that's when I almost lose it. That's when I almost forget about trying to be calm and am tempted to just scream my goddamn head off.

But screaming will only draw attention to the mess I'm in,

attention neither Macy, nor I, is currently equipped to deal with. So I force myself to swallow down my horror as I scrub my face over and over. I have this sick feeling I'm never going to feel clean again.

I continue rinsing the rest of my body as I tell an impatient Macy about my trip down through the tunnels to the art cottage.

"But I swear, Mace, the last thing I remember is gathering up paint to work on my project. I was in the art supply closet, and I had a really strong vision of what I wanted to do on my canvas, so I picked up gray and green and blue paint and then went into the art room and started painting, for what felt like hours."

An idea suddenly comes to me.

"Wait a minute." I turn to Macy as I try to puzzle this out. "Did Jaxon say *where* Cole was attacked?" If this happened because he saw me go into the art room and came after me, then maybe it wasn't the cold-blooded attack it looks like.

Maybe it really *was* self-defense.

Please, please let it have been self-defense.

Then again, how on earth could I actually defend myself against a werewolf? Or end up without a scratch, for that matter? My only power right now is the ability to turn to stone, and though I can see that as a benefit when actually being attacked—as long as my attacker doesn't also have a sledgehammer—I have no idea how it works in an offensive situation.

Like, how could I possibly have drawn this much blood from anyone while doing my best impersonation of a garden gnome?

"He didn't say." Macy hands me my phone. "Maybe you should ask him."

"I'll ask him when I see him." I shudder as I reach for a pair of sweats and a T-shirt. "I have to go talk to your dad anyway. But first I need a shower."

Macy looks grim even as she nods. "Okay, you shower and I'll brush my teeth. Then we'll go see my dad together. "

"You don't have to do that," I tell her, though I'll admit that I really, really don't want to face this alone.

She rolls her eyes. "What's that old saying? One for all and all for one?" She plants her hands on her hips. "You're not going down to my father's office and confessing to whatever the hell this is without me."

I start to argue, but she shoots me a death glare so intense that I end up just snapping my mouth shut. Macy may be the most easygoing person I've ever met, but she definitely has a spine made of steel under all that fun exterior.

Macy is still getting ready when I finish my shower, so I grab the bloody clothes off the floor and shove them in an empty bag I have lying around. It's one thing to tell Uncle Finn what I think happened. It's another to parade what looks an awful lot like evidence of my guilt in front of the entire school. I also grab my notebook, just in case, and shove it into my backpack as well before slinging it over my shoulder.

Once we leave the room, I expect Macy to head for the main stairs that deposit us close to her dad's office. But she turns left instead, winding her way through two separate hallways filled with dorm rooms before finally stopping in front of one of my least-favorite paintings in the school—a dramatic rendition of the Salem Witch Trials, which shows all nineteen victims hung at once while flames engulf the village behind them.

Still, the last thing I'm expecting is for Macy to whisper a few words and then wave a hand that makes the painting vanish entirely.

She turns to me, her expression grim again. "Things are going to be in an uproar in the main rooms." Then she does the unexpected. She smiles. "So let's take a shortcut."

Seconds later, a door appears out of nowhere.

20

Karma's a Witch's Cousin

Unlike the other doors at Katmere, this one is bright yellow and has rainbow stickers all over it—which says everything it needs to about who has claimed ownership of it.

Macy puts her hand on the door and whispers something that sounds like "locks" and "doors" in an almost melodic cadence. And then the door opens.

"Come on," she entreats, beckoning urgently with her hand as the door swings farther inward. "Before anyone sees."

She doesn't have to tell me twice. I follow her through the door, and I don't even squeak as it shuts itself behind us with a quiet *swish*.

Of course, once the door closes, we're standing in total darkness, which freaks me out for a whole bunch of other reasons. With my heart beating unsteadily, I fumble for my phone to turn on my flashlight app.

But Macy is on it, and before I can so much as get the cell out of my pocket, she murmurs something about "light" and "life," and a line of candles along the left side of the passage flares to life.

It's the coolest thing ever, and the more of Macy's powers I see, the more impressed I get. But as my eyes adjust to the soft light and I finally see our surroundings, I can't help but grin.

Because *of course* Macy's secret passage is nothing like every other secret passage in the history of castles and secret passages and scary books. It's not musty, it's not overly narrow, and it's definitely *not* creepy. In fact, the whole thing is pretty much the antithesis of creepy. And also, it's totally kick-ass.

Just like the dungeons downstairs, the walls here are made of large and craggy black stones. But randomly placed amid the rocks are beautiful crystals and jewels in all the shades of the rainbow and then some. Polished pink quartz glitters next to sky-blue aquamarines, while a large citrine glints just above a gorgeous rectangular moonstone.

And those aren't the only gems. As far as the eye can see, the passage is lined with them. Emeralds and opals and sunstones and tourmalines... The list goes on and on. And so does the secret passageway.

Who makes a hidden corridor like this? I wonder as we start down the hall. *Filled with all these jewels and crystals that will never see the light of day?* I remember that dragons are known for their love of treasure, but this takes it to a whole new level.

There are stickers here, too, just like in the library. Big ones, small ones, colorful ones, black-and-white ones, and for the first time, I wonder if Macy is the one responsible for the decorations in the library that I liked so much. Or if she and the librarian, Amka, just happen to have the same aesthetic.

On a different day—if I'm not kicked out of Katmere and thrown in some paranormal prison somewhere for attempted murder—I want to come back and read every single one of these stickers.

But for now, I settle for reading the few that are right at face level as we continue along the shadowy passageway.

Why, yes, I can drive a stick, with a picture of a witch's hat and broom.

Karma's a witch, with a crystal ball in the background.

And my personal favorite, *100% that witch*, surrounded by a bed of flowers and sage.

I can't help laughing at that last one, and Macy shoots me a grin as she reaches over and squeezes my hand. "It's going to be okay, Grace," she tells me as we go around a curve. "My dad will figure out what happened."

"I hope so," I tell her, because being a gargoyle is one thing. Being a violent monster who blacks out and then tries to murder people in the bloodiest way possible is something else entirely.

For the first time, I really wonder if Hudson is actually *dead*. More, I start to wonder if maybe I killed him. Everyone seems so sure that I wouldn't have returned to Katmere if I thought Hudson was still a threat, so I've been operating under the assumption that either I left him locked up in some between space, unable to get out, or he figured a way to get free and I came back to help find him.

But if I can half drain an alpha werewolf of blood without having a clue I've done it—although I still have absolutely no idea how that could be possible—what makes me think I didn't do the same to the guy who tried to murder my mate?

Is that why I have no memory of the last four months? Because being a murderer was so traumatic to me that my mind blocked it out? And now it's blocking it out again?

Macy steers me down another long corridor and then a long set of narrow but winding stairs, then whispers, "We're almost there."

Fantastic.

"Almost there" means it's time to face the consequences of what happened to Cole.

"Almost there" means it's time to find out if I really have become the monster I'm afraid I have.

"Almost there" means things are about to get really real and really scary, really fast.

"Okay," Macy says as we finally stop in front of a door painted in rainbow stripes. Big surprise. "You ready?"

"No. Not even a little bit," I answer with a shake of my hand.

"I know." She hugs me tight for just a few seconds before pulling away. "But suck it up, buttercup. It's time to figure out what the actual hell is going on."

She grabs the door handle and gives me her best attempt at a smile. "I mean, how bad could it possibly be?"

I don't have an answer for her, and that's probably good, because the next thing I know, she's throwing the door open—and I'm staring directly at Jaxon and Uncle Finn.

21

Keep Your Enemies Close, Unless They Bleed a Lot

Jaxon turns to me and frowns. "What are you doing here, Grace? I told you where I was so you wouldn't worry. I've got this."

"No, you don't." I shake my head and try to figure out how to explain how I woke up this morning.

"Sure I do." For the first time, he looks uncertain. "I didn't have anything to do with Cole, and Foster knows it."

"I know you didn't hurt Cole." I take a deep breath. "I know you didn't, because I'm pretty sure I did."

For long seconds, neither Jaxon nor my uncle says anything. They just kind of stare at me like they're replaying my words in their heads over and over again, trying to make sense of them. But the longer they're silent, the more confused they look—and the tenser I get.

Which is why, in the end, I don't wait for them to say anything. Instead I pour out the whole story, starting with the trip to the art cottage and ending with my blood-soaked clothes, which I pull out of my bag and hand to Uncle Finn.

He doesn't look excited about taking them, but then, who would? Especially when I just dumped a problem of massive proportions right onto his sturdy wooden desk.

"Are you okay?" Jaxon asks the second I finally stop talking. "You're sure he didn't manage to hurt you somehow? You're sure he didn't bite you?"

I freeze at the urgency in his tone. "Why? What happens if he bites me? I don't turn into a werewolf, do I?" Because that would just make the clusterfuck that's become my life complete.

A gargoyle werewolf? Or a werewolf gargoyle? Weregoyle? *Garwolf?* I *do* not want to be a garwolf.

Then again, who cares what the proper term is? I shake my head to clear it. I just know that I really, really, really don't want to turn into one.

"No," Uncle Finn interjects in a voice meant to talk me off whatever ledge I'm dangling on—which, okay. Fair enough. "It doesn't work like that. You aren't going to turn into a werewolf or anything else."

"So how does it work? And while we're at it, how can I have possibly beaten up Cole and taken it? It doesn't make any sense. Why don't I remember it? How could I have just gone to bed covered in blood and not even noticed?"

Uncle Finn just sighs and runs a hand through his sandy-brown hair. "I don't know."

I give my uncle a disbelieving look. "You're the headmaster of a school filled with paranormals. How can 'I don't know' be the best answer you've got?"

"Because I've never seen anything like this before. And by the way, the whole gargoyle thing is as new to the rest of us as it is to you. We've been learning while you were gone, of course, but there's still a lot we don't know."

"Obviously." I don't mean to sound snarky; I really don't. I know he just wants to help. But what am I supposed to do here? I can't just go around assaulting people. The whole I-don't-remember thing is going to get old fast. God knows it's already old for me.

Macy steps between us. "So what do we do, Dad? How do we stop this from happening again?"

I wrap my arms around my waist and hold on tight. "You're not going to call the police, are you? I didn't mean to hurt him. Honestly,

I still can't figure out how I *did* hurt him. He's—"

"No one's calling the police, Grace," Jaxon tells me firmly. "That's not how we handle things here. And even if we did, you can't be held responsible for something you did when you weren't aware. Right, Foster?"

"Of course. I mean, we're going to have to watch you, make sure this doesn't happen again. You can't go around assaulting other students."

"Even if they deserve it," Macy interjects. "I know it's wrong, but after everything Cole did to you last semester, I'm having a hard time feeling sympathy for the guy."

Jaxon snorts. "I should have killed him when I had the shot. Then this never would have happened."

"No, you shouldn't have," I scold him. "That's a horrible thing to say."

"Horrible," Macy agrees, "but also a little bit true."

I shoot her a what-the-hell look, but she just kind of shrugs, as if to say, *What did you expect?*

With no help from her or Jaxon, I turn to my uncle. "How is Cole, anyway? Is he going to be okay?"

"He'll be fine. He got a couple of blood transfusions this morning and will probably spend the rest of the day in the infirmary resting, but he'll be fine tomorrow. Good thing about paranormals? We bounce back quickly, especially with a little help from our healers."

"Oh, thank God." I slump against Jaxon as relief sweeps through me.

Defending myself against Lia when she was trying to kill me was one thing. Deliberately going out of my way to try to hurt Cole for no reason is something else entirely. I'm pretty sure Cole is going to think so, too.

"Has he said anything?" I ask after I give myself a chance to wallow in the relief that I didn't do any permanent damage. "I mean, he has to know that I'm the one who attacked him, right?"

"His story is he doesn't know who attacked him," my uncle answers. "Which may or may not be true."

"It's a bunch of bullshit," Jaxon says flatly.

"We don't know that," Uncle Finn admonishes. "And if he doesn't know it was Grace who attacked him, I'm not about to spread the word. At least not until we figure out what's happening to her."

"He knows," Jaxon says. "He just doesn't want to say, because then he'd have to admit to the whole school that he got beaten up by a girl."

"Hey!" I give Jaxon a grumpy face.

"His thinking, not mine," Jaxon clarifies, dropping a kiss on the top of my head. "I saw what you did to Lia—and Hudson. No way would I want to mess with you. But Cole doesn't think like that. He can't.

"Because if the alpha werewolf admits to getting the crap kicked out of him by *anyone* while he was conscious, then he might as well hang it up. He'll spend the next month fighting off every werewolf in the pack who thinks they have a shot at alpha status." Jaxon glances at my uncle. "Right, Foster?"

Uncle Finn nods reluctantly. "Pretty much, yeah. After what happened with Jaxon in November...he has to be very careful how he plays this."

"Which means you've got to be careful, too, Grace." Macy speaks up for the first time in several minutes. "Because if he knows you're the one who did this...the one who has threatened everything he's been working for, he's going to come after you. He won't do it blatantly, because Jaxon would gut him, but he will find a way. That's who he is."

"A coward." Jaxon sneers.

Uncle Finn holds my gaze. "But that only makes him more dangerous, Grace. Because he's not me. He's sly and crafty, and he knows how to bide his time. I would talk to him, but if I do that, he'll know that you must have told me what happened. And then he'll be wondering who else knows. And how long it will be before everything blows up in his face."

"You really think he'll try something?" I ask, my gaze darting between Jaxon and my uncle.

"Not if he's half as bright as Foster's giving him credit for," Jaxon tells me. But the look in his eyes says something different.

"Oh, he'll definitely try something," Uncle Finn tells me. "The only question is when."

I don't know what to say to that, don't even know what I'm supposed to feel. Except tired. So tired.

I barely made it through the last homicidal maniac who was gunning for me, and now, here comes another. I mean, yeah, I obviously did something to provoke this one, but that doesn't make any sense to me, either. Why would my gargoyle try to murder Cole when I have no reason to do so? I mean, I've let what happened last semester go. Or at least I thought I had. This whole thing is scary as hell.

When is this new life of mine going to feel normal? When is it going to feel less like the Hunger Games and more like high school? My wrist starts hurting, and I reach down to rub it, only to realize I'm rubbing the scars from Lia's bindings. And that Jaxon, Macy, and my uncle can see exactly what I'm doing.

I drop my hand, but it's too late. Jaxon wraps his arms around me from behind and rests his hands on mine, his thumb gently stroking my wrist.

"He's already proven he's willing to kill to get his way," Macy says after an awkward pause that makes me feel even worse. "And that was before his reputation was on the line. Now that he stands to lose the only thing that matters to him? Yeah, he'll try something. We just have to be ready for it."

"We *will* be ready for it," Jaxon tells me, his midnight-sky eyes never leaving mine. "If he actually comes after you, I'll—"

"Let me handle it," my uncle interrupts. "I gave him another chance after everything that happened with you because of extenuating circumstances. But if he tries anything else, he's gone."

"What about me?" I finally ask my uncle when I can actually think past the throbbing in my head.

"What about you?" he answers.

"I'm the one who caused this problem. I'm the one who went after Cole for no rhyme or reason that I can figure out. You said he'll be expelled if he comes after me. But what about what I did? What's going to happen to me?"

22

Family Is My
Favorite F-Word

"Nothing," Jaxon grinds out. "Nothing is going to happen to you. This isn't your fault."

"We don't know that," I answer him, pulling out of his arms. "We don't have a clue why I attacked Cole."

"You're right, we don't," Uncle Finn says. "And nobody is doing anything until we figure out what's going on with you."

He wraps an arm around my shoulders and squeezes reassuringly. "I'm not in the habit of kicking students out who are struggling with their powers, Grace. Or who make bad choices with their power for the right reasons. That's why Flint is still here, even after everything that happened last semester. Jaxon, too. And it's also why Katmere has the best healers around. So that when mistakes happen, we can fix them."

"We don't know this was a mistake—"

"Did you want to hurt Cole when you left your dorm room?"

"No."

"Did you make a plan to hurt or kill him during the time you were gone?"

"Of course not." I pause, rethink it. "I mean, I certainly don't *remember* doing something like that."

"Okay, then. I'm going to operate under the assumption that what happened with Cole last night was some kind of slipup with your new powers. And we're going to treat it as such. I already called a couple of the gargoyle experts who consulted about your case earlier, hoping they could give me some advice about your missing memories. But now that this is going on, I'll see if I can talk one of them into coming to Katmere this week to work with you." He gives me a reassuring smile. "I promise you, we'll get to the bottom of this, Grace."

My eyes burn a little at this new proof that Uncle Finn has had my back all along, that he's been moving so many pieces around in the background, trying to figure out the best way to help me.

It's not quite like having my parents back—nothing will ever feel like that again. But it's something good in the middle of all this mess. And it's a lot better than the lost and lonely feeling I had when I first got to Katmere four and a half months ago.

"Thank you," I murmur when I can finally squeeze the words past the giant lump in my throat. "All of you. I don't know what I would do without you."

"Yeah, well, that's a good thing, considering you're stuck with us," Macy says, moving in for a hug just as the chimes ring, signaling the first class of the day.

"I'll take you," I answer, hugging her back.

"All right, all right," Uncle Finn says, and I could be mistaken, but I'm pretty sure he sounds like his throat is a little tight, too. "Get to class. And for the love of Salem, all of you try to stay out of trouble."

"Where's the fun in that?" Jaxon murmurs in my ear as he walks me through the door into the hall. We're going out the normal exit this time, not the secret passage.

"The fun is I don't wake up covered in werewolf blood ever again," I answer him and shudder. "Which is pretty much a win-win for everyone, don't you think?"

"I think you forget that you're talking to a vampire," he teases, and his mouth is still close enough to my ear to cause all kinds of shivers in all kinds of places. I lean in to him, and for a beat, we both just enjoy the way it feels to rest against each other, the hardness of his body cradled by the softness of mine.

But then he shifts a little, leaning down as if to kiss me, and I freeze up all over again. Again I try to hide it, but Jaxon notices—of course he does. Not for the first time, I wonder how long it's going to take my gargoyle side to accept a vampire for a mate. Or why my gargoyle side even has an issue with vampires in the first place.

I don't try to make an excuse this time. Instead, I just smile sadly at him and mouth, *I'm sorry*. He doesn't answer, just shakes his head in a "don't worry about it" kind of way. I can see that it hurts him, though, even as he shifts to drop a kiss on my forehead.

"Can I walk you to class?" he asks as he pulls back.

"Of course." I wrap an arm around his waist and squeeze him extra tight before looking around for Macy's hot-pink hair as we fold into the crowds. I don't want her to feel left out.

But, per usual, she's already up ahead of us, talking animatedly to Gwen and another one of the witches who are making their way to class.

As we start to walk, I lean away again, grab hold of Jaxon's hand, and thread our fingers together. I may not be able to kiss him right now, but that doesn't mean I don't love him. And it doesn't mean I don't want to be with him any way that I can.

Jaxon doesn't say anything, but he doesn't object, either. And when I look up at him, I realize that the small smile he's got on his face has an extremely goofy tint to it. Because of me.

I'm the girl who turns badass vampire prince Jaxon Vega goofy.

Not going to lie, it feels good.

"So where am I walking you?" Jaxon asks as we finally reach the main hallway.

"I don't know. They switched my science class. I went from basic Chem to the Physics of Flight, but I don't know why."

"Really? You don't know why?" Jaxon asks, brow raised, a teasing glint in his eyes.

"No." I shrug. "Do you?"

"I mean, I can't say for sure, but I'm guessing it has something to do with the big, beautiful wings your alter ego carries around."

"My alter— Ooooh." That has my eyes going wide. "You mean the Physics of Flight is about actually being able to fly?"

"Yeah." He looks at me incredulously. "What did you think it was about?"

"I don't know. Airplanes, I guess. That's why I was so confused."

"No, Grace. At Katmere, the class about flying is *actually* about flying."

"I just— That's— I mean…" In the end, I just shake my head. I mean, what else is there to say about that? Except: "Flight class. They think I should be in flight class." What on earth am I supposed to do with that?

"Well, wings are pretty much a prerequisite for flying," Jaxon teases as we turn down another hallway. "And so is figuring out how to use them."

"Oh yeah?" It's my turn to raise a brow at him. "Because I'm pretty sure *you* can fly without them."

He laughs. "Oh, hey! I've got a new joke for you."

"A new joke?" My brows hit my hairline as a grin splits my face. "Awesome. Lay it on me."

The look he gives me is suddenly steaming hot, and it says *very clearly* that there's a whole lot he wants to lay on me, and very little of it has to do with the cheesy jokes I love.

There's a part of me that wants to look away, that feels uncomfortable with the sudden intimacy of the moment. But that isn't fair to him—isn't fair to either of us, really—so I keep my gaze steady on his, even as heat and uncertainty surge in equal parts through my body.

For a moment, just a moment, I think Jaxon is going to follow up on the feelings I don't even try to hide, his midnight eyes turning to a deep, unrelenting black as his jaw goes tight.

But then the moment passes, and I can see him make the choice to let the tension, and everything that comes with it, slip away.

I don't know if I'm relieved or disappointed. Probably a little bit of both. But when Jaxon takes a very deliberate step back, physically and emotionally, it seems only fair to go with it.

"So." He grins down at me. "What sound does a gargoyle make when he sneezes?"

"A gargoyle joke? Seriously?" I roll my eyes at him.

He laughs. "What, too soon?"

He looks so pleased with himself that I can't deny him anything. "No, go ahead."

"What does a gargoyle say when he sneezes?"

I eye him warily. "I'm afraid to ask."

"Stat-choo!"

"Oh my God. That's awful."

He grins. "I know, right? Want to hear another one?"

"I don't know," I answer, skepticism ripe in my voice. "Do I?"

"You do." He squeezes my hand. "Why don't gargoyles go out during the day?"

"I don't want to know." I brace for his answer.

"Because they're too stoned."

"Oh my God!" I make a face at him. "That one was bad."

"It *was* awful," he agrees.

"And you obviously loved it. I've created a monster," I tease, shaking my head in mock horror as I lean into him.

But Jaxon's eyes are shadowed now, the laughter slipping away as easily as it came.

"No." Jaxon watches me with an intensity that shakes me to my very bones. "I've always been a monster, Grace. You're the one who's made me human."

My stomach sinks like a stone.

Because while Jaxon is definitely becoming more human...I'm deathly afraid that I'm turning into the real monster at Katmere Academy.

23

Saturday Morning Cartoons Never Prepared Me for This

Jaxon's words stay with me all day, melting me whenever I think about them. About him. Making me more determined than ever to find my way back to him, fully.

With that thought in mind, I decide to skip lunch—both Jaxon and Macy have study-group plans anyway—and head straight for the library, where I'll have a couple of hours of uninterrupted time to research gargoyles.

To research myself.

Which I really, really need to do, considering my knowledge on the subject is incredibly limited. And when I googled them last night, all I got was an architecture lesson when what I really need to know is why I am apparently prone to bloody attacks and amnesia.

I should probably set up an appointment with Mr. Damasen, see what information he can give me on gargoyles that doesn't involve pages upon pages about how they're really good waterspouts and gutters.

I mean, I didn't know that much about vampires, dragons, or witches when I got here, but I had a basic understanding of what they were and how things worked for them—though Jaxon, Macy, and Flint have still blown my mind on several occasions.

But gargoyles? I've got almost nothing. Except that they don't seem to like vampires much.

In fact, the extent of my knowledge about *myself* pretty much comes from studying the Cathedral of Notre-Dame in art class and from what I can remember of the *Gargoyles* TV show reruns I watched when I was little. My mom always got a little agitated when she found me watching that show... Now I can't help but wonder if it's because she and my dad knew what was coming.

It's a horrible thought—the idea that my parents deliberately kept who I really am from me my whole life—so I shove it to the back of my head and force myself not to think about it. Because learning that I'm a gargoyle is bad enough. Learning that my parents didn't care enough to prepare me for this? That's unforgivable.

Or it would be if they were alive. Now that they're dead...I don't know. Something else to go in my growing "Shit I Don't Have Time for Today" folder. Because dwelling on it now definitely isn't going to help me.

Instead, I paste a huge smile on my face—a smile that I'm far from feeling right now—and walk straight up to the circulation desk in the center of the library.

Amka is there, thankfully, and she smiles at me just as widely—hers looks genuine, though, which is nice. "Grace! It's so good to have you back." She reaches across the desk and squeezes my hand. "How are you?"

I start to give her a trite answer—*I'm good, thanks*—but the warmth and concern in her eyes get to me, even though I don't want them to. So instead of lying, I just kind of shrug and say, "I'm here." Which isn't exactly what I'm feeling, but it's close enough to get the point across.

Her smile turns sympathetic. "Yeah, you are. And I'm really glad about that."

And there she goes again, putting things in perspective for me really quickly. "Yeah. Me too." My manners kick in a little belatedly. "How are you?"

"I'm doing well. Just getting the library in shape for the Ludares tournament. Teams like to meet in here to strategize before the big day."

"What's Ludares?" I ask. "And is that what that's for?" I point to the table now taking up space in the center of the library. I didn't get a good look at it on my way in, but I plan on checking it out later, when I need a research break. From what I saw, it's filled with all kinds of interesting and magical objects.

"Originally, it was designed as a Trial to compete for spots on the Circle—the governing body for supernaturals—but…since no one on it has died in a thousand years, there haven't been any new openings to compete for. Which means for now, it's just a sporting event.

"Of course, the version of Ludares that's the actual Test is a lot more dangerous than what we play now—and the odds are way stacked against the challenger's success. Now it's more for fun and to promote interspecies relations, since the teams are made up of all four of Katmere's factions." Her eyes twinkle. "It's the highlight of every school year."

"So how do you play?"

"You wouldn't believe me if I told you. It's something you have to be a part of to understand."

"That's so cool. I can't wait to see it."

"See it?" Amka laughs. "You should compete in it."

"Me?" I'm aghast. "No way can I compete against a bunch of vampires and dragons. I mean, what am I going to do? Turn to stone? I'm pretty sure that's not much help in a competition."

"Don't be so negative. Gargoyles can do a lot more than turn to stone, Grace."

"They can?" Excitement bubbles up in my voice. "Like what?"

"You'll figure it out soon enough."

I'm a little annoyed—that's not much of an answer—and my shoulders sag, but then she turns around and points to one of the heavy wooden tables in the corner of the library. There are about three dozen books piled into several haphazard stacks, plus a laptop sitting right in front of a comfortable-looking armchair in a patchwork of colors.

"I took the liberty of pulling every book we have about gargoyles. The piles on either side of the laptop are the ones I think you should start with—they approach things pretty broadly and give a good overview. The back piles are more nitty-gritty research-oriented stuff and will answer more specific questions you might have as you learn more.

"And the laptop is already signed in to the top three magical databases in the world. If you have any questions about how to use them to research, let me know. But to be honest, they're pretty self-explanatory. I think you'll do fine."

Despite not being a crier—I've never been a crier—I can feel tears burning the back of my throat for, like, the third time today. I hate it, absolutely despise it, but I can't seem to help it. I feel so topsy-turvy, and realizing so many people have my back…it's just a little overwhelming.

Or a lot overwhelming. I haven't decided yet.

"Thank you," I tell her when my throat finally relaxes enough for me to speak. "I…I really appreciate it."

"Of course, Grace. Anytime." She smiles. "We bibliophiles need to stick together."

I grin back. "Yeah, we do."

"Good." She reaches behind her to the small, stickered refrigerator she keeps next to her workspace and pulls out a can of lemon La Croix and a Dr Pepper and hands them to me. "Researching is thirsty work."

"Oh, wow." I take the cans from her with suddenly shaky hands. "Thank you so much. I don't even know what to say."

"Don't say anything. Just get to work," she says with a wink.

"Yes, ma'am." I give her one last smile and then head toward the table in the corner.

My fingers are itching to dive in to the books—and so is the rest of me, to be honest—but I take a few minutes to get situated before

I start. I pull out the notebook I've designated just for my research and a handful of my favorite pens.

I put in my earbuds and get my favorite playlist going before pulling out the pack of M&M's I bought at the vending machine in the student lounge on my way here. Then, and only then, do I settle into what very well might be the most comfortable chair in existence... and finally reach for a book.

I just hope it has some of the answers I need. And I wouldn't mind a good memory retrieval spell, too...

24

Go Smudge Yourself

"**G**ra-ace. Come on, time to wake up." A familiar voice penetrates the hazy fog of sleep that surrounds me. "Come on, Grace. You need to get up." Someone taps my shoulder.

I swipe a hand across my face. Then roll over and curl up into a ball.

"I don't know what to do." This time I'm conscious enough to identify the voice as Macy's, even though I have no idea who she's talking to or even what she's talking about. Nor do I care.

I'm so tired, all I want to do is sleep.

"Let me try." This time it's my uncle Finn who bends over me and says, "Grace, I need you to wake up for me, okay? Open your eyes. Come on. Right now."

I ignore him, curling into an even tighter ball, and when he runs a comforting hand over the top of my head, I moan and try to pull my pillow over my face. But there's no pillow under my head and no covers for me to yank up and hide beneath.

I'm almost conscious enough to recognize this as strange— almost—and when someone shakes my shoulder more forcefully this time, I manage to crack my eyes open just enough to see Macy, my uncle, and Amka staring down at me, all with worried looks on their faces.

I don't have a clue what Uncle Finn or Amka is doing in our room, and at the moment, I don't actually care. I just want them to leave so I can go back to sleep.

"There you are, Grace," my uncle says. "There you go. Can you sit up for us? Maybe let us get a good look into those pretty eyes of yours? Come on now, Grace. Come back to us."

"I'm tired," I whine in a voice I'm sure I'll be embarrassed about later. "I just want to—" I break off as pain registers for the first time. My throat is so dry that every word I speak feels like a razor blade scraping against my voice box.

Screw mornings. And screw three-person wake-up calls.

I close my eyes again as sleep continues to beckon, but apparently my uncle has had enough. He starts shaking me gently so that I can't even curl up in peace now. "Come on, Grace." His voice is firmer than it was before, more no-nonsense than I have ever heard it. "You need to snap out of this. Right now."

I sigh heavily, but I finally manage to roll over to face him. "What's the matter?" I rasp, forcing myself to speak, and to swallow, despite the pain. "What do you want?"

I hear a door open and close and then rapid footsteps coming closer. "What's going on? Is she all right? I came as soon as I got Macy's text."

The worry in Jaxon's voice finally manages to do what the coaxing and shaking couldn't. I push myself into a sitting position and this time actually manage to pry my eyes all the way open.

"Can I have some water?" I ask through lips that feel absurdly parched, considering I'm not wandering the Sahara.

"Yeah, of course." Macy grabs something from her backpack and hands it to me—a stainless-steel tumbler with the lid off. I take a long drink. Then go back for two more as my throat finally begins to feel human again.

As does the rest of me.

The cold water has the added benefit of getting my brain going, and as soon as I've slaked my thirst, I turn to Jaxon with what I'm sure are still sleep-fogged eyes.

"What's going on?" I ask. "Why is everyone in Macy's and my room?"

There's a weird silence as the four of them look at one another, then back at me.

"What?" I ask again.

Macy sighs. "I hate to break it to you, Grace, but this is definitely not our room."

"Whose room is it, then?" I ask, looking around. And that's when panic hits me, because I realize Macy is right. This isn't our room. It isn't Jaxon's room. In fact, I'm pretty positive it isn't even a bedroom, unless the person furnishing it is a huge fan of Scary Dungeons 'R' Us.

"Where are we?" I ask when I can finally find my voice again.

Amka steps in before Jaxon or my family can answer. Squatting down next to me—and for the first time, I realize I'm on the floor—she asks, "Where do you think you are?"

"I don't know." I look around again, this time hoping to find a clue as agitation builds inside me. I'm just beginning to realize that not only do I not know where I am, but I also have absolutely no idea how I got here.

And can I just say, this is seriously getting old?

The last thing I remember is sitting down to work in the library, with a sparkling water and some M&M's. After that...nothing. It's a blank. Again.

"Is someone hurt?" I demand, panic roaring through me. "Did I do it again? Did I attack someone?"

"No, Grace. Everything's fine." Amka puts what I know she means to be a calming hand on my shoulder, but it doesn't work. It just makes me more freaked out, as does the low, soothing tone of her voice.

"Don't do that. Don't try to placate me." I push away from her, leap to my feet...and turn to Jaxon. "Please, please don't lie to me. Did I hurt someone? Did I—"

"No!" He says it much more vehemently, voice adamant and eyes steady as he stares into mine. "You didn't hurt anyone, I swear. You're the one we're worried about right now."

"Why? What happened?" I believe Jaxon, I do, but the memory of waking up covered in blood this morning is so strong that I can't help looking down at my hands, my clothes, just to make sure. Just to feel safe.

I'm not bloody, thank God. But the sleeve of my blazer is ripped all to hell. Because that's not terrifying at all, considering it's just now reaching a high of freezing outside.

Suddenly, the concern on everyone's faces makes a lot more sense. They aren't worried that I hurt someone. This time, they're worried that I'm the one who's gotten hurt.

I swallow the fear exploding inside me like a hand grenade and try to breathe. I *am* going to figure this out. It's bad enough that I lost four months to this mess. No way am I going to just accept that I've brought it back with me. No way am I going to let this become my new normal.

"Where am I?" I ask for a second time, because I am absolutely positive I've never been in a room with a crystal ball before *ever*, let alone at Katmere Academy. And I've certainly never been in a room with a candle collection that rivals Bath & Body Works—if Bath & Body Works was into carved-up ritual candles and enough incense to cover Alaska twice over.

"You're in the casting tower," Macy tells me.

"The casting tower?" I didn't even know there was such a thing.

"It's on the opposite side of the castle from my room," Jaxon adds in what I assume is an attempt to help me get my bearings.

"Oh, right. The smaller tower on the gazebo side." I shove a hand—one that I'm working overtime to keep steady—through my curls. "I guess I just always assumed it was somebody else's dorm room."

"Nope." Macy shoots me a grin that almost touches her eyes. "Your boyfriend is the only one who rates a tower. This one belongs to *all* the witches."

Of course it belongs to the witches. If it belonged to anyone else, I'd be really concerned. Especially since I just looked down and realized that I am standing dead center in the middle of a giant pentagram.

And not just any giant pentagram. The giant pentagram that makes up the center of an even more giant casting circle...

Oh, hell no. Lia cured me of *ever* wanting to be anywhere close to the middle of another spell. Ever.

I take several big steps backward, not because I want to get away from Jaxon or Macy or the others but because I am getting the hell out of this circle. Now.

Call it an overabundance of caution, call it PTSD, call it whatever the hell you want; I don't care. No way am I spending another second in a circle surrounded by red and black candles.

No, thank you.

The rest of them follow me, because of course they do. Each of them takes a step forward for each step I take back. My uncle and Amka look really concerned, and Macy looks curious. But Jaxon... Jaxon's got a small, rueful smile on his face that tells me he knows exactly what's got me so freaked out. Then again, he's the only one here who was down in that tunnel with me.

With everything that happened to him that day, too, I'm surprised he hasn't run screaming from this room. God knows I'm considering it.

"Grace?" Macy asks as I continue to step backward. "Where are you going?"

"Out of, ummm..." I break off in frustration as I realize I'm *still* in the circle. "How big is this thing anyway?"

"It takes up most of the room," Uncle Finn answers, looking even more confused. "We have a lot of witches who need to fit around the circle. Why?"

But Macy seems to have finally clued in. "Oh, sweetie, the circle isn't cast. Nothing can hurt you right now. And in here we do magic that does no harm anyway. There's nothing to be afraid of."

"Of course there isn't. I know that. I'm still just going to…" I use my thumb to point backward over my shoulder.

"Would it make you feel better if we left this room completely?" Amka asks.

I focus on her as relief sweeps through me. "So much, I can't even tell you."

"Okay, then let's go." Just that easily, Uncle Finn starts herding everyone toward the door. "There's something you need to see in the library anyway."

"In the library?" Now I'm even more confused. "You mean the gargoyle books Amka got out for me? I saw them earlier, and I'm planning on working my way through them."

"No. Something else. We'll talk about it when we get there."

That doesn't sound ominous at all. I'm about to press for details, but my uncle looks grim. Really grim, and it scares me more than I want to admit.

Before Katmere, I never imagined I'd be afraid of walking into a library. Then again, before Katmere, I never imagined a lot of things.

25

And the Blackouts Just Keep on Coming

As soon as we get outside the casting room, Jaxon stops me with a light hand on my wrist.

"What's wrong?" I ask, more than willing to take as long as possible to get to what I'm rapidly beginning to think of as the library of doom. "Do you need something?"

"No, but I'm pretty sure you do."

I wait for him to elaborate, but he doesn't. He just tilts his head to the side—and listens like he's waiting for something. A minute later, Mekhi is standing before me. And holding a large black jacket that I recognize as Jaxon's.

He grins at me and bows, presenting the jacket as if to royalty. "My lady."

For the first time since I woke up in a giant magical circle, everything seems like it might be okay. Mekhi isn't treating me weirdly. He's grinning at me like he always does. And I can't help but grin back.

I give a mock curtsy and take the jacket from his hands. "My liege."

"I'm going to want all the details later, but I've got to book it to my next class right now. See ya, Grace!" And with that, he vanishes. I don't think I'll ever get used to how fast vampires can move.

"You didn't have to ask Mekhi to do that." I take off my ripped-up blazer and don Jaxon's jacket, inhaling his scent as I do.

"I know." He watches me carefully. "I like taking care of you."

My already battered heart aches a little more at his words and the look in his eyes. I just wish I knew how to respond. There's a part of me, a big part, that wants to lean in to him and press my lips to his. But I also know my gargoyle won't let me yet, which is super frustrating on pretty much all the levels.

I mean, why let me kiss him that first time when I just got back to school, only to make sure I never let him near me like that again? It bothers me, and I can only imagine that it bothers Jaxon, too, even though he doesn't say anything. In the end, I do the only thing I can do. I hold his gaze, hoping he can see in my eyes just how much his caring means to me.

"Come on, let's go," Jaxon finally says, and there is a gruffness to his voice that isn't usually there. He holds a hand out to me.

I take it, and the two of us head down the winding steps together.

"Do you know what Uncle Finn wants to show me in the library?" I ask as we make it to the correct floor.

"No." He shakes his head. "I got a frantic text from Macy telling me that you were missing, so the guys and I started looking, along with Finn and her. They texted us that they'd found you in the tower, but that's all I know."

"I don't understand," I tell him, a shiver running down my spine as we finally make it to the hallway the library is on. "I went to the library to research gargoyles around noon, but I don't remember doing any research. I don't remember anything, actually, after I sat down to work."

"It's five o'clock, Grace."

"But I was in the library. Did Amka know when I left?"

"You would think, but I don't know. Like I said, she called your uncle and Macy, not me." There's something in his voice that I can't quite identify, but he doesn't sound impressed.

Apparently, Jaxon feels like he deserves to be notified about things related to me. Which is annoying, because he doesn't actually own me. And yet, I think about how I would feel if something happened to him... Yeah, pretty sure I would want to be notified, too.

He holds the library door open for me, and then we walk inside, only to find a conspicuously empty open glass case. Whatever item was displayed there is gone, the bed of purple velvet empty in that one spot.

"Is this what you wanted to show me?" I ask my uncle. "I don't know what happened. It was fine when I was here earlier."

And if anyone had actually tried to break into it when I was here, I would have seen them. So would Amka. The exhibit is diagonally across from the table she set up for me and directly in front of the circulation desk.

"What *do* you remember from when you were here earlier, Grace?" Amka is the one asking me questions now, my uncle hanging back and following her lead.

"Not a lot, honestly. I remember our conversation and sitting down to work, but that's it. Did something else happen?"

"You don't remember working?"

"No. I remember getting ready to work, but I don't remember opening a book or taking any notes. Did I do that?"

"You took all the notes." She picks up a notebook from her desk and hands it to me.

I flip through it, and she's right. It's more than half full already, with information about gargoyles that I have no recollection of but am now itching to sit down and read.

"I did all this in five hours?" I ask, surprised by how thorough the note-taking is, when usually I hit only the highlights and rely on my really good memory (present situation obviously not included) to fill in the blanks.

"Actually, you did all that in an hour and a half. At one thirty, I closed the library for a few minutes and ran out to my cottage to get some medicine for a sudden headache. You said you were doing well, so I left you working, but when I came back, you were gone. And the Athame of Morrigan had been stolen."

Horror moves through me as all the threads of the story start to come together in one glaring realization. "You think I did this?" I ask. "You think I stole the…" I wave my hand in the air.

"Athame," Macy fills in. "It's a double-sided ceremonial blade for witches. This particular one has been in our family for centuries."

I want to be outraged that they think I could do this. But the truth is, they have every right to suspect me. Especially since I have absolutely no idea what I was doing during the time Amka left the library.

"We don't think *you* stole it," Uncle Finn tells me in a voice I recognize as deliberately soothing. "But we do think something is going on inside you that makes you do these things, and that's what we want to try to figure out so we can help you."

"Do we really know?" I ask, my voice coming out higher and louder than I want it to. "I mean, are you sure I'm the one who did this?" It's not even that I doubt them, it's just that I don't *want* to believe them. Because then I have to start wondering. What kind of powers does this gargoyle inside me have? And why is it using me to do these terrible things?

Jaxon wraps a supportive arm around my waist, then rests his chin on my shoulder as he whispers in my ear, "It's okay. We've got this."

I'm glad he thinks so, because right now, it doesn't feel like I've got anything.

"That's why we wanted you to come here, so we could all rewatch the footage together. See if we can figure out what's really going on." My uncle walks behind the circulation desk.

"Nobody blames you, Grace," Macy says with a reassuring smile. "We know something else is going on."

My knees get weak at theirs words—there's *footage*?—and at the grim look on my uncle's face. Because if they've seen the footage already, then they know for sure that I'm the one who stole the athame.

The knowledge hits me like a body blow.

I know it's naive, but I think I've been holding out hope all day.

Hope that there was another explanation for the blood on my clothes this morning. Definite hope that someone else attacked Cole, and now hope that someone else stole the athame.

Because knowing that it's me, knowing that I did all that and have no recollection of it whatsoever, is beyond terrifying. Not just that I can't remember but that I really don't have any control over what I do when I'm like that.

I could actually kill someone, and I would never know.

Panic starts to bubble up in my chest, my breath coming out in shallow puffs. I count to ten…then twenty. My heart is beating so fast, I start to feel light-headed. I don't take my gaze from my uncle as he fiddles with the computer on the circulation desk and then turns the monitor around to face me.

"It's okay," Jaxon says again, even though it's not. Even though it's about as far from okay as it can possibly get. "I promise you, Grace, we'll figure this out."

"I hope so," I answer as we all crowd around Uncle Finn to watch the video footage. "Because how long can this go on before I end up in prison…or worse?"

My stomach sinks as I watch a recording of me on the screen—doing things I don't remember doing.

According to the time at the bottom of the footage, I got up from the table where I was reading and taking notes at exactly one thirty. I went over to Amka and said something to her. She nodded with a strange look on her face, and less than a minute later, she got up. But instead of leaving, like she'd said earlier, she walked over to the glass case housing the athame and several other precious magical items, all of which, it turns out, were under a protection spell, my uncle explains.

And at 1:37, the librarian went ahead and opened the case like it was nothing. Then she walked out of the library and didn't come back.

"What just happened?" I ask, looking from Jaxon to Amka to my uncle and then back again. "Did I use some kind of special gargoyle power?"

Amka shakes her head as the video continues to roll, and I watch as I reach into the case and scoop out the athame, snagging my jacket on the way out. "I have no memory of doing that, of unlocking the case."

"Hudson," Jaxon says, voice low and vehement and maybe even a little...scared? Which messes me up in all kinds of ways, because Jaxon is almost never scared.

"What?" my uncle Finn demands. "What about Hudson?"

"When we were kids, he used to do that. He has to speak directly to the person, but he can persuade anyone to do anything for him with merely his voice."

"Do what?" I ask as razor-sharp talons of fear rake through me. "What did Hudson do, Jaxon?"

Jaxon finally manages to pull his haunted gaze from the video. "Use his power of persuasion to get people to do whatever he wanted."

26

Possession Is Nine-Tenths of the Law

Jaxon's words hang in the air between us for several seconds, the power and horror of them an actual physical presence that has my body tensing and a chill running over my skin.

"What does that mean?" I finally whisper, the words falling like grenades into the silence between us. "Is Hudson here? Did I bring him back with me? Is he persuading me to do things?"

"He's definitely here," Uncle Finn agrees. "The only question is what we do next."

"Well, where is he, then?" I demand. "Why haven't we seen him?"

I look from my uncle's sad face to Jaxon's enraged one, from Amka's quiet compassion to the distress Macy tries to hide but simply can't, and a weight starts to grow in my stomach. A weight that gets heavier and heavier with every second that passes.

A weight that nearly pulls me under as the truth crashes into me.

"No," I tell them, shaking my head as panic and disgust and horror wrench through me all at the same time. "No, no, no. It can't be."

"Grace, it's okay." Jaxon steps forward, lays a hand on my arm.

"It's *not* okay!" I all but shout at him. "It's the opposite of okay."

"Breathe," my uncle says. "There are things we can do to try to fix this. "

"Try to fix it?" I answer with a laugh that even I can tell borders on the hysterical. "I have a monster living *inside me*."

"There are options," Amka says, her voice deliberately soothing. "There are several options we can try before we start to panic—"

"Not to be rude, Amka, but I think you mean before *you* start to panic. Because I'm already there."

Panic races through me, and this time I'm pretty sure I'm not going to be able to stop the attack. At this point, I'm pretty sure not even a dump truck full of Xanax would be able to stop it. Not when my head is swimming and my heart is pounding out of my chest.

"Grace, it's okay." Macy reaches for me, but I step backward and hold my hand up in the typical gesture for *give me a second*.

Thankfully, everyone does. They give me more than a second, in fact, though I don't know how much more. Eventually, my now-familiar defense mechanisms slide into place.

I'm nowhere close to being okay—at this point, I can't even imagine what okay would feel like—but I shove my panic down deep inside me and focus on keeping my mind clear.

I need to be able to think.

I need to figure out what to do.

Scratch that, *we* need to figure out what to do, because as I stare at the four concerned people looking back at me, I realize that just because it feels like I'm alone—more alone even than the day my parents died—I'm not.

Jaxon and Macy and Uncle Finn and even Amka aren't going to let me do this alone, even if I wanted to. And the truth is, I really, really don't want to. I wouldn't even know where to start.

"So," I manage to say after a few attempts at clearing my throat. "I have a favor to ask."

"Anything," Jaxon tells me, and he reaches a hand out, grabs on to mine. It's only after our palms connect that I realize how cold all this has made me. Jaxon's palm feels burning hot against my own.

"Can you say it?" I ask.

Jaxon's grip tightens on my hand. "Say what?" he asks, but the look on his face tells me he already knows.

"I just need you to say it so I don't feel like there's something really wrong with me. Please."

Jaxon is looking more haunted than I have ever seen him. Normally, I'd be the one to comfort him when he looks like this, but I can't. I don't have it in me. Not now. Not yet.

"Jaxon," I whisper, because I don't know what else to do. "Please."

He nods jerkily, his eyes a burning-hot obsidian that sizzles along every inch of my skin as he looks at me.

"The reason we haven't been able to figure out what happened to Hudson," he says in a voice that tears like broken glass. "The reason we haven't been able to find out where you left him, or where he went, is because he's been here all along."

I lock my knees in place so I don't crumble, then wait for him to drop the bombshell that's been living in my head the last several minutes, the bombshell that I don't want to hear—don't want to know—but that I all but begged him to let loose.

"The reason we haven't been able to figure out where at Katmere Academy Hudson is hiding is because all along, he's been hiding inside you."

27

When the Evil Within Really Needs to be the Evil That's Out, Out, Out

His words—expected and yet a total shock—go off inside me like a bomb. Like a nuclear reactor at the most dangerous stage of meltdown. Because this can't be happening. This just can't be happening.

I can't have Jaxon's evil brother inside me.

I can't have him taking control of me whenever he wants.

I can't have him wiping my memories out of existence.

I just can't.

And yet, apparently, I can. I do.

"It's okay," my uncle tells me. "As soon as I get back to my office, I'm going to make some calls. I'll find someone who knows how to deal with this and get them to Katmere as soon as possible."

"And I'll start doing research," Macy adds. "Like Amka said, there are some spells that might work, so she and I can contact several different covens and see what we can find out. Plus, we'll keep researching. We'll find a way to get Hudson out of your mind. I swear."

Her words reverberate in my head, spinning around and around and around as I try to grapple with this new nightmare. As I try to figure out if I can actually feel Hudson inside me, his oily fingers on my heart and mind.

I try and try and try, but I can't find anything. No thoughts that aren't my own. No feelings that don't belong to me. Nothing out of the ordinary except, of course, the whole body-snatching routine he's doing.

As I'm trying to come to terms with this nightmare, this new and horrible violation, the conversation rages around me. Jaxon, Uncle Finn, Macy, Amka, all throwing their two cents in about how to fix this.

About how to fix me.

Everyone giving their opinion on what, to me, is the most personal problem of my life. The most personal problem anyone could ever have—someone else living inside your skin, taking you over whenever they want, making you do horrible things you would never willingly do.

"What about me?" I ask when I can't stand the discussing/bickering for one second longer.

"I promise we'll fix this," Uncle Finn says. "We will get him out of you."

"That's not what I meant," I tell him. "I meant, what do *I* do? While you four are all trying to figure out how to save me, what can *I* do to save myself?"

That gets their attention, has them eyeing one another as they try to figure out what I mean. Which is just proof that there's a problem, right?

"Grace, honey, there's nothing for you to do right now." My uncle addresses me in the deliberately calm tone of someone who expects the person he's using it on to go hysterical at any moment.

But the hysteria is gone. Not forever, as I'm sure it will be back before this nightmare is over, but for now. And in its place is a determination not to be placated, a determination to never be placed in a situation like this one ever again.

"Well, then I guess we'd better find something for me to do," I tell him. "Because if we're right, if Hudson is actually living inside me like some kind of parasite, there is no way I'm just going to sit back and wait to see what you guys come up with. Doing that is what's gotten me into every terrible situation I've been in since I got to Alaska."

The words are harsh and, in another situation, another reality, I would never have said them. But in this situation, in *this* reality, they needed to be said.

And the people I'm talking to need to listen to them...and to me. Because there is no way I'm taking a back seat for one more second. No way I'm just going to sit around and let them prevaricate and tell me half-truths and hide things from me in the name of *protection*. Not now. Not anymore.

"Yes, I want to know what I can do to get Hudson out of me," I tell them. "But since that seems like it's going to be a process, I need some stopgap measures to help me out. Like what I can do, right now, to ensure he can't make me hurt anyone else. Not what *you* can do but what *I* can do.

"Because I am not going to just sit here and let him take control of me whenever he wants until all the experts can figure things out. He is never going to use me as a weapon again—not against Cole, not against Amka, and definitely, definitely not against Jaxon."

"Hudson can't use you against me—" Jaxon starts to interrupt, but I cut him off with a hand.

"He already has," I tell him as my brain races through different scenarios and things start to fall into place. "Why do you think I'm so uncomfortable with you right now? Why do you think I back away every time you try to kiss me? Maybe you haven't gotten around to putting that together yet, but it's becoming crystal clear to me."

I can see from the look in Jaxon's eyes that I'm getting through to him, that he's going back over every interaction we've had the last two days and trying to see what was me and what was Hudson. Not that I blame him—I've just done the very same thing...and I really, really don't like what I've found.

"I'm done, Jaxon. I'm done, Uncle Finn. I'm not waking up covered in someone else's blood ever again. Or in the middle of a casting circle, missing with ripped clothes. And I am not giving a murderer free range over my body or my head for one more second than I have to."

My chest is tight and my hands are shaking, but my mind is clear, and I know—I *know*—that I'm doing the right thing.

"Either you talk to me and help me figure out what I can do, or I swear, I'm going to walk back to that stack of books over there. I'm going to read every single one of them until I figure out how to turn myself back into a gargoyle. And this time, I'm going to stay that way until Hudson can no longer hurt anyone."

Jaxon opens his mouth to speak, but I shake my head. I'm not done yet.

"And if that means staying a gargoyle *forever*, then that is what I'll do. It's not what I *want* to do," I tell them as they all start to protest. "But it's what I will do, because no one—*no one*—is going to use me as a pawn ever again."

It's why I nearly died when I got here and why Jaxon and Flint nearly died, too. If they had just told me the truth when I first arrived, I wouldn't have had to spend my first four days at Katmere bumbling around trying to figure things out as people tried to kill me. I wouldn't have trusted the wrong people.

And maybe, just maybe I wouldn't have ended up in those tunnels with Lia, and Jaxon wouldn't have nearly died, and we wouldn't be right here, right now, with Hudson taking some kind of psychotic vacation *in my goddamn body.*

Just the thought makes me sick, makes me want to cry. Makes me want to scream.

I want him gone, want him out of me right the hell now.

But if that's not a possibility, I need to know how to keep myself and the people around me safe from him, no matter what.

I look from Jaxon to Macy to my uncle to Amka, only to find

them all staring back at me with a grudging respect in their eyes. Which means it's time to ask the question burning a hole in my chest. "Do I need to turn into a gargoyle again, or is there a way to block him out?"

Suddenly, I feel something flutter inside that feels an awful lot like a scream—of rage or agony or terror, I don't know which. But it's definitely a scream... And it's definitely not coming from me.

28

Sometimes Girls
Just Wanna
Take Charge

I barely have time to figure out what that means, if it means anything, when Jaxon says, "I'm taking you to the Bloodletter."

"The Bloodletter?" I repeat, because it's not a name I've ever heard before. And also because it's not one that sounds particularly... inviting. I mean, in a world full of paranormals who don't bat an eye at blood loss or near-death encounters, what kind of monster do you have to be to be called the Bloodletter?

It's freaky as hell.

"The Bloodletter?" Uncle Finn repeats with the same skepticism I'm feeling. "Are you sure that's a good idea?"

"No," Jaxon answers. "In fact, I'm pretty sure it's a terrible fucking idea. But so is Grace turning back into a gargoyle for who knows how long." He looks at me, and his face is full of worry and love and a touch of fear that he's trying really hard not to let me see. "I don't know if the Bloodletter can help figure out a way to quarantine Hudson in your head. But I do know that if anyone can, it's her."

"Who is she?" I ask, because I feel like I at least need to have some clue of what I'm walking into if I do this.

"She's an Ancient," Jaxon tells me. "A vampire who has been alive longer than almost anything on the planet. And she...*lives*...in an ice cave it doesn't take that long to get to from here."

I turn his words over in my head, trying to find a deeper meaning to them. I know there is one—it's obvious from the way looks are flying between my uncle and Amka. Macy seems oblivious, but that's obviously because she's as in the dark about this subject as I am.

"She's brutal," Amka says after a second. "Completely terrifying. But if anyone knows how to help you, she will."

I've got to admit, "brutal" is not exactly a word that evokes confidence in me. Then again, neither is "terrifying." And considering I'm standing in a room with one of the most powerful vampires in existence and no one here is the least bit afraid of him, I shudder to think of what this Bloodletter person might be like.

Especially since even Jaxon seems nervous at the idea of taking me to her.

"Do you know her?" I ask as apprehension fills me. "I mean, will she try to kill us on sight or will she at least listen to what we have to say?"

"She's brutal but not completely psychotic," Jaxon tells me. "And I do know her, yes. She raised me."

He doesn't say anything else, just kind of drops it out there, like being raised by the most terrifying vampire in existence is a totally normal thing. He might as well have pulled out a full-on *South Park* impression and said, *Move along, people. Nothing to see here.*

Which only convinces me more that there's a lot Jaxon's leaving out. And more concerned that what he's leaving out is really, really bad.

But if seeing this Bloodletter person will help get Hudson out of my head, and maybe even give me a glimpse into Jaxon's childhood, then I'm all in.

"How long does it take to get there?" I ask. "And when do we leave?"

"A few hours," Jaxon replies. "And we can leave now if you want."

"Now?" Uncle Finn asks, sounding less than impressed. "Why don't you at least wait until morning, when it's light out?"

"And give Hudson another chance to try to body snatch me again?" I ask, and I don't even have to pretend to be traumatized crush

at the thought. "I'd rather not."

Not to mention, I'm too freaked out to sleep tonight—and maybe ever again. The fact that Hudson is inside me is terrifying and gross and weird. Can he read my thoughts, too? Like, is he in my head right now, hearing everything I'm thinking? Or are his talents limited to just taking over my body? *Just.* Give me a break.

How did my life get to this? Five months ago, I was in San Diego, and my biggest decision was where I was going to go to college. Now, I still have to decide that—or at least I think I do (do gargoyles even go to college?)—plus deal with evil alpha werewolves trying to take me down and psychopathic vampires living in my head.

If it wasn't for Jaxon, I'd be pretty positive that I've traded down... way, way down.

Deciding the best way to circumvent Uncle Finn's objections is to simply act like this is a done deal, I turn to Jaxon. "Do we need to call first and let her know we're coming? I mean, if she has a phone in her"—I can't believe I'm saying this—"ice cave?"

"She doesn't need a phone. And if she doesn't already know we're coming, she'll figure it out long before we get there."

Because that's not creepy at all. "Awesome." I smile at him. "I'll go get changed and meet you at the front entrance in fifteen minutes?"

Jaxon nods. "Make sure to layer up. We'll be out in the cold for a while."

By "a while," I assume he means the whole time, considering the Bloodletter lives in an ice cave. Which is another weird-as-hell thing that I want to hear more about—including whether or not Jaxon grew up in the ice cave we are going to visit or if he grew up somewhere else and moved there after. I mean, because nothing says "retirement" like carving out a home for yourself in the middle of a frozen Alaskan cave.

"Give her at least thirty minutes, Jaxon," my uncle says with the air of a man who knows when he's been beaten.

"I'd rather get started as soon as possible," I object.

"And I'd rather you had something to eat before you go." He gives me a hard look that lets me know in no uncertain terms that this is one thing he is not budging on. "It's not like you can just drop into a restaurant out there in the middle of the Alaskan wilderness, and the Bloodletter definitely isn't going to have anything *you* might want to eat. So stop by the cafeteria before you go. You can grab a sandwich to eat now, and I'll make sure they also pack you some food to take with you—since I assume you'll be staying overnight."

I hadn't thought that far ahead—hadn't thought about anything other than getting Hudson out of me—and I'm grateful that Uncle Finn has. Especially considering I skipped lunch today, and my stomach is currently reminding me of that in no uncertain terms.

"Thanks, Uncle Finn." I go up on tiptoes to kiss his cheek.

He responds by patting my back a little awkwardly, even as he says, "Be careful out there. And let Jaxon take the lead with the Bloodletter. He knows her better than anyone."

I nod, even as I wonder what he means—and what it means for Jaxon that the person who raised him, the person he knows best in the world, is also a woman known for her viciousness.

"Come on, Grace. I'll help you pick out what you need to wear," Macy says as she starts bustling me toward the exit.

I go along with her, glancing back only to give Jaxon a wave and to mouth, *Thirty minutes*, at him.

He nods back, but I can see the upset in his eyes. And I get it. I do. I'm trying my best not to freak out about Hudson, too, but the truth is, I'm hanging on by a small freaking thread. Jaxon has to be feeling the same way, with an added dose of feeling responsible for the situation, because he's Jaxon and that's how he deals with every situation—especially ones that involve me.

"You ready?" Macy asks, watching as I turn from Jaxon to head up to our room.

"No," I answer. But I keep walking forward. Because some days, what a girl wants to do and what a girl needs to do are two very different things.

29

I'm Too Sexy for
My Coat...and So
Is Everyone Else

"**N**ice coat," Jaxon says when he sees me thirty minutes later, and the painfully tight line of his mouth curves upward.

I'm dressed in about six layers to protect me from the wilderness—including a hot-pink puffer coat that predators can probably see from fifty miles away—but when Macy proudly laid it on my bed, I didn't have the heart, or the energy, to say no.

"Don't start," I say, then look him over for something to make fun of as well. Of course, there's nothing. He's dressed head to toe in all-black winter wear and he looks good, really good. Nothing at all like an escapee from a cotton-candy factory.

As we walk down the front steps of the school, I expect to see a snowmobile parked at the bottom of them. But there's nothing, and I look at Jaxon in confusion, even as I duck my face a little deeper into the wool scarf that covers me from cheekbone to chest.

"The temperature is going to drop at least twenty degrees in the next couple of hours," he tells me as he pulls me close. "I don't want you out here any longer than you have to be."

"Yeah, but won't a snowmobile help with that?" I ask. I mean, it's got to be better than hiking, right?

But Jaxon just laughs. "A snowmobile will only slow us down."

"What exactly does that mean?"

"It means we're going to fade."

"Fade?" I have no idea what that means, but it doesn't sound particularly appealing. Then again, what about this situation is appealing? Visiting an ancient vampire and hoping she doesn't kill us? Living with a psychopath inside my head? Having no memory of the last four months?

Screw it. Whatever fading is, whatever Jaxon has in mind, has got to be better than anything else we're dealing with right now.

Which is why I just nod when Jaxon explains that fading is a vampire thing and it involves moving very, very fast from one place to another.

I start to ask how fast is fast, but does it matter? As long as we get to the Bloodletter and figure out what to do about Hudson before he decides to turn my life into a fictional TV show called *Bodysnatched*, we could swim to the Bloodletter's cave and I wouldn't care.

"So what exactly do I need to do?" I ask as Jaxon moves in front of me.

"I pick you up in my arms," he answers, "and then you hang on tight."

That doesn't sound too bad. Almost romantic, even.

Jaxon leans forward and sweeps me off my feet, one arm under my shoulders and the other under my knees. Once I'm safely balanced in his arms, he looks down at me and winks. "Ready?"

Not even close. I give him a thumbs-up. "Yeah, absolutely."

"Hang on!" he warns, then waits until I wrap both my arms around his neck as tightly as I can.

Once I do, he shoots me a grin. And then he starts to run.

Except it's not like any running I've ever experienced before. In fact, it's not like running at all. If I had to guess, it's more like we're *disappearing* from one place to the next in rapid succession, too fast for me to get my bearings on the new location before we *disappear* again.

It's strange and terrifying and exhilarating all at the same time, and I hold on as hard as I can, afraid of what will happen if I let go, even though Jaxon has his arms gripping me tightly against his chest.

As he fades again and again, I keep trying to think, trying to focus on what I want to say to the Bloodletter or how I can lock Hudson out of my mind, but we're going so fast that real thinking is impossible. Instead, there's only instinct and the most basic follow-through of thought.

It's the strangest feeling in the world. And also one of the most freeing.

I don't have a clue how long we've been traveling when Jaxon finally stops at the top of a mountain. He sets me down slowly, which I'm grateful for, since my legs suddenly feel like rubber.

"Are we there?" I ask, looking around for a cave entrance.

Jaxon grins and, not for the first time, I realize how nice it is that Jaxon doesn't have to cover every inch of exposed skin the way I do when we're outside. I like being able to see his face, like even more being able to gauge his reaction to my words. "I wanted to show you the view. And I thought you might like a break."

"A break? We've only been moving a few minutes."

His grin becomes a laugh. "It's been more like an hour and a half. And we've gone almost three hundred miles."

"Three hundred miles? But that means we've been traveling at close to—"

"Two hundred miles an hour, yeah. Fading is more than just movement. I don't know how to describe it; it's kind of like flying—without a body. Every vampire starts practicing it at a young age, but I was always very, very good at it." He looks like a little kid, absurdly proud of himself.

"That's...incredible." No wonder I was having such a hard time holding on to images and thoughts as Jaxon faded. We weren't so much moving as bending reality.

As I turn all this information over in my head, I can't help thinking about a book I read in seventh grade, *Fahrenheit 451* by Ray Bradbury. In it, he talks about people driving cars superfast on the regular highways—like 130 miles an hour fast—and the government condoning it, because it keeps people from thinking. They have to concentrate on driving, and not dying, to the exclusion of everything else.

It felt a little like that when Jaxon was fading. Like everything else in my life, even the bad stuff, just disappeared, leaving only the most basic survival instincts in its place. I know Bradbury meant his book to be a warning, but fading is so cool that I can't help wondering how Jaxon feels about it.

I wonder if it feels for him the way it did for me, or if vampires are more able to handle it because they're built to go those kinds of speeds. I almost ask him, but he seems happy—really happy—and I don't want to ruin that with questions that might be hard to answer.

So I don't say anything at all, at least not until Jaxon turns me around and I get to see the view from the very top of this very tall mountain. And it is breathtaking. Massive peaks as far as the eye can see, miles upon miles of snow packed onto the tops and sides of mountains in a kind of frozen wonderland made even more precious by the fact that we really might be the only two people to ever stand here.

It's an awe-inspiring feeling...and a humbling one, which only grows as astronomical twilight closes in around us, turning the world to a faint purple.

The aurora borealis isn't out yet, but some of the stars are, and seeing them against this gorgeous, seemingly never-ending horizon helps put everything I'm going through in perspective. I can't help comparing what one human life—one human's problems—is in contrast to all this, just like I can't help wondering, for the very first time, what immortality feels like. I mean, I know what *I* feel when I'm standing here. Small, insignificant, finite. But what does someone like Jaxon feel, not only with the knowledge that he can climb—and conquer—this impossible mountain in minutes, but also with the knowledge that *he will be here as long as this mountain is*.

I can't imagine what that feels like.

I don't know how long we stand there staring off into the ever-darkening distance. Long enough for Jaxon's arms to creep around me and for me to relax against him.

Long enough for the last little bit of sun to sink down below the mountains.

More than long enough for the cold to seep in.

Jaxon notices my first shiver and pulls away reluctantly. I know how he feels. Right now, I'd be okay with spending eternity up here on this mountain, just him and me and this incredible feeling of peace. I haven't experienced anything like it since before my parents died. And maybe not even then.

Peace can't last with Hudson inside you, a voice in the back of my head says, shattering the feeling of contentment. Could it be my gargoyle side again, warning me? I wonder. Obviously Hudson wouldn't warn me about himself.

Another question for my research, I decide, if my life ever slows down enough for me to actually get some done. Which reminds me, I need to set aside some time when I get back to Katmere to review the notes on gargoyles that Hudson apparently took. Another shiver races down my spine as I wonder what he was looking for about me.

"We need to go," Jaxon says, unzipping my backpack and pulling out a stainless-steel bottle of water. "But you need to drink something before we do. These altitudes can be brutal."

"Even on gargoyles?" I tease, leaning in to him again because it feels right.

"Especially on gargoyles." He smirks as he holds the bottle out to me.

I drink, more because Jaxon is standing there watching me than because I'm actually thirsty. It's a small thing, not worth arguing about, especially when he knows more about this climate than I do. The last thing I need is to add dehydration on top of everything else going on inside me right now.

"Can I have a granola bar?" I ask when I hand him the bottle to put back in my pack.

"Sure," he says, digging in the backpack to find me one.

After chewing a few bites, I ask, "How long until we get to the Bloodletter's cave?"

Jaxon lifts me into his arms again, considers it. "That depends."

"On what?"

"On whether or not we run into any bears."

"Bears?" I squeak, because nobody said anything about bears. "Aren't they still hibernating?"

"It's March," he answers.

"What does that mean?"

When he doesn't answer, I poke him in the shoulder. "Jaxon! What does that mean?"

He shoots me a wicked grin. "It means we'll see."

I poke him again. "What about—"

He takes off, full fade, before I can finish the thought, and then it's just Jaxon and me flying down the side of a mountain. Well, Jaxon, me, and, apparently, a bunch of bears.

I so didn't sign up for this.

30

Winner Winner
Bloodletter's
Dinner

I t seems like only a few minutes before Jaxon stops again, but when I glance at my cell phone, I realize that another hour has gone by. That means that if we traveled at the same speed we did during the first half of the trip, we must be about five hundred miles from Katmere.

"We're here," Jaxon says, but I figured as much. It's in the tightness of his mouth, the sudden tenseness of his shoulders.

I look around, try to find the ice cave where we're supposed to meet the Bloodletter, but all I see is mountain in every direction. Mountain and snow. Then again, I'm not exactly an expert on ice caves.

"Is there anything I need to know?" I ask when he takes my hand, starts to lead me closer to the base of the mountain.

"Honestly, there's so much you need to know that I'm not sure where to start."

I laugh at first, because I think he's joking, but a quick glance at his face tells me that I've misread the situation. In response, the ball of tension in my stomach gets just a little tighter.

"Maybe the abbreviated version?" I suggest as we come to another sudden stop, this time right in front of two giant piles of snow.

"I don't know how much good it'll do, but I can try." He shakes his head, runs a gloved hand up and down his thigh in the most nervous gesture I've ever seen from him as the silence goes on and on and on.

I've just about decided that he's changed his mind, that he's not going to tell me anything, when Jaxon says in a voice that's more wind than whisper, "Don't get too close to her. Don't try to shake her hand when you meet her. Don't—"

He breaks off, and this time he runs a palm over his face instead of his thigh and, though it blends in with the howl of a nearby wolf, I swear I hear him say, "This is never going to work."

"You don't know that," I answer.

His head snaps up, and this time the obsidian gaze he focuses on me is like nothing I've ever seen from him. Silver flames dance in the depths of his eyes, and there is a mountain of despair there as well as a host of other emotions that I don't recognize or understand.

"You realize she's a vampire, right?"

"Of course." I don't know where he's going with this, but they were pretty clear back at the library.

"If she hasn't eaten in a while," Jaxon says, mouth twisted in a grimace I could never have missed, "she'll probably have a food source there."

"A food source?" I repeat. "You mean a human?"

"Yeah." He swallows hard. "I want you to know that I don't do what she does. I don't feed from people the way she does. I don't—"

"It's okay," I tell him as I realize that he's as nervous about what I'm going to think of his upbringing and the woman who raised him as he is about my safety and the fact that his brother is now hanging out inside me somewhere.

It's a shocking revelation about a guy who has never appeared anything but confident, and it warms me even as it makes me nervous.

Jaxon nods. "Sometimes she lures tourists in. Sometimes other paranormals bring her 'gifts' for her assistance." He holds my gaze. "Not me, though."

"Whatever happens in there is okay," I tell him, leaning forward so that my arms are wrapped around his waist and my chin is resting on his chest. "I promise."

"'Okay' is a bit of an overstatement," he tells me. "But she is tens of thousands of years old, so it is what it is." He hugs me back, then steps away. "Also, you need to let me do most of the talking in there. If she asks you a question, answer, of course, but she doesn't particularly like strangers. Oh, and don't touch her or let her touch you."

Okay, now the warnings are just getting weird. "Why would I touch her?"

"Just give her a wide berth, I mean. She doesn't like people very much."

"I never would have guessed that, considering she lives in an ice cave in one of the most remote areas of Alaska."

"Yeah, well, there're a lot of reasons people live where they do. It's not always about choice."

I start to ask him what he means, but he might as well have hung a No Trespassing sign on that statement. So in the end, I don't push. Instead, I just nod and ask, "Anything else I need to know?"

"Nothing I can explain to you in a couple of minutes. Besides, it's getting colder. We should go in before you freeze."

I am cold, my teeth all but chattering despite the many, many layers of clothing I'm currently wearing, so I don't argue. Instead, I just step back and wait for Jaxon to lead the way.

And though I think I'm ready for anything, I have to admit the one thing I don't expect is for Jaxon to raise a hand and lift an entire bank of snow several feet into the air. But as he does, he reveals a small opening in the base of the mountain: the entrance to the ice cave.

Jaxon drops the snow behind us, then moves his hands through the air in a complicated pattern. I try to watch what he's doing, but he's moving so fast that his hands are little more than a blur. I start to ask, but he's concentrating so hard that I just stand there waiting for him to finish instead.

"Safeguards," he tells me as he takes my hand and walks me into the cave.

"To protect people from wandering in?" I ask.

He shakes his head. "To keep my father out."

Jaxon's jaw tightens, and I get the sense he really doesn't want me asking more questions. So I don't.

Besides, it's taking every ounce of concentration I have to keep from slipping and sliding down the steepest, narrowest, *iciest* path I have ever seen. Jaxon holds my hand tightly all the way, using his strength to steady me several times as we descend.

He's got his phone in his left hand, the flashlight app on to illuminate our path, and we stop several times so that I can get a better foothold. Those are actually the times I like best, because they're the only times I finally get to really look around the cave we're walking into...and it is absolutely gorgeous. Everywhere I gaze are beautiful ice and rock formations—some sharp enough to impale a person, others stripped away by time and water to reveal their very origins.

Those are some of my favorites.

Eventually, we get to a fork in the path but continue down the right side.

There's a second fork at the bottom of that path, and this time Jaxon takes us to the left. We go through another set of safeguards and then suddenly, everything flattens out. We're in a huge room, filled with so many lit candles that, after the dark, I have to blink against the glare of them all.

"What is this place?" I whisper to Jaxon, because it seems like the kind of place that demands a whisper. Wide open, with high ceilings and brilliant rock and ice formations in all directions, it's the most stunning natural wonder I've ever seen.

The place feels like a dream...at least until I glance toward one of the corners and realize there are chains and cuffs jammed into the ceiling—right above a couple of bloodstained buckets. There's no one in the cuffs right now, but the fact that they exist at all takes away my awe at the beauty of the room.

Jaxon sees where I'm looking—it's hard to be subtle when you imagine humans being hung and drained of their blood—and steps forward to deliberately block my view. I don't argue with him; I already have a pretty good idea I'm going to be seeing that setup in my nightmares for some time to come. I don't need to see it in real life again. Ever.

Jaxon seems to feel the same way, because he's tugging me over to the largest arch pretty quickly now, even though the floor is still slippery and uneven.

"Ready?" he asks, right before we get there.

I nod, because honestly, what else am I going to do? And then, with Jaxon's arm wrapped tightly around my shoulders, I walk straight through the archway to meet the Bloodletter.

31

Welcome to the Ice Age

I don't know what I'm expecting when I walk through that frozen archway, but the perfectly put-together living room in front of me is. Not. It.

The room is gorgeous, the ceiling and walls decorated with more rock and ice formations...and behind glass, one very large expressionist painting of a field of poppies in all the shades of red and blue and green and gold.

I'm transfixed by it, much the way I was by the Klimt I saw in Jaxon's room when I first got to Katmere. Partly because it is beautiful and partly because the closer I get to it, the more convinced I become that the painting is an original Monet.

Then again, when you've been alive for thousands of years, I guess it's easier to get your hands on the works of the masters—maybe even before they became masters.

The rest of the room looks like any living room anywhere—with an upgrade from standard to absolutely stunning. A gigantic rock fireplace dominates one of the side walls. Bookshelves line the room, filled with books bound in cracked and colorful leather, and a giant rug that looks like a bouquet of flowers exploded stretches across the massive floor.

In the center of the room, facing away from the fire, are two large wingback chairs in the same red as the poppies in the painting. Across from them, separated by a long rectangular glass coffee table, is a comfortable-looking sofa in harvest gold.

And sitting on the sofa, legs curled under her with a book in her lap, is a very sweet-looking old woman, with short gray curls and colorful reading glasses. She's dressed in a silk caftan in swirling shades of blue, and her light-brown skin glows in the candlelight as she closes her book and deposits it on the glass table.

"Four visits in as many months," she says, looking up at us with a soft smile. "Careful, Jaxon, or I'm going to start getting spoiled."

Her voice sounds like she looks—sweet, cultured, calm—and I feel a little like I'm being punked. This is the most dangerous vampire in existence? This is the woman Jaxon refers to as the *Bloodletter*? She looks like she'd be more at home knitting and playing with her grandchildren than she ever would hanging people upside down from the ceiling to drain their blood.

But Jaxon is moving us toward her, his head angled down in the most submissive gesture I have ever seen from him, so this has to be her, fuzzy slippers and all.

"You could never be spoiled," he answers as we come to a stop right in front of her. Or rather, Jaxon comes to a stop in front of her. I come to a stop several feet back, as Jaxon has deliberately angled his body between us. "I like the new color scheme."

"I was overdue for a change. Spring is a time for renewal, after all." She smiles ruefully. "Unless you're an old vampire like myself."

"Ancient isn't the same as old," Jaxon says to her, and I can tell from his voice that he means it. And also that he admires her a great deal, even if he doesn't trust her completely.

"Always such a charmer." She stands up, her gaze meeting mine for the first time. "But I'm guessing *you* already know that."

I nod, more cognizant than ever of Jaxon's warning to let him do the talking. Because while the Bloodletter might look like the sweetest grandma ever, her green eyes gleam with shrewdness—and more than a little bit of avarice—as she looks me over. Add in the fact that I can see the tips of her fangs glowing against her bottom lip in the firelight, and I'm beginning to feel a little bit like a fly to the proverbial spider.

"You brought your mate," she tells him with an arch look, one that speaks volumes I don't begin to understand.

"I did," he replies.

"Well, let me get a look at her, then." She walks forward, pressing a hand to the side of Jaxon's biceps in an effort to guide him over a few steps.

Jaxon doesn't budge, which makes the Bloodletter laugh, a bright, colorful sound that echoes off the vaulted ceilings and ice-hard walls. "That's my boy," she says. "Always the overprotective one. But I can assure you this time, there's no need."

Again, she presses on his biceps in a very obvious "scoot over a little" gesture. Again, he doesn't move so much as an inch.

Annoyance replaces amusement in her bright-green eyes, and she sends him a look that, not going to lie, has me shaking a little in my shoes. Certain that she can smell it, I tamp down the small quiver of fear and meet her curious gaze with one of my own.

I can tell she likes that, just as I can tell how unhappy she is with Jaxon's refusal to bend to her will. Deciding to take it out of both their hands, I step forward and smile at her. "I'm Grace," I say, and though convention suggests that I offer my hand, Jaxon's earlier warning still rings in my ears. "It's really nice to meet you."

She gives me a delighted smile in response but makes no move to touch me, either—even before Jaxon lets out an obvious sound of displeasure.

"It's wonderful to meet you, too. I'm glad everything has…worked itself out with you."

Surprised by her words, I glance at Jaxon. He doesn't take his eyes off the woman who raised him, but he does answer my silent question. "She knows you're a gargoyle. I came to see her twice when you were locked in stone."

"He left no stone unturned, as it were, when he was looking for a way to set you free. But alas, gargoyles haven't been my specialty in quite a long while." Her gaze seems to go far away as she continues. "I did hope to change that once, but it was not to be."

Even though I already know that Jaxon did anything and everything he could to help me when I was trapped as a gargoyle, it still warms me to hear it—especially from this woman he very obviously respects.

"Thank you for trying to help me," I tell her. "I appreciate it."

"There wasn't anything for me to try," she answers. "Much to your mate's chagrin. But I would have helped him if I could. I suggested he bring you to me, in fact. I'm glad he's finally taken my advice."

She moves a few steps back, gesturing to the two red chairs before once again settling herself on the couch.

"I always planned on bringing Grace to meet you eventually," Jaxon says.

Her eyes soften at that, and for the first time, I see genuine affection in her expression as she looks at Jaxon. I find myself relaxing just a little at the sight of it—not because I think she won't hurt me but because I'm pretty sure she won't do anything that would harm Jaxon.

"I know." She leans forward and pats his hand. As she does, I see a softening in Jaxon, too, a momentary dropping of his guard as he looks at this woman he obviously loves but just as obviously doesn't trust.

It's such a weird dynamic that I can't help feeling sorry for the both of them, even as I wonder what it's like. Before their deaths, I trusted my parents implicitly—it never occurred to me not to.

And though I've found out things about them since they died— things like my father was a warlock and maybe they knew about the gargoyle thing all along—at least I still know, even if they lied to me, that they would never have hurt me.

Jaxon's mother scarred him. His brother tried to kill him. And this woman, who obviously had a major impact on his life and who obviously loves him, has Jaxon so tense, so on edge, that I'm afraid he might shatter at the first wrong move.

Silence stretches between us before Jaxon finally says, "I'm sorry to do this on the first night that you meet Grace, but we need your help."

"I know." She looks from Jaxon to me and back again. "And I will do what I can. But there are no easy solutions to what plagues you. There are, however, many, many chances for things to go wrong."

32

One Person's Reality Is Another Person's Total Mind F*ck

That sounds...awful.

I'm more than a little freaked when I turn to Jaxon, but he just gives me a reassuring look as he rubs the back of my hand with his thumb before turning back to the Bloodletter.

He does an amazing job of relating the events since I've come back, so much so that the Bloodletter's eyes glaze over only once in the telling. When it's done, she stares at me for a few beats, then asks me to take a walk with her.

I look to Jaxon—not for permission so much as reassurance that she's not taking me to some inner cavern to drain my blood—and he gives me a slight nod. It's an uneasy nod, but it's a nod nonetheless.

Not the most reassuring thing in the world, but it's not like I really have a choice at this point.

The Bloodletter smiles when I get up and beckons me closer with one beringed hand. "Don't worry, Grace; we won't go far. I do my best thinking while I walk."

The Ancient vampire leads me through a double arch into another, darker room. But the second we walk in, the room springs to life. The sun is shining, the sand beneath my boots is sparkling, and in the distance, I can see, and hear, the roar of the ocean waves.

"How—" I stumble to a stop and stare at the familiar blue of the

Pacific Ocean. And not just any part of the Pacific, but my beloved La Jolla Cove. I recognize it from the tidal pools around the sides of the relatively small beach and the way the ocean washes up on the sand and the rocks in a rhythm as familiar as my own breathing.

"How did you do this?" I ask, blinking back the rush of homesick tears from my eyes. The Bloodletter has given me a gift beyond measure. No way am I going to waste one second of my time here crying. "How did you know?"

"I know a lot of things, Grace, and I can do almost as many." She shrugs delicately. "Come on. Let's go walk by the water."

"Okay," I agree, even though I know the water isn't real. Even though I know I'm in the middle of a giant illusion. The fact that it feels real is enough for me right now.

We don't talk as we make our way up the beach to the slowly rolling waves.

"If you want your mind and body back, my darling—" She stops to stare out over the vast ocean for what feels like an eternity before turning to face me, her eyes swirling that eerie electric green again. "It's going to require sacrifice. Probably more than you're willing to give."

I swallow. "What does that mean exactly?"

But she pats my hand and simply says, "That's something for you to learn another day. For now, why don't you take a moment and feel the water?"

I look down and realize we're near where the ocean should be kissing my toes if I were to move just a few more inches to the side.

"But it's not real," I tell her. "There's nothing there."

"'Real' is in the eye of the beholder," she answers. "Feel the water."

"How are you doing this?" I gasp as I let the water run through my fingers. The feel of it gets me in the gut, even though I try not to let it. But how can I not when it reminds me of all the times I was there with my parents or Heather?

"A good illusion covers all the bases," she tells me. "A *great* illusion makes it impossible to tell where reality leaves off and deception begins."

She waves her hand, and just like that, we're in the middle of the desert, sand where there was only ocean before.

I swallow my instinctive protest, my urge to beg her to bring the water back. To bring my home back. And instead plunge my hand into the sand right in front of me.

I come away with a handful of it, just as I knew I would, and when I let it leak through my fist back onto the ground, some of it sticks on the wetness of my fingers so that I have to brush it off against my ski pants.

"I don't understand what's happening here."

"Because you don't believe what you see," she snaps.

"But I can't believe it. It's not *real*."

"It's as real as you want it to be, Grace." Another wave of her hand and a sandstorm kicks up, hard and fast. Grains of sand whip against my face, fill my nose and my mouth until I can barely breathe.

"Enough," I manage to wheeze out between coughs.

"Is it enough?" the Bloodletter asks in a voice as cold as the Alaskan wilderness she has made her home. "Do you understand what I'm trying to tell you?"

No, I don't. Not even a little bit. But I'm afraid if I tell her that, I'm going to end up buried under a thousand pounds of sand, so I just nod.

But I do try to focus, not just on what she's saying but on the deeper meaning of what she wants me to understand.

Her gaze holds mine, her green eyes urging me to think beyond my simple understanding of the world. To recognize that some things have to be believed to be understood instead of the other way around.

It's a leap of faith, one I'm not sure I'm comfortable making after everything that's already happened. But what other choice do I have? I can believe or I can get swept away—not just by the sand she is continuing to blow my way but by Hudson's dark and overwhelming will.

I swallow, knowing there really is no other option for me. And so I close my eyes, lower my defenses just a little, and let her words swirl in my mind, settle in my bones, become my reality.

The moment I do, the illusion of this world fades into something that feels even more right. Something that feels like coming home.

Suddenly, there's another voice in my head, and it's not the one I'm used to, the one that warns me of bad things to come. No, this voice is low and sardonic. It's also familiar—really familiar.

"Well, it's about time."

"Oh shit." My stomach bottoms out. "Did you hear him?" I demand of the Bloodletter. "Tell me you heard him."

"It's okay, Grace," she answers. And if she says any more, I don't know because—just like that—the world around me goes completely black.

33

It's Hard to Pick My Battles When My Battles Keep Picking Me

*S*omething isn't right.

It's the first thought I have as I slowly open my eyes. My head hurts and my stomach is roiling like I'm going to throw up. I notice I'm lying on a bed, in what I think is a dimly lit bedroom. Which doesn't make sense, because the last thing I remember is talking to the Bloodletter—right up until I heard someone in my head with a British accent.

My eyes fly open as I remember Hudson, and I bolt upright, then wish I hadn't as the room spins around me. I do my best to breathe through the nausea and focus on remembering what's important. Namely, Hudson, and what he did or didn't do.

Did he take control of my body again?

Did he hurt Jaxon or the Bloodletter, and is that why they're not here?

Worse, did *I* hurt them?

I glance down at myself, checking for blood—something I'll probably do every time I wake up for the rest of my life now, courtesy of Hudson's little werewolf-hunting expedition. So, thanks for that, Hudson. I appreciate the mental scars.

"Sorry, I didn't think he'd bleed so much. It was just a little prick. Then again, so is he."

Oh God. I didn't imagine it. Damn. I close my eyes and lie back down, praying that none of this is actually happening. That it's all just a really bad dream.

"Stop talking to me!" I order.

"Why on earth would I do that now that you can finally hear me? Do you have any idea how boring it gets in here? Especially when you spend so much of your time mooning all over the place about my loser brother. It's nauseating, really."

"Yeah, well, feel free to leave anytime you want," I suggest.

"What do you think I've been trying to do?" Exasperation colors his tone. *"But you got pissed off about that, too, even though it was your idea. No offense, Grace, but you're a hard woman to please."*

This isn't happening. It can't be. The body snatching was bad enough, but now I have to deal with this disembodied voice in my head, too? And not just any disembodied voice but one that belongs to a psychopath with a full-on British accent? *How is this my life?*

"Hey now, I resent that. I'm not disembodied. At least not completely."

"I see you're not even going to argue about the psychopath part." I shake my head in astonishment.

"It's called picking your battles. You should try it sometime. You might end up in the infirmary less. Just saying."

The fact that he might be right about this one specific comment only annoys me more. "Is there a point to this conversation?"

"Grace," he says softly. *"Open your eyes."*

I don't want to do it. I don't even know why, except that I really, really don't want to.

But at the same time, it's sort of a compulsion. The kind that I know is going to hurt later—like when I chipped my tooth in seventh grade and couldn't resist touching it with my tongue, even though I knew it was so sharp, it would cut me. That's what it feels like listening to Hudson tell me to open my eyes.

"Wow, so I'm a toothache now?" He sounds insulted. *"Thaaaaanks."*

"If you were a toothache, I'd go to the dentist and let her drill you out of my head," I tell him, my voice filled with the frustration I can't get away from. "Without novocaine."

"You've got quite the mean streak in you, Grace. Does it make me a masochist if I admit that I like it?"

Ugh. Seriously? I can stand the voice in my head. I can maybe even put up with the fact that that voice belongs to Hudson. But the sexual innuendo is going to make me vomit.

I finally stop fighting myself and decide to open my eyes if it means it will shut him up, even for a second. Then really wish I hadn't because—

Holy hell. He's right there, one wide shoulder resting against the icy wall near a lamp, long legs crossed at the ankle, obnoxious smirk on his ridiculously pretty face. He's got the signature Vega high cheekbones and strong jawline, but that's where the similarity to Jaxon ends. For where Jaxon's eyes may be as black as a starless night, Hudson's are an endless blue sky. Thick eyebrows, the same shade of rich dark brown as his short hair, slant downward, his gorgeous eyes narrowing as he takes in every detail of my reaction. And that's when I realize, Jaxon might ooze power and danger in his every movement, but Hudson has always been the real one to fear. Jaxon was a blunt weapon next to his brother, who seems to be cataloging my every weakness, every nuance and emotion, with surgical precision. This guy would know exactly how to hurt you the most—and you'd never see it coming.

Nothing in the world could have stopped the shiver that slides down my spine.

I wouldn't be surprised if he turned around and there was a sign plastered across the back of his silver-gray dress shirt spelling out villain in huge black letters.

That's how perfect he is at looking bad. At *being* bad. And that's before I even notice that his free hand is shoved negligently into the pocket of a pair of expensive-looking black dress pants.

Because of course it is. Looks like the devil really does wear Gucci...

"These are Versace," he answers, indignation ripe in his tone.

"Who cares?" I demand as my brain finally catches up with my observational skills. "Have you been standing there all along?"

"Yes, Grace, I've been here all along," he tells me with a long-suffering sigh. "No offense, but where else would I be? We're kind of attached, in case you didn't notice."

"Believe me, I've noticed."

"Then why ask a silly question?"

I roll my eyes at him. "I'm so sorry. I'll stop asking silly questions if you stop—oh, I don't know—hijacking my body to try to kill people."

"I already told you, it was just supposed to be a little prick. It is not my fault werewolves have such abysmal tempers." He lifts one dark, perfect brow. "But I've got to say, you are a feisty one. Do you really think Jaxon can handle you?"

"It's none of your business what Jaxon can and can't handle."

"So that's a solid no, then?" This time, he flashes a sly little smile that should be obnoxious but somehow only ends up making his already perfect face look even more perfect.

"Aww, you think I have a perfect face?" He turns his head to the side to emphasize his sky-high cheekbones and chiseled jaw. "What's your favorite feature?"

"You weren't supposed to hear that."

"I'm in your head, Grace. I hear everything."

"But I see you over there, and your lips are moving." All of a sudden, his words register. *"Everything?"*

He holds up one finger. "First, only you can see me. Your mind is manifesting me. And two..." His smile gets even slyer. *"Everything."*

I duck my head so he can't see the heat scorching my cheeks. "I have no idea how to respond to that."

"No worries." Hudson winks at me. "I'm used to girls being speechless around me."

I groan. "I wasn't worried." *And are you* really *going to keep doing this?*

"Doing what?" He pastes a mock-innocent look on his face.

"Commenting on my thoughts, even when I'm not talking to you." I groan again and flop back onto the bed.

He grins. "Consider it extra motivation."

"For what?" I demand.

"I don't know." He pretends to study his nails. "Getting me out of your head, maybe?"

"Believe me, I don't need any extra motivation. The sooner I get you gone, the sooner I never have to see you again."

I brace myself for his next sarcastic remark, figuring it will be a doozy. But for long seconds, he doesn't say anything at all. Instead, he pulls a ball out of thin air and starts tossing it up in front of his face and then catching it again.

Once, twice, then again and again. At first, I'm grateful for the silence—and the peace that comes with it. But the longer it goes on, the more antsy I become. Because the only thing worse than knowing everything Hudson is thinking is knowing *nothing* that he's thinking. I can't help but guess he's plotting to murder me like I'm plotting to murder him right now.

Eventually, though, he turns his attention back to me. "See," he says with another of those deadpan looks of his, "I told you, you had a mean streak."

Then he tosses the ball up in the air yet again.

"Yeah, well, I'd rather have a mean streak than an asshole streak," I tell him.

"Everyone has an asshole streak, Grace." He looks me straight in the eyes when he says this, and for the first time, it feels sincere. *He* feels sincere. "The only difference is whether or not they're honest enough to let you see it. And those who aren't? Those are the ones you need to watch out for."

"Why does that feel like a warning?" I wonder aloud.

"Because you're not some pathetic little human anymore. You're a gargoyle, and when it comes to how people feel about gargoyles—knowing one, owning one, possessing one—nothing and nobody is quite what they seem."

"Including you?" I shoot back, even as a shiver works its way down my back at his warning.

"Obviously me," he agrees, sounding bored and annoyed. "But my point is, I'm not the only one."

I don't know how to respond to that, don't know if he's just messing with my mind or if there really is some truth to what Hudson is saying. Before I can decide, he steps away from the wall. But instead of coming toward me, he moves farther back into the shadows of the room.

"Here comes one now," he whispers deep in the recesses of my brain.

"What do you mean?" I ask, just as softly.

He shakes his head, refuses to say anything else.

And it's not until I turn away, not until the Bloodletter calls my name, that I realize that the ball Hudson tossed up in the air? It never came back down.

34

This Place Isn't
Big Enough for
the Both of Us

"Grace, are you awake yet?" The Bloodletter's voice seems farther away than expected.

"I'm awake," I tell her, pushing myself into a sitting position and leaning back against the pillows. "I'm sorry. Hudson..."

"What about Hudson?" the Bloodletter asks, leaning forward with watchful eyes.

For the first time, I realize that the shadows were hiding bars that are between her and me. Even worse is the realization that *I'm on the wrong side of those bars*.

I bolt upright then, my gaze searching the shadowy darkness until it collides with Jaxon's. "What's going on?" I demand in a voice made shrill with fear. "Why am I in a cage?"

"It's okay," he soothes.

"It's *not* okay. I'm not some animal in the zoo, Jaxon. Get me out of here. Now."

I start to reach for the bars, then think better of it, since they've got this weird, electric glow to them and I can't help wondering what that means...not to mention what it will mean for me if I touch them.

"We can't do that, Grace. Not yet," the Bloodletter answers.

"Why not?" For the first time, I start to wonder if Hudson's words were actually true. If he wasn't just saying those things to mess with me.

"Much as I enjoy messing with you, Grace, I'm not in the habit of issuing warnings for no reason," Hudson admonishes from the shadows.

"Stop talking to me!" I practically shout back. "Can't you see I'm in trouble here?"

Jaxon and the Bloodletter exchange a surprised look.

"Who are you talking to, Grace?" Jaxon asks.

"They can't hear me," Hudson reminds me, and I clamp my jaw tight.

"It's okay," the Bloodletter says. "I know Hudson is in there with you. I'm the one who put you to sleep when I realized just how strong Hudson's hold on you is."

Part of me wants to ask how she knows, but then I figure, why wouldn't she? What's the point of being that old if you don't know a lot about a lot?

"Oh, please." Hudson lets out a long-suffering sigh and steps away from the shadows again to pace in the narrow space next to my bed. "She makes me sound like a cult leader. I haven't forced you do anything you didn't want to do."

I turn to him in shock. "You mean besides stealing the athame and trying to kill Cole? Oh, and the fact that I've now blacked out *three times* in as many days?"

"To be fair, Cole deserved it. And we didn't *try* to kill him."

I watch as the Bloodletter grabs Jaxon's arm and pulls him away from the cage bars to tell him something privately. Fuck my life. More secrets.

But I use the space to hiss quietly back at Hudson. "You're right. *We* didn't do anything. *You* did."

He sighs and leans against the ice wall again. "Potato, po-tah-to. But back to the situation at hand. I warned you not to trust her."

"You warned me *after* she'd already put me in a cage. What good is that?" I snipe back.

"And besides, you're the reason I'm even in this cage, so you're the one I should be blaming."

"Yeah, yeah, yeah. Same song, different singer." He waves a careless hand.

"I have no idea what that means."

"It means more powerful people than you have bent over backward trying to absolve my little brother of guilt. I don't even know why I'm surprised that you've turned out to be just like the rest of them."

"I'm not trying to absolve Jaxon of anything!" I whisper-shout. "I'm just trying to get out of this damn cage. How did you come back without a body so that I'd be lucky enough to have you trapped in my head in the first place?"

"I came back with a body." He shakes his head and glances at Jaxon, still conversing with the Bloodletter. "I was confused, too, but I know that much. The last thing I remember is my brother trying to kill me and I was moving on instinct, fading toward him to protect myself. When you turned to stone, I'm pretty sure you took my faded body that was still re-forming with you. And, well"—he spreads his hands wide—"here we are."

That makes a twisted kind of sense to me, even though I don't want it to be true. But what else could have happened? I didn't shift to my gargoyle form on purpose—I didn't even know it was possible. But if he was fading into me at the exact same time, maybe it messed with how I shifted. Or maybe I messed with how he faded. Either way, it really might be *my* fault that he's trapped in my head. Ugh. So not what I wanted to realize.

I turn back to the Bloodletter with that knowledge churning in my head and try to get her attention again. "What do I need to do for you to let me out of here?"

The Bloodletter and Jaxon walk back to the cage bars. Jaxon's face looks extremely worried, and I suddenly have the urge to hug him, to tell him everything is going to be all right.

"You're the one in the cage, and you want to ease *his* suffering.

Point fucking made," Hudson growls, but I ignore him, holding Jaxon's gaze instead.

The Bloodletter interrupts. "You need to let me teach you how to build a wall so you can lock Hudson out. You have to put a barrier between the two of you, Grace. Hudson can't be trusted."

"I know that."

"Do you?" she asks. "Do you really? Because I don't think you can fully understand until you know him. Until you see how he operates, up close and personal. You may not believe it, but the time will come when you want to empathize with him."

"I would never—"

"Oh yes, you would. You will. But you can't. You have to stay strong, to be on your guard at all times. No one in your world is more dangerous than Hudson. No one else can do what he can. He'll tell you anything you *need* to hear, everything you *want* to hear. He'll lie to you, he'll trick you, and when you lower your guard, he'll kill you. Or worse. He'll kill everyone you love, just because he can."

Hudson stops pacing, his face turning to stone as he waits for my reaction. Only his eyes are alive, a vivid, storm-tossed blue that delves into the very heart of me.

"I won't let that happen. I swear," I tell her, even as panic races through me. "How can I lock him out?"

"That's what I want to show you," she says. "If you'll let me."

"Of course I'll let you. I thought that was the whole reason we were here—so you could teach me how to get rid of him. I just don't understand why you felt like you needed to lock me up." I turn to Jaxon. "Or why *you* thought it was okay to let her."

He looks sick. "I didn't—"

"He doesn't have a choice. And neither do you. It's bad enough that Hudson could take over your body. But now that he's started talking to you, we have to find a way to create a partition between you and him before it's too late. This cage will give us the freedom to do that, since he's behind bars, too."

I notice that she doesn't mention that it protects anyone *inside* the cage from his power—namely me—but I don't call her on it. Not when my stomach is doing a triple somersault in the worst possible way and I have bigger, more important things to question her about. "Too late?"

"Yes, too late," she reiterates. "The longer we wait, the greater the chance that the next time he takes you over..." She pauses and glances at Jaxon before turning back to me. "The next time, you might not be able to find your way back."

Her voice echoes ominously throughout the cavern, her warning hitting me like a wrecking ball. "That can't really happen, can it?" I whisper through a throat tight with horror.

"Of course not!" Hudson starts pacing the room again. "I mean, seriously. Who would actually choose to spend their life as a Jaxon Vega fangirl?"

I ignore him.

"It's absolutely possible," the Bloodletter assures me. "And the longer he stays in you, the harder it's going to be for you to get him out—especially if he decides he doesn't want to go."

Hudson runs a hand through his hair, his fingers tangling in the longer, wavy strands on top. "Believe me, that will not be a problem, Grace. I want out of you at least as much as you want me out."

"What happens if he decides to stay?" I ask. "I mean, how does it happen?"

The Bloodletter studies me for several seconds, as if weighing how much she wants to say. "First, he'll start to control you more often—and for longer periods of time. When he lets you go, it'll be harder for you to remember who you are, harder to fit back into your everyday life, until it will seem easier to just let him take over. Until one day you just give up completely."

"I wouldn't do that to you, Grace. You have to trust me." Hudson sounds almost as frantic as I feel. "Don't build the wall. Don't let her lock me up."

I turn and stare into Hudson's eyes. He's stopped pacing now, and we both just hold the other's gaze for what seems like minutes. I can't tell what he's thinking, but as he's proven, he can hear every one of my thoughts. *I wish I could trust you, but you know that's impossible.*

His shoulders slump, but he nods. *"I know."* He must think the words this time, because his lips don't move, yet I hear each one like a gunshot.

"Don't listen to him," Jaxon tells me urgently. "Whatever he's saying to you is a lie. You can't trust Hudson. You can't—" He breaks off all of a sudden, his eyes wide with shock as he presses a hand to his chest.

"Stop him, Grace." The Bloodletter's voice slices like a lash.

"Stop what?" I demand as Jaxon stumbles forward a few steps before falling to his knees.

"You're killing him," she answers hoarsely, and that's when I realize my hand is outstretched toward Jaxon, power like I've never felt before racing through my body.

I gasp, drop my hand. But Jaxon continues to clutch at his chest.

"Stop it!" I yell at Hudson. And when that doesn't work, I beg. "Please stop! Don't hurt him. Please don't *make* me hurt him."

And just like that, the flow of power evaporates.

"Jaxon?" I whisper as he slowly drops his hands back to his sides. "Are you all right?"

"You're a coward," he answers, looking at me with such contempt that it bruises something deep inside me. At least until I realize it's Hudson he's talking to, not me. "Hiding inside a girl who doesn't even understand her own power yet, using her to do your dirty work. You're pathetic."

"Fuck you!" Hudson snarls, and he sounds like a totally different person—one more than capable of doing all the terrible things Jaxon once told me he did. "You don't know anything about me!"

I don't repeat what he said to Jaxon. In fact, after what he just used me to do, I refuse to acknowledge him at all.

"How did he get through the cage?" Jaxon demands as he turns on the Bloodletter. "You said we had to put Grace in the cage to neutralize his powers. How did he get through?"

"I'm not sure, though I would imagine it has something to do with the mating bond. Even magic this strong"—she gestures to the bars between us—"can't neutralize the bond completely. He must have found a way to use it to reach you."

"But walling him up will stop him, right? He'll never be able to hurt Jaxon like that again?" I choke out the words.

"It will stop him," the Bloodletter answers. "For at least a week, maybe even two. Hopefully it will be long enough for you to do what needs to be done to banish him completely."

"Don't do it, Grace," Hudson tells me. "You can't trust her."

Maybe not, but I can't trust you, *either, so I'm going to go with the person who can help me the most.*

"This is not how things were supposed to happen." He shakes his head. "Why won't you trust me?"

Maybe because you're a raging psychopath, and I am tired of doing your bidding.

I turn to the Bloodletter. "I'm ready. Show me how to build the wall."

35

I'm Going to Wash That Psychopath Right Out of My Hair

The Bloodletter assesses me for several seconds before she answers. "Every single paranormal finds a different way to build a shield inside them. They do what feels natural—what feels right—to them as they explore and grow into their powers.

"At a different time, that's how you would learn to build *your* wall. As a shield to keep your powers from adversely affecting the people around you."

"But I don't have any powers," I tell her, more than a little confused. "I mean, except the ability to turn to stone. I'm still skeptical on the flying part."

She smiles a little at that and shakes her head. "You have more power than you know, Grace. You just have to find it."

I have no idea what that means, but at this point, I'm willing to try anything. Especially if it means Hudson can't hurt Jaxon again—or anyone else. "Is that how I build the wall or the shield or whatever you want to call it? By channeling my power?"

"Not this time. Because you're not trying to keep your powers in. You're trying to separate yourself and your powers from Hudson and *his* powers. So while we would normally be talking about a shield, right now, we have to talk about a wall."

"Inside me."

"Yes. It won't last forever—as you just saw, Hudson's power is too great to be contained for long, and eventually he *will* break the wall down. But hopefully we'll be able to buy you some time before that happens. Maybe a week or two, I'd guess."

I look from her to Jaxon. "Time to do what?"

Now Jaxon is the one who answers. "Time to get what we need to perform the spell that will get Hudson out of you once and for all."

"There's a spell for that?" Relief swamps me, and I sink back onto the edge of the bed. "Well, why don't we just do it right now?"

"Eager much?" Hudson drolls.

Once again, I ignore him. He's not worth talking to, especially not after the shit he just pulled.

"Because, like all magic, it has a price," the Bloodletter tells me. "And that price includes certain accoutrements that you don't have yet."

"What kind of *accoutrements* are we talking about here?" I ask as I picture eye of newt and wing of bat and God only knows what else. Then again, before Katmere Academy, most of my knowledge about witches came from *Hocus Pocus* and *Charmed*, so maybe I don't have the clearest picture of it all. "And where do we get them?"

"When you were…gone, and I was looking for a way to help you, I found the spell Lia used to bring Hudson back," Jaxon says. "She had the items she needed, but they didn't hold as much power as she needed them to. Plus, she had to bring him back from the dead and not just re-form him from fading, which is all we've got to do.

"Lia didn't have enough power on her own to get the job done, so she needed mine to complete the spell…of course that definitely would have killed me. So this time, I'm all for finding the most powerful objects we can, just to make sure no one has to die. Except maybe Hudson, but I'm okay with that."

"I'm fine doing it Lia's way," Hudson interjects. He's back to lounging indolently against a wall near the bars.

"That *is* shocking," I agree, then get mad at myself for answering him, giving him the attention he obviously wants. Especially since he's now got a ridiculously smug look on his face.

"Yeah, well, Lia was totally unreasonable when it came to Hudson, even when he was alive," Jaxon mutters. It takes me a moment to figure out what he's talking about, but then I realize he thinks my last comment was to him. "But she knew how to do her research. The full spell calls for at least four powerful items."

Four items. That doesn't sound so bad.

The Bloodletter adds, "Well, four to bring him back as he was, a vampire. Five if you want to bring him back as a human, stripped of his powers."

Even better. "So how do we get all five?" I ask.

"Wait a minute!" Hudson is up and pacing again, indolence replaced by a quiet kind of desperation. "You don't need five to get me out of here. You only need four."

Maybe, but five will make sure you never hurt anyone again, and right now, that sounds pretty good to me.

"You don't get to make that choice!" Hudson tells me.

Considering you just used your powers to attack my boyfriend and you're in my head…yeah, Hudson, I'm pretty sure I do.

But I *am* curious. "Why five items to bring him back human but only four to bring him back?"

The Bloodletter narrows her eyes on me, clearly not enjoying being questioned.

"If you wouldn't mind," I tack on nervously.

Which must do the trick, because she answers. "To strip a paranormal of their powers requires the magical consent of all five ruling factions, by covenant. But simply bringing him back as a vampire, since he's already crossed into the mortal coil again, requires only power. Enormous power. And that power can be found in magical objects."

Jaxon nods. "Every faction has magical objects that hold the most power, so we'll need at least four from the different factions to have enough power." But then his eyebrows shoot up, and he pivots to the

Bloodletter. "Wait. How can we have an item from all five factions if Grace is the only gargoyle in existence?"

As though she'd been expecting this question, she continues. "The four items needed to bring him back are the eyetooth of an alpha werewolf. The moonstone from a powerful warlock. The bloodstone from a born vampire. And the full bone of a dragon. Which combined should have enough power." The Bloodletter's eyes take on that eerie electric-green glow as she mentions the last item we need. "But you'll need the heartstone a mythical Unkillable Beast protects to have enough power to *break* the covenant and strip Hudson of his powers."

Jaxon doesn't seem to notice the change in his mentor. "We can get some of the items at school," he insists. "A couple of the other ones we'll have to travel to find, though."

"And I can ensure the bloodstone comes to you," the Bloodletter promises.

"How are you going to do that?" Jaxon turns to her and asks. "Bloodstones are incredibly rare."

The Bloodletter shrugs. "People owe me favors."

"That's not an answer," Jaxon insists. Her only response is an attempt to stare him down, holding his gaze with the green ice of hers. Somehow, Jaxon doesn't flinch under her glacial stare.

"Looks like they're going to be at that for a while," Hudson says with an exaggerated eye roll. "I say we make a break for it."

"Yes, because the only thing worse than having you trapped in my head is having you trapped in my head while I wander the Alaskan wilderness, freezing and alone." The *thanks but no thanks* is implied.

"No pain, no gain." He chuckles.

"Easy for you to say when you'll be getting all the gain and none of the pain."

"I wouldn't be too sure about that." There's an inflection in his voice that has me wondering what's up. But when I glance back at him, his face is as blank as the snow Jaxon and I traversed to get here.

Still, Hudson has a point about what looks to be turning into the world's longest staring contest between the world's two most stubborn people. If I don't break it up soon, I'm pretty sure we'll be here all night.

"So this wall thing I need to build," I say into the tense silence that blankets the cavern. "How exactly do I do that? Because I am more than ready to take a break from Hudson Vega."

36

DIY Exorcism

"You already started," the Bloodletter tells me, "before I put you to sleep. You started laying the groundwork instinctively."

"But how did I do that? How do I build this mythical, mystical wall? And what makes you think I've already started?" I ask, more confused than ever.

"I knew you'd started the minute you began hearing Hudson's voice. Because he didn't talk to you when he was free to take control of you. It's only after you started to impede that freedom that he had something to say."

"That's not true!" Hudson throws his hands up. "I've been trying to get your attention all along. You just couldn't listen until Yoda here taught you how to make an illusion real."

"Wait a minute." I turn to the Bloodletter in horror. "You mean I'll still be able to hear him, even after I wall him up?" Just the idea turns my stomach. "I thought the whole point was to get rid of him."

"The whole point is to make sure he can't take you over anymore. The wall will prevent that, at least for a while. But now that he's figured out how to get your attention..." She shakes her head. "I don't think we'll be able to do anything about that."

Jaxon balls his fists at this statement, but he doesn't say a word.

I sigh. "Well, this day just got a whole lot worse, didn't it?"

Hudson shakes his head. "You really think it's any better for me? At least you haven't been able to hear me for the last two days. I've heard every thought you've had, and let me tell you, they weren't all gems. Especially the hours you spend thinking about my *dreamy* baby brother," Hudson tells me. "Not fun. Not fun at all."

"Then do us both a favor and get out!" I turn and yell at him, not caring that Jaxon and the Bloodletter hear me. I'm more than a little embarrassed at the idea of Hudson being privy to *all* my thoughts, especially the ones about Jaxon.

"What the everlasting bloody hell do you think I've been trying to do?" he answers. "You think I decided to pick a fight with an alpha werewolf just for fun? Believe me, there are better ways for me to get my kicks—even when I'm locked up with you."

Hudson keeps talking about how miserable it is to be locked up inside me—like I don't know that already—but I stop listening as I try to work through everything he just said about the fight with Cole.

None of it makes sense, unless— "Jaxon? What are the five things the spell says we need to get Hudson out of my body for good again?"

"Four," Hudson snaps. "You need four things. One, two, three, four. Even a kindergartener can count that high."

"Temper tantrums are so unbecoming," I throw at him over my shoulder without taking my eyes off Jaxon.

"Yeah, well, so is ignorance, but that doesn't seem to be stopping *you*."

That gets my attention, and I turn to Hudson and smile. "Maybe I can sew up your mouth while I'm walling you away. Surely there's a spell for that somewhere." I keep my voice saccharin sweet.

"Yeah, because I'm totally the one with the temper here." He rolls his eyes.

Jaxon's gaze darts between me and roughly the direction I've been looking in for a few seconds before he decides to settle back on me. "The first thing we need is a vampire's bloodstone," he tells me. "That's a stone that's formed when droplets of a vampire's blood are put under extreme pressure. Like how a diamond is made."

Wow. If that doesn't give a whole new kind of horrific meaning to the term "blood diamond," then I don't know what does. "So there are a lot of these stones out there, just floating around?"

"That's the thing. There aren't that many of them at all. It's a really difficult process to get right, so very few vampires have them. I mean, my family has several—including the ones in the king's and queen's crowns—but they're very closely guarded. Which is why I'm worried about getting my hands on one to—"

"I already told you that I'll find a way for one to come within your grasp," the Bloodletter interjects. "We're vampires, for God's sake. Getting a bloodstone is the least of your problems."

"So what's the worst of our problems, then?" I ask, because I'd rather have the bad news first. And I'm tired of hearing everything piecemeal. For once, I'd like the whole picture up front.

"Dragon bone," Hudson and Jaxon both say at the exact same time.

"Dragon bone?" I repeat, mind boggled. "Like a real, live dragon bone?"

"Actually, a real, *dead* dragon bone," Hudson answers, poker-faced. "Considering most live dragons tend to be using their bones, and nobody likes a grumpy dragon."

"Where would we find *dead* dragon bone?"

Jaxon gives me a weird look at my emphasis on the word "dead," but he answers, "Dragon Boneyard," at the exact same time that Hudson does—again.

"Dragon Boneyard?" I repeat. "That doesn't sound terrifying at all."

"You have no idea," Hudson says. "I keep trying to figure out how we'll navigate the boneyard. It's going to be a disaster."

"I don't think I even want to know yet. One problem at a—" I freeze as something occurs to me. "Hey, wait. You really *do* know what we need to perform the spell."

"Nothing gets by you." Hudson gives me a fake, wide-eyed look, then growls, "No shit, Sherlock."

"You know, you really don't have to be so intolerable all the time," I admonish.

"And here I thought you liked intolerable guys. You *are* dating Jaxy-Waxy, after all."

"Your brother's not intolerable," I tell him, a little offended on Jaxon's behalf.

"Says the girl who's known him less than two weeks."

I ignore him—not because there's a part of me that thinks he might be right but because I don't have time for this right now. We have things that need to get done, and they have nothing to do with my and Jaxon's relationship.

"So we need a bone from a dead dragon and a bloodstone from the vampires," I tell Jaxon. "We already have something from the alpha werewolf. And the athame of a powerful warlock, courtesy of Hudson, although actually, not sure why we needed that. Wasn't the warlock thing supposed to be a stone?"

Jaxon's eyes widen as he realizes where I'm going. "You think that's what Hudson was doing when he..." He trails off, like even saying the word is too much.

"Body snatched me? It would seem so."

"The spell only calls for a tooth, though," Jaxon says. "Why all the excess blood?"

"I already told you Cole's got an attitude problem," Hudson answers. "And apparently a chip on his shoulder a mile wide when it comes to you, Grace."

"Hudson says Cole freaked out and the extra blood was an accident." I pause, unsure if this next bit sounds like I'm defending him. "Cole and I haven't exactly had the best relationship since I got to Katmere."

Jaxon nods. "That's an understatement. Although did Hudson really have to nearly kill him?"

"Tomato, to-mah-to," Hudson answers with a negligible little shrug that does nothing to hide the satisfied gleam in his eyes, one that reminds me an awful lot of Jaxon after he, too, nearly drained Cole dry.

I wonder what Hudson—what either of them—would do if I told them that they have way more in common than they could possibly imagine.

Probably scream at the messenger, and who's got time for that? Especially when Jaxon already looks so tense that I fear he might start shaking the ground at any moment.

So instead, I content myself with saying, "You're terrible, you know that?" to Hudson before turning back to Jaxon. "So does the athame help?"

"Actually, no," Jaxon answers, a contemplative look on his face. "The fourth item is a talisman from one of the seven main covens. I'm not sure why he took the athame."

"Because at the center of the athame's hilt is a talisman—a moonstone," Hudson answers in a voice that clearly says how he thinks Jaxon is a child. "You're welcome."

"Which you're going to share the location of immediately." I don't even bother to make it a question.

"Of course, Grace." He gives me the most condescending smile in existence. "How can I resist when you ask so nicely?"

I relay what he said about the talisman to Jaxon and pretend I don't notice the way my boyfriend's eyes narrow at the in-his-face knowledge that I'm carrying on a full-blown conversation with Hudson at the same time I'm talking to him.

"The *fifth* item is near the North Pole," Jaxon continues with a deliberate sneer on his mouth as he says it—definitely rubbing in the whole "we're going to make you human and you have no say in it" thing to Hudson. Which, not going to lie, is totally well deserved after everything Hudson did.

"The North Pole? What's there? I mean, besides Santa's workshop?"

Jaxon and the Bloodletter both kind of raise eyebrows at that, so I give them a sheepish smile. "Not the right time for levity, huh?"

"I thought it was funny," Hudson says. "Besides, I bet you'd look cute in one of those tiny little elf costumes with the bells on the toes."

"Excuse me?" I say, not sure if he's making fun of how short I am or if he's implying something lascivious and inappropriate. Either way, I'm really not okay with it.

For once, Hudson is mysteriously silent. The jerk.

"The Unkillable Beast," the Bloodletter finally answers, and there's something in the way she says it that has me looking at her more closely. Something that has the hair on the back of my neck standing up and the rest of me trying to figure out just what feels so off about the voice she used.

But her face is impassive, her eyes placid pools of green, so I decide I must have imagined it. And focus instead on what she said and not how she said it. "Unkillable?" I repeat. "That sounds very... not good."

"You have no idea," the Bloodletter agrees. "But it's the only way to break the covenant and take Hudson's power away for good."

I expect Hudson to protest the idea—maybe something snarky about no reason to get ourselves killed on his account when he's quite happy keeping his power—but he doesn't say a word. He just stares at the Bloodletter with his sharp, watchful gaze.

When I turn back to Jaxon, it's to find him and the Bloodletter watching me expectantly. "I'm sorry, did I miss something?" I lift my brows in question.

"I asked if you wanted to try the wall thing," Jaxon says.

I don't even pause to give Hudson a chance to react. "Good God, yes."

Because a thought is starting to take form in my head that has dread pooling in my stomach. If Hudson already knew how to get out and was taking control of my body to make that happen... What was he planning on doing once he *was* out? Kill them all?

"There's that mean streak in you again, Grace."

It's only after Hudson walks into the shadows and disappears that I realize he never answered my question.

37

Sweet Dreams Are Made of Anything But This

Turns out, building a mental wall isn't as hard as I thought it would be. Just placing individual bricks around a part of my mind. And the Bloodletter was right: my own defense mechanisms had gotten started all on their own, so the only thing I had to do was finish piling them higher and mortar them in place with sheer grit and determination.

Several hours later, after the Bloodletter had satisfied herself that the wall would hold, she lowers the bars and sets me free again.

I all but run out of the room and throw myself into Jaxon's arms. No offense to the Bloodletter and her ice cave, but I can't get back to school soon enough. Something about being trapped in a frozen cage and having no control over my life or my fate just does that to me. Shocking, I know.

Turns out, leaving isn't quite possible yet, though, not when Jaxon has gone to the trouble of setting out the meal Uncle Finn had insisted we pack for me.

"Thank you so much," I tell him as I all but devour the turkey sandwich and chips he's arranged on a napkin beside a thermos of water. "This might be my new favorite food in the world."

Jaxon raises one eyebrow. "And what would your old favorite food have been?"

I laugh. "I'm from San Diego. Tacos, of course."

Now that I've eaten, I can feel, maybe, a little bit more hospitable to the woman who kept me locked in a cage all night. *Maybe*. So I force myself to smile and say, "Thank you for all your help."

She waves in the general direction of the cave entrance. "It's time for you two to be leaving."

And just like that, we've been dismissed. Which is fine with me. I'm more than eager to finally say goodbye to these caves and this strange, ancient vampire who seems to have more secrets than I ever want to know.

The trip back isn't quite as exhilarating as the trip to the Bloodletter's cave—partly because we're both so tired and partly because Hudson keeps up a running commentary in my head that makes it hard to concentrate on anything Jaxon has to say. I know I'm going to have to figure out what to do about that sooner rather than later, but for now I just concentrate on keeping the peace.

Because wrangling what amounts to a shit ton of testosterone with fangs is not exactly easy.

I'm completely exhausted by the time we make it back to Katmere. Hudson seems to have fallen asleep again, thank God, and I know Jaxon wants me to come to his room for a while, but all I want is my bed and about twelve hours of uninterrupted sleep. But since we have class tomorrow, I'll settle for eight.

And Jaxon looks plenty fatigued himself, with dark circles under his eyes I'd only ever seen on him once before, when he first showed up in Uncle Finn's office. I don't know why I ever assumed Jaxon's power was infinite. Of course it isn't.

Still, he walks me to my room—of course he does—and once we get there, I go up on tiptoes and hug him as hard as I can.

The embrace startles him. Maybe because more often than not, lately, I'm backing away from him. Still, it takes only a second for him to wrap his arms around me and lift me off the ground in return.

As he does, he buries his face in my neck and just breathes me in. I recognize the move, because I'm doing the exact same thing to him. Even after hours of fading, he smells so good—all fresh water and oranges and Jaxon.

Then, just as suddenly, he's several feet away, walking backward down the hallway while his eyes blaze with a dark fire that has my breath evaporating in my lungs. "Get some sleep," he orders, "and I'll meet you in the cafeteria tomorrow for breakfast."

I nod and force my brain to work just long enough to string two words together. "What time?"

"Text me when you get up and let me know what works for you."

I nod and turn to go inside, closing the door softly behind me.

"You're back!" Macy exclaims, bouncing off her bed. "How was it? Was the Bloodletter as scary as everyone says? Is Jaxon really not afraid of her? Did she help you get rid of Hudson? Could she—" She breaks off as she gets her first good look at me. "Hey, are you okay?"

"Yeah, of course. Why wouldn't I be?"

"Oh, I don't know." She grabs on to my shoulders and turns me around to face the mirror on her closet door. "Maybe because you look like that?"

"Oh." My cheeks are flushed, my curls are wild, and dark circles ring my eyes and make me look feverish. "I'm fine. Just exhausted."

I walk over to my closet and shuck all my snow gear.

"So can I assume Hudson is gone, then?" she asks tentatively, sitting down on the edge of her bed.

"You would assume wrong," I say, collapsing on my own bed in my long underwear and turtleneck. I know I need to take a shower, but right now I have no motivation to do anything other than sit right here and pretend the last two days—and the last four months—have just been a really long nightmare that I'm about to wake up from any second.

"What do you mean?" Macy's eyes go huge. "He's still in you?"

"Ugh. Please don't ever say it like that again." I rub a hand over my very tired eyes. "But yes, Hudson is still in my head. The Bloodletter showed me how to wall off his powers so he can't control me anymore, but he is definitely still in there."

"How do you know? If he's not taking you over—"

"Because he has a new trick. He talks to me now."

Macy looks at me like she isn't sure *how* to process that new information. "He..."

"Talks to me." I roll my eyes. "Non. Stop."

"Like, he just *talks* to you?" Macy asks, and when I nod, she continues. "I mean, what's he saying right now?"

"He's asleep right now, but I'm sure when he wakes up, he'll have something to say."

"About?"

"Anything. Everything. He's definitely a vampire with opinions. Not to mention delusions of grandeur."

Macy laughs. "That's pretty much every vampire everywhere. They aren't exactly known for their humble natures."

I think of Jaxon and Lia, Mekhi and the other members of the Order. Macy might have a point there.

"Sooooo..." Macy pauses like she doesn't want to ask the next question but someone has to. "How are *you* dealing with having someone so evil inside your head? Are you okay? I mean, I know you said he can't *do* anything in there anymore, but still..."

To be honest, I don't have the energy to go down this rabbit hole right now. And I don't know, maybe I never will. Heather's mom told me after my parents died that it was okay not to focus on the pain, not to discuss the trauma, until I was ready. So that's exactly what I plan on doing now.

The loss of control, the sheer violation on the deepest level, plus what it means to have another person in my head...much less a murderer... Well, I'm not ready to even think about any of that yet. So instead I'm going to do my best Dory impersonation and just keep swimming, just keep swimming. And—in this one instance—lie. "About like you would expect me to feel. Nauseated but it's manageable."

"What are you going to do?"

"Besides cry and eat a boatload of Cherry Garcia ice cream?" I offer flippantly.

"I'm thinking two boatloads, but yeah. Besides that?"

I tell her about the spell and the five things we have to get to turn Hudson human again.

"So that's why Hudson made you take the athame?" she asks, astonished. "He wants out, too?"

"That's what he says. Although he was only going for the four items. He has no interest in being turned human."

She looks alarmed. "We can't let him out if he still has his powers. You know that, right?"

"Believe me, I know. I'm just not sure how long I can handle having him in my head."

"I can only imagine." She moves to my bed and sits down next to me so she can wrap an arm around my shoulders. "But don't worry. We'll get started tomorrow on figuring out how to get the last three things. And we should probably rope Flint in. I bet he'll have some ideas about how to get the dragon bone."

"I don't— You don't—" I break off, not sure how to say all the things I'm feeling right now.

"I don't what?" she asks.

"You don't have to do this with me. I mean, it sounds like at least two of the tasks are going to be really dangerous, and I don't want anything to happen to you."

"Are you kidding me right now?" Macy demands, and she looks outraged in a way I've never seen from her before. "You really think I'm going to let you do this by yourself?"

"I won't be by myself. Jaxon—"

"Jaxon won't be enough. I know he's like super powerful and all that," she says, waving her arms in a woo-woo kind of gesture. "But even he can't take on the Unkillable Beast and win—even if you *are* there to help him. There's a reason the thing is called 'unkillable.' I've heard stories about it since I was a child. To be honest, I didn't think it was a real thing. More like the monster your parents warn you about so you don't venture far from home. But if it's real, I've got your back in defeating it."

"Macy." There are so many things I want to say, so many things I want to tell her, but I can't get any of them out. I can't organize my thoughts, and I definitely can't squeeze them through my too-tight throat. Finally, I settle on the one thing I can say. "Thank you."

She grins. "You're welcome."

Then she reaches behind me and fluffs my pillow. "Let's both get some rest. Tomorrow sounds like it's going to be a big day."

I couldn't agree more. My eyes close the second my head hits the pillow, and just as I'm drifting off to sleep, I swear I hear Hudson say, "Sweet dreams, Grace."

38

Take Me Under Your Dragon Wing

"**H**ey, New Girl! Wait up!"

I roll my eyes at Flint but move to the side of the hallway to wait for him anyway. "It's March. When are you going to stop calling me that?" I ask when he finally catches up to me.

"Never," he answers with his usual grin. "I have a present for you..."

He waves a packet of Pop-Tarts in the air above my head, but I easily jump up and snag them. I overslept this morning and am so hungry because of it that I almost pat the familiar silver foil wrapping and whisper, *My precious.*

As we weave around the rest of the students in the crowded hallway on our way to History of Witchcraft, I quickly open the packaging and take a huge bite of the first pastry I pull out before sighing happily. Cherry. He knows me so well.

"So...evil brother in your head?" Flint asks warily. He must see the question on my face because he quickly adds, "Macy told me."

I glance around the halls, note everyone who—per usual—is staring at me. As I do, I can't help but wonder if Macy told the whole school. I mean, the other students have been staring at me since I first arrived at Katmere, so it's hard to tell if I'm just the new gargoyle attraction...or the new gargoyle attraction with a healthy side of psychopath. Either way, a weight presses down on my chest, making it hard to breathe.

"Hey, hey," Flint says and places a strong hand on my back. "I didn't mean to upset you. Macy just told me so you didn't have to go through the trouble. On strictest confidence. I swear."

The skin around his mouth is pulled tight, and I suddenly remember what Macy told me several months ago—that Flint's brother was one of those killed in the tug-of-war between Jaxon and Hudson last year—and I feel like a total jerk. He must be as freaked out as I am that Hudson is back, and Macy figured she should warn him so he had a chance to process it in private.

"It's okay," I tell him as we make our way through the door to class and slide into our seats in the middle of the room. "He can't hurt anyone anymore."

"How sure are you about that?" Flint asks, an urgency in his voice that I've never heard from him before, even when he was trying to stop Lia. "You don't know him, Grace. You can't make blanket statements like that about someone as evil and powerful as Hudson Vega."

He's deliberately kept his voice low, but obviously not low enough, because several people turn to look at us in alarm when he says Hudson's name.

"Evil and powerful, hmm?" Hudson strides into class and plops down into an empty seat on the other side of Flint, then proceeds to stretch...loudly. "I like the sound of that."

Of course you do, I think. *Which says everything about you that I need to know.*

"I wouldn't be too sure about that," he shoots back as he rolls his shoulders. "How long was I asleep, anyway? I feel amazing."

I lift one brow. *That makes one of us—your snoring kept me up half the night.*

"That's ridiculous! I do *not* snore." He sounds so indignant that it's all I can do not to laugh.

Yeah, keep telling yourself that.

"Hey, Grace. What's going on?" Flint whispers as Dr. Veracruz walks to the front of the classroom, her five-inch heels making a clicking sound with each step she takes. "You're just staring at an empty seat."

"Oh, sorry. I got…distracted."

Now he looks even more confused, not to mention a little annoyed. "By what?"

I sigh and decide to just break the news to him. "By Hudson. He's sitting in the seat next to you, all right?"

"He's sitting *where*?" Flint jumps out of his desk, much to my chagrin…and the amusement of most of the other students. "I don't see him."

"Of course you don't. Sit down, will you?" I hiss. When he doesn't budge, I grab his hand and pull until he finally acquiesces. "It's fine," I reiterate. "It's just a mental projection of his ghost that's currently taking up residence in my head."

Hudson interrupts. "Hey now, I'm not a ghost."

I ignore him and keep my gaze on Flint, who looks skeptical but slides back into his seat, then leans over and whispers, "How could you possibly be fine with *that* in your head?"

"Wow, Montgomery. Don't hold back," Hudson drawls. "Tell me how you really feel."

Will you please shut up? I snarl at Hudson but still keep my gaze trained on Flint. "Trust me. He's been neutered. Nothing more than a Chihuahua in my head, all bark, no bite."

"Wow, thanks. I am *not* a neutered pet," Hudson says with an offended sniff.

Keep it up and I'll figure out how to actually *neuter you.* I turn and hold his gaze so he knows I mean it.

"There are the claws I'm so fond of." He grins at me. "You really do have a bit of the badass in you, Grace, even if you don't believe it."

Flint touches my arm to get my attention again. "How do you know?" Flint whispers as the teacher gives us the not-so-side-eye. "How can you be so sure he's not a threat?"

"Because, for now, the only power he's got is to talk me to death. Plus, I'm sure Macy told you we've got a plan to get him out of my head and make him completely human."

"It's a bad plan," Hudson interjects.

"Yes, she did, and count me in," Flint says, even as Dr. Veracruz starts making her way toward us, her heels hitting the ground like shots from a gun in the now-quiet room.

"For what?" I ask.

"For whatever plan you've got to take the fangs out of Hudson," Flint answers. "Because I am totally down for that."

"Oh, hell no." For the first time, Hudson looks totally alarmed. "No way am I putting up with Dragon Breath over there while we try to figure shit out."

I smile at Flint. "That's a really great idea. I would love your help. Thanks."

"It's a really terrible idea," Hudson grouses as he settles back in his seat with his arms crossed in front of him. He looks like a three-year-old on the verge of throwing a temper tantrum, full-on pout definitely in evidence. "Dragon Boy has a ridiculous temper."

Dr. Veracruz walks back to the front of the class and starts writing dates on the chalkboard. With Flint focused on taking notes, I turn my head just slightly toward Hudson.

That's a little stereotypical, don't you think?

"I wasn't talking about all dragons," he says with a roll of his eyes. "Just this dragon in particular." For the first time ever, Hudson looks... ashamed? "Let's just say I know the family."

"Miss Foster!" I jerk to attention as Dr. Veracruz all but shouts my name.

"Yes, ma'am?"

"Are you planning on answering my question or are you going to spend the whole class period staring at an empty seat?"

"I wasn't—" I break off as my cheeks flood with heat, because what am I going to say? That I wasn't actually staring at an empty seat, I was just arguing with a voice in my head?

Yeah, because that sounds like a totally rational argument...not to mention a one-way ticket to social suicide.

"I'm not just a voice in your head!" Hudson snaps indignantly.

"Yes, Miss Foster?" Dr. Veracruz's voice slices like a guillotine. "What exactly is it that you weren't doing? Besides not paying attention in my class?"

"I'm sorry," I tell her, giving up because there's no reasonable explanation I can put forth. And because the sooner I humble myself, hopefully the sooner she'll go back to the front of the class and leave me alone. "I won't let it happen again."

For long seconds, she just stares at me. Then, just when I think she's going to turn away and head back to the front of the classroom, she says, "Since you seem so eager to make up for your lackadaisical attitude so far in this class, why don't you explain to us about the true enemies of witches during the Salem Witch Trials."

"The true enemies of witches?" I ask faintly, because I have absolutely no idea how to answer that question. Everything I was ever taught in school told me that there were no real witches in Salem. Then again, everything in my old life told me witches don't exist. So maybe she has a point.

"Um, witches during the Salem Witch Trials..." I mumble, hoping for divine inspiration before I make an even bigger fool of myself in front of the class. Unfortunately, nothing is coming.

At least not until Hudson says, "Tell her the real culprits of the Salem Witch Trials weren't the Puritans."

What do you mean? Of course they were.

"No, they weren't. The Witch Trials were a power play by vampires, plain and simple, and the people who died there were pawns in a petty battle that a lot of people hoped would spawn the Third Great War—including my father. But they were wrong."

39

Salem WTF Trials

My mind is blown, completely blown, by this alternate version of history that Hudson provides. Part of me thinks it's total BS, but with Dr. Veracruz standing right in front of me looking like she plans to turn me into something slimy if I don't answer her soon, I decide to just go for it.

I repeat what Hudson explained to me—minus the whole "my father" reference—and one look at her stunned face tells me everything I need to know. Namely that Hudson didn't lie *and* that Dr. Veracruz didn't expect me to know anything about the trials.

The rest of class passes in a blur, largely because Hudson is in a very talkative mood this morning. And since I'm the only person who can hear him, I'm the lucky one who gets to hear all the things about all the things. Lucky, lucky me.

I pack up quickly when the bell rings, determined to get to my Physics of Flight class on time. It turns out Flint is in the advanced class right across from mine, so we end up walking together. Something that, for no reason I can ascertain, makes Hudson cranky as hell.

"Do we really have to spend all day talking to Dragon Boy?" he complains. "What could you two possibly have in common?"

"Oh, I don't know. How about the fact that we both despise you?"

I fire back, not caring that Flint has an amused expression on his face as he watches me chew out the air next to him.

"Believe me, that's not exactly an exclusive club," Hudson answers with a snort.

I roll my eyes. "Which should tell you something about your people skills."

"All it tells me is that people are even more small-minded than I imagined."

"Small-minded?" I ask incredulously. "Because they didn't go along with your little 'conquer the world' plan? How shortsighted of them."

Flint barks out a laugh but doesn't seem to mind that he's only privy to my side of this ridiculous argument.

"Hey, the world could do a lot worse than to be ruled by me," he says. "Look around."

"Wow. Arrogant much?" I ask.

"It's only arrogant if it's not true," he answers and nods toward the stairs that lead to Jaxon's tower.

I don't have a clue how to respond to that, so I don't. Instead, I turn to Flint and ask, "What's this class about anyway? I mean, is it just the science behind flying or do we learn how to fly? How scared should I be?"

"Most of us learn how to fly long before we get to Katmere," Flint explains. "So this class deals more with the why than the how of flight. They call it a physics class, but there's a lot of biology, too, because we learn about the structure and makeup of different wings. And we even dissect a few."

"You mean they aren't all the same?" I ask, a little surprised by the idea that wings are so different at the core. I guess I thought it was like anything else—hair, eyes, skin. They're available in different colors, but when it comes down to important things, they're the same. They're all made up of the same biological matter and they all function the same way. The idea that wings aren't like that is surprisingly fascinating.

Then again, judging by the look on Flint's face, he's even more surprised that I assumed they are. "Of course they're different," he says. "Dragon wings have to support a creature that weighs thousands of pounds. Pixie wings support creatures who can fit in the palm of your hand. And it's not just about size—we fly completely differently, too."

"What do you mean? Isn't flying flying?"

"Not even a little bit. Pixies can hover over whatever they want for long periods of time. Dragons' wings are built for speed and distance, while pixies' wings are built for easy maneuverability. Because pixies are so much smaller and slower—even though their wings flap faster—they can change direction on a dime, while it takes us time to slow down enough to bank hard left or right."

"So," I say as we turn down a fairly empty hallway. "I have a question."

"Will I help you learn to fly? Of course I will. It'll be so much fun." Flint grins. "Plus, we still have those pictures for Mr. Damasen to finish."

"Oh, right. I'm sorry; I totally blanked on that." I roll my eyes at myself. "Too much going on in my head, I guess. Maybe we can do it this weekend?"

"Yeah, sure. Just let me know what works for you."

"Great, thanks. And I'm sure I'll want to take you up on the flying lessons." I mean, I still can't believe that I can *fly*. Me. Under my own power. Because I'm a gargoyle, I mean. When the whole "I have wings" thing came up earlier, the implication of being able to fly was there. But to think about it, to imagine Flint giving me lessons on how not to die while doing it... It's more than a little overwhelming.

Instead, I focus on something else. Giving the idea time to settle can't be a bad thing.

"But speaking of flying, I actually had a different question," I say to Flint.

He turns amused eyes my way. "Yes?"

"You mentioned pixies. How many other species are out there? Are there a lot of other creatures that aren't at Katmere, ones that I don't even know exist?"

"Definitely." He grins. "More than you could ever imagine."

"Oh." I'm not sure what I'm supposed to do with that.

My surprise must show, because Flint lifts a brow at me. "Was that not the answer you were looking for?"

"I don't know—I just... What other kinds of creatures are there? And why aren't they at Katmere?"

"Because Katmere's teachers specialize in dragons, werewolves, vampires, and witches," Flint tells me. "There are other schools out there that specialize in other magical creatures."

There goes my mind, blowing up all over again. "Like...?"

"Like in Hawaii, there's a school that specializes in water shifters."

"Water shifters?" I repeat.

"Yes," Flint answers with a laugh. He must know what I'm thinking, because he adds, "Mermaids are real. So are selkies and nereids and sirens, among other things."

"Seriously?" I ask.

"Seriously." He shakes his head in obvious amusement. "You look dazzled."

"I feel dazzled."

"Vegas has Ceralean," Hudson adds from near my head. "It's a school for succubi, among others."

Out of all the mythological creatures, that's what you come at me with? I give an exaggerated eye roll. *A creature known for its sexual appetites?*

"Hey, I was just adding to your knowledge base." The look he gives me is so innocent that I'm amazed he doesn't have a halo sparkling... right around his feet. "You're the one who asked."

I don't even bother to say anything this time. I just roll my eyes again...at least until I realize Flint is staring at me like he suddenly thinks something is really wrong with me. I'm proven right when he asks, "Umm, do you have something in your eye?"

"Yeah, I just got some dirt in there or something." I rub my eye. "All better."

"Really? Dirt in your eye?" Hudson makes a disgusted noise. "Nice to know where I stand."

Somewhere below an eyelash and above pink eye.

He cracks up, and the sound of it nearly stops me in my tracks. For a guy who's such a jerk, he's got a surprisingly nice laugh.

Flint and I turn one more corner, and I'm so busy arguing with Hudson in my head that I don't realize Jaxon is waiting by my classroom door until I almost run into him.

"You okay?" he asks at the same time Flint says, "Whoa."

"I'm fine," I tell them both a little heatedly, annoyed at the way they keep frowning at me in concern. They should try balancing multiple conversations at the same time—especially when one is in their head, where no one else can hear it or keep up.

"Let's be real," Hudson says. "It's not like either of them would be able to keep up even if they could hear. The two of them are more brawn than brain, if you ask me."

It's so blatantly untrue that I don't even bother to get offended. Instead, I poke him back because I can...and because riling him up is too much fun not to at least try. *You're just jealous because you don't have any brawn at the moment.*

"Yeah, *that's* what I'm jealous of."

There's something fleeting in his tone that gives me pause, but it's gone so fast that I don't have a chance to figure out what it is.

Plus, Flint chooses just then to say, "I've got to get to class. But hit me up about those flying lessons soon. You're going to need them for Ludares."

I wave at Flint, then lean forward and slide my arms around Jaxon's waist and smile up at him as he does the same. "Sorry I missed out on seeing you at breakfast this morning. I was so tired, I didn't wake up until fifteen minutes before class started."

He smiles back. "That's actually why I stopped by. I thought you might want to meet me at the library after art. I have to make up a midterm from yesterday during lunch today, but I thought we could spend some time tonight researching how to kill the Unkillable Beast."

"Awww, how cute. Little Jaxy-Waxy wants a study date." Hudson sneers.

"Are you serious right now?" I demand. "Leave your brother alone."

Jaxon looks over his shoulder at the empty hallway I'm currently yelling at and then raises an eyebrow at me.

I shrug and just say, "Hudson."

Jaxon's eyes narrow, but he nods. What else can he do?

Hudson leans against the stone wall, next to another huge tapestry depicting an army of dragons in massive metal armor soaring over a small village. It's terrifying and exhilarating at the same time, and I make a mental note to look at it more closely after class.

"I've got a better idea," Hudson says as he readjusts, crossing his arms and resting the bottom of his foot against the wall. "Why don't you leave my brother alone for a little while? Watching the two of you make goo-goo eyes at each other is nauseating."

"Give me a break. Pretty sure you need a body to be nauseated."

Hudson shrugs. "I guess that just goes to show how disgusting the two of you really are."

Refusing to be drawn in to yet another argument with Hudson, I refocus on Jaxon, only to find him staring at me with a frown on his face. "Sorry," I tell him sheepishly. "Your brother has a big mouth."

"That's an understatement if I've ever heard one," Jaxon agrees with a nod of his head.

A random thought occurs to me. "Hey, I've been meaning to ask you… Why does Hudson have a British accent but you don't?"

Jaxon shrugs. "Our parents are British."

I wait for him to say more, but he doesn't. Which says everything, I suppose. What must that feel like, to have had so little to do with your parents that you don't even have the same accent? I can't imagine, and it breaks my heart for him all over again.

"Of course. We should all feel bad for the boy not raised by the two most vain people on the planet," Hudson snarks.

I ignore him, then change the subject with Jaxon. "I would love to meet you in the library after I'm done in the art room. Does six o'clock work?"

He nods. "Sounds perfect." But when he leans down to kiss me, Hudson makes such an obnoxious gagging sound that there's no way I can actually go through with it.

I duck my head and Jaxon sighs, but he doesn't say anything. Instead, he presses a kiss to the top of my head and says, "I'll see you then."

"Okay."

I watch him go, but the second he makes it around the corner, I turn on Hudson. "Seriously? Was the gagging really necessary?"

He resorts to the British stiff upper lip. "You have no idea how necessary."

"You do realize that you are completely ridiculous, don't you?"

Hudson looks like he doesn't know what to say about that—or even how to feel about it. Half offended, half amused, all intrigued— it's an interesting look on him, even before he says, "Well, that's a new one. No one's ever called me *that* before."

"Maybe because they've never actually met you."

I expect a snappy comeback, but instead there's a contemplative silence for several seconds. Eventually, though, he murmurs, "Perhaps you're right."

I don't know what to say after that, and I think maybe he doesn't, either, because silence stretches between us—the longest silence there's ever been, in fact, when one of us isn't sleeping.

I do an about-face and head into class, leaving Hudson still leaning against the wall.

Something tells me the Physics of Flight isn't exactly going to be the class I excel in, so I find a seat at the back of the classroom. I wait for Hudson to join me, but he actually does what I asked for once and leaves me alone.

Too bad.

40

Survival Is So Last Year

"**Y**ou should absolutely compete." Class is nearly over, so I'm shocked when I hear Hudson's voice next to me. "Thanks for saving me a seat, by the way."

I'm sitting in the back of the room because the last thing I want is to draw attention to myself in a class I'm two months behind in— and definitely not because there are empty seats on both sides of me.

"Compete in what?" I mutter to him under my breath, but I'm not really paying attention to his answer. I'm too busy trying to scribble down notes that might as well be another language.

"Ludares. Although, it's really just an excuse for everyone to try to kill one another doing really dangerous stuff." He does a quick, "people are weird" eyebrow lift. "Most popular day of the year here at Katmere. Especially among the shifters."

"Well, of course. I mean, when you put it like that, who wouldn't want to take part in it? I mean, survival is so last decade."

He laughs. "Exactly."

I try to get back into Mr. Marquez's lecture, but by now I've lost even the faint thread of what's going on, so I decide to just snap a few pics of the lecture notes instead of actually trying to decipher them. If I can't figure them out on my own later, I'll ask Flint for help.

"Or you could ask me?" Hudson says a little sardonically. "I may be a"—he moves his fingers in the universal symbol for air quotes—"'psychopath,' but I'm a psychopath who got a ninety-eight in this class."

"You took this class? Why?" A thought occurs to me. "Can you fly like Jaxon?"

"You make him sound like Superman." Hudson rolls his eyes. "He can't actually fly."

"You get what I mean." I wave a hand. "Whenever he does... whatever it is he does. If you don't call it flying, what do you call it?"

"He's got telekinesis. He floats. You know, like a blimp."

That startles a laugh out of me. I mean, the description is awful, but it's also kind of hilarious imagining Jaxon just floating around the top of sports stadiums like the Goodyear Blimp.

"It's a good picture, isn't it?" Hudson smiles slyly.

"It's an absurd picture and you know it. Your brother is *amazing*."

"So you keep telling me."

The bell rings, and I pause our conversation long enough to pack up my things and make my way into the hall. It's lunchtime, and normally I'd try to find Macy, but the thought of going into the cafeteria right now is too much for me.

Everyone staring at me. Judging me. And finding me wanting. At this rate, I'm probably going to have to repeat my senior year, too.

The whole thing sucks. It just sucks. And I think about getting it over with. Just walking into the cafeteria, standing on a table, and announcing to everyone that I'm responsible for Hudson being back. Oh, and by the way, the rumors are true. I totally make a kick-ass statue.

It would probably be better to just get it over with quickly, kind of like ripping off a Band-Aid. But I'm so tired right now and everything that's happened is pressing down on me, making me feel like I might crumble at any second.

I hesitate in the hallway, my gaze meeting Hudson's, and it seems like he doesn't know what I should do, either. His uncertainty has me wobbling on my feet before I shake it off and turn in the other direction.

I grab a pack of peanut butter crackers out of the nearest vending machine and head out to the art studio to get to work on my painting that I'm behind on now. Hopefully, a few extra hours down there will help me kick my funk mood, too.

The rest of the afternoon goes by pretty uneventfully, as long as you count Hudson talking nonstop uneventful. He's got an opinion on everything—even things no normal person should have an opinion on.

He thinks the art teacher looks like a flamingo in her hot-pink dress. And while he's not wrong, it's hard to focus on what she's saying with that picture in my head now.

He's convinced T. S. Eliot shouldn't be included in British Literature because he was born in Missouri—I get an hour-long diatribe about that particular offense.

And right now...right now he's arguing about the way that I mix black paint.

"I'm in your head so I know you're not blind, Grace. How can you possibly think that's an attractive shade of black?"

I stare at the color in question and then mix just the barest hint of blue into it. Partly because I want to and partly because I know it will upset Hudson even more. And after the last four hours, I'm all about pissing him off any way I can. Payback's a bitch like that.

"It's subtle and I like that." I dab a little on my canvas, and it's still not quite where I want it, so I go back and add just a touch more of midnight blue.

Hudson throws his hands into the air. "I give up. You're impossible."

Thankfully, I'm the only student left in the art room, so I don't have to worry about other people thinking I'm talking to the stool next to me. "*I'm* impossible? You're the one throwing a hissy fit about my painting."

"I am not throwing a *hissy fit*." I can tell he's offended—all the crisp British syllables are back in his voice, even as he stretches his legs out in front of him. "I am merely trying to provide some artistic feedback based on my long history of art appreciation—"

"Oh, here we go again." I roll my eyes. "If you bring up the fact that you're old one more time—"

"I am not old! I'm *older*. Vampires are immortal, in case you've forgotten, so you can't judge our age the same way you judge human age."

"Sounds to me a lot like a justification for getting around the fact that you're old as dirt." I know that I'm poking a caged bear, know that he's going to end up taking my head off if I keep needling him, but I can't help it. He totally deserves it after everything he's done to annoy me.

From the beginning, he's had the upper hand during most of our arguments, and now that I've found something that bugs him, I can't help rubbing it in a little. That probably makes me a terrible person, but I've had a psychopath inside my head for nearly four months, so I figure I can't totally be to blame for this new mean streak of mine.

"You know what? Do whatever you want with the black. The fact that it's dull and is going to ruin your painting is your problem—"

"I'm sorry, could you say that a little louder, please?" I put a hand to my ear in the universal "I can't hear you" gesture.

"I said it's dull."

"No, not that part. The part about it being my painting. Mine. Can you say that again?"

"Whatever," he huffs. "I was just trying to help."

"Yeah, I know. What is it about guys that always makes them want to help—even when no one is asking for it?"

"Do what you want," he answers, and when he doesn't say anything else, I think maybe I've gone too far. But when I sneak a quick peek at his face, I realize he's working almost as hard as I am not to grin. Which is absurd, I know. I want him out of my head more than anything, but I have to admit that now that he can't take control of my body anymore, arguing with him is a ridiculous amount of fun.

With that thought in mind, I grab the darkest red I can find and mix a glob of it into my black. And then wait for the explosion.

It takes about five seconds, which is four seconds longer than I expected, but then Hudson all but screeches, "Are you kidding me with this? Are you trying to blind me?" and I know I've scored a direct hit. Another point for me.

Sure, the tally currently looks something like this: Grace 7, Hudson 7 million, but I'll take the win.

At least until I remember that I've got something to ask him.

"Oh, hey. I've been meaning to ask. Now that we're actually working on the spell to get you out of my head... Where did you put the werewolf canine and the athame?"

"Top shelf in your closet. In a bag, far right."

"Up there? Why would you hide them there?"

"Because I didn't want you to find them somewhere and totally freak out before you knew where they came from."

"Good call," I admit grudgingly.

I keep painting, ignoring Hudson's objections. I'm still not sure what I'm painting yet, but I know that there's a compulsion inside me to get it on canvas. Part of me wonders if it's a memory from those four months I was trapped in gargoyle form, if it's something important that I don't remember. But another part of me figures that's just wishful thinking. That I'm so desperate to regain that piece of my life that I'm seeing portents of good things, even if they don't actually exist.

Delusional much, Grace? Why, yes, I am. I step back and look at what I've done so far.

The background is complete, and looking at it feels strange because it's unfamiliar but also good—because something deep down inside me is whispering that I've gotten it just right.

And to be clear, that something isn't Hudson. It's deeper, more primal, and I keep hoping if I paint enough, it will unlock everything else.

I'm cleaning the black off my brush, thinking about what comes next, when a text hits my phone. My hands are covered in paint and I almost don't get it, but I change my mind at the last second.

And then gasp when I see the text is from Jaxon—and that I'm nearly an hour and a half late for our date.

41

Turns Out the Devil Wears Armani

Unfortunately, there's a whole a string of texts from Jaxon—several from six thirty, one from seven o'clock, and then three that just came in.

Jaxon: Running late? I've got a table set up at the back of the library, near the study rooms

Jaxon: Why are vampires like wizards?

Jaxon: Because they're neck-romancers

Jaxon: Sorry, I couldn't resist

Jaxon: You okay? Did you fall asleep?

Jaxon: Hey, I'm not sure if you fell asleep or if you're painting, but I've found some interesting stuff

Jaxon: Can you text me when you get the chance, just so I know you're okay?

Jaxon: Miss you

I feel awful. I can't believe I forgot to meet him. I was looking forward to seeing him all day, and then I got so wrapped up in my painting that it totally slipped my mind. I tell myself it's because my brain is on overload and the last thing I want to do is spend a bunch of time trying to figure out how to take on the Unkillable Beast and how not to die. To be fair, it's a valid argument, but that doesn't mean I feel any less shitty about not showing up.

"I'm sure baby brother will survive being stood up," Hudson tells me, and there's an edge to his voice that wasn't there just a few minutes ago. "You should keep painting. You're really on a roll."

"Despite the fact that I used the wrong black?" I answer, barely paying attention as I fire off a text to Jaxon, apologizing and telling him that I'm coming.

"Sorry to be so particular, but Armani black is a very specific color." He looks like he swallowed a lemon and it would be funny if I wasn't in such a hurry.

I shove my phone in my backpack and start cleaning up as fast as I can. Which isn't nearly fast enough, considering how big of a mess I've made mixing paint. "Who said I was even thinking about Armani black?"

"Sorry. I just…" For the first time since I first saw him, he looks totally discombobulated. Like he's said too much but also not enough. I almost ask him what's wrong, but then I remind myself that we're not friends. That he's just a guy squatting in my brain for a while, and he's not even a very nice one. I don't actually owe him anything.

I speed up my cleaning, determined to get to the library before Jaxon totally gives up on me. I expect Hudson to snark the entire time—it *is* his favorite pastime, after all—but he's strangely silent after the Armani comment. Which I'm grateful for, because it lets me focus entirely on getting the supplies put away.

I'm just about done when the door to the art room flies open on a gust of wind. Cold air fills the room, and I whirl around, wondering what new threat I'm facing—only to find Jaxon standing there, watching me with a small smile and unfathomable eyes.

"I'm so sorry!" I tell him, rushing forward to greet him as he slams the door closed behind him. "I totally got carried away with my painting and I lost track of time. I didn't mean to—"

"Hey, don't worry about it." He looks me up and down, his smile growing as he takes in my paint-covered artist's smock. "I like this look."

I give him the same kind of once-over he just gave me, taking in the frayed jeans and the black designer T-shirt. "The feeling is definitely mutual."

"Oh yeah?" He wraps me in his arms, and I feel a warmth deep inside me—sexy and comforting and exciting all at the same time. "I'm glad to hear that."

"You smell good," I tell him, burying my nose in the bend between his neck and his shoulder for several long seconds. And he does, fresh and bright and so, so amazing.

"Yeah, well, I can say that feeling is mutual, too." He scrapes a fang across the sensitive skin beneath my ear. "Very, very mutual."

"Tell me you're not serious," Hudson says with a yawn. "Tell me this isn't the pinnacle of your scintillating conversations."

Why don't you take a nap or something, I hiss at him even as I pull away from Jaxon.

"You ready to go?" Jaxon asks.

"Yeah, just give me a minute to get the rest of the supplies put up." I take off my apron and store it in my cubicle, then finish putting the bottles of paint back in the cabinet.

Five minutes later, we're walking through the tunnels—tunnels that seem nowhere near as frightening when Jaxon is by my side, talking about what he's found in his hour-and-a-half search through the library's magical databases.

"I've spent most of tonight trying to identify what the Unkillable Beast is," he tells me as we make it to the rotunda with the huge bone chandelier hanging from the ceiling. "There are so many different versions throughout the last several hundred years, almost like it's more fairy tale than real monster, that it's hard to get a read on what we'll be facing if we go up there. Except for the fact that almost no one makes it back alive—and those who do can't agree on what they've seen."

"Is there anything similar in the different accounts?" I ask, focusing on the conversation and not on the fact that I'm about to pass the tunnel where Hudson's ex-girlfriend tried to murder Jaxon and me. "I mean, besides the 'everyone gets dead' thing?"

I think about asking Hudson what he remembers about that night—if anything—but decide it doesn't matter. Besides, what if he wants to take a field trip to the scene of his reincarnation? Show-and-tell isn't really my thing, especially not down here.

"I don't remember anything," Hudson tells me quietly as he strides alongside us, one hand casually sliding along the stoned and jeweled walls. He's a few inches ahead, so I can't really see his face. "I didn't put her up to it, if that's what you're thinking."

I'm not thinking anything, I answer, though that's not quite the truth. It's hard not to be afraid of Hudson when I'm down here, harder still not to be angry with him. Maybe what happened wasn't his fault, but it's hard to imagine that he and his persuasive power didn't have some small role to play in the fact that Lia was obsessed with bringing him back.

"The stories do have a few things in common," Jaxon answers, his arm tightening around me as if he senses my disquiet.

Which only makes me feel worse about being such a baby, so I swallow the lingering fear. I shove it down deep inside me and concentrate instead on something I do have the power to change. "Like what? Have you figured out exactly how to find it yet?"

I remember him saying in the caves that the Beast is somewhere near the North Pole. Though I don't see why he couldn't have a nice summer home somewhere in Greece or Egypt, L.A. or Miami? Anywhere that has warm weather and a beach would be good with me right now, because after that trip to the Bloodletter's, I am ready to get away from the snow for a while.

"That's actually the one thing every account agrees on," Jaxon tells me. "The Unkillable Beast lives somewhere near the Arctic Circle. Seems everyone is happy to share approximately where to find it—just so you can plan a trip avoiding it at all costs."

"I'm with them," I tell him, making a face. "Taking on the North

Pole sounds hellish enough without also taking on a monster that can't be killed. Are we sure it doesn't spend March in Tahiti?"

Jaxon looks confused at first, but then he gets it. "I'm sorry. When this is all done and we've graduated from Katmere, I'll take you someplace warm and sunny, I promise."

"I'm going to hold you to that promise," I tell him. "I cannot spend every day for the rest of my life in freaking Alaska."

"Nothing says we have to live in Alaska after graduation. I know you were planning on doing the college thing before your parents died and you ended up here. We can still do that if you want."

"I don't know what I want, to be honest." It sounds bad when I say it like that, especially considering I'm only three months from graduation. But the plan I had before my parents died seems like it belonged to a whole different person.

"What do you want to do?" I ask Jaxon, because I figure any plan I have for the future is going to include my mate.

"I don't know that I really had a plan for after graduation, to be honest. When you're immortal, you've got a lot more time to think things through."

"Especially if you're a prince and have already been alive a couple of centuries." I make a mental note to ask him later about the whole "vampire aging" thing. I mean, I know he's centuries old, but I also know he's only about eighteen in human years. I sincerely hope I'm not dating someone who was in diapers and sucked his thumb for a hundred years.

Hudson snort-laughs, so I know he heard that last thought, but he doesn't turn around. I can't help a smile spreading across my face at the image of a twenty-year-old *Hudson* in said diapers.

This finally gets his attention, and he shoots me a raised eyebrow over one shoulder. "Very kinky, Miss Foster."

My face turns beet red, but Jaxon doesn't seem to notice.

"I'm not sure what my plans are, but we have the rest of our lives to sort it out," Jaxon finally replies and squeezes my shoulder.

We make it out of the tunnels and through the creepy dungeon area, and I feel myself relax the second the cell door clangs closed behind us.

"What else did you learn about this monster?" I ask as we make our way toward the staircase that leads to the library. We pass through the lounge on the main floor, and while a few people turn to stare, it's a lot less than it was a couple of days ago.

Maybe they really are getting used to having a human/gargoyle around. Now, if I could just get used to the gargoyle portion of that equation myself, I'm pretty sure everything would get a lot easier.

"It's big. Like, beyond-measure huge. Twenty, thirty stories, some say. And it's very, very old."

"Well, that sounds encouraging," I say, tongue firmly in cheek. "I mean, who doesn't want to fight a monster who's been around forever and is the size of a mountain?"

"Right? Although I don't think it's quite that big. More like the side of a mountain."

"Well, that makes it so much better," I tease as we finally make it to the library. But as Jaxon reaches for the door handle, I realize it's almost completely dark inside. "Oh no! Did Amka close while you came to get me? I'm so sorry—"

"Relax," he says with a grin, bending down to drop a quick kiss on my lips. "I've got it covered."

Hudson steps aside as Jaxon opens the door and gestures for me to precede him. But I'm only a few steps into the library's main room before I realize that I've messed up a lot more than an evening study date. I've messed up a *date* date, because sitting in the center of the room is a small, round table covered with a tablecloth, candles, and one of the most gorgeous bouquets of flowers I have ever seen.

"Well, well, well," Hudson says, sauntering into the room, his hands shoved into his front pockets. "Isn't this cozy? Tell Jaxon I'm overwhelmed, but he really shouldn't have."

42

Ben & Jerry Are the Only Two Guys I Want to Fight Over

"**O**h, Jaxon. You didn't have to do this." I walk toward the table, feeling more than a little bit fluttery as I take in the candles and the sparkling water on ice and the *flowers*. The really beautiful flowers. "They're gorgeous."

"I'm glad you like them."

"I love them," I correct him, burying my face in the white, lavender, and purple blooms. "They smell amazing." I hold them out to him.

"I smelled them when I picked them out," he says. "And it's not that big a deal."

I melt all over at his words, because it's a huge deal for so many reasons.

One, he went through the trouble of organizing a dinner like this for me because he thought I would like it.

Two, he went through the trouble of finding flowers in the middle of Alaska and picked them out himself.

Three, he did this even though ours is the first real relationship he's ever had—the first time he's allowed himself to feel in more than a hundred years. How could I not fall for Jaxon when he reminds me, over and over again, just what good care he will take of me?

"They're flowers, not a trip to Paris," Hudson says as he grabs a book off the circulation desk and thumbs through the pages. There's such annoyance in his movements that I totally ignore him. The night is young. There's more than enough time for him to rain on my parade before I have to go back to my room.

"It's a huge deal," I answer them both, wrapping my arms around Jaxon's waist and squeezing him tightly. "And I'm so sorry I forgot. I feel awful."

"Don't." He gives me a soft smile as he brushes a curl back from my face. "You've had a rough few days. And there's a microwave next to Amka's desk. Your dinner is easy to reheat if we need to."

"What did you get me?" I ask, my suddenly growling stomach a reminder that I've had very little to eat today.

Jaxon laughs at the rumble. "Come on, let's get you seated and you can find out."

He escorts me to the table, and I realize he's done more than just candles and flowers. He's gotten me street tacos in the middle of Alaska that look just like the ones from my favorite taqueria in San Diego. "How did you do this?"

"I can't tell you all my secrets," he answers with a grin.

"Yeah, but you definitely have to tell me *this* secret." I pick one up and take a bite, relishing the way the familiar flavor explodes in my mouth. "I'm going to have to get these again soon." I take another bite, so excited about this little taste of home that I'm not even pretending to have any restraint.

"Or you could keep me around, and I could get them for you anytime you want," Jaxon suggests as he settles down next to me.

"Yeah, I could totally do that." We grin into each other's eyes for long seconds, my breath catching in my chest for all the right reasons this time—at least until Hudson walks over and interrupts with a disbelieving laugh.

"Meat? My brother got you meat as a gift?" He snorts as soon as Jaxon gets up to turn on some music.

I glare at Hudson and whisper-shout, "They're not meat. They're tacos. And—"

"Which are made up of meat, am I correct?" He starts circling the table like an attorney hell-bent on cross-examination. He even looks the part in his flawless dress shirt and dress pants.

"Okay, yes. But there's nothing wrong with that. I love tacos." I deliberately turn away from Hudson and back to Jaxon, who is fiddling with his iPhone.

"And I love human blood. Doesn't mean I want it as a present." Hudson comes close now, bracing his hands on the back of my chair and leaning down so that he's all but whispering in my ear when he continues. "But it's good that you have such low expectations. You're going to need them with Jaxy-Waxy."

"Will you stop calling him that?" It takes every ounce of willpower I have not to whirl around and shout at him—but apparently that's exactly what he wants, so I refuse to bite. Instead, I swallow back the string of sharp retorts I want to throw at him and focus as much attention as I can muster on Jaxon instead.

He finally settles on Savage Garden's "I Knew I Loved You," and my heart stutters in my chest, even before he turns and gives me a look that makes me feel all kinds of delicious things.

The look in his eyes tells me he knows exactly what I'm feeling… and he likes it. A lot.

"You're going to have to tell me where you got these," I say to Jaxon when he makes it back to the table. I take another bite of the taco Hudson is working overtime trying to ruin for me. After I've swallowed, I continue. "I'm going to need them again, like, tomorrow."

"I could probably arrange that."

"Oh, really?" I lift my brows questioningly.

He shakes his head in response, obviously amused. "Grace, there isn't much I wouldn't do to make you happy. I can't give you Tahiti for a few more months, but I can absolutely get you tacos every day, if that's what you want."

"I don't need tacos." I reach for his hand and squeeze it tightly. "I just need you."

"I need you, too," he answers before nodding at me to keep eating.

It's as I pick up my second taco that he switches the subject. "Tell me about the art project you're working on. I'm dying to get a look at it."

"Yeah, me too," I tell him with a little snort.

He looks intrigued. "What does that mean?"

"It means I have no idea what I'm working on. Usually I know exactly what I'm going to paint, but this time I'm just painting like my life depends on it, but I don't know what it is I'm painting. Weird, right?"

"Genius is weird," Jaxon answers with a shrug. "Everyone knows that. I say keep embracing it, see what happens."

"That's what I figure, too. The worst thing that can happen is it's trash, so where's the harm?"

"It's not trash," he tells me.

"How do you know?"

"Because I know you."

It's such a simple answer, but it has me swooning a little anyway, because it's just what I need to hear right now.

"You're entirely too charming," I tell him with a soft smile. "You know that, right?"

Jaxon just grins and leans in for a kiss before sitting back down, and Hudson gags. Again. And I can't stop myself from turning to glare at him.

"Hey, is Hudson still talking to you?" Jaxon asks, and he doesn't sound happy.

"He's always talking to me," I look at Jaxon and complain with a roll of my eyes. "I swear, he never shuts up."

"You know, that mean streak of yours is getting a lot wider recently," Hudson grumps.

"It's because you're rubbing off on me," I shoot back. But the second the words are out, I can feel myself blush scarlet. "I didn't mean—"

"I know what you meant," Hudson interjects, but the grumpiness is gone, replaced by a slyness in his dark-blue eyes that makes me distinctly nervous, though I'm not sure why.

"My brother sure knows how to ruin a mood," Jaxon mutters as he gets up to clear my dinner away.

"Thank you," Hudson answers. "I do what I can."

"Could you please just shut up for five minutes?" I demand as I stand to follow Jaxon.

"Now, where's the fun in that?" Hudson walks across the library and climbs on top of one of the shorter bookshelves, dangling his feet down the side as he picks up the mini gargoyle Amka has sitting on top of it and loosely wraps his arms around the statue. "Besides, if I'm quiet, who's going to point out the error of your ways?"

"Wow, condescending much?" I stick my tongue out at Hudson, who pretends to catch it like I blew him a kiss and dramatically holds it up to his heart before I can turn away.

"I'm sorry," I say as I catch up to Jaxon and wrap my arms around his waist from behind. "I know you wanted tonight to be special, and Hudson keeps messing it up."

"Don't worry about it," he answers, turning around so he can hold me, too. "It's not your fault."

"It feels like my fault." I squeeze him more tightly.

"Well, it's not." He leans down a little, brushes a kiss over my temple. "But since our date isn't exactly turning out as planned, why don't we at least do something useful with the time?"

"Like what?"

"Like find out more about gargoyles? I know you were trying to do that before everything went wrong with Hudson the other day."

"Nothing went wrong with me," Hudson growls at him. "I was trying to help her."

"That sounds amazing," I reply to Jaxon, and he gestures for me to sit back at the table while he fetches the books from the back table where Amka left them for me.

I turn to glare at Hudson. "Because body snatching is so helpful?"

"Are you back to being mad at me about that again?" He sighs. "Even now that you know why I had to get the athame?"

"I'm never not going to be mad at you about that," I shoot back.

"It figures. I was trying to help, and this is what I get."

"Trying to help?" I make a disbelieving noise in the back of my throat. "Trying to help *yourself*, don't you mean?"

"Are you ever going to get tired of making me the bad guy?" he asks softly.

"I don't know. Are you ever going to get tired of *being* the bad guy?" I answer.

In the middle of all this, Jaxon walks back to the table and deposits three books I remember from the pile set aside for me. My fingers are itching to read them, and I quickly grab the top book, *Magical Creatures Big and Small*.

Jaxon doesn't sit down like I expect but instead walks over to the bookcase where Hudson is perched and bends down to grab a book from the bottom shelf. For just a second, it looks like Hudson is going to kick him full-on in the face—completely unbeknownst to Jaxon, of course.

Don't you dare, I mouth at Hudson.

Hudson gives me an arched brow, but in the end, he leaves Jaxon alone. "Overprotective much?"

I narrow my eyes at him. *From a murderer? Damn straight.*

"You do know that Jaxon's the one who killed *me*, right?" He shakes his head as he hops off the shelf, turns away, and mutters, "This is my limit for abuse for one night. I've got more important things to do."

And just like that, he disappears down one of the narrow rows between shelves toward the back of the library. It takes a minute for me to realize he's following the same gargoyle path that I did the first time I'd entered the library. The first time I'd met Lia...

43

Even Homicidal Maniacs Have Their Limits

More important things to do? The words ricochet in my head. "What does that mean?"

Hudson doesn't answer.

"I'm serious, Hudson. What exactly are you planning to do?"

Still no answer. The jerk.

I try one more time, yelling down the aisle toward where Hudson disappeared. "You can't just go around saying things like that and expect me to—"

Jaxon sits down and sighs. "Maybe we should do this another time."

"Why?" I snap, my anger exploding out at him.

He raises a brow at my tone but keeps his voice mild when he answers. "I was asking if you want to try out the research thing another time, since you seem a little…preoccupied…yelling at my brother."

Just like that, my anger drains away. Because it's not Jaxon's fault his brother is a douche who will use any means necessary to get his way.

"No, of course not. I'm so sorry. I think researching gargoyles is a great idea. I've been wanting to do that since I got back."

"Are you sure?" Jaxon rests his hand over mine and squeezes gently. "I understand if you need to—"

"I need to be with you," I answer, ignoring the residual tightness in my stomach left over from Hudson's assholery. "And researching gargoyles—and how to get your brother out of my head once and for all—sounds like a really good idea right about now."

"To be fair, figuring out how to get Hudson out of your head sounds like a really good idea to me all the time," Jaxon tells me with a rueful shake of his head.

I laugh as I slip my hand out from under his. "You're not wrong about that."

I flip to the index at the back of the book and start looking for any topic that might be able to help us.

"So do you know anything about gargoyles?" I ask as I pull my notebook out of my backpack before settling down next to Jaxon. "I mean, surely some things are common knowledge, right? Like how even people who don't believe in them know that vampires can't come into a room uninvited or dragons like to hoard treasure." I pause as I rethink what I said. "Actually, I guess I don't know for sure that's true about dragons—"

"Oh, it's true," Jaxon tells me with a grin. But the grin fades pretty quickly into a thoughtful look as he taps his fingers on the table and stares off into space for several seconds.

"There are a lot of stories about gargoyles from the old days," he says eventually. "I'm not old enough to have met any—my father killed them all long before I was born."

His last sentence falls on the table like a grenade, one that takes a full three seconds before it explodes—and takes me with it. "Your father *killed* them?" I ask, and I can't keep the shock out of my voice.

"Yeah," he answers, and I've never seen him look more deeply ashamed.

"How?" I whisper.

I meant how did he kill them *all*, but Jaxon takes my question literally. "Gargoyles *can* die, Grace. Not easily, but they can. Of course, for the gargoyle *king*, he decided to kill him personally with an eternal bite."

Eternal bite? A shiver skates along my spine. "What's that?"

Jaxon sighs. "It's my father's gift. One bite is deadly. Absolutely no one has ever survived. Not even the gargoyle king himself."

I make a mental note to not get within biting distance of the king. Ever. "But the rest he just slaughtered the good old-fashioned way?"

"Well, his armies did, yes." He chuckles, but there's no humor in it. "Apparently a predilection for genocide runs in my family."

The word "genocide" slams into me with the power of a set of brass knuckles. I can't imagine anything worse for Hudson to have done, can't imagine how depraved—how downright evil—

"Oi, you can bugger right off with that!" Hudson suddenly shouts, coming back into the main area from the shadowy aisle.

The sudden towering rage in Hudson's voice has my eyes going wide and my heart pumping way too fast. It's so huge, so overwhelming, that I can feel it threatening the barricade I put up in my head. Can feel the cracks deep inside as the wall trembles.

"Hudson?" I manage to choke out. "Are you—"

But he's not done yet, his voice—and his insults—getting more British by the second. "Don't you fucking come at me with that bullshite, you fucking wanker! You're a daft bastard, and I'm fucking sick of you swanning around like the bloody little fucking bastard that you are!"

Again, the wall trembles. Again, more cracks spring up, and I try desperately to patch them even as I work to calm him down. "Hudson. Hey, Hudson."

He ignores me. He's pacing back and forth in front of the circulation desk as he yells more insults at Jaxon—who is completely oblivious to the fact that his older brother has just called him a rat-arsed git.

Jaxon gets to his feet now—I guess it's hard to miss that something is wrong as I chase Hudson around the front half of the library—fists clenched and eyes wild with concern as he stares at me. It's obvious he's trying to find a way to fight his brother without hurting me, but he can't figure it out...because the only place Hudson really exists right now is inside me.

When he looks like he's going to say something else, I hold up a hand to settle him back down. The last thing we need is for him to say something else that sets Hudson off again.

He doesn't look happy, but he nods and slowly unclenches his fists. Convinced he isn't going to say anything else, I turn and walk over to Hudson.

"Hey, now. Hey, look at me." I put a hand on his shoulder. "Come on, Hudson. Take a deep breath and look at me, okay?"

He whirls around then, and the look he turns on me is filled with such fulminating fury, such absolute, abject betrayal, that I can't help but stumble back a couple of steps.

I don't know if it was the stumble or the look on *my* face, but whatever it is, it brings Hudson back down in an instant. He doesn't apologize for his outburst, doesn't try to explain it. But he stops swearing, stops looking like he wants to tear the entire library—and Jaxon—apart. And skulks off to sit in one of the chairs by the window, his back to me.

I turn around to find Jaxon staring, and there's an edge in his eyes that has a chill working its way down my spine. Not because I think he'll hurt me—Jaxon would never do that—but because it makes him feel far away from me, distant in a way I didn't expect and don't know how to handle.

"I'm sorry," I whisper. "I don't mean to hurt you. It's just hard to ignore someone throwing a tantrum in my head. I wish I could," I tell him. "Even more, I wish he wasn't there at all. But he is, and I'm trying, Jaxon. I'm really trying."

The ice in his gaze melts at my words, and his whole body softens. "I know." He reaches for my hand, pulls me close. "You're handling so much right now. I wish I could take it all away from you."

"That's not your job."

"I'm your mate." He looks vaguely insulted. "If it's not my job, whose is it?"

"Mine," I whisper, going on tiptoes to press my lips, very softly, to his. "You're just the moral support."

He gives a startled laugh. "That's the first time I've ever been given that role."

"I bet. How does it feel?"

To his credit, he thinks about it for a moment before saying, "I don't like it."

I shoot him a fake shocked look, and he just laughs. Then says, "Do you want to hear about gargoyles or not?"

"I absolutely do."

Jaxon leads me back to the table and we settle into our seats again, reaching for the books we'd started to read before Hudson's outburst.

"Like I was saying, gargoyles are old—although not as old as vampires. No one knows how they were created—" He breaks off, thinks about it. "Or at least, *I* don't know how. I just know that they didn't exist before the First Great War but were around by the time of the Second. There are all kinds of origin stories, but my favorite ones always revolve around the witches bringing them into existence in the hopes of saving themselves and humans from another great war. Some say they used dark magic, but I never believed it. I always thought they asked a higher power for help, and that's why gargoyles have always been protectors."

Protectors. The word settles on me. It sinks into my bones, flows through my veins—because it feels right. It feels like the home I haven't had in four long months and, conversely, the home I've been looking for my entire life even though I didn't know it.

"What are we supposed to protect?" I ask, blood humming with the promise of what's to come.

"Magic itself," Jaxon tells me. "And all the factions who wield it in all their different ways."

"So not just witch magic, then."

"No, not just the witches. Gargoyles kept the balance among all the paranormals—vampires and werewolves, witches and dragons." He pauses. "Mermaids and selkies and every other not-just-human creature on the planet—and also humans."

"But why did your father kill the gargoyles, then? If they were the ones keeping everything balanced, why would he want to get rid of them?"

"Power," Jaxon says. "He and my mother wanted more power, power they couldn't just take with the gargoyles watching. And now they have it. They sit at the head of the Circle—"

"Amka mentioned the Circle to me. What is it?" I ask.

"The Circle is the ruling body that governs paranormals all over the world. My parents have the highest positions of power on the council, positions they inherited when my father instigated the destruction of all the gargoyles," Jaxon explains.

"He instigated the *murdering* of all the gargoyles," Hudson says from where he's still near the window, "because he convinced his allies that the humans were planning another war, used the Salem Witch Trials to prove his point. And gargoyles were going to side with them."

"He killed them all because of a war that never happened?" I whisper, horrified.

Jaxon turns the page in the book he's currently thumbing through. "Well, this is what some people believe, yes."

"He killed them all because he is an evil, selfish, power-hungry, cowardly arsehole," Hudson corrects. "He's drunk his own Kool-Aid and truly believes he's the savior of our kind."

I'm a little shocked—and a lot horrified—at how Hudson, of all people, describes his and Jaxon's father. Hudson is the one who wanted to wipe the other species out of existence, so why does he sound so judgmental over the fact that his father did the same thing?

"I am *nothing* like my father," Hudson grinds out, sounding more offended than I have ever heard him. "Nothing!"

I don't contradict him, even though it seems absurd for him to try to pretend away the similarities in his agenda and his father's. Sure, they went after different factions in their search for supremacy, but that doesn't make them different. It just makes them two sides of the same coin.

And I would do well to remember this before I get us all killed.

Because Hudson won't be in my head forever. And what he will do when he's out is anyone's guess.

Jaxon must be thinking the same thing, because he leans forward and says, "No matter what we have to do, we can never let my brother loose on the world with his power. My father killed the entire gargoyle race. Who knows what Hudson will do?"

44

Two Heads Aren't Better than One

I wait for Hudson to explode, but he doesn't say a word. In fact, he's so quiet that after several minutes of silence, I'd think Hudson had fallen asleep if I didn't see the way his foot is tap-tap-tapping on the ground as he stares out the window.

I don't know why he doesn't respond to Jaxon's words—maybe because he realizes everything Jaxon said about him is true. Maybe because he's embarrassed. Maybe because he got his burst of anger out earlier. I don't know. I just know that I expect some kind of response from him.

I've known Hudson for only a few days and already I know that it's not like him to be quiet. And it's definitely not like him not to have a comeback or six...

A sudden sadness swamps me, along with a wave of exhaustion that has me fighting back a yawn. Jaxon sees it, though—of course he does—and says, "Come on, the rest of the research can wait until tomorrow. Let's get you back to your room."

I want to argue, but I'm fading fast, so I just nod. "Don't we need to clean up first?" I gesture to the table where the candles still burn.

"I can walk you to your room, then come back and clean up." Jaxon starts gently herding me toward the library door.

"Don't be ridiculous. It'll take ten minutes, and then we can head back to my room."

Turns out, it barely takes five minutes to get everything picked up and put away before we're on our way to my room. When we get there, I know Jaxon expects to be able to kiss me like he did yesterday, but Hudson isn't asleep now. He's not talking to me, but he's very definitely aware of what's going on, and I can't just make out with Jaxon when his brother is watching—especially not when he's watching from inside my head.

The last thing I want is for him (or anyone) to know what I'm thinking when Jaxon kisses me...or worse, what I'm feeling. It's personal and private and nobody's business but mine.

So when Jaxon moves to set the huge vase of flowers on the floor beside my door, I put a hand on his arm to stop him. "Three's a crowd," I tell him.

He looks confused, but my meaning must register because he nods and steps away. "I'll see you tomorrow, then? We can meet for breakfast at ten, then research at the library after that, if it works for you?"

"I can't think of a better way to spend a Saturday morning than with you," I tell him.

"Good." He starts to hand me my flowers, but I wrap my arms around him in a huge hug first, pulling his face down to mine so I can give him a superfast peck on the lips.

"Thank you for tonight. It was awesome."

"Yeah?" He looks embarrassed but also a little pleased. I'll admit it's an adorable look on him.

"Yeah. You're..." I trail off as I struggle to put my thoughts into words.

Jaxon leans against the doorframe then, a shit-eating grin on his face and a huge vase of flowers in his arms, and somehow still manages to look sexy as fuck. "I'm what?" he asks, making a ridiculous face.

"A total dork," I answer after I burst out laughing.

He laughs, too. "Not quite what I was going for, but I'll take it." He hands me my flowers, then bends down to kiss my cheek.

"Because I'll take you."

My heart turns into an actual puddle—there's no other word for it. "Good," I answer. "Because I'll take you, too."

And then Jaxon is opening the door and I'm floating inside, heart and head full of this boy, this powerful, perfect boy who makes me feel things I never imagined possible.

Macy's not here—probably out with some of the witches doing witch things—so I put the flowers on my desk before flopping down on my bed. A couple of minutes later, I turn on my favorite playlist and grab the book off my nightstand. But it's the same book I was reading four months ago when I turned into a gargoyle, so I can't follow the plot.

Three minutes and five pages later and I put the book down. I consider streaming something from Netflix, but nothing sounds good, and eventually I end up wandering around my room, touching everything as I look for something to do.

Turns out, there's nothing to do—it's been a long time since I've been in my room alone, and it feels so awkward, I almost can't believe I'm in the right place. I don't know what's wrong with me, considering when I got to Katmere Academy, all I wanted was to be on my own, and now I feel like I'm about to jump out of my skin.

Finally, I decide to take a shower so I can go to bed, but I'm halfway to the bathroom, pajamas in my hand, when I realize I can't do that. Last night when I showered, Hudson was asleep. Tonight, he isn't.

He's being unnaturally quiet and hasn't said a word to me since Jaxon's outburst in the library, but he's sprawled out on Macy's bed reading—I stretch a little bit to get a look at the front of his book—*Crime and Punishment* by Dostoevsky, and I wonder idly if he relates to Rodion, who ends up killing people for his own selfish needs.

I hesitate. I want to wash my hair, but there's no way I'm going to strip naked and take a shower with him watching me, whether he seems like he's reading or not. How could he not see me naked if I can see myself naked? I mean, he's *in* my head.

"I wouldn't do that." I nearly jump when Hudson finally speaks to me out of the blue. He's still on Macy's bed, with his ankles crossed and his arms folded beneath his head, but now his book is lying across his chest.

There are a million other questions I want to ask him—namely what made him so upset that he shut down to begin with—but I settle for asking about his immediate statement first. "What do you mean?"

"I wouldn't watch you take a shower or get undressed. You don't have to worry about that."

"Yeah, but how could you *not* watch? You're literally in my head, even though it seems like you're over there on Macy's bed." I tap my head. "You're still right here."

"I don't know. The best I can do is close my eyes and go deep inside my own mind so I'm not really active in yours at the time. I guess we'll see. But take your shower. You don't have anything gross to fear from me."

"Is that what you did at the end, in the library? Went deep into your own mind?" I don't know why it matters, don't know why I don't just take the win and be happy he left me alone for as long as he did. But I don't feel particularly happy, and I want to know what shut Hudson down to begin with.

"No," he answers after a second. "I've been here all along. I just…"

"What?"

"I don't know." He shakes his head. "I guess I just wanted to think for a while."

"I can understand that."

He smiles, and for the first time tonight, it's not mocking. But it's not happy, either. It's just kind of…sad. "Can you?"

It's a good question, one I don't know the answer to. I think I have a lot on my mind—pun maybe, kind of, totally intended—but for the first time, I wonder what it must be like to be Hudson. Trapped in the head of a girl you barely know and who has made no secret of the fact that she doesn't like you, stuck there until she can figure out how to not only get you out of her head but also to make you human, something you've never been in your life.

I know how alienated and strange I feel knowing that a part of me is gargoyle, not human. How much more awful must it feel to be a vampire and know that by the time you're free, you will have lost the most basic building block of who you are?

It's a terrible thought, the idea of being responsible for stripping Hudson of his very identity. But at the same time, what's the alternative? Set him free and hope he doesn't decide to use his very formidable powers to launch a war on the entire world?

He's done absolutely nothing to earn the kind of trust that would require.

"You're right," he tells me after a second.

"About what?"

He rolls over on the bed, gives me his back. And says, "You don't have a clue what it's like to be me."

It's a true statement but also a hurtful one, and for long seconds I stand there wondering how to respond. But in the end, there is no response—or at least no *good* response—and I decide now might be the perfect time for me to take that shower. In the mood he's in, I'm pretty sure Hudson will have absolutely no interest in breaking his promise.

"I wouldn't break my promise anyway." The comment slides insidiously into my mind, so slowly and quietly that it takes me a moment to even recognize it for what it is.

But once I do, I can't help answering back: *I know*. Because I do, even though I don't know how I know.

It's only later, after I'm washing the conditioner out of my hair, that something occurs to me. It wasn't that I was bored when I first got to my room. It wasn't that I didn't know what to do with myself that made me unable to settle.

It was the fact that Hudson wasn't there, in my head, saying all the ridiculous, snarky, hilarious things that he normally says that had me so discombobulated.

It doesn't make any sense, but somehow, in the space of only a couple of days, I've grown used to having his voice in my head. I've grown used to his running commentary and his puffed-up opinions and even the way he pushes at me to get me to admit what I really think and feel.

I don't know how it happened when I hate the guy and everything he stands for—everything he once did. But it did happen, and now I don't have a clue what to do about the fact that maybe, just maybe, I'm beginning to think of Hudson as something more than an enemy. Not a friend—I'm not childish enough to lower my guard that much—but something that isn't entirely hateful, either.

It's not the best description ever, and I expect a snarky comment as soon as I make it, but nothing comes. Because Hudson is doing what he said he would—giving me the privacy I need.

And that just makes me more confused.

I get out of the shower and dry off so quickly that my PJs are still sticking to damp spots when I brush my teeth and finally head to bed.

As I slide under my covers, I glance over at Macy's side of the room and realize Hudson is gone. He's so quiet that I figure he must be asleep. Which is probably a good thing, considering I have to think, really think, and the last thing I need right now is him peering over my shoulder while I do.

Because the truth is, I can't just sit around waiting for him to do something awful. I can already feel cracks in the shield I put up to keep him locked away, and who knows what he'll do once it's weak enough for him to get through?

Now that it's the weekend, I've got to step up my search for the objects I need to get him out of my head. Jaxon reminded me just how dangerous and untrustworthy he is. Add that to the cracks in the wall…and suddenly it's beginning to feel like it's going to be days, not weeks, before he breaks through.

And then we'll all be screwed.

45

Leave Your Daddy
Issues at the Door

I wake up to a screaming alarm and sunlight filtering in through the one window in our dorm room.

"Turn it off," Macy complains from her bed, where she's busy shoving a pillow over her head. "For the love of God, turn it off."

I do, but then I roll out of bed because it's nine fifteen and I have to be in the cafeteria in forty-five minutes. Which shouldn't be such a chore, but I had a hard time sleeping last night, and today I am dragging already.

I make my way to the bathroom as quietly as I can to splash water on my face and brush my teeth, but Macy rolls over after a minute and asks, "Where are you going?"

"I'm meeting Jaxon for breakfast; then we're going to the library to research." I stare at her sleepy eyes. "You do remember I have a vampire in my brain and my walls won't hold him in check forever, yes?"

Macy groans and whines into her pillow for a minute, but then she pushes back her covers and sits up, feet on the floor.

I burst out laughing at my first good look at her, and she gives me a disgruntled pout in return. I try to apologize, but I can't. Every time I look at her, I end up grinning, because she looks ridiculous.

Her hot-pink hair is sticking up in what looks like a rooster comb

and her eye makeup—which she must have gone heavy on last night—
has smeared all over her eyes so that she looks like a raccoon. An
adorable raccoon, but a raccoon nonetheless.

"Why are you getting up?" I ask as I make my way to my closet.
"Go back to sleep. You look like you need it."

"You have no idea. One of the wolves had a party last night, and
it got a little out of control." She waves a hand up and down in front
of her face. "Hence the old-hag look."

"That's not quite how I would describe it, but okay." I grin at her.
"So that begs the question, why are you getting up when you have all
day to recuperate?"

"Because I'm going with you, silly."

"What? No, you don't have to do that. We're just going to sit
around and read dusty books all day."

"I can sit around with the best of them." Macy pushes to her feet
and stumbles her way over to the bathroom. "Besides, I'm really good
at research. Like, wicked good, even without the spells. So I'll help
you until I have to meet Gwen at two."

"There's a spell to help you research?" I ask, fascinated at the idea.

She rolls her eyes—or at least, I think she does. The insanely
heavy, smeared eye makeup makes it impossible to tell. "There's a
spell for everything if you look hard enough."

"Everything?" I ask, but she's already shut the bathroom door
behind her. Seconds later, I hear the shower go on.

"Everything," Hudson answers. "Witches are nothing if not
practical creatures. Why do something the hard way if you can hack
it?"

He's sitting on the floor near the door, knees up and arms draped
over them. For the first time since he showed up in my head, he's
dressed in a pair of faded jeans. They're ripped at the knees, frayed
around the bottom, and somehow manage to look amazing on him.
As does the white T-shirt he's wearing.

"What about vampires?" I ask, because I'm curious. And because

I'm anxious to distract myself from the fact that Hudson looks good—and that I've noticed that fact. "Are they practical, too?"

He snorts. "Only when it comes to who they're going to eat."

"That's awful!" I tell him, but I'm laughing just a little.

"Yeah, well, awful and true usually go hand in hand." He runs his palms over his knees in a gesture that looks an awful lot like nerves. "Or haven't you figured that out yet?"

That he believes this says a lot about Hudson. But he's not usually so brutal, and I can't help wondering what happened in the middle of the night that turned him so massively bitter. I think about asking him, but things are relatively peaceful right now, and I'd rather try to keep it that way. Especially since I'm meeting up with Jaxon in less than an hour.

"I'm going to change, okay?" I tell Hudson as I cross to my closet to pick something to wear.

He waves a hand in that negligent "do what you want" way that he has, but he also tilts his head back against the wall and closes his eyes.

"Thank you," I tell him as I start to browse through my clothes.

He doesn't answer.

I move to pull out one of the outfits Macy got me when I first moved here, but in the end I settle on a turquoise tank top and black yoga pants from my old life. Because I now live in a sometimes-drafty old castle in Alaska and I don't want to spend the next ten hours of my life freezing, I layer my favorite cardigan over the tank top. As its worn softness settles around me, I feel more like myself than I have since I turned back from being stone.

It's a good feeling.

"I'm done," I tell Hudson softly, and he nods, but he doesn't open his eyes.

And as I stand here with this unique, unprecedented chance to study him uninterrupted—usually he's wide awake and trading barbs with me every time I so much as get a glimpse of him—I can't help but realize how tired he looks.

I get it. I've had two solid nights of sleep and I still feel like I've been run over by a semi. But his tiredness looks edgier, harder, more soul deep, and I wonder what's going on in his head. I wonder what he's feeling, if anything.

Four days ago, it would have been impossible for me to imagine that I would worry about Hudson, even for a second. I still can't believe it now. Not after everything he's done, to Jaxon and to everyone else here at Katmere. Not after everything he wanted to do to the world.

I wonder if this is what Stockholm Syndrome feels like? Despite everything your captor has done, all the horrible things they are, you start to identify with them anyway? God, I really hope that's not the case.

"I think you should be more concerned about whether reverse Stockholm Syndrome is a thing, don't you? Considering you're the one who has been holding me captive for almost three and a half months?" The crisp British accent is back, and when he opens his eyes, so is the superior smirk that makes Hudson...Hudson.

My eyes go wide. "Me? You're the one who won't leave my head!"

"Won't leave your head?" he scoffs. "Do you know how ridiculous that sounds? I'm desperate to leave your head. You're the one who wastes time going to classes and painting pictures—oh, and kissing my brother—when you should be looking for a bloodstone!"

"I'm sorry that me *living my life* is such a waste of time for you, but I can't just drop everything and run around the world to stop you from having a temper tantrum," I shoot back.

"Temper tantrum?" His voice is dangerously low. "That's the second time you've accused me of having a temper tantrum when I've expressed legitimate concerns about your attitude. I put up with it the first time, but now I'm warning you. Don't do it again."

I take exception at the warning, not to mention the look in his eyes when he issues it. "Or what?" I ask, my entire body crackling with outrage.

Suddenly he's up and across the room, his face several inches from mine. "Or I'll stop playing nice, and that's something I'm not sure you—or your precious little mate—can handle."

"You think taking over my body and leaving me covered in blood is playing nice?" I screech, about half an octave shy of the pitch needed to actually break glass. "You think making snide comments about your brother every second I'm with him is *playing nice*?"

His eyes narrow to slits. "Compared to what you're doing to me? Hell yeah, I think I'm playing nice."

"Doing to you? *Doing to you?*" I throw my hand in a "step right up" kind of gesture. "Please, feel free. Tell me exactly what it is that I'm doing to you that's so awful besides trying to find a way for you to live outside of my head?"

"You—" He breaks off, fists clenched and jaw working as he stares me down. "I—" With a roar, he whirls around and punches a fist straight through the nearest wall.

I rear back, shocked at the depth of his fury. Shocked even more by the fact that there's an actual fist-size hole in the wall next to my head. I look down at my hands, wondering if maybe he took over my mind long enough for me to somehow punch the hole.

But my hands are fine, and the knuckles aren't the least bit red. So no, I didn't punch the wall. Hudson did. The only question is *how*?

Fear races through me at the idea that he can wield that kind of power even when he's bodyless. Even when he's inside me. I know his main power is that of persuasion, and for the first time, I wonder if he's using it on me without my knowledge.

Maybe that's why I feel bad for him sometimes. Maybe that's why, last night, I thought that maybe he wasn't quite the enemy I'd been afraid he would be. Maybe that's why—

"Could you just stop?" Hudson whispers, and he looks weaker and more sickly than I have ever seen him. "Not forever, but just for a few minutes. Could you please just stop?"

46

Gargoyles Need a Little Glamour, Too

"Stop what?" I ask, baffled, as he turns away.

His shoulders sag.

"Hudson?" I prompt when he doesn't answer, but he just shakes his head as he walks over to the window so he can look out at the snow. "Stop what?"

He laughs, but it's not his normal sarcastic laugh. Instead, it's just…sad. "The fact that you don't know says everything."

I'm not sure how to respond to that, so I don't say anything. Silence billows around us like a piece of the shiny tissue paper my mom always wrapped my presents in—weightless and so, so fragile— and the longer it goes on, the more I'm afraid to break it. The more I'm afraid that if I do, I'll also break the weird truce that Hudson and I have had going on for the last two days.

And if I do, what happens then?

Thankfully, Macy comes to the rescue—as usual. At nine forty-five, a full fifteen minutes before I have to meet Jaxon at the cafeteria, she comes bopping out of the bathroom looking a million times better than when she went in.

"Give me five minutes to find my shoes and do a quick glamour, and we can be on our way," she says as she walks to her closet.

"Why do you always get the glamour, and I always have to look like this?" I ask, waving a hand in front of my face.

"Because you have the gorgeous hair. And you look fine. Honest."

She wiggles her hands in front of her face and chants a few words under her breath, and suddenly her hair is dry and her face looks a little brighter, a little smoother, a little more beautiful.

"You're disgusting," I tell her.

"Fine, fine, fine." She rolls her eyes. "Come here and I'll do one on you."

Excitement flutters in my chest. "Really?"

"Really. I would have done one before, but you never seemed interested. It's easy-peasy."

Normally, I'm not interested—I'm pretty resigned to my cute-on-a-good-day looks. But after everything that's already happened with Hudson and what I'm afraid is still to come once Hudson and Jaxon are back in the same room together, I could use the extra armor.

So I cross the room to Macy, tilt my face up to hers—since she's eight inches taller than I am, which is also totally not anything I'm jealous about—and wait for her to work her magic.

"Close your eyes," she tells me, so I do and wait for her to finish. And wait. And wait. And wait.

"Do I need that much work?" I joke, cracking my eyes open when Macy lets out an impatient sigh.

"You don't need any work," she answers. "Which is a good thing, because my glamour isn't working on you."

"What do you mean, it's not working on me?"

"I mean, it's not working." She looks baffled. "I don't understand. The third time I tried, I even used a more complicated one, but it didn't work, either. And it always works. I don't understand."

"Obviously it's because I'm already too glamorous," I tease. "I mean—" I wave a hand up and down myself in a "look at me" joke.

"Right?" Macy agrees. "That must be it."

I laugh and bump her gently with my shoulder. "I was just joking, you dork."

"I know." She winks at me. "But you're adorable, so…"

"Adorable sometimes," I agree with a sigh. "Glamorous? Absolutely never. Even your magic knows that, obviously."

She rolls her eyes a second time. "Give me a break. I just wish I could figure out what's going on."

Me too. I wonder if it's some weird gargoyle thing we haven't figured out. Some rule like Stone Shall Never Be Glamorous or something like that… Just my luck.

She reaches a hand across the room to her closet and murmurs something under her breath. Seconds later, her favorite pair of Rothy's floats right into her hand. "So my magic isn't on the fritz." She turns to me with a shrug. "I don't get it."

"Yeah, me neither." I wait for Hudson to chime in—having lived several hundreds of years, he knows a lot more than either of us about magical things—and usually can't wait to make me feel naïve by pointing out what he considers obvious. But he is still looking out the window…and being stubbornly silent.

"I'll ask my dad the next time I see him. In the meantime, I guess you're going to have to settle for being adorable instead of glamorous. Think you can handle it?"

It's my turn to roll my eyes. "Semi-adorable, and I handle it every other day of my life, don't I?"

"Whatever." Macy crosses the room to get her phone and then gasps when she comes face-to-face with the hole Hudson left in the wall.

"What happened?" she asks, her gaze darting back and forth between the hole and me. "My dad is going to flip!"

"Hudson and I were having a fight, so…"

"So you punched the wall?" Her eyes are practically popping out of her head.

"Of course not! *He* punched the wall." I hold up a hand to stop what I'm sure is about to be a million questions. "And before you ask me, no, I have no idea how he did it. We were arguing, he got mad, and then I watched him punch the wall. When he pulled back, boom.

There was a hole directly where he punched."

"I don't understand how someone without a body could do that. I mean, does he still have access to his powers?" She looks horrified at the very idea.

"I don't think so. Wouldn't I know if he did?" But just the idea has me worrying even more than I already was. What if he's been persuading me all along and I just didn't know it?

"Jesus, I haven't been persuading you," Hudson snaps. "Can you please give it a rest? I'm not actually Satan."

"I never said you were!" I snap back, doing my best to ignore the relief I feel in the pit of my stomach over the fact that he's talking to me again. "But do you blame me for wondering?"

Macy, obviously realizing I'm fighting with Hudson again, rolls her eyes and starts gathering up her class supplies into her backpack.

"You're bloody right, I do!" The fact that the Britishisms are coming back tells me just how upset he actually is. "Don't you think things would look a lot different if I was actually using my gift on you? You'd be doing whatever I tell you to instead of arguing with me until I want to pull my bleeding hair out."

"Well, excuse me for remaining a sentient being with thoughts and ideas of my own. So sorry to inconvenience you."

Is it a bitchy response? Yeah. Do I care? Not even a little bit. He deserves it with his silent treatment one second and his "lord of the manor" attitude the next.

"You've been inconveniencing me since the day I laid eyes on you," he growls. "Why should today be any different?"

"You know what? Why don't you bite me?" I shoot him a mock-innocent look. "Oh, wait. I forgot. You can't."

Hudson's growl becomes a snarl, and he finally turns from the window and stalks across the room toward me. But then he stops several feet short of me, hands shoved into his back pockets as he stares me down with narrowed eyes. "You're going to push too far one of these days. You know that, right?"

"And then what? You're going to punch another wall?" I narrow my eyes right back. "Don't threaten me. I'm not some scared little girl who's just going to fall in line. If you wanted that, you should have holed up inside some sweet little human's brain instead of mine."

"Some sweet little human?" he repeats, and just like that, his anger is gone, replaced by an amusement that's almost palpable. "So the gargoyle thing is starting to grow on you, hmm?"

I don't know what to say to that, don't even know how I feel about what I just said. So I do the only thing I can do in this situation—I ignore his question completely.

"Come on, Macy. We need to get to the cafeteria. Jaxon's going to think I forgot about him—again."

"I'm ready," my cousin answers. She grins. "I've just been waiting for you and Hudson to stop tearing into each other. I gotta say, your face was priceless."

"How did I look?" I ask as we close the door behind us and start walking down the hallway.

"Like you wanted to murder a small village. Or, you know, a major metropolitan area."

"Now you're talking my kind of fun," Hudson joins in. "Just tell me when and where and I'm there."

"Wouldn't you be there anyway? Considering we are currently attached?" I raise my brows at the fact that the worst seems to be over—at least for now.

"It was a figure of speech. You know what those are, right?"

"You mean like verbs? Nouns? Adjectives?" I tease him, because of course I know what a figure of speech is. I also know what colloquial phrases are, which is what he actually threw at me.

Hudson rubs his eyes. "You scare me sometimes, you know that? You really do."

I laugh, then throw him a colloquial phrase right back. "Baby, you haven't seen anything yet."

He sighs. "Don't I know it."

47

Are you Bloodstoned?

"So I have a question," I tell Macy as we walk to the cafeteria.

"Sure." She looks at me quizzically.

"How obvious was it that I was fighting with Hudson back in our dorm room? Because if people can tell, I'm sure they're thinking there's something seriously wrong with me."

"Umm, too late for that," she teases. But when I shoot her an exasperated look, she relents. "I think you forget where you are. Last year, a witch turned herself invisible for almost six months. People spent a semester walking around looking like they were talking to the walls. Weird shit happens here every day. Nobody even blinks most of the time."

"Yeah, well, they blink at me. All the time."

"We've been through this. Dating Jaxon means half the school hates you and the other half wants to be you. That's just how it is. Add in the gargoyle thing and it's not the talking to Hudson that's going to make people stare at you. So relax, okay?"

I turn her words over in my head. "Yeah, okay."

Jaxon is walking into the cafeteria just as we get there—and at least half of the Order is with him: Mekhi, whom I haven't seen since he brought me Jaxon's jacket, and Luca and Rafael.

All three grin at me like I'm Christmas—or at least Halloween.

"About time you decided to show your face down here," Mekhi tells me as he wraps me up in a huge, ocean-scented hug. "We've been bugging Jaxon about when we were going to get the chance to see you."

Luca's and Rafael's hugs are more restrained—we don't know each other as well—but they both welcome me back enthusiastically.

Jaxon gives them a couple of minutes, then elbows his way through the group to pull me out and get things moving. "Hungry?" he asks as we walk toward the main cafeteria line.

"I am, actually." I'm a little surprised by the fact that I'm starving again. Either fighting with Hudson burns a ton of calories or I'm still making up for the fact that I went fifteen weeks without food.

I grab a tray, pile it high with eggs, toast, and hash browns. Jaxon adds a packet of cherry Pop-Tarts with a wink, then heads off to get his own breakfast while I pour myself two of the world's largest cups of coffee.

Macy—who is a self-proclaimed caffeine addict—gives me a wide-eyed look when I reach for the second cup, but she doesn't say anything. A girl's got to do what a girl's got to do, after all.

It's not long before we're seated at a table. Jaxon and the other vamps are all drinking their breakfast out of stainless-steel tumblers—a concession to the fact that I'm new to watching the whole blood-drinking thing, I'm sure—while Macy and I drink our coffee like we're mainlining it.

My bizarre life is definitely catching up with me, and right now I feel like there's not enough caffeine in the world. Jaxon must feel the same way, because he's looking a little haggard, too.

"You okay?" I whisper, sliding my hand into his as the others laugh and joke around us.

"Yeah." He smiles back. "This is the first time I've fed in a couple of days, and I think it's wearing on me. Especially after the trip to the Bloodletter."

"Jaxon, you can't do that! I know you've been worried about me, but you need to take care of yourself, too."

I burrow into him, and as I do, I feel that same warmth glowing inside me...and between us. *The mating bond?* I wonder. Most of the time I barely notice it—maybe because I still don't know as much about it as I should—but right now I can feel a connection between us, bright and lovely.

I lean into it a little, loving the way it feels. Loving even more the way Jaxon feels at the other end of it—warm and welcoming and strong and steady.

I don't know what I'm doing, don't know, even, how to interact with the bond. But Jaxon looks so soft and sleepy and unlike himself that I can't help reaching out. Can't help closing my eyes and putting a hand across his heart, on this space where it feels like something exists between us, and smiling at him warmly.

Jaxon's cheeks start to have a little more color in them, and his eyes look more alert, so I pull back even as I squeeze the hand I'm still holding in my own.

His midnight eyes heat up at the connection between us, his brows quirking in a sexy way that has me burrowing even deeper into his side and whispering, "Later," into his ear.

As I relinquish the last of my hold on the bond, Hudson flops down in an empty spot at the table and snarls, "At least warn me the next time you're going to do something so completely nauseating," he orders. "I can go look out a window or something."

He's my mate. I'm allowed to fawn all over him if I want to.

Hudson's only response is a narrowing of his eyes and a growl so intense that it actually sends a shiver down my spine.

"You're really going to spend the afternoon jumping off the castle?" Macy is asking the vamp contingent at the table.

Jumping off the castle? I mouth to Jaxon, who just inclines his head in a "what can we do?" way.

"Got to start practicing for Ludares, don't we?" Mekhi answers her. "It'll be here before we know it."

"So you guys are really going to compete?" I ask, looking at Jaxon.

"I heard it was dangerous."

The entire table turns to stare at me, eyebrows raised.

"So what if it's dangerous?" Rafael answers. "It's our last year at Katmere—been waiting for the chance to dominate the tourney forever. Damn straight we're going to compete."

"Besides, there's danger, Grace, and then there's *danger*." Mekhi grins at me. "No one's actually died from competing in the Ludares."

"*Nobody's died?* Are you kidding me with this? How is the fact that nobody's died *yet* a ringing endorsement for this game?" I look to my cousin for a little solidarity, but she's right there with the others, a patronizing look on her face, like *I'm* the one who doesn't understand.

And that's when it dawns on me. "Wait a minute, Macy. You're not actually going to compete in a game where danger is the first adjective that comes to everyone's mind, too, are you?"

"'Danger' is the second adjective," Luca tells me with a grin. "'Fun' is the first."

"Oh, well, in that case, of course we should all compete," I tell him. "Wouldn't want to miss out on a good time."

"Exactly!" Rafael says with a wink. "Plus, you know, if any of us ever hopes to end up on the Circle, well…training starts now!"

"You mean that's still a thing?" I ask. I vaguely remember Amka mentioning something about how Ludares originally wasn't a game but a trial to end up on the Circle, but to be honest, I haven't thought much about it. "You play a game to become a Circle member? What if you suck at sports?"

Jaxon chuckles. "Ludares started out as a competition for the strongest mated pairs. If you survived the test, you earned a seat on the Circle."

Mekhi smiles. "Can you imagine how brutal it was? One mated pair against *eight* kick-ass opponents? I would have loved to have seen Jaxon's or Flint's parents compete to be on the Circle. It must have been *wild*."

Umm, yeah, *so* not my idea of a good time. At all. "So only mated pairs can sit on the Circle, then?" I didn't expect that, but I probably should have, considering both of Jaxon's and Flint's parents are on it.

Jaxon nods. "Pretty much—it takes at least two people to survive the Trial, or so they say." He squeezes my hand, his gaze holding mine. "I keep thinking we should do it one day. The Circle needs someone to lead it who won't let that happen."

"Us? Why? I thought you hated all the prince stuff?" I mean, being queen certainly isn't on my agenda. I'm more interested in art school, even if I have to do a gap year because of the whole "trapped as a gargoyle for four months" mess that screwed up college apps and everything else in my life, apparently.

"I do," he assures me. "But there's been a Third Great War brewing for a long time, and Hudson only exacerbated it with the shit he pulled before he died."

"Yes, let's blame me for the fact that Dad and the wolves are teaming up with made vampires so they can wipe everyone else out of existence." Hudson rolls his eyes. "What a wanker."

"What does that have to do with *us* being the head of the Circle?" I ask Jaxon, though I definitely want to follow up on Hudson's comment later, because it sounded very different from anything else I've heard.

"Gargoyles are peacekeepers," Mekhi interjects. "If you and Jaxon take his parents' place, you have a much better chance of keeping shit under control. Between Jaxon's power and your ability to chill things out—"

"I can do that?" I interrupt.

"That's what the old stories all say," Rafael tells me. "Gargoyles were created to keep the balance among the factions."

"Exactly. So when my parents abdicate, we can take their place and get things going back in the right direction," Jaxon says seriously. "Which definitely includes avoiding war."

"Yeah, like that's going to happen." Hudson rolls his eyes. "First of all, the only way dear old Dad would abdicate is if you severed his head from his body and then burned him, twice. And even then I'm not so sure. And secondly, who says sitting on the Circle is a good thing anyway? Jaxon may suddenly have this starry-eyed vision of how easy it will be to stop a war, but the truth is, it's hard and it's bloody brutal." He speaks with assurance, like he knows what he's talking about.

"Besides, it's not like being on the Circle is such a good thing. I'd rather stay off the damn council and keep my mate safe than be on it and always have to worry about someone trying to kill her to take our place. Trust Jaxon to not give a shit about that part."

"What if someone's mate dies?" I ask. "How does that work?"

"Usually, that only happens if someone murders them," Macy says. "Vampires are the only immortal creatures, but the rest of us tend to live a really long time."

"You wouldn't have to worry about that," Jaxon insists. "No one will ever try to touch you once we lead the Circle. No one would dare."

I don't know how I feel about any of this, including the fact that Jaxon has apparently been making plans in his head for our future without consulting me at all. And the fact that he seems to think it's going to be his job to take care of me for the rest of our lives. I mean, I'm okay with taking care of each other, but I'm not okay with being some kind of burden he's responsible for.

No effing way. I'll just have to double my efforts researching gargoyles. I don't want to be anyone's burden. I want to take care of myself.

Jaxon turns to discuss some particularly cool strategy with Mekhi, and I can't stop my gaze from seeking out Hudson's to see if he agrees with Jaxon that I need protecting.

"You could kick all our asses, Grace." Hudson's fathomless blue eyes never leave mine. "And then some."

I laugh. I can't help it. I don't believe him even a little, but the tightness in my chest eases a little bit, anyway. I mean, if *Hudson* thinks I'm kick-ass, that's gotta count for something, right?

"Damn straight it does." Hudson grins at me, and I realize I've missed it in the time he's been so quiet.

Before I can think much about that, though, Macy complains about a wolf she wants to teach a lesson. When she doesn't elaborate, I remember she never answered my earlier question. "Macy? You're not really competing, are you?"

Macy's whole face lights up. "Of course I'm competing! This is the first year I *can* compete, and I can't effing wait!"

"You go, girl," Flint says as he drops down onto a chair at the end of the table beside Hudson, who gets up and leans against a nearby wall. "This year's tournament is going to be epic."

Flint holds a hand out for a fist bump, and Macy nearly swallows her tongue. Right before she bumps his fist hard enough to give herself a bruise. Apparently, some things never change...

"Completely epic," Jaxon agrees. "When do we need to register our team by?"

"This Wednesday," Flint says. He waits for a few seconds, then says oh so casually but not actually casually at all, "Do you guys have your team together yet, Jaxon?"

Jaxon eyes him for a few seconds, and at first I'm confused by what's going on—if Jaxon is going to do this, isn't he going to compete with the Order? But then I remember what Hudson told me yesterday about how the game fosters interspecies relationships...and injuries, apparently.

"You want to team up?" Jaxon asks, just as casually but not really.

"I was thinking about it. Eden and I were going to partner up with Xavier, but we still need to add some vamps and witches." He looks at me. "And maybe a gargoyle?"

When hell freezes over.

48

Win, Lose, or Die

"What? Me?" I ask, my eyes going huge. "I mean...I don't think... Can gargoyles really compete?" I know Amka said I could, but I thought she was just teasing me.

And, by the way, please let the answer be no. Please let the answer be no. I'm not fabulous at sports to begin with, let alone paranormal sports where the goal is not to die, but there is no guarantee. Not to mention the fact that I have no idea what my powers are yet... I mean, besides turning to stone, which doesn't seem very helpful in a game anyway.

"Ludares is open to every junior and senior in the school," Flint tells me. "So, hell yeah, you can compete. Plus, I'm totally down with having a gargoyle on my team. Who knows what you can do?"

"Nothing," I answer. "I can do nothing. That's the problem."

"That's not true," Hudson tells me from where he's still leaning against the wall. "You can do things. You just don't know what they are yet."

"How do you know?" Equal parts terror and excitement thrum through me as I lean forward. "Did you see me do something when we were together?"

The whole table is staring at me again. I ignore them because apparently this is my life for now. I hadn't meant to ask the question out loud, but sometimes I get so caught up or invested in the conversation that I don't realize what I'm doing.

I vaguely register Macy telling everyone that I can see and talk to Hudson—at least I think that's what she says because suddenly everyone in the Order tenses up and turns to Jaxon, who just shrugs. Which is fine with me, since right now I'm more interested in hearing what Hudson has to say than I am worried about Jaxon's friends staring at me.

"You mean besides keeping me trapped in stone with you for nearly three and a half months?" He raises one brow.

I sigh and throw my hands up. Because I already know that. "Yeah, that's basically my point. I can't imagine being much help on a team when all I can do is turn to stone. It's kind of easy to catch me that way."

Hudson chuckles. "There's more, you know. Like, the wings aren't for decoration only—you just need to figure out how to use them."

That's true. And Flint did offer to teach me—maybe I should take him up on those flying lessons sooner rather than later. I mean, if I can even turn back into a gargoyle again. I haven't felt so much as a tingling over the last four days.

"I think I'll sit the game out," I say to the table at large, who are all still gaping at me—well, except for Flint and Macy, who are reminiscing about past Ludares tournaments. "I mean, you make it sound like so much fun, but—"

"No way!" Flint pauses with his fork in midair. "You have to play. Besides, your uncle mentioned that the prize this year is kick-ass."

"Oh yeah?" Macy bounces excitedly. "What is it? He hasn't even told me yet."

"I was in his office when he got the call yesterday; that's the only reason I know," Flint tells her. "It looks like Byron's parents have decided to donate the prize this year."

"Really?" Mekhi looks surprised.

Actually, everyone at the table does. I remember Jaxon telling me Byron was the Order member whose mate was killed by a few members of Cole's pack. Though, for a while at least, Byron seemed to think Hudson had somehow influenced the wolves to do what they did.

Hudson raises his brows. "Do I just get blamed for *everyone's* deaths now?" He clenches his jaw and turns to read tomorrow's menu posted on the wall.

"Stop taunting us and just tell us what the prize is, Flint." Macy's voice—a little whiny and a little annoyed—is what draws my attention back to the conversation this time.

Well, that and Jaxon shifting so that he's pressed against my back, his chin resting on my shoulder.

I turn my face to the left so I can smile at him, and he winks back, then gives me a sexy little eyebrow raise that makes me think all kinds of things I shouldn't be thinking about in the middle of the cafeteria—especially not when Jaxon's brother is in my head, watching the whole thing.

"I'm not taunting you!" Flint sounds indignant now. "You guys are the ones who wouldn't stop talking long enough for me to tell you."

"Well, we've stopped talking now," Luca says. "So spill it."

"Byron's parents have decided to donate…" He does a little drumroll on the dining table. "A bloodstone! And not just any bloodstone. It's one of the queen's favorites, from the royal collection, that she gifted his parents on the eve of his mate's death."

Everything inside me stills as I remember the Bloodletter telling us that she would take care of getting the bloodstone to us. This must be what she meant. A glance at Jaxon's face tells me he thinks so, too—and that he isn't the least bit surprised by this bit of news, either. He obviously had a good idea what the Bloodletter would do.

Which also makes his interest in playing Ludares right now—in the middle of everything we have going on—make so much more sense. If the only way to get the bloodstone is to win the tournament, then it looks like hell really has frozen over.

I just need to figure out how not to be a total burden—and, oh yeah, how not to be the first death—on the Ludares field in the history of Katmere.

49

Teamwork Makes the Dream Work... (or it Gives You Nightmares)

"Hey, Jaxon, wait up." Flint jogs up behind Jaxon, Macy, and me as we walk out of the cafeteria.

Jaxon turns, brows raised. "What's up?"

"I was just wondering..." Flint trails off, and if I didn't know better, I'd think he was panicking, though I don't know why. I do know that he's floundering, though, mouth opening and closing like he's searching for words but has forgotten how to actually make sounds.

"Are you okay?" I ask, leaning forward to rest a hand on his arm. "You don't look so good."

"Oh, yeah. I'm fine." Flint focuses on me for a beat, seems to catch his breath. Then says, "Sorry. Too many thoughts going through my brain at the same time." He shoots me his ten-thousand-kilowatt grin.

I smile back—it's impossible not to when Flint gives you that look—and tell him, "Yeah, that happens to me, too, sometimes. So what do you need?"

"Oh, right. I was just wondering if you wanted to spend some time practicing for Ludares today?" he says to Jaxon, then turns to me again. "We could even get that flying lesson in, New Girl."

"Flying lesson?" Jaxon repeats, looking like he wants to say something.

"If it doesn't get me punched this time, I thought I'd take New

Girl up, show her some moves," Flint tells him with a shit-eating grin. "Plus we still have that project for Mr. Damasen to finish."

"And by moves, you mean how not to die in the air, right?" Jaxon gives him a look that's half funny and half very definitely not.

"Absolutely. I'm not going to hurt her, Jaxon." He holds Jaxon's gaze as he says it, and his usual smile is completely MIA.

"Yeah, I've heard that before," Jaxon shoots back.

"Stop it." I bump him with my shoulder, even as I roll my eyes at Flint. "Ignore him. I'm really looking forward to learning to fly. But today we were going to do something different."

"Oh yeah?" Flint looks interested. "Like what?"

"Nothing that requires an entourage," Jaxon interjects.

"Who are you calling your entourage?" Flint demands with a wide grin. "Maybe you and Grace are Macy's and *my* entourage. Right, Mace?"

For a minute, I think my cousin is going to swoon right here in the middle of the hallway. "Yeah, absolutely," she tells him, and I swear the only thing more obvious than the stars in her eyes is the drool on her chin. "I think Jaxon would make a great entourage."

Flint guffaws at that, even as Jaxon gives me a "what the fuck" look. I shrug back, because seriously, what is there to say? Except, "We're going to the library to grab some info on gargoyle powers and the Dragon Boneyard. Then we thought we'd head up to Jaxon's room and hang out as we research."

"Oh, come on," Hudson says, annoyance coloring every British syllable. "We don't need Dragon Breath to find out what we need to know."

Right. Because there's no way an actual dragon might know anything about the Dragon Boneyard.

"The Dragon Boneyard?" Flint looks intrigued. "What do you want to know about it?"

"Everything," I answer, linking one arm through Jaxon's and the other through Flint's. "So why don't you come, too? You can help us figure out what we need to know."

"Yeah, sure. What do you need?"

"We'll tell you all about it when we get to Jaxon's room," I promise. Then I glance behind me at my cousin, who looks like she doesn't know if she should follow us or not. "Come on, Mace. We need all the help we can get."

"Awesome. Just let me text Gwen and tell her I'm not going to be able to hang out later."

"Oh, never mind," I tell her. "I forgot you had somewhere to be. Jaxon, Flint, and I can totally handle it."

Macy shoots me a "stop talking now" look, then fires off a series of quick texts. "Too late," she says, and then she's darting in front of us to lead the way to the library.

It doesn't take us long to gather what we need, partly because Amka has the books ready for us—at Jaxon's request—and partly because she's willing to loan us two of the library laptops so we can access the magic databases from anywhere in the castle and not just the library.

Flint helps by grabbing a few books on dragons that he thinks will help, while Macy runs back down to the cafeteria to gather snacks for our "marathon research sesh," as she keeps calling it. In the meantime, Hudson just lounges around on whatever open chair he can find, calling out book titles that he thinks might help us.

"Where was all this information last night?" I ask him after my third run to the stacks at the back of the library.

"Last night I was too busy—"

"Trying not to vomit," I fill in for him. "Yeah, yeah, I know the routine by heart by now."

"Just because I've used it a few times doesn't make it any less true," he tells me with a definite tone to his voice.

"True, but it does make it lose its impact. At the moment, I'm pretty convinced you have the weakest stomach of anyone I've ever met, which is particularly interesting considering you don't even *have* a stomach."

"Sure I do," he responds, and to prove it, he lifts up his T-shirt, revealing—not going to lie—one of the best sets of abs I've ever seen. Seriously. Which…I'm not quite sure how I feel about that. I mean, it shouldn't matter. And it doesn't. But…wow. Just wow. I'd have to be blind not to notice.

Hudson shoots me a smug look but doesn't say anything as he lets his shirt drop back down. Then again, he doesn't have to. The argument over whether or not he has a stomach has most definitely been settled…and I most definitely lost.

"You ready?" Jaxon asks as he comes up behind me with a giant armful of books.

"Yeah, of course. Can I help carry some of those?"

"I've got them," he says with a grin, and he does—at least partly because his abs absolutely give Hudson's a run for their money.

"I call bullshit," Hudson grumbles as we leave the library. He's walking a little bit ahead of us, but he's turned around to face me as he walks backward. Not going to lie, there's a part of me that would love nothing more than for him to trip and fall on his ass.

Petty? Yes. Mean? Absolutely. But I'd still pay good money to see it. Maybe landing on his ass will take him down a peg or ten, which is something he definitely needs. Arrogant prick.

"Don't hold back," Hudson says, and in the blink of an eye, he's suddenly right behind me, his arrogant, smarmy voice right in my ear. "Tell me how you really feel."

"I always do," I shoot back as a shiver runs down my spine.

By the time we get to Jaxon's tower, Macy is already there with a bag full of the least nutritious stuff Katmere has to offer. Chips, popcorn, and even a pack of ten-dollar Oreos.

"I stole them from my dad's stash," she says as she drops them on the table in the antechamber to Jaxon's bedroom, where he does most of his studying.

The last time I saw the place, it was a total mess—Lia made

sure of it before she dragged our drugged asses to the tunnels so she could torture the both of us. But sometime in the three and a half months I was gone, Jaxon not only put it back together, but he actually redecorated the place.

I stroll around the room, vaguely paying attention as Jaxon explains to Flint and Macy fully about what the Bloodletter said we need to do to get Hudson out of my head. Flint has some succinct words about the Unkillable Beast—and the Bloodletter, for that matter—but he's obviously into it. He's hanging on Jaxon's every word and even offering a ton of suggestions.

For once, nobody's paying any attention to me as I run a hand along Jaxon's bookshelves and take in all the new decor. And can I just say I like it? The lack of attention *and* his decorating choices...

Now, instead of a couple of big, comfy chairs dominating the sitting area, there's *one* big, comfy chair and a huge, overstuffed black couch that is definitely large enough for two people to stretch out on. There's a new coffee table—which looks a lot sturdier than the one he turned to kindling during one of his telekinetic losses of control—and in the corner, under the window that nearly killed me when it shattered, is a big table with four black upholstered dining chairs positioned around it. Because of course everything in Jaxon's tower is black. Of course it is...

Except for the books. They're every color under the sun, and they *are* still everywhere—on the bookcases, stacked on the floor in the corners, stacked on the coffee table and underneath the big table, piled up in random places throughout the room—and I love it.

I love even more that there are books I've never heard of mixed with books that are old favorites of mine mixed with classics I've always wanted to read. Add in the artwork on the wall—the Klimt sketch that made me swoon the first time I came up here along with a few other haunting paintings—and this room is pretty much my favorite place on earth.

Then again, how could it not be? Jaxon is here.

I expect Hudson to make a ton of snide comments about the decorating, but he's strangely quiet, staring intently at something on one of Jaxon's shelves, a carving of a horse from the looks of it. It's not a super-intricate carving, but clearly it's something Jaxon loves, the edges smooth and shiny as though his fingers have spent hours rubbing each curve of the horse's neck or body.

Just when I start to wonder what's so interesting about the horse, Hudson shoves his hands deep into his pockets, shaking his head as he walks away. I think I hear him mutter, "Loser," but it's so faint that I can't be sure.

Hudson has been in a weird mood since breakfast, and I refuse to let him ruin my focus again. I'm determined to not wait for Jaxon to take care of me anymore. I need to step up and figure out how to solve my own problems.

Jaxon piles the books on the main table, and I pick one up called *The Myth and Mayhem of Gargoyles*. I don't know why I chose it, except for the fact that I like the idea of causing a little mayhem—me, Grace Foster, pretty much the most un-mayhem-like person on the face of the earth. As I flip it open, I can't help but wonder for a second—or several seconds, if I'm being honest—what it would feel like to just give in to the havoc. To say whatever I want instead of always filtering it, to do what I want instead of what I think I should do.

Then again, now's not exactly the time for that. There's too much going on right now to shake things up just to do it. So I stretch out on Jaxon's very inviting couch and start reading, while everyone else claims their own separate corner of the room.

Flint settles at the main table and flips open one of the laptops, announcing he plans to start researching the Dragon Boneyard—how to get there, the best time of day to go, and how to get out alive, because apparently not getting out alive is an actual thing. Yay.

Macy picks up a book on the magical nature of gargoyles, curls up in the comfy chair across from me, and dives in while nibbling on a giant stack of Oreos.

And Jaxon—Jaxon grabs the other laptop after offering it to me and settles down at the end of the couch to do more research on the Unkillable Beast.

I look around at my friends, all of whom are spending their Saturday cooped up inside looking for information to help me, and my heart swells. They could be doing anything right now, and instead they're doing this.

Hudson can call me emotional, he can call me naïve or overly sentimental or any number of other things, but I still have to blink back tears of gratitude that these people have found their way into my life. I came to Katmere Academy at the lowest point in my life, desperate, miserable, sad. I figured I would just get through the year and then get the hell out.

And while nothing here has been what I expected—I mean, a gargoyle, really?—I can't imagine going back to a life without Macy's enthusiasm or Jaxon's intensity or Flint's teasing (though his murder attempts I can definitely do without).

Sometimes life hands you more than a new hand of cards to play—it hands you a whole new deck, maybe even a whole new game. Losing my parents the way I did will forever be one of the most horrible and traumatizing experiences of my life, but sitting here with these people makes me feel like maybe, just maybe, I've got a chance of coming out the other side of it.

And that is more, so much more, than I imagined just a few short months ago.

"Hey, look at this!" Macy sits up abruptly. "I think I just figured out why the glamour didn't work on you this morning. It wasn't me. It was you!"

"Why? Can't do glamours on stone?" I guess, because that feels about right.

"No." She shoots me a "you're being a dork" look, then flips the book she's reading so I can see. "It didn't work because it says right here that you're immune to magic!"

50

It's Getting Crowded
Under the Bed

"Immune to magic?" Flint asks, closing his laptop and coming over to check out Macy's find. "Really?"

"And to dragon fire, vampire and werewolf bites, siren calls—the list goes on and on. Basically, gargoyles have a natural built-in resistance to nearly all forms of paranormal magic. That's—" She holds her hand up to her temple and mimes her brain exploding.

"No wonder Marise always had such a hard time healing you," she continues. "We put it down to you being completely human, but it must have been the gargoyle thing all along."

"She had trouble healing me?" I ask, because I don't remember that at all.

"Yeah, she did," Jaxon says, a contemplative look on his face. "The first time when she tried to break down my venom and also later, after what happened in the tunnels. With her help healing you, she thought you'd bounce back fast once you got the blood transfusion. But she couldn't get her powers to work on you the way she thought they should. Everything took longer than it would have with—" He breaks off.

"You can say it," I tell him. "With a real paranormal."

"I wasn't going to say *real*," he tells me with a frown. "I was going to say with one of the *usual* paranormals. Big difference."

"Small difference," I answer, but with a smile to let him know that I'm not actually holding it against him. "But whatever. It doesn't matter. Because I know I'm not—" I break off as my cheeks start to heat up.

"You're not what?" Macy asks.

"Umm, well." I glance anywhere but at my friends. The wall. The wall looks interesting. "It's just that I know I'm not immune to all of those things."

"I don't agree," Macy says, leaning forward. "I mean, how do we know that Lia's spell would have even worked if Jaxon didn't get involved? You can't use her as proof that you're not immune."

"Well, she sure went through a hell of a lot of pain for nothing," Jaxon says.

"No shit," Flint agrees. "That was awful."

"Seriously?" Jaxon tells him, and the fact that his voice is mild makes it all so much worse. "*You're* going to complain *to us* about what happened in the tunnels being awful, when Grace still has scars from your talons?"

"That's what those scars are from?" Hudson demands, a sudden glint in his eye that doesn't bode well for anyone. "*Flint* gave them to you?"

"I thought I was doing the right thing, Jaxon." The look Flint sends him is pleading. "I thought I was stopping a new effing apocalypse by preventing Lia from bringing Hudson back."

"The apocalypse? Seriously?" Hudson leans against the wall, arms crossed over his chest and an incredulous look on his face. He hasn't said a word in what feels like forever in Hudson time, but this comment has definitely woken him up with a vengeance. "You people really think I'm the fucking harbinger of the apocalypse?"

"You don't really want to get into that right now, do you?" I turn and ask.

"Hell yeah, I want to get into it. I'm bloody well sick of being cast as the bad guy."

"Like I said before, maybe don't *be* the bad guy, Hudson," I snap. "You don't get to have it both ways."

"We're getting off track here," Macy says, waving the book in our faces. "Are you going to tell us why you're so convinced this is wrong?"

I don't want to—it feels like giving everyone here a look into something they have no business knowing about—but at this point, I kind of have to. Plus, I do want to know the answer, and maybe one of them has it, even though Jaxon is currently looking as confused as everyone else.

"It's no big deal," I tell them. "It's just that I happen to know for a fact that I'm not immune to vampire bites."

"How would you know that?" Macy demands. "Has someone tried to bite—" She breaks off, her eyes going wide as understanding dawns. "Ooooooh. So that's how. Niiiice." She gives Jaxon an approving look.

Suddenly Flint is looking anywhere but at the two of us. "Oh, right. Well, then..." He coughs a little, clears his throat, and looks incredibly uncomfortable as he continues. "Maybe the book is wrong, then?"

"The damn book isn't wrong," Hudson snarls. "There are different kinds of bites."

"It's not wrong," Jaxon unconsciously echoes his brother. "If I was trying to inject my venom into you to kill you—or to change you—it probably wouldn't work because I'd be using my powers. But the times that I've bitten you...that's not what I'm doing. Hurting you or changing you is the last thing on my mind. I'm trying to—"

He breaks off, like he hasn't already said too much. But it's too late. All three of us know how he was going to finish that statement—with some variation of the fact that his biting me had nothing to do with pain and everything to do with giving me pleasure.

Which it did. Does. A lot. But no one else needs to know that. Not Flint, who seems strangely disturbed by the image. Not Macy, who has all but turned into a heart-eyed emoji. And definitely not Hudson, who seems to be getting colder—and more pissed off—with each word any of us says.

Macy's going to demand details the second I'm alone—it's written all over her face. And now that I'm thinking about what she's going to ask, I'm also thinking about how I'm going to answer. Which means I'm thinking about Jaxon biting me and—

"Enough already," Hudson growls as I can't help remembering the last time Jaxon did that to me. "You don't have to be so graphic. We get it."

"I wasn't being graphic at all," I answer. "What is your problem today, anyway?"

"I don't have a problem!" he snaps back. "I just think some things should remain private."

"Yeah, well, me too. But here you are." I glance back at Jaxon, who's got his eyebrows raised, like he wants me to tell the whole room what Hudson is saying. I give a quick shake of my head. I just want this entire conversation over.

As if sensing how embarrassed I am by his nondisclosure disclosure, Jaxon pushes us back to the original topic with sheer willpower and a whole lot of royal attitude. It's funny how I forget how well he plays the prince because he does it so rarely—unlike Hudson, whose whole demeanor pretty much shouts, *I'm royalty and you're not fit to lick my boots.*

Hudson's voice is as dry and British as my mother's favorite shortbread cookie when he answers, "To be fair, a lot of people aren't."

I roll my eyes and flick my gaze back to him. "You need to be careful, or people are going to start believing you mean the ridiculous things you say."

"Good."

I just roll my eyes again, then focus on Jaxon, who is quizzing people in a round-robin format on what they've found so far. Not for the first time, I'm grateful that I'm mated to someone like Jaxon, who not only doesn't try to insert himself into my conversations with Hudson but who also steers attention away from the fact that a hundred-years-old vampire is yammering in my head whenever I need him to. Some of these conversations are bad enough the first time—I couldn't imagine having to repeat them to Jaxon. He doesn't need to know all the weird little side trips my brain makes, especially with Hudson egging me on.

Feeling like I've dodged a bullet, I settle back down on the couch and continue reading. Sadly, I haven't really learned anything new at all. Certainly nothing of the scintillating "mayhem" I'd been promised. In fact, the most exciting thing the book has mentioned so far is that gargoyles can stand as sentries for months on end, without a need for food or sleep as long as they are stone.

Just as I suspected, I make an excellent garden gnome. Paint me pink and stand me on one leg and I might even be able to pull off yard flamingo. Fantastic.

I'd feel useless, except Flint hasn't learned anything yet, either, about the actual Dragon Boneyard that he didn't already know.

"The only other thing I learned," Macy says when Flint is finished, "is that gargoyles are supposed to have the power to channel magic. It's weird. Magic doesn't work on them, but they can—supposedly—borrow magic from other paranormals and use it themselves."

"What does that mean?" I ask, intrigued at the idea of having some power, any power, that actually does something. I mean, turning to stone is cool and all if you want to spend your life as a tourist attraction, but it's not very exciting. Neither is being immune to other powers.

Yeah, it's a great defensive gift, but it doesn't let me actually *do* anything. And considering the company I'm keeping, that seems totally unfair.

"I think it means that if I share my power with you, you'll be able to use it," Jaxon tells me.

"If that's the case, we have to try it!" Macy says, jumping out of her chair. "Me first!"

51

Get Your Magic On

Jaxon shakes his head, amused, but does a go-ahead hand gesture as he settles into the couch to watch what happens.

"Okay, cool." She looks at me. "I'm going to send you some fire energy. See if you can light one of the candles on the bookshelf."

I look at her like she's gotten a little too close to her own fire and singed a few brain cells. "You don't actually think I can light a candle without a match, do you?"

"Of course you can! It's easy." She holds an arm out—palm facing up—and focuses on a black candle on the top shelf of the bookcase. Then she curls her fingers into her palms, and the candle wick catches flame. "See? Easy-peasy."

"Easy for you," I tell her. "If I try that, one of two things is going to happen. Either nothing will happen *or* I'll set the entire bookcase on fire—neither of which seems like the outcome we're going for here."

"Yeah, well, better here than at the Dragon Boneyard, don't you think?" Macy says, a rare hint of exasperation in her tone as she looks at me, eyes narrowed and hands on her hips. "Now, come on. Hold your hand up and let's try it."

"Okay, fine," I tell her, standing up even as nerves drop the entire bottom out of my stomach. "But if I set your hair on fire, I don't want to hear about it."

"I am a witch, you know. If you set my hair on fire, I'll just grow it back." She grins, moving to stand about three feet from me. "Now, come on. Arm up."

"Okay." I take a deep breath, then blow it out slowly as I do what she requests. "Now what?"

"I want you to try to open yourself up so that I can send some power your way."

I shake my head. "I don't know how to do that."

"Just breathe. And try to reach out for me." She holds her arm out straight at me, but where mine is palm up, hers is palm down. "Okay, Grace. Lower your guards and reach."

I have absolutely no idea what that means, but I figure, *What the hell.* The worst that will happen is I'll look like a total dork and hey, everyone here has already seen me do that at least once.

So I take another deep breath and then try to do what Macy asked me to—I reach for her, trying to will a tiny spark of her magic into me.

"Do you feel anything?" she asks, and her eyes are glowing just a little, in a way I've never seen before.

"No. I'm sorry."

She smiles. "Don't be sorry. Just try again."

I do, and this time I try really hard, but still nothing happens.

"Third time's the charm," Macy says with a grin. Then asks, "Feel it?"

She seems so sure, I can't help wondering if I'm just missing something. "I don't know if I do or not," I answer after trying for several seconds to feel something. Anything.

"You don't," Hudson tells me, not even bothering to look up from the book he's been reading all afternoon.

"How do you know?" I demand.

"Because I'm in your head and *I* don't feel anything? Plus, I have power and I know what you're supposed to feel, and that's definitely not happening right now."

"Of course it's not," I whine. "I'm destined to live my life on the side of a museum—as the world's most unaccomplished waterspout."

A bubble of panic forms in my chest as I realize everyone is staring at me, varying degrees of pity in their eyes. Well, except Hudson. For once, my complete humiliation appears to not be of any interest to him.

Probably sensing my frustration, Jaxon tries to tease me out of my growing anger. "Hey, don't worry. We can figure this out another day." He smiles encouragingly. "Rome wasn't built in a day."

I sigh. Maybe he's right. This paranormal stuff is all new to me. Maybe it's perfectly natural that I can't do even the most basic gargoyle things yet.

Hudson sighs, carefully closing his book and setting it on the cocktail table near his chair in the corner. "Rome wasn't built in a day, but this is going to be." He stretches like a cat, his hands so far above his head that the bottom of his T-shirt lifts up to expose those ridiculous abs again.

He catches me looking and raises a brow, right before he says, "You can do this; it's just clear you need someone with a little more… expertise."

Screw the candle. My face feels like it's on fire.

"Grace, are we doing this or not?" Macy asks.

"Not," I answer. "I can't figure out what to do."

"Nobody knows how at the beginning," Hudson says as he walks over to stand a foot to my side. "You can do this. I promise."

I turn to face him more fully. "You can't promise that. You don't know—"

He gives me a soft smile. "I *do* know."

"How?" I ask, my voice breaking.

"Because I won't let you fail." He nods to Macy. "Tell her to try again."

I hold his gaze, then take a deep breath. I swivel my head toward Macy. "Hudson says we should try once more, Mace," I tell my cousin. "And then I'm calling it quits."

"O-kay," she says, clearly not sure if she should be glad Hudson is encouraging me to try again or not. "Once more." And then her eyes do that weird glowy thing as she sends another burst of power my way.

"Ready?" Hudson asks, a grin slowly spreading across his face that sets butterflies loose in my stomach.

"Ready for what?"

He snaps his fingers. "For this."

Come on Baby, Light My Candle

Just like that, there's a weird feeling deep inside me. A spark of heat, of light, of energy that is both familiar and completely foreign at the same time.

"Go ahead," Hudson tells me, his voice little more than a whisper. "Reach for it."

So I do, hand outstretched and everything about me open wide. And then it's there, right there inside me. Arrowing into me. Lighting me up from the inside. Making every nerve ending in my body come alive like I've never felt before.

"Do you feel it now?" Macy asks, voice raised excitedly.

"I do," I tell her, because this has to be it. This brilliant feeling that's warm and bright and airy and light has magic written all over it.

"Good," Macy continues. "Now hold it for a minute, get used to it. Feel it moving through your body."

I do as she says, letting the warmth and the light burn through me.

"What do I do now?" I ask, because while it feels amazing to have this feeling inside me, it also feels unsustainable—like it'll burn right through me and then disappear if I don't know what to do with it.

"Focus your mind," Macy says, "on lighting the candle. Imagine it. And then just do it."

I stare at the candle as hard as I've ever stared at anything in my life. I imagine it lit, a flame burning along its wick. And then I try to light it.

Nothing happens.

"Don't worry about it," Macy says. "You're so close, I can feel it. Just try again."

So I do, again and again, and still nothing happens.

I can feel the light flickering inside me, feel it starting to dissipate, and I'm so afraid that it'll go away that my hands start to tremble and my chest starts to ache.

Macy must see my distress, because she says, "It's okay. We can try again later."

"Don't listen to her," Hudson tells me, moving to stand right behind me now, both our gazes focused on the candle, so close that I can feel his breath against my ear. "You can do this."

"I can't do this. It's leaving. I can feel it—"

"So draw it back," he orders. "Don't send it out like Macy told you to. Pull it back, concentrate it into one ball of energy, of power, and *then* let it go."

"But Macy said—"

"Fuck what Macy said. Everyone wields their power differently. I can feel it in you. It's right there, ready to be used. So use it."

"I can't—"

"You can."

"It's okay," Jaxon tells me. "We'll practice a little bit each day until you get it."

"Don't listen to him," Hudson orders. "You've got this."

"I don't have it. I don't."

Hudson leans forward, braces his arm under mine, and grabs onto my hand. "Focus," he tells me. "Send every ounce of the magic you feel inside you right here, to where I'm holding you." He squeezes my hand for emphasis. "Pull it back from wherever else you sent it and put it all right there."

I take a deep breath and let it out shakily. Breathe in a second time and let it out. The third time I breathe in, I hold it for long seconds as I try to do what he asks. The light has made a trail through me, so I grab on to one end of it and start to pull, rolling it back, back, back until it's right there in my chest, my shoulder, my arm. Until finally, I can feel it in the palm of my hand.

"Feel it?" Hudson asks.

I nod, because I do. It's so strong, it's like it's going to burn a hole right through me.

"You've got it now," he tells me.

"I do. I've got it," I whisper.

"I know. Now, open your fist." He lets go of my hand slowly, gently unweaving our fingers even as he keeps his arm directly under mine.

"Aim," he says, his voice and his body a solid presence behind me. Holding my feet to the flame and my palm to the power. Not letting me back up so much as an inch.

And then he's right there—chin near my shoulder, mouth pressed to my ear—as he whispers, "Now let it go."

So I do. And then let out a little scream as every single candle on Jaxon's bookcase bursts into flame at exactly the same moment. Oh my God. I did it. I really did it!

"Holy shit, New Girl!" Flint yelps. "What the hell was that?"

"I don't know." I turn to look at Hudson, and for a second, just a second, he's right there, his face barely an inch from mine. Our eyes lock and power—pure, unadulterated power—sizzles between us. At least until he steps back, putting several feet of distance between us in an instant.

"How much power did you give her, Macy?" Jaxon asks, looking from the bookcase to my cousin and back again.

"That wasn't me," Macy answers. "I can barely do that now with all my power, let alone with the little bit I was siphoning off for Grace."

"Then where did it come from?" Jaxon demands. "Power like that doesn't just—"

He breaks off as it hits him, which is just about the same time it hits me. No wonder the power felt strangely familiar. It's been there, lurking inside me, for nearly four months.

"Hudson." Jaxon says his brother's name like it leaves a bad taste in his mouth, nose up and mouth curled into a small sneer while I simply whisper it.

But when I whirl around to confront him, determined to find out what and how and why he did what he did, he's gone. And not "hiding in a corner, pouting" gone, either. He's *gone* gone, and I have absolutely no idea what to do to bring him back.

53

Everybody Wants to
Rule the World

"I don't know what happened," I tell Jaxon for what feels like the thousandth time. "He helped me feel the power, helped me focus it, helped me use it, and then he just disappeared."

"How can he disappear?" Jaxon answers, shoving a hand through his already messed-up hair. "I thought he was trapped in your head?"

"He *is* trapped in my head," I soothe. "Sometimes he just goes to a part I can't access very easily."

"How does that even work?" Flint asks, his voice going up an octave on the last word, and for the first time I realize he's almost as stressed out as Jaxon. "He's just running around in your head, and you hope he's not screwing up anything important?"

I start to take offense—it's not like I have absolute control over Hudson, but I feel like he and I have been bumping along pretty well since the body-snatching incidents—at least until I remember that Flint's older brother died because of Hudson. It's what put such a strain on his friendship with Jaxon, and it's what led to the weirdness that's between them today.

"It's not like that, Flint. We have different times when we give each other privacy—like when I'm in the shower, for instance—where we don't know what the other person is doing. He's still trapped in here with me; he's just out of touch for a little while. He'll be back."

Jaxon looks sick. "I never thought about you taking a shower or getting dressed with him around. How come I never thought of that?"

"Because it doesn't matter. We have a system worked out."

"Is this part of your system?" Flint asks, and the tone he uses gets my back up. "Him directing his power through you and then disappearing while you take the consequences?"

"The consequences?" I answer. "You aren't my teacher *or* my parents. There are no *consequences* in us having a discussion, no matter how unhappy you are.

"Plus." I shoot him a narrow-eyed look. "I don't even know what you're so upset about. You wanted me to channel magic and I did, so back off a little, will you?"

"That's not what I meant, and you know it," Flint shoots back. "I just meant that you're the one who's going to have to fix things if he messes them up, and that doesn't seem fair to you."

His explanation takes a little of the fight out of me, and I slump down onto the back of the couch. "I get that you want answers, guys. I want answers, too. But there are times when something upsets me, and I want to be alone. I owe Hudson that same courtesy."

Besides, after everything that happened, I want some time alone, too. Some time to process everything that happened and just sit with it for a while. So I'm in no hurry for Hudson to come back. Once he does, I'm pretty sure everything is going to get even more complicated.

Flint relaxes a little at my words, and so does Jaxon, but they both keep wary eyes on me. As does Macy, who has been uncharacteristically quiet since the whole magic-channeling thing happened. And while I appreciate the fact that all three of them are only looking out for me in their own ways, I also have to admit that the overprotectiveness is going to exhaust my patience sooner rather than later.

Macy must sense it, because out of the blue, she suddenly suggests, "Hey, why don't you guys go flying?"

"Flying?" I ask, because just the thought of it makes me nervous.

"Yes, flying. It's another one of those powers gargoyles have," she tells me. "And the one power we knew about before we even started researching. So why don't you take Flint up on his offer to teach you and just go for it?"

"I don't know, Macy," Jaxon says out of nowhere. "Grace has already had to deal with a lot today and—"

Just that easily, I make my decision. Maybe it's contrary—okay, it's probably contrary—but Jaxon doesn't get to decide what I do or when I do it. The guy is a bulldozer, especially with the people he feels responsible for. If I give him an inch, he'll take seven miles... and then start inquiring about mineral and air rights.

"I'd love to go flying, Flint!" I say with an enthusiasm that is at least partially fake. "But I think we should come up with a plan before we do anything else."

"I think that's a good idea," Macy agrees. "I mean, how many days do we have left before Hudson gives up on wandering to other parts of your brain and decides to just go back to doing his 'adventures in vampire body snatching' thing?"

It's a legitimate question, considering Hudson has already gained enough strength to punch a hole in the wall. I didn't tell Jaxon about that—he's already so worried that giving him more to stress out about seems like a bad idea—but we're running out of time. I know it and so does Hudson.

And while there's a part of me that wants to believe he would never do that to me again now that we've gotten to know each other a little, there's another part that's smart enough to recognize that Hudson will do whatever he needs to do to get out of my head. That right now he's going along with me because he knows I'm actively working for the same thing. I don't know what he'd do if I changed my mind.

"I feel like we have at least a few more days," I settle for telling everyone. "But I'm not sure about much more than that."

"Which means we need to get this show on the road," Flint says. "I have a general idea of where the Boneyard is and how to get there. I just need to get my hands on a map so we're not wandering around forever trying to find the right spot."

"Good plan," Jaxon says dryly.

Flint pauses. Then he shoots me—and Jaxon—his typical goofy grin. "I've already texted my grandma about the map, told her I needed it for a school project, and she promised to text me a pic when she gets back to her lair tonight. Then we should be good to go."

"That's awesome!" I tell him. "So we have the Ludares tournament on Wednesday, and that will get us the bloodstone. So we can go to the Dragon Boneyard on Thursday? Or should we go before?"

"Definitely not before," Flint answers in an "obviously" kind of tone. "The Boneyard is dangerous. If one of us gets hurt, we'll risk losing Ludares. No way am I going to let that happen."

"Good point," Macy says. "If we lose, we don't get the bloodstone."

"Pretty sure Flint is more worried about the bragging rights than the bloodstone," I tease. "But either way, I agree. We can't risk being hurt going into the tournament."

"But we can risk being hurt in the Dragon Boneyard?" Macy asks. "I mean, not to sound like a baby, but what kind of hurt are we talking about? A broken finger or full-on dismemberment? Because I can deal with a couple of broken bones, but I need my limbs."

Jaxon laughs. "Pretty sure we all need our limbs, Macy."

"Yeah, but now that Grace is a gargoyle, I have the highest chance of actually losing a limb in this whole group. And I just want to go on record as saying, I'm not okay with that," Macy says.

"Fair enough," Flint tells her. "Ludares and then a trip to the Boneyard with absolutely no dismemberment. I think we can pull that off."

"So Boneyard on Thursday night," Jaxon says. "And if no one loses a leg, we can plan on going after the Unkillable Beast on Friday or Saturday—depending on what shape we're in?"

"Do we even know where the Unkillable Beast *is*?" Macy asks. "I mean, you mentioned it's somewhere near the North Pole, but the Arctic is a huge area. And not exactly hospitable. We don't want to be bumbling around in freezing temperatures."

"Actually, I kept researching and discovered it's on an enchanted island in the Arctic off the coast of Siberia," Jaxon adds.

"It's on an enchanted island?" I ask. "Seriously?"

"That's what the legends say," Flint agrees.

"Not a legend if it's true," Jaxon says. "I spent the last several hours looking for info on the Unkillable Beast's location, and I think I've found it. I'm going to do more research tonight and tomorrow, just to make sure I'm right. But if I am, I say we aim for Saturday."

"So...Ludares Wednesday, Boneyard Thursday, and Beast on Saturday." Flint recites the plan, a questioning look on his face. "Everyone good with that?"

"I am," I tell him, although the truth is that my hands are shaking a little at the thought of that lineup.

"Me too," Macy agrees.

Jaxon nods.

"Awesome. Can't wait." Flint rubs his hands together, then waggles his brows at me. "So how about that flying lesson now?"

54

Who Needs a Magic Carpet When Your Bestie's a Dragon?

"So there's one big problem with flying lessons for me," I tell him ten minutes later, after I've run back to my room for all the cold-weather clothes I need to survive stepping outside in Alaska in March. Which, it turns out, are pretty much the same ones I needed in November, so yay me for missing the really cold months. At least there's one point in the gargoyle column. "I don't know how to shift, which means I have no wings. No wings, no flying." I glance around. "But maybe we could get some of those assignment pictures over for Mr. Damasen?"

I try to hide how positively scared witless I am at letting him take me up in the air in something even less secure than the puddle jumper that brought me to Denali to begin with.

He smiles ruefully. "You know, we don't have to do it if you don't want to. I honestly thought it might be fun, might give you a different perspective than before. We can do something else, but eventually you're going to have to get in the air."

My stomach is tied in all kinds of knots—most of them falling somewhere in the range of mildly scared to full-blown terrified. And yeah, there's definitely a part of me that wants to back out of this mess. But Flint looks so dejected at the perceived rejection that I just can't do it.

"No, that's okay. Let's do it."

He stares at me through narrowed eyes. "Yeah?"

I take a deep breath, then blow it out slowly as I gather every ounce of my courage. "Yeah."

"Awesome! You won't regret it."

I bite my tongue to keep from telling him that I already do.

"You ready?"

"Ready is a bit of an overstatement, but yeah. Sure. Why not?" I wave my hands expansively.

"Don't sound so enthusiastic," he says with a laugh.

I roll my eyes. "Dude, this is the best you're going to get."

"We'll see."

He takes a couple of steps back, which makes me move several more feet in the other direction. More than several, really, because if there's one thing I've learned at Katmere Academy, it's that you really can't be too careful when it comes to personal safety.

And then, just like that, Flint does it.

He drops down to all fours and, as I watch, stunned, the very air around him forms a kind of funnel. I'm not sure what's happening, but I know something is, because the air surrounding him is starting to blur.

Caution has me taking another couple of steps backward, which turns out to be a good thing because the blurring is followed by a bright flash of light that nearly blinds me. Seconds later, a shimmer of rainbow colors engulfs him for five, six, seven or so seconds and then—standing right in front of me is a giant green dragon. And when I say giant, I mean *gigantic*. And also incredibly beautiful.

I didn't really appreciate Flint in his dragon form when he was trying to kill me, but now that he's staring down at me with what I'm pretty sure is the dragon version of his ridiculous grin, I can't help but notice that he is a really, really good-looking dragon.

He's tall and broad and muscular, with long, sharp horns that curve upward just a little and a ton of gorgeous frills of differing lengths around his face. His eyes are the same striking amber they are in his human form but with a cool, serpentlike slit down the middle, and his wings are enormous—the kind of enormous where several adult humans could take shelter under one. And his scales…I mean, I always knew he was green, but now I realize that he's actually all the shades of green mixed together, each scale a different color overlapping in a pattern that makes him look like he's shimmering, even when he's just standing here in front of me.

Flint waits patiently while I look him over, but eventually he must get bored because he lowers his head and shows me his really wicked-looking teeth in a way that is definitely designed to get me moving. Which, okay, I get. But I'm beginning to realize we should have talked about a few things before he shifted, because it's becoming more and more obvious that there's at least one really big problem.

"We both know you're gorgeous, so I'm not going to waste a lot of time telling you that," I say as I slowly, carefully cover the ground between us. His eyes track my every move, though my compliment seems to appease him, because he finally hides those wicked teeth of his again.

"But I do have a question for you," I tell him, even as I contemplate reaching out to pet him.

"You do know that he can't talk like this, right?" Hudson asks from where he's sitting on the front stairs, his sudden appearance startling me slightly. I guess "alone time" is done.

I give him a narrow-eyed look. "Of course I know that."

"So how do you expect him to answer you?" Hudson asks. "Sign language? Interpretive dance? Smoke signals?"

"You could shut up and let me talk for a minute." I snark. "How about that?"

Hudson holds a hand up in a "feel free" motion.

I turn back to Flint. "I'm not sure how you're going to answer my question, but I guess we're going to have to figure that out."

He snorts a little, then tilts his head in a gesture I can only describe as royal. As in the royal "go ahead" decree.

"You said before that I could ride on your back. But..." I look him up and down, which pretty much amounts to looking up, up, and then up some more. "How am I supposed to reach your back? You're gigantic. I mean, this is definitely not going to be like riding a horse."

He snorts again, and this time there's a whole lot of insult in it. Turns out dragons—or at least this dragon—are a lot more expressive than I ever imagined.

Flint eyes me for another couple of seconds, just, I think, to make sure I understand how insulted he is to be compared to a horse. Then he slowly lowers his head and nuzzles my shoulder with the bridge of his nose.

And just like that, I melt. Because when he's not trying to kill me in his dragon form, Flint might actually be the most adorable thing I've ever seen.

"Yeah, yeah, yeah," I tell him, even as I reach up to stroke his nose and a few of his frills.

He makes a little noise, then presses closer, and I can't help but laugh. "You made it very clear you don't want to be called a horse, but you're acting like a giant puppy dog right now." To prove my point, I bring my second hand up to scratch the top of his head. I swear to God, Flint grins in response—or comes as close as a dragon can to smiling, super-sharp teeth and all.

I pet him for a couple of minutes, and I enjoy it at least as much as Flint does. But I'm also conscious of time quickly moving along, so finally I pull my hands back and step away.

The dragon snorts and moves forward to nudge me—a very clear signal that he wants more—but this time I give him only a cursory pat on the head. "You know, I would stand here all day and pet you if I could. I swear. But we have an assignment to do, and you still haven't explained to me how I'm supposed to get on your back."

Flint snorts again, then heaves a ridiculous sigh as he lowers himself to kneel on the ground.

"Yeah, that's great. But there's still no way I'm going to manage to make it onto your back." Even kneeling, belly to the ground, his back is still a good eight to ten feet off the ground. I can't even reach to the top of his back, let alone swing myself up onto it.

Flint tilts his head again, like he can't believe we're even having this discussion. I'm also pretty sure he rolled his eyes at me—which, not going to lie, doesn't feel good. I mean, it's one thing having a human Flint roll his eyes at me. It's a whole different feeling when a dragon does it. I don't know why, but it is.

This time, when he leans down and nudges me, I don't even bother to pet him. "I'm serious, Flint. We need to figure this out."

"You could always throw a saddle and some really big stirrups on him," Hudson suggests.

"If you're not going to help, I don't want to talk to you right now," I retort before Flint nudges me again, a little more forcefully this time. "Hey! That hurt!"

He does it again. And then again, this time hard enough to leave a bruise.

"Flint!" I scowl at him as I stumble back a little more. "Will you please stop fooling around? You're hurting me."

He sighs, and it is the longest-suffering sigh I have ever heard from an animal—or a human, for that matter—in my life. This time when he lowers his head, he doesn't nudge my shoulders. Instead, he nudges my thighs.

"Okay, look! That's it! If you keep this up, I'm going back—" I break off on a scream as Flint finally manages to get his head between my knees.

"Now there's something you don't see every day," Hudson comments wryly.

"Don't start!" I snap, because the only thing worse than dealing with the fact that

a guy who isn't my boyfriend very unexpectedly *has his head between my legs* (even if he is in dragon form) is dealing with it while

Hudson looks on.

I start to say something else but end up letting out a little scream as Flint tosses me up and back a little, so that I land, ass first, on the center of his neck.

Seconds later, he's lifting his head, and I'm trying not to scream as I slide down, down, down his neck, over spikes that turn out to be not that spiky at all only to slam, face-first, onto his back.

55

Ain't Nothing but a Wing Thing

I just lay there, arms wrapped around his sides, and try to come to grips with what just happened to me. Eventually, though, Flint gets restless and starts to stand up, even though I am in no way seated appropriately.

"Wait, wait, wait!" I cry out as I try to shift myself around on a moving dragon—which, as it turns out, is even harder than it sounds. Especially when Hudson is laughing his ass off at me.

This time Flint's snort sounds a little more like a growl.

"Okay, okay, I'm sorry," I tell him as I finally manage to get myself situated properly, facing forward with my legs straddling his back and my arms wrapped around his neck.

He snorts again, obviously unimpressed with my apology. "Look, I said I was sorry. Now it seems really obvious what you were doing. But at the time, it didn't. So I'm sorry I thought…whatever it was I thought."

Flint twists his head around just enough for me to see the disdain on his features.

"You know what? Enough is enough. You want to be annoyed with me, fine. But how was I supposed to know? I've never ridden a dragon before. I've never even been this close to a dragon before except, you know, when you were digging your talons into my back. So let's just call it even and get on with the lesson, okay?"

No snort this time, but he does give a regal head toss that tells me my apology is sorely lacking. And also that he's over it, which is good, because so am I.

Seconds later, Flint bucks his head back in a warning that I don't understand and then shoots straight into the sky.

I scream again, louder this time, then wrap my hands around Flint's throat in what could probably best be described as a death grip. If I don't loosen up soon, it will probably end badly for both of us, but as he zooms to the very top of the castle, there's nothing I can do about it.

So I just close my eyes, hold on, and pray I don't fall off.

"Bugger this!" Hudson growls, and I realize he's now sitting right behind me.

"What are you doing here?" I demand, even as a scream rises in my throat. "I thought you were comfortable on that step."

"You do realize I'm actually in your head, right? So where you go, I go. It's kind of a thing."

"I know that. I just didn't expect you to decide to ride Flint along with me. It doesn't really seem your style."

"As it turns out," he answers stiffly, "I've never ridden a dragon before. I thought it would be..."

"Terrifying?" I ask as Flint does a vertical spin as he continues to fly higher.

"Fun." The word comes out a little breathless, which I can totally understand. My breath is in my throat, too.

Thankfully, it turns out Flint can breathe even with my death grip, and he takes a few loops around the castle and the sky above it. It's not exactly a flying lesson, but now that my brain is functioning again, I realize he's just trying to relax me a little. Get me used to flying, even if it is on a dragon.

I'm positive it won't work—it's super scary flying around this castle that's built on the side of a mountain—but eventually I manage to keep my eyes open for an extended period of time. And when I do, I nearly squeal in delight because, scary or not, it's absolutely, breathtakingly beautiful up here.

The sky is crystal blue, the mountain is covered in glistening snow, and the castle looks like something out of a movie...or a dream. Its gray and black stones provide a startling contrast to the white snow, its parapets and towers stretching high into the bright blue sky.

Flint turns his long, majestic neck so he can glance back and check on me, and I hold on tight, expecting us to quickly drop back down to the ground.

But I totally underestimated Flint—big surprise—because instead of heading for the ground, he takes a tight turn in midair and heads straight up, up, up into the sky.

"Oh my God! What are you doing?" I screech, but he doesn't so much as look back at me. Instead he just goes faster.

I expect Hudson to complain, but when I glance at him, he's got a full-blown grin on his face. Then again, it's not like he's got the same fear of dying that I do...

We're back to flying vertically now, and I bite back a scream as I hold on as tightly as I can with both my arms *and* my legs. Not going to lie, it's completely terrifying. But it's also exciting and exhilarating and the view—when I finally manage to pry my eyes open—is absolutely breathtaking.

A few years ago, I watched a documentary called *The Art of Flight*. It was about snowboarding in the most difficult and breathtaking locations in the world, and Denali was one of the places spotlighted in the movie. They took a helicopter up to some of the areas that are off-limits to normal climbers and skiers and made a big deal about walking in places where no other human being had ever been.

At the time, I hadn't understood what the big deal was. But now, holding on to Flint as I get a dragon's-eye view of those very areas, all I can think is, *Of course*.

Of course they wanted to see this place that so few people have ever seen.

Of course they wanted to capture it on film so others had a chance to feel what they felt.

Of course it's worth anything—worth everything—to get here. Right here.

And suddenly, something wild inside me breaks free. It claws its way out of the deepest part of my soul, yearning toward the sky, toward the snow, toward freedom.

I gasp, because for that one second, my body wasn't under my control. It belonged to something—to someone—else, and I don't have a clue how to find my way back.

Of course, Flint chooses that moment to change direction, going into a deep dive that has the wind in my face and my heart in my throat. We're racing down even faster than we came up, and as terror whips through me, whatever raised its head inside me settles back down.

I want to follow it, want to figure out if it's the gargoyle or something else—something worse—but I can't when every ounce of concentration I have is focused on hanging on to Flint and praying that we don't crash.

We don't, but because he's Flint, he can't resist doing a series of loop-the-loops in the middle of our dive. I'm not sure what it says about our speed that I don't even have to worry about falling off, even when we're upside down, because centrifugal force keeps me plastered to his back the entire time.

In fact, by the time his third set of somersaults comes around, I don't even have to close my eyes. Instead, I just laugh with Hudson and enjoy the ride.

Eventually, he starts flying slowly by various architectural elements I recall from Mr. Damasen's list. I pull my phone from my coat pocket and quickly snap several pictures of each feature as we fly by.

When I finish taking the last picture, I put my phone back in my pocket and zip it up. Flint gives me another quick look over his shoulder and, I swear, shoots me a surprisingly wicked grin, considering he's a *dragon.* That's the only clue I have to grip his neck tightly before he's soaring back up into the sky again, spinning a bit as we go.

And then, when I think we can't go any higher—he stops flapping his wings entirely.

We freeze in the sky for a split second without his strong wings pushing us forward, and my breath catches in my throat. I have an idea what he's about to do next, and I can feel the scream building in my chest. But before I can open my mouth and set it free, Flint flips his large body in midair, and suddenly...we're diving straight for the ground, wings tucked tight against his body as we continue to pick up speed.

I'm screaming like I'm on the scariest roller coaster ride in existence. Even Hudson gives a shout from behind me, his arms reaching around my waist and tugging me against his chest as though to protect me. And just like that, the wild thing deep inside me is set free again, and I'm laughing so hard, I can barely catch my breath.

At least until we get closer to the ground, because Flint's showing absolutely no sign of slowing down despite the fact that the tree line is looming awfully close. My stomach clenches, and a quick glance behind me shows that even Hudson looks a little nervous. But Flint hasn't steered us wrong yet, so I just take a deep breath and wait for whatever he's going to do next.

What he does next, in fact, is pull up at pretty much the last second, sending us screaming back to the top of the castle as I laugh and laugh and laugh. Now Flint looks back at me, laughter in his own eyes as we do two quick spins around the school before finally coming in for the smoothest landing ever.

I manage to get off him pretty much the way I got on but in reverse, and seconds later, I'm back on the ground, standing on my own shaky legs.

There's another shimmer, another air funnel, and a few seconds later, Flint is standing next to me in what's left of his school uniform—which now is little more than a pair of ripped-up pants and half a button-down shirt missing all the buttons.

I take one look at him and start laughing, partly because of his clothes and partly because of the goofy smile on his face. It doesn't take long before he's laughing, too.

"So what'd you think?" Flint asks.

"It wasn't quite the flying lesson I was anticipating," I answer with a grin. "But it was so much fun." And it's true. For the first time since I turned human again, I feel completely, 100 percent myself. It's a good feeling, one that has me holding on to Flint's arm because I don't want him to go. I don't want him to take this feeling with him. "Did you have fun?"

"I really did. And you're a natural."

"Yeah, right. You rolled your eyes at me."

He very deliberately rolls them again. "You couldn't figure out how to get on my back."

"Well, it's not like dragons come with an instruction manual. It was difficult."

"Apparently." I stick my tongue out at him, but he just laughs. "Wanna do it again sometime?"

"Absolutely." I take a second to go over my schedule in my head. Then suggest, "How about tomorrow morning? We could get the whole Ludares team together to meet and maybe practice for the tournament? And you can show me how to fly, using my own wings this time."

"I like the way you think, New Girl. Meet you on the practice field at nine?"

"Make it ten. Macy's not a morning person."

He shakes his head. "Witches and vamps, man. They never are." He glances toward the school. "You need me to walk you back to your room?"

"Nah, I'm good. But thanks, Flint." I give him an impulsive hug. "You're the best."

"Not so much, New Girl." This time his smile is tinged with just a little bit of sadness. "But I can't wait to see you fly tomorrow. See if you can give me a run for my money."

"Pretty sure a F-35 couldn't give you a run for your money, but thanks for the compliment." I give him a little wave, then head toward the stairs that lead up to the front entrance. As I go, I can't help wondering what it is that keeps making Flint seem so sad when he thinks I'm not looking.

56

Just Shut Up and Dance

I'm exhausted by the time I get back to my bedroom around eight. Macy tries to convince me to go hang out with some of her witch friends—they're getting together for Netflix and facials—but the truth is, I'm too nervous about tomorrow to think about anything else.

I'm going to meet the whole Ludares team tomorrow—Flint and Macy worked on rounding it out today, and they think they've finally got the team we need to win. And we *need* to win, at least if we're going to get the bloodstone we need to force Hudson out of my head and turn him human. Without it, we're totally screwed.

But how am I supposed to compete in this game I still know next to nothing about? I mean, I know it takes place in the Katmere athletic complex—a place I've never even set foot in before. I also know that it's a strange hybrid of Keep Away and Hot Potato and that every member on the team has to control the ball for at least one part of the game.

All of which translates to me having to keep the ball away from the other team with my nonexistent skills.

I mean, yeah, I can turn to stone with the ball, but that isn't going to get it across the finish line. Supposedly, I can fly, but that would require shifting into my gargoyle form, which I've yet to do again. Well, that and actually flying. And as for the channeling-magic thing… I don't know. How much of that was me this afternoon and how much of it was Hudson? It's a question that's haunted me since I realized it was his power, rather than Macy's, that I was directing.

Nervous, frustrated, and more than a little freaked out, all I really want to do is bury my head in a good book and pretend the rest of the world doesn't exist—even if part of that world is actually sharing my headspace with me.

But ten minutes into that plan, I realize it's a bust. I'm still way too hyped-up from a combination of nerves and residual energy from what was probably the most amazing flying lesson in the history of flying lessons to just sit around on my bed.

Maybe I should have gone to girls' night with Macy after all. At least I'd have something to do besides watch my own fears chase one another around and around in my head all night. But if I'd gone, I'd be forced to make small talk with people I don't know, and that's a whole different level of stress. Especially since I've never been very good at small talk even at the best of times.

In the end, I decide to take a quick shower, hoping that will settle me down. But that doesn't work, either—I'm still bouncing off the walls even after I dry my hair and straighten up my side of the room.

I think about calling Jaxon, but he'd looked really tired when we parted tonight. He'd mentioned going to bed early. If he's actually done that, I don't want to be the one to disturb him.

The best thing I can do for me is also to sleep—my mind has been through a lot over the course of the last several months. Too bad sleep currently feels about as foreign as a walk on the moon.

With nothing else to do, I gather up Macy's and my dirty laundry and head down to the laundry room on the second floor. I've never used it before, but I know where it is because it's attached to one of the student lounges where Macy gave me a tour my first couple of days at Katmere.

Normally I'd do only my laundry—I'm not sure how witches normally handle things, and the last thing I want is to upset the status quo—but since I've heard Macy bemoan being short on tights three different days this week, I might as well help my cousin out. It's the least I can do after everything she's done for me.

It's not until an hour later, as I'm loading clean clothes from the washer to the dryer, that Hudson finally shows back up again with a "Boo!" so loud, I swear it shakes the rafters.

I've been expecting him and still he startles me so much that I drop my wet clothes all over the place—and nearly scream loud enough to be heard in the art cottage.

I bite the scream back at the last second, but it still takes me a little bit to get my breath back. "You know you're a jerk, right?" I snarl at him when I can talk again—and after I've picked up all the clothes he made me drop.

"You're just saying that because you missed me," he tells me from where he's perched on the lid of a washing machine several washers down.

"Missed you or wanted to make sure you weren't somewhere plotting world domination? It's a fine distinction, really."

"But an important one," he says with a grin that lights up his whole face.

I immediately distrust it. "Exactly what are you so smiley about this evening anyway?"

"Can't a guy just be happy for no reason?" he asks with an arch of his brow.

I throw the last of the clothes in the dryer and slam the lid with a solid *thud*. "Not when the last time he was happy, he was plotting a hostile takeover of half the paranormal world."

"You wound me. It was at least three-quarters."

"Remind me. How'd that work out for you again?" I ask as I empty out the lint trap and hit the start button.

"Pretty well, considering I'm sitting here tonight with a superhot gargoyle's panties on my shoe." He holds up his left foot and sure enough, my black lace panties are dangling from the toe of his merlot suede Armani loafers.

"How is that even possible?" I demand, leaning down to yank them from his foot. They come off, but when I look at my hand, there's nothing there.

I mean, of course there isn't. Just because I can see him sitting on that washing machine doesn't mean he's actually there. Any more than it means my panties were actually dangling from his shoe. Except I *saw* them.

"Abracadabra," he answers, complete with full-on magician hand gestures. Which...

"Oh my God. Are you high?" I ask.

"I'm inside your head, Grace. If I were high, wouldn't that mean you are, too?"

"Yeah, well, maybe *I* am," I mutter as I gather up my laundry supplies, because I cannot think of another scenario on the planet where Hudson would behave in such a bizarre manner. The fact that the whole routine is just a teeny, tiny bit charming is also of paramount concern.

"Or maybe you're just coming around," he shoots back, his eyes shining a deep indigo in the bright lights of the laundry room.

"What exactly am I coming around to?" I ask. "Thinking you need a tranquilizer...or possibly seven?"

"More like the idea that all this doesn't have to end as badly as you seem to think it will."

I shoot him a baffled look. "I...don't have a clue what that means."

"Don't you?" He watches me closely.

"Not even a little bit, no."

For long seconds, he doesn't say anything. Then, just when I think he's going back to his normal, sarcastic ways, he lifts a hand and circles his index finger in a little loop that makes no sense to me at all—at least not until Flo Rida's "Good Feeling" starts playing—out of nowhere.

"What. Is. Happening?" I look around the laundry room a little wildly, at least half of me wondering if I'm being punked. Because *what even is happening?* "Why are you playing Flo Rida?"

"Why not?" he answers, then grabs my wrist just as the refrain starts. Then, before I can register what's going on, he gives one solid yank, and I fly straight into his hard chest, squawking like an angry pterodactyl the whole way.

"What the hell, Hudson?" I demand, shoving at his chest until he finally lets me put some distance between us. "What's wrong with you?"

"Why does something have to be wrong?" he answers.

"Because we hate each other. And because happy music isn't exactly your style. And because the last thing I want to do right now is hug you."

This time, both brows go up, marking the return of the superior look I know and hate so well. "Who said anything about hugging?" he asks, right before he spins me out in what I can only assume is supposed to be some kind of dance move.

"Hudson," I say, but he ignores me in favor of pulling me back in and then spinning me back out in the opposite direction.

"Hudson!" I repeat a little louder. "What are you doing?"

He gives me a "what the hell" look. "*We* are dancing."

"No," I correct him. "*You* are dancing. *I'm* beginning to feel a dislocated shoulder coming on."

"And whose fault is that?" he asks. "Dance with me, Grace."

"Why?"

"Because I asked you to." He spins me out again, but this time the move is a lot gentler.

"But why did you ask me to?" I quiz when he pulls me back in. "What's going on, Hudson?"

"Grace?" he says, looking deep into my eyes, and for the briefest moment, I see something there that makes me catch my breath. And also wonder if I'm imagining it.

"Yes?"

He circles his finger again, and the music switches from Flo Rida to the opening lyrics of Walk the Moon's "Shut Up and Dance."

And it's so clever, so ridiculous, so Hudson, that I can't help bursting into laughter. Right before I decide, *screw it*, and let him dance me from one end of the laundry room to the other.

When the song finally comes to an end, Hudson lets me go, and we both stand there grinning at each other.

As we do, I can't help but wonder what someone would think if they'd walked into the laundry room a few seconds ago and found me dancing around the machines by myself, singing to a song only I can hear. Probably that it's just another weird human thing...or an even weirder gargoyle thing...which I guess it is, now that I think about it.

Still, I'm a little hot, a little breathless, but a lot more relaxed than I was when I got to the laundry room, and maybe that's why I finally ask him, "How did you know I love that song?"

And just that easily, his smile fades away, leaving nothing there but an emptiness so stark that I feel it deep in my chest. Even before he answers, "So you really remember nothing of the time we spent together?"

57

Pulling all the (Heart) Strings

Confusion swamps me. "I don't... I mean... I told you..."

"Never mind." He shakes his head, rubs a hand over his hair. "I don't know what I was thinking."

"I don't know what you were thinking, either," I tell him. "That's kind of the point of a conversation."

"Maybe." He shrugs.

"Maybe? What does that mean?" I feel like I'm missing something important here, but I don't have a clue what it is. Even worse, this damn amnesia makes it impossible to figure out.

This time when his eyes meet mine, there's so much intensity there that my mouth goes desert dry. "It means I guess I saw what I wanted to see this afternoon."

I don't have a response to that, so I just stand there, watching him, even as a small frisson of...*something* works its way down my spine. I can't identify it—and if I'm honest, I don't want to—but it scares me a little. Even as it makes me more determined than ever to regain my memory of what happened in those three and a half missing months.

Because for a moment, during the whole magic-channeling portion of the afternoon, I realized that it didn't feel absolutely awful having Hudson stand right behind me. In fact, it almost felt kind of...nice.

I shook the feeling off because just the idea is absurd, but now that he's standing here in front of me, a vulnerable look in his eyes for the first time ever, I can't help but wonder if this afternoon was an anomaly or a memory of a friendship so unimaginable that I've somehow managed to forget it.

"Hudson…"

"Don't worry about it," he tells me, and the softness that's been here since he showed up this morning is effectively gone. As I watch the Hudson I've come to know and despise over the last few days come to the fore, I can't decide if I'm relieved or sad. Or maybe a little of both…

"So why'd you decide to do laundry tonight, anyway? I thought you and Lover Boy would be cuddled up in his tower."

"Is that why you stayed away?" I ask as I open up the dryer to check my clothes. Sadly, they're still very much wet, but I grab a few things I don't want to overdry and shrink and throw them in my basket before I close the door and flip the timer on again. "Because you wanted to give me some privacy?"

"I stayed away because I had some things I needed to do. But you dodged the question, which makes me wonder if there's an actual reason you're here doing laundry." He narrows his eyes at me. "So spill."

"It's nothing."

"You hate doing laundry, so I don't believe for a minute that it's nothing." He snatches my favorite sweatshirt out of the dryer and dangles it just out of my reach. "Spill or you'll never see this hoodie alive again."

"It's nothing," I tell him a second time. Then screech a little as he balls my damp hoodie up and prepares to make a three-pointer into the trash can.

"Last chance, Grace."

"Okay, fine. I'm nervous."

"Nervous?" He looks confused as he lowers the hoodie. "About what?"

"We're all supposed to meet tomorrow morning on the practice field and start preparing for Ludares. I'm supposed to try to fly for the first time, and I have no idea how that's going to work. Or even if I'll be able to turn into a gargoyle. Everyone else will be doing their thing, and I'm either going to be a useless human or an even more useless statue."

Hudson laughs. He actually laughs, and I have the sudden urge to punch him.

"Thanks," I tell him with the nastiest glare I can muster. "You pushed me to tell you, and now you're laughing at me. You suck."

"I'm not laughing at you, Grace," he manages to say between laughs. "I'm... Yeah, I can't even lie with a straight face. I'm totally laughing at you."

"You know, this may be funny to you, but if we don't do well as a team, we don't get the bloodstone. If we don't get the bloodstone, we don't find a way to free you and you're stuck inside me forever until, you know, we both die. So I have no clue why you're so amused."

"I'm amused," he answers with a shake of his head, "because you're going to do fine."

"You don't know that—"

"I *do* know it, and you would, too, if you would just get out of your head for a minute and let yourself breathe."

"I'm trying to get out of my damn head!" I fire back. "So sorry that I'm struggling with it, but it's kind of hard to do with you in here demanding my attention all the time! It's even harder to do when I can't remember anything. I don't know what I can do, so how can I have any faith in myself? How can I 'breathe'?"

"Yeah, well, I know what you can do. I'm the one who was trapped with Gargoyle Grace for more than a hundred days, and I'm the one who remembers every damn minute of it. So listen to me, stop worrying, and just trust your instincts. You're going to do great."

His words give me pause, precisely because they aren't the ones I expected him—or anyone—to say. "What does that mean?" I ask after several seconds pass. "When you say you were there, what does that mean?"

"It means four months is a long time to just stand around somewhere." He shifts uncomfortably. "We weren't just frozen in time while you were gone, Grace. You were a gargoyle, and one of the things you spent that time doing was figuring out what that means."

His words have my hands trembling and my heart pounding triple-time as I realize he knows more about me than I ever imagined.

I guess I thought we were enemies when we were together, but he makes it sound like that wasn't the case. Or at least, not the whole case.

Did we talk? Did we laugh? Did we fight? The latter seems the most likely, but the look in his eyes doesn't make it seem like he hated every second. "You remember what I was doing during those months?" I whisper.

For the first time, he looks wary, like he's afraid he's said too much.

And I get it, I do. I know everyone is worried that I have to find my memories in my own time, but I just want to know now.

He doesn't answer my question, but he does say something even more interesting. "You love being a gargoyle."

Now his words have my palms dampening and my stomach roiling with excitement. "What did I learn?" I ask.

The need to know is a physical ache inside me.

"What can I do?" I ask him.

"Pretty much anything you want to," he finally answers. "And if you want to prove it to yourself, you could just shift right here. There's plenty of room."

"What do you mean? *Here* here?" I ask, looking around. "Where anyone could come in?"

"I guarantee you, Grace, no one is coming in. You're the only one in the entire school doing your laundry on a Saturday night. Honestly, I don't know whether to be impressed or embarrassed for you."

"Wow." I glare at him. "That's a great way to motivate someone."

"It's not my job to motivate you," he shoots back. "That's your job.

I'm the enemy, if you remember correctly."

"I do remember," I snap. "And if I didn't, God knows it would only take a minute with you to figure it out."

"Exactly." He looks me over with that cold smile of his that doesn't quite meet his eyes. "Now, are you going to do something, or are we just going to stand around here all night while you feel sorry for yourself?"

Those words piss me off more than any others he might have used, and I have to force myself not to scream when I answer, "I'm not feeling sorry for myself!"

He looks me over from head to toe and says, "Okay."

That's it. Just a simple *okay*—and somehow he has me seeing red. "What do I need to do?" I grit my teeth, hating having to ask him. But pride is one thing. Naïveté is another. "What do I have to do to shift?"

"You've already got the answer to that."

"Yeah, but I can't remember the answer! So will you please help me out instead of just standing there voicing platitudes in my head?" I throw my hands wide in the air.

For long seconds, he looks torn. Like he doesn't know how much to say. But eventually his need to get the hell out of my head must supersede everything else, because he says, "You told me once that being a gargoyle was the most natural thing in the world for you. Like, you couldn't imagine how you'd spent seventeen years of your life not feeling it, because it felt like home."

I roll his words around in my mind, weighing them against everything that I'm feeling now, and they make no sense. "I really said that?"

"You really did."

How did I go from that to feeling like being a gargoyle is the most unnatural thing in the world for me? Could I really forget that much, I wonder, even as I stand in the middle of the room with my eyes closed and try to look inside myself.

But there's nothing to see, except the yawning emptiness that has been there all along. "This is hopeless."

Hudson shakes his head and reaches down to pick up my hands. "You're trying too hard." Our gazes meet, and I get lost in the tumultuous blue waves in his eyes. "You don't have to learn how to *be* a gargoyle. You *are* one. It's a part of you, of who you are. And no matter what—no one can take that from you."

I feel like he's talking about more than just my being a gargoyle. "What does that—"

He stops me. "Not now," he says. "For now, close your eyes." He waits until I do before continuing. "Take a deep breath, let it out. And reach for that part of yourself that's hidden. The part you keep a secret from everyone else."

When I do, I can't help but see all the different threads inside me, each one a string that leads to a different piece of me, a different person or thing that makes me.

On the plus side, all I have to do is lay hands on the individual strings to realize what I'm dealing with. Bright orange for my love of reading. Soft blue for the ocean. Turquoise for my mother's laugh. Hot pink for Macy. Black for Jaxon, along with a single two-toned thread that starts as a medium green and keeps getting darker and darker until it fades into black. One look and I'm nearly positive that this is our mating bond, though I don't know how I know that. Red for my art. Brown for Saturday-morning walks with my father. There's even a brilliant emerald-green string, almost shimmering, it's so iridescent. I start to reach for that one, but a voice warns me to stay away from that string. Before I can really give it more thought, I get distracted by a gorgeous cerulean string, which I instinctively know is my mother. A deep russet string, my father. Even an aquamarine string for La Jolla.

The list goes on and on, and so do the colored strings, and I sort through them all—even ones I don't recognize yet—until I finally find a shiny platinum one buried deep in the middle of all the others.

Instinctively, I know this one is it. My gargoyle.

Not going to lie, I'm a little scared of it and what it can do. But being afraid never got me anywhere, and it's definitely not going to solve this problem, so I just reach for it, breath held and heart beating way too fast.

The moment I touch it, I feel something resonate deep inside me, kind of like I did with Hudson's magic earlier. But this is deeper, stronger—a tidal wave where that was just a drop—and I can feel it sweeping over me. Roiling around me. *Burying* me in its power and its presence.

There's a part of me that wants to pull back, that wants to protect myself more than it wants anything else. But it's too late. Everything is crashing in on me now, and all I can do is hang on and wait to see what happens.

It doesn't take long, maybe a second or two, though it feels like an eternity. It starts in my hands and arms, a heaviness that feels completely foreign and yet completely right all at the same time. Once it reaches my shoulders, it spreads like wildfire down my torso to my hips and legs and feet before finally sweeping up my neck to my jaw and cheeks and the top of my head.

At the same time, there's a burning in my back, and it scares me a little until I remember—my wings. Of course.

And then it's done and I'm standing in the middle of Katmere's laundry room in my gargoyle form—and nothing has ever felt so weird. Really, really weird.

Now that I've shifted, I keep holding on to the string deep inside me, but I let go when Hudson tells me to.

"What's wrong?" I ask as he grins down at me. And, on a side note, can I just say how goddamn unfair it is that I'm short, even as a gargoyle? I mean, I just turned to stone for God's sake. Can't I at least grow a few inches along with the transformation?

"You're never going to stop complaining about that, are you?" Hudson asks.

"Never!" I answer immediately. But I've got bigger things than my height to worry about right now. "Why can't I hold on to the string?"

I mean, it's no big deal—it's not like it's burning my stone hands or anything. I'm just curious.

"Because I'm pretty sure the longer you hold the string, the more like a statue you become. But shifting to right here, to this point, lets you move and walk and *fly*," he tells me.

"Oh! So pretty important, then, huh?" I joke, right before I decide to see if Hudson is right.

Turns out, he is. I *can* walk. I can also dance and spin in circles and jump so hard, I shake the whole floor. And it is absolutely amazing!

There's a part of me that wants to see if I can fly—I've already wiggled my wings and they work—but there are a couple of problems with that. One, we're inside, and if I can't stop, I really, really don't want to explain to Uncle Finn why I've either knocked myself senseless or crashed through one of the castle walls.

And two, which is really just a sidebar of number one, I have *absolutely no idea* how to work these things. I'm pretty sure one day in my Physics of Flight class does not qualify me to operate wings, even if they are on my own back.

Suddenly, I remember the pic Macy showed me and I reach up... Sure enough, there are the horns. Sigh. At least they don't feel that big.

I don't know how long I walk and stomp and twirl around as a gargoyle, but I know it's long enough for my laundry to grow cold and wrinkle.

Long enough for Hudson to give up chasing me and slump down in the corner to watch, a non-sarcastic grin on his face.

More than long enough for my muscles to grow tired and shaky. Turns out it takes some serious effort to move this much rock.

I don't want to turn back yet, though. I don't know why or how, but there's something ridiculously freeing being in this form. I thought I'd feel trapped or weighed down or claustrophobic, but instead I just feel...content. Like I've found a giant piece of myself that I didn't even know was missing.

Eventually, though, I know I have to turn back to my human

form. It's late, Macy will probably be back from girls' night soon, and I don't want her to think I ditched her just to go hang with someone else. Plus, I have an early day tomorrow—we arranged to meet on the practice field at nine, and I want to get some sleep, maybe give myself a chance not to make a total fool of myself. Plus, Jaxon will be worried if he thinks I've disappeared again.

"Jaxy-Waxy keeps a tight rein on you, huh?" Hudson says, sarcasm back in full force now that he's used up his decency quotient for the year—maybe even the decade.

I don't answer him until I've changed back to human form—a process as easy as reaching for a bright gold string, which must be human Grace, and willing myself into my human body again. My clothes, which had turned to stone, shift back to cloth as well. "*Jaxon* worries ever since half the school, *and* his brother, tried to kill me."

Hudson yawns. "To be fair, I was trying to kill *him*. You just got in the way."

"Wow, I'm sure that makes both of us feel so much better."

He shrugs. "Didn't know making you feel better was my job."

And just like that, I'm totally exasperated with him again. Also very confused. I mean, what was going on in his head earlier, when he burst in here and twirled me around the room like we were best friends or something? And what's changed to bring him back to his oh-so-un-lovable self?

Not that I'm complaining. This Hudson I know how to handle. The other one completely freaked me out.

"Huh." Hudson snorts from where he's leaning a shoulder against the wall. "That's what I get for being nice."

"Yeah, you probably shouldn't do that," I agree. "It's not a good look on you."

"Please. Everything's a good look on me and you know it." He emphasizes the point by giving me what can only be described as a "male-model catwalk" look.

I burst out laughing—I can't help it. And though Hudson pretends to be thoroughly disgusted with me, I've gotten to know him enough to recognize the gleam of humor deep in his eyes.

"I'm going to bed," I tell him when I finally stop laughing.

"Is that an invitation?" he asks.

Suddenly my cheeks are burning and everything feels too hot. "To not be a total douche for the next six hours so I can sleep? Yes. For anything else? Not a chance in hell." And with that parting shot, I pick up my laundry basket and head back to my room.

"Good. I didn't want to break your heart anyway." But he's whistling as we make our way up the stairs, and it's only after we get back to my room that I realize the tune is Flo Rida's "Good Feeling."

I don't know why that makes me smile, but it does.

Which is probably why, when I slide into bed a few minutes later, I whisper, "Thank you, Hudson. I really appreciate all your help today."

There's a long silence, so long that I would think he'd fallen asleep if I couldn't see his eyes. Eventually, though, he sighs and says, "Don't thank me, Grace."

"Why not?" I roll over so I can get a better look at his face as he leans up against the side of my bed.

"Because," he tells me, indigo eyes burning hotly with a myriad of emotions I can't begin to decipher, "if you do, I'm going to do something that you'll regret."

58

Always Look on
the Bite Side

"What do you get when you kiss a dragon?" I ask as soon as Jaxon answers his door. I reach up and idly twist the pendant he gave me in my hand. I've been wearing it nearly every day since I got back, but this is the first time it's not buried under a ton of clothes.

He looks at me with sleepy eyes and says, "Nausea?"

"Close. Burned lips." I hand him the tumbler full of blood I picked up for him at the cafeteria. "Here. Drink up."

He takes it, a small grin playing around his lips. "Thank you." Then he leans forward and takes my mouth in a short but powerful kiss. "I think I'll skip the burned lips and kiss a gargoyle instead."

"Good plan." I put my own hot-chocolate-filled tumbler on the table next to his door, then wrap my arms around his neck as I pull him down for a longer, more satisfying kiss of my own.

Jaxon makes a sound deep in his throat as he moves closer. He kisses the corners of my mouth, then drags his tongue along the line of my lower lip before wrapping his arms around my waist and pulling me close. "What about Hudson?" he whispers, his breath hot against my ear.

"He's still asleep. It's why I decided to meet you up here instead of in the foyer."

"I like the way you think," Jaxon tells me, even as he turns us so that I'm sandwiched between him and the wall. Then he runs his lips along the edge of my jaw and down my neck until he gets to the hollow of my throat.

"And I like the way you do that," I answer, tangling my fingers in the cool silk of his hair as I arch against him.

"Good." He skims lower, nuzzling the collar of my shirt down a little so he can kiss along my collarbone. "Because I plan on doing it for a long time to come. Mate."

"Jesus. Corny much?" Hudson butts in out of nowhere. He looks as sleepy-eyed as Jaxon, and half his hair is sticking straight up. But— per usual—his sarcasm is absolutely on point. "I mean, seriously. Surely my brother can come up with a better line than that. Or is he just planning on stamping his name on your ass and calling it a day?"

I pull away from Jaxon with a groan before turning to face Hudson, who's now leaning against the doorframe. "You know what? Bite me."

"I'd love to," he fires back, his midnight-blue eyes burning hotly into mine as he leans in close and shows a fang. "Any particular place you have in mind?"

Out of the blue, a not-altogether-bad shiver makes its way down my spine, which in turn freaks me out so much that I jerk back so quickly—from both of them—that I nearly fall flat on my ass.

"Hey, you okay?" Jaxon asks, reaching a hand out to steady me.

"Yeah, of course. I just..."

"I think I know." He lifts a brow. "Hudson's awake?"

"Something like that, yeah." I bend forward, rest the top of my head against his chest. And whisper, "I'm sorry."

"Never apologize," he answers. "At least not for that." Then he steps back into his room, gesturing for me to take a seat on the couch while he heads toward his bedroom. "Give me a couple of minutes to brush my teeth and get dressed. Then we can go."

"No hurry. We've got time," I call out as he closes his door. Mostly because I'd planned for us to have a few more minutes before we went down to hang with the others...and before Hudson woke up. Apparently, I should have skipped the cafeteria run. But Jaxon looked so run-down all day yesterday that I wanted to make sure he got something to eat.

"Drink." Hudson flops down onto the chair facing the couch. He slouches into the seat and stretches his long legs out in front of him, arms tightly crossed. His jaw is clenched. And he sounds pissier than I've ever heard him—which is saying something.

It's also fine with me, because I'm feeling pretty damn pissy myself. "What are you talking about?" I ask flatly, as I have no interest in being cordial right now.

"He drinks, not eats."

"Whatever." I glare at him. "And will you please stop eavesdropping on my thoughts!"

"It's not eavesdropping when you're projecting them through your whole head like a bloody carnival barker," he shoots back. "No offense, but it's pretty hard not to listen. It's also nauseating as fuck."

"You know what? You're being a jackass and I don't even know why. Or did you just use up your entire niceness quotient for the month yesterday?"

"Don't you mean the year?" he asks with an obnoxious smirk.

"More like the decade, apparently." I stand and make my way to the table by the door to pick up my hot chocolate—and a book. Because there is no way I'm going to spend the next however many minutes listening to Hudson whine.

"Make sure to check the shelves at the back of the room. I'm pretty sure there's a book of fairy tales in there somewhere. I mean, if you want to keep telling yourself a bunch of lies."

"Oh. My. God!" I whirl on him, my fists clenched and a scream building in my throat. "What is your problem? You're acting like a douche!"

At first I think he's going to answer me—it certainly looks like he's got a lot to say when he gets up in my face—but then he just stares at me, eyes blazing and mouth pressed into a line so tight and straight that it has to be painful.

Long seconds pass, and the tension ratchets up between us more and more until it feels like the top of my head is going to explode. Just when I'm about to lose it or scream at him—or both—Jaxon walks out of his bedroom, black jacket in hand.

"I didn't know if you remembered to bring a coat," he says, holding the jacket out to me. "The playing field is heated, but the walk there takes a few minutes."

Hudson turns away, muttering something obscene-sounding under his breath, and there's a part of me that wants to grab his arm. That wants to demand we finish this argument that makes no freaking sense.

But Jaxon is waiting for me, looking sweet and also sexy as hell in a pair of slim-fit black track pants and a black compression shirt that shows every muscle he's got. And he's got a lot of them.

"I brought one," I tell him, nodding to the back of the couch where I dropped my coat when I first got here. "But thanks. I appreciate it."

"Of course." He grins as he grabs an empty backpack and stuffs it full of water bottles—then reaches into the closed cabinet under one of his bookshelves and pulls out a box of my favorite granola bars and adds a couple to the bag.

"Where'd you get those?" I ask, a little surprised and a lot touched.

"I ordered them when we first got together, along with some Pop-Tarts in case you're ever hungry when you're hanging out here. They came when you were..." He waves a hand to encompass everything that happened. "So I put them away for when you got back—and here you are."

"Here I am," I repeat, nearly swooning at the way he takes such good care of me, even when I don't know he's doing it. "Thank you," I say again.

Jaxon rolls his eyes. "Stop saying that," he tells me as he zips the backpack before picking up my coat and helping me into it. "None of this is a big deal."

"That's not true," I say, snagging his hand when he would have started for the door. I wait until he turns toward me to continue. "It's a very big deal to me, and I appreciate it."

He gives a little one-shouldered shrug, but I can tell he's pleased by my words. Still, looking at him out here in the light, I also realize the tiredness I saw on his face from earlier wasn't just sleepiness. He's feeling drained, even though he won't say so. I can tell, from the open books scattered all over the table by the window, he's been burning the candle at both ends researching the Unkillable Beast. We know it's on an enchanted island in the Arctic, but he wanted to learn more about it to help us prepare. Plus, he'd mentioned earlier trying to find a weakness.

My chest tightens. I know the horror is weighing on him of what Hudson could do if we bring him back with his abilities.

"Ready?" he asks, taking a step back. "It's almost nine."

"Almost ready," I answer, wrapping my arms around his waist. As I do, I reach for the mating bond, which is easy to find after last night, when I discovered all the different threads inside me.

"What are you doing?" he asks.

Instead of answering, I grab on to the black string with green streaks and start channeling a bunch of energy down the mating bond and straight into him.

"Stop!" Jaxon pulls away. "You don't have to do that."

"I don't have to do anything," I answer. "But I'm doing this." And now that I can hold the mating bond in my hand, it doesn't matter if I'm touching Jaxon or not. I'm not letting go of it until it looks like Jaxon has all the strength and energy he needs.

"What are you doing?" Hudson demands. "You can't just send all your power into him! What are you going to do when you need it?"

I smile at Jaxon, but I'm answering them both. "I can do anything I want—and what I want is to take care of Jaxon."

Hudson throws his hands in the air. "Maybe you'll feel differently when you get your ass handed to you on the practice field today."

My breath hitches. I know he meant to hit back at me, but I'm still surprised when I feel the punch in my chest. Just a reminder I'd started to let my guard down around Hudson, started to believe he really thought I was stronger than everyone else gives me credit for. And I have no idea why finding out that he doesn't suddenly makes me so sad.

Besides, he's completely wrong. We have a plan, and now that I can shift into my gargoyle, I know it's going to work.

Win the Ludares tournament and get the bloodstone.

Grab a bone from a graveyard.

And well, yeah, stealing the Unkillable Beast's heartstone feels a little iffy, but Jaxon is positive we can do it.

Once we do all that, we'll get Hudson out of my head once and for all—and he won't be able to hurt anyone else. Jaxon can finally get some sleep and we can maybe, maybe have a normal end to our senior year.

Or, you know, at least completely doable.

For the first time since I learned Hudson is stuck in my head, I can't help the smile spreading across my face. We've got a plan: Win the game. Get the bone. Kill the beast. As Macy likes to say, easy-peasy. We've totally got this.

Jaxon and I head out of his room hand in hand, a lightness in my step that's only marginally dimmed when I think I hear Hudson mutter, "We're all doomed."

59

Jaxon and I are the first to make it to the practice field. Because I'm bundled up in four layers of clothing, he insists I strip off the top two layers—which doesn't sit well with me, considering I'm still freezing from the walk through the forest, but he says if I start to sweat, it will make the walk back a million times worse.

I mean, the temperature isn't *terrible*—at least not by Alaska's standards—but something tells me *I'll* still be cold here in the middle of July.

"So what are we going to work on today?" I ask as I strip out of my coat, my hoodie, and my ski pants. The fact that I'm still wearing my fleece pants, leggings, a tank top, and a long-sleeve thermal shirt makes my head spin—and I'm pretty sure it always will. I guess it really is true that you can take the girl out of San Diego, but you can't take San Diego out of the girl…

"I thought we'd see what you can do," Jaxon says. "And I know Flint wants to get everyone talking strategy for the game."

"He's really taking this seriously," I comment as I start to stretch. "Especially considering we only have a couple days to train and the stakes are so high."

"Oh, I think he's got a lot of reasons he wants to win," Jaxon tells me with a look I can't quite decipher. "Plus, I don't think you get what a big deal Ludares is here. The whole school looks forward to March for the tournament, and the winners get bragging rights for the rest of the year. And there's also the fact that Flint's team came in second last year, and I'm sure he's planning on making sure this year is different."

I bend over and put my hands flat on the ground as I stretch out my legs. "Thankfully, considering this is our best shot at a bloodstone."

Jaxon makes a sound of agreement deep in his throat, but when I peer around my thigh at him, there's a gleam in his eye that says he's focused on something else entirely: namely my butt as I bend over to stretch.

"Hey! We're supposed to be talking about the competition," I tell him as I open my legs wider so that I can stretch from side to side.

"Get first place, win the bloodstone, vanquish Hudson. I got it," he says, but he still hasn't lifted his eyes from my ass.

"Jaxon!" Heat rushes to my cheeks, but it makes me happy that he gets as much pleasure looking at me as I do looking at him—after all, I've been enjoying the sight of him in that compression shirt since I first saw him in it this morning.

"Sorry," he says, coming closer to rub a hand up and down my back. "Sometimes it hits me in the face how lucky I am to have you."

His honesty makes my knees tremble. But when I stand up, I'm still determined not to let him see how much—at least not until he leans forward and drops a kiss on first one cheek and then the other. "You're beautiful, Grace, inside and out. And I'm so grateful you found me."

This time there's no hiding it as I full-on melt. "I'm really glad I found you, too," I say as I wrap my arms around his waist and hug him close. "And ignored you every time you told me to get the hell out of Katmere Academy."

He pulls me even closer. "I don't know what I was thinking."

"Yeah, me neither." I press a kiss to his collarbone before pulling back. "Then again, you might have had a point. Considering the whole

Lia thing and now the whole Hudson thing... I mean, I'm glad I didn't know this was coming, because I would have run as far and as fast as I could. And then I would have missed out on you. On us. But your warning *does* make a lot more sense in retrospect."

I expect him to laugh with me, but he doesn't. Instead, he gets that tortured look on his face that I hate, the one that says he's beating himself up over things that are completely beyond his control.

I think about trying to coax him out of the mood, about doing what I usually do and try to talk some sense into him. But the more I learn about Jaxon, the more I've learned that that doesn't always work on him. So instead of sitting him down for a heart-to-heart, I do the only other thing I can think of.

I pull away and say, "Catch me if you can."

One incredulous eyebrow goes up. "What did you just say?"

I take several big steps backward. "I said, catch me if you can."

"You do realize I'm a vampire, right?" Now both his eyebrows are raised almost to his hairline. "I mean, I can just..." He fades the distance between us. "Catch you."

He goes to wrap his arms around me, but I push him away. "Not like that."

"You mean there's another way?"

I wiggle my brows at him, even as I take several more steps back. "There's always another way."

"Oooookay. I'll bite—"

"Not if I can help it, you won't." And then I do what Hudson taught me yesterday in the laundry room. I reach down deep inside myself for all the colored threads and wrap my hand around the bright platinum one. When my fingers wrap around it, I feel that same strange heaviness coming over me.

"Grace, are you okay—" Jaxon breaks off, eyes widening in shock as I start to turn to stone right in front of him. But unlike that time in the hallway, I don't hold on until I'm a statue. Instead, I let go as soon as it feels like the shift is complete.

And it works! Just like last night, I'm a gargoyle, but I can still move around. I can still talk. I can still be Grace, just in gargoyle form.

"Oh my God!" Jaxon says, coming closer again. "Look at you."

"Pretty cool, huh?" I hold a hand out for him to examine. "I mean, except for the horns." I run a self-conscious hand over one of them.

"I like the horns," Jaxon tells me with a grin. "They give you character."

"Oh yeah. Sooooo much character."

"I'm serious. They look good. You look good."

"Yeah?" I hate how vulnerable I feel when I ask that question, hate that I need to know Jaxon loves this side of me, too. Which gives me a whole new appreciation for how Jaxon felt when he was waiting to see how I would react to him being a vampire.

"Yeah," he says as he reaches out and runs a finger down the back of my hand from wrist to fingertip.

It feels good. *We* feel good.

"So, have you been practicing shifting into your gargoyle form?" he asks as we walk a little ways together. "You did it so easily."

"Just last night, Hudson helped me—"

I break off as Jaxon's face goes completely blank. "Hudson helped you?" he repeats.

"Yeah, just for a few minutes when I was doing laundry," I tell him, suddenly feeling the need to babble to get the words out faster. "I mean, it was no big deal. I was nervous about today, so he explained to me how shifters do it. Turns out, it works the same for gargoyles."

"Wait a minute. So you were nervous about coming out here with everyone?" Jaxon's jaw tightens, regret and self-disgust swirling in the depths of his eyes. "Why didn't you tell me? I would have brought you here alone first and worked as long as you wanted to. Or told them we couldn't come. I'd never force you into something you felt weird doing."

"I *know* that. I just…" I drift off with a shrug, not really sure what I want to say or how I want to say it.

"Just what?" he demands.

"It's embarrassing, okay? Everybody here make it looks so easy to be a paranormal, and it's humiliating to admit how freaked out I was about consciously shifting for the first time. I didn't want to make a fool of myself in front of everyone."

"First of all, there's nothing for you to be embarrassed about. Most people are nervous about their powers as they learn to use them. It's totally normal, and I would have said that to you if you'd asked me. And second, it's *humiliating* to admit that to me, but not to Hudson? Are you fucking kidding me?"

"Come on, Jaxon, that's not what I meant at all. I just want you to see me as strong, you know?" I go to run a hand through my hair, totally forgetting that it's stone as well, so I end up just patting my stone hair instead. Because that isn't awkward at all.

"I don't need to see you that way, Grace. You *are* that way. You're strong and powerful and amazing and no one knows that better than I do—you saved my life twice."

"That's not what I meant."

"I know, but that's what I see when I look at you. So if you need help for once or feel uncertain for a little while, why wouldn't you come to me? Why would you go to Hudson of all people?"

"Damn it, Jaxon. I didn't *go* to Hudson with anything, but it's not like I had a choice. I can't get away from him, so what am I supposed to do?"

Jaxon's eyes go watchful. "What does that mean exactly, that you don't have a choice? What don't you have a choice about?"

I can practically see the wheels turning in his head as he tries to reason this whole thing out, and it suddenly occurs to me that telling him that Hudson knows everything I'm thinking is akin to walking through a minefield without a metal detector. Terrifying, dangerous, and potentially very, very messy.

But it's obvious from his face—and his questions—that it's too late to step back now, and I'm not sure I would anyway, because lying to my mate seems like a really bad idea. Then again, so does jumping down her throat when she makes a simple comment about a simple choice she made for herself about her own power...

Which is why I don't backtrack and why I don't apologize or try to prevaricate. Instead, I take a deep breath in an effort to beat back the annoyance and the anxiety that are building inside me—and then tell Jaxon as much of the truth as I understand myself. "It means he knows every single thing I'm thinking. Not just what I'm doing, but if I'm hungry or what pair of underwear I'm thinking about wearing or that I really don't understand aeronautical physics at all.

"So yeah, he knew that I was nervous about shifting again—who wouldn't be, considering I don't even remember doing it the first time? Or, for that matter, how I shifted back to my human form. I was worried about not being able to turn into a gargoyle. I was worried about not being able to shift back again. I was worried about it all. Every single part of it, even though I was doing laundry late at night because I was trying *not* to think about it so I could actually sleep."

I'm all worked up now, so I start to pace—which, it turns out, feels oddly different from when I do it in my human form but also oddly the same. It's something to think about, but at a different time, when Jaxon isn't looking at me like his head might explode at any second.

"So yes, Jaxon," I continue, "Hudson helped me out. Not because I had anything against you, but just because he was there."

Jaxon holds my gaze, and I watch a muscle in his jaw tick, but he doesn't say anything.

I can't help the sadness creeping in to fill the void where my anger had been. This isn't Jaxon's fault any more than it's mine. I sigh. "Fucking Hudson."

"Ouch. Don't hold back, Grace. Tell me how you really feel," Hudson says from where he's suddenly sprawled out on the Astroturf right behind Jaxon, a copy of Sartre's *No Exit* open in his hands.

60

Paranormal Telenovelas Are a Lifestyle Choice

"**A**re you kidding me?" I turn and yell at Hudson, sadness disappearing under the reservoir of annoyance he so easily taps into. "You decide to show up *now*?"

"I've been here awhile, but it was starting to get uncomfortable listening to the two of you fight." He yawns and stretches a little, which just pisses me off more—exactly as I know he intends. "And by uncomfortable, I mean really fucking boring."

"Oh, I'm *so* sorry to hear that. Since, you know, I live to serve your every whim."

"I do know," he agrees. "And I have to say I appreciate it, which was why I'm letting you know that this whole back-and-forth thing with Jaxon really isn't working for me. But no worries. I know you'll fix it for next time."

I am well aware that he's just messing with me, know that he's trying to get me upset, and still I fall into the trap because how can I not? "You're awful, you know that? Like really, really, 'slugs crawling on your skin' awful."

He yawns again. "Old news, Grace. Try to keep up."

"Is this actually happening right now?" Jaxon's voice slices through the air between us. "I'm talking to *you* and you're talking to *him*?"

"I don't have a choice—" I start to say.

"Don't," he says, gaze like black ice. "Don't lie to me and say you aren't doing it willingly. You *turned* to face him. I'm sorry he's so much more interesting than I am—"

"He's not, Jaxon. Of course he's not."

"Now, now, Grace, my brother asked you not to lie," Hudson admonishes me. "But cut him some slack, will you? It's not his fault he's so damn boring."

I glare at Hudson. "Stop it! He is *not* boring!"

"Could have fooled me." Yet another yawn. "And here I thought you were supposed to be practicing the whole gargoyle thing this morning? Though, I have to admit, I like what you've done with the horns."

"The horns?" Instinctively, I lift a hand to my left horn and feel it. "Oh my God, it's bigger. How can it be bigger?"

"Now there's a question I'm sure Jaxon's never heard," Hudson says dryly.

"I'm still here, you know," Jaxon grinds out. "I'm right fucking here."

"I know. I'm sorry, Jaxon. I'm so sorry. But he's the most annoying person on the planet, and he refuses to shut up."

"Careful, Grace. Keep that up and you're going to hurt my feelings," Hudson mocks.

"I couldn't get that lucky!" I snap before turning back to Jaxon, who's got a half-angry, half-amazed look on his face.

"Is this what he does all day?" he finally asks. "Just badgers you until you look like you're about to explode?"

"He does it until I *do* explode, but yes. This is what he does. Over and over and over again."

"Wow, snookums. You make me sound so powerful." Hudson bats his eyes at me, but there's a gleam of remorse in them, like maybe he thinks he's gone too far. I don't trust it, but then, I don't trust anything about him. He's probably just sad Jaxon and I are no longer at each other's throats.

"Again, ouch."

"Again, bite me."

He's not smiling, but I can see two fangs gleaming. "You keep offering that, and someone's going to take you up on it."

"Yeah, well, someone already has," I retort.

"Don't remind me."

The usual amusement is gone from his tone. Everything is gone, and all that's left is blankness—blank voice, blank face. I'd say blank body language except he lies back down on the field, kicks one ankle over the other knee, and holds *No Exit* up in front of his face as he starts to read.

It's blatant—the "I don't have a care in the world" and "fuck you very much" body language rolled into one—and I don't have a clue what to say about it. Or how to feel about it.

Before I can figure it out, Jaxon says, "I'm sorry," and he walks over and wraps his arms around my waist from behind.

I stiffen instinctively, then force myself to relax, even as I shift back to my human form. Because there's no use being angry with him for being angry about this situation. Does it suck for me? Yes. Would I be pissed as hell if he had some girl in his head taking all his attention away from me, who knew everything about him before I did and worked really hard to make me feel completely out of the loop? Hell yes, I would.

So I bury my annoyance deep and wrap my arms around his body as I lean in to him. "No, *I'm* sorry. I know this can't be easy for you."

"None of this is easy for either of us," he answers as he bends down and drops a soft kiss on the side of my neck. "I think I need to remember that more."

"We both do," I answer. "I'm sorry I get caught up in fighting with Hudson and I forget sometimes."

"Don't be sorry. Being annoying is my brother's singular talent."

"Whatever," Hudson growls, and he sounds even more pissed than he did this morning. "It barely cracks the top ten of my talents."

It takes every ounce of willpower I have, but this time I ignore him, keeping my attention completely focused on Jaxon—or at least as focused as I can considering Hudson is yammering away at me in the background.

"Thank you for understanding how hard this is for me. I know it's hard for you, too, and I appreciate how much you're trying to make this as easy for me as possible."

Jaxon sighs, his arms tightening around me just a little as he responds. "Thank you for understanding my side of this mess, too. I promise, we'll get him out of your head as soon as we possibly can."

"Sooner than that would be better," I joke, and it works. Jaxon laughs.

He holds me for several seconds longer, until we can see Flint and Macy entering the practice field with two other people I don't know.

Jaxon drops another kiss on my neck before pulling reluctantly away. But just before he lets me go, he leans down and whispers, "Does he really know what underwear you're wearing?"

"Black with white polka dots," Hudson answers without looking up from his book.

I sigh. "He really does."

Jaxon looks disgruntled, but he doesn't say anything, thankfully.

Hudson, however, has no such qualms. "You should wear the red ones with the white flowers tomorrow, though. They're my favorite."

Before I can think of a comeback to that, Flint sneaks up behind me and grabs me in a giant bear hug. And as he swings me around—chanting "Grace, Grace, Baby" much to my chagrin—I can't help but notice that Jaxon is showing a lot more fang than he usually does.

Then again, so is Hudson...

Forget YA novel, I'm living in the middle of a paranormal telenovela, and what happens next is anyone's guess...

Fuck. My. Life.

61

The Monster Mash-Up

"**Y**ou ready to show these guys how it's done, Grace?" Flint asks when he finally drops me back on my feet.

"How what's done?" I ask, surreptitiously checking to make sure all my clothes are in all the right places. Flint is a *very* enthusiastic hugger.

"How to fly, baby!" He throws his arms out and does a really bad impression of wings and flying as he zips around me like a three-year-old pretending to be an airplane—cute, sweet, and absolutely ridiculous.

"I'm ready for *you* to show them how it's done," I tell him.

"No way! We're in this together. Well, you, me, and Eden." He turns to the girl behind him with a grin and beckons her forward.

She gives him a look when he waves, like there's no way she's going to give him the satisfaction of responding to such a plebian method of communication. But after making him wait just long enough that everyone knows she's moving only because she wants to, she swaggers toward us, all glorious hair and "don't mess with me" attitude.

"This is Eden Seong," Flint tells me when she finally reaches us. "She's one of my closest friends and also happens to be fire with a Ludares ball."

"And everything else," she drawls, and somehow even her voice is cool.

I can't believe I haven't noticed her around school before, because she's totally not the type to blend in. She's tall like Macy, with straight black hair that falls all the way to her butt and thick, severely cut bangs that hit below her eyebrows to the very tops of her *purple* eyes. I look closer, sure that they're just really blue, but nope. They're totally purple and the coolest eyes I've ever seen.

She's dressed completely in white—white workout pants, white tennis shoes, and white tank top that shows off a wild Korean dragon tattoo that stretches across her shoulders and down both her arms. So she's a dragon like Flint then. Badass.

She's got multiple piercings—several in her ears, plus her nose and her eyebrow—and each piercing is adorned with a glittering gemstone in a different color. She's also wearing close to a dozen flashy jeweled rings on her fingers, but instead of being overkill, it all just kind of works together to make her sparkle even more.

Not going to lie, I love her already, even before she thrusts out a hand to shake mine and says, "Being a gargoyle is the most kick-ass thing I have *ever* heard of. Good job."

I laugh. "It's not like I had a choice in the matter."

She shrugs. "No one actually gets a choice of what they are at the molecular level, Grace. It's what you do with it that matters, and so far everything you've done is pretty badass."

"I don't know about that."

"I do. And you should listen to me. Everybody does."

Again, she should come off as completely arrogant, but instead it just kind of screams of charming and total rock star. No wonder Flint adores her.

"It's true," Flint tells me as he drapes an arm around her shoulders and squeezes tight enough to make Eden glare at him. "She gives the best advice."

Eden shoots him a "why are you touching me" look, which only makes him squeeze her harder. But when he reaches up to ruffle her hair, she ducks out from under his arm and twists it behind his back hard enough to have him squealing—not to mention coughing out a couple of pathetic blasts of ice—which has Jaxon, Macy, and the guy who came on the field with Eden, who I don't know yet, cracking up.

"Are you done?" Eden asks, eyes narrowed.

"For now." Flint gives her his most charming grin, and she just rolls her eyes. But she also lets him go.

"Anyway," Flint continues, "this is Eden. And this"—he turns to the white guy dressed in navy track pants, a gray compression shirt, and a navy baseball cap—"is Xavier. He's a wolf, but we try not to hold it against him."

Xavier cheerfully flips him off before nodding my way. "Nice to meet you, Grace. I've certainly heard a lot about you."

He doesn't tell me from where, and I don't ask. If he's a wolf, I'm not sure I want to know anyway.

"Nice to meet you, too," I answer with a smile. He's got laughing green eyes and a wide smile that makes it impossible not to grin back at him. Eden may be cool, but this guy is F.U.N. It's written all over him.

Add in the fact that my cousin keeps glancing at him out of the corner of her eye, and I'm only more interested in getting to know this guy.

"Is this everyone?" I ask, because I thought Flint mentioned there being eight people on a team.

"Mekhi will be here any minute," Jaxon tells the group.

"And Gwen had a makeup test this morning," Macy says. "But she'll be here as soon as it's over."

I'm super excited that Mekhi's going to be on our team—and just as excited that Macy chose Gwen to play with us instead of one of her other friends. Gwen was definitely the nicest when I met her whole friend group a few months ago. Somehow I can't imagine Simone agreeing the way Gwen and everyone else had when Jaxon explained just why we needed the bloodstone.

It still feels strange to think of that time being a few months ago, since for me it feels like it's been only a few weeks. But I'm trying to get used to it, just like I'm trying to get used to my memory likely never coming back. I hate the thought of never remembering those months, but I'm tired of worrying about it, tired of beating myself up over it.

"I hate that you can't remember, too," Hudson says, but it's a soft tone, not his usual sardonic one. He wanders over to check out the wolf, no longer pretending to be captivated by his book.

I want to ask him what happened, want to beg him to forget what everyone says is good for me and just tell me. But now isn't exactly the time, and how do I know I can trust what he tells me anyway?

"So what are we doing first?" Xavier asks, bouncing up on his toes like he's ready to take off at any second. Take off for where, I don't know, but I'm betting he'll be an impressive sight.

"I think we should probably divide into teams and see what we can do together first," Flint says, pulling a medium-size ball out of the duffel bag he'd dropped on the ground. "Macy, you want to enchant this thing for us?"

He tosses it to my cousin, who pulls out her wand and aims it at the ball as she murmurs what I assume is a spell.

"What's she doing?" I ask Jaxon, completely lost.

"Ludares is half Keep Away, half Hot Potato, but with a bunch of magical twists. The first twist is that the ball burns hotter and hotter the longer you hold it, so you've got to get rid of it after thirty seconds at the most or you're going to end burned right up. And shocked, because it vibrates, too."

"It vibrates and burns you?"

"Yeah, which is why teamwork makes the dream work," Flint adds. "The ball resets itself every time a new player touches it, so you have to move it around a lot. The only surefire way to lose the game is to try to do everything yourself. You can't do it, at least not without causing some pretty serious damage to yourself."

"How is this even a game?" I ask, baffled. "Let alone one they let high school students play."

"It's the best game ever," Xavier chimes in. "Especially when you fall through a portal."

"A portal?" I turn to Jaxon. "What's a portal?"

"It's a magical passageway or door to somewhere else," he explains.

"I know what *a portal* is," I tell him with a roll of my eyes. "I mean, what is a portal in Ludares?"

"Exactly the same thing," Eden tells me. "When you're up here so close to the North Pole, several portals exist anyway, in nature. Ludares kind of takes advantage of that. Some of the school staff taps into the same kind of energy that opens portals between the poles and the sun and channels it into portals all over the arena that you can fall into."

"Ours don't take you to the sun, though," Macy finishes. "They just take you around the arena. But each one is different, and you don't know where you're going to be when you enter a portal. You may end up at the finish line, or you may end up all the way at the other end of the field and you have to start over."

"So I just jump into a portal over there"—I gesture to an area right inside the field's boundaries—"and I could end up all the way over there?" I point to the goalpost.

"Exactly!" Eden tells me with a grin that lights up her whole face. "Or you could end up over there." She points in the opposite direction. "With half of the opposing team crawling up your ass."

"That does sound like fun," I say, tongue totally in cheek, but the others just laugh.

"Once you play it, you'll see how cool it is," Xavier assures me. "Especially since everyone gets to use their magic however they want— so the game gets really wild sometimes."

"Right?" Eden agrees. "Remember sophomore year, when Alejandro turned everyone on the opposing team into turtles and then he and his teammates just ran the ball all the way down the field?"

"Well, until the witch used up all her energy and couldn't block the opposing wolves who broke free and ran them down," Xavier adds with a gleam in his eyes.

"I remember Sancha turning herself into a giant snapping turtle and nearly snapping Felicity's hand right off. That was something to see," Flint says.

"Or when Drew turned the entire arena into a lightning storm and Foster nearly got struck?" Jaxon reminisces.

"My dad was so mad. He walked around with his hair sticking up for three days straight." Macy giggles.

"So yeah," Jaxon tells me. "Lots of wild times on the Ludares field."

A horrifying thought occurs to me. "Can't the dragons just burn everyone on the other team?" And then another thought. "Can't the vamps just fade to the end and win in thirty seconds?"

Xavier's grin gets even wider. "I like how this one thinks."

But Jaxon shakes his head and clarifies, "There are magical safeguards that prevent any spell or speed burst lasting more than ten seconds. Think of it as everyone wearing a personal handicap device. Our abilities are tempered." Jaxon winks at me. "Otherwise, obviously, I'd win in seconds."

Everyone laughs at his joke.

Everyone except Hudson, who turns his attention from studying Xavier to Jaxon, his eyebrows raised. "And I thought *my* ego was huge."

"So how do you win?" I snark. "Whoever's not dead or a turtle by the end?"

"We're not quite that sadistic," Eden says with a laugh, "but I like your style."

Xavier picks up where Macy and Eden left off, his green eyes dancing with excitement. "Whoever gets the ball over the other team's goal line first wins. No excuses. No second chances."

"That's it? You just run the hot ball down the field and cross a goal line with it?" I ask.

"Don't forget the 'try not to die' portion of that equation," Jaxon tells me.

"Yeah," Eden agrees. "And believe me, that's easier said than done at least half the time. Especially since this is the big magic show of the year—everyone is using their powers at the most spectacular level trying to shock and awe the other team."

"And everyone else in the arena," Xavier adds.

"True dat," Flint agrees with the biggest grin I've ever seen from him, and that's saying something.

"So, just to be clear, there're a bunch of portals you can wander into all over the stadium."

"Yeah." Flint grins. "I mean, not now. They set them up the day of the event, but yeah. It's super fun."

I nod. "And even if you're almost at the goal line, if you fall through a surprise portal the last couple of seconds, then you could be totally screwed." I shake my head. "That's diabolical."

"It is, absolutely," Jaxon agrees.

"It's also the most fun you can have with a hot ball ever," Xavier says.

"I don't even want to know what that means," I tease.

Xavier just winks at me in response, which makes me laugh and roll my eyes at the same time. The wink doesn't affect me at all—I've got Jaxon—but I'd be lying if I said I didn't notice how attractive the look is on him. No wonder Macy keeps glancing his way. It's ridiculous how even the goofy boys at this school have game.

"Are there any other rules I should know about?" I ask, just as Mekhi walks up to join us. He grins at me, and I wave back, excited to see him. Things have been so busy since I got back that we haven't had much of a chance to talk.

"The ball has to keep moving the entire time. If you have the ball and pause for longer than five seconds—even if you've just come out of a portal and have no idea where you are—then it's an automatic turnover," Xavier tells me.

"And every player has to have the ball at least once," Eden adds. "If not—"

"The other team wins. Apparently, if you breathe the wrong way, the other team wins," I say, totally disgusted.

"Yeah, but look at it this way," Mekhi tells me as he starts to stretch. "The other team's playing by the exact same rules."

I nod. "Fair enough."

"All right, enough talking!" Flint claps his hands to get everyone's attention. "We're dividing into teams, so for now, it'll be Jaxon, Grace, and me against the rest of you. When Gwen shows up, she can join our team."

He turns and wiggles his brows at me. "Ready to fly, Grace?"

"Not even a little bit." Still, I reach for that platinum thread, and seconds later I'm a gargoyle again, complete with kick-ass wings.

Which they all spend the next five minutes gawking over. As they should. They're totally awesome. Xavier asked how concrete wings fly and Flint smacked him. "Obviously magic."

My grin widens. I've got magical wings.

"We call the ball first," Eden says.

"Why should you get the ball first?" Flint asks indignantly. "There are only three of us!"

"Yeah, and one of you is Jaxon Vega while the other is a gargoyle made out of stone—which, you know, is impervious to heat. Pretty sure you've got a couple of big advantages over there already."

"But you said it vibrates," I tell them. "I'm not immune to that."

Everyone cracks up, even Jaxon. It takes me a second to realize what they're laughing at, and then I blush nonstop.

"So what am I, chopped liver?" Flint jumps in to save me, making a show of going from indignant to *really* indignant in the space of three seconds flat.

Eden looks him over with a huge smirk on her face. "You said it, not me."

"Oh, that's it. Fine, take the ball." He grabs it from Macy and fires it. "I'm going to be feeding it to you in five minutes flat."

"Oh yeah? Try it." She opens her mouth and shoots a giant stream of lightning straight at him. It doesn't hit him, but it does burn off the bottom half of his workout shirt.

Flint yelps and jumps, while the rest of us burst out laughing. Though the female contingent of the group also totally checks out Flint's very nice abs—Eden very much included.

Or maybe not just the female contingent of the group, I realize when I glance over at Jaxon, who is paying pretty close attention as his ex-best friend strips what remains of his shirt off and drops it on the ground, and everyone scatters to take up positions on the field.

"It's a good look for him," I tease.

"What?" Jaxon asks, seeming a little confused.

"I saw you checking him out." I nod toward Flint. "No worries, though. Believe me, I get it."

"I didn't—I wasn't—"

I just laugh and take a note from Flint's playbook and waggle my brows at him.

But when things finally quiet down again and we start to take sides, I lean in to Flint and ask, "Shouldn't I at least *practice* flying before we start actually playing the game?"

62

Gravity Bites

"**D**on't worry about it, Grace," Flint says with a grin. "You've got this."

"I most definitely don't have this!" I yelp. "I've never even tried to fly before!"

"Yeah, but you saw me fly. It's easy." He's taking such long strides that it's hard for me to keep up, but if he's going to throw all these ridiculous pronouncements out, he's at least going to look me in the eye when he does it.

I run to catch up, something that isn't easy to do as a gargoyle, apparently, and finally manage to get in front of him while Jaxon—and Hudson—look on in amusement. The jerks.

"Are you smoking something?" I slam a hand on his chest to make sure I get his attention. "I mean, seriously, are you *actually* high right now? I can't fly, Flint. I've never even *used my wings before*. There is no way you're going to just throw a hot ball at me and tell me to fly and think I'm going to just take off.

"So park your ego at the door for ten minutes, give me some flying pointers and a few minutes to practice, and *then* let's ground them into dust. Otherwise, I'm leaving and I'm not coming back."

Flint's eyes keep getting wider and wider the longer I talk, and by the time I'm done, he's actually looking a little shamefaced—an expression that only gets worse when he realizes Jaxon watched the entire exchange.

"Yeah, of course. I'm sorry, Grace. Eden and I have this competitive thing going and it gets the best of me every time."

"Don't worry about it." I smile to soften my earlier frustration. "Just tell them we need fifteen minutes and then teach me how to fly, okay?"

Jaxon laughs. "I'll go tell them they get to try to beat just me for now," he says with a surreptitious wink at me, "while you two figure out how to defy gravity."

Flint watches him go, a pensive frown on his face. But when he turns back to me, he's all smiles. "So, flying's easy. You just need to think—"

"Happy thoughts?" I ask dryly.

He cracks up. "You're a gargoyle, not Peter Pan."

I roll my eyes at him, but I don't think he sees it, as we're hustling to the other side of the field now. "*That* was pretty much my point."

"What I was going to say is that you need to *think* about flying."

"So, like, I think about flapping my wings?" To my amazement, they flap back and forth even as I say the words.

"Oh my God, Flint!" I grab him, stopping him from taking another step, and jump up and down. "Did you see that?"

He's grinning hugely now. "Of course I saw it!"

I crane my neck around so I can see it, and then I do it again. And again. And again. "Oh my God! They work! They really work!"

Flint is full-on laughing his ass off now, but I don't care. I'm so excited that my wings work that I keep hopping around and making them flap as hard as I can.

Even Hudson is laughing now, but it's *with* me, not at me. "You look good flapping your wings like that."

"I do, don't I?" I flap them again, just because I can. "I have wings, Hudson! And they work!"

"Hell yeah, they do." He shakes his head with a big smile.

I turn to Flint. "Okay, now what do I do?"

"You just flap super hard until you get off the ground."

"Really?" I ask, my eyes going wide as I start to try that.

He bursts out laughing, so hard that for a moment he can't even talk. I'm not sure what the joke is until he finally recovers enough to put a hand on my shoulder. "No, stop," he says. "I was joking, Grace."

"Oh." I blush a little, but I'm having too much fun to be embarrassed for long. *Plus, I want to fly!* "So tell me what to do. For real this time!"

"Okay. What you want to do is think about flying. Not about falling, not about being able to move your wings, not about getting off the ground. Just think about flying. About catching the wind."

He looks around, then seems to get an idea, because he reaches out and grabs my hand. "Let's go to the bleachers."

"Are you kidding me? I'm not jumping off the bleachers the first time I try to fly! No effing way."

"We're not jumping from the bleachers, for God's sake. You're not a baby bird."

Hudson snort-laughs at this, then fades ahead of us, so that he's lounging on the bleachers with a huge, shit-eating grin before we even get close.

Once we're there, Flint stops at the railing right in front of the first row of bleachers. "Although, to be fair, if you did jump off the bleachers and started to fall, Jaxon and I would absolutely have your back. So there's nothing to worry about, right? Just a simple walk in the park...but, you know, in the sky," he teases.

My eyes go wide. "Says the guy who five minutes ago told me I'd figure flying out in the middle of the game."

He waggles his brows. "To be fair, I still stand by that analysis. But let's try this instead."

Then, with absolutely no warning at all, he picks me up and puts me on top of the railing in front of the first bleacher. Unlike when I'm in my human form, lifting me like this actually strains his biceps and has him grunting a little.

Which only makes it worse when he lets go of me—keeping my balance on a railing is one thing. Keeping my balance when I'm stone is something else entirely. And it's only sheer strength of will that stops me from shrieking when he lets go. But I manage it, because there's *no way* I'm going to act like a hysterical little human caught in the middle of a bunch of big, bad paranormals.

Jaxon deserves better for a mate, but more importantly, I deserve better, too.

So instead of letting out the scream that wells in my throat the second I'm standing on my own, I swallow it down deep. Then ask, "What next?"

Flint looks more than a little uncertain when he says, "Jump?"

"Is that a question or a command?" I ask.

"Umm, both?"

"I thought you said you'd give me flying lessons! This"—I gesture around me—"is not flying lessons!"

"I meant once you were in the air. I do the best triple loops in the school." He grins.

I shake my head. "Yeah, because triple loops are what I need right now, Flint."

"Look, I'm doing my best, okay?" He chuckles and steps back a few steps. "Now, will you at least try it my way?"

I place my hands on my hips and raise one pointed brow. "And what way is that exactly?"

"Just jump and then..." He gestures with his arms.

"Flap my wings?"

"Yes. But don't think about your wings. Think about—"

"Flying." I sigh. "Yeah, I got that much before." I look out at the field and the others who are kind of practicing but mostly just looking at me.

Okay, what the hell? Better to fall on my ass than never give it a shot. I take a deep breath, close my eyes.

"Remember, think about flying," Flint tells me, and he's a little farther away than he was a minute ago. I'm not sure if that's because he thinks I'm going to fly or if it's because he thinks I'm going to crash and wants to be out of the blast radius.

It doesn't matter, I tell myself as I try to focus. Nothing does but thinking about flying. The fact that I have no idea how I'm supposed to do that doesn't matter at all.

I'm flying. I'm flying. I'm flying. Flint told me to think about flying, so I'm thinking about flying. I'm flying. Like a bird. Like a plane. Like…okay, bad analogy. I'm flying. I'm fly—

I jump and…land on my stony ass—which, it turns out, doesn't hurt nearly as much as when I fall on my human ass. Thankfully. Though it is definitely more jolting.

"It's also definitely not flying," Hudson teases from where he's still lounging a few feet up on the bleachers.

"Are you okay?" Jaxon asks as he comes jogging over to help me up. "I'm sorry, I was too far away to catch you."

Of course he would think he was supposed to catch me. I shake my head and smile. "No worries. Stone is a good shock absorber."

He laughs. "No, it's not."

"No, it's not," I agree, brushing the grass off my fleece pants. "But I swear it didn't hurt. I'm all right."

"Good." He nods to the railing. "You want to try it again?"

"Not even a little bit."

He lifts a brow. "Going to do it anyway?"

I lift my chin. "Abso-freaking-lutely."

63

There Aren't Enough
Happy Thoughts
in the World

Jaxon holds out a hand. "Let me help you up."

I think about arguing, then decide, why would I? I have no interest in hauling my stony self on top of a three-foot railing. To be honest, I'm not sure I could get my regular self on top of the railing, either.

Two minutes later, I'm back on the ground, and this time my ass *does* hurt.

Three minutes after that, my ass *and* my pride hurt.

"Are you sure I *don't* need to think happy thoughts?" I ask Flint.

He grins. "I mean, you can try, but I don't think that will help, either."

"Yeah, well, the grumpy thoughts sure aren't cutting it."

"No shit." Hudson shakes his head and leans even farther back, placing both his hands behind his head. "Although the entertainment value is priceless."

Flint helps me up this time. "So, fourth time's the charm?"

"Fourth time is let's try something different," Jaxon interjects, taking my hand and pulling me toward the center of the field.

"How am I going to fly out here?" I ask. "Don't I need to start from someplace higher?"

He grins at me. "You *are* going to start from someplace higher."

And then he lifts us up, up, up, until we're hovering close to the roof of the practice field.

"Umm, while I appreciate the ride, it's not flying if you're lifting me up." I have to bite back an honest-to-God snicker as I imagine the two of us floating around up there like a few blimps. Hudson would never let me live it down.

"Guess you'd better fly, then, huh?" Hudson says. "Otherwise, I'm going to live off this for days…"

"Trust me, I won't be lifting you up for long." Jaxon pulls away a little, floating backward until we're no longer touching. "Now, try."

I look down at the ground about fifty feet below and wonder if I really want to try from this height. But trying on the ground didn't work at all, and if there's one thing I do know, it's that Jaxon won't let me fall. So what do I have to lose?

With that in mind, I close my eyes and think *happy thoughts* about flying. I'm not saying it worked, but I am saying that for the first time, my wings start to move—and they do it without my consciously deciding to move them.

It's a weird feeling. Not a bad one, but definitely a weird one. On the ground, I didn't feel much of anything when I was moving my wings, but now that I'm up here, it's a very different story. There's pressure underneath them that I didn't expect, and each time my wings push through, it gives me a little jolt.

"You're still holding me, right?" I ask Jaxon as I start to move forward.

"Absolutely," he answers with a grin that he's trying really hard to hide.

I know it's because I look ridiculous—I keep catching myself stroking my arms out in front of me like doing the breaststroke in midair is actually going to get me somewhere or something.

The absurdity is made worse by the fact that the faster I get my wings to go, the more likely I am to end up bobbing up and down. Which means if I don't get this whole thing figured out soon, I'm going to find myself swimming through the air, all while looking like I'm practicing bizarrely timed evasive maneuvers anytime I want to fly.

Probably not the way I want to go, considering even my mate can't keep a straight face. I can only imagine what Flint and Macy and the others are thinking down below.

"I think we should quit," I tell Jaxon after a few more minutes of attempting to stay semi-vertical and also fly. "I'm never going to get this."

"That's not true. You're already so much better than you were."

"Considering my worst was plummeting off a railing, I feel like you're sugarcoating things."

He grins at me, and though he's several feet away, I swear I feel him caress my face. "One more time," he says. "For me. I've got an idea."

"What's your idea?"

"I'll tell you after. Just go ahead and try."

"Fine," I agree, "But after this, I'm done being today's entertainment. I'll have to find another way to contribute to the team…like being the water/blood girl."

He laughs. "I'm sure it's not going to come to that."

"I'm not."

But I said I would give it one more shot, so I will. I get my wings up to speed, and then I concentrate on moving forward, sans breaststroke.

For a minute, it looks like I'm about to go backward, and then suddenly, I jerk forward. "Oh my God!" I screech, beyond excited… until a few seconds later, I plummet about fifteen feet straight down.

Jaxon catches me, just like he said he would, and then suddenly, I'm flying. Forward. In a straight line.

"I'm doing it!" I shout to Jaxon, who is grinning hugely about twenty feet behind me, still hovering where we started.

"I can see that," he answers.

"I'm flying, Flint!" I shout down below me.

Flint gives me a big grin and a double thumbs-up in return.

"Hudson! I did it! I'm flying!" I whisper excitedly, knowing he can hear me at any distance.

"Yeah, you are." Suddenly, he's floating on his back next to me. "Wanna race to the end of the field?"

"Only if you don't 'let' me win."

He lifts a brow. "Do you know me at all?"

"Good point." I flap my wings extra hard, just to see what will happen. Then squeak with delight as I move ahead.

Hudson laughs, then pulls back even with me a few seconds later. "Ready?" he asks.

I nod. "On your mark."

He rolls over. "Get set."

I get myself into position, then yell, "Go!"

We shoot through the sky, and though a part of me knows he's not actually flying next to me, for these few seconds it feels like he is—and it's amazing. Exhilarating. Intoxicating.

We race through the air, going faster and faster and faster, until we hit the finish line together. I pull up, do a quick loop-the-loop that leaves me breathless and laughing, while Hudson does a front somersault.

Down below, Macy and Flint and Mekhi are cheering, and so is everyone else. I wave to them, then glance back at Hudson to share my joy, only to realize that he's gone. Or, more accurately, that he was never there at all.

Suddenly, the race doesn't feel quite so amazing. And neither does anything else, though I have no idea why.

"Hudson?" I reach out, wondering if he's gone back to wherever he goes when he doesn't want to talk to me.

"I'm here," he answers in my thoughts. *"You looked great out there."*

"*We* looked great out there."

"Maybe."

I can feel him starting to say more, but before he can, Jaxon is right in front of me, wrapping his arms around me in a celebratory hug. "That was awesome!"

I gaze up at his face beaming down at me. "It was, right? I can't believe I did that. Can you?"

"Of course I can. I'm beginning to figure out that you can do anything, Grace."

"Umm, no. But tell me the truth. How much of that was me and how much was you?"

Jaxon grins. "That was one hundred percent you."

"At the end?" I ask, eyes wide as I think about the loop-the-loop I turned.

"No, the whole time. It was all you. That was my last idea. To let you go and see what happened if I wasn't holding you back."

64

Pardon My Existential Crisis

There's something in the way Jaxon talks about holding me back—or, in this case, not holding me back—that makes me nervous. I don't know what it is, considering he's never been anything but supportive, but it niggles at me for the rest of the afternoon as Flint and the others teach me Ludares's rules and tactics.

Or, should I say, attempt to teach me, as every single person on the field has their own idea of the right way to play the game—which, I figure, should make for a really interesting team strategy.

"It's all about the portals," Xavier tells me at one point. "Sure, they're going to screw you over sometimes, but you've got to use them. You hit the right one and you win the game, just like that." He snaps his fingers to illustrate. "Plus, the crowd loves it!"

"The crowd also loves when you end up surrounded by the enemy and all alone as the ball burns the shit out of you," Eden contradicts with a hard eye roll. "It's about getting the ball down the field, Grace. You do that and they'll love you, no matter what. And portals may be flashy, but a straight shot makes one hell of an impression, too."

"For now," my cousin tells me when we're walking to our positions later in the afternoon, "the most important thing is that we work together and build a team. If we do that, the rest will come."

"No mercy!" Flint tells Jaxon, Gwen, and me as we get into our last huddle of the day. Gwen joined up after her test, and I have to admit, I'm grateful to have a witch on our side now. Thoughts of Macy turning all of us to turtles have been dancing in my head for hours. "When it comes to Ludares, mercy is for weaklings. We're going to go into these last plays and *crush* them into dust."

"What if I don't want to crush them into dust?" I ask, winking at Jaxon, who is rolling his eyes behind Flint's back.

"Do it anyway," Flint orders. "Just stomp those pretty gargoyle feet of yours all over them."

Yeah. I don't bother to tell him that's not going to happen, but I'm pretty sure he can tell from my face. And from the fact that, by the end of that round, Eden stomps her Nikes all over *him*.

We play all day—turns out Flint charmed a few witches in the kitchen into making us a picnic lunch—and by the time it gets dark, I'm exhausted and limping more than a little. But I'm also feeling pretty good about my ability to fly a ball down the field, so I'm definitely calling it a win.

Jaxon walks Macy and me back to our room around nine, and I start to invite him in to watch a movie or something. But he's looking a little worse for wear, the energy burst I gave him this morning having obviously worn off.

Because I know him and his ridiculous pride, I don't offer to give him another boost. Instead, I wait for Macy to slip into our room before I hug him close, kiss his neck, and send a spurt of energy down the mating bond before he even knows what I'm doing.

He pulls away immediately. "You've got to stop doing that."

"I'm not going to stop doing that. Not when you so obviously need it."

"I'll be fine," he tells me, resting his forehead against mine. "This isn't the first time in my life I've been tired and had a lot on my mind."

I know he's thinking of the time he and Hudson fought, and my chest feels tight. "This time, things will end differently. I promise."

Jaxon gives a not-altogether-pleasant laugh and says, "Yeah, well, let's hope, for his sake."

"Besides, I need you in tip-top shape," I tell him, sliding my hands into the back pockets of his jeans as I snuggle close.

"Yeah?" He grins. "Me too." And then he leans down to kiss me, but just before our lips connect, Hudson groans dramatically.

"I keep trying to change the channel, but it won't work."

Even though I know it's a ploy, I can't help biting anyway. That's the magic—and the horror—of Hudson. *Change what channel?* I demand.

"This one." He mimes pressing the button on a remote. "So much kissing, when what I could really use is a good old-fashioned car chase. Or an assassination attempt. Or, you know, 'a plague on both your houses!' Something, anything, but this"—he waves his hand at Jaxon and me still snuggled up together—"all day, every day."

Seriously? This is where you want to go after that No Exit *BS you pulled on the field?*

"I don't see what the problem is," he says loftily. "It's a great piece of literature."

Yeah, 'cause that's why you were reading it. I pull away from Jaxon with a regretful smile. "Apparently Hudson has decided to rejoin the party."

For just a second, Jaxon looks angry. Like, really angry, but then it melts away and he gives me a rueful smile. "I'm really looking forward to the day he disappears for good."

"Yeah, me too," I answer. And I mean it, I do. I really am looking forward to having my mind and my body back for my exclusive use. But still, there's something in Jaxon's statement, and his voice, that doesn't feel quite right. I just can't put my finger on what it is.

Maybe that's why, when he leans in to drop a quick kiss on my lips, I dodge and give him a big hug instead. Or maybe it's just my overactive imagination, because when he hugs me back, arms so tight around me that for a minute—just a minute—I feel safe and whole and right, something I haven't felt in far too long.

I glance at Hudson and notice fury in his gaze before he has a chance to hide it. He's angrier than I've ever seen him. Angry and something more—hurt. His gaze narrows on Jaxon just as Jaxon seems to almost stumble, reaching out to put one hand on the wall beside him.

"Whoa." Jaxon gives me a half smile. "I think I'm more tired than I thought."

Something isn't right. I can feel it. But before I can ask him, he straightens and gives me a confident smile.

"See you in the morning?" he asks me when he finally pulls away.

"Yeah. I'll meet you guys in the cafeteria for breakfast before class."

"Sounds good." He starts to turn away but stops at the last second and says, "Give this to Hudson for me, will you?" And then he flips up his middle finger.

"Very mature," Hudson drawls, still leaning against the door.

"You just did," I tell Jaxon.

"Oh yeah?" The news gives him a little bounce in his step. "Then here's a couple more." This time he uses both hands to flip his brother off before finally turning and walking away.

I watch him go, and Hudson pretends to play some very sad music on an air violin in the background. "And the villain fades away into obscurity, never to be seen or heard from again..."

"He's not the villain of this story." I frown. "You are. And Jaxon's not going anywhere."

"Yeah." Hudson heaves an exaggerated sigh and steps away from the door. "That's what you keep telling me."

"Aren't you tired?" I ask him as I let myself into my room. "Go take a nap or something."

"Not tired at all. I napped all day just so we could spend the evening together." He gives me a shit-eating grin. "I feel great."

And just like that, all the puzzle pieces fit together and I figure out the horrible truth of what just happened to my boyfriend. "You're draining Jaxon's energy, aren't you? How are you doing it?" I demand, but then it comes to me. "Oh my God. You're using my mating bond to drain my mate? Are you serious?"

He holds both hands up. "It's not like that."

My stomach rolls. How could I not have guessed it before now? I can't believe I missed it. I was actually starting to *trust* Hudson. I feel light-headed and queasy.

"I don't have a choice. This whole *me being alive but not actually alive yet* means I have to take energy from somewhere, and for whatever reason the universe hooked me up to your mating bond. Probably so that I could take energy from both of you instead of just you, so I wouldn't overwhelm your system."

"Wait a minute." His explanation is yet another shock to my system. "So you're feeding off me, too?"

I'll give him credit. He doesn't lie. Instead, he looks me straight in the eye and says, "Yes."

"This whole time?" I ask, incredulous. "You've been feeding off Jaxon and me since we got here?"

"Pretty much, yeah. But I'm taking way more from him than I am from you."

"You say that like it's a good thing...and not an absolutely terrifying one." I shake my head to try to clear it. "Why would you do that? Why would you risk hurting him like that?"

"Because he has more to spare. And I'm not hurting him." He sighs. "I'm just borrowing some of his life force so I can stay alive."

"Which means what? That you're pulling his life force out of him... like Darth Vader?" I demand. "Oh my God. You're deliberately hurting him and it's all my fault."

"It's *no one's* fault," he answers. "Jaxon has more power than you do, so I automatically get more power from him."

"What about what just happened?" I demand, eyes narrowed. "When he stumbled? I know you did something to him. What did you do?"

He sighs. "I took an extra burst of energy. It wasn't even a big one."

I narrow my eyes at him. "It felt like a big one. I thought he was going to fall in the hallway."

He doesn't answer for the longest time, and when he does, he sounds totally cavalier. "Normally I'm careful not to take too much from either of you. Maybe this time I wasn't so careful."

"I knew it!" Anger rockets through me. "Why would you do that to him?"

"He's fine," Hudson tells me, voice and eyes completely flat.

"How do you know?"

"Because he has more power. He can take it."

"Because you say so?" I demand, furious and scared at the same time. What if something happens to Jaxon and it's because of this? Because of me? It's a terrifying thought.

"Would you rather I fed off all of *your* energy?" Hudson asks, brows raised. "Or would you rather I didn't feed at all and just died?"

I don't answer him, but that just means he draws his own conclusions, his eyes going bleak for one brief second before his normal sardonic look returns. "I guess that's exactly what you'd prefer. Too bad we're tied together, then, huh? All your problems would be solved if you could just let me die."

65

No Exit: A Biography

It's the first time Hudson's death has ever been put so starkly before, and I don't know what to say to him—or even what to feel. I mean, Jaxon's arguments for killing him were real and valid and important, and I understand why he did it. I also understand that it was the hardest thing he's ever had to do, whether he admits it to himself or not.

"Oh yeah. Of course. Let's feel sorry for *Jaxon* in this equation. I'm so sorry it hurt his *feelings* to murder me."

Everything about that sentence sets me off, because no. Just no. He doesn't get to play the victim here.

"You really should stop trying to rewrite history," I tell him. "It's not like Jaxon just woke up one morning and decided to kill you. You caused hundreds of paranormals to attack one another. For *fun*. For some ridiculous plan of born-vampire supremacy."

"No." Hudson glares at me. "No, no, no. I have done a lot of shitty things in my life, and I take responsibility for every single one of them. But I *do not* take responsibility for that." He begins pacing around my room.

I don't have the energy to process what he just said. My mind is still racing, remembering all the times over the last few weeks that Jaxon's looked tired. And all because of Hudson feeding on him, using the mating bond. I know he doesn't mean to hurt Jaxon or me, but that doesn't make it any easier to hear. Not when I'm responsible for the fact that something—someone—is hurting my mate right in front of me. I suddenly feel sick and stumble over to sit on the edge of my bed. I have to fix this.

My head feels like it's going to explode. Then again, for the first time, so does my heart. I close my eyes and reach inside me for the dual-toned mating bond string I've become so familiar with over the last few days. I take it into my hand and squeeze, sending wave after wave of energy to Jaxon, remembering every single time he had dark circles under his eyes and I'd thought he just needed sleep. The tight lines I'd ignored around his smile. The faded black of his bottomless eyes.

This was all my fault. So many times I'd focused on my own problems instead of seeing how my mate was suffering and trying to hide it—*right in front of me.* And that's when I realize something else... Jaxon knew Hudson was feeding on the bond. And he didn't say anything.

My chest feels cleaved open. *He didn't want to make me feel guilty. And more, he didn't want to make me have to choose.*

"You need to stop."

I don't think I can. Because this is bad. This is really, really bad.

"Grace!" Hudson's voice thunders through my head with an urgency I can't ignore. "Stop!"

"You're the one who got me thinking about all of this and now you want me to stop?" I demand incredulously. "Screw you."

"I mean the energy!" he tells me as he puts an insistent hand on top of mine. "You can't give him any more or you're going to be drained. You need to stop."

He's right. I feel like I could sleep for a year. So I let go of the black-and-green string, though it leaves me feeling even more bereft.

"Goddamn it," Hudson growls. "You're going to kill yourself if you're not careful. You can't just play around with this stuff."

Before I can answer, he feeds me a burst of his own energy to make up for some of what I gave Jaxon.

"You didn't have to do that," I tell him, even as I feel his power surging through my veins, grounding me. Making me feel solid again.

"Someone has to," he snarls, "since you seem incapable of thinking of yourself in any given situation."

"That's not true!" I tell him.

"It sure feels true. And the fact that my brother lets you get away with it is a bunch of bullshit on his part, too. That's not what the mating bond is supposed to be about."

"Oh, really?" I stare at him incredulously. "Taking care of each other *isn't* what the bond is about?"

"Each other being the operative words in that sentence," Hudson snaps.

My phone dings, and I pull it out of my pocket and read the message from Jaxon:

Jaxon: Please don't ever do that again.

Three dots blink and then disappear, then start blinking again, as though he's reconsidering what he was about to text. Finally, my phone dings again.

Jaxon: Thank you

I text back a quick love you and good night, then put my phone away.

"He *thanked you* for giving him your strength?!" Hudson throws his hands in the air. "Quite the mate you've got there, Grace."

I whirl on him. "You know what, you've got a hell of a lot of nerve talking to me about the mating bond when you were okay with letting your mate *die* to bring *you* back."

Rage explodes within me, pure, towering rage that threatens to melt every single part of me. It's mind-numbing, stroke-inducing, completely catastrophic, and for a brief moment all I can think about is tearing the world apart.

Seconds later, it disappears, just like that. And that's when I realize, it wasn't my fury that I was feeling at all. It was Hudson's, and it was incandescent.

It takes a few more seconds before he's willing—or able—to talk, and when he does, it's in a voice that is eminently reasonable and twice as terrifying because of it.

"First of all," he tells me, "I didn't ask Lia for a damn thing. Do you think, for one second, I wanted to end up here, like this? A prisoner in your head, a front-row spectator to whatever the hell it is you and Jaxon have going on? Alive but not?

"Second, Lia *was not* my mate. And third, you have a hell of a lot of nerve accusing me of anything when you have no fucking clue what you're talking about."

And just like that, my brain melts all over again. This time, it's not from anger, though. This time, it's because the pain underlying all that fury is all-encompassing—and impossible to witness without flinching.

It burns away my own anger, leaves me feeling bereft and anxious and like there's something I just don't understand.

The fact that I want to understand is shocking enough. The fact that I want to help is mind-blowing. Except, also not.

"Hudson?" I reach out quietly, hoping to find a way to break through the pain.

But even as I call his name, I know that he won't answer. I know that, trapped in my head or not, he's already gone.

66

Frenemies Are Forever

Once Hudson disappears, I'm at loose ends. I have so many thoughts, so many feelings, that I can't process them all, so I end up pacing around my dorm room for, like, ten minutes. Eventually, I figure out that he's not coming back anytime soon, so I do the only thing I can think of to help myself get to sleep. I take a hot shower, hoping, if nothing else, that I can drown all the bizarre feelings roiling around inside me.

After a long shower that does absolutely nothing to settle my nerves or my stomach, I put on a tank and pajama shorts before heading back into the bedroom. Macy's there, sitting cross-legged on her bed with her earbuds in and a notebook open on her lap. She waves at me but doesn't try to talk, which means she must be studying.

It works for me, because I don't have much to say right now. I have so many emotions whirling around inside me that it's a miracle I can even think, let alone speak.

But then I realize Hudson must have come back while I was in the shower, too, and somehow that makes the emotions better and also worse at the same time. I don't question it, though. Not now.

He's slouched in the chair by my desk, the book he was reading earlier open on his lap but his gaze trained on my every movement. He looks wiped, and one glance tells me he feels the same way I do—too raw to want to discuss what was said earlier.

"So, *No Exit* isn't quite the scintillating blockbuster you made it out to be?" I ask archly.

Hudson shoots me a relieved look. "I've already read it. Several times. Existentialism is so…"

"Last century?"

"Please, have you seen the world news lately?" he asks dryly.

"Good point," I agree as I walk over to the bathroom sink and squeeze toothpaste onto my toothbrush.

When I've finished brushing my teeth and putting my dirty clothes in the hamper, I gratefully flop myself down on the bed. Training for the Ludares tournament with the others was more fun than I've had in a long time. But now, after that and sending Jaxon energy, I'm totally exhausted.

And I'm pretty sure I have a couple of major muscle groups that are going to hurt a whole lot tomorrow. Flying definitely uses muscles I didn't even know I had.

"Did you have fun?" Macy asks, taking off her headphones the second I get settled.

"So much fun. Did you?"

"Oh my God, yes! I can't believe I'm on a team with Jaxon and Flint and Gwen and Mekhi! I never imagined I'd find myself on such a badass team my first year being able to play. We're totally going to win this tournament."

"We *have* to win the tournament," I remind her. "We need that bloodstone."

"We will. Don't even worry about it." She pauses before clearing her throat. "So did you, umm…" She coughs. "I mean, did you…" She coughs again, then finally manages to ask, "What did you think of Xavier?"

And because Hudson's diabolical nature has obviously rubbed off on me, I respond with, "Xavier who?"

Hudson snort-laughs but must realize I plan to chat with my

cousin for a bit because, with an arched brow, *No Exit* magically appears in his hands once more, and he opens it up to somewhere in the middle.

Macy's mouth drops open at my question. Like, literally drops open, and she sits there for what feels like ten seconds just staring at me, mouth ajar. "Xavier!" she finally says. "You know, the guy in the gray shirt? With the green eyes and the funny jokes?"

"No." I shake my head, give her a puzzled look. "Doesn't ring a bell."

"How can it not ring a bell?" She sits up, all aflutter. "We just spent, like, ten hours with him! Xavier."

"You know, you're a terrible person," Hudson says with a very British sniff as he continues to read. "Truly horrible."

"Xavier," I say musingly. "Xavier. Xavier. Xavier."

"Yes!" she squawks. "Xavier! You know—"

"Do you mean the great guy with the gorgeous face who you were making googly eyes at all day?" I ask slyly. "The one who spent an awful lot of time showing off his muscles right in front of you? Yeah, I might have a general idea of who Xavier is."

"Oh my God!" She throws a pillow at me, and when I dodge, she follows up with a stuffed animal, another pillow, and then one of her favorite bear slippers. "How could you do that to me! I thought you really hadn't noticed."

"How could I *not* notice him?" I chuckle. "He spent the whole day making everybody laugh and trying desperately to impress you."

"He wasn't actually trying to impress me," she says, looking shy for what might be the first time since I got to Katmere. "Was he?"

"Oh my God, yes. At one point, Hudson and I were both convinced he was going to strip down and start flexing his abs right in front of you."

"His abs and everything else," Hudson adds dryly, looking up long enough to wink at me.

"Really?" Macy leans forward excitedly, even as she clutches another pillow on her lap. "You think so?"

"I know so. He was totally showing off for you. And I told you, I wasn't the only one who noticed. Hudson asked several times if we were sure he was a wolf and not a peacock."

My cousin laughs delightedly, then says, "You mean Jaxon."

"What?" I ask, confused.

"Jaxon said all those things, right? Not Hudson."

"No," I tell her, even more confused by the question. "It was definitely Hudson, not Jaxon, who was paying attention to what was happening between you two—and who made all the comments."

"Oh." She gives me a weird look. "I didn't realize you and Hudson..."

"What?" I ask when she trails off, looking awkward.

She clears her throat the way she always does when she's nervous. Then says, "I guess I just didn't realize you and Hudson had gotten so...close."

67

Talk Darcy to Me

"Close?" I repeat as her words send a shock wave of...something through me. I croak out, "We aren't close."

"You aren't?" she asks, and now she's the one who sounds confused. "Of course not!"

"Ouch!" Hudson says, turning a page in his book.

"Hush," I snap back before focusing on Macy. "I mean, we talk, but that's because he never shuts up."

"Umm, double ouch," Hudson interjects, slamming the book closed and walking over to the window. Suddenly, I'm worried our mutual truce might disappear again, and I honestly don't have it in me to go another round with His Royal Snarkiness. At least not right now.

"I mean, yeah, he makes me laugh sometimes," I blunder on. "And is strangely charming on occasion. And he notices everything about me and the world around us. And yeah, sometimes he helps me when I'm least expecting it, like when I was nervous about changing into a gargoyle or when I couldn't figure out how to light the candles in the library or when I was—" I break off as I realize what I'm saying. What I sound like.

And that Macy is staring at me all over again, the surprise and discomfort replaced by abject, slack-jawed shock. It doesn't help that Hudson has suddenly gotten just as quiet. More, I can sense him deep inside me, still and silent and *listening*.

"It's not what you think," I tell her finally.

"Okay," she answers with a nod, and it's totally not what I'm expecting. Then she stands up and crosses over to her pajama drawer. "I think I'm going to take a shower, wash off some of today's grime."

"You don't want to talk about Xavier some more?" I ask as she heads toward the bathroom.

She smiles at that, a quick grin that lights up her whole face and finally breaks through the seriousness that's been there for the last couple of minutes. "There's not much to say yet," she tells me. "Except...you liked him, right?"

"I really did. He seems great. And perfect for you."

"Yeah." She nods, the smile slowly dropping off her face. "I think so, too."

As the bathroom door closes behind her, I go over our conversation in my head, wondering what could possibly have made Macy act so strangely. But there's nothing there, except for her weird reaction to the fact that Hudson and I talk.

But seriously, what am I supposed to do? The guy lives in my head. Should I just ignore everything he says?

"*Please* don't do that," Hudson tells me from his favorite spot near the window. I think he likes it there because it makes him look like a brooding Brontë hero.

"As if," he answers with another one of those proper British sniffs. "Brontë heroes are weak and pathetic and strange. I'm definitely an Austen hero." He gives me an arch look as he lifts his chin and sticks out his chest. "Mr. Darcy himself, perhaps?"

I crack up, exactly as he intends, because how can I not? He looks so ridiculous posing there that I can't help laughing and laughing and laughing. Especially when he adds a mock-offended face.

"Don't tell anyone," I say when I finally stop laughing. "But I've never been a Darcy fan."

"What? That's blasphemy, I tell you, blasphemy!"

And now he's laughing with me, his face all lit up, blue eyes shining. And I don't get it. I just don't get it.

"What don't you get?" he asks, the laughter fading away to be replaced by a serious look that I can't quite interpret. Then again, maybe he feels the same way about me.

"The fact that you can be like this with me and yet also be so evil. It doesn't make sense."

"That's because you don't want it to make sense," he tells me, and this time there's no mocking in the offended look he gives me as the rest of my sentence must register. "*Evil?* You think I'm fucking *evil*?"

And just like that, our mutual decision not to have this conversation fades into mist. "Well, how else would you describe what you did?"

"Necessary," he answers, shaking his head like he can't even believe we're having this conversation. Then again, maybe I can't, either.

"Necessary?" I repeat flatly. "You really think killing all those people was necessary?"

"Don't do that," he tells me. "Don't judge me when you don't know what you're talking about. When you weren't there. Am I proud of what I did? Not even a little bit. Would I do it again? You're damn straight I would. Sometimes you have to do horrible, awful, terrifying things in order to prevent something even worse from happening."

"Is that what you think you were doing?" I ask.

"I know that's what I was doing. The fact that you don't believe me doesn't make it any less true. It just means that you don't know shite." He shoves a hand through his hair and turns to look back out the window. "Then again, why should I be surprised? My baby brother doesn't know anything, either, and yet you trust him over me every single time."

"What do you want me to say? That I trust you more than Jaxon? That I believe you over my mate?"

"Your mate." He gives a sharp bark of laughter that sends chills down my spine, though I don't know why. "Yeah. Why would you believe me over *your mate*?"

"You know what? That's not fair. You want to pretend that it's just your word versus his, but the whole school was so scared of you that they were literally plotting to kill me at the mere idea that Lia might be able to bring you back from the dead. People don't do that just because they don't like somebody, no matter what you want me to believe."

"People fear what they don't understand. They always have and they always will."

"What does that mean?" I whisper, willing him to turn around and face me. "*Tell me*, Hudson."

He does, but when our eyes meet, there's something terrible in his. Something dark and desperate and so blindingly painful that I feel it nearly tear me in two.

"You think *Jaxon* has power?" he whispers to me in a voice that somehow fills up the whole room. "You don't have a clue what real power is, Grace. If you did, if you knew what I could do, you wouldn't have to ask me these questions, because you'd already know the answers."

68

The Truth Hurts

My heart wedges in my throat at the certainty in his voice, at the darkness and the horror he doesn't even try to hold back.

There's a part of me that wants to ask him to explain, but there's another, bigger part of me that's terrified of the answer.

So I don't say anything. Instead, I just lay on my bed, Macy's forgotten pillow clutched to my chest, and listen to the sound of the water running in her shower.

For the longest time, Hudson doesn't say anything, either. He just stands by the window, looking out at the dimly lit grounds.

Silence stretches between us, as fraught and frozen as the tundra in winter, untouched by even the smallest ray of light or warmth. It's so cold that it's painful, so empty that it echoes inside me, reverberating off every part of me until there's nothing that doesn't ache.

Nothing that doesn't burn.

I'm close to the breaking point, desperate to say something—anything—to shatter the icy desert between us, but Hudson cracks first.

"You know, you really were adorable when you were five."

It's the last thing I expect him to say, and it has me shooting up in bed as surprise replaces the strange hurt I've been wallowing in. "What does *that* mean?"

"It means you looked adorable when you smiled with your two

front teeth missing. I love that the first one fell out but that you knocked the second one out when you went head over handlebars two weeks later."

"How do you know that?" I whisper.

"You told me."

"No." I shake my head. "I never tell anyone that story." Because if I did, I'd have to explain about how that same front tooth ended up growing in really strange and gnarly because the baby tooth was knocked out too early, and before I got braces, everyone used to make fun of me for it—which is why beavers are still my least favorite animal to this day.

"Well, you told *me*," he answers, sounding incredibly pleased with that fact. "And now I'm watching the home movies, live and in color."

"What kind of home movies?" I ask warily.

"The kind where you look adorable in that navy polka dot dress you used to love to spin around the living room in. I particularly like the matching bow."

Oh my God. "Are you in my memories?"

"Yes, of course." He shakes his head, but his eyes are soft and the smile on his mouth is even softer. "You really were an incredibly cute kid."

"You can't do that!" I tell him. "You can't just go into my memories and look at whatever you want."

"Sure I can. They are just lying around, after all."

"They're not just 'lying around.' They're inside my *head*!"

"Yeah, and so am I." He holds his hands up in an *obviously* kind of gesture. "So you see what I mean about them just being here, right?"

"Seriously?"

"Umm, yeah. The bunny outfit when you were six is also one of my favorites."

"Oh my God." I pull Macy's pillow tightly over my head and wonder if it's possible to actually smother myself with rainbow fur. Not that that seems like such a bad idea right now.

"Why are you doing this to me?" I groan as I rack my brain, trying to imagine what horrible, humiliating memories he might run across at any second. I know there aren't actually that many, but right now it feels like the supply is limitless.

"I don't know, even I have to say that you've got a few doozies," he tells me. "That one with the chicken when you were in third grade was pretty embarrassing."

"First of all, it was a rooster. And second of all, he was rabid."

"Chickens can't get rabies," Hudson tells me with an amused smirk.

"What? Of course they can."

"No, they can't." He laughs. "Rabies only affects mammals. Chickens are birds, therefore no rabies."

"What do you know anyway?" I demand, flopping over on my side. "What are you, the Chicken Whisperer all of a sudden?"

"Yes," he answers, totally deadpan. "That's me, absolutely. Hudson Vega, world-renowned chicken whisperer. How did you know?"

"Oh, shut up," I groan and throw the pillow at him, but it doesn't actually connect. Of course it doesn't, because he's not really standing by the window. He's in my head, watching *home movies*. I grab another pillow to dive face-first into and moan, "You're such a pain in my ass, you know that? Giant. Enormous. Massive."

"Wow. How did I miss the memory of you swallowing a thesaurus? I should probably get right on finding that one. Maybe it's next to the one where you lost your bikini top at La Jolla Cove? You remember, right? You were thirteen and had to get your mom to bring you a towel while you waded neck-deep in the water."

"I hate you."

He grins. "No, you don't."

"Yes, I do," I insist, even though I know I sound like a cranky toddler.

His laugh dies away. "Yeah, maybe you do, at that." He sighs and seems to consider his words carefully before he continues. "You know I'm only looking at the memories you already shared with me, right?"

"That can't be true," I answer. "There's no way I tell anyone about my tooth. Or the bikini top. Or—" I stop myself before I can blurt anything else out.

"Or the time you threw up all over your kindergarten teacher's shoes?" he asks quietly.

"Why would I tell you these things? I don't tell them to anyone. Not even Heather or Macy know about most of them."

"I think that's something you need to ask yourself, isn't it? If you hate me this much, why would you tell me all these things?"

I don't have an answer for him. Hell, I don't even have an answer for myself. Maybe that's why I roll over and face the wall. Because suddenly, it feels like there's a whole lot I don't know.

The darkness is back, the yawning chasm that I've been trying to push my way through since I became human again. Only this time, I don't just see the emptiness. Instead, I see the wreckage, the destruction, the total wasteland of what is…and more, what could have—maybe even should have—been.

It hurts so much more than I expected it would.

Hudson doesn't disturb me again. But he does finally walk away from the window and slump down on the floor next to me, his back resting against the edge of my bed.

I keep my eyes closed, and suddenly, right behind my lids, a different memory begins to play. This one is of two dark-haired little boys, the older no more than ten years old, and both dressed in what look to be period costumes in the middle of a dark, tapestry-filled room. A giant table dominates the center of the space, with huge, elaborately carved wooden chairs tucked in all around it.

Standing beside the table is one of the little boys, his blue eyes filled with tears as he begs, "No, Mummy, no! Please don't take him. Please don't take him! Please don't take him!" He just keeps saying it over and over, and I can feel my chest growing tighter with each word.

"I have to take him," she answers in a cold, clipped voice. "Now, stop your crying and say your goodbyes, or we'll leave without them."

The little boy doesn't stop crying, but he does stop begging as he walks across the room to the younger boy—this one with dark, confused eyes. The blue-eyed boy hugs him and then fades across the room to grab something from the table before fading back to the other boy, a small, wooden horse gripped in his tiny hands.

He gives the other boy the toy and whispers, "I made him for you and named him Jax, so you wouldn't forget his name. I love you." He glances up at his mother before adding in a voice so raw, my heart breaks, "Don't forget me, Jax."

"Okay, that's enough," his mother tells him. "Go finish your studies. I'll be back for dinner, and I'll quiz you on them."

His mother and the dark-eyed boy turn and leave the other little boy all alone in the room. As the door clicks shut behind them, he falls to his knees, sobbing the way only a child can. With his whole body and heart and soul. The devastation, the pain, tears through me like an avalanche.

Just then, a man in a suit walks into the room and towers over the boy. Then smiles. "Use the pain, Hudson. It will make you stronger."

The child turns to look at the man, and a chill suddenly slides down my spine. The hatred in his gaze should belong to someone much older, and it has my breath catching in my throat. The boy narrows his eyes on his father, and everything goes still—the man, the child, the very air they breathe. And then everything explodes into particles. The table. The chairs. The rug. Everything but the man, whose smile grows wider.

"Fantastic. I'll tell your mother to get you a puppy tomorrow." And then he turns and leaves the room, leaving the boy on the hardwood floor, with the carpet disintegrated now, the splinters cutting into his knees.

He could have destroyed his father as easily as the chairs, but he couldn't bring himself to do it. He wouldn't be what his father wanted him to be. A killer.

And then the memory fades away as easily as it came.

Oh my God. "Hudson—"

"Stop," he tells me so matter-of-factly that I almost start to doubt what I just saw. At least until he says, "I don't have many childhood memories, at least not ones that a human would understand, so my pickings were fairly slim. But it only seemed fair that I show you something after all the ones that you've shown me. I mean, you've seen it before, but you don't remember, so…"

"You showed me this before?" I ask him as I surreptitiously wipe the tears off my cheeks.

He laughs, but there's no humor in the sound. "I showed you everything before."

The emptiness in those words echoes inside me, and I close my eyes, unsure of what to say to him. Unsure, even, if I can believe him, though I find myself wanting to. Badly.

"Hudson—"

"You're exhausted, Grace," he tells me as he stands up, and I would swear that I felt his hand brush across my hair. "Sleep now."

There's so much I want to say to him, words on the tip of my tongue that I suddenly don't know how to voice. So I do what he says. I close my eyes and let myself drift away.

But right before sleep claims me, I find a way to say at least one of the things that I want to. "You know I don't want you to die, right?"

Hudson freezes, then sighs wearily. "I know, Grace."

"But I can't let Jaxon die, either," I tell him. "I can't."

"I know that, too."

"Please don't make me choose." My eyes are closing, and I'm starting to drift off.

But I still hear him when he says, "I'll never make you choose, Grace. How could I when I know that you'd never choose me?"

69

To Bite or Not to Bite

"**O**h my God, Grace! Get up!" Macy's squeals echo through our dorm room before light has even begun to filter through our window.

"Not yet," I groan, rolling over and burying my head under my pillow for the second time in eight hours. "Still dark."

I burrow deeper into my blankets, start to fall back into a dream about a little blue-eyed boy and his horse, when Macy shakes me. "I'm serious! You need to get up."

"Make her go away," Hudson groans from what *sounds like* the floor next to my bed.

Macy's phone rings, and she gives up trying to get me awake while she takes the call.

I peek over the edge of my bed and, sure enough, he's sprawled on the floor. He, too, buries his head under a pillow—one of my hot-pink pillows, to be exact.

"Don't judge me," he complains. "It's slim pickings in this room."

I smile. "Yeah, but I've got to say, hot pink might just be your color."

"You know I bite, right?" he growls as he pulls the pillow tight around his head.

"Yes, because I'm *so* scared you're going to bite me." I roll my eyes. "While you're—you know—in my head."

He doesn't answer, and I'm just about to congratulate myself for winning this round when I feel his fangs scraping gently down my neck. They don't stop until they get to my pulse point, and then they hover there for one second, two.

Unexpected heat races through me at the familiarity of his touch, followed closely by an icy blast of panic—because he's *not* Jaxon. "Hey! What are you doing?" I start to push him away, but he's already gone.

"Showing you that even if I'm in your head, I can still bite you anytime you want me to."

"But I don't want you to!" I all but screech, even as my body still resonates from his touch. "That's my whole point."

"I know," he answers calmly. "That's why I didn't do it."

My hand goes to my neck, and I realize he's right. There's not even a tiny scratch. Thank God. "Don't ever do that again," I tell him, just to make sure he gets the message. "I don't want anyone but Jaxon to bite me. Ever."

His smile turns mocking and maybe even a little grim, but he doesn't argue with me. He just nods and says, "Message received. I promise I won't do that again."

"Good." Still, I run my fingers over my neck one more time, strangely disturbed by the warmth I feel under my skin despite the fact that Hudson never actually did anything to me. "Thank you."

"Of course." He grins slyly. "I mean, at least not until you ask me to."

"Ugh." I hit him with my pillow. "You're disgusting, you know that?"

"Because I told you I wouldn't touch you without your permission?" His look of wide-eyed innocence isn't nearly as good as he thinks it is. "I was only trying to be a gentleman."

"You know what? Bite me." As soon as the words are out of my mouth, I realize what I've said. Even before Hudson leans forward with a wicked glint in his blue eyes. I throw a hand up and block his mouth. "No! I did *not* mean that in the good way."

"That's okay, Grace." He gives me a look that I'm pretty sure would melt my panties off my body *if* I wasn't mated to his brother. "I don't mind being bad."

"Yeah, I've heard that about you."

I throw back the covers—determined to end this conversation even if it means running away to the shower—and realize that Macy is off her call and speaking to me.

"I'm sorry," I tell her, trying to figure out why her eyes are so big and her face is so pale. "I was still asleep, so I didn't hear what you said. What's going on?"

"The Circle!" she tells me. "They're here."

"The Circle?" At first, her words don't make any sense to my sleep-addled brain, but when Hudson curses low and long in a corner of my mind, it registers who she's talking about. "Jaxon and Hudson's parents are here?" I whisper, horrified at the thought.

"Yes! The king and queen, plus the other three mated pairs showed up at five this morning. No advance warning, no call ahead. Just eight of them at the front gate, demanding entrance. My dad is beyond pissed."

"Why are they here?" I ask, shoving my super-obnoxious curls out of my way.

"Officially?" Macy answers. "For their twenty-five-year inspection. Which they scheduled at this time to support the Ludares tournament in order to promote interspecies cooperation and friendship."

"And unofficially?" I ask, a little afraid to hear the answer.

"They want a look at you," Hudson and Macy both reply at the exact same time.

"Me?" Okay, that was unexpected. "Why me?"

I mean, I get why maybe Jaxon's parents would want to meet me—seeing as how I'm mated to their only living (that they know about, at least) son. But why get the rest of the Circle involved in what should be a personal family matter?

When I say as much to Macy and Hudson, they laugh—*at* me this time, definitely not with me.

"This isn't about you being mated to Jaxon," Hudson tells me. "I don't think they care, one way or the other, about that—unless they think it threatens their power. What they do care about—what I guarantee you all members of the Circle care about, even the non-power-hungry ones—is that you're the first gargoyle to be born in more than a thousand years."

"Why does that matter? What is one lone gargoyle going to do to them? And a not very powerful gargoyle at that?" I say to the both of them.

"First of all," Macy says emphatically, "you're a new gargoyle, but that doesn't mean you're not a powerful one. It means you've got to take some time to figure out what's up. You don't even know all the things a gargoyle can do yet, let alone what you specifically can do.

"So yeah, of course they're scared. If they weren't, the king wouldn't have murdered all the gargoyles on his last horrific rampage and the Circle sure as hell wouldn't have let him get away with it. They may be cowards, for the most part, but normally they wouldn't be okay with full-on genocide unless it actually served them."

"Damn, Macy, tell us how you really feel!" Hudson exclaims. Then adds to me, "What she said."

I laugh a little bit at that, which leads to a questioning look from Macy. "Hudson approves of your summation," I tell her.

"That's because my summation is right-on. And his father is an asshole." She gives me a look that speaks volumes. "Like father, like son, apparently."

Hudson rolls his eyes but surprisingly has nothing to say in response. Which might actually be a first, now that I think about it. He does, however, sit up and lean against the side of my bed, then runs a hand through his short, tousled hair. I know he's not really real—so why is he sleeping in just a pair of flannel pajama pants and no shirt? Did he take off his shirt, or am I just—inexplicably—choosing to imagine him without one?

And of course, he hears that stray thought and winks at me over one bare shoulder. "I'll let you decide."

I ignore the heat stinging my cheeks and focus on Macy.

"So why exactly does the fact that the Circle decided to pay us a not-so-auspicious visit mean that I have to get up at"—I glance at my phone—"dear God, five fifteen in the morning?"

"Because, apparently, they've called a before-school assembly. And that means we all have to be in the auditorium at six thirty in full dress uniform."

"Full dress uniform? You mean the skirt, tie, and blazer?" I think I've worn the whole uniform only once the entire time I've been here.

"Not the blazer," Macy says with an exaggerated sigh. "The robes."

"Robes?" I look toward my empty closet. "There's no robe in there."

"No, but I have an extra—from when I was shorter, thankfully. Otherwise, you'd fall on your face."

"So skirt, tie, robe?" I ask, making sure I've got it.

"Yeah."

"Like graduation robe?" I ask, just to be clear. Because right now I'm kind of picturing a room full of students in fuzzy black bathrobes. Not that that would be a bad thing...

"More like ceremonial robes." Macy sighs.

Which puts all my senses on red alert. "Not like human-sacrifice robes, right?"

Macy narrows her eyes at me. "No one's going to sacrifice you, Grace."

Easy for her to say. I tamp down the little spurt of annoyance and lead with humor instead. "Says the spider to the fly..."

Macy laughs, just as I intended her to. Which eggs me on. "I'm just saying, no one gets to criticize me for being skittish until they've had to fight off a homicidal bitch with talons through their arms, a dislocated shoulder, a concussion, and gaping wounds on their wrists and ankles from clawing their way out of shackles. On an altar. Surrounded by blood. In the dark. While drugged."

Macy looks at me, completely deadpan, and says, "Well, who hasn't? I mean, really."

I burst out laughing, like full-on belly laughter, because the delivery was just too perfect. "Is that your way of telling me I'm being too much of a drama queen about the whole near-death-experience thing?"

"Are you kidding me? It's my way of telling you that I would like nothing more than a chance to dropkick that bitch straight to hell a second time." She crosses to her closet and pulls out two dark-purple robes. One she tosses on her bed and one she hands to me.

"It's purple," I tell her.

"Yeah," she says.

"The robe is purple."

She nods. "Pretty much, yeah."

"I'm going to look like Barney if I put that on."

She grins. "Welcome to Katmere Academy." And then, while I'm still eyeing the giant purple monstrosity that is supposed to be my ceremonial robe, she steals the freaking bathroom right out from under me.

70

When the Devil Comes Up to Denali

I've been in auditoriums before. I mean, I *am* an American high school student. But nothing could prepare me for what the Katmere Academy auditorium looks like.

Huge, with ceilings that are probably close to thirty or forty feet high and creepy-looking carved spires everywhere, it looks more like a Gothic church than it does a meeting room for students.

Stained-glass windows depicting various paranormal scenes, check.

Carved black lancet arches hovering over every walkway, double check.

Elaborate and semi-creepy engravings on pretty much every available surface, triple check.

Seriously, I'm pretty sure the only thing missing is an altar.

In its place is a round stage in the center of the room, surrounded by hundreds of chairs in the same deep purple as our robes. So as the students filter in and find their seats, the whole front of the room looks like an eggplant exploded—or, more accurately, about a thousand eggplants.

The House of Usher has nothing on this place. Edgar Allan Poe, eat your heart out.

I turn to my left to share the joke with Hudson but realize he didn't walk in with me.

Uncle Finn is on the stage already, but nobody else is, despite there being eight intricately carved (big surprise) chairs set up in a row directly behind the microphone and sound system that my uncle is currently messing with.

I have to laugh as I watch him, because here in the middle of this auditorium that looks like a horror story waiting to happen, my uncle is doing the same thing that every high school principal or vice principal in the history of high schools does before a schoolwide assembly. The abject normalcy of the whole thing amuses me, but it also makes me just a little homesick.

Not necessarily for the life I used to have but for the girl I used to be. Normal. Human. Average.

I mean, in my head I'm the same old boring Grace I've always been, but at Katmere Academy, I'm abnormal. An anomaly. Someone to be stared at and whispered about. Most of the time, I ignore it—I mean, I'm the girl mated to Jaxon Vega while Hudson Vega lives in her head. And, oh yeah, I have a pesky habit of turning to stone whenever I want.

Honestly, who wouldn't stare?

"Let's sit over there," Macy says, pointing to a couple of empty seats near the very front. "I want a good view of this mess."

I'm not normally a very front-of-the-room kind of girl, but of the things I feel like I might have to argue about today, where I sit doesn't even blip on the radar. Besides, at least this way I'll get a good look at Jaxon and Hudson's parents.

"No!" Hudson's shout reverberates in my head, so loud and vehement that it actually brings me to a stop, eyes wide, as I look around, wondering what kind of attack I should brace for.

But everything looks normal—or as normal as it gets at Katmere Academy, considering a group of witches is bouncing a ball all around the auditorium using nothing but a few flicks of their fingers.

What's wrong? I demand, my heart beating out of control.

"Don't sit up front. Don't get anywhere near them."

Near whom? I ask, again looking around for a threat I have yet to recognize.

"My parents. They would love for you to sit that close so they can get a good look at you."

I feel like that's normal, under the circumstances, I tell him with a shrug. *And I want a good look at them, too.*

Macy's gotten a little bit ahead of me, since Hudson's shout stopped me in my tracks, and I weave around a couple of groups of students in an effort to catch up to her.

"Damn it, Grace! I said no!"

Excuse me? I ask, shocked and more than a little annoyed. *Did you just order me not to do something?*

"You can't trust them," he tells me. *"You can't just put yourself up there in front of the king and queen and think nothing's going to happen."*

We're in the middle of a crowded assembly! I shake my head in amazement. *What are they going to do to me?*

I wave to Gwen, who is sidling up to Macy, already sitting in the front row. I'm still seven or eight rows back, so I skirt around a few students in an effort to weave my way to them.

"Anything they want! That's what I'm trying to tell you. My father is the head of the Circle because he has killed, literally, everyone who might possibly be any kind of threat to him. And he has done that continuously for two thousand years. Do you think for one second that he's going to hesitate to kill you, too?"

In the middle of a school function? Sure, he's going to try to kill me with my uncle, all the Katmere Academy teachers, and the entire student body looking on. Not likely. So will you please chill out and let me take an effing seat?

I move down a couple more stairs and then freeze, not because I want to but because my feet won't move. At all.

I start to panic, wondering what on earth can be wrong, but then it hits me. *Don't you dare! Hudson! Let me go right now!*

"Grace, stop for a second!" Hudson's voice is deliberately soothing, which only makes me that much angrier. *"Just listen to me."*

No! No, no, no! I'm not going to listen to you when you are controlling my body. What the ever-loving fuck is wrong *with you?*

"I just need you to think for a minute."

And I just need you to let *me go. If you don't release me right this second, I swear to God, Hudson, when I finally get you out of my head, I will murder you. I will literally make you human and then stab you through your fucking black heart until you die right in front of me! And then I'll stab you some more.*

Hudson walks "us" off to the side, weaving around students rushing to grab their own seats, then eventually slips us between two panels into a hidden alcove. And I'm not going to lie, having someone else take control of your body, with you stuck in the passenger seat, might be one of the worst experiences of my life. The violation, the fear, the anger swirling inside me right now are all building into a storm of epic proportions.

Once we're hidden, I can feel him struggling to give up control of my mind. It's like trying to walk through wet mud, but eventually the resistance gives way with a little pop, and I'm free. I feel *myself* rush in to fill the emptiness, and I can't fight the shiver of panic that overtakes my body.

When he moves around to face me, panic gives way to white-hot anger. He holds his hands up. "All right, all right. I'm sorry."

I take a deep breath, fight for calm. And then say *screw it*, latching on to the part of me that I've pushed down for so long. "Fuck. You."

"Feel better?" Hudson asks. "Now, can you just listen for a moment?"

Is he for *real*? I am beyond mad, well into a full-blown rage. "I am *never* listening to you again. *Never!*"

My heart is racing like I've run down twenty flights of stairs, double-time, my head whirling at the knowledge that Hudson must already have punched through the wall the Bloodletter helped me build. How is it possible for him to be that strong? How can he be knocking it down when it's been less than a week?

Am I really that weak? Or is he just that strong?

He's standing there perfectly still, his face pleading as he tries to get me to listen to him. "I'm only trying to help you, Grace. I only want—"

"Help me?" I hurl at him like a berserker, my rage so overwhelming that it's all I can do not to claw his goddamn smug face off. Only the knowledge that he isn't actually standing in front of me keeps me from punching him right now.

"By violating my *trust* and taking my *free will*? How can you *possibly* think that's helping me?"

"It isn't like that—"

"Well, that's what it feels like!" I'm furious, absolutely furious, and I know it shows because Hudson's eyes are wide with what looks like actual despair. I almost feel bad. Almost. But since Hudson has made it very obvious that not only will he *not* respect the sanctity of my right to do what I please with my body, he won't even respect my right not to have five minutes without him yammering in my head.

So instead of heading to where Macy is waiting for me, I grab my phone and text her that I'll be right back. Then I put my hands on my hips, so I can have this out with Hudson once and for all.

71

Revenge of the Body Snatched

"Grace, I'm sorry." Hudson must finally realize the full weight of my fury, because he rushes in to try to calm me down. "I didn't mean to take your choice away from you—"

"Yeah, well, that's exactly what you did, and I am not going to put up with it for one more minute. Not from you, not from anyone."

Rage at everything that happened over the last five months wells up inside me, and I let Hudson have every single bit of it—partly because he deserves it and partly because I can't hold it in for one second longer. "Ever since I first heard of this ridiculous school, my right to choose how to handle my own life has been almost nonexistent."

"Grace, please—"

"No! You don't talk now." I point my finger in his face. "You don't pull what you just pulled on me and then think we're going to go back to the way we were. I've had you yammering in my head for nearly a week but *you* are going to listen to *me* now.

"I take back what I said before. My control over my life didn't end when I got here. It ended even before I got to this school—*because of you*. Because of your psychotic, twisted, *fucked-up* ex-girlfriend. She was so in love with you that she *murdered my parents*. She murdered them, just so I would have to come to this school. Just so Jaxon could find his mate. Just so she could use his power to bring *you* back.

"I know everybody laughs; I know it's a great big joke in my friend group now that I was almost a fucking human sacrifice, but think about that, will you, please? Just think about it. A regular, human girl from San Diego ends up in fucking Alaska, tied up on an altar so that an evil, heinous bitch could bring back her genocidal asshole of a boyfriend."

Hudson's eyes are going wider and wider with each word that I shout at him, and he looks absolutely devastated. But I don't actually care right now. I've been devastated for months. He can handle it for five damn minutes.

"Even before that, things weren't exactly rosy, were they? People tried to kill me left and right, all because they were afraid of you! So there I am, mated to a vampire—a *vampire*—when I didn't even know they existed two weeks before that. And that's great, actually. He's wonderful and kind and I love him and yay for us.

"But I don't even get to enjoy that, do I? No, of course not, because we're barely recovered from Lia's attack when you show up out of nowhere and try to murder my mate. So I step in and save him and now I'm locked up with you somewhere for three and a half months. Three and a half months, mind you, that I can't even fucking remember."

My hair has fallen in my face, so I pause in my diatribe just long enough to shove my ridiculous, out-of-control curls away and try to ignore this additional thing I can't tame.

"And then you do what you do. Body snatch me and turn me into an attempted murderer and a thief, leave me to wake up *covered in someone's blood*." I poke his chest with each of those words for emphasis. I will *never* get over that experience, and he needs to know it. "You live in my head for days without my permission, and then you think *I'm* crossing the line for freaking out when you take control of my body because you don't like *where I want to sit*? Who the *hell* do you think you are? You may think you're trying to protect me, but I've got to say, every single bad thing that's happened to me in the last five months can be traced directly back to you.

"So instead of asking me to think for a minute, why don't *you* think instead? Why don't *you* listen for a minute and figure out why anything you have to say should matter to me at all?"

By the time I'm done, Hudson's face is ashen. And now that I've gotten out all the bitterness and rage and pain inside me, I know that mine is, too. I hate losing my temper, hate yelling at people, because nothing good ever comes of it. And I've never in my whole life lost my temper like I just did. Is it any wonder my head now hurts like I've been on a week-long crying jag?

But at the same time, being nice wasn't cutting it with him. He was going to keep rolling right over my objections like the steamroller he is, and I'm not about to let that happen. I won't let him take control of my body ever again, and he needs to understand that.

"I don't—" He breaks off. "I didn't mean—" He breaks off again. "I'm sorry. I know it doesn't mean anything to you and it probably shouldn't, but I am sorry, Grace."

"Don't be sorry," I answer with a sigh. "Or be sorry, it doesn't really matter anymore. But don't ever do that again. *Ever.*"

He starts to say something else, but I'm done listening. The assembly is about to start, and I don't have any time or interest in listening to him say he's sorry again or offer platitudes about why he did what he did…or worse, start back on me again about where I sit or who I should be afraid of.

I'm not naive, either, even though Hudson doesn't seem to believe that. So I turn away from him and head back into the auditorium, but as I walk toward the center aisle, instead of turning left, I turn right… and walk up to the third-from-the-last row and sit down behind two huge dragon males. I can still see the stage, a little, and can still hear everything that's being said, but I'm pretty sure it will be hard for anyone to see me.

With that thought in mind, I pull out my phone and text Jaxon a quick note, telling him I'm sitting alone near the back because I have a headache and might need to leave early.

It's not a lie, considering my head *is* killing me, but I don't want to get into everything in text right now, either. Plus, I don't want him to come looking for me. I figure I can stay inconspicuous only if I'm not actually sitting next to their son.

"Thank you," Hudson tells me as he slides into the seat next to me, but I don't answer him. Not because I'm still angry but because I don't have anything else to say to him. Not right now, and maybe not ever if he doesn't get his act together.

I wait for him to say something obnoxious or try to argue with me, but he doesn't say a word. Maybe he's learning after all. I guess time will tell.

Jaxon texts back, asking if I need anything. When I tell him no, he explains that he's backstage right now—a command performance with the king and queen.

Maybe I should be disappointed, but I'm not. Him being away from me is that one extra layer of anonymity I was looking for.

And as the king and queen and the rest of the Circle file onto the stage, my palms begin to sweat. I'm not ready to forgive Hudson yet, but I can't lie that there's a part of me very grateful I am very, very far away from his parents as I watch both of them scan the audience while they take their seats.

It's obvious they're looking for someone...and it's not their son, as he was just with them backstage. But the longer they search, the more convinced I become that they really are looking for me. And after seeing Hudson's memory of his parents last night, I'm more than happy to make sure they don't find me. At least not until I'm ready for them.

72

Welcome to the Paranormal Jungle

I start to text Jaxon again, but before I can figure out what to say, Uncle Finn turns on the microphone. He talks for a few minutes about the Ludares tournament, laying down the rules, talking about how many teams have signed up (twelve) and how the brackets are going to be run.

When he gets to the prize for winning the tournament, he turns toward the dignitaries seated behind him in ornate chairs—I snort; who am I kidding? Those are thrones and they want everyone to know it—and announces, "To discuss the prize for this very special Ludares tournament, we are incredibly lucky to have none other than King Cyrus and Queen Delilah from the Vampire Court here to announce the very special prize. Please join me in welcoming them and several other members of the Circle." He starts off the applause, but soon the auditorium is filled with the sound of respectful clapping, which amuses me because in my experience, so few things at this school have ever engendered such a tepid response.

Apparently, there are very few members of my generation who actually have any interest in the Circle—and especially the vampire king and queen—at all. Not that I blame them, but it's still interesting to see. And even more interesting to watch as that knowledge hits Cyrus full-on.

He tries to hide it, but I'm watching closely from a little spot between my two shields, and he. Looks. Pissed.

He doesn't say anything, though, as his eyes scan the crowd. He's smiling and waving as the queen moves to the microphone, but he's not missing one face. I slink down lower in my seat and all but feel Hudson's relief.

The queen introduces herself in a melodic British accent and with a smile that looks surprisingly sincere as she thanks everyone for such a warm, warm welcome. Even as her gaze—like her husband's—moves from face to face in the crowd, I can feel people opening up, see their shoulders relaxing and their bodies leaning forward as if they're suddenly afraid of missing even one word that falls from her bloodred-painted lips.

Her eyes are the same near-black as Jaxon's, and her skin has the same unique—and slightly odd—olive and alabaster tint to it. Her features are sharp, angled, and it's suddenly obvious just where the Vega cheekbones and jawline that I love so much come from. The long, lithe build and dark hair, too, though the queen wears hers in a long braid wrapped around the crown of her head—and then balances her gold-and-jewel-encrusted crown on top of it, just in case someone at Katmere doesn't know who she is.

She makes a striking picture, no doubt, and her sons are the spitting image of her, though Hudson's eyes are a different color. And like them, there's a regality—an expectation of how things should be—to her that simply can't be taught.

This is a woman who was born to rule...and to do it warmly, in such a way that nearly everyone watching her somehow feels like they have a connection to her. That she is speaking directly to them. No doubt, it's a spectacular talent.

I just don't know if I buy it.

Because I still can't forget that this is the woman who slashed Jaxon's face so severely that she *scarred a vampire*. The woman who took him away from Hudson without a backward glance even as

Hudson sobbed for the little brother he loved.

And yet she is winking at the crowd. She is smiling and thanking people by name and even cracking a joke or two just to make her public adore her a tiny bit more.

It's such a strange dichotomy that I'm reminded of an Andy Warhol painting. He did the same image in four different—usually tertiary—colors because each person's brain sees colors differently, and it is up to the brain to make its color perception fact. Looking at this woman, watching her after seeing the way she was in Hudson's memory yesterday, makes me wonder which shades of her my brain is really seeing…and which one I should make my reality.

Until I can figure out the answer, I think it behooves me to stay very, very far away from the queen. I'm guessing her name isn't Delilah for nothing.

Eventually, she manages to thank everyone in existence, but it's not until she starts talking about the prize that I lean forward, breath held and eyes peeled. *Let it be the bloodstone*, I beg the universe. *Please, please, please let it be the bloodstone. Don't let Byron's parents have changed their mind.*

"I know that the usual prize for the annual Katmere Ludares tournament is a trophy and a small monetary prize to be divided among the winning team." She smiles at the audience and seems to enjoy the sudden uptick in enthusiasm that seems to fill the auditorium. "But this year, we thought we'd do something a little different, a little bigger"—she waits for the spontaneous applause to die down—"since we have a big *occasion* to celebrate as well." She pauses to lean in herself, like she's about to share a secret with her most favorite loyal subjects. My stomach bottoms out, partly because I realize I might be the occasion she's referring to and partly because it terrifies me to see just how anxious everyone is to know what she has to say.

"Of course," she continues with a big, wide smile, "you already have up-close-and-personal knowledge of the occasion I'm referring to—the discovery of the first gargoyle in a thousand years!" Again she looks around the crowd, and again I slump a little farther down in my seat. "The Circle and I are thrilled to welcome Grace Foster into our world.

"Welcome, Grace. I want you to know how very excited the Circle is to meet you." She lifts her hands in the gesture for applause, and the audience gives her what she's after, even though it's suddenly nowhere near as enthusiastic as it was. Which is okay with me, honestly.

Again, she waits for the noise to die down before continuing. "Now, let's talk about the prize—everybody's favorite part, including mine."

She reaches into the box and pulls out a large, deep-red geode, as richly colored as the blood that formed it. It glows—whether from the light reflecting off its angles or from within, I'm not sure—but it is absolutely breathtaking. "For the team that wins this year's very special Ludares tournament, we offer up this rare and beautiful bloodstone, donated by the distinguished Lord family, in fact originally gifted to them from our own personal royal collection!"

The auditorium goes wild, teenagers and faculty alike applauding and stomping and cheering her generosity. She loves it, of course, and so does the king, who sweeps in to take the microphone from her.

Looking at him up there, I realize he's nearly as tall as Jaxon and Hudson, and probably as muscular, though the three-piece suit in bright blue that he's wearing makes it hard to be sure. But that's where the similarity ends. Sure, Hudson gets his blue eyes from his father, but while they are the exact same shade of cobalt, they couldn't be more different. Hudson's are warm and alive, dancing with humor and intelligence even when he's angry with me. Cyrus's eyes are just as alive, but they are constantly moving, constantly observing, constantly helping him calculate and adjust.

Everything about Cyrus screams that he is as much a showman as his wife. But unlike Delilah, who works the audience, Cyrus seems happy just to bathe in their adoration. And unlike Delilah, I don't have to think about who this man is or what he wants. Even without living through Hudson's painful memory last night, I know Cyrus is a textbook narcissist, one who cares about nothing more than his own power and prestige.

One who is willing to turn his own son into the greatest weapon the world has ever seen if it means he can use him to increase that adoration.

Delilah fascinates me even as I refuse to trust her. Cyrus just disgusts me.

My gaze darts to Hudson, concerned about what he must be thinking or feeling. But he might as well be watching the Home Shopping Network for all the emotion he's displaying. On a day when they're selling cookware or something equally as useless to a vampire.

I turn back to Cyrus—who is like a cobra, because it serves everyone best if you don't take your eyes off him for longer than a second or two—just as he starts to speak. But even as I do, I reach for the armrest between our seats and lay my hand next to Hudson's, so that just our pinkie fingers are brushing.

Touching but not.

"What an incredible prize we have for you!" He moves across the stage like he owns it, like he was born for this, his accent adding a sophistication to his words I know he doesn't deserve. Suddenly he pauses and sweeps his hand in front of him to encompass the entire audience. "As you all know, a bloodstone is an incredibly rare *and* powerful magical object. But I want to let you in on a little secret. This is not just any bloodstone!" He holds the collective breath of everyone in the palm of his hand, and he knows it. He even goes so far as to wink at Delilah before continuing, "As my beautiful wife Queen Delilah mentioned, this particular bloodstone was gifted to the Lords from our personal royal collection. Truly a prize beyond measure for our winning team this year because"—he pauses as the auditorium erupts in cheers again, a wide smile never wavering on his ndsome face—"because *this* bloodstone is in fact the most *powerful* dstone to ever exist."

He leans forward, his whole demeanor changing as he grips the microphone with both hands and his tone grows somber. "As you all know, we lost our firstborn son sixteen months ago. Hudson was a lot of things—a misguided youth, to be certain—but also the joy of his mother's and my life. And he was also the most powerful vampire ever born."

He smiles softly, as though remembering Hudson fondly. But I've seen the real Cyrus. He's not proud of his son. He's proud that *he* created him. "I still remember the first time he used his gift to persuade the kitchen staff to swap out my evening blood for Kool-Aid." He chuckles now and shakes his head, as though a loving parent were remembering his child's antics, and the auditorium laughs with him, surely just as he planned.

Hudson, meanwhile, is eerily still during this recitation, and I have the distinct feeling Cyrus isn't sharing the full story with his audience.

"He wasn't as amused then, as he's implying, huh?" I venture a guess.

Hudson snort-laughs. "Sure. If you consider banning me from feeding for a month as amused."

My jaw falls open as I gasp. "He *starved* you for a *month*?"

His gaze never leaves his father. "It's no big deal. We're immortal, so it's not like I was going to die. It's just not very comfortable."

Without thinking, I lay my hand on his, but this time he flinches and pulls away. I watch as he crosses his arms over his chest, like just the suggestion of openness is too much for him right now.

Not that I blame him. His father is as close to a monster as I can possibly imagine.

Cyrus, meanwhile, is having a great time as he continues. "When Hudson was born, we all knew he was special. So we had his blood stored in a bloodstone for eternity—the very bloodstone, in fact, that the Lords have donated for this year's tournament!"

He pauses, arms up, as he waits for the audience to erupt. A portion of them do, cheering and whistling at his words. Others slouch down in their chairs, try to look invisible, like they're terrified of attracting his or his dead son's attention. I expect that to piss him off, but Cyrus pauses, stands up to his full height again, and bathes in their adoration *and* their terror. It doesn't seem to matter what kind of attention he's getting, as long as he's getting a lot of it.

It's the most bizarre and terrible thing I think I've ever seen.

"What better way to celebrate this amazing tournament?" Cyrus continues. "And also, of course, to welcome the newest member of our paranormal community—the first gargoyle born in over one thousand years. Mate to my son, niece to our amazing headmaster. How lucky are we to be here to witness this miracle? I can't wait to meet our young Grace."

Where Hudson was still before, now he has a violent reaction to his father's words, everything in him rising up to reject what Cyrus said, especially as people around the audience start looking for me.

"Get down, Grace," he hisses. "Pull your robe up around your face. I don't want him to see you."

"If I pull my robe up around my face, I'm going to look a lot more obvious than I do now," I shoot back. "Just chill. The assembly is almost over."

On the stage, Cyrus is introducing Nuri and Aidan Montgomery, a mixed-race couple who I realize with some astonishment are Flint's parents. The witches, Imogen and Linden Choi, are next, followed by werewolves Angela and Willow Martinez.

As I stare at the eight people onstage, I realize for the first time that each is with their mate. "I forgot only mated pairs can be on the Circle," I whisper to Hudson. "I can't remember, is that a law?"

"Pretty much," he answers, completely disgruntled. "You don't have to be mated to get on the Council, but you have to pass a Trial that is impossible to pass by yourself. And since the only person who can help you in the Trial is your mate...you see the conundrum."

"All mated pairs on the Circle."

"Exactly. And if you get on as a pair and your mate dies, you stay for one more year until a new mated pair can compete to replace you."

I have more questions for Hudson, but Cyrus is wrapping up the assembly, and Hudson is pushing at me to "get the hell out." I still think he's overreacting, at least until Cyrus says, "Thank you all for coming. Have a great day. And, Grace Foster, if you don't mind, can you please come up to the stage for a few minutes? We really are eager to meet you!"

Hudson curses and I freeze, neither of which is a particularly helpful strategy for dealing with the fact that the king has just pretty much ordered me to the stage. "What do I do?" I ask Hudson once I absorb the shock.

"Get up, get out, and don't look back," he tells me.

"Are you sure?" But I follow his directions, all but diving into the throng of students crowding the walkway.

"Very sure," he answers. "An empty auditorium when everyone else is in class is not the time to face my father. Now go, go, go."

I do as he says, making a beeline for one of the auditorium doors. Just before I reach it, I turn around to get a glimpse of what Cyrus is doing and what he's planning to do if I don't show up.

It's a bad move on my part, though, because the second I turn, our gazes collide. And recognition flashes on his face, along with the knowledge that I am very deliberately not following his directions.

I expect him to get mad, to order me to come down. But instead he simply inclines his head in an "all right, if you say so" gesture that chills me to the bone. Because it's not acceptance that I see in his eyes. It's slyness, combined with a whole lot of strategy.

For the first time, I think Hudson may be right. Maybe I really don't have any idea who or what I'm dealing with.

73

Live and Let Love

I spend the next two days going to class, dodging the vampire king and queen, training with my team for the tournament, and trying to sneak small moments of time with Jaxon, who it turns out is as freaked out about me meeting his parents as Hudson is, mostly because he wants me to have absolutely nothing to do with his mom.

And I have to admit, I'm a little freaked out by the fact that both brothers have apparently been traumatized by a different parent. Like, what kind of monsters are these people—besides the obvious—that their two (very) badass sons each consider them, if not the devil, then at least one of his closest minions?

So far, Jaxon has been putting his parents off by citing a brutal training schedule for the tournament (which isn't actually too far from the truth), but that excuse is finite, and I'm not sure what's going to happen when the tournament is over.

When Wednesday, the day of the tournament, dawns bright and beautiful, I can't help but feel a biting chill in the air. Of course, it won't matter in the arena, since it's a climate-controlled dome, but still, it feels like the world is warning me not to get out of bed today.

I'm up early, too nervous about winning the games and the stone to get much sleep, even though Macy and Jaxon don't seem to be having any problem. We don't have to report to the arena until ten, but I know if I sit around the room for the next three hours and stare at my sleeping cousin while obsessing over messing up the tournament, I'll end up bouncing off the walls.

Not even Hudson is around to distract me, telling me earlier he had something he had to do and would be gone for a few hours, but he'd be back in time for the tournament. I asked how he could possibly go *anywhere* stuck in my head, but he was already gone before I got the whole question out. Which isn't scary at all...

So after getting layered up and leaving a note for Macy—I didn't want to text her and risk waking her up—I grab a yogurt and a couple of granola bars and make my way down to the arena.

I honestly don't know what I plan to do there—beyond practice my flying some more and maybe walk the field, just to get a feel for what it's like. I figure I'll be alone for at least an hour or so, but the second I pass through one of the arena's ornate entrances—and the twisted passageways that lead to the seating—I realize that was a pipe dream. There are players all over the huge field. Not hundreds or anything like that but definitely at least ten or fifteen—one of whom is Flint.

Guess I'm not the only one on my team excited-slash-nervous-as-hell about today.

His back is toward me, but I'd recognize his Afro and broad shoulders anywhere—plus he's already wearing one of the super-colorful jerseys Macy got for each of us so we could all match on the field. I don't know much about the rest of the teams we're competing against, but I can guarantee no one else out here has a jersey like ours, with its wild kaleidoscope of colors, much like one of my favorite Kandinsky paintings.

I walk deeper into the arena, marveling at how amazing it looks already. Like everything else at Katmere, it has a decidedly Gothic spin to it—black stones, lancet arches, intricately carved stonework—but the design of it is all Roman Colosseum. Three stories high with fanned amphitheater seating, VIP boxes at the top, and all the gorgeous and imposing walkways imaginable. It's the most intimidating and impressive high school arena I have ever seen.

And it's already decorated for the game—interspersed among the regular Katmere Academy flags are pennants from each of the individual teams competing today.

When Macy first mentioned having flags for our team, I thought she was just being my fun-loving, colorful cousin. But as I spot our banners in all their brightly colored glory mingling around the stadium with the darker, more boring ones of the other teams, I can't help being impressed with just how on top of things she really is.

If it had been left up to the rest of us, I don't think we'd even have one flag in the arena, and Macy has ensured that we have *hundreds*. And while it's probably ridiculous, seeing them all over the place does exactly what it's designed to do—it gets me excited and makes me even prouder to be playing on my team.

It also makes me believe that maybe, just maybe, we really will win.

Determined to get down to the giant oval field so I can warm up and practice a little, I make my way back through the passageways until I come to the entrance closest to Flint. He's still stretching, so maybe we can warm up together.

I'm planning to sneak up on him, but I barely get within ten feet before he turns with a grin and says, "Hey, you."

"No sneaking up on a dragon, huh?"

"There's a reason 'ears like a dragon' is a saying," he tells me.

"But it's not a saying," I answer, confused.

"No? Well, then it should be." He offers a halfhearted grin and grabs a stainless-steel tumbler off the nearest bench and guzzles from it. "So what are you doing here so early?" he asks.

"Probably the same thing you are."

He lifts a brow. "Exorcising demons?"

I laugh. "No, silly. Getting in some extra practice."

I expect him to laugh with me, but when he doesn't, I realize there was nothing joking about his last statement. "Hey." I put a hand on his shoulder. "You okay?"

"Yeah, I'm fine." But this time, his patented Flint grin doesn't reach his eyes. When I keep looking at him, concerned, he shrugs.

"What's going on?" I drop my bag on the field and then take a seat on the bench, gesture for him to do the same. "Are you nervous about the game?" I don't even know how to process a nervous Flint. He's the epitome of optimism.

Oh no. If *Flint* is having doubts... I almost choke on my next words. "If you're anxious...that must mean you think we're all going to die gruesome deaths today, don't you?" I can feel the bubbles of panic start to rise in my stomach. "What was I thinking, that I could help us win? I've been a gargoyle all of six seconds. I'm like a weight around the team's necks." Sheer panic has me firing questions at Flint like a machine gun. "Can I quit the team? Will you get penalized if I throw myself down the stairs and break a leg? Is there someone available who can replace me on short notice?"

He reaches for my shoulders, but I barely notice. "Grace—"

"If the team only has seven, will they adjust the magical restraints? Can Jaxon use more of his strength without me?"

"Grace—"

"What if I develop a sudden shellfish allerg—"

"Grace!" Flint's voice finally seizes my attention, and I stop talking and blink up at him. "I've met someone."

Of all the things he was going to say, that is definitely not even top-twenty material. I swallow. "So you're not nervous I'm an anchor, destined to drag the team down?"

He chuckles. "Not remotely."

Okay. Then why the doom-and-gloom version of Flint? "Um, that's great that you met someone, isn't it?"

"Yeah." He looks away, pulling his hands back into his lap.

"What's her name?" I ask, trying to encourage him to talk. It's clear he has something he needs to get off his chest, but I have no idea what it is. "I mean, you don't have to tell me if you don't want—"

crush

I break off when he laughs, because it's a low and painful sound. "I'm gay, Grace. I thought you'd figured that out by now."

"Oh!" Now that he says it out loud, I feel like a horrible friend. All the times I'd seen girls coming on to him—even Macy, God bless her—and he'd never shown any interest. Was I really so caught up in my own life that Flint and I had never stopped to talk about him?

Not to mention, yeah, Jaxon gets jealous sometimes when I hang out with Flint, but I always thought that was ridiculous. There's no chemistry between the two of us at all—even when I thought he was hitting on me in the library that time, it felt off. Like something wasn't right. Like he was trying too hard.

Because I only saw what I wanted to see, and apparently, so does everyone else around this place. Yeah, I'm the worst.

But that doesn't matter now. All that matters is the fact that Flint is staring at me, waiting for some kind of reaction from me, and I can't mess this up.

"That's awesome!" I squeal, throwing myself at him, wrapping my arms around his wide shoulders in a huge hug.

His arms go around my waist, but he doesn't really hug me back. "Wait. Awesome?" he repeats, confused.

"Of course. Why wouldn't it be?" I pull back and give him a once-over. "I mean, look at you. Of course there's a guy interested in seeing you. You're smart, gorgeous, funny… It's the trifecta, right?"

He laughs, but there are tears in his eyes, and it breaks my heart. "Oh, Flint. Please don't cry. There's nothing to cry about in being gay. You know that, right? You are who you are. You love who you love. Besides, I think the Circle could use a really kick-ass gay dragon couple on it, don't you? Give those asshole werewolves a run for their money."

"Oh my God, Grace." He rubs a hand over his face, and then he's hugging me, too. For real this time. Eventually we both get all the hugging out of our system and he leans back again. "I figure once we start dating, well, everyone's going to know. But you're the first person I've told, and that was not the reaction I expected."

"What?" I ask. "Is it not normal for me to hope you show the werewolves up in all the ways? Every werewolf I've met so far—with the exception of Xavier—is fucking awful. I say take them down with your awesomeness."

He's laughing full-out now, which is exactly what I was hoping for. "I love you, Grace." He chuckles again when I raise a brow. "Not like *that*."

"So this is all amazing news. And you've met someone." I shake my head. "I've gotta be honest—I'm not seeing a problem here. I'm all for finding your mate!"

He sighs, and it's like he's trying to dislodge the weight of the world. "For what feels like my whole life, I've been in love with the same guy. But he was emotionally unavailable. And, well." He laughs, but there's absolutely no humor in his next words. "Now he's *really* emotionally unavailable."

I'm starting to see where this is going. "So you're giving up on him, aren't you?"

"Yeah," he says. "It's time. I always thought, if he could just let his guard down a crack, the magic could get in and he'd see we were destined to be mated. I just knew in my bones he was my mate." Flint shakes his head. "I was so wrong."

I feel awful for Flint but also, I'm curious how this mating-bond magic works—since I'm currently a happy victim of it. "I'm confused. The mating bond doesn't always mate soul mates?"

Flint shrugs. "No one knows exactly how the magic works, but we do know it's sentient—for lack of a better word. It won't mate pairs too young, for instance, or same-sex pairs before both are self-aware of their sexuality. Or if you never meet. In fact, the bond only snaps in place when you touch your mate." He gives me a rueful smile. "But hey, the good news is the magic also allows for you to have more than one mate in your lifetime—and a few times it's even been between more than just two people."

He waggles his brows at that last statement, and I laugh. "Gives a whole new meaning to the saying 'the more the merrier,' eh?"

I finally get a smile from Flint that reaches his eyes. "Definitely."

"So…you're going to open yourself up to the magic finding you another mate, is that it?" I reach over and rest a hand on his arm. "I think that's a great idea, Flint."

"Yeah. Like I said, I've met this great guy now who likes me back, and he deserves better than a lovesick dragon pining for someone who's never going to notice him that way. But, well, it's hard. I'm afraid I'll forever be split in two. The guy who loved this one person most of his life and this new person. Even if he didn't return my feelings—he was constant, you know? He was *my* constant."

Flint's voice breaks, and his beautiful eyes begin to water again. His heartbreak is like a gaping, jagged wound, and I want to hunt down whoever this asshole is who didn't recognize how amazing Flint is and kick his ass. Twice. Instead, I do the only thing I *can* do: I slide over and wrap my arms around Flint's waist and give him another hug. "He doesn't deserve you."

His big arms tighten around me. "Probably not."

"I say focus on the person who sees you for who you really are, and if you love him with all your heart, you can never go wrong." I squeeze him again.

"I'm sorry," Flint says, wiping his eyes in that "I'm not crying, just got dirt in my eye" sort of way. "I never meant to start this now. We have a game… But he's asked if he can come watch, cheer for us, for me, and, well, yeah. I had to shed some weight first."

He breaks off, his focus snagged by something across the field. And even before I turn to look, I know who I'm going to see.

Jaxon. Of course. Walking across the field with the rest of our team, all of them decked out in the colorful, cheerful jerseys that feel really out of place right now.

I figure I should probably disengage from the hot dragon before Jaxon gets jealous, and I glance up at Flint to share the joke, but his gaze isn't on mine.

And suddenly I see *everything* I was too determined not to see before.

Seconds later, when Flint has his trademark goofy grin in place, I wonder how it's taken me this long to catch on to three very important facts: One, Flint uses that grin as a shield. Two, he lets real emotion break through that shield only when he can no longer contain it— namely when one certain person is around. And three... I swallow the lump in my throat, rub at the sudden ache in my chest. And three, the emotionally unavailable guy he's giving up on, the one he's waited so long for, is Jaxon.

74

A Whole New Kind of March Madness

My newfound knowledge is reverberating in my brain like a gong that's been hit way too hard as I walk over to Jaxon, a fake smile on my face. I'm focused on him, and on everything I just learned, but the building noise in the stadium makes me realize that while I was talking to Flint, the whole arena has filled up. It's not time for the tournament to start, but teams are warming up and orders are being picked.

"It works the same way the human March Madness does," Jaxon tells me as we line up to sign in. "But on a smaller scale. We start with sixteen teams randomly assigned to play each other, and the winners of those games go on to play one of the other winning teams, and we keep doing that until we win or get eliminated. Which means—"

"If we want to claim the bloodstone, then we need to win four games today," I finish for him, even though I'm only half listening. Most of my brain is still focused on Flint and how just my existence is breaking his heart wide open right.

It kills me, makes me feel helpless in a way that scrapes me raw on the inside. And having to hide what I know from Jaxon somehow only makes it worse.

Especially as he grins down at me. "Exactly. Easy, right?"

I roll my eyes and try to focus on him, for no other reason than to give Flint an extra layer of protection for his feelings. "Sooooo easy." Yeah, right.

"Not even a little bit," I answer as my stomach churns with nerves. About the game, about Flint, about everything I've learned and everything I still don't have a clue about.

Jaxon laughs and hugs me close, but that doesn't stop the nerves. In fact, it only makes them worse because I can see Flint looking at me out of the corner of his eye. But when I try to catch his attention or smile, he ducks his head or pretends to be looking somewhere else.

Eventually, I stop trying, but when Jaxon gets busy talking to Mekhi and Luca, who is on the team behind ours, I bump my shoulder against Flint's. He looks startled at first, but eventually he grins and bumps me back just as gently.

"You okay?" I ask.

"I'm good," he answers, and since he isn't wearing that grin of his—and is instead looking as sincere as I have ever seen him look—I decide to believe him. Or at least not to keep poking at what I can imagine is an unbelievably painful subject.

When we finally get to the front of the line, I realize it's Uncle Finn who's checking us in. He gives us a huge smile and hands each one of us a plastic bracelet we immediately slide on our wrists. Macy explained to me last night that these bracelets are charmed to prevent serious injury during an otherwise intensely rough game, so I tug on mine a couple of times, just to make sure there's no chance it will fall off during the tournament.

Uncle Finn wishes us all luck. It's the same thing he says to each of the teams, but I think it's pretty obvious that he's rooting for us, especially when Macy pops colorful star stickers in the center of both his cheeks.

After we all sign in, Jaxon holds out a black box to Flint and says, "Team captains need to draw."

"We don't really have a team captain," Flint starts, but Jaxon looks at him like he's got two heads.

"Dude, this is all you," he says as he claps him on the back. "You're the team captain. Now, draw the number."

Flint swallows hard at Jaxon's words—or actions, I can't tell—then nods and reaches into the box. He pulls out a little round ball with the number eleven written on it.

"What does that mean?" I ask.

Jaxon points to a huge whiteboard free-floating on the sidelines, right in the center of the field. "It means we play team four first," he answers with a huge grin as he points to a team dressed in black T-shirts.

"Liam and Rafael's team," Mekhi whoops from behind us. "It's going to be fun kicking their asses."

Liam and Rafael are looking right back at us, shaking their heads. "You're going down, Vega!" Liam shouts.

"I'm so scared," Jaxon shoots back. "Can't you tell?"

"Children," Hudson says. "They're all children." But he's grinning almost as widely as his brother.

"You need a star sticker," I tell him. "For spirit."

"You mean like one of these?" Hudson turns his head, and I can see he's already got one on his left cheek. Which I totally wasn't expecting.

"Looks good on you," I tell him.

"Everything looks good on me," he answers, but the sparkle in his eyes makes it a joke.

"So what do we do now?" I ask the group at large.

"Now, we find a shady place in the stands and kick back to watch the action," Eden tells us. "We'll be playing fourth, and I can't wait to watch some of these people out here get their asses kicked on the field."

"And by that she means, she can't wait to kick their asses herself," Xavier interprets as we follow behind her.

"Yeah." I laugh. "I got that."

He smiles and makes a show of bumping fists with me before

jogging to the front of our group, so he can walk next to Flint...and Macy.

Once we're settled, I reach into my bag for a granola bar—I need the energy even if my stomach may be in knots right now—but Macy stops me. "They'll be around with much better stuff in a few minutes."

I'm not sure what she means until I realize several witches from the kitchen are buzzing up and down the field with huge containers strapped in front of them—kind of like the ones vendors wear at football games, only much smaller.

"Hot dogs?" I ask, a little surprised because they seem like such an incongruous food to be eating in the middle of Alaska.

Macy laughs. "Not quite."

It takes a few minutes, but eventually one of the witches makes her way to us. Turns out she's selling funnel cakes in the shape of the Katmere Academy crest. They're smothered in strawberries and whipped cream and they look absolutely delicious.

Flint orders about fifteen of them for the group. I figure she's just going to take our order, but then she reaches into her box and keeps pulling them out, hot and fresh and dripping with strawberries.

The next vendor who comes along is selling fresh lemonade, and Xavier gets what feels like several gallons of it as we settle in to watch the first match.

Cyrus—in a fitted, three-piece pinstriped suit, hair tied back into a tiny ponytail at the nape of his neck and bloodstone ring glowing under the stadium lights—saunters his way to the center of the field, a microphone in his hand. Once there, he throws his arms wide and welcomes us all to the annual Ludares tournament, then goes through the rules "for anyone who might need a refresher."

Every player must hold the comet (a large ball about six inches in diameter that magically vibrates painfully and heats the longer a player holds it) at least once in every match.

There are magical handicaps in place so that yes, one player can be faster or stronger than another, or be able to turn them into a turtle even (everyone laughs at that joke), but no spell or burst of speed or supernatural strength lasts more than ten seconds.

The only exception is flight, which can last up to twenty seconds at a time. So clearly a team with good flyers is going to have a slight advantage. I glance at Flint, and we fist-bump on that one.

All abilities that time out recharge every thirty seconds. I can tell from this rule, timing of when to use your speed or strength or flight or whatever so you have it when you need it is going to require a lot of strategy—and luck.

Everyone has been given a magical bracelet to prevent any serious injury. Dragon fire or ice, vampire bites, wolf claws and bites, and even witch's spells can all still hurt like a bitch, but there's no actual damage.

And of course, a player in mortal danger would immediately be magically transported to the sidelines and marked as permanently out of that match.

Despite all the rules, the actual game play is pretty simple. Get the comet across your goal line before your opposing team does the same—without breaking the rules.

Cyrus finishes his recitation of the regulations and then postures on for a while about interspecies cooperation, like he invented the game himself—which is made more entertaining by Hudson's snarky comments about Cyrus liking the sound of his own voice more than anyone else in the entire stadium. He's sitting directly behind me, the only one in the whole row, and I can tell he likes it that way. Even before he stretches out on the bench, sunglasses on, and heckles his father.

His insults are so inventive that I'm a little sad I'm the only one who gets to enjoy them. Then again, I'm pretty sure they'd get our team ejected from the tournament if anyone else heard him call the king a slack-jawed numby, so there is that...

Eventually, Cyrus calls the first two teams down to the field and blunders through introductions because he never bothered to figure out how to pronounce their names before he called them down. It's the most arrogant—and also the most normal—school thing I've seen the whole time I've been at Katmere. I mean, besides having watched my uncle fidget with the sound system as he tried to get it to work.

Once the teams are introduced—I decide I'm rooting for team two, because it's got Luca and Byron on it—Cyrus opens up the case that's been lying at the center of the field since I got here this morning.

He announces into the microphone that Nuri—Flint's mom—is going to be in charge of this tip-off, and we all have to wait while she walks out from the sidelines. I grin as I realize she's dressed much more casually than Cyrus in a pair of jeans and a black turtleneck, and it only makes him look like more of a tool. Not that he needs much help in that department.

Cyrus motions to the box with a flourish but makes no move to pick up the comet.

Nuri leans over and picks up the black and purple object—and can I just say it's a lot more interesting-looking than I anticipated, a shiny black ball inside a purple metal netting—and holds it up in front of her. The entire stadium screams and cheers until the whole place feels like it's shaking with excitement.

The playing field is completely empty of markings except for a small box directly in the center of the grass and two purple lines—one on either side of the box—about ten feet away from it, which run the vertical length of the field.

The longer she holds the comet, the louder everyone cheers. This goes on for at least two minutes, and then she walks to the box at the center and steps on the raised platform, the comet still in her hand. I genuinely don't think the crowd can get any louder.

But when she holds out the ball—that has now turned a bright red—to the spectators as if offering it, her gaze going back and forth from one side of the arena to the other, challenging each and every person, the screaming becomes positively deafening. Students are stomping now in addition to yelling, and I'm certain the entire arena is going to collapse around us. It's thrilling and awe-inspiring and my face aches with the giant smile plastered on it.

It doesn't take long before I'm screaming and stomping right along with everyone else, but I have to admit, I have no idea why we're all so excited. Maybe this is tradition?

Hudson chuckles in my head, where I can hear him over the crowd. *"Did you forget the comet gets hotter and vibrates at excruciating speeds the longer you hold it?"*

My eyes go wide. *Ohhhhh.* She's been holding it for at least five minutes now. Jaxon had told me the longest he'd ever held it was two minutes before the pain became so unbearable, he couldn't survive it. *Five minutes…?*

"Flint's mom is scary as fuck." The awe in Hudson's voice matches my own.

A quick glance at Flint shows him beaming with pride.

Finally, Nuri seems satisfied she's made her point and raises the comet above her head. And everything instantly goes dead silent.

The teams are lined up along both lines, and I notice that Rafael is directly in the center of his line, along with a short Black girl named Kali, whom I've never met but am pretty sure is a witch. On the other side are two warlocks: Cam—Macy's ex, and James, his friend with the creepy wandering eyes—another reason I'm not rooting for team one.

"The two in the center for each team are the ones who go for the ball," Hudson tells me quietly. Now that his father is done talking, he's leaning forward, elbows braced on his knees, so he can talk to me.

"Do they run for it?" I ask, because this isn't something we practiced—or even discussed, I realize now.

"Not exactly," Hudson answers, and he nods toward the field. "Watch and see."

And so I do, eyes wide as a whistle blows and Nuri throws the ball up as high as her dragon strength will let her. It soars straight up, up, up, almost to the top of the dome, and no one goes for it. No one tries to touch it at all. But the second it begins to fall, it. Is. On.

Rafael uses every ounce of vampire strength he has to jump

straight at the ball, while Kali shoots flames out of her fingertips straight at where she assumes James and Cam will be. But they have tricks up their sleeves, too, and they're already under her blast radius. In the meantime, James sends a powerful cyclone of water straight toward Kali and Rafael, while Cam uses a wind spell to knock the ball several feet back from where it should be falling.

It's the most amazing thing I've ever seen, the byproduct of power flying this way and that as the four players battle for control of the ball. It's about a million times more exciting than the tip-off at the beginning of a basketball game, and I can't even begin to imagine what an NBA stadium would look like if this kind of action went on.

Probably a lot like this one, actually, with its crowds of students yelling and stomping in excitement.

Rafael overshoots because of Cam's wind spell and misses the ball, which falls straight toward James. He jumps, prepared to catch it, but Kali swoops in with an air spell of her own and yanks it away at the last second. She fires it straight at one of the other girls on her team, who catches it.

And the game is on.

The girl runs for about ten seconds, and then she just disappears.

"Where'd she go?" I demand, leaning forward and searching the field—like every other person in the entire arena.

"Watch and see," Hudson repeats, which is absolutely no help at all. I turn to Jaxon, but he's shouting encouragement to his friends.

Seconds later, the girl pops back up—all the way at the opposite end of the field from where she needs to be to win.

"Portals are a real bitch," Xavier says with a shake of his head. "Especially since her team isn't anywhere near her—"

He breaks off as Luca fades across the field to her in less than the blink of an eye. She tosses him the comet, and he fades right back to the other end of the field.

Except one of the dragons from Cam's team is there waiting, and as soon as he gets close, she sends a stream of fire at him that has him jerking to the right to avoid her...and falling straight into another portal.

This time, he pops up several seconds later at center field with the ball glowing bright red. He sends it soaring up and over to Rafael, who jumps to get it—but misses when one of the wolves intercepts it and takes off right back down the field.

"This is unbelievable!" I shout to be heard above the crowd, and everyone on my team grins at me.

"You haven't seen anything yet," Hudson says. "This is just the beginning."

"What does that even mean?" I ask, right before Rafael and a vampire from the other team fade straight at each other.

They collide with a huge *thump* that can be heard around the stadium, then go down in a tangle of limbs and fangs. Rafael pops up seconds later with the ball and disappears into another portal.

The game goes on like this for the next twenty minutes, until Kali finally crosses the finish line, the ball burning bright red in her hand.

The crowd goes wild, and I slump back in my seat, already worn out just from the adrenaline pumping through me.

"That was the most intense thing I've ever seen," I tell Jaxon, who grins at me.

"Just wait," he says as he leans forward to drop a kiss on my lips that makes me really, really uncomfortable, considering everyone who is watching.

"For what?" I ask. "I thought the match was over."

"For our turn," Eden answers for him. "If you think watching is intense, just wait until you're on the field."

I know she's right, and I can't help wondering what it's going to feel like, though I don't want to ask.

Hudson answers anyway. "Like you're caught in the middle of a tornado. Everything goes really slow and also superfast at the same time. And you're just along for the ride, waiting to see what part of the storm is going to kick the shit out of you."

A whole new flush of adrenaline surges through me. "Which part usually does the kicking?"

"In my experience?" he asks, brows raised.

"Yeah. I mean, who do I need to watch out for?"

"The dragons," he answers with a disgusted shake of his head. "It's always the bloody dragons who have the most tricks up their sleeves."

75

Now You See Me, Now You Don't

By the time our turn comes an hour later, I'm about to jump out of my skin.

"Break a wing," Hudson tells me as we head down to the waiting area while the refs and teachers reset the field, realigning the portals to come out different places than they did in the previous games, so that no one who's been trying to keep track has any extra advantage.

"Excuse me?" I answer, super offended. "Why would you wish that on me right before I go out to play the most important game of my life? Especially when I need to fly?"

He laughs. "I meant it in the break-a-leg context," he tells me with a shake of his head.

"Well, maybe be more specific next time," I answer. "Because it sounded like you meant it in the break-a-hip context."

"What are you, ninety?"

"What are you?" I snipe back. "Three hundred?"

"Age is just a number," he answers with a sniff.

"Yeah, that's what I thought." I roll my eyes.

"Don't be nervous," Jaxon says, taking my hand and squeezing it so tightly that I'm not sure he hasn't broken something.

"I don't think I'm the only one who's nervous here," I tease.

"Just excited." He grins. "I can't believe I'm actually going to play

Ludares. This is going to be so kick-ass."

My chest squeezes as I remember the Jaxon everyone knew before I got to Katmere. So certain he couldn't show an ounce of joy or weakness for fear a war among the species might break out. I'd forgotten this was the first time he'd allowed himself to compete.

"I know, right?" I start to say more, but Flint is in the middle of his team-captain-slash-cheerleader tour, where he gives every player a clap on the back and some encouraging words, and apparently it's Jaxon's and my turn.

"You've got this, okay?" he tells us. "Jaxon, don't be afraid to shake this shit up, *literally*, and you—" He gives me a mock-serious look that has me struggling to keep a straight face. "You just get up in the air and fly your little heart out. You're our secret weapon. Every other team only has two flyers, but we've got three—four if you count Jaxon."

"Yes, by all means, count the blimp," Hudson drawls.

Stop it, I hiss, but honestly, it takes every ounce of self-control I have not to laugh. Which only encourages Hudson more.

"Too bad there's a roof on this place. If we were lucky, he could just float away."

Stop, I say again as we start to walk out onto the field. *I actually have to pay attention now.*

"Okay, okay." He stops at the sidelines and watches as we head, single file, onto the field. We're almost to the purple line when he calls, "Hey, Grace?"

"Yeah?" I turn toward him instinctively.

He gives me a little chin nod. "Break a hip."

I burst out laughing all over again, and as I do, my stomach unclenches and the last of my nerves dissolve.

This time it's Aiden who marches onto the field with us and takes his place in the box. He's a lot more serious than the other members of the Circle—though not quite as serious as Cyrus—so there are no encouraging smiles from the dragon and no wishing of luck.

He just stands there waiting as team four lines up across from us. Liam is in the direct center of the lineup, and so is a dragon I've never met before. Flint calls him Caden, and the two do a little friendly trash-talking, but it's obviously all in good fun. That, combined with the fact that Rafael and Liam are on this team, convinces me that, while the competition might be fierce, it will probably also be fair.

One of the great things about my friends is they tend not to associate with assholes—which is a good quality to have in friends, if you ask me. Flint and Gwen line up in the center of our group with Jaxon next to Gwen and me next to Jaxon. Xavier is on my other side.

"You okay?" Jaxon asks as Aiden gets a new comet out of the center box.

"As ready as I'm ever going to be," I answer, suddenly uncomfortably aware of just how wet my palms are.

I surreptitiously rub them on my pants—hard to catch a ball with sweaty palms—and hope no one notices. But Xavier grins down at me and says, "Don't worry, gargoyle. Jaxon and I've got your back." He looks all proud wolf as he says it, head up, chest out, body loose and ready for the fight.

And though I know I should be grateful for the support, I can't help firing back, "Don't worry, wolf. I've got *your* back." And then I smack him right in the center of his shoulder blades, just because I can.

He looks startled but not mad, and then he tosses back his head and lets out a loud, excited howl that gets the entire stadium on their feet. I don't speak wolf, but I don't have to, to know that howl was a challenge and a statement of intent at the same time.

Especially when one of the wolves across from us howls back—though his isn't nearly as impressive as Xavier's.

Aiden just shakes his head, but for the first time I see a gleam of excitement in his eyes. Right before he throws the comet straight up.

For a second, it feels like everything is frozen as we all tilt our heads back and watch the ball go up, up, up. It finally reaches its ultimate height and hangs there before it eventually starts to come down.

And that's when it feels like the gates of hell open up around me. Flint shoots straight into the air, partially shifting as he goes so that he can use his wings to propel him upward. But the other dragon is doing the exact same thing, while Rafael jumps and grabs on to Flint, using his super-vampire strength to hold Flint back.

Flint roars in disapproval, shooting a stream of fire straight at the other dragon in an effort to slow him down even as he kicks Rafael in the face. Rafael's strength is dampened ten seconds faster than Flint's ability to fly, so Flint is eventually able to shake him off and use his powerful wings to propel him away from the other team before he's grounded for thirty seconds.

"Oh my God," I tell Jaxon and Xavier. "This is terrifying."

"No, this is amazing!" Xavier answers as, in the middle of the melee, Gwen quietly casts a spell and nets the ball right out from in front of the other team's dragon. Then she yanks it down and straight into her arms and starts to run for the nearest portal.

"Come on, Grace!" Jaxon shouts, and then we're running right along with Gwen. I have no idea what I'm supposed to be doing as Gwen dives headfirst into a portal, but I'm beginning to figure out that's part of the challenge, and the strategy, of the game.

Especially with the portals involved, no one knows exactly what's going to happen next, and the players who are the best at thinking on their feet are the ones who have the best shot of getting something done.

With that thought in mind, I stop running so fast and instead concentrate on watching as much of the field as I can, waiting for Gwen to pop back out of the portal.

She finally does, about halfway down the field from where the rest of us have managed to run. The ball is starting to glow red-hot, though, and I know she's going to need to get rid of it soon.

Eden figures it out, too, because she swoops down and grabs the ball in her talons. But her thirty seconds as a dragon are almost up, so she drops it to Flint, who rockets down the field with it.

But one of their witches casts a spell that binds his wings to his body, and he starts freefalling toward the earth. Macy counteracts the spell with a flick of her wand and some words I can't hear. Then snatches the ball away from him and takes off toward the goal line.

Rafael fades straight for her and I hold my breath, because I know she doesn't have a chance.

Jaxon must know, too, because he fades to her in what feels like the blink of an eye. She tosses him the ball, and then he takes off fading the short distance to the goal line. He's so close, I think he's going to make it. But then Rafael comes out of nowhere and slams into him so hard that they both go flying...and so does the ball, straight into the air.

Flint, Eden, and the two dragons on the other team go racing for the ball, but it looks like they're on as big of a collision course as the vampires were. Which means I might have a chance to swoop in and steal it.

I shift into my gargoyle form before I even finish the thought and take off flying. On the sidelines, I can hear Hudson shouting for me, but I don't have time to pay attention to that. Not when the four dragons are closing in on the ball like their lives depend on it. I only have thirty seconds of flight available, and I'm determined to reach the comet with a few seconds to spare.

Suddenly, Flint and Eden both disappear into two camouflaged midair tunnels—which leaves me the only one on the team with any chance of retrieving the ball. I lay on the speed, and since the other team's dragons make the mistake of thinking the threat is gone now that Flint and Eden have disappeared, I swoop in from behind and underneath them and steal the ball right out from in front of their noses...and claws.

I get a swipe across my wing for my trouble, but there are perks that come with being made of stone. And while it sets me off-kilter,

I manage to recover.

Part of me wants to make a run for the goal line, but I know that when it comes to speed, I'm no match for two dragons. So I swoop toward the ground and drop the ball into Xavier's waiting hands.

He takes off with it, but it isn't long before the vampires are on him, so he moves toward Jaxon, who has gotten back to his feet, and tosses the ball straight into his waiting hands.

Rafael makes a lunge for him, but Jaxon avoids him and fades his way straight to the goal line.

The whole match is over in less than two minutes, and no one is more surprised than I am that I actually played an important part in helping us win.

Once I'm down on the ground, Macy throws her arms around my shoulders and shouts, "One down, three to go."

"Three to go," I echo, grinning from ear to ear. Maybe this won't be so bad after all...

76

From Jock to Cock-a-Doodle-Doo

The rest of the day passes in a blur of excitement and anxiety, exhaustion and adrenaline rushes.

Our second match takes more than twenty-five minutes and nearly destroys us, while our third match is even worse. We pull it out, though, then watch in disgust as team twelve beats team three in a game that stretches forty-five minutes long and leaves the team led by the alpha wolf, Cole, as the only other one standing.

"Oh shit," Xavier snarls, and there's a wealth of rage in those two words. He drops back down onto the bleachers as Cole runs the ball across the goal line, much to the excitement of half the stadium.

The other half groans in dismay, and I groan right along with them. Considering our history with Cole, that wolf is going to be out for blood.

Normally, it would be strange for Xavier to have the same feelings I do, since Cole is technically his alpha. But Xavier is a relatively new transfer to Katmere, too—he's only been here about a year—and as I've learned over the last couple of days, not a big fan of the school's alpha.

Not that I blame him. Cole is a total jerk, and that's putting it mildly. Then again, stealing a guy's canine will likely piss off even the best person, and Cole is definitely not that.

"He's a total arse," Hudson says. "Personally, I think someone should have challenged him a long time ago."

"Give Xavier time," I respond. "I'm pretty sure that's coming before the end of the year."

He grins. "I knew there was a reason I liked that wolf."

"Look at it this way," I tell Xavier as I reach over and grab his hand in solidarity. "After today, he's going to be so humiliated that everything else that happened before isn't even going to register."

"You mean like when Jaxon drained him in front of the whole school?" Xavier says, with a wicked gleam in his eye. "Or like when someone else drained him in the middle of the night? Or—"

"Yes," I tell him. "Yes, that's exactly what I mean."

"Oh, goodie." He grins. "Please, universe. Please let me be the one to plow my elbow straight down his throat in the middle of a pileup."

"I was thinking your foot," I tease him. "But if you want to go small..."

His smile turns into a full-on belly laugh as he holds a hand up for a high five. "Girl, I like your style."

"Good," I tell him as I slap my hand against his. "Because you're pretty much the only one in this whole school who does."

"That's totally not true," Eden says, dropping back to wrap a hand around my shoulder. "Any girl who can keep Jaxon *and* Hudson Vega in line at the same time is a girl I can get behind."

I just shake my head. "You've got a very broad definition of 'in line.'"

"Hey!" Jaxon yelps. "What's that supposed to mean?"

I roll my eyes at him teasingly. "It means that I'm not sure who's more trouble. You or your brother."

"My brother," he and Hudson say at the exact same time.

"I rest my case."

"You know," Flint tells Xavier quietly as the mandatory fifteen-minute rest period kicks in for the other team, "if you need to kind of chill out this game, so you don't piss off your alpha, we get it."

"Umm, no, we don't," Macy grumps. "Cole's got a solid team. We're going to need every single one of us."

"I don't understand, either," Xavier answers, looking completely affronted. "What kind of asshole do you think I am?"

"The kind who has to live under this alpha for at least another year," Flint tells him. "We can still kick their asses, even if you need to hang back a little."

"I'm not hanging back!" Xavier looks seriously pissed as he goes into full peacock mode. Chest out, feathers up, and eyes wild with a vicious annoyance. "Give me half a chance, and I'll be the first one to kick that guy's ass, alpha or not."

"Okay, okay." Flint holds up a conciliatory hand. "I just thought I'd offer."

"Yeah, well, don't do me any favors," Xavier tells him, and it's obvious he's still pissed.

I wait a few minutes before I move over to sit next to him. "You know Flint didn't mean any harm, right?" I say quietly.

"I'm not a punk," he fires back. "I didn't come this far with you guys just to sell you out to make things easier for myself. That's not who I am."

"I know," I tell him as Macy moves to sit on his other side.

"I think you're super brave going against Cole," she tells him, and I swear he puffs up a little more right in front of us. And since he's in good hands with Macy, I move back to Jaxon—just in time for the bell to go off, warning us to get to the field.

"You've got this," Jaxon tells me, giving me a hug for luck as we move toward the field. "You're a badass, Grace, so just go for it."

Once we're there, it's to see that Cyrus himself is waiting to escort us onto the field. Of course he is. No way would he let the final match go on without him.

I've managed to avoid him since he arrived, so this will be the first time I'll get the up-close-and-personal introduction. Super excited... not. #ratherhavearootcanal

He smiles when he sees Jaxon, but there's no warmth in it at all. And the cold blue eyes he runs over me might be the same shade as Hudson's, but the look in them gives me the creeps in a really big way.

I try to ignore him—and the stakes of this final game—but as I line up on the purple paint between Xavier and Macy, my stomach goes from tight to doing backward somersaults.

Because while this might just be a game to everyone else in the arena, for me this means a whole lot more. I lean forward to look at Jaxon, maybe even try to catch his attention, but he and Flint are in an intense eye fight with the guys on the other team directly facing them. Any other time, I'd be amused at their intensity, but right now, I'm trying not to vomit up funnel cake and humiliate myself in front of my mate.

"You've got this," Hudson tells me. *"Just fly your badass heart out and you'll do great."*

I don't know about that. I look across at Cole's team, which is made up of some of the biggest assholes in the school—big surprise. I glance at Jaxon, who's been holding his own all day but is definitely showing signs of fatigue, although far less than I'd have imagined with Hudson still feeding on the mating bond. *I have a feeling I'm about to get my ass handed to me.*

"Look at it this way," he tells me with a wicked grin. *"At the end of the day, there are way worse asses that you could have in your hands."*

Wow. Those are your words of wisdom?

"I'm not old enough to be wise, so yeah. Pretty much." I can sense his smile fade. *"Also, this isn't the only bloodstone in the world. It's the easiest to get our hands on, but it's not the only one. So whatever happens in this game, it's going to be okay. Okay?"*

The tightness in my chest eases. *Thank you.*

"Good. Now go kick that smug werewolf's ass, will you, please?"

I grit my teeth. *I'll do my best.*

I take a deep breath and stare back across the line at Cole's team. They still look like the biggest assholes in the school, so that hasn't changed.

But the knot in my stomach is a lot looser, and Hudson's words keep playing in my head. No matter what happens here, everything is going to be okay. I can work with that.

"Ready?" Flint asks from where he and Jaxon are lined up in the center of our team.

When we all nod, he grins and says, "Okay, then. Let's kick some alpha werewolf ass."

Two seconds later, the whistle blows.

Cyrus definitely has the same strength his sons do, because the ball goes up, up, up until it nearly touches the stadium's ceiling. Still, the second it starts to fall, all hell breaks loose.

Or at least, that's what it feels like when you're in the middle of a vampire, a werewolf, a dragon, and a witch all racing for the same ball.

Flint lets out a billow of ice straight at Cole and his teammate, a witch by the name of Jacqueline. The ice hits her, and she freezes for ten seconds, but Cole jumps over the blast as he dives for the ball. Jaxon's there before him, though, his telekinesis knocking the ball out of Cole's range. But he blasts it so hard that he sends it spinning straight up at the roof again.

The crowd groans at the mistake, and so do I as I send him a little "you've got this" vibe down the mating bond. He sends a laugh back, and that's when I realize it wasn't a mistake at all. Because Flint's partially shifted, and he's already up there waiting to snatch the ball right out of the air.

Cole bellows in rage as Flint snags the ball and fully shifts in midair, now flying straight toward the goal line as fast as he can go. He's been air-bound about ten seconds, and he likely can make it to the goal in the twenty seconds of flight he has left, but the ball has started burning red in his hands. And by the time he's halfway to the goal, he can't disguise the ripples of pain echoing through him. He has to toss the ball to Eden, who's launched herself into the air after him.

She reaches for the ball, a huge smile on her face as she realizes just how close to the goal line they are. Even I hold my breath, wondering if this match is really going to be over this easily.

But out of nowhere, one of the vamps on Cole's team jumps and intercepts the ball.

It's Flint's turn to shout as the vamp hits the ground with a solid *thud* and starts fading toward the opposite goal line. He's almost there, and now I've gone from excited to totally freaking out, thinking there's no way we're going to catch him. But then Mekhi pops out of a portal a few feet from the goal line and charges straight into him.

Yay!

I'm so excited that I start clapping, even as the ensuing crash makes a deep crater in the field. The crowd gasps, thinking one of them might be hurt, but Mekhi just rolls through it, picking the ball up from under the other vampire as he does. And disappears straight into another portal.

This one lets him out at center field, but the ball is already starting to glow red-hot. Mekhi's grimacing as he looks around—for Jaxon or Flint, I assume—but they've both fallen through portals in their race to get to the other vampire.

Xavier races up behind him, though—Cole hot on his ass—and grabs the ball before somersaulting through the air and literally diving into the closest portal, one hand holding the ball tucked up close to his side.

"Where is he; where is he?" Macy shouts as she looks wildly around the field, but none of us has an answer for her because he's not out yet. The seconds tick by, and I start to panic, because if someone isn't close to him when he finally makes it out of the portal, we are totally and completely screwed.

I glance at the clock on the side of the field. It reads twenty-seven seconds when Xavier finally emerges from the portal, which means he has three seconds to give the ball away before it starts to burn him. And I'm standing exactly three feet away from him.

Shit.

He throws the ball at me and I fumble it, nearly drop it as nerves race through me. The crowd goes nuts, but I'm beyond listening as I struggle to hold on to the edge of the ball as Cole comes barreling straight at me.

Shit. Shit. Shit.

After several hours of playing, I'm not ashamed to admit I'm feeling the strain. I need to get the ball and shift fast, but I hesitate, worried it'll take the last of my strength and Cole will finally get his revenge. But I clench my jaw and narrow my eyes on the ball. I've got this.

I manage to get a grip on it at the exact same time Cole launches himself at me, and I shift on the run, shoot straight into the air the second I've got my wings. Cole manages to grab on to my foot, though, and he's so strong that I can't shake him off.

Which means I'm basically flying through the stadium with Cole hanging off me. Which, okay, except the ball is really starting to vibrate, and I'm going to have to land soon, something I won't be able to do with a werewolf attached to my damn foot.

Thankfully, Eden is racing toward me, her purple dragon wings catching huge air, but the ball is starting to vibrate so hard that I don't think I can hold on much longer. Plus, I'm a little afraid I'm going to lose a finger. But this is for the bloodstone. This is to get Hudson out of my head. So I do the only thing I can think of, the only thing that will get Cole off me. I lift my other foot up and kick Cole straight in the face as hard as I can.

He screams, but he lets go, falling about fifteen feet to the ground below, and I turn around and throw the ball straight at Eden.

She catches it with a dragon's roar and a thumbs-up, and then she's racing toward the finish line. She's almost there and the crowd is on their feet, chanting for her—and so are we—when one of the witches from Cole's team hits her with a spell that has her spinning wildly toward the ground.

Shit!

Fear grips me by the throat as I worry about her getting hurt—dragon or not, that's a really long fall, and if it's a nearly fatal one, she'll be disqualified and magically removed from the game—but Jaxon blasts out with his telekinesis and keeps her from slamming into the ground. Before one of us can get the ball from her, though, the other werewolf on Cole's team swoops in and grabs it.

Macy and I race toward him, but he dives into a portal right before one of us gets there. To my surprise, Macy dives in after him. Twenty-five seconds later, they finally emerge, but he's lying stunned on the ground and she's got the ball. It's burning red-hot, though, so she throws it to Xavier, who catches it on the fly.

The only problem? They're all the way at the other end of the field again, and Cole's entire team is between them and the goal line. Then again, so are we.

Xavier runs for twenty seconds, dodging hexes and dragon fire and even a vampire bite to the shoulder as Mekhi and Jaxon try to fight off a witch and a dragon so one of them can fade to him.

Gwen and I race forward, happy that everyone else is occupied, but before either of us can get to Xavier, Cole brings him down with a body slam about halfway up the field. Xavier's not going out with a fight, however, and he rolls away, clutching the ball to his chest as it burns hotter and vibrates so hard, I can hear it halfway across the field.

Just then, Cole slices a massive claw straight toward Xavier's arm. I wince in anticipation of how much it's going to hurt, even if Xavier's magically protected from the claw piercing skin. But at the last second, Cole flicks his wrist and the claw misses Xavier's arm entirely.

But it turns out Cole wasn't aiming for the arm at all. Everyone in the stadium gasps as, instead, he slices the magical bracelet on Xavier's wrist clean off. We watch it fall to the ground as if in slow motion. Xavier's eyes widen when he finally realizes what the rest of us have already caught on to. Cole's next blow, his clawed hand already arcing above Xavier, is headed straight for Xavier's unprotected throat.

My heart stutters in my chest. Gwen is pretty close, but not close enough to help Xavier. And neither am I. No one is.

The whole stadium is on their feet as Cole's razor-sharp claws close the distance with Xavier's neck in the blink of an eye. There is a collective gasp. It's a death blow. There's no way—

There's a huge roar from the crowd because... I blink... Blink again... Wow. Not a death blow after all, because Cole is now...a fluffy white chicken. His soft feathers gently caress Xavier's neck as his small chicken body falls the three feet to the ground to squawk angrily.

My gaze darts around the arena until I connect with Macy, who obviously popped up through another portal about thirty feet from Xavier in the middle of all the drama. She looks as white as a sheet. Also hella pissed. And deeply satisfied at humiliating Cole for such a cowardly, and almost deadly, move.

But we don't have time to savor the image of Cole clucking, because the spell won't last much longer and Xavier is on his feet in a split second, the comet still burning bright in his hands. The stadium erupts in cheering and foot stomping.

Quickly looking around, he spies Eden and tosses her the comet as she swoops in from behind. She's climbing now, her powerful wings taking her fifty feet in the air in seconds. But Cole's team isn't out, and one of the witches slams Eden with a lightning bolt and Eden is tumbling from the sky, the comet no longer in her hands and falling as well.

I launch myself into the air after it. The only problem is that one of their dragons has done the same thing, so we race each other to the ball. My heart is pounding faster and faster the closer we get, and I'm determined to win the race as another burst of energy from Jaxon via the mating bond sizzles along my skin.

I fly faster than I've ever flown, but he still gets there first.

Well, what's the point of being a gargoyle if you can't turn someone into stone every once in a while? Praying this works, I grab on to his wing with one hand and pull on the platinum string deep inside me with the other. He changes instantly...and without the wing design to carry a large dragon *made of heavy stone*, well, he starts to drop like a stone.

I flip the ball right out of his stone hands and then let go of the platinum string when we're about twenty feet off the ground.

He changes back to a living dragon instantly, and he is beyond pissed. He hits me with every ounce of fire he's got, but hey, gargoyle, baby. I don't feel a thing. So I wave goodbye and then somersault backward—straight into a portal that I did not see coming.

And holy hell! It feels like I'm being pulled apart, my entire body being stretched from end to end like I'm one of those rubber toys you get at arcade games as a kid. It doesn't hurt, but it feels really strange, and it's all I can do to hold on to the ball as even my hands start to stretch.

Still, there's no way I'm coming out of this portal without this ball. No way in hell. So I dig down deep and hold on as tight as I can. That's when the pain starts—when I resist the stretch—but I don't care. I am not messing this up, not when we're so close.

And then, suddenly, the pain is gone and the portal is vomiting me back onto the field. Unlike everyone else, I can't keep my footing, and I end up rolling straight onto my back like a turtle. But I've got the ball. That's all that matters. Even if it is vibrating so much that my fingers feel like they're starting to crack.

I roll over, looking for someone to throw the thing to, and Jaxon lands right in front of me with a grin and a wink. I toss him the ball, and then he's fading away, running full tilt toward the goal...at the other end of the field. Again.

Seriously, these portals completely suck.

I race behind him—well behind him—not sure what else I can do at this point. I won't be able to fly again for another thirty seconds. But then Cole and the other werewolf start to pass me in wolf form, heading straight for Jaxon. I can't take down both of them, but I sure as hell can take down one, so I throw myself sideways straight into Cole.

He snarls like a rabid dog, his teeth closing on my hand. But again, stone, so it doesn't hurt. But for the second time today, he's not turning loose, so now he's dragging me like a rag doll down the field by one arm.

Not quite what I was going for with what I hoped would be a heroic save. Not sure what else to do, I reach up with my other hand and pull his tail as hard as I can.

He screams like a pissed-off child, which means he lets go of my hand just long enough for me to yank it away. But he's furious now and focused completely on me and not the ball. Which seems like it could be a problem.

At least until Xavier swoops in with a snarl—also in wolf form—and backs him down and away from me.

Cole turns and runs straight toward Jaxon like he's just remembered the ball, but I know the truth and so does Xavier. We saw his face when he ran. He was scared of Xavier, which I'm afraid is going to have ramifications way beyond this game.

But for now, Jaxon is almost to the finish line. Thank God! I don't think my nerves can handle much more of this.

Before he can get there, though, one of the vampires throws himself right in his path and shoves him back just as his foot is about to cross the goal. Jaxon goes flying and so does the other vampire, both of them spinning out of control through the air.

Jaxon lands on his feet, but he's cursing, the ball so hot, it's practically incandescent at this point. He has no other choice but to drop it. Luckily Gwen is close, and she swoops in to pick it up. Then she's running back toward the goal. One of the dragons is hot on her heels, so she lifts a hand above her head and calls the elements.

A powerful gust of wind swirls through the field, knocking the dragon out of the air and sending him careening into the witch who thought she was sneaking up on Gwen, wand raised.

But then, out of nowhere, the other vamp slams into Gwen. They fly sideways into a portal and are gone for about ten seconds, though it feels like forever as the timer on the side of the game crawls past twenty-seven seconds. Eventually Gwen staggers out a few feet from me, the red-hot comet clutched in her hands. But she's banged up pretty badly and she's clutching her ribs.

I'm worried about her, but the ref has her, so—grateful that my flying time-out is over—I race forward, grab the comet, and then fly straight toward the goal line with every ounce of strength and speed I have. Cole is racing along behind me, howling with rage, but I don't look at him. I don't look at anyone or anything but the goal line. This is our last shot to win this, and I am not going to screw it up.

Out of the corner of my eye, I see both dragons from the other team racing straight for me. I can't stop them, so I don't worry about them. I just fly. And right before they overtake me, I reach inside myself and pull on the platinum string again, forcing more of my body to turn to stone, and then I instantly drop fifteen feet straight down from the extra weight. And they collide overhead like an explosion.

But that doesn't matter, because I'm at the goal line. I release the string and yank on my human golden string, shed the extra weight, then fly straight over the goal and drop to the ground just before my thirty seconds of flight are up.

77

Comet Me, Baby

"We did it!" Flint crows for what has to be the hundredth time since we won the tournament earlier this afternoon. He shoots me an excited grin as he drops a few six-packs of soda on the table in Jaxon's tower antechamber.

"Damn straight we did!" Xavier echoes, crossing to meet him so the two of them can engage in the typical backslapping and chest-bumping celebration that comes with winning a sporting event. "Cole who?"

"That's what I'm saying," Eden agrees from where she's sitting on the couch, her scuffed purple combat boots propped on Jaxon's coffee table. "Swear to God, the best part was his face at the end. He couldn't believe they'd used all the dirty tricks and still lost."

"Dude. In what universe is a werewolf *ever* going to beat a dragon?" Flint scoffs.

"Excuse me?" Xavier asks. "What am I?"

"I haven't figured it out yet, actually," Flint answers, looking him up and down. "Maybe a weredragon? Or a dragonwolf?"

"Let's go with *wolf*dragon," he tells Flint with a grin.

"I could get behind that," Eden agrees, making grabby hands at Macy as she rounds the corner from the top of the stairs carrying a truly impressive number of pizza boxes from the cafeteria.

"How's Gwen?" I ask Macy.

"Her girlfriend texted me, told me they gave her a bunch of painkillers and she's sleeping in the infirmary right now. But she should be okay in a few days." She plops the boxes down on Jaxon's coffee table. "What are we debating now?"

"He's more dragon than wolf, so dragon should go first," Flint continues, grabbing a box off the top of the stack...and then keeping it for himself. "I mean, Xavier here's not a douche, is he?"

"True that," I say. And since—gargoyle or not—I don't have the amazing metabolism that comes with the ability to scarf down an entire pizza or three, I grab a much more sedate two pieces out of the communal pepperoni box before settling on the floor at one end of the coffee table.

"Not all wolves are douches," Xavier answers, right before he also grabs his own personal pizza box. "Just the ones at Katmere."

"You can say that louder for the people in the back," Mekhi tells him from his seat next to me.

"Like alpha, like everyone," Jaxon agrees. "That's why you should challenge him, Xavier. Once he's gone, the rest of the wolves will knock all their shit out."

"Pretty sure our boy already challenged that jackass on the Ludares field today," Flint answers. "You owned his ass before it was done. He was clucking long before Macy turned him into a chicken."

"We owned *all* their asses today," Eden says right before shoving half a piece of pizza into her mouth. "Every single one."

"But seriously? Best play of the game *has to* go to Macy. Not only did she save dear Xavier's life, but did everyone see Cole's tiny chicken body plop to the ground and cluck around for what felt like the happiest ten seconds of my life?" Mekhi laughs so hard, there are tears in his eyes. "And close second is when Grace was just flying down the field with Cole hanging off her foot." He brings his fingers and thumb together to mimic Cole biting me.

"Oh yeah," I tell him, totally deadpan, as the others crack up.

"That was sooo hilarious."

"Maybe not for you," Jaxon tells me with the grin that always sets butterflies off in my stomach. "But it was pure gold for the rest of us."

"I actually really liked it when you turned Seraphina to stone," Eden tells me. "It was the coolest move I've ever seen on a Ludares field."

"Yeah, it was," Flint agrees. "And did you see when…"

He keeps talking, while I turn to Jaxon beside me. "Are all dragons such braggarts?" I whisper.

"You haven't seen anything." He doesn't bother to whisper as he rolls his eyes. "Once Flint gets going, it takes hours to wind him back down again."

"I'm not a cuckoo clock, you know," Flint tells him, and though he's wearing that goofy grin of his, there's a flash of something that looks an awful lot like hurt there, too. "You can't actually wind me up."

"It's not the winding *up* I'm interested in," Jaxon responds, and suddenly I feel really awful, as I can't help thinking about what Flint told me on the field this morning.

"Anybody need another drink?" I ask as I stand and head over to the table near the window. Eden and Flint both ask for a soda, while Macy requests a sparkling water.

I take my time gathering everything up, mostly because I need a minute before I head back over there.

I get that Flint doesn't think I've connected the dots, and I know his heart is breaking over Jaxon, but there's a part of me that wishes he hadn't chosen me to be that person there for him this morning. Jaxon's my mate. How am I supposed to feel except guilty as hell that he's hurting and I'm the reason? Especially since they've known each other way longer than Jaxon and I have.

I'm the interloper. I'm the one who came along and probably messed everything up in Flint's mind. But what am I supposed to do? Just give up my mate? I couldn't even if I wanted to, and I most definitely don't want to. Which leaves us where? With me breaking one of my closest friends' hearts just by existing? Or me watching while he breaks that heart on Jaxon over and over again?

It's awful just to think about, my soul hurting for Flint in a way that makes me ache deep down inside. I just wish there was something, *anything* I could do to make this better.

"There's nothing," Hudson says in a surprisingly serious voice as he walks over and flops down against the wall next to Jaxon's bedroom, about as far from the group as he can possibly get and still be in the same room. I'd wondered where he went during the game, figured maybe he'd stayed away so I could focus. But now, I stare at the dark circles under his eyes, the fatigue hunching his shoulders, the hollowness in his cheeks, making his cheekbones look even sharper.

My chest is so tight, I can barely breathe. I glance from him to Jaxon, who is laughing at something Mekhi is saying, the picture of health and energy, and then at Hudson, gaunt and exhausted. And I know Jaxon wasn't the one giving me his energy on the field. It was Hudson.

I'm about to mention it when I see his expression shift. He doesn't want me to make a big deal about it...so I don't.

Instead, I forget the drinks and walk over to where Hudson is and sit down next to him. I want to send him some of my energy, but I know he won't accept it. So instead, I pick up our conversation again.

"But I want to do something..." I search for the right words. "I feel like I should be able to fix this."

"Flint knows it's too late, Grace. Now he's just trying to figure out how to deal with the disappointment. Let him."

There's a layer of undercurrent there that I can't even begin to unpack right now. Lia? I wonder. How weird must it be to know that your mate loved you so much that she died to bring you back? But also, how awful.

"I already told you—she wasn't my mate." Hudson's voice cuts like a switchblade. I wait for him to say more, but he doesn't. At least not about Lia. "You're right, though. Flint probably shouldn't have brought you into his mess."

"It's not a mess. It's how he feels," I say, looking around to make sure no one can hear me. They're all used to watching me talk to empty space and pay me no mind. Still, I keep my voice extra low. "He can't help how he feels."

I'm still wondering about all the weird vibes I'm picking up from Hudson about Lia. Not that I'm going to push or anything. One painful relationship confession a day is already more than I can take…

"The two aren't mutually exclusive, you know," he says in the super-snooty British accent he gets only when he's trying to make me feel childish…or trying to piss me off. "Emotions are absurdly messy all the time."

"Is that why you don't let yourself have any?" I shoot back. "Because they're too messy for you?"

There's another long silence. Then, "Do try to keep up, Grace. I have plenty of emotions. Mostly loathing, at the moment, but a feeling's a feeling."

I roll my eyes. "You're never going to change."

"Oh, if only that were true." He quirks a brow. "Better hurry with those drinks. The hoard is getting restless."

Before I can answer, Flint calls, "Hey, do you need some help?" Or, in other words, *Where's my drink?*

"Nope, I've got it," I tell him, grabbing a Dr Pepper for myself before piling all the drinks up and carrying them back over to the coffee table.

"So the assembly to get the bloodstone is tomorrow afternoon," Macy says once I'm settled back down between her and Jaxon. "Next item is the dragon bone. We should get that before the assembly starts."

"If we go tomorrow, Gwen won't be able to join us," Mekhi says. "I stopped by the infirmary to check on her before we came up here and she's doing better, but Marise says she is definitely out of commission for a day or two."

"Poor Gwen," I commiserate. "Her arm looked awful."

"It was awful," Mekhi agrees.

"She'll hate missing the Boneyard," Macy says. "But we need to get this done so we can move on to the next item."

"Wait a minute, go back." Eden looks at Flint. "Is this why you were asking about the Boneyard?" When he nods, she asks, "What do you need a dragon bone for?"

I think about blowing off her question, but the truth is all eight of us won the bloodstone. If only a few of us claim it for a prize, we're going to look like real jerks.

Jaxon must feel the same way, because he answers, "We entered the tournament because we need the bloodstone for a really important spell. But we also need a few other things as well—including a dragon bone."

"A dragon bone," Eden muses before she turns to Flint with wide eyes. "From the Boneyard? You're actually *taking* them to the *Boneyard*?"

"They have to go," he tells her. "What am I supposed to do? Just let them wander around down there and hope they don't die?"

"Wander down where?" Macy squeaks, and now she's the one with wide eyes. "What kind of place are you taking us to?"

"The magical kind that doesn't want non-dragons to visit," Eden answers. "Or even *dragons*, for that matter."

"Yeah, well, unfortunately, we don't have a choice," Jaxon tells her grimly, and then he fills the whole group in on the details of my situation.

"So," Xavier says, leaning forward so our gazes are locked. "He's in there right now?" He taps the side of my head gently.

"Does he think he can shake me out?" Hudson asks dryly. "Or is he just trying to stare longingly into my eyes?"

A little bit of both, maybe? I answer, because seriously. Who does that?

"Yes," Jaxon says, sliding forward so he can stop Xavier before he gives me a concussion. "He is. And the only way to get him out is with these five objects."

"But do we really want him out?" Mekhi asks. "I mean, it didn't go so well for everyone the last time he was free."

"And it's not going so well for my mate now that he isn't," Jaxon snaps and Mekhi—along with everyone else—kind of sits back a little at his tone. Now that Jaxon's more approachable, I think people tend to forget he's still Jaxon, still the dark prince, and I think he must have reminded them.

"He took her body over more than once," Jaxon continues. "He knows her every thought, has access to our mating bond. So yeah, he has to go. As soon as possible."

"Yeah, he does," Xavier agrees, looking a little horrified at Jaxon's listing. Plus, he's not pounding on my temple anymore.

"Well, then, I'm in," Eden says.

"In what?" I ask, a little baffled.

"In for the Boneyard and whatever else you need to do."

"Yeah, me too," says Xavier. "Hijacking a girl's body like that just isn't cool. What a douche canoe."

I glance over at Hudson, who's now got his head tilted back against the wall, eyes closed. I can feel his exhaustion from here. "Everyone's a critic," he mutters.

"Count me in, too," Mekhi says. "You know I've always got your back, Jaxon. And yours, too, now, Grace."

"My dad is going to flip if he finds out we got three more of his students involved," Macy says. "I talked to him, and he's agreed to keep the Circle busy and out of our hair tomorrow morning while we sneak down to the Boneyard, but he's not happy about us going alone. He's really not going to be happy about us taking all of you."

"Plus, it's dangerous," I tell them. "Really dangerous."

"Umm, pretty sure I'm the one who just said that," Eden answers with a shrug. "But you know, sometimes a girl's gotta do what a girl's gotta do. And apparently, what your girl needs to do is kick a homicidal maniac out of her head."

"Cheers to that," Flint says, raising his soda. "Besides, sometimes—"

"Careful just doesn't get the job done," Jaxon joins in with a huge grin.

"Damn straight." Flint nods with satisfaction at what must be an inside joke between the two, before clapping his hands together. "So, just to be clear, we're doing this thing tomorrow morning?"

"Damn straight," Eden agrees, and everyone nods.

"Wait a minute—aren't we getting ahead of ourselves?" I ask. "I mean, we don't even know where the Boneyard is yet, do we?"

"We do," Flint says, exchanging a glance with Eden. "I talked to my grandma about it, but I also asked Eden to talk to *her* grandma the other day when you asked me, and she got the deets."

"The good news is, we won't have to travel very far," Eden says. "The bad news is, Grand-mère says only someone with a death wish would go there. Almost no one makes it out alive."

78

Talk About a Bone to Pick

"**N**o one makes it out alive?" Macy says, eyes wide. "Wow, that sounds like fun."

"Don't worry, Mace," Xavier answers. "We can handle a bunch of old bones."

"It's a little more complicated than that," Flint tells him.

"But we can do it," Eden says. "I know it."

"On the plus side, it can't be worse than going after a beast that's impossible to kill," I interject. "Just saying."

"Love that optimism," Mekhi tells me. Then looks out at the group. "I say we go for it."

"Tomorrow, five a.m.," Jaxon orders before asking Flint and Eden, "Where do we need to meet?"

"The tunnels," Flint answers, and my stomach drops. But it is what it is. Sometimes you just have to put your head down and get the bad stuff done, even if you don't want to.

"Sounds good to me," Xavier says as he picks up his box and soda can and throws them in the recycling container at the top of the stairs. The rest of us follow suit, and the party breaks up soon after.

The tournament took a lot out of all of us, and no one wants to stick around for a late night. Except me... Hudson is sound asleep now, so spending a little time with my mate without his brother butting in every ten seconds sounds like heaven.

I wait until Flint leaves—no reason to rub things in—before I settle on the sofa next to Jaxon and lift his hand to my mouth. He watches me with blazing-hot eyes for several seconds, then wraps his arms around me and pulls me against his body.

We both sigh at the contact. "You feel really good," he tells me.

"So do you." I lift my head and wait for him to kiss me, but he just drops a peck on my lips. Which is nice, but definitely not what I'm going for here.

I stretch up and kiss him this time, but again he pulls away after a second.

I can't decide if he's doing it on purpose because he's trying to be funny or if there's a problem I don't know about. But when I search his face, he smiles warmly, like he's having a great time.

And that's when I decide to take matters into my own hands. Standing up, I hold out a hand to him and say, "Come on, let's go"—I add air quotes for what I'm now thinking should be our forever secret code for "make out"—"watch the aurora borealis."

He looks confused. "You want to go see the northern lights? Now?"

"Yes, now!" I would stomp my foot like a petulant child, except I'm afraid the sudden movement will wake up Hudson. And that's the last thing I want.

"O-kay." Jaxon gives me a weird look as we move toward his bedroom—and the parapet outside his window. "Any particular reason why? I mean, I'm fine with it. I just—"

I grab him by the sweater and yank him down toward me so that I can slam my lips onto his.

"Oh," he murmurs in surprise. Then a deeper, "Oh," as he wraps his arms around me and picks me up and carries me to his bed, our mouths still locked together.

He turns so that he's the one who hits the bed first, and I land on top of him. I straddle his hips with my knees and start kissing my way along his neck, relishing the way he feels against me. Hard. Strong. Perfect.

Jaxon groans and tilts his head back to give me better access, even as his hands mold my hips. "Wait," he gasps as I kiss the razor-sharp edge of his jaw. "What about Hudson?"

"Asleep," I answer, my hands sliding underneath his shirt to stroke the warm skin of his stomach.

He groans and then rolls us until I'm stretched out underneath him. "Why didn't you say so?" he asks, leaning on his elbows right above me.

"I tried. What do you think the whole 'aurora borealis' thing was all about?"

He looks confused. "What do you mean—" He breaks off as understanding dawns. "Wait a minute. That was your *move*?"

"I wouldn't exactly call it a move." I frown at him, but he's already shaking his head and laughing.

"I never would have guessed it. The aurora borealis as a move." He gives me a nod of respect. "That's smooth. I like it."

"Obviously not *that* smooth," I tell him, "since we're talking about it instead of kissing under it."

"Well, by all means, let's get back to it, then. I'd hate to disappoint you." He waves a hand and his curtains slide out of the way, showing the aurora borealis shimmering just beyond his window.

And then he's kissing me and it feels so good. So right. His mouth moving on mine. His hair tickling my cheek. His hands slipping under my sweater and sliding against my skin.

I arch in to him, tangling our legs together as he skims his lips down my neck and across my collarbone. I tilt my head to the side, offering him my neck—offering him my vein—and his fangs scrape gently against my skin.

Anticipation slides down my spine. I've missed this so much. I move against him, tangle my hands in his hair, and—my phone alarm goes off, blaring obnoxiously in the silence.

Jaxon pulls away with a groan. "What is that for?"

"I'm supposed to FaceTime with Heather tonight." I sit up and pull my phone out so I can swipe off the alarm. "Let me just text her and say I'll call in a little—"

"It can't be morning already," Hudson complains with a groan.

"And fuck, just fuck. Hudson's up." I flop back down on the bed and stare up at the ceiling.

Jaxon takes one look at my face and does the same. "He always was a light sleeper. Even when we were kids."

"Yeah, well, it comes from never knowing if your father was going to come into the room and try to kill you or your younger brother," Hudson snipes back, his voice a little stiff as he must figure out what was going on while he slept.

"That's awful," I whisper, my opinion of Cyrus—and Delilah—sinking even lower, and honestly, I didn't think that was possible.

I can feel Hudson shrug in my mind.

"What's wrong?" Jaxon asks, rolling onto his side so he can get a better look at my face. "Are you nervous about tomorrow?"

I take the out, not willing to betray Hudson's confidence. "I am, actually. What if it's as bad as Eden's grandmother says?"

"Don't worry about it," Jaxon answers with a confident smile. "I'll protect you."

"That's not the point." I sit up, annoyed by his sudden "I'm the guy; I've got this" attitude. "The point is we're asking a lot of people we care about to risk their lives to help me. I don't want to see anyone get hurt."

"I'm telling you, I've got this," Jaxon says. "I can protect all of you. It's what I do."

"And *I* keep telling you that I don't *want* someone to protect me. I want to stand on my own two feet, *beside* my mate, not behind him—" I break off as the FaceTime ring starts coming from my phone.

"What?" Jaxon asks, looking confused.

I don't answer him. Instead, I hold my phone up and say, "I've got to take this. I haven't talked to Heather in forever." I drop an absent-minded kiss on the top of his head before walking through the alcove toward the stairs. "I'll see you tomorrow."

"I've gotta say, Grace," Hudson tells me as I swipe to answer Heather's call, *"you never cease to surprise me."*

79

Talk About a
Trust Fall

The next morning, I fire off a couple of quicks texts to Heather as Macy and I hustle down the last hallway toward the tunnels.

Me: So good to FINALLY talk to you last night

Me: Can't believe your parents bought you a ticket to Alaska for your bday!!!!! Can't wait to see you xoxoxo

It was so good to talk to her last night that I never wanted to hang up. I miss her so much and can't believe she forgave me for my four-month absence as easily as she did. I was totally prepared to grovel.

Instead, I found out she's going to come visit me for spring break… if I survive the next few days, anyway. *And* if I can figure out how to break the news to her that paranormals exist and that I'm a gargoyle. I could try to hide it, but there's no way I'm bringing her here and treating her the way they treated me when I first got to Katmere. No damn way.

Heather: Me too!! Also, calculus sucks balls

"We're here," Macy says, just as she and I step into the dungeon where Eden had texted everyone to meet her. I'll admit my heart stuttered last night when I realized that must mean the Dragon Boneyard was beneath the school—near the dungeons.

Although honestly, once I thought about it, it wasn't entirely unexpected. I mean, I'd already guessed Katmere was more closely tied to the dragons than any other faction, what with the jewels embedded in the tunnel walls and bone corridors. In one of my hours of research in the library, I'd stumbled upon a whole history of the school.

Turns out Katmere hadn't always been a school.

It had started as a dragon lair.

And not just any dragon lair but the original ruling family's lair. They'd sided with Cyrus in the Second Great War, though, and as a concession after their loss, the lair had been claimed and Katmere established to foster interspecies relationships by making all the factions school together.

I'd asked once what happened to the original family, since I knew it wasn't Flint's parents, but Flint just shrugged and said most of them died in the war, and no one really knew where the rest scattered.

So much loss and tragedy in this supernatural world. And for what? So one group is in charge and another isn't? Is it really all about power?

"It rarely is," Hudson says, and I walk over to where he's idly running his fingertips along the jeweled walls. He's been in a funk all morning, and I'm going to need him to check his attitude at the door if I hope to keep my wits about me in the Boneyard. Hudson can make me forget everything else in a blink when he pushes my buttons. Zero to sixty in 2.8 seconds.

"What are you, a Bugatti?" he asks. "That's the only car in the world that can go that fast."

"When you start bugging me, yeah," I answer, and he groans.

"Worst. Pun. Ever."

"I do what I can," I tell him with a grin before glancing back at the group. Jaxon and Flint are discussing potential issues before we enter the Boneyard, Macy is checking her wand and swapping small potion bottles back and forth from her backpack to a pouch wrapped around her waist, and Eden and Xavier are betting each other over who can carry back the heaviest bone. My heart fills with pride at my newfound family.

At least until Xavier demands of Macy, "Are you wearing a fanny pack?"

Macy doesn't even spare him a look as she answers, "It's my potion accessory kit."

"Don't you mean your potion ASSessory kit?" he shoots back with a sly, wolfish smile.

We all laugh, even as I turn to Hudson and say softly, "You know we're risking our lives for *you*, right?"

"Yeah, that's why you're all doing it," he scoffs. "More like to stop me from feeding on your precious Jaxon."

I shake my head. "Well, it's why *I'm* doing it."

That makes him pause. He stares at me for several long seconds, his indigo eyes blazing into mine with a dozen emotions I can't begin to name. I wait for him to put a voice to one of them, wait for him to say something—anything—that will help me understand why he's being so difficult right now.

And for a minute, it looks like he's actually going to do it. Like he'll open his mouth and say something that has some emotional depth to it.

But in the end, he just shakes his head and looks away. Shoves a rough hand through his hair. Does anything and everything but actually talk to me about something that matters.

He does, however, say, "Then by all means let me get my pom-poms ready."

And there we go. Zero to one hundred and *sixty*. "Fine. And to get you out of my damn head so I don't have to listen to you ruin my mood ever again." I huff and give him my back. We're all very likely about to die. Would it really kill him to just say thanks?

Jaxon motions everyone over, steps into the first cell, and starts to plug the code into the door so we can get to the tunnels. But Flint stops him with a hand to the shoulder.

"That's not how we get to the tunnels that lead to the Boneyard."

"What do you mean?" Macy asks. "I thought you said the only way to find it is through the tunnels."

"It is." Eden grins. "Just not those."

Flint motions for all of us to join him at the back of the cell, where one of the walls appears to have several gemstones embedded in a crude circle of emerald, ruby, sapphire, obsidian, amethyst, tourmaline, topaz, and citrine. He taps each gem as though entering a safe code, then steps back.

A couple of seconds later the floor under my feet rumbles ominously, and then the huge stones inside the circle of gems move back one by one, until we're all staring at a small, round tunnel in the middle of the wall.

"So who wants to go into the creepy hole first?" Macy jokes, and everyone laughs, but no one rushes to raise their hand.

"Well, you're all in luck, because I think it's going to have to be a dragon." Flint's eyes twinkle with devilish excitement. He turns to Eden and asks, "Should we tell them what's on the other side? Or more specifically, what's not?"

Eden rolls her eyes at him. "Yeah, I'm not risking a werewolf bite or fang to the neck in panic." She turns to address us. "As you know, these tunnels were built for dragons…who can fly. So on the other side of this tunnel…there's no ground for a bit. For Grace, who can fly—and Jaxon—when it launches you into the air, obviously, do your thing and you'll be fine. For the rest of you, just count to thirty before each person goes in, and Flint or I will catch you on the other side."

She nods as though that's that, grabs the small ledge above the hole, and swings her whole body inside in one fluid motion, feet first. And then disappears.

Flint jokes, "I love this part," before he, too, jumps into the hole and disappears.

The rest of us just stand there, looking from one to the other, wondering if they're messing with us or if we're really expected to just jump and let gravity do its thing. Either way, none of us is particularly excited about being the first one to jump.

Jaxon grabs my hand and says, "Hey, no worries. I'll catch you."

Before I can point out that I actually have wings and can "catch" myself, thank you very much, Xavier responds with, "Dude, she *has* wings. You better catch *me* instead. No way do I want a dragon's talon through my heart."

Everyone nervously laughs, and we tacitly agree as a group that yeah, Jaxon should be the one to "catch" everyone without wings, so he jumps in the hole next. I wait to hear a scream or a splat or something, but this is Jaxon, so...nothing.

Since I'm the last one of those left who can fly, I take a deep breath and walk up to the hole and peer in. It goes down pretty far pretty fast... My heart starts racing for all the wrong reasons.

"Don't worry," Hudson says with a deliberately smug look on his face from the spot where he's been leaning against a wall the whole time, "*Jaxon* will catch you."

And that does it. I glare at him and lift my chin right before I turn back to the hole and jump straight in.

80

A Gargoyle's Guide to Antigravity

I try to play it cool, but it's a long, long, long way down, and I end up screaming before I hit the first turn. Beneath me, the stone is smooth and slick, and that only helps me pick up speed as I zip around each crook and bend, still heading on a massive descent. Honestly, it kind of reminds me of a slip-and-slide water park in San Diego, and I'm grinning madly by the end...at least until the bottom gives way and the tunnel ejects me out into a dark and yawning void.

Black hole anyone?

My lungs—and everything else—tighten up as terror rips through me, but somehow I manage to shift in midair, my wings catching me before I fall more than a couple of feet. I can tell the cavern is small in the near-pitch-darkness, because I can hear the echo of our wings flapping, but not much else. Also, there must be water somewhere nearby, because wet, musty air coats my skin within seconds.

I can feel Flint and Eden hovering next to me, but I can't see them all that well as a shiver of fear skates along my spine. This place does not want me here; I can feel it in my bones. My inner voice is all but begging me to get the hell out of here, and I've never wanted to listen to it more.

I'm pretty sure I spot Jaxon standing on a path off to the side, so I maneuver to him, land, and shift back. He pulls me in for a hug, but his focus never wavers from the hole from hell. As Mekhi, Xavier, and Macy pop out one by one, he floats them easily to the ground.

Mekhi is teasing Xavier that he screams like his sister's banshee best friend when Eden and Flint shift three feet above the ground and land on solid feet next to us, both shaking their heads.

"What, no one trusts a dragon to catch them?" Flint jokes, but he doesn't seem to mind as he turns to Eden and confides, "Man, that ride never gets old, does it?"

"Wait, I thought you'd never been to the Boneyard before. Is that not where we're going?" I ask, genuinely confused.

"Turns out the Boneyard is not too far from the horde, which I most definitely have been to." He waggles his brows at me comically and I laugh.

"Okay, I'll bite. What's the horde?"

Flint's tone turns almost reverent as he answers simply, "Treasure."

"You need a napkin to mop up some of that drool, man?" Xavier asks.

But Jaxon grins and shakes his head. "Dragons." As if that says it all.

"Anyway," Flint continues, "the Boneyard actually isn't too far from here. Just down a side corridor. Follow us."

Eden sets off after Flint into the near darkness, and we fall in behind them. I can't see much—apparently gargoyle eyes aren't anything special despite what that old TV show said, so I pull out my cell phone and tap the flashlight app. No way am I walking around creepy tunnels in the near dark.

Hudson chuckles beside me. "Chicken."

"Shhh," I tell him and focus on making sure there actually *is* ground in front of me before I take each step. "I'm concentrating on not falling."

He chuckles again but thankfully doesn't comment.

We walk for another fifteen minutes through a maze of tunnels, pausing occasionally for Eden and Flint to argue over a direction. I've about decided we're completely lost when Flint looks over his shoulder and shouts, "We made it!"

And then he and Eden turn sharply left...and disappear.

81

One Hundred Percent That Witch

Jaxon and I rush to the last place we saw the dragons, but all that's there is a solid wall. We start pressing our hands on the jagged edges of the stone surface, thinking maybe there's a secret latch or something.

All of a sudden, my hand touches flesh, and I scream and jump back. It's Flint.

"How—?" I start to ask.

"What are you guys doing?" he asks as he walks straight out of the solid wall. "Come on, stop messing around. What's the holdup?"

"Well, we don't seem to be able to walk through solid stone walls." I raise one eyebrow as Xavier pats his hand against the wall to show Flint.

"Oh, damn. We didn't think of that." He calls over his shoulder to Eden. "Apparently only dragons can pass through."

Eden walks through the wall now, too, and yes, it's just as creepy when she does it. "Huh. Grand-mère didn't mention that would be a problem. I wonder if she doesn't know. Any ideas?"

Jaxon steps forward and says, "Move back a little and let me try." Then he spreads his legs and places his hands out, like he's going to physically move a bed or something, but focuses on the wall about five feet in front of him.

"Oh, this I've got to see," Hudson snarks and positions himself beside his brother. "Baby brother is going to start moving rock...in a tunnel."

His words don't register until I feel the ground start to rumble, small pebbles and dust falling from the ceiling all around us.

"Stop!" Macy shouts, and thankfully Jaxon does. "I don't think it's safe for us to try to break this wall down, Jaxon. It may be an illusion for the dragons, but it is very real to the rest of us. You might end up causing a cave-in."

"So how are we going to get through it, then?" Xavier asks.

"Now, I'm just spitballing here," Hudson says as he wanders over to the wall and leans a shoulder against it. "But it seems that maybe the best way to take out a magical wall is with...magic." He cocks one brow at me. "If only we had a witch handy..."

I stick my tongue out at him because, really, sarcasm is what we're missing right now? Then I turn to my cousin and ask, "Macy, do you think you can break through the wall's magic?"

Her eyes narrow as she thinks about it, but then she squares her shoulders and says, "You bet I can."

She pulls her backpack off her shoulder and starts rummaging through it. "Grace, can you help me with these?" she asks as she pulls out eight candles and places them equidistant in a large circle. "Okay, everyone, stand inside the circle."

Once we're all inside the protection of the circle, she casts her spell, and the candles begin to burn. Once she's satisfied with their flames, she points her wand at the wall and calls the elements. The wind comes slowly, blowing softly and gently down the tunnel. Macy starts to chant, her voice getting louder and louder with each line of the spell. The wind picks up, and at one point, I even feel a fine mist of water spray across my skin.

The wind picks up again, the flames on the candles growing higher and higher, and the very earth beneath our feet starts to tremble.

That's when Macy raises her wand, her arms open and face raised to the ceiling, and says, "Illusions great. Illusions small. Find a door within this wall."

The wind picks up even more, howling through the passageway so hard and fast that I'm sure it's going to knock us down. The flames on the candles shoot straight up to the ceiling.

"Good job, Macy." There's a grudging respect in Hudson's tone that's usually absent when he talks about my cousin—or about anyone, for that matter. And that's before she lifts her wand above her head and points it straight up as she chants so low and fast that the only words I can make out are "heat," "cleanse," "burn."

All of a sudden, lightning flashes down, and I scream as it connects with Macy's wand. But my cousin doesn't even flinch. Instead, she just stands there, seconds ticking by as her wand absorbs every molecule of energy the lightning bolt can deliver.

Only when the lightning has dissipated and the wind and rain and fire have died down does Macy point her wand straight at the part of the wall where Eden and Flint say the Dragon Boneyard should be. And with a flick of her wrist, she unleashes every ounce of the power she's just absorbed.

The ancient stone rumbles and creaks as it trembles under the incredible power Macy is directing at it. For several seconds, I think the ancient dragon magic is going to hold, but then the first rock falls. Soon, the entire wall starts to crumble away, huge pieces of rock and stone raining down around us.

As the first stone threatens to hit us, Eden and Flint throw their arms up to protect their heads. But Macy's magic is too strong, her power resonating throughout the entire passageway and sealing the circle—and everyone in it—from harm.

More rocks and stones fall, littering the ground all around us. But not one pebble makes it through Macy's barrier; not one stray rock so much as touches the fire that encircles us. And when the lightning finally dissipates, when Macy's spell finally winds down and the dust from the falling rocks finally clears, the wall is gone.

And in its place is the opening to a giant glowing cavern.

82

Ride or Die

Macy quickly closes the circle with a gratitude to the elements, and then we walk through the craggy opening in the wall that Macy just created.

"What the hell is this place?" Xavier demands as we all look around in a combination of fascination and horror.

"Salvador Dali's wet dream, apparently," Jaxon answers, wrapping an arm around my waist and pulling me close.

"Right?" I agree. "I'm just saying, the second I see one of those creepy clocks, I'm out of here."

We're standing in a small alcove at the edge of a cliff overlooking a massive cavern. The cavern itself is about three hundred feet across and appears bottomless. And if that's not terrifying as fuck, it's also super dark. But there's just enough light coming from whatever is beyond it for me to see the sharp and craggy rock formations jutting out from both sides.

"You definitely don't want to fall into that," Mekhi comments as he peeks over the edge.

"Not even a little bit," Macy answers.

I step closer to the edge, too, and something about the change in perspective makes me realize that the glowing area across the cavern is actually an island and the cavern is a bizarre kind of moat surrounding it.

More, the island itself is filled with massive—and I mean *massive*—white bones. Which is creepy, yes, but what else do you expect when you sign up to go to a Dragon Boneyard? But what's really fascinating about the whole thing, what has all of us staring at it like we can't believe our eyes, is that the bones are so huge that they provide an enormous reflective surface when the dim light hits them. It is that reflection that makes the island look like some kind of paranormal nuclear reactor.

It's beautiful and terrifying at the same time.

"The Boneyard is right there," Flint says, as if the giant skeletons aren't enough of a tip-off.

"I'm okay as long as there are no rats," Macy says, stepping a little closer to the edge of the deep, yawning abyss in front of us as she strains to see across it. "Tell me there are no rats."

"Pretty sure if there were rats, they would have fallen in by now. And been, you know…" Xavier mimes being impaled, complete with tongue hanging sickly out of the corner of his mouth.

"Now, there's something you don't see every day," Hudson comments dryly.

"Pretty sure we could have done without the visual aid," Eden says to Xavier.

"I don't know. I think it adds a certain *je ne sais quoi*," Mekhi jokes, right before he picks up a large rock from the ground and throws it as hard as his vampire strength will let him. It barely makes it a third of the way across the divide before falling down, down, down…

We wait silently to hear it land, but it just keeps falling. Which isn't concerning at all.

Then again, I suppose it's no more concerning than the long, sharp rock spikes protruding from the walls and, presumably, the ground.

"So, you know what I'm thinking?" Xavier says as he claps Flint on the back.

"That you really don't want to fall in?"

"Obviously. But I'm also thinking that it's finally the dragons' turn to save the day."

"Finally?" Eden shoots back. "Don't you mean always?"

Flint holds his hand up for a fist bump, which she delivers...right before she shifts in a colorful shimmer of light. Flint follows suit only a few seconds later.

Dragon riding absolutely solves the problem of crossing the divide, but it leaves the area where we're standing right now really, really crowded. I'm currently uncomfortably close to the edge, and that discomfort is growing exponentially, considering the added weight of the dragons is cracking the ground beneath our feet and making the edges crumble into oblivion.

Then again, that's probably the point.

"Who's riding which dragon?" I ask even as I inch toward Eden. Not that I mind riding with Flint, but one fall from this height above the craggy floor will mean certain death, and he's a bit too much of a daredevil for my current liking.

Before anyone else can pick their ride, we all turn as one just to the right of the island as we hear a high-pitched howling that chills my bones. The noise gets only louder until a huge gust of wind races across the cavern and knocks me back a few steps. Macy stumbles, too, and teeters next to the edge.

My heart jumps into my throat as I dive for her, but Xavier gets there first, wrapping an arm around her waist and pulling her forward, away from the edge, in a yank-and-swoop move for the record books. All that's missing is the backward dip and kiss, but judging from the looks on both their faces, it isn't far behind.

"What the hell was that?" Mekhi demands, looking at the ravine like it's suddenly been possessed.

"Wyvern wind," Jaxon and Hudson answer at exactly the same time.

I start to ask what that means, but the truth is I'm not sure I want to know. Especially since it comes again about forty seconds later, clearly circling the island, just as Jaxon is helping me up onto Eden's back. It slams into me, has me grabbing on to Eden's neck in a desperate effort not to fall off.

"There's no way we're going to make it before the next gust of wind," Xavier says, looking out across the chasm.

Flint snorts like Xavier's personally insulted him.

"I'm just saying, man, it's a long effing way."

Flint snorts again, and this time it's obvious he is very insulted.

"I think they've got it," I say, wrapping my arms tight around Eden's neck as Jaxon climbs up behind me, followed by Mekhi. "We've just got to time it right."

"Exactly," Macy agrees as she settles in behind Xavier on Flint. "We can go the second the next blast hits."

"We will," Jaxon says. "But I've got a backup plan, too. Just in case."

"Oh yeah?" Xavier says. "Want to let the rest of us in on it?"

Before he can answer, another gust of wyvern wind comes howling around the island and straight at us.

"Too late," Macy shouts as she grabs on tight to Flint.

I hold on tight, too, because the second the wind sweeps across us, Flint and Eden launch themselves straight into the air.

It's abrupt and fast and scary as fuck, so scary that Macy screams for the first ten seconds straight. Which I totally get. If my vocal cords weren't paralyzed, I'd be screaming, too.

Of every terrible and bizarre thing that's happened to me since I got to Katmere Academy, this is one of the most terrifying. Especially as we come up on thirty seconds and the cavern continues to stretch endlessly in front of us. There's no way we'll get to the island in less than ten.

Flint and Eden must have reached the same conclusion, because I can feel them bracing themselves even as they rocket forward faster and faster.

My vocal cords unfreeze themselves just long enough for me to let out one wild yell, and then the wind is screaming straight toward us. Flint and Eden barrel-roll away from the wind while still going close to what has to be a hundred miles an hour.

Macy's back to screaming, and so is Xavier, but the wind misses us. Which means we have forty more seconds to get to the other side. Eden puts her head down and races forward, and I squeeze my eyes shut as tightly as I can, even as I count to forty. No way do I want to see what happens next.

Sure enough, I can hear the wyvern wind whistling as it races toward us. But this time, when Eden tries to evade it with another side roll, it doesn't work. The first edge of the wind clips her left wing as it starts to slide toward the rest of us, and I have one second to think that we're totally screwed. No way are we going to make it out of this alive.

But Jaxon throws a hand out and slaps the wind back before it can touch us. And then, using every ounce of power he's got, he pushes it back and then holds it there, just long enough for Eden to right herself and go slamming across the edge of the island onto what looks to be some sort of landing pad.

And as she skids to a fast and rocky stop, I manage to suck in the first real breath I've taken since I climbed on Eden's back.

Flint lands right next to us, and after we slide off the dragons' backs, we all collapse on the ground.

83

Sometimes Homecoming Really Does Mean Coming Home

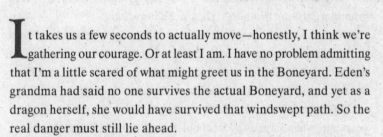

I t takes us a few seconds to actually move—honestly, I think we're gathering our courage. Or at least I am. I have no problem admitting that I'm a little scared of what might greet us in the Boneyard. Eden's grandma had said no one survives the actual Boneyard, and yet as a dragon herself, she would have survived that windswept path. So the real danger must still lie ahead.

Jaxon takes hold of my hand and gently tugs me to my feet and down the path leading away from the cliff's edge. The others follow right behind us as we walk down into the Boneyard.

I gasp when we finally make it to the entrance, because OH. MY. GOD.

"Holy shit," Hudson says, 100 percent echoing my thoughts as I scan from one side of the fifty-foot-high cavern to the other.

"Are these all dragons?" I whisper, staring out at the piles and piles and *piles* of bones. Rib bones rise twenty feet in the air like massive monuments, testament to these majestic beasts the rest of the world only remembers now in fairy tales. Shattered leg bones the length of trucks. Cracked skulls the size of cars. Just everywhere you look…bones.

"Yeah." Flint sounds more somber than I've ever heard him, and when I glance at him out of the corner of my eye, I realize he's crying.

Not full-on sobbing or anything, but there are definitely a few tears running down his cheeks.

A quick look at Eden shows she's having exactly the same reaction.

"I didn't expect there to be so many," I say, reaching out to grab Flint's hand with my free one. "It's..." Terrible and beautiful and awe-inspiring all at the same time.

"Home," Eden whispers as she takes the final step over the threshold. "It's home."

"Every dragon really gets called back here when they die?" Mekhi asks. "Every dragon in the whole world?"

"Every dragon," Flint tells him. "My grandparents, my great-grandparents, my brother... They're all here."

And suddenly, I'm deeply ashamed. When we decided to travel to the Dragon Boneyard for a bone to get Hudson out of my head, not once did I consider that we'd be *robbing a grave*. That that bone is someone's sister. Someone's father. Someone's *child*.

"My mom's here, too," Eden says reverently. "She died a couple of years ago, when I was away at school. I never thought I'd get the chance to come here. I never thought I'd get the chance to say goodbye." The last couple of words come out thick and painful, and I feel them all the way down deep inside me.

It devastated me when my parents died—there's a part of me that's still devastated now and will be for a long time to come. But at least I got to say goodbye to them with a formal funeral. At least I have a place where I can go to feel close to them. I can't imagine how I'd feel if they just disappeared one day, and I never even knew where they ended up.

"I'm sorry, Grace," Hudson says beside me, and for once there's no artifice to the words. No sarcasm or layers of protection or hidden agenda. Nothing but raw, honest truth when he continues. "I'm so sorry Lia did what she did to bring me back. And I'm so sorry that what she did hurt you so badly. I'd take it all back if I could."

And shit, now I'm crying, too. Because what am I supposed to say to that? How am I supposed to feel?

"You're supposed to hate me," he answers. "God knows, I hate myself."

"It's not your fault," I whisper, and though it hurts to say it, for the first time, I actually believe it.

Whatever he did, whatever his reasons, I know that Hudson didn't mean for anything to end this way. He wouldn't ever have wanted my parents to die to save him. I don't know how I know this, but I do. Sometimes, you just have to offer someone your blind trust. Take the leap.

And so it's not his fault.

It just is.

Our gazes connect, and it's like the wall that separates our minds and souls has been lifted. Suddenly, I'm feeling everything he's feeling. The anguish. The guilt. The self-hatred. All of it.

I'm drowning in despair so overwhelming, I can't catch my breath. And then it's gone. The wall is back in place, and I take a deep breath. And then another. But the ball of anger I didn't even know I'd been carrying around with me at the unfairness of what Lia did to my parents is also gone.

Thank you.

He doesn't reply. There's nothing more to say. He already said it all in that one vulnerable act.

"Can we go in?" Xavier asks quietly, and this is the first time I've seen him without his snapback on. At first, I think he's lost it, and then I recognize the outline of it shoved in his back pocket.

For respect, I realize as he runs a nervous hand over his shaggy black hair. He's taken the hat off as a sign of respect before we enter the Boneyard.

"Yeah," Flint says, dashing a quick hand across his cheek. "Let's do this and get the hell out of here. It's time to go home."

84

Two Vampires, a Witch, and a Werewolf Walk into a Boneyard...

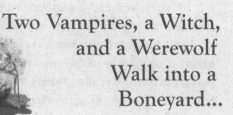

"Where do we start?" Mekhi asks as we gingerly pick our way down the entrance path. Unlike human cemeteries, here there doesn't seem to be any rhyme or reason. Fragments of bones are strewn across every surface—including the path we're walking on. And none of them seems to belong to the same skeleton.

"We need to find a complete bone," Jaxon tells us. "Which doesn't look like it's going to be as easy as we thought it would be."

He, too, looks around at the shards of bones lying everywhere.

Mekhi sighs. "Not to sound like an ass here, but not only do we have to find a complete bone, we have to find one that we can actually get back to Katmere. I mean, these things are huge. And while I know we can carry it together, or Jaxon can use his telekinesis to move one, what exactly are we going to do with it when we get back to school? Most of these fragments won't even fit in our dorm rooms."

He's right, I realize as we get farther into the Boneyard. Most of the dragon skulls alone are at least five feet tall. And the rib and leg and neck bones are way bigger than that.

"Well," Macy adds, "I for one do not want to do that dragon flight again with a giant leg bone in tow. Why don't I work on a spell to open a portal to get us back to school, while you guys search for a bone? I set things up before I left—just have to see if I can get it to work."

I raise my brows. "You can create a portal? Why not one to get us here?"

Macy shakes her head. "I can only create a portal to a place where I have an anchor. I've never been here before, so... But I've got your backs now. So go find a bone before something terrible tries to kick us out of here."

"Nah." Xavier grins. "I think that's the worst of it. In fact, this looks like it's going to be a lot easier than we thought. What's a bunch of bones going to do to us anyway?"

Even Flint's signature grin slides from his face as we all stare at Xavier in shock.

"Dude, did you just jinx us?" Flint asks.

Xavier shakes his head. "You guys worry too much. Trust me. My wolf is super chill, so this place must not have any booby traps or anything. We're good to go. Now, how do we find a bone we can carry that's still solid?"

"Well, some of the tailbones are pretty small," Flint suggests. "At least if you get one from the end of the tail."

"Oh, that's a good idea," Macy tells him. "So we just have to find a tail."

Again, we look around. And again, I'm overwhelmed at the magnitude of the task in front of us. Because, unlike human remains, these dragons aren't grouped by individual skeleton. Bones lay wherever and belong to whomever. Very few of the fragments I'm looking at seem to belong to the same bone, let alone the same dragon.

"I think we need to split up if we have any hope of actually finding something," Jaxon says, and I have to agree with him. This place is massive, nearly two hundred yards wide, with some of the bone piles two stories high.

"Macy and I will take this section over here," Xavier says, pointing to the front right half of the cavern that will also allow Macy to finish creating the portal back to campus.

"Flint and I will take the front left," Eden tells us before heading that way.

"I guess that leaves the back right to Jaxon and Grace," Mekhi suggests to Jaxon. "While I take the back left."

"Actually, why don't Hudson and I take the back right, while you and Jaxon head to the back left," I suggest, and everyone turns to look at me. "Look, he's here whether we want him to be or not, and he has just as much at stake in helping us find a bone. I say we use him."

Jaxon's jaw clenches and unclenches for a few seconds, and I can tell he wants to protest. But some of what I've talked to him about these last few days must have finally gotten through, because he just nods. "You're right," he says before turning to Mekhi. "Let's go." Then they both fade away.

Everyone else gets busy searching, but Hudson is just standing there staring at me. "What's wrong?" I ask.

He shakes his head. "What's going on? You know I can see only what you see, right? I'm not really here, Grace."

Actually, I think I'd forgotten that. The moment we'd shared earlier had seemed so real, so tangible, that I'd genuinely forgotten *he* wasn't. I glance at Jaxon in the distance, wondering what he was thinking when I even suggested this. I'm about to tell him I've made a mistake when Hudson pipes up. "Hey, I think I found one!"

I quickly turn and realize he's pointing at the rib we're currently standing under. It's the size of a house and not something I could even move, let alone lift.

"Great choice." I roll my eyes at him but don't try to fight the half smile turning up one corner of my mouth. "Now, let's see you carry it."

He grins. "You know I'm more like management, right?"

"Yeah, that's what I thought. Come on, let's go find a bone Flint or Jaxon can actually carry."

As we start searching, I think about going over to Jaxon and telling him what happened between Hudson and me. But he and Mekhi are in the middle of digging through a giant pile of bones, and this doesn't seem like the time. Besides, it's not a big deal. It can wait until we're back at school. Jaxon will just be glad to hear I've made my peace with what happened to my parents.

I turn back to Hudson, feeling lighter than I have in a very long time. "All right, smart-ass," I tell him, "let's see who can find a bone first. And hurry, okay? I want to get out of here before a swarm of locusts decides to suddenly attack us."

Because whether Xavier's wolf senses are chill or not, I know Eden's grand-mère was right. My inner voice is begging me to leave this place as quickly as possible.

85

Dust and Dragon Bones

Now that I'm focused, I start searching through the piles of bones like a woman on a mission. I'm determined to get this done—while we managed to sneak off campus pretty easily, I'm not so sure we'll be able to get back on with the same ease. Not with the way the Circle is sniffing around.

"What does a dragon tailbone look like anyway?" I ask Hudson as we finally get to the back right quadrant of the room.

"I have no idea," he answers. "My plan is to find any intact bone that we can, period, and get it to the front of the room. If it's small, great, we're out of here. If it's not, then we have a backup in case things go to shit."

"Yeah, good point."

There are a bunch more bones scattered around where we're standing, so I bend down to check them out. Hudson does the same, and it isn't long before we develop a system for searching.

We pick a small ten-foot-by-ten-foot area, and I walk all the way around it as quickly as possible; then we start combing it from different sides until we meet in the middle. If we don't find anything, we move on to the next area. As Hudson explains, he's more looking through my memories than looking at the actual bone piles, but, well, it works.

"You mentioned something in the tunnels, when I was thinking about the original dragons. I said that was a lot of death just for someone to gain more power, and you said it's rarely all about power." I frown. "But I've met your dad, your *real* dad, in your memories. And it was clear that man *is* driven by power."

Hudson sighs. "I can't believe I'm going to defend that asshole— but his almighty quest for power has a purpose more than just feeding his ego. People don't follow him solely because he's got boatloads of charisma, Grace. His agenda has a thread of truth to it."

I have no idea what he's trying to tell me. I know what it *sounds* like his point is, but no way am I willing to accept that the Hudson I've gotten to know would ever agree with Cyrus there, no matter what Jaxon thought sixteen months ago. "That born vampires are a superior race and deserve to rule? You *agree* with that?"

"Hell no," Hudson barks out, shuffling around to get another view of a pile of bones. "But it is true that it's not fair paranormal creatures have to live in the shadows, always fearful of humans discovering us and trying to destroy us."

I blink back at him, my eyebrows shooting up into my hairline. "But your kind *feeds* on humans, Hudson. Shouldn't we have the right to protect ourselves?"

"Did you enjoy your dinner last night, Grace?" he asks out of the blue. "The pepperoni on your pizza?"

Understanding dawns. "No way. I know where you're going with this, and just no. Even though I can't entirely agree with our right to kill animals for food, there's no way that's the same as vampires hunting down *humans* as food."

He raises an obnoxious eyebrow. "And yet your kind has no issue with the hunting of deer to thin a population, for the good of the whole herd, yes?"

"That's different!"

A smug smile tugs up one corner of his mouth at my outburst. "Of course. 'Cause humans definitely don't have issues with overcrowding or limited resources."

"But— But—" I sputter because okay, maybe he has a tiny point there.

"It's about balance, Grace." He shoves his hands deep into his pockets. "Did you ever consider maybe the Creator had a plan for us, too? That we were created for a reason? That we weren't just some horrible cosmic joke?"

His endless blue gaze holds mine, so many emotions swirling just beneath their depths that I feel like they might pull me under. Because while we've been talking about Cyrus, I know that last bit was really about him. Is that what he truly thinks? That he's a horrible mistake? It's a devastating emotion to witness. But then he blinks and it's gone so fast, I have to wonder if I imagined it.

"Agree or disagree, Grace, that's how Cyrus is able to get so many people to follow him. Leaning in to thousands of years of perceived persecution and fear and anger, telling them humans are to blame for their lot in life, that gargoyles are standing in their way, that even their neighbors could be the enemy.

"Yes, I hate my father. But can you really blame someone for following the devil himself if he promises a better world for their children? Even if it requires walking through a river of someone else's blood?" He laughs, but there's no humor in the deep timbre. "Just because Dad doesn't care about a better world for *his* kids doesn't mean he doesn't believe in the cause. And it definitely doesn't mean he doesn't enjoy being the savior. Because the only thing he likes more than power is adoration."

"Is that why you did what you did?" I ask him. "Because your father twisted you up with his words until you couldn't tell right from wrong? Until you believed what he had to say?" "Is that what you really think of me?" he shoots back. "That I'm so weak?"

"You can't just rewrite history, Hudson," I tell him. "It's not like Jaxon woke up one morning and just decided to kill you. You were planning on exterminating made vampires simply because you don't like them. That's genocide, in case you don't recognize the definition."

Hudson glares at me. "I told you before, I have done a lot of shitty things in my life, and I take responsibility for every single one of them. But I do not take responsibility for that. I stamped out made vampires and others because they were my father's allies, he was building an army, not simply because they were made vampires. They had pledged their allegiance to him and were plotting to wipe out everyone in their way to finally bring paranormals out of the shadows. You have no idea how close we were to a Third Great War. I couldn't let that happen.

"So if you want to come at me for murder, go ahead. I made a horrible decision to stop an even more horrible outcome. But genocide is somebody else's sin, and I am not going to take responsibility for it. Don't be like my brother. Don't judge me until you know both sides of the story."

His words resonate inside of me—not just the ring of truthfulness I could hear when he was talking, but also the vehemence and the indignation and the rage that he can't even begin to hide.

Which leaves me...I don't know where. I mean, I don't believe for one second that Jaxon would kill his brother without being sure that it was the only option. At the same time, though, Hudson has lived in my head for days, and I'm beginning to recognize when he's full of shit and when he's telling the truth.

This latest diatribe of his smacks of the truth.

What I'm supposed to do with this version of the truth, I don't know. And I don't have a clue how I'm supposed to reconcile it with Jaxon's version. Either way, I'm not sure this changes my feelings on if Hudson can be trusted to come back with his powers.

He pauses, then shakes his head with a pissed-off laugh. "Why am I not surprised?" He stands up to his full height, hands on hips, gaze holding mine in its punishing depth. "I know how much you love to lump everyone and everything into just two groups, Grace. Good versus evil. But don't you think it's about time you grew up?"

He shakes his head and leans over another pile I'd looked at earlier. I'm about to argue that I *am* grown up, thank you very much, and also that I was starting to think maybe Hudson was trying to protect humans with his killing spree—which no one has once considered—when he lets out a celebratory whoop. "I found one!" he shouts, pointing to a bone the size of his arm.

"That's fantastic!" I rush around to look at the bone myself and confirm it's whole and small enough that we can carry it out. "Let's go round up the others."

I pick up the bone and take only a couple of steps toward Jaxon and Mekhi before a pile of bones directly behind us starts to rustle.

"What's that?" I ask, whirling around as my imagination runs wild. Honestly, at this point I wouldn't be surprised if an army of angry pixies flew out of the center of a pile of bones and tried to set us on fire.

"I don't know," Hudson answers. "Stay near me."

I don't bother to point out how ridiculous that statement is. One glance at his face spells out just how clearly he gets it and how frustrated he is by it.

As we head to the front, a second bone pile starts to shudder, bones clacking together in an almost songlike rhythm. An eerie-as-fuck song, mind you, but a song nonetheless.

Hudson and I look at each other, eyebrows raised, then start moving faster as we head to the front of the cavern. And when a third pile of bones starts to rumble, he urges, "We need to move!"

But before we take more than a couple of steps, a giant leg bone falls from the ceiling and crashes into the spot right beside us.

It shatters as soon as it hits the ground in a thundering explosion, bone shards flying like mortar shells in all directions. One slices me right beneath my left eye, and blood starts pouring down my face.

"Fuck!" Flint yells from across the cavern. "A dragon must have just died! I think the Boneyard is calling the bones home."

"You *think* that's what's going on?" Xavier shouts as he grabs Macy's hand and they make a mad dash for the landing pad area where she'd been working on building a portal earlier.

Moments later, the other leg bone falls—about six inches from where Xavier and Macy had been searching.

"We've got to go," Flint yells. "Now!"

"We can't go now," Eden tells him. "We don't have a bone yet."

"Hudson and I found one," I say, holding up our find as a giant rib bone falls in the back of the cavern.

"Then let's blow this pop stand!" Xavier yells as he and Macy make a beeline for the cavern entrance.

"I'm with them," Mekhi says, right before he fades to the front of the Boneyard—and doesn't stop until he's on the safe side of the entrance.

"Me too," Jaxon agrees just as what I think is a tailbone comes crashing straight down at us.

Jaxon throws an arm up at the last second and uses his telekinesis to send the bone spinning to the back of the chamber. Then does the same again and again and again, as more and more of the tail starts to fall, faster and faster. Flint and Eden are almost at the front now, where Macy and Xavier are standing just outside the Boneyard, Macy wringing her hands as she watches the carnage unfold.

A neck bone suddenly comes flying at Flint out of nowhere, and Jaxon turns and sends it soaring away.

But the split second it takes to help Flint leaves Jaxon vulnerable, and when the next bone comes flying down—an absolutely massive rib bone—he isn't fast enough, or strong enough, to stop it.

At the last moment, he shoves me away as hard as he can, and I end up tumbling butt-first into a pile of bones, just as the colossal rib bone crashes into Jaxon and slams him to the ground hard enough to knock him out.

86

Grace Under Fire

"**J**axon!" I scream, scrambling up from the pile of bone shards he knocked me into in order to save me. My hands and arms are scraped to hell, but I barely register that as I race across the distance between us. "Oh my God, Jaxon!"

"Look out," Hudson snaps, and I pull back just as a giant bone—I'm too close to tell what it is—crashes in front of me and explodes into thousands of fragments that have me dropping the bone and covering my face with my arms.

"Okay, go," Hudson says when it's safe again, and I finish the dash to his brother just as another bone comes flying at me. It's a smaller one, and I brace myself for impact, but it explodes moments before it strikes me.

Bone shards fall everywhere.

Seconds later, the same thing happens to a bone that's about to fall on Jaxon.

I don't know what's going on, and I don't care. As long as bones keep exploding, that means they aren't landing on one of us, and that is something I can get behind.

I drop to my knees next to Jaxon and start trying to tug the bone off him, but it doesn't budge. It's too big, and I'm not strong enough, even when I put my back against it and try to use my legs for leverage.

"Jaxon!" Flint yells and races back toward Jaxon and me.

Mekhi beats him to it—but only by a couple seconds—and then the two of them pick up the bone like it's nothing and send it flying.

But Jaxon is still out, and when I feel the back of his head, there's a giant bump there. Huh. Who knew vampires could get concussions?

All around us, bones keep falling in giant, thunderous explosions. I remember watching this documentary once on World War II and how the soldiers suffered PTSD for the rest of their lives from the experience of surviving mortar fire, and now I get it. I really, really get it.

It starts with the sound of something falling from the sky. Then a quick, desperate look up, only to realize that the sky is vast and the sound could be coming from any direction. So you turn, try to identify the source of the sound as it gets louder and louder, only to realize it could actually be coming from the opposite direction you're looking in and you'll never even see it before the blast hits you.

The sheer panic of not being able to tell from what direction danger is coming completely steals your ability to even try to save yourself. And in that moment, you feel utterly powerless. Utterly vulnerable. Utterly alone.

Surviving soldiers say they would just run blindly toward what they hoped was safety, never knowing if their next step would be their last.

And now I have an inkling of what they went through, and it is the most terrifying experience of my life because of the total and complete inability to guess where the next hit is coming from.

What happened with Lia was frightening, but this is devastating. Completely soul-crushing.

One after another, bones fall from the cavern ceiling, no rhyme or reason, no pattern, nothing. It's utter chaos. As each bone slams into a bone pile, fragments fly in all directions, and before long, Mekhi, Flint, and I are cut all to hell.

Still, no bone has fallen on us, so I count it as a win.

But I know it's only a matter of time. We need to get the fuck out of here—now.

"Can you carry him?" I ask Mekhi. "Just fade to the front of the Boneyard with him over your shoulder?"

"Yeah, of course."

Mekhi grabs Jaxon and fades toward the front of the Boneyard, while Flint and I both shift. Then we take to the air and race toward the entrance.

"Get moving, Grace!" Hudson growls as another bone comes crashing toward me.

I'm trying, I snap, pushing my wings as hard as I can.

"Try harder," he snaps back. *"Or you'll die in here."*

Like I don't know that?

Flint deliberately pulls above me—I think to block me from flying bones, which I hate because it means he's made himself more vulnerable. That knowledge has me struggling to go faster, and we plow through the air, desperate to get to the exit.

But bones are falling in earnest now, from every direction, and shrapnel is flying up every time a bone crashes to the ground. The noise is deafening, and fear is a metallic taste in my mouth. The need to survive is a visceral tug deep inside me, a desperation that claws at me right beneath my skin.

The fact that there is nothing I can do about it makes everything worse. No choice I can make that might make it better, no path I can try that might lessen the gravity of the danger. I have no choice except to pray that I get out of this alive.

So in the end, I do the only thing I can. I take a deep breath and surrender to the lack of control. Let it beat against my heart like a wild thing. And then I just fly.

Flint drops behind me right at the end, and the two of us shoot through the narrowing entrance of the Boneyard—one after the other. We collapse on the ground near the landing pad—where everyone else is waiting…also on the ground.

I can barely breathe. My heart is about to pound out of my chest, and I've never been so exhausted in my life. A glance at Flint, and everyone else, shows they aren't doing much better.

Jaxon is starting to stir on the ground, thank God, and as soon as I can breathe without coughing, I crawl over to him.

"Are you okay?" I ask, smoothing his hair back from his face.

He shakes his head like he's trying to clear it. "Yeah, I think so." Things must come flooding back, though, because he sits up in a rush. "Are you all right?" He glances around, then demands, "Is everyone okay? What happened?"

"You got hit in the head with a bone the size of a house and passed out," Mekhi jokes.

Jaxon looks stunned…and also mortified and furious with himself. "I *passed out*? In the middle of all that? How could I do that to you guys?"

"Umm, you didn't do anything. You got hurt," I answer him. "It happens to the best of us."

"Not to me. It's my job to protect you."

"It's our job to protect one another," I tell him, waving an arm to encompass everyone.

He looks like he wants to say more, but finally he just shakes his head like he gives up. Which is probably the smartest move at this point, since he's dealing with six other paranormals—all of whom are used to holding their own in any given situation.

"It's not that you aren't a total badass," I tell him with the best straight face I can manage. "It's just that we're all badasses."

"Amen to that," Eden says from where she's slumped next to Mekhi.

"And it's a good thing," Xavier says. "Because we're going to have to do this whole thing again tomorrow."

"What? Seriously?" Macy rests her head against her drawn-up knees.

"We didn't get a bone?" Jaxon groans.

"We didn't get a bone," Xavier confirms. "Being under fire from a dragon skeleton changed everything really fast."

"Shit, I had one. I must have dropped it when I fell." Or maybe it's when that first bone almost took me out. I can't remember. All I know is I had a bone and now I very much do not.

Jaxon looks completely embarrassed as he says, "I'm sorry, guys. We dragged you along on this expedition from hell for nothing."

"First of all, you didn't drag us along," Flint says. "We came willingly. So stop beating yourself up. And secondly…" He reaches into his pocket with a wicked grin and pulls out a delicate-looking bone about the length of a pencil. "Toe bones still count as bones, right?"

"Hell yeah, they do!" Eden tells him with a whoop of delight. "You did it!"

"Umm, I think you mean *we* did it." Flint shoves the bone back into his pocket for safekeeping, then reaches down and helps Jaxon to his feet. "And not to sound too much like a giant baby, but can I suggest we get the hell out of here before the next we're-all-gonna-scream-and-die activity begins?"

Macy giggles and says, "I'm with you on that one. Luckily, I've already got"—she pulls out her spell book—"a portal back to school ready and waiting. Before we left, I made sure to do the spell that opens up our dorm room as the other side of the portal, remember? Because honestly, I don't think I could do that dragon ride again, guys."

"I could literally kiss you, Macy," Xavier says, and I can tell my cousin has no idea how to reply…even though she is suddenly all smiles.

87

All the Right Moves

I wake up to Macy dancing around the room with her headphones in. She's still in her pajamas, and I can see a ton of cuts and bruises on her arms and upper back—thank you, Dragon Boneyard—but she looks happy. Really happy, and I don't blame her.

Last night was terrifying, and I'm feeling pretty glad to be alive, too, even though we're both running on fumes after—I glance at the clock—only about four hours of sleep. Maybe that's why, instead of rolling over and going back to sleep, I convince her to switch to her phone speaker and then dance around the room with her.

We're laughing at each other as we shimmy and shake our hips, but it doesn't even matter because we're alive...and because we got the dragon bone.

We. Got. The. Dragon. Bone.

That means we've got all four things necessary to get Hudson out of my head. I mean, yeah, we still have the Unkillable Beast to get through, but we're almost there. Why shouldn't we celebrate?

"Oh, I don't know," Hudson interjects from behind me, sitting up and leaning against the wall on my bed. "Because the Unkillable Beast is going to kill you, perhaps?"

"Hush!" I tell him as I collapse next to him, out of breath as the song ends. Macy plops down on her own bed as well. "Don't be raining on my parade this morning."

"Is that what I'm doing?" He looks somber, but there's an underlying note of something in his voice that has me narrowing my eyes.

"You're happy," I accuse.

"Excuse me?" Immediately, the tone is gone, replaced by his normal sardonic one.

"You are," I tell him as surprise courses through me. "You're actually happy for once."

He sniffs but doesn't say anything else, which means I'm right. The knowledge only makes me grin more widely. A happy Hudson can only be a good thing.

"Xavier held my hand last night," Macy says, and now she's smiling up at the ceiling she's been contemplating so hard for the last couple of minutes.

"What?" I shoot up in bed. "When?"

"When we were walking back from the Boneyard."

"How did I miss that?" I demand. "I was right there, wasn't I?"

"You were one of the first to go through the portal, with Flint and Jaxon. Xavier and I were walking together at the back and..." She pauses, a dreamy smile coming over her face. "About halfway back to school, he told me to watch out for something in the tunnels and tugged my hand to pull me away. And then he just never let go."

"Seriously? That's great. I mean, if you like him?"

"I do, actually." She rolls over on her bed and hugs her pillow to her chest. "He gives me butterflies. Not like the 'oh my gosh, the most popular boy in school is in my room' butterflies, but real butterflies. Because of *who* he is, not because of what he is."

"Oh, Macy, that's awesome. That's how I feel about Jaxon, actually."

"Really?"

"Yeah. Like it doesn't matter that he's this badass vamp. It only matters that he's Jaxon."

"You certainly know how to kill a mood, don't you?" Hudson

snarks from where he's sitting on top of my dresser. "I think I need a dose of insulin after all that sweetness."

"Bite me," I answer with a roll of my eyes in his direction, and Macy grins.

"If you keep saying that, one of these days I'm going to take you up on that offer," he tells me.

"I'll worry about that after you actually get some teeth," I shoot back.

"Wow. Looks like you don't have that problem," he tells me, all mock hurt. But there's a glint of amusement in his eyes that he doesn't even try to hide. "Maybe I'll borrow some of yours. Sounds like you've got plenty of teeth to go around."

"Yeah, I do." I snap said teeth at him. "My gargoyle fangs may not be as badass as yours, but they get the job done. You should probably remember that."

"I remember everything about you," he tells me, and there's something in his voice, and his face, that has me turning toward him, wanting to ask...I don't know what exactly. But definitely something.

"Okay," Macy says with a groan that breaks the sudden tension between Hudson and me. "Class starts in half an hour, so it's definitely a glamour day."

I smile at her, relaxed and happy for the first time in weeks.

At least until Macy sticks her head around the wall that separates the sink from the rest of the room and says, "Don't forget we have that assembly today."

"What assembly?" I ask as I reach for my uniform skirt and a purple tank top.

"The one where we get the bloodstone, silly." She peeks around the wall that separates the bathroom from the rest of the room. "The vampire king wants to do it with all the pomp and circumstance."

And just like that, my good mood shatters. And so does Hudson's, if the very British curses he's tossing out are any indication...

88

Subconsciously Yours

Several hours later, it's time for art class, and I can't help the bounce in my step. I've been itching to finish the painting I started when I first got back. I still have no idea where it's going, but it's calling to me. And so is the fact that I need a finished product for my midterm grade.

Before I start, I do what I always do. I arrange my tools exactly how I like them, small, fine ones near the front; bigger ones near the back; all the colors of the rainbow right in front of me. And then I start to paint.

At least today I have a picture in my mind of what I want to paint. Before, it was just a desperate drive to get the background colors right. But today...today I have an image. I don't know where it came from or where I've seen it before—or if it's something from the three and a half months I have no memory of—but wherever it's from, it's clear as day. I don't need answers to the other questions yet. Not when I can simply paint what I see.

And so I do, mixing color after color, shade after shade, until all the variations of blue and gray and black and white combine on the canvas in front of me. I layer the shades carefully, one tiny color distinction after another, until they form a picture so tightly painted that one tone is practically indistinguishable from another. Until trying to get through the painting means unraveling every single shade of every single color.

I work for hours—well after art class is over—until my hands are sore and my shoulders and biceps are on fire. And still I keep going, still I keep painting, layer after layer after layer, until the picture in my head slowly comes to life on the canvas.

Hudson wakes up from a nap in the middle of the painting, and I expect him to argue with me about the right shade of black again.

But he doesn't. Instead, he just watches me with unfathomable eyes...and an oddly gentle look on his face.

When it's finally complete, when I'm finally convinced I've done the picture in my mind justice, I put down the paintbrushes. And nearly weep with the relief that comes from lowering my arms.

I stretch out all the kinks, then close my eyes to give my tired brain a break. But when I finally open them, it's to find Hudson looking straight at me.

"So you remember?" he asks in a tone so tentative that I can't believe it even came from him.

"No." I glance back at the painting, my stomach clenching a little at the idea that I might have *finally* remembered something...even if I can't identify it yet. Even if it's just my subconscious poking at me, trying to tell me something. Trying to get me to do what I so desperately want to do—remember. "Do you recognize it?"

"It's impossible." Hudson shakes his head as if to clear it. "You couldn't possibly have painted this if you don't remember. Not this accurately. Not this perfectly."

"I felt it," I tell him, struggling to find a description that will make sense to both of us. "I don't know how else to describe it. From the moment I've been back, this place has been building in my head until I couldn't *not* paint it. From the moment I picked up my paintbrush, it was the only thing that felt right."

I don't say anything else—there's nothing else for me to say—and for long seconds, neither does Hudson. Eventually, though, he inclines his head and says, "It's perfect."

"You know where it is." It's not a question, even though my voice is quieter than his.

"Yes," he answers.

My breath catches in my chest, my throat. Finally, I'll know something. Finally, I'll have one memory to hold on to. It's not much, but it's more than I had when I woke up this morning. More than I had when I brushed my teeth or took a shower or picked up my favorite Pop-Tarts in the cafeteria.

But the seconds tick by, and still Hudson doesn't say anything until, finally, I feel like I can't take it anymore. Until I feel like even my skin doesn't fit.

"Are you going to tell me?" I demand, after time has passed and done nothing to alleviate the nerves.

Another silence, this one even longer than the one that came before it. "It's my lair," he answers, and there's a lifetime in those three words.

89

Bend Till You Break

"**D**on't be nervous," Jaxon tells me several hours later as I fiddle with my uniform tie for what feels like the hundredth time. But I can't help it. My stomach's been churning since Macy told me about the assembly this morning. That feeling only doubled when Hudson told me I'd painted his lair from memory, until right here, right now, I feel like exploding.

"Be very nervous," Hudson tells me from his spot lounging against the door. "In fact, maybe you should just call in sick."

Jaxon's phone rings—his mom is calling—and he walks into his bedroom to answer it.

"I think you're the one who's nervous," I answer as soon as Jaxon is out of earshot.

"Umm, yeah. Because, you know, at least two people in that room want to kill you. Probably more." Hudson pauses and thinks. "Yeah, definitely more."

"Well then, it's sad for them, isn't it, that I have no intention of dying today. Or anytime soon."

"Yeah, we'll see," he mutters.

"You need to be a little more positive, you know that?" I'm so annoyed that I say this louder than I intend as Jaxon strides back over to me.

"What did I do?" Jaxon asks, looking very confused.

"That wasn't to you," I explain. "That was to your brother."

"Oh." Jaxon rears back, like he forgot Hudson exists. Or like he can't believe I might be talking to both of them at the same time. Like I haven't done that every day since I made it back to my human form or anything.

"What's he saying?"

"That it's a bad idea to go to this assembly. But he said it about the last one, too, so I don't have a lot of faith in his opinion. Besides, how else are we going to get the bloodstone?"

"There are eight of you," Hudson tells me testily. "You could let any one of the other seven pick it up."

"And let Cyrus know I'm afraid of him?" I shake my head at Hudson. "I don't think so."

"You *should* be afraid of him. And even if you're not, you should act like you are. Anything else will just piss him off."

"Apparently everything is going to piss him off." I put both my hands on my hips. "So why does it matter what I do?"

"You're right, it probably doesn't. Which is another reason why you shouldn't go!" Hudson practically growls with aggravation.

"Why don't you go visit someone else for a while? Bring your doom and gloom there?" I make an obnoxious face. "Oh wait, you can't. That's why we need to get the stone."

He arches a brow. "You know that joke was old the first time you told it, right?"

"Yeah, well, you—"

"Not to interrupt what I'm sure is a scintillating conversation," Jaxon says so coolly that I feel the chill in my bones, "but I thought maybe you might like to talk to me instead of my brother. I mean, since you're actually in my room."

Of course. Because what I need today is for both the Vega brothers to freak out on me, even if it is for different reasons.

"Yeah, well, I wouldn't have to freak out if you would take your own safety a little more seriously," Hudson tells me. "I can't help you if you won't help yourself."

I didn't ask you to help me! I answer in my head so Jaxon doesn't get upset.

"Maybe you should," he shoots back.

"Seriously?" Jaxon says. "You can't stop talking to him for two seconds? I'm trying to have a conversation with you here."

"Of course I can. I'm sorry." I take a deep breath, blow it out slowly. "What do you want to talk about, Jaxon?"

"Has he always been this whiny?" Hudson demands. "Honestly, I don't know how you stand it."

"Stop," I tell him and intentionally give him my back, determined not to engage with him any more right now.

But he's not having it. He walks around Jaxon so I'm facing both brothers now. "I'm only trying to be helpful, Grace. I know better than most just how spoiled Jaxon can be."

He's not spoiled. I jump in to defend Jaxon instantly and then realize, almost as quickly, that I've just been totally played. Hudson was trying to get a rise out of me. *You're kind of a jackass. You know that, right?*

"Know it?" He looks down his nose at me in a kind of snooty, kind of playful manner. "I pride myself on it."

Yeah, but—

"So." Jaxon looks really nervous. "What do you think?"

"About what?" I ask before I can think better of it.

"You weren't listening?" He looks vaguely homicidal. "You didn't hear anything I said?"

"I did. I just—"

He sighs disgustedly. "What I said was that there's another way to get Hudson out of your head. Besides the spell with the five artifacts."

"Seriously? And you're just bringing this up now?" I grab on to his hand. "What is it?"

"It's fairly drastic—"

"Yeah, because going up against something called the Unkillable Beast isn't drastic at all," I answer, totally deadpan. "Why didn't you tell me earlier? I mean, we already have all four of the necessary—"

"Five," Jaxon growls. "We need five items. There's no way we're bringing him back if he's not human. No way."

I think back to what the Bloodletter said, to what everyone has said about Hudson—except Hudson. Every time I start to think that maybe he's not so bad, I force myself to remember what it felt like to be standing in that assembly with him and be unable to move. "Okay, okay. I know you're right about the whole power thing. So what is this other way?"

Jaxon looks a little sick, and this time he's the one taking the deep breath. Which makes my stomach plummet.

"What is it?" I ask, suddenly a lot more frightened than I was just a minute ago.

"We could break the mating bond."

The words fall like a nuclear bomb between us, the shock and pain of them radiating through me in a way nothing ever has in my whole life—even my parents' deaths.

"I don't— I can't—"

"Holy shit. Exactly how much does my brother hate me?" Hudson whispers.

I take a moment to answer Hudson and…also try to figure out how to breathe. *Seriously? That's what you're asking now? I would assume a lot, since he, you know, killed you.*

"Killing is pretty normal in our world. Trying to break a mating bond? That's unheard of. Mainly because it's literally impossible. Trust me, if it were possible, my mom would have definitely divorced *her* jackass mate." Hudson starts to pace. "This must be some scary-as-shit magic if it can sever a mating bond."

Wow. Okay, then.

I press a hand to my stomach, still trying to absorb the blow of Jaxon's words. And worse, the fact that he brought this up at all.

"So..." I have a million things I want to ask but no idea how to ask them. So I start with the most basic. "You don't want to be mated to me anymore?"

"Of course I want to be mated to you!" he exclaims, and this time he's the one who grabs my hands. "I want it more than anything."

"Then why would you even suggest..." There's a strange ringing in my ears, and I shake my head to clear it. "I thought mating bonds were unbreakable."

"I thought so, too. But I asked the Bloodletter—"

"You asked her? When we were there?" The pain deep inside me gets worse and worse. "When? When she put me to sleep? When she locked me in that cage?"

"No, not then. Of course not." He gives me a pleading look. "It was way before."

Somehow, that sounds even worse. "How 'way before,' considering I was here for a week, then gone for nearly four months, then here for a few days? When exactly did you ask her? And why?"

"I asked her after you first got here and I realized we were mated. I'd nearly killed you with the window... It just seemed like a really bad idea to be mated to a human who might die because of me. So I went to her and asked for a spell to break the bond."

There's so much to unpack there that I don't even know where to start. And for once, Hudson is completely silent, absolutely no help at all. The traitor.

I still can't believe Jaxon didn't tell me up front that we were mated. I mean, I get why he didn't say anything that first day, but why not after the snowball fight or when we started dating?

But I also can't believe he was going to break the bond—without even asking me. He was going to do something so irrevocable, so painful, so terrible, and he wasn't even going to get my opinion on the matter. It would have affected me, too, I'm sure of it, and he wasn't even going to ask?

And now, after we've come so far, he brings up breaking the bond again because having Hudson in my head is an inconvenience to him? Even though we're so close to getting him out another way? A way that leaves the bond completely intact?

"Did she give you the spell?" I finally whisper, because there's so much to say, I don't know where to start.

"She did," he tells me.

My breath catches. "Seriously?" It feels like he just hit me again. "And you took it?"

"I was scared. I'd nearly killed you. I didn't want to hurt you, Grace."

"Yeah, because this is a picnic." I look wildly around his room. "Where is it? Where are you keeping it?"

I don't know why it matters, but it does. If he knows where it is, if it's right at his damn fingertips...

"I threw it away."

"What?" That's not the answer I was expecting.

"I threw it away the same day she gave it to me. I couldn't bring myself to do it, Grace. To either of us. Not before we'd even had a chance to try. Not without your permission."

I blow out a breath slowly as the pain finally ebbs. It doesn't go away completely, but it slowly dissipates. Because he couldn't do it. He couldn't break what was between us before it even got started, and especially without telling me. That makes a difference. If he could, if he'd kept it...I don't know if I'd ever be able to get past it.

"We're not breaking the mating bond, Jaxon."

"It could starve him. Without the energy from the bond to feed on, he would die quickly, right? I think you'd be okay in that scenario. It's the draining that is slowly killing us all."

His words poke at all my still-tender spots. "And I'd have to sit by and watch him die. While also being traumatized at the loss of my mate."

"You wouldn't lose me. I'd still be here—"

"Just not my mate anymore." I look at him with what I know is my heart in my eyes and whisper, "Is that really what you want?"

"Of course it's not what I want!" he practically shouts.

"Good. Then don't bring it up again."

"Grace—"

"No." I want to throw myself at him, to wrap my arms around his waist, but I'm still aching.

"I'm sorry." He pulls me close, holds me as tightly as I wanted to hold him. "I was only trying to make things better for you."

"I don't need that kind of help," I answer, even as I wonder if that's really true. If making things better for me is the only reason he brought this up.

"I'm sorry," he says again. "I'm so sorry."

I don't know if it's enough. Honestly, I don't know what would be enough right now, but it's a start. That has to count for something.

"Okay," I tell him, even though I'm feeling anything but. Still, we're out of time. We have to get to the assembly.

Maybe if I just breathe for a little while, the pain will go away. And so will the sense of betrayal that's ricocheting through me.

As I head for the door, I dread having to field Hudson's snark in the middle of all this. But for once, he doesn't make a sound.

90

Fire and Bloodstone

I'm still reeling ten minutes later as we make our way to the ceremony. I tell myself that it's no big deal, that everything is going to be okay—with Jaxon, with the ceremony, with the Unkillable Beast. But how okay can I convince myself things are going to be if Jaxon was willing to sever our mating bond?

Everything feels wrong now, off-kilter. And the fact that Hudson is back to haranguing me definitely doesn't help.

"Which part of *my father murdered every gargoyle in existence* do you not understand?" Hudson demands as we make our way down to the auditorium. "Do you think he killed all of them in secret? He did it right out in the open and dared anyone to question him. And if they did, he killed them, too—or at least discredited them. You think he can't make one silly little girl go away?

"His words, not mine," he hastens to add when I turn on him, infuriated. "I'm just saying, that's what he'll be thinking. It's not true, but that's how he'll see it."

"Yeah, well, that's ridiculous," I mutter and glance up at Jaxon talking to Mekhi.

"Absolutely. But he's a ridiculous man. Evil. Monstrous. But ridiculous. You'll do well to remember that."

He doesn't say anything else, but then neither do Jaxon, Mekhi, or I as we take the last flight of stairs two at a time. The others are waiting for us at the bottom, looking a million times happier than I feel. Then again, the king probably doesn't want to kill *them*.

"Looking good, Grace," Flint tells me, holding up a hand for a fist bump.

"You're looking pretty good yourself," I tell him, because it's true. All the guys look amazing in their dress uniforms, especially since they get to wear blazers tonight instead of those absurd purple robes.

"Everybody ready for this dog and vampire show?" Mekhi asks as he holds an arm out for Eden. She looks a little surprised at the gesture—I'm guessing the combat boots and kick-ass attitude tend to limit the gallant gestures aimed her way—but then she smiles wider than I've ever seen her.

"Damn straight!" she tells him, taking his offered arm.

Xavier offers his arm to Macy, and she giggles like a schoolgirl before she also takes it. But I can't help grinning at the way she and Xavier keep stealing glances at each other out of the corners of their eyes when they think the other one isn't looking.

"Guess that leaves you and me," Flint says to Gwen with a waggle of his eyebrows.

She looks at him like he's a little strange, but she nods as she gingerly takes his arm. She's doing so much better, but her arm is still badly bruised and cut up.

Jaxon reaches up and smooths my curls off my face. "It's going to be okay," he tells me. "I promise, I won't let anything happen to you."

"I know you won't," I answer as he takes my hand in his. But his words from earlier keep playing in my head.

Sometimes it feels like Jaxon tries to protect me from everyone but himself.

But as our palms meet, I can't help but realize how drained he is. I fed him energy down the mating bond right after we got back from the Boneyard earlier, and he seemed to be doing better, but right now I'm not so sure.

We have to get the last item. We don't have any time to waste.

"So anxious to get me out, huh?" Hudson asks.

So anxious to get your brother back to normal, I answer. *It's not the same thing.*

I wait for the obnoxious comeback, and it doesn't take long. "Jaxon doesn't do normal, or haven't you noticed?"

Says the guy who lives in my head, I shoot back, fed up with everyone at the moment. *Hate to be the one to break it to you, but he's not the abnormal one here.*

Hudson starts to say something else, but he stops as we walk into the auditorium, which is already half filled with students, many of whom turn to look at us as we start toward the back row of seats.

There's a purple carpet—*a purple carpet!*—lining the walkway up to the stage. It's obviously for us, and I feel completely ridiculous walking down it, even though everyone else seems to think it's totally normal.

Uncle Finn is waiting when we get to the stage, once again fiddling with the sound system. He grins at all of us and goes out of his way to send an encouraging little wink to Macy and me.

Still, there's something in his eyes—they're so serious, despite his smile and wink—that makes my stomach clench.

"Is it too late to run?" I ask, and I'm only half kidding. Something about this just feels off. Jaxon squeezes my hand.

"I told you not to come," Hudson hisses at me. "I told you something bad would happen."

Nothing bad has happened yet, I try to soothe, but my heart has started beating out of control.

Even Jaxon looks like he thinks running might be a good option, especially as the assembly hall doors swing open and the members of the Circle come parading up the walkway on the opposite side of the auditorium from where the rest of us entered.

Cyrus heads to the podium with all the pomp and flair of Mick Jagger at a Stones concert. Today he's dressed in a black pinstripe suit with a purple-and-black tie and, not going to lie, he looks like a million bucks. Of course, his eyes are gleaming like a zealot's, so it takes a little away from the whole picture.

As soon as the other members of the Circle find their seats, he starts the assembly with a, "Thank you, Katmere Academy, for the most exciting Ludares tournament we have ever experienced. It was truly a delight to preside over such an incredible event."

The room falls silent as he looks the audience over, and I'm not sure what's scarier, the serious looks on their faces or the sound of the locks as the doors slide shut.

I swallow the panic rising in my throat as I give the audience a shaky smile. What I really want to do is race down the aisle like a K-pop fan after my favorite idol, but instead I stay where I am as the king turns back to the audience and continues what I now know—what all eight of us now know—is a total fucking farce.

"First on the agenda is celebrating the win of this amazing team up here. They played an incredible game of Ludares, didn't they? That moment when Grace dodged the two dragons was breathtaking. And when she turned one of the dragons to stone?" He shakes his head. "Absolutely captivating."

The audience claps more enthusiastically than I expected.

"So, with no further ado, let's bring them up to accept the special prize donated this year—a bloodstone from the royal collection."

Delilah is also at the front of the stage, though it's clear she plans to let her husband do all the talking today. She's dressed head to toe in white, and she looks chillingly beautiful. Her crimson lips are turned upward in a perfect smile—that appears genuine as long as you don't look at it too closely.

Cyrus motions toward our team at the back of the auditorium. "Can our Ludares winners please come forward together and take a bow?"

The group of us exchanges uneasy glances—but Jaxon squares his shoulders and walks in front, with all of us following behind reluctantly and single file.

"Take your bow," Cyrus instructs as we come to a stop on the stage, and we do as the audience applauds.

Cyrus walks behind us now and pats everyone on the back as he calls their name. I'm at the end, though, and he stops when he gets to me.

"Grace." Cyrus hands me the box with the bloodstone in it, looking me up and down, and it totally squicks me out. Not because the look he gives me is lascivious—it's not—but because it's avaricious. Like he wants me, but only because he's already figured out how to best use me to serve his interests.

"It's so lovely to meet you," he tells me, coming around to my side and opening both arms in some kind of bizarre facsimile of a social-distancing hug. "My son's mate, a gargoyle." He shakes his head. "It's unfathomable but so, so exciting."

"So exciting," Delilah echoes, and her perfect crimson smile never wavers.

Cyrus continues. "I can't tell you how impressed we were by your performance during the tournament."

"My entire team did very well," I agree.

Delilah cocks a brow in exactly the same way as both her sons do but says nothing.

"So they did. But *you* were their secret weapon. We all saw Grace Foster's performance at the Ludares tournament yesterday, correct?" Cyrus's voice booms through the auditorium and elicits cheers in response. "We saw the amazing things she could do, didn't we?" More cheers.

"But we also saw how vulnerable the poor girl is," Cyrus adds, shaking his head. "We saw her struggle, we saw her dragged across the field by a werewolf, we saw her nearly die between two dragons. Grace, our only gargoyle in more than one thousand years."

Where's he going with this? I ask Hudson as he continues to list the many things that have happened to me since my parents died.

"Nowhere good."

Cyrus pauses, and it's like the whole room forgot how to breathe. He turns to his wife and motions her over. "Would you like to deliver the good news, Delilah?"

The queen continues to smile as she walks forward, but it's not a happy smile. It's rigid, brittle, and I wonder how long she can hold it before shattering. Wonder how long she can wear this facade before she breaks completely.

Long enough, I guess, because she doesn't break as she steps forward to take the microphone. As she turns to the audience and says, "It is with the *utmost pleasure* that I share some exciting news."

She faces me, and I don't know whether it's Hudson or me who's more anxious about what she's going to say. Probably me. As her smile grows wider, my heartbeat pounds in my ears so loudly, I'm not sure I'll be able to hear the words.

"The Circle has voted and agreed. King Cyrus and I will be taking Grace home with us to the Vampire Court."

Huh. Turns out I definitely heard that...even though I wish I hadn't.

91

Family Feud **Has Nothing on Us**

"**F**uck, no!" Everything within Hudson instantly repudiates his mother's words. Then again, everything inside me does the same thing.

"Don't worry, Grace. I won't let that happen," Jaxon whispers as his hand tightens on mine, but I only vaguely register his words.

I think I'm in shock. My palms are sweaty, but I can't hear my heartbeat anymore. It's pounding so fast, it's just one continuous hum in my head.

"It was a grave and difficult decision," Cyrus takes the microphone back and adds. "But in a four-four decision—with my lead vote breaking the tie—the Circle has agreed that we must take Grace back home to London with us, where we can train her to defend herself, and protect her until she can protect herself."

The audience of students begins to clap at his words, though not as enthusiastically as before, but he doesn't seem to notice or mind. "I know you all care for Grace as we do, and I am so glad you agree that this rare creature, this new hope for our battered world, must be guarded at all costs."

"You can't do that!" Jaxon growls at his father.

Cyrus turns from the mic and tells his son in a low, contemptuous voice, "Stay quiet, boy. You won't like what lies down that road if you don't."

"I don't care—" Jaxon starts, but he breaks off when I squeeze his hand hard enough to almost break it. Because Hudson is yammering in my head, screaming at me to stop Jaxon, that he has another plan.

Cyrus takes Jaxon's pause as acceptance and turns back to his audience and continues his speech, but I'm not paying attention to what he says.

"Wait," I whisper to my mate. "Just give Hudson a second to talk to me."

"Hudson?" Jaxon asks, his face twisted in disbelief. "You're going to believe *him*? My parents' perfect little minion?"

"It's not like that," I tell him, but when he starts to argue, I hold up a surreptitious hand to stop him.

"Challenge for inclusion," Hudson tells me. "Do it loud and make sure it's on the record."

Inclusion? What's that?

"Just do it before they close the assembly. You don't have much time."

"Wait," I shout, and Cyrus turns, a furious set to his normally placid face at being openly challenged.

I take a deep breath. Am I really going to trust Hudson?

"Do you have a choice?" he huffs.

I don't. So I shout out as loudly and as clearly as I can, "I challenge for inclusion."

And the room goes eerily quiet. *Oh fuck. What have I done?*

"The only thing you could," Hudson replies, but he's not looking at me. He's looking directly at his father, a sly smile curving his lips, like he just called checkmate before his dad even knew he was on the board.

"Inclusion?" Cyrus hisses at me with murder in his eyes.

His reaction only spurs me on. "Yes," I say again. "I challenge for inclusion."

"On what grounds?" he demands as the other members of the

Circle start to exchange looks.

Yeah, Hudson, on what grounds?

"On the grounds that gargoyles have a rightful seat on the Circle and held one all the way up until their extermination. But don't use that word because it will just set my father off more."

What? That's what inclusion is? I'm calling for a seat on the Circle? I don't want that!

"It's that or live in my parents' dungeon forever. I've spent a lot of time down there myself, and I have to say, it's not a place you want to call home."

"On what grounds?" Cyrus thunders again, and when I don't immediately answer, he gives a twisted little smirk and turns back around to face the audience. "Inclusion den—"

"Gargoyles are an equal ruling faction on the Circle by law," I tell him. "Now that a gargoyle exists again, I have the right to representation. And since I am the only gargoyle in existence, I challenge for inclusion."

The other Circle members exchange another look, and some of them—like Flint's parents—are nodding. Even Delilah looks a little pained.

"Do you even know what the challenge is?" he demands.

"It's a..."

"Trial," Hudson supplies.

"Trial," I call out. "It's a test I have to pass." *Oh shit*, I realize. This is what everyone told me about. The reason Ludares came about to begin with.

What have you gotten me into? I demand of Hudson.

"It's a trial no one ever takes alone, one that only mated pairs can take," Cyrus tells me. "Therefore—"

"Good thing she has a mate," Jaxon says, stepping forward. "And we challenge for inclusion. Together."

Cyrus looks like he's going to explode and kill us both on the stage, consequences be damned, but then Imogen—one of the witches on the

Circle—stands up. "They should have the right to challenge," she says.

Her mate stands with her. "I agree."

"So do we," Nuri and her partner stand as well.

It won't be enough, I tell Hudson. *There won't be enough votes without the wolves.*

"You have a right to a seat by law," Hudson tells me. "It isn't up for a vote."

"By law, a gargoyle has a right to a seat on the Circle. This isn't up for debate. Or vote." I hold Cyrus's gaze and can tell he's debating his next move carefully.

"Fine," Cyrus says, the word crackling with rage and indignation. "Your challenge stands. The Trial will take place two days from now at dawn in the arena."

"Tell him you need more time," Hudson says urgently. "No way can you be ready in two days—"

"I need more time!" I say.

Cyrus shoots me a malicious look and says, "There is no more time. The Circle cannot afford to linger here as long as your heart desires. It is either two days from now or not at all. You choose."

"I guess I'll see you in the arena, then," I tell him.

He nods, his face once again carefully blank. "That you will."

As we leave the stage, the audience seems as mixed up as I feel. Some students are clapping and whistling, while others are whispering behind their hands or actively ignoring us—which is a new experience for me here at Katmere, but one I can definitely get behind.

The fewer people who are looking at me, the better. Especially now.

"Well, that went better than expected," Hudson comments.

"We're fucked, aren't we?" I ask.

Both Hudson and Jaxon reply at the same time. "Definitely."

92

Is It Really a Throw Down if it Makes You Want to Throw Up?

"What did I just do?" I demand as soon as we leave the ceremony and make our way up to Jaxon's tower. Panic is a living, breathing beast within me, making my hands shake and my brain feel like it's about to explode. "What did I just do?"

"It's fine," Hudson says quickly. "You're fine."

"You agreed to compete in the Trials," Jaxon tells me. "Everyone who gets on the Circle has to compete—and win. That's why it's always done as a mated pair, because it's dangerous." He pauses. "It's really dangerous, Grace. And usually deadly. No one has won a seat in a thousand years. Don't you think people have tried to remove Cyrus before?"

"Of course it's dangerous," I answer. "I mean, what exactly about your world *isn't* deadly?"

"It's your world, too," Hudson reminds me, and for once he doesn't sound cavalier. In fact, he sounds concerned, and not in a snide way.

Which, now that I think about it, might be what's freaking me out so much. Well, that and my having just agreed to participate in some twisted paranormal version of reality TV—sudden-death edition.

"And I say you might as well be in charge of it instead of crushed by it," he adds.

"You shut up!" I tell him, and I'm so annoyed that I end up

practically yelling it. Out loud. "You're the one who got me into this mess!"

"Me?" Jaxon looks insulted. "I'm just trying to help get you *out* of this mess."

I don't bother telling him I'm talking to Hudson. Not when I've got enough anger to go around. "By signing up to die with me? I'm glad that feels like helping."

Now he just looks pissed off. "Should I have left you to go it alone when I can help you? We are mates, you know. That's not just in name only."

"Unless you decide otherwise," I snark, and I know it's a low blow, but I'm still hurting big-time from what happened before. Then to add this whole Trial thing on top of it, followed by the fact that the only help with it can come from my mate? The guy who just told me that, for a while at least, he didn't even want to *be* my mate?

It's like rubbing salt in an open wound—followed by a lemon juice and vinegar chaser.

"Okay, look," Macy steps in. "This is bad. No doubt about it. But we have too much to do in the next two days to start sniping at one another. So can we just settle down and make a plan?"

"I'm pretty sure Cyrus already made a plan." I sigh and run a hand through my hair. "And it ends with me in chains or dead."

"Yeah, well, that's not going to happen," Xavier tells me, hands on hips like he's ready to battle now. "Not if we have anything to say about it."

"Can someone tell me exactly what this Trial is that I've just signed myself up for? I know Ludares was based on it, but what exactly does that mean?"

"It's basically Ludares without rules. Or safety bracelets. No-holds-barred, free-for-all till the death," Jaxon tells me. "And instead of eight-versus-eight teams, it's the two challengers against eight champions picked by the Circle."

"So Ludares on steroids?" I ask as a whole new brand of horror sweeps through me. "And I'm supposed to play by *myself*?"

"With your mate," Jaxon reminds me. "I've got your back, Grace."

I sigh, because as mad at him as I am—and I am really, really mad—I know that's true. Jaxon would never leave me hanging when I need him. Especially not when there's a way for him to help me. It's as I remember this that the last of my anger leaves me. Because Jaxon has always tried to do what is right for me—no matter how misguided—and that outweighs everything else.

"So," I say when I can finally think through the panic. "We have two days to get Jaxon and me in shape for the Trial. Fantastic. Any ideas?"

It's a sarcastic question, but judging from the contemplative looks on everyone's faces, they're actually trying to answer it. So many reasons why I adore my friends.

"Well, I think we should talk about the fact that we have to get Hudson out of your head before you get on that field," Flint says. "Otherwise he's going to keep draining you and Jaxon, and then you'll both lose—and possibly even die."

"He's right," Macy agrees. "We've got to get him out as soon as possible."

"Which means getting to the Unkillable Beast as soon as possible," Jaxon says. "We can't let him out until we have the heartstone the beast is guarding."

"What is it with my brother's determination to die?" Hudson grumbles. "You don't need a heartstone. You just need to get me out so I don't put any more strain on the mating bond. And you already have everything you need to do that."

"Yeah, well, you don't get a vote," I tell him as Jaxon and Flint start arguing over the best way to go about killing the beast.

"Of course I don't. Why should I, when I'm the one most affected by it?" He rolls his eyes.

Ugh. I'm frustrated and freaked out, and the last thing I need is Hudson's martyr complex right now.

"Martyr complex?" he almost roars. "Are you kidding me? I'm the *only* reason you're not in chains bound for my parents' dungeon, and *I* have a martyr complex? Seriously?"

I sigh. "You weren't supposed to hear that."

"News flash. I'm in your head," he snaps and paces in front of Jaxon's bookcase. "I hear everything. Every snarky little thought you have, I know about it. Every fear, I see it. Every random thought is front and center in my brain, so I get that you're afraid. And I get that you don't want to trust me because of what everyone else has told you.

"But could you please, for one minute, just listen to me? Just think this through. I swear, I'm trying to help you. I swear, that's all I'm trying to do, Grace. All I've done since I've come back is try to help you."

I want to believe him, I do. So much so that it surprises me. But I'm scared. I've made mistakes before, trusted people I shouldn't. Look at what happened with Lia.

"I'm not Lia," he tells me. "I never would have asked for this. I never would have even dreamed of putting you through what she did. What happened with her is one of the biggest regrets of my life and if I could take it back, I would—"

"Take what back?" I ask, shocked at how tortured he looks, how remorseful. Usually, those are the last two adjectives I'd ever use for Hudson.

"I made a mistake," he tells me. "I teased her one day, not long before I died. Told her she'd love me forever. I was joking, just playing around, but..." He shakes his head. "I don't get to do that, because my power makes it true. I knew better, but I forgot for one second, and all this happened." He holds his hands out helplessly.

His words make everything inside me sit at attention. Because maybe Lia wasn't as evil as I thought. Maybe she was just one more victim of power beyond someone's control. It's a hard thought to swallow after everything that's happened, so I file it in my "Shit I Don't Have Time For Today" folder and promise myself I'll get back to it when I have more time.

"I'm trying to fix what I can," he tells me. "I swear, Grace, the last thing I want to do right now is hurt you—or anyone. You just have to trust me. And if you try to kill the beast before the Trial, you're going to die. If not by it, then by the Trial when you drag your broken ass into the arena."

I can feel his despair, feel his agitation, and despite everything, I believe him. More, I realize, I've believed him for a while now.

"That's not true," I tell the group. "We have the four items. We could let Hudson out right now. That would give us two days to recover all our strength and train really hard, so we'll actually have a chance of not dying." I nod. "It's the best option."

"Over my dead fucking body," Jaxon replies, ice dripping from every word he bites out.

93

Betrayal Is a Four-Letter Word

"**B**est option for whom exactly?" Flint demands, jaw tight and eyes blazing. "Not for the rest of us, that's for damn sure."

"I'm with Flint," Eden says. "We can't do that. We can't let Hudson, with his power of persuasion, out in the world again. We just can't."

"I understand that you're scared—" I start.

"We're not scared," Macy says. "We're practical. We lived through Hudson once, until Jaxon and the rest of the Order finally found a way to bring him down. There's no way we can risk letting him loose again. No way we can justify risking so many people's lives just because it's expedient for us."

"What about risking *our* lives?" I ask. "Going against the Unkillable Beast won't be easy. One of us could die—"

"It's worth it," Xavier says quietly, his voice and eyes as serious as I've ever seen them.

"Dying is worth it?" I repeat flatly. "Seriously?"

"Do you know how many people he killed?" Mekhi asks. "How many wolves and made vampires died because of Hudson? Because he thought born vampires were the most important species on the planet? His gift of persuasion is just too powerful."

"That's not what happened," Hudson tells me, and there's an underlying urgency in his voice. "I told you that, Grace."

A memory of the scene with his father scratches at my mind. *Why does everyone keep mentioning your gift of persuasion but not the fact that you can literally destroy matter with your mind? What about the memory with your dad? No offense, the fact that you can disintegrate things with a mere thought seems even scarier than the persuasion thing.*

"Because they don't know about it. No one does." He sighs. "Well, except my parents. But my father believes the gift is unusable. That his attempts to force it to grow unfettered didn't make it stronger, it made it go dormant."

Why?

His impenetrable blue eyes hold mine, not a flicker of emotion moving in them. "Because he ran out of things to threaten that I love."

The fact that he says it so simply, so emotionlessly, only makes it worse. Every word slams into me like a bullet, and I sink down on the couch, slowly bleeding out.

Finally, I whisper, connecting all the dots, "So he thinks when he couldn't make you use it anymore, it just slowly atrophied?"

Hudson nods. "Why do you think he eventually let me leave the Vampire Court and attend Katmere? I was no longer of use to him."

My heart breaks wide open for the little boy in that memory. And for the guy standing in front of me, too. But I don't have time to analyze my feelings right now. I need to convince everyone that the devil they fear doesn't exist.

I don't bother to answer Mekhi. Instead, I plead with the group, "Are you really sure that you've got the full story? I know what you believe, but have you ever stopped to ask why he did what he did? Have you ever stopped to wonder if there was a justifiable reason?"

"For murder?" Jaxon narrows his gaze on me. "You're starting to believe whatever lies he's been feeding you. Grace, you know he can't be trusted."

"I *don't* know that," I answer with a shake of my head.

"What if we bring him back and it turns out he's been planning to start his evil crusade all over again?" Gwen asks. "How do we live with ourselves?"

"Yes, because that's what I've been doing. Plotting for months on how to destroy the world." He shakes his head. "Who do they think I am? Dr. Evil?"

I ignore him because I know I have only a couple of minutes to make my case or they're going to move on, whether I want them to or not. So I look from person to person and try to explain. "Cyrus was organizing an army of made vampires, and others, to start another war. Hudson was only trying to prevent an even bigger catastrophe. I'm not saying I agree with his methods, but I believe him when he says he was doing the right thing. He only turned Cyrus's allies against one another."

Flint looks like I hit him with a truck. "Are you blaming *my brother* for what Hudson did?" I have never seen Flint really mad before, and as he raises up to his full dragon height, I have to say, I hope I never see it again. He's not threatening me in any way, but yeah. He is *pissed*. "Is he telling you my *family* was aligned with that fucking power-hungry monster?"

"Your brother most certainly was," Hudson replies, but I ignore him. "Had a nasty temper and hated being boxed in by humans."

"That's not what I'm saying, Flint." I try to calm him down. "But I *am* saying there may be more to this story than you know. I believe him. Doesn't that count for anything?"

"You don't know what you're talking about," Jaxon finally chimes in.

"Excuse me?" I stare at him. "What exactly does *that* mean?"

"You have Hudson whispering in your head, trying to trick you—"

"You really think I'm that silly? That I don't know my own mind?" I ask.

"I think you're human—"

"But I'm not only human," I shoot back. "Am I? At least, not any more than the rest of you. So why does my opinion matter less?"

"Because you weren't there," Jaxon tells me, and he sounds exasperated. Which is fine with me, because I'm way beyond exasperated at this point. Not that that seems to matter to him. Either because he doesn't know that he's offended me or he doesn't care—neither of which is particularly okay in my opinion. "You didn't see what we saw."

"Maybe not, but none of you has seen what I have, either. Hudson has been in my head for a week and a half, twenty-four seven. You think I don't know who he is now? You think I can't recognize a psychopath when I see one?"

"It doesn't matter if you think he's innocent," Flint says. "The risk is too great. We can't let him have his powers. Who knows what he'll do with them next?"

"So you think we have the right to play judge and jury?" I ask. "I think he deserves a chance."

"The truth is, Grace, it doesn't matter what you think," Jaxon tells me. "Because you're outvoted, seven to one."

I stare at him incredulously for long seconds, then glance around the room to see if anyone else thinks he sounds as autocratic as I do. But they all just look back at me solemnly. Which just pisses me off more.

I take a deep breath, try to calm down enough to be rational. Which is hard when my friends are all looking at me like I'm being ridiculous. Worse, like I'm a non-paranormal.

Though I'm not surprised by their stance. Not really. If I'd lived through what they did, I'd likely feel the same about a new girl at school who wants to set free the psychopath who gives them nightmares. But that doesn't mean it doesn't hurt me that Macy and Jaxon—*Jaxon*—are taking sides against me on something so important.

My heart is breaking, and I'm fighting tears as I finally choke out, "Are you seriously not even going to consider what I'm telling you, Jaxon? Are you really not even going to try to see your mate's point of view?"

Jaxon looks as bad as I feel as he reaches for my hands, pulls them close to his chest. "I love you, Grace. You know that." His words are raw and gravelly, like they're being wrenched from deep inside him. "But I can't give you this. Anything else, but not this." He gazes down at me, and there is a wetness in his own eyes that looks a lot like tears as he continues. "I can't afford to put myself first. Or my mate. It's my responsibility to keep everyone safe. Their lives are in *my* hands. So how can you ask *me* to choose?"

"Because I'm right, Jaxon." I turn to the rest of my friends. "I know you don't believe me, but I am. I know Hudson isn't going to hurt anyone again."

"And if you're wrong?" Xavier asks. "What then?"

"I'm not wrong," I tell him as I turn to Jaxon and lay my final card on the table. "And if I say I won't fly off on Flint's back to this mythical Arctic island with you?" I ask softly. "What then?"

"Then we go without you." Jaxon swallows but holds my gaze. "This is more important than any one person. Even you, Grace."

Pain swamps me, threatens to drag me under, and I don't have a clue what to say. Because there is no way to solve this dilemma, no way to find common ground among us, even though the stakes are death.

Or maybe because they are. I don't know anymore.

I'm not sure I know anything anymore. Except that there really is no changing Jaxon's mind.

Not on this.

Tears slide unheeded down my cheeks.

Poor reluctant prince.

Poor beautiful boy.

I glance around, see the closed looks on all my friends' faces, and realize that I really am outvoted. I really can't change their minds. And if I walk away now, if I refuse to go because I know they're wrong, then I'm lowering their chances of succeeding...and worse, *surviving*, as they face this Unkillable Beast.

The knowledge wounds me like few things ever have, and all I want to do is scream.

And that's when I hear Hudson deep in the recesses of my mind. *"It's okay, Grace. Whatever you decide, it's okay."*

You don't mean that, I tell him.

"If it gets you to stop crying, then you're damn right I mean it," he answers. *"This isn't something you can fix. It's just something you have to endure. Whatever happens next, I promise I won't blame you for it."*

It's not fair, I tell him. *It isn't fair what they're going to do to you.*

His laugh, when it comes, is straight out of a tragedy. *"Life isn't fair, Grace. I thought you'd know that better than most."*

I'm sorry, I tell him as tears slide down my cheeks.

"Don't be," he answers. *"None of this is your fault."*

The fact that he's right doesn't make me feel better. In fact, it only makes me feel worse, even as I reach up and cup Jaxon's face so he knows that I understand. So he knows that I feel the weight of the world he carries on his shoulders and that I won't add to it. Not right now. Not over this.

"Fine," I whisper, even though I know, deep down, that it's the wrong thing to do. "I'll go with you. But you have to promise me something in return."

"Anything," he answers as his hands tighten on my own.

"If we actually manage to get the heartstone—and survive—you have to promise me that we'll have this conversation again before we use it. You have to promise me that you'll give me one more chance to change your mind."

"You can have as many chances as you want," Jaxon answers me as he brings my hand to his lips. "I won't change my mind, but I'll listen to what you have to say. I'll always at least listen, Grace."

It's not enough. Not close to enough. But it's all he can give me. So I'll take it for now and hope for a miracle.

94

Some Days the Glass Really Is Half Empty

"I've got bad news and more bad news. Which do you want first?" Xavier says the following night as soon as he enters Jaxon's tower where the rest of us have gathered. Unfortunately, there's absolutely no levity in his face as he asks.

"Is that even a real question?" Macy rolls her eyes. "If things are that bad, just tell us."

"Okay, bad news it is, then." He runs a hand over his face, as if bracing himself to deliver the worst. "I was just making the rounds, checking things out. And there's absolutely no way we're getting off campus tonight."

"What do you mean?" Jaxon demands. "We have to get off campus. We need to find the heartstone tonight, or we won't be able to free Hudson before the Trials."

"Yeah, no shit," Xavier answers. "That's why I called it bad news."

"There has to be a way," Flint says. "The tunnels—"

"I was just down there," Xavier answers. "They've got them closed off, with armed fucking guards standing at every single exit."

"Armed?" I ask, startled at the image of weapons here at Katmere. "Armed with what?"

"Magic," Jaxon answers quietly. "It's all they need."

"What about the battlements?" Macy asks. "The dragons—and

Grace—can fly off the towers—"

"Yeah, they've got people up there, too. A lot of them." Xavier slumps down against the wall and says, "We're fucked."

"We can't be fucked," Flint says. "We have to do this, so let's figure it out and get it done."

"That's what we're trying to do, dragon. Do you have any more suggestions, or do you just want to bitch about it?" Mekhi asks.

"I don't see you with any better suggestions, *vampire*. And I was just trying to make a point."

Mekhi snorts. "The point has already been made. So either put up or shut up. We don't have time for any more shit."

Flint holds a hand to his ear, pretends to listen really hard. "And what's your plan again?"

"Can you give us the rest of the bad news?" I ask, hoping to break up the insult trading before we have an all-out brawl on Jaxon's floor.

"What do you mean?" asks Eden from where she's sprawled across the end of the couch.

"Xavier said he had bad news and more bad news." The room goes silent as we all look at him. "So what other bad news is there?" I ask a second time.

"Oh, I heard the Circle called for champions to play in their stead, some of the fiercest warriors in the world, but your uncle Finn threw down. Said if Cyrus had the balls to accept a challenge, then he could damn well fight himself."

The churning in my stomach rises tenfold. I groan. "That's not just more bad news. That's awful, horrible, we're-all-gonna-die news."

Xavier grins now. "Oh, sorry, no, that's *not* the bad news. Apparently the king is scared shitless to meet Jaxon on the field—for good reason—so he still insisted on champions. And your uncle agreed...but they have to be Katmere students."

Okay, yeah, that's pretty bad news. I don't want to fight for my life against other teens. But at least we won't be facing off against Jaxon's parents. Or Flint's mom, who is a complete badass.

"So who did he pick?" Jaxon asks, and he sounds as grim as I feel.

"Cole was the first to agree," he answers, "and he's out for blood... of course."

My stomach drops. Why is it always Cole? I've never done anything to that jerk, at least not intentionally, and he's been gunning for me from the moment I got here. I've never really wished ill on anyone before—except Lia when she was trying to murder me—but I am really sad I stopped Jaxon from finishing Cole off when he had the chance.

Jaxon shakes his head and looks disgusted, and I'm about 99 percent positive he's having the exact same thoughts I am.

But all he asks is, "Who else?"

"He's picked Marc and Quinn as his additional wolves. And—"

"That's three wolves," Mekhi interrupts. "Why does he get three of them on the team?"

Xavier looks at him like he's not paying attention. "Do you know any vamps in the school who think it's a good idea to be on a team whose sole purpose is to let the king take Grace back to his dungeon, thereby separating Jaxon Vega and his mate?"

"Fair point," Mekhi agrees.

"What about the witches?" Macy asks, fingers nervously twisting the bottom of her sweater.

"From what I hear, it's going to be Simone and Cam, for sure. No one knows if it's going to be the witches or the dragons who have a third player, too, so the rumors are flying."

"I knew it!" Macy throws out a hand, and an entire row of books falls off the nearest bookshelf. "The traitor! When I get through with him, he's going to have lice and acne and a serious case of the bubonic plague! He's such a douche. I knew he was pissed when we broke up, but this is seriously gross behavior."

"The dragons are just as bad," Xavier continues. "The two definites are Joaquin and Delphina."

"Delphina, really?" Flint looks a little sick at the thought, which makes my already shaky stomach just flat-out revolt. If it does one more somersault, I swear I'm going to throw up, right here in the middle of our meeting. I don't know who Delphina is, but if she can make Flint look like that, I'm perfectly happy never meeting her.

"And the hits just keep on coming," Eden growls. "Can we get back to the more pressing issue at hand, though? How on earth are we going to get out of Katmere if they have all the exits blocked?"

"There has to be a way out they don't have covered," I say. "There has to be."

"If so, I don't know what it is," Xavier answers.

"Well then, what's even the point of going to school in a magic castle?" I complain, throwing up my hands.

"There's nothing actually 'magic' about the castle itself," Jaxon says in a voice meant to calm me down. "Just the people in—"

"Actually, that's not technically true right now," Macy says, sitting up like her hair is suddenly on fire. "Oh my God, I think I know what to do!"

95

Second Star to the Right and Straight On Till Siberia

"We're almost there," Macy says as we walk single file down the dorm hallway. Flint, Jaxon, and Xavier are talking loudly and joking around, trying to act like it's totally normal for us to all be wandering the halls together at eleven at night, half of us with backpacks over our shoulders.

It's a good effort, but the truth is, I think anyone from the Circle who sees the eight of us together is going to know there's a problem. Which is probably why the rest of us are walking around like we're scared of our own shadow.

Well, not Eden. She looks like she's ready to punch anyone who glances at us twice. Then again, the more I'm around her, the more I'm beginning to realize that's her normal modus operandi.

My stomach is churning, partly from the fear of getting caught, partly from nervousness over the Unkillable Beast, and partly because Hudson has gone radio silent. He's never quiet, and I know his nerves must be triple mine, 'cause we're either both going to die or half of who he is will no longer exist after today. I refuse to focus on either outcome.

Still, I'm trying not to show how anxious I am, and I think I must be doing an okay job of it, because Jaxon doesn't seem any more concerned than usual—and neither does Macy.

"Okay, we're here," my cousin says as we stop in front of the yellow door leading to her secret passage. She waves her hand in front of the door and whispers the same spell as last time, and then we're inside.

It's just as cool as I remember, with stickers and jewels and scented candles to lead the way. Everyone else seems to think so, too, because—despite the circumstances—there are a lot of oohs and aahs going on.

"I can't believe you kept this place a secret," Eden tells her as she stops to examine a sticker that reads, *Life's a Witch, Then You Fly.* "It's amazing."

Macy shrugs. "I don't know. I found it when I was a kid, and it's kind of always been my place. I used to hide from my dad in here when it was bedtime."

"Well, I, for one, plan on visiting a lot more once we get the Circle the fuck out of Katmere," Xavier says with a wink at Macy. "It's really cool."

"It could use a dragon sticker or two," Eden tells her as we wind our way around one of the twists and turns.

All of a sudden, Xavier leans over and licks Macy's cheek. She shrieks and shoves at him, and a glance around tells me everyone else is about where I am—doubting what we just saw with our own eyes.

But Xavier just shrugs and points at a sticker directly above her head. "I was just following orders."

I move closer and see that it reads, *Get a Taste of Religion: Lick a Witch*, and I can't help it. I burst out laughing. Macy and Eden crack up right after me, followed quickly by the others. Xavier, the giant goofball, looks exceptionally pleased with himself, though I don't know if it's because he managed to get all of us to loosen up or if it's because he licked Macy and didn't get punched.

The last traces of tension are completely gone as we wind our way down the hallway until it dead-ends at a short ladder, right in front of a trapdoor at the top of the wall. "Next stop, planetarium," Macy says as she scoots to the front of the group and climbs up the ladder. Seconds later, she pushes open the door and crawls forward a few feet before she disappears with a loud squeak.

Xavier bounds up the ladder after her. "Macy? Are you okay?" Suddenly, he falls through the hole, too—though the noise he makes is more of a yelp than a squeak.

The rest of us kind of look at one another in a "who's next?" kind of way, but none of us actually makes a move for the ladder. Facing the Unkillable Beast, sure. Falling through a floor...maybe not.

Eventually, though, Eden rolls her eyes and mutters, "What the hell," right before she charges up the ladder, two rungs at a time. A little more cautious than the other two, she sits on the top of the ladder and slides in feetfirst. Seconds after her head disappears, we hear a soft thump on the other side of the wall, followed by another, louder yelp.

"Think she landed on Xavier?" Mekhi asks, brows raised.

"Oh yeah," Jaxon answers. "No doubt."

Jaxon seems determined not to go before I do, so I climb the ladder next. I slide my feet in first, just like Eden did, then close my eyes and call out, "Incoming," right before I let myself drop straight into darkness.

My feet hit solid wood and not werewolf, thank God, but it's so dark, I can't see two inches in front of my face. I do have the presence of mind to shuffle several feet away from the gaping hole above my head, but after that, I'm left fumbling for my phone as I call for my cousin.

"Right here!" she answers a little breathlessly, and when I finally get my flashlight app open and focused on her face, it's hard to miss the fact that her lipstick is smeared in all the right places. Looks like Xavier found more to lick than just her cheek...

I gesture for her to wipe her mouth just as Jaxon comes through the hole and lands like a cat next to me with barely a sound. Flint slides through after him, whooping like he's on a ride at Disneyland. Then again, when *isn't* he whooping like he's on a ride at Disneyland?

Mekhi brings up the rear, and then—flashlights out—we're

stumbling around, looking for a light switch.

Xavier hits the switch to turn on the giant star dome above us. Suddenly, all the constellations are rotating over our heads and it's strangely cool to be in this room, with these people, as all the stars float by above us.

It reminds me of the night Jaxon first kissed me, when he took me out on the battlements to watch a meteor shower. I glance over at him, feeling all warm and fuzzy on the inside, only to find him already watching me, a soft smile lighting up the hard planes of his face. So I'm not the only one remembering that night.

"So, wanna tell us why we're in the planetarium, Macy?" Flint asks.

She gives him a huge grin. "Well...I was practicing how to build portals with Mr. Badar, our Lunar Astronomy teacher, because I figured we might need one to get back to campus after the Boneyard. Anyway, Mr. Badar was demonstrating how to build a portal leaving campus instead of just returning, and so he built this one..." She holds her hands wide like she's revealing a magic trick. "And he left it up so I could come back and study it!"

"Way to go, Macy." Flint offers her a high five, and now we're all grinning.

"Only thing is that portals tend to move a few inches with the rotation of the Earth, so this one could have moved." She points to a corner in the room. "Last time I saw it, it was over there."

I turn and take a few steps back, so I can see around the telescope to where she's pointing, then scream as I feel myself falling, falling, falling for the second time in less than a week.

96

Get Fanged

No matter how hard I try to right myself as I tumble through the vortex—determined not to make the same mistakes this time—I end up falling out of the sky and flat on my face. It turns out, hitting the ground hurts even more than slamming into the planetarium stage did, and it knocks the breath out of me.

Still, I scoot along the ground, trying to get out of the way of the portal before someone else comes shooting through after me. Sure enough, I still haven't managed to take a full breath before Jaxon lands on his feet nearby. The jerk.

"Are you okay?" he asks, crouching next to me.

I nod as my lungs finally start working again. "One of these days, you're going to need to teach me how to do that without nearly dying," I gasp.

He grins. "I'll see what I can do."

Seconds later, the portal drops Macy out—and she, too, manages to land on her feet. It's a shakier landing than Jaxon's, but that's not saying much, since I'm pretty sure the moon landing was shakier than his.

I look around and realize we're in the forest beyond the cottages. I wish I could see a bit more as I wait for everyone else to make it through the portal. But it's dark and there isn't much to see.

Once everyone arrives, Flint and Eden change into their dragons. Flint lowers his head and I'm just about to climb on the way he showed me—much to Jaxon's chagrin—when we're suddenly surrounded by about twenty Circle guards in their black uniforms—several of whom have partially shifted into their werewolf or dragon forms.

The others—vampires and warlocks—stand shoulder to shoulder with them. And every single one of them looks like they mean business.

"You need to come with us," the vampy-looking one with the most stripes on his shoulder says.

Jaxon steps forward, gives him a sardonic look. "You know that's not going to happen, Simon."

The fact that Jaxon knows his name surprises me, until it registers that these are his father's guards. "The king has given orders that anyone trying to leave campus be detained and brought to him immediately," the guard responds.

"My father doesn't get to make those decisions at Katmere and you know it, Simon. The Circle doesn't run this school."

Jaxon takes another step forward, angling his body so that he's blocking as many of us from the guards as he can manage, while also keeping me firmly behind him.

"Yes, but I take my orders from your father, and I will follow them. He thought you and your mate might be too afraid to show up tomorrow, so we've been on the lookout for you all night. And here you are." He doesn't finish the sentence with *like the cowards you are*, but his voice says it for him.

"We're not running away," Jaxon tells him in the most reasonable tone I've ever heard from him. "We're out here practicing for the Trials tomorrow. My mate was nervous and wanted to do one more practice session."

"Well then, I'm sure the king will understand when you explain it to him." Simon grins coldly. "But you will be explaining it to him. Tonight."

His voice is sharp as steel and filled with resolve, but that's not what has my breath catching in my throat and my blood turning to ice.

It's the malice in his eyes—it's obvious he's been looking forward to this for a long time, and he isn't going to be talked out of it. Which means we're about to be hauled in front of the king before we get the heartstone, or we're about to put up a fight. Either isn't optimal right now, especially not this close to the school and the hundred or so other guards the Circle brought with them.

"You need to shift." Hudson's voice comes, loud and urgent, from deep inside me. *"There's going to be a fight, and you're way too vulnerable as a human."*

If I shift now, I'll take any element of surprise away from Jaxon.

"Jaxon can handle himself and so can the others. If you don't shift now, it will be too late."

My friends and I talked about this the other night, what to do if we ended up getting caught on school grounds. Jaxon was adamant about us leaving him, but now that we're faced with that decision, there's no way I can do it. A glance at the others' faces—especially Mekhi— tells me the same thing. None of us is going anywhere without Jaxon.

And so I do almost what Hudson suggests. I reach for the platinum string and hold it gently in my hand. I don't close my fist around it quite yet, but I prepare myself to be able to in a split second.

"Shift, damn it!" Hudson is frantic now. *"You don't know my father. You don't know what he's capable of—"*

Can you please be quiet? I urge. *I can't hear with you shouting in my head. Just give me a minute to think, will you?*

"Simon, we both know this isn't going to end well for you and your little band of misfit toys." Jaxon's voice snaps like kindling. "Which means you've got two choices. You can go on your way and pretend you never saw us out here practicing." He holds up his backpack as proof of our late-night practice routine. "Or you can get your ass kicked. Now, I don't care which one of those you choose, but it is going to be one of those two choices. So take a minute, talk it over, and let me know what you guys end up deciding."

A couple of the other guards laugh, a sound that's immediately quelled when they find themselves the object of Jaxon's own ice-cold stare. Though, to be honest, I'm shocked they can even meet his gaze. I'm his mate, and if he ever looked at me like that, I would *die*.

At first, it feels like they're going to back down. A couple of the guards shift their feet; a couple others look anywhere else but at Jaxon. And still others—warlocks, all of them—lift their hands away from their wand holders, a clear sign that they aren't looking to get in a full-on battle tonight.

But then something happens—the crack of a twig in the forest, a sudden movement from Flint behind me in his dragon form, a slight shift of Jaxon's feet so he could block me just a little more completely. I don't know—I'll probably never know—but out of nowhere, one of the guards at the very edge of their circle leaps straight at Mekhi, shifting in midair.

Jaxon shoves me into Flint—for protection, I think—and then moves to intercept the guard, but Mekhi is on the other side of the group, and the split second he took to shove me into Flint cost him. Worse, it costs Mekhi, as Jaxon is half a second too late as the guard sinks his werewolf teeth straight into Mekhi's throat, going for the jugular.

97

Another One Bites the Dust

Macy screams as Jaxon rips the wolf off Mekhi's throat, and for one second, two, time seems to stand still. And then all hell breaks loose.

Mekhi drops to his knees, clutching his throat, as blood pours onto the ground around him.

I'm desperate to reach him, but every time I try, Flint wraps his tail around me—my own personal dragon armor—and holds me tight even as he shoots fire straight at the contingent of guards rushing toward him.

But I'm not weak, human Grace anymore, and while he is busy par-broiling one of the werewolves, I grab hold of my platinum string as tightly as I can.

"Get to Mekhi," Hudson urges. He appears behind me as the shift comes over me. "We can still save him, but it has to be now."

I don't question him—not about this and not when time is so precious. Instead, I shoot straight up in the air to disentangle myself from Flint's tail.

He's either too busy to notice or he trusts gargoyle Grace in a way he doesn't trust my human form. Either way, he doesn't come after me as I fly straight up, high above the melee.

Blood and destruction are everywhere—broken branches litter

the ground, several trees are either uprooted or on fire, and people and animals are locked in hand-to-hand combat or lying dazed and injured on the ground.

A quick scan of the area shows that Mekhi is the only one of my group who is injured, thankfully. I race to him, dropping into a crouch beside him and shielding him with my wings as the fighting continues to go on around us.

Out of the corner of my eye, I see Jaxon trying to get to us, but guard after guard is grabbing on to him, fighting him, trying to tear him apart. They aren't having much luck—my mate is way too powerful for that—but they're slowing him down, and every second they cost him could cost Mekhi his life.

"No, it won't," Hudson tells me. "We've got this."

"How?" I ask even as I press a hand to Mekhi's throat in a vain effort to stop the bleeding. I'm willing to do whatever he wants but unsure of what we *can* do. Mekhi's already lost so much blood. I know he's not human, but I can't believe he's got much time left.

"Break off a piece of your stone," Hudson tells me.

"A piece of my stone?" I repeat, glancing down at myself and the thick, heavy pieces of stone that make up my entire body now. "How do I do that?"

Mekhi gasps and clutches at me, his hand wrapping around my arm and squeezing hard. At first I think he's trying to break the stone off me, but then I realize he's shaking his head, mouthing *no, no, no* as he grows more and more sickly looking.

"I have to, Mekhi," I tell him. "You'll die if I don't."

He shakes his head again, continues mouthing *no* to me, even as he runs out of air and starts to be strangled by his own blood.

"I don't understand," I tell Hudson, close to tears as I try to find a balance between what Mekhi wants and what I know is the right thing.

"It's because you're Jaxon's mate," Hudson says grimly. "He knows you're going to be queen one day and, close friends or not, he can't allow you to sacrifice a piece of yourself for him. It's an etiquette thing, ancient rules that don't matter until we get to a situation like this."

"Fuck ancient rules," I spit as I reach up and break off a piece of my horn. God knows I hate the damn things anyway.

Mekhi's eyes widen, but I lean down and whisper, "I won't tell if you don't. Now, shut up and let me do what I can before it's too late." I turn to Hudson. "Tell me what to do. Please."

"Cup the stone between your hands," he tells me, "and let me do the rest."

I don't know what he means, but now isn't the time to argue, so I do as he says. Seconds later, I feel a strange heat running down my arms and through my fingers.

A few seconds after that, Hudson says, "Okay, that's enough."

I lift my hand to find a fine stone powder cupped in my other palm. I want to ask how he did it—because I know, deep inside, that this was Hudson and not me—but there's no time. "What now?" I beg.

"Pour it across his throat, covering the wound. Then hold your hand over it until you feel it set."

If someone had told me an hour ago that I would be pouring stone into an open wound as a means of healing someone, I would have told them they were out of their ever-loving minds. But every hour in this world brings something new and exciting and terrible, and apparently right now is no different.

So I do what Hudson tells me and pray the whole time that I'm not making things for Mekhi a million times worse.

"Hold his throat," Hudson tells me as soon as the last of the ground stone falls into his cut. "Don't let go until I tell you."

I nod. "Okay."

All around me, there are horrible noises. Battle noises. People screaming, the squish of flesh as bodies batter against each other, the roar of dragons and howls of enraged wolves. I want to look, want to make sure that Jaxon and Macy and Flint and Eden and Xavier—that all my people—are okay.

But Mekhi's eyes are wide and afraid in a way I've never seen from him before, and there's no way I'm looking away, even for an instant. No way I'm leaving him alone in this for one single, solitary moment.

And so I lean down and whisper all kinds of things to him. Things that make no sense to me, let alone him, but that bind us together with their extreme lack of importance and their utter humanity at the same time.

Things like how much I like his locks, and how I think he and Eden would make a good couple, and how much I appreciated his friendship my first couple of weeks at Katmere. And also what my favorite vampire movie is—*The Lost Boys*, obviously—and why being a gargoyle is the strangest feeling in the world.

Finally, after what feels like hours but is probably only three or four minutes, I feel the heat under my hand start to dissipate. Mekhi's eyes go wide, and suddenly he takes a long, deep breath for the first time since I landed beside him.

"You did it," Hudson tells me, and there's pride in his voice as well as something that sounds an awful lot like awe.

"I did it?" I repeat, a part of me unable to believe that this bizarre act might actually have worked.

"Take your hand away," he says, and I do, astonished to see that where a gaping wound was only a few minutes ago, there is now only smooth, sleek stone.

"According to the books I've read on gargoyles, the stone patch-up won't last forever," Hudson continues as I reach down and pull Mekhi into a sitting position. "But it should last more than long enough for him to get himself to the infirmary to be looked at."

I grin as I tell Mekhi what Hudson said, finally allowing myself to hug him now that I know my handiwork won't fall apart in the next two minutes and take Mekhi with it.

But Mekhi shakes his head as soon as I mention getting him to the infirmary. "No way!" he grinds out in a voice that's both lower and rustier than his usual tone. "I need to go with you. The plan—"

"Screw the plan," I tell him as Jaxon finally shows up beside us. He's a little bloody and a lot bruised, but he's alive and in one piece and that's good enough for me. "You're going to the infirmary."

"Damn straight he is," Jaxon agrees. And so do the others as they gather around us, too.

And that's when I look up and realize that despite insurmountable odds, we've won this round. The entire contingent of Circle guards is lying on the ground in various states of unconsciousness or injury, and every single one of my friends is still standing. Except Mekhi, obviously, but he's alive and that's more than good enough for me.

"We need to go," Eden urges. "They won't be down for long, and they've probably already called for help. If we have any chance of actually getting out of here, now is the time to go—before reinforcements show up."

Her nose starts bleeding as she talks, and she wipes the blood away with the back of her hand.

"But we have to get Mekhi to the infirmary," I protest. "We can't leave him out here alone."

"There's no time," he tells me. "I can hear them coming."

"We all can," Xavier agrees. "We've got to go, Grace."

I turn to Jaxon. Surely he gets that we can't just leave his best friend here in the middle of this mess. But he, too, is shaking his head. "We're out of time, Grace. It's now or never."

I want to say never, but I know I can't. Not now that we're so close.

"I'm strong enough to fade because of you, Grace. Now, go." And just like that, Mekhi's gone, fading into the forest.

"Let's go," Flint says grimly, and then he's shifting back into his dragon form. I shift back to human at the same time, and now,

Jaxon doesn't wait for me to climb on under my own power. Instead, he all but throws me on top of Flint and climbs on right behind me.

Next to us, Xavier and Macy are climbing onto Eden.

And then we're off—bruised, bloodied, battered, but not broken (yet)—in search of a monster that absolutely no one has ever been able to kill.

Piece. Of. Cake.

98

Fly by Night

"We have a problem," I tell Jaxon about ten minutes into our flight.

"I know," he agrees but then doesn't say anything else. Nothing at all, even though I wait several more minutes.

"Are we going to talk about the problem?" I finally ask, not because I'm trying to be obnoxious but because I really think we need time to plan. And yes, we've got a couple-hours flight ahead of us, but who knows how long it's going to take to figure out what we're going to do now that our plan is down a person. And not just anyone—one of the most important people, considering Mekhi's power is hypnotism.

"You could still turn back, you know," Hudson says quietly in the corner of my mind.

You know he won't listen. So if you aren't willing to help, just go back to sulking and let me figure out what to do.

"I wasn't sulking earlier," he tells me, then seems to think better of it. *"Okay, yes, I was sulking, but I'm over it."*

Glad to hear it. But seriously, any suggestions on how we can do this now that we're down to six people?

"Besides turning around?"

I purse my lips at him in annoyance. *Yes. Besides that.*

"Well then, I go back to my idea from the other day, which is to

tell you not to try to kill the beast."

I already told you we're not going home.

"I'm not saying you need to go home. I'm talking about going in there and attempting to have a conversation with the Unkillable Beast before you try to kill it...and lose."

You don't know that we'll lose, I tell him.

"Oh, you're all going to die a most horrible death. You really think six high school students, no matter how powerful they are, are going to just waltz into a cave and defeat a beast that lore claims people have been trying to kill for two thousand years?" He laughs in my head, but there's very little humor in the sound.

Well, what are we supposed to do? We need this heartstone it's apparently protecting. How else are we going to get it if we don't kill it?

"Honestly? I don't know." He shakes his head. *"But I do know that going in, powers blazing, is only going to piss it off. And I don't want to see that happen—to any of you."*

And going in with our hands up isn't going to get us killed, too? I shake my head.

"I don't know. But I do know not every monster is what they seem."

His words hit home, probably because I know he's not just talking about the Unkillable Beast.

I don't know. I don't know what to think. I don't know what to believe. I sure as hell don't know if he's right. We aren't even sure if this monster can communicate. And what if the time it takes to try to reason with it is all it needs to kill my friends?

My cell phone goes off in the middle of my mental debate, and it's Macy texting me, because obviously she and Xavier are having the same conversation that Hudson and I are having—and that Jaxon is currently avoiding.

Macy: Any ideas?

Me: None

Macy: Yeah. Us either

"You know I have a dozen other ideas, too, right? Virtually any

idea I come up with will be better than my brother's plan to just go in, guns blazing, and kill a monster with 'unkillable' literally in its name."

He accompanies his last statement with a massive eye roll and I can't help taunting him a little. *Careful, you keep rolling your eyes like that and they're going to get stuck that way.*

He snorts. *"I should be so lucky. At least then everyone will know how I really feel."*

I laugh despite myself. *You're what my mother would have called a "piece of work," you know that?*

"Yeah? Because you're what my mom calls 'dangerous.'"

I think back to my meeting with the vampire queen and answer, *I'm pretty sure your mother doesn't think there's anything dangerous about me.*

"That's where you're wrong," he tells me. *"Both my parents are terrified of you. If they weren't, they'd be back in jolly old London right now."*

Before I can ask what he means by that, Macy texts me again.

Macy: X says we need a new plan

Me: No shit

Macy: How do we get into the cave?

Macy: If Mekhi isn't around to hypnotize it, how do we distract it?

Me: Get a banjo and dance the hula?

Macy: You aren't Timon or Pumbaa and this isn't the Lion King.

She follows it with an eye-roll emoji.

Me: I know that. I meant YOU

Macy: I'm not Timon either. And I'm sure as shit not Pumbaa

Now it's a string of eye-roll emojis, which makes me laugh. If Macy and Hudson are rolling their eyes at me like that, then I must really be on a roll tonight.

I start to say as much to Hudson, but Jaxon finally stirs behind me.

"We need to set a trap," he says.

"What do you mean, a trap? Like a *bear* trap?"

"Something a little less gruesome, hopefully," he answers. "But don't you think that's our best bet? Home-turf advantage is a real thing. You never attack on your opponent's home turf if you can avoid it, because it's the territory they're most familiar with and therefore most able to defend."

"And also because it's the territory they're most likely willing to die to defend," I add, thinking back on everything I've learned in history class through the years.

"Exactly. Now, we don't have the time or the resources to lure the monster off its island—so that's out. But we *can* lure it out of its comfort zone, away from its cave or wherever it's living." He pauses, and I can practically hear the wheels turning in his brain as he continues to plot.

Suddenly, I feel bad about turning to Hudson earlier when I thought Jaxon just wasn't going to engage with the situation. I should have known better—no matter what he says or does, Jaxon has always made my safety and everyone else's a priority from day one. And that includes making sure we have the best shot he can give us against an unkillable monster.

"When we had Mekhi," he continues, "it was okay to take it at its home because we could manipulate the odds with Mekhi's ability to hypnotize, but with him gone…it's just too risky."

He shakes his head, then focuses on me instead of the horizon. "What do you think?"

"I think it looks like baby brother is finally starting to use his brain for once," Hudson comments. *"I'm impressed."*

I ignore the sarcasm of that last comment and focus instead on the realization that I have the two most powerful vampires of my generation currently focused on solving the same problem at the same time. Surely that's enough to get something important done.

"I think it sounds like the beginning of a plan," I say as I text Macy what's going on so she and Xavier can get in on the planning session. "So what do you think we should do first?"

"Hopefully not die," Hudson replies, and I have to admit, he's summed it up nicely.

99

With Baited Breath

We finally arrive at the island and realize it's not an island as much as a volcano, partially sticking up out of the ocean. There is a huge crater at the top, but its craggy sides jut straight into the water. Which means, the monster must be inside the crater…and there's nowhere to land except inside the enclosed space the beast calls home. I can't help but shake the feeling this is about as ridiculous as fighting a tiger at a zoo—in *his* cage.

Flint and Eden circle the opening several times, but all we can see from this height, with the bottom of the crater hundreds of feet below the opening, is surprisingly dense forest areas and huge piles of boulders. But no Unkillable Beast.

A thought suddenly occurs to me. "Did any of the books or databases say how *big* this beast is supposed to be? Should we even be able to see it from the sky?"

Jaxon leans forward so I can hear him over the wind rushing past us. "The stories vary, but most of them say it is massive. Several stories high."

"Then why can't we see it?" An uneasiness creeps into my bones as we both stare down into the crater again and still see nothing but trees and rocks. Everything in me says it's a very bad idea to land inside this crater. We need to turn around. Now.

"Let's go ahead and land!" Jaxon shouts to Flint, and my stomach pitches as Flint swiftly moves in for a quick descent.

I start to beg Jaxon for us all to turn around and go home, but he squeezes my waist and says, "Everything's going to be okay."

I've never wanted to believe anyone more in my life.

By the time we touch down inside a clearing in the crater, it's at least three o'clock in the morning, when everything is completely still and quiet. Normally, I like being the only one awake in the middle of the night—there's something about the silence that usually speaks to my soul.

But here, on the Unkillable Beast's island off the north coast of Siberia, the stillness just feels eerie, in the most disturbing way. I know it's probably just me projecting my own fears on an innocent, nearly uninhabited island, but the truth is, from the moment Flint lands on the soft, moss-covered strip of land, I know something is very, very wrong. It's like the island is speaking to me.

I almost laugh at my silliness. Of course the island isn't *trying to tell me something*. And so I ignore the voice deep inside warning—no, begging—me to leave.

Instead, I remind myself that the voice wasn't particularly happy about the Boneyard, either, and that turned out okay. Besides, it's not like my friends are about to change their minds now, so I try to shake off my uneasiness as I step away from Flint and Jaxon so Flint can shift back to his human form.

Hudson is walking around the edge of the forest about twenty feet away, trying fruitlessly to peer into the darkness. I think about reminding him that if I can't see in there, he certainly can't, but I know he's just trying to occupy himself doing *something*. He feels as antsy as I do.

Xavier, Macy, and Eden join us a few seconds later, and under the dim light cast by Macy's wand, we start to search the crater for the den of the Unkillable Beast. We may not have any plans for going in there at the moment, but it's pretty hard to lure someone or something someplace if you don't know where the starting point is.

But the more we explore the interior of the crater, the more apparent it becomes that the place is enchanted. It's March, which means the temperature on one of these islands should range anywhere from fifteen to forty-five degrees, depending on the day and the kind of winter/spring we're in store for (thank you, Google). And while it definitely felt about thirty-five degrees at the opening, the area inside the crater is a near-tropical climate that has me sweating inside my many layers of clothes.

So yeah, definitely magical is the consensus, and that's before we discover a waterfall and hot springs that seem to appear out of nowhere and cast an eerie light within the crater. It's like the water itself is enchanted, its soft blue depths glowing so brightly, the entire area is lit like early morning, revealing trees, tall and green, with big, strangely shaped leaves that look more like they belong on a tropical island than this close to the Arctic Circle. Hibiscus and bromeliads envelop the forest in their sweet scents, and giant boulders are scattered randomly around the nearby clearing.

"This is where it lives," Jaxon says as we walk closer to the water, even as he keeps his eyes peeled for the monster.

"How do you know?" I ask.

"Where would you choose to live?" Jaxon counters. "In the pitch-black forest on the other side or near this glowing hot bath and fresh water?" He motions with his head just past us and grins. "Also, there's a cave on the other side of the waterfall."

"What do we do?" I ask, my gaze fixed on the waterfall now.

"We back away slowly," Xavier whispers. "And try to figure out what trap we could possibly set."

"Obviously, we need bait," Eden tells him as we move back toward the dark forest, to hide in the shadows and plan. "Really good bait."

"What kind of bait?" I ask even as the voice inside me whispers over and over, *Leave.*

"I'll be the bait," Xavier volunteers. "Once we decide the best place to set up the trap, I can go in and lure it out. No way is it going to put up with having some interloper in its cave."

"But we don't even know what the beast looks like yet," Macy complains. "What if it's small and faster than a wolf? Or is twenty feet tall with eight long, octopus-like arms that you can't avoid?"

I know she was just offering some extreme examples, but I find myself nodding to each one. They all sound plausible to me right now.

"We just have to lure it out of its cave and keep it trapped or distracted," Xavier reminds us as we start looking around for a good place to set our trap. "The heartstone is probably kept right at the back of its cave where the Unkillable Beast can protect it."

Hudson catches my eye and mutters, "And this is your genius plan? To catch a beast when you have no idea what it looks like or what its powers are? And when you have no idea if your trap is the right size or strength of magical constraint? And you thought *my* idea was out there..."

I roll my eyes at him but turn to the group and ask, "Do we have any idea what this beast is? How big it is? How strong it is? If it's magical? I mean, how could we possibly know what kind of trap will keep it, well, caught?"

"It's obviously got to be magical," Macy says. "There's no other way to be prepared for whatever comes barreling out of those caves after us."

Everyone nods. Makes sense, I guess.

"Yeah, but what are we talking about here?" Eden says. "A spell? And if so, which one?"

"I could fry it," Flint suggests with a grin. "Pretty sure it wouldn't come back for more after that."

"Yeah, but what if it's wearing the heartstone and you fry it, too? What are we going to do then?" Macy asks. "Whatever the trap is can't be that violent."

"So you want to give the Unkillable Beast a chance to get a second wind?" Flint asks incredulously.

"No. I think I should put it to sleep," Macy suggests. "I have a spell for that, and I think it will work."

"You *think* it will work?" Eden asks, both brows raised.

"Well, I can't guarantee it, since I have no idea what the Unkillable Beast is, but yes. It should work. I looked it up on the way here, just to be sure."

"And if the sleep spell doesn't work?" I ask tentatively, not wanting to set Macy off, but not wanting to be caught without a backup plan, either.

"Then I say Flint freezes it. Xavier and I discussed it on the way here, and it seems like the best move," Jaxon volunteers. "It won't fry any stone the beast might have on it, but it will give us a couple of minutes to think things through once we know what the beast is and what it can do. Acting is always better than reacting, anyway."

Hudson snort-laughs at this. "The day my brother thinks first, then leaps second, I'll eat my shorts."

You're not wearing any shorts, I remind him.

He turns and winks at me. "Why, Miss Foster, have you been peeking?"

I know he's trying to distract me; he must sense my nerves are about to snap like a piano wire, but I blush all the same. *You're obnoxious.*

He simply bows at me before turning back to the half-baked plan we're currently cooking.

"So where are we setting up?" Xavier asks, looking around. "The beast'll be coming out along this path, right?" He points to the broken stone path that leads around the water's edge and then straight across the lake, with large, flat boulders, to meet the waterfall. "So how far out from them do we want to bring it before we spring the trap?"

"Not too far," Eden suggests. "We need cover, and there isn't much except this forest once you get away from the clearing."

"I agree," I tell them, thinking back to playing paintball with my dad as a kid and all the lessons he taught me about ambushes. Now that I think about it, I can't help but wonder if he knew I would need the information someday. Maybe not to fight an Unkillable Beast but because he came from this paranormal world and he knew just how dangerous it was.

"Flint should hide up there." I point to a small ledge a quarter of the way up the inside of the crater wall. "You can still reach the beast if you shoot ice from there, can't you?" I ask.

He measures the distance with his eyes. "Yeah, I should still have reach."

"Good. And Macy needs to be closer—"

"How much closer?" Xavier asks, and he doesn't look happy.

"As close as I need to be," she answers him with a glare before glancing around. "If it's coming down this path, I can get a really good shot at it if I'm sitting in that tree." She points to a huge coniferous tree about thirty feet away from the waterfall.

Xavier looks like a thundercloud at the very thought, and I have to admit, having her that close to the walkway doesn't make me feel particularly good, either. I mean, if the beast can jump, it could be on her in seconds, and there's nothing we could do to stop it.

"I'll be fine," Macy says, as if reading my thoughts.

"Maybe we should rethink—"

"I'm doing it," she tells me as she jogs toward the tree. "Besides, no guts, no glory, right?"

"The saying could also go, no guts, no terrifying death," I tell her.

She turns back just so I can see her roll her eyes. "I can do this, Grace. You need to trust me."

She's right. I know she's right, and still it's hard for me to watch her swing herself up into the tree and then find the branch with the heaviest foliage to hide on.

"I think we should have Eden as backup, too," Jaxon says as Flint gives me a quick wink before flying up to the ledge we decided on.

"I'm not sure how much help I'll be," she comments. "I only shoot lightning. If I aim at the beast, I *will* electrocute it."

"Which is why you're going to be Flint's backup," Jaxon tells her. "Worst-case scenario only."

"I can do that." She glances around. "Where do you want me?"

"Probably as close to the mountain as you can get," I tell her, "but on ground level. That way if Macy and Flint miss, you can come in behind him and do what you need to do."

"How about over there?" She points to a small alcove carved into the actual mountain that's only a couple of feet from the entrance.

"That's really close." I look around for someplace else. "How about something a little farther away?"

She grins at me. "Don't worry, Grace. I got this."

"I know you do, but—"

"Don't worry," she repeats. "Just make sure you don't get eaten, okay?"

"Yeah." I smile sickly. "That sounds like a plan."

When all three of them are in position, Jaxon looks at Xavier and me. "Ready?" he asks.

Not even a little bit. I don't say that, though. I can't. So instead, I just nod before shifting into my gargoyle form. It's past time to get this show on the road.

100

Carpe Slay-Em

Xavier, Jaxon, and I walk through the craggy rock entrance to the beast's oasis like we own the place—partly, I think, to shore up our own nerves when it comes to being bait and partly because it never hurts to look more confident than you feel.

"What do you think it is?" Xavier asks as the path we're on winds past the hot springs.

"I'm less concerned about what it is right now than *where* it is," Jaxon answers as he sweeps his head back and forth, checking out every single hiding spot we can find.

Thank God the water is glowing so brightly, or we'd be fighting this monster in the pitch dark. And most likely all about to die.

Stop! The voice inside me is growing more insistent with each step I take toward the Unkillable Beast.

It's creepy as fuck, and I can't help wondering if my gargoyle knows something I don't. If its senses are picking up on the danger I know is here but can't quite pinpoint yet.

Unlike my gargoyle, Hudson is oddly silent. He stopped asking me to reconsider right about the time we got everyone in position, and I thought at first that he went away to pout the way he sometimes does.

But I can feel him inside my mind, senses on high alert as he looks out at the world through my eyes, trying to spot the beast, too.

Trying—I know, even though he won't admit it—to help Jaxon and me any way that he can.

Which is the dichotomy of Hudson and always has been. He's capable of doing such horrible things that his own brother wanted him dead—or human—but now he's here, doing his best to defend Jaxon against a threat he doesn't even think we should be facing.

"You *shouldn't be facing it,*" he tells me. But he doesn't say it with his usual snark—for once, he's not trying to pick a fight. Instead, he's quiet. Sad, almost, like he knows what's coming and has given up any chance of stopping it.

A sudden noise cuts through the night air, a clanging of chains that has all three of us freezing in our tracks.

"What the hell was that?" I ask, whirling toward a sound I think is coming from behind the waterfall.

"Sounded like chains to me," Xavier answers, his werewolf ears working overtime.

The clang of chains comes again, more enthusiastically, and this time it's very obvious where it's coming from.

"Chains?" I murmur to Jaxon. "What's that about?"

He shakes his head. "I don't know."

The voice inside me is screaming now. *Go back, go back, go back!*

It's beyond scary, has me pausing for several seconds to draw in a shuddering breath as panic takes root deep inside me. But it's too late now. We're here and the clock is ticking away. We need to get this done.

So we exchange one long look among the three of us before squaring our shoulders and heading toward the cavern, where the clanging continues to grow louder and louder.

Not going to lie, I'm terrified. Terrified of what awaits us in that cave—I mean, what kind of monster uses chains to fight?—and terrified of what we have to do. I've never deliberately killed anyone or anything in my life (I even relocate bugs outside when I see them), and the idea of coming all the way up here to kill this monster and take a heartstone it clearly doesn't want us to take—when it has done nothing to me or any of my friends—doesn't feel right.

But what's the alternative? Leave my friends to continue alone? There's no right answer here, nothing to do but forge ahead and somehow hope that everything turns out okay, though I don't know how that's possible right now.

Jaxon looks at me questioningly, but I just nod. And then the three of us walk toward the cave and the Unkillable Beast, whatever that might be, heart pounding in my chest. Palms sweaty. And a sick feeling growing in my stomach that something truly horrible is about to happen.

The cave is dark as we approach, and we're all on high alert, waiting for something to attack us. But the closer we get to the cave, the harder it is to ignore the clanging sound, to not focus on that to the exclusion of everything else.

Add in the low, husky growls that have started coming from deep inside, and it takes every ounce of courage I have to keep going—and that's before I look down at the ground and see the plethora of bones lying around. Some long and in perfect shape, others broken clean in half, but all recognizable as *human* bones.

People, I can only imagine, who had come before us and failed to do what we have to do.

When we get to the entrance, Jaxon holds a hand up to stop Xavier and me, then takes the first step into the cave himself. The chains go wild, but nothing else happens. Even the growls seem to have quieted.

Jaxon takes another step into the cave. I follow right behind and Xavier follows me.

I shine the flashlight on my phone around the darkened cave, but I don't see anything—and neither does Xavier or Jaxon, apparently, because seconds later, their flashlight beams follow mine.

We look around, though there's not much to see. I don't know what I was expecting, but not this barren cavern. There's nothing here, just rocky walls and bones scattered all around—skulls and leg bones and rib cages still intact.

"Where is it?" I whisper, because there are no rocks in here, nothing at all for a monster to hide behind.

At first, I'm afraid that there are more rooms, that the cavern extends the way the Bloodletter's does. But more sweeps of our flashlights reveal that this is it. This one room, with rocky, bloodstained walls and a rough dirt floor.

And huge, thick chains anchored into the ceiling and the back wall.

"I don't understand," Xavier says. "I know the noise came from here. I know it did. So where the hell is this thing?"

Finally, another low growl sounds, and we spin into a protective circle, our backs together as we sweep our flashlight beams all over the cavern.

The voice inside my head warns. *Leave, leave, leave.*

I can't leave! I tell it. *It's too late.*

Way too late.

Seconds later, another, louder growl sounds as the chains in front of us start to clank. And the wall itself begins to move.

101

Heaven on My Mind

"**W**hat the fuck!" Xavier exclaims, stumbling back, as the wall seems to come alive.

It growls once, long and low and loud, and the chains all but scream as it launches itself straight toward us.

Jaxon grabs me and shoves me behind him as he blasts out with every ounce of telekinetic power he has. It stops the thing—whatever it is—in midair, for a moment or maybe two. And then it just keeps coming, landing on all fours in front of us.

As I get my first good look at the beast, I can't help thinking it's like something out of a fantasy novel straight from hell. It's huge—the hugest creature I've ever seen in my life—and made entirely of craggy rock that's sharp and broken in a ton of different places, moss growing haphazardly all around.

Its eyes glow red and its teeth are vicious in a mouth that looks like it could swallow all three of us whole in one gulp. And it's advancing on us, one slow step at a time.

Jaxon lashes out again, throwing everything he's got straight at the monster. But all that does is make it angry, and it retaliates by striking with one massive hand (paw?) and sends him flying against a stone wall so hard that the cavern shakes.

"Jaxon!" I scream, grabbing Xavier and taking to the air as the thing turns and takes a swing at us as well.

I manage to dodge it, but the ceiling isn't high enough for me to get out of its reach, so on its second swing, it catches Xavier and me, and we go flying toward the opposite wall.

We hit hard, so hard that my teeth rattle and my brain feels like it's going to explode right out of my stone skull. I'm a little dazed, a little out of it, but Hudson is in my head, screaming at me to get up. Screaming at me to *move, move, move.*

I do, one second before a giant fist comes down, right where I had just been lying.

"Xavier!" I scream, but he's already up and in wolf form, jumping straight over the monster's shoulder and landing next to Jaxon, who has also gotten back to his feet.

The beast roars and charges straight at them. As it does, I notice for the first time that the chains aren't its weapons. They're shackles, keeping it tied to the wall.

"Run!" I yell to Jaxon. "If we get out of the cave, maybe it can't reach you."

But this is Jaxon Vega we're talking about, and there's no way he's leaving his mate behind with this monster, something that I'm both grateful for and infuriated by at this moment when I need him to save himself.

Instead of lashing out and trying to blast the monster back like he did the first time, though, Jaxon focuses his power straight into the ground. A giant earthquake hits the cave, causing rocks and bones to fall from the walls and the very floor beneath our feet to buckle even as it rises up.

The creature screams, low and loud and agonizing to hear, and as it reaches out and picks Jaxon up, I'm sure that this is it. I'm sure that this is where it crushes Jaxon into dust right in front of me.

But it doesn't crush Jaxon. Instead it throws him straight at the cave entrance, so hard that Jaxon flies right out of the cave and keeps going until I can't see him anymore.

"Go, Grace!" Hudson screams at me. *"Get out now, while it's distracted."*

But I can't get out, because the thing distracting the beast is Xavier, and he's heading straight for him.

"Hey!" I yell as loud as I can. "Over here! Come get me over here!"

The beast ignores me, laser focused on Xavier, who has hopped onto one of the rock formations in the wall, waiting—I think—for his chance to leap past the beast.

But he doesn't have my vantage point, can't see what I can, which is that there's not enough room for him to clear it. Anywhere he goes, the monster will get him—if not the second he leaps, then the second right after.

Can't die, can't die, can't die. The gargoyle in my head starts to chant and, right this second, it kind of makes me want to scream. Because my head is a pretty fucking crowded place as it is, with Hudson screaming at me to run, my own thoughts going wild, Jaxon shoving energy down the mating bond toward me, and now my goddamn gargoyle telling me that I can't die.

Which, no shit. I'm not planning on dying today.

But I can't just leave Xavier to fight it alone. So I do the only thing I *can* do—I get back in the air and fly straight at the Unkillable Beast's head. If I can distract it even a little, maybe Xavier will have a chance to get away.

Get away, get away, get away! My gargoyle chants its new mantra even as I dive-bomb the monster's head. At first, it ignores me, still so focused on Xavier that it barely acknowledges I exist. But when I get close enough to kick it in one of its bloodred eyes, it turns on me with a roar that echoes off the walls and shakes me down to my toes.

"Run, Xavier! Get out of here, now!" I yell as the beast faces me. Our whole plan was to lure the beast out of the cave, and if Xavier will leave, I think I can fly past it and hopefully its chains are long enough it can follow us outside to where Macy is waiting to put it to sleep.

I fly away as fast as I can, determined to stay out of its reach long enough for Xavier to have a fighting chance. But I've barely made it halfway across the cave before the beast grabs me in its massive rock fist and sends me spinning toward the wall Xavier was just standing on. I bounce off and land in a heap on the ground.

Xavier at least managed to get down in the ensuing chaos, but he didn't leave. Instead, he switched back to his human form and landed on the wall where the chains are embedded.

As the beast reaches for me a second time, Xavier grabs on to the chain that binds its arm and pulls with every ounce of werewolf strength he has.

It doesn't do much, but the resistance surprises the monster enough that it turns its head to glare at Xavier for a split second. And that's all it takes for me to roll away.

The beast yanks its arm forward hard enough to send Xavier ricocheting off the wall, but then screams when it realizes I'm not where it left me. As it whirls around with a giant growl, Eden, Flint, Macy, and Jaxon must have given up on Xavier and me luring it out, because they suddenly storm the cave.

Eden and Flint are in their massive dragon forms, and as they circle around the beast like it's an airplane tower, I realize just how big it really is. Because Eden's and Flint's dragons are *huge*, and they look like nothing more than hummingbirds buzzing around its head. It must be...eighty stories tall. And growing, if my eyes aren't deceiving me.

Eden hits the stone giant with a blast of lightning that has it bellowing in rage, but this attack barely slows it down. Flint follows with a stream of ice so powerful that the entire cave freezes around us, icicles dripping off everything.

And still the monster barely seems to notice. It just keeps fighting, just keeps snarling and smashing and throwing *us* until rocks are tumbling down from the walls all around us, pieces flying everywhere and slicing us to ribbons.

Go, go, go! Don't die, don't die! The gargoyle in my head is screaming now, so loud I can barely concentrate on anything else. Until a wrench on the mating bond has me gasping and nearly falling right out of the air.

"Jaxon!" I scream, whirling around just in time to see my mate fall to his knees. His complexion is gray, his eyes dull, and though he throws a hand out and manages to catch himself before he pitches forward onto his face, I know it's a close thing.

I can see it. More, I can feel it.

I dive down, racing to him as fast as I can—trying to get there before the beast sees just how weak and vulnerable Jaxon is.

And I get it. He's already used up so much of his finite energy today—the guards at school, the telekinetic attacks on the beast, the energy burst he sent me a little while ago while he was racing to get the others. Between all of that and what Hudson drains from him, Jaxon's got nothing left to fight.

I manage to get to Jaxon just as the beast knocks Eden clear out of the sky. She hits the ground so hard, her dragon screams, and when she tries to get up, she can't. She stumbles, falls, and I realize in horror that her wing is broken.

I throw myself in front of Jaxon, and as I do, I get a chance to look around at my friends who are valiantly fighting and realize that there's no way we can win. The beast isn't even winded, and we're in pieces.

Eden with her broken wing.

Jaxon with his awe-inspiring power almost completely depleted.

Flint shooting fire as the monster corners him but limping along in human form with what looks like a compound fracture to his leg.

Macy's okay, thank God, but she's poised with her wand up as she sends spell after spell spinning toward the giant. They hit—I know they hit—and yet nothing happens. Not one makes an impact.

And Xavier...Xavier is limping, too, though not as bad as Flint. He's currently circling around behind the beast, poised to go for the back of its knee in a last-ditch attempt to slow the monster down, but I already know that it isn't going to work. Nothing we do is going to work.

"You need to stop this!" Hudson begs as he walks over to where I'm leaning on a rock wall, trying to catch my breath. For the first time, he sounds panicked—really, really panicked. "You have to call them off, Grace. No one else will do it, so you have to."

"I don't know how!" I yell back at him. "Even if I try to call them off, even if they listen to me, the beast isn't going to just let us go. How do I get them out of here without us all being killed?"

"Talk to him," Hudson tells me.

"Talk to *him*? Talk to who?" I shriek.

"The Unkillable Beast. Can't you hear him? He's been talking to you all along—you need to answer him. You're the only one who can."

"Talking to me? Nobody's been talking to me!"

"I hear him, Grace. I know you hear him, too. That voice telling you to go, telling you not to die. That's him."

"No. You're wrong. That's my gargoyle."

"I'm not wrong. You need to trust me, Grace."

"I don't believe—"

"Goddammit!" he yells as he falls to his knees, tears in his eyes, face twisted in agony. "I've fucked up, okay? A lot. I know that. You know that. But I'm not fucking this up. I know that's his voice. I know you can talk to him. I know you can stop this. You're the only one who can. Just fucking listen to me for once in your whole fucking life like you did when we were together."

He's screaming now, begging, and I want to believe him. I do. But if I'm wrong— "No!" I scream as the beast turns toward Macy with a roar.

I shoot straight up in the air, race to get to her before he reaches her, but even as I fly faster than I ever have in my life, I know I'm not going to be fast enough. I know I'm going to be too late.

Xavier gets there a split second before I do. He throws himself in front of Macy, sends her careening to the ground behind him and takes the blow meant for her.

I can hear the bones shatter from where I am, can feel his skull crack and cave in even before he flies straight into the wall. He hits the ground with a sickening *thud*, but the beast doesn't care. He reaches for Xavier's leg, starts to pick him up, but it's my turn to throw myself in front of Xavier.

I land between them, and I do what Hudson's been begging me to do. I throw my arms up in the universal gesture for stop and scream, "No!" from the very depths of my soul.

102

We Are the Monsters

The Unkillable Beast rears back like I've struck him, so hard that he ends up stumbling and falling to the ground with a loud bellow that shakes every bone in my body. Shakes the very walls of the cavern.

But even as he screams, there's that voice inside me again, telling me, *No hurt, no hurt*, and I realize Hudson is right. That voice I've been hearing since I got to Katmere, that voice that warned me every time trouble was coming, that voice that I was certain was my gargoyle, was actually the Unkillable Beast all along.

I have no idea how. I have no idea why. But right now, all I care about is saving my friends.

I rub a hand over my eyes to wipe the tears away and then look at it, really look at this stone giant, for the first time since I got here.

I look at the craggy, broken rocks of his exterior.

At the stone rubbed smooth beneath the iron shackles.

At the top of his head and the one broken remnant of a horn that rests there, and I realize what I should have known all along.

The reason Macy's magic didn't work on him.

The reason Jaxon's telekinesis didn't, either.

The reason Eden's lightning and Flint's ice didn't so much as faze him isn't because he's all-powerful. It's because, like me, he's totally immune to magic.

Because he's a gargoyle.

Not unkillable at all. Just a gargoyle—the last in existence besides me—chained up for a thousand years, if the lore is to be believed.

As I stare at him, this poor gargoyle, this poor, giant monster of a man—I put a hand to my own head, to the horns that have grown larger every time I've gained power, and look at him with new eyes. How many battles must he have survived, how many opponents must he have defeated to have grown as large as he is now?

The answer is unfathomable.

And we've only added to his agony.

Oh my God. What have we done?

What have we done?

I'm sorry, I say. *I'm sorry. I'm so sorry.*

I don't know if I'm saying it to him or to Xavier or to Hudson or to all three. I just know that it's my own hardheadedness that has brought us here, my flat-out refusal to listen to Hudson even when he begged me to, that led us to this exact moment in time. My inability to see anything in terms beyond black or white, good or bad. Savior or monster.

And now a moment I can't change or take back, no matter how much I wish I could, stretches before me.

Behind me, Macy screams in agony, and I know what I'm going to find even before I look. Still, I turn around—keeping one arm extended to the beast to show that I mean him no more harm—just as she sinks to her knees, sobbing, beside Xavier.

I watch as she gathers him up in her arms and rocks him back and forth, back and forth, back and forth.

"No!" Flint yells as he tries to limp over to where we are. "No! No, don't tell me that, please don't tell me that. No!"

Eden's back in human form, tears streaming down her face and Jaxon…Jaxon looks broken in a way I've never seen before.

Sorry. Sorry, sorry, sorry, the voice inside me says. *Wolves are bad. I must protect her. I must save her.*

I don't know who he's referring to and right now, I don't think it matters. All that matters is that Xavier is dead. He's dead and this poor, broken soul killed him, not because he wanted to but because I wouldn't listen. Because I refused to see.

The horror and the grief turn my knees to nothing—just like the rest of me—and my legs go out from under me.

I hit the ground hard, my shin scraping against a slab of rock that fell from the walls, but I barely notice. How can I when Xavier is right here, his sightless eyes staring into the distance?

He was alive. Two minutes ago, he was alive, and now he's not. Now he's gone, and I could have stopped it all if I had just listened to what Hudson had tried so desperately to tell me.

This is my fault. This is all my fault.

Eden drops to her knees behind Macy, wraps her arms around my cousin, and holds her while she sobs. I should be doing that, should be doing something, anything to fix this mess that I've created. But I can't move. I can't think.

I can't even breathe.

"You have to finish it," Hudson tells me. "You have to get everyone home. You have to let Xavier go and save the people you can save."

"I don't even know how to get home," I whisper, and it's true. Neither Flint nor Eden is in any shape to fly us back to Katmere.

And the Trial is in less than four hours. I have to be there, or we will all suffer more than we already have. The king and queen are just the type to punish all my friends—and Jaxon—for my perceived indiscretions.

Ironic, really, considering the many mistakes I've made here tonight, and they're going to punish me for missing a mere *game* to see if I'm worthy. For being a gargoyle. For dating their son.

The hits just keep on coming.

"I'm sorry, Macy," I choke out as I crawl to my cousin, hug her, and press a kiss to the top of her head.

"I'm sorry," I whisper to Hudson as I climb slowly to my feet.

I'm sorry. I'm so, so sorry, I tell this ancient gargoyle as I cross the distance between us and put my hand on his giant foot.

He roars at first, tries to pull away, but he doesn't try to hurt me again. He doesn't do anything but watch me out of those centuries-old eyes and wait to see what I'm going to do next.

Who did this to you? I ask, running a hand over the shackle on his ankle. *Who locked you up like this and made you into the Unkillable Beast?*

He screeches a little at the name, and I don't blame him. For centuries upon centuries, he's been in this crater, hunted by all kinds of magical creatures trying to steal some precious object he only wants to protect.

The horror of it, the unmitigated depravity it takes to do something like this... I can't even imagine.

I have to save her, he tells me. *I can't die. I have to save her. I have to free her.*

Who? I ask. *Who do you have to save? Maybe we can help.*

I don't know why he would believe me, considering my friends and I just tried to kill him, but I have to try. I owe him that much. The world that did this to him and perpetuated it for a millennia owes him so much more.

I look behind me at my friends, all of whom look like they've been to hell and back. All of whom are shell-shocked and bleeding and as devastated as I feel. I owe them, too.

At first the beast—no, the gargoyle—doesn't respond to my offer. Not that I blame him—I wouldn't, either. But then slowly, so slowly that I'm not sure I'm not imagining the whole thing, he lifts his wrist up and looks at the shackles.

Oh, of course. *Of course we'll let you go.*

I turn to my friends—my broken, bloody, devastated friends—and though it kills me, I have to ask them for one more thing. "I'm sorry. I'm so sorry, but I need your help."

Flint looks from me to the gargoyle, and I can see what he's thinking. Why should he help the monster who just murdered his friend?

"Because it's not his fault," I whisper before he can even formulate the question. "We came and attacked him. We tried to hurt him like so many of the people who have come before us. None of this is his fault. And because he's a gargoyle like me."

Everyone blinks at me, unsure how to process this revelation.

Macy is the first to move. She stumbles to her feet, mascara running in tear-streaked rivers down her face, and aims her wand at the gargoyle. At first, I think she's going to attack him again, and I put a hand up, try to ward off her magic—and the ensuing rampage such a move might cause. But then she surprises me, my cousin—with her kind heart as big and fierce as any dragon's.

She whispers a spell under her breath and shoots a bolt of lightning straight at the chain tethering the gargoyle to the wall.

103

Going Through
the Potions

The chain doesn't break, so she blasts it again. And again. And again.

Each time, the chain shudders and groans, but no matter what she hits it with, it continues to hold.

Soon, Flint joins in, shooting ice at the chain to make it brittle, and I pick up a giant rock and, flying, try to smash the frozen chain to bits. But again, no matter how hard we try or how much the chains protest what we're doing, they stay exactly where they are.

Finally, Jaxon staggers to his feet. He's wan and a little gray-looking and in almost as bad a shape as he was that day in the tunnels with Lia. And still he tries to help, too, putting every ounce of strength and power he has left into pulling the chains straight out of the wall.

The wall creaks, and cracks start appearing deep inside it, but the chains continue to hold.

Jaxon starts to try again, but he's swaying on his feet, and I'm terrified that using any more power will injure him permanently.

And so I turn to the Unkillable Beast—this gargoyle who doesn't deserve what my friends and I tried to do to him—and my heart breaks just a little bit more to see his head low, his shoulders hunched, like he knew all along that this was going to happen.

I'm sorry, I tell him again. *I'm sorry I can't take you with us right now. But I promise, we'll come back for you. We'll find a way to set you free, and we'll come back.*

He studies me for long seconds, those bloodred eyes growing more human and less animalistic by the second. And then he asks, very simply, *Why?*

Why will we come back? To free you—

No. Why did you come to begin with?

Oh. I look down, embarrassed by what I've done. Embarrassed by the hubris that thought it would be okay to take something from this creature who has already suffered so much and embarrassed by all the other mistakes I made that led us here, to this moment.

We needed a treasure you protect. A heartstone, I tell him. *I'm sorry. We thought we could just take it from you. It was wrong of us. We're so sorry.*

Heartstone? He cocks his head to the side, like he's trying to figure out what I'm talking about.

Yes, heartstone, I repeat.

Slowly, so slowly that I think I must be imagining it at first, the gargoyle's chest starts to glow a dark, deep red. He looks down at the color and so do we, more than a little shocked by what we're seeing.

You need heartstone? he asks, and then he pats his chest.

Oh my God. The heartstone isn't a jewel he's protecting. It's his *stone heart*. And after everything we've done to him, he's still willing to give it to us for no other reason I can guess than that we stopped trying to kill him.

I fall to my knees again on a painful sob. Who *did this* to him? Who could be so cruel?

The gargoyle taps his chest again. *Need heart stone?*

No, I answer. *No, I don't. But thank you.*

We've crossed too many lines to get here, sacrificed far too many things. Lost Xavier. I'm not going to compound that by killing this innocent creature, too.

I ruined everything because I didn't fight harder for what I believed in, for what I believed was true. I knew that it was wrong to take away Hudson's vampire nature. I knew it was wrong for us to sit in judgment of him. And I knew it was wrong to risk all our lives because I wasn't strong enough to convince anyone that they were wrong, too.

So many wrongs that have led us here that I don't know how to make right. I don't know how I'll ever make my way home again.

"Grace." Jaxon leans against the wall to steady himself. "I know you're upset, but you need to take it."

"I'm not taking it," I tell him, bowing my head in a silent thank-you to my kin. "I'm not killing this gargoyle, Jaxon."

"When you calm down, you're going to regret this."

"There are many things I regret, but this decision will never be one of them," I reply without turning to look at him. Instead, I lower my head and rest it against the side of the gargoyle's foot as I shift back to my human form. *Thank you, my friend. For everything*, I tell him. *I promise I'll be back.*

When I pull away, it's to find that Jaxon has picked up Xavier's body and is fireman-carrying him out of the cave. Macy is helping Flint hobble back over the rough ground and Eden is walking behind them, her right shoulder slanted down in a way that looks incredibly painful.

I hurry to catch up—we still need to find a way back home—but I pause at the mouth of the cave to wave at the gargoyle one more time. And I smile when he waves back.

Time is ticking away as we wind past the hot springs and back to the clearing, where the temperature has dropped several degrees and the aurora borealis dances across the sky in shades of green. The Trial is supposed to start in a little more than three hours, and neither Jaxon nor I am in any shape for it. Not to mention I have no idea how we're going to get home. The dragons are both claiming that they can fly, but Flint's bone is sticking through his leg, and I saw what Eden's wing looks like.

No way is she going to be able to support a dragon's weight on that wing, let alone the rest of us.

Macy doesn't stop walking until she's only a couple of feet from the water, and we all trail along behind her, lost and confused and more than a little scared. She settles Flint on the sand, then drops to her knees and starts rustling in her backpack. She doesn't stop until she's pulled out a handful of crystals and a spell book.

In the meantime, Jaxon lays Xavier's body on the ground several feet from Flint before collapsing on the sand, and Eden drops down between them. She's trying to keep her face neutral, but I can see the pain in her eyes as she looks at Xavier, and I know that only half her agony is physical.

My own anguish is pressing in on me, making it nearly impossible for me to breathe as I face my friends—really face them—for the first time since Xavier died.

I feel so guilty, I can barely look them in the eyes, but they deserve that from me and a lot more. So I meet each of their gazes in turn as I tell them, "I'm sorry. I never should have dragged any of you into my problems."

I look at Xavier's broken body and nearly choke on my own grief. "There's nothing I can do to bring Xavier back. I would change places with him—or with any of you—in a second if I could. I'm sorry. I'm so, so sorry."

"This isn't on you," Jaxon tells me, voice hoarse and eyes bruised with pain and exhaustion. "I pushed for this. I insisted that we come. I didn't listen to your doubts. This is my fault. If I had just—"

"Stop it, both of you," Macy snaps, even as she drags her hands across her face to wipe the tears away. "It's not up to either of you to apologize. We all made the decision to come. We all knew what the risks were—probably more than Grace, as we've all grown up with stories of the Unkillable Beast. And we came anyway."

Her tears keep falling, so she clears her throat several times as she, once again, wipes them away. "We flew all the way up here and attacked that poor creature, because we told ourselves we were preventing a greater atrocity. We told ourselves we were doing the right thing even though everything about it was wrong. And that, too, is on all of us.

"We play with magic our entire lives. We do spells and shift forms and even move the earth"—she looks at Jaxon—"when we want to. But the world we live in—the privileges we enjoy—come with responsibilities and consequences that we learn about in school but never truly think about until we have to."

She looks at Xavier, and it seems like she's going to break down completely, but then she squares her shoulders and looks everyone in the eye except me. "We—all of us—are the ones who lost sight of those lessons when we decided to come here and play God with Hudson and the beast and even with our own lives—even after my cousin *begged us* not to. And that's on every single one of us; it's something we're going to have to live with, a lesson we are all going to agonize over for a long time to come."

She clears her throat. "But we owe it to Xavier and to that poor gargoyle in there and to all the people back at school—all the paranormals in the world who don't understand what the Circle has become or what it is doing—to learn from this mistake and to do whatever we must to stop them. It won't right this wrong, it won't fix this mistake, but it might keep others from making worse ones."

She points at me. "And that means getting you to that Trial and getting you on the Circle and doing whatever else we need to make things better. So all of you need to stop blaming yourselves. You need to stop wallowing in guilt and sadness and anger and help me get us back to Katmere before it's too late to stop what the Circle is trying so desperately to set in motion."

For long seconds, none of us moves. Instead, we stand transfixed by the power and the responsibility of her words. At least until she raises an eyebrow and says, "Or do I have to do this all by myself?"

104

Because We Could Not Stop for Death

"**W**e're in," Flint says, trying desperately to push himself back to a standing position. It's painful to watch, at least until Jaxon rests a hand on his shoulder, then leans over and speaks quietly to him. I don't know what he says, but Flint settles back down and doesn't try to get up again.

"What do you need?" I ask as I scramble over to where Macy is once again kneeling in the sand.

"Give everybody a crystal and have them face north, south, east, and west respectively," she answers, pointing in the right directions as she reads over a page in the spell book several times before closing the book with a snap and shoving it in her backpack. "Then lay the fifth crystal on Xavier's chest."

I do as she says, my throat tightening a little as I place the crystal in the center of Xavier's Guns 'N' Roses T-shirt. I whisper a quick prayer for him, then head back to Macy to see what else I can do to help.

Jaxon must have the same thought, because he asks, "What do you need from us?" as he staggers over to where we're standing.

I grab on to his hand, send him a stream of energy through the mating bond.

"Stop," he tells me, pulling away. "You can't afford that right now."

"Yeah, well, I can't afford to have my mate get sick, either. So let me do this right now. We'll figure out the rest when we get back to school."

He doesn't agree, but he doesn't argue anymore, so I feed him a little more energy. Not enough to weaken me significantly, but enough that he doesn't look quite so gray and pallid.

"Just stand over there, where Grace put you," Macy answers as she slides her backpack onto her back.

"Now what?" I ask Macy as she turns to face the ocean.

"Now I'm going to try a spell Gwen told me about when I was preparing for tonight. I've never done it before, so all I can say is it's either going to work and get us back to school, or it's going to fail and splinter us into a thousand beams of light." She looks over at me. "So here's hoping."

"Umm, yeah," I answer, eyes wide and stomach flipping all the different ways. "Here's hoping."

She hands me one of the crystals and says, "Hold this for me, will you, please? And check to make sure everyone is where they need to be."

"Of course." I do as she instructs, glancing at the others before wrapping my fingers around the crystal as she pulls her athame out of her pocket instead of her wand and holds it dagger-side up. "Ready?" she asks as she grabs on to my hand.

"To splinter into a thousand beams of light?" Flint asks. "Sure. Why not?"

"That's what I was hoping you'd say," she answers and then tilts her face to the sky. "Here goes everything."

I hold my breath as Macy lifts her arms to the sky in a circular pose worthy of a ballet dancer. Her athame is in her right hand and she points it straight at the heart of the aurora borealis dancing above us as she moves her other hand in small, circular motions, over and over again.

At first nothing happens, but slowly—so slowly that it takes me a few seconds to realize what's going on—the crystal in my hand starts to pulsate against my palm. A quick look shows me that the others' crystals are doing the same thing, glowing brighter and brighter as they begin to vibrate in their hands.

I look to Macy, but she is so focused on the sky that she doesn't so much as glance my way. I think that means she can't see, so I start to lift my hand up, to show her what the crystal is doing, but a small, nearly imperceptible shake of her head has me freezing in place.

But as the crystals continue to vibrate, to glow brighter and burn hotter, Macy's circular hand motions get bigger and bigger and bigger, until she seems to be encircling all of us with the gesture, wrapping her magic and her protection around the whole group of us even as she continues to channel energy from the sky.

All of a sudden, Macy gasps at the same time the crystal in my hand starts to burn superhot. I cry out, trying to hold on to it, but the heat gets more and more severe with each second that passes, until I have no choice but to open my fingers. For one second, two, the crystal lays flat against my palm and then it starts to rise, floating higher and higher above our heads until it floats into the athame's path.

The others' crystals do the same thing until they line up between the athame and the sky in rainbow order. The second the last crystal slides into place, lightning shoots through the sky and slams straight into the crystals and through them into Macy's athame.

I cry out at the sudden flash and heat of it, but Macy doesn't so much as gasp. She just holds the athame steady even as the lightning links up to it and then shoots out, making a giant circle that wraps around us all.

Sand and water rise up around us, a sudden wind whipping them into a tornado until we're surrounded on all sides by sand and water and wind and lightning—all four of the elements coming together through Macy.

She starts to shake, her entire body lighting up with the strength of the elements whipping through her. Soon her clothes are plastered to her body, her hair stands on end, and her very skin seems to be glowing from within. She reaches out to me then, grabs my hand, and I feel it, all of the energy from the elements—from the natural world around us—flowing from her into me.

It's powerful, painful, so overwhelming that I nearly break away from her—until I realize that she needs me. That the energy is too much for her to contain on her own and she's funneling it through me, through my gargoyle, because I can absorb it, the power of the magic sliding through me but not hurting me at all.

So I hold tight to her hand, let her funnel everything that she needs to straight into me. And when a second blast of lightning cracks across the sky, I don't so much as flinch, even when it links up with the first.

Seconds pass, filled with incredible, unbelievable power, and then there's another giant flash. This one lights up the entire sky, spreads over the water, over the clearing, over us, until there is no more crater.

Until there is no more rock.

Until there is no more *us*, only the light and energy and air that we've become.

105

Fall from Grace

We hit the ground screaming, every single one of us, as the light molecules we traveled on band together to re-form our bodies. It's painful and weird and a little bit terrifying, but it takes only a few seconds, and then I'm struggling to absorb the pain and get my breath back.

"What time is it?" I demand as I stagger to my feet and look around at my friends, all of whom are still curled up and moaning on the snow. I reach for my phone, but it's dead. I throw it and scream, "What time is it, goddammit?"

Rosy streaks of dawn are starting to work their way across the sky, and panic is a living, breathing animal within me. I didn't come this far just to fail because we're too late. We can't be too late.

Please God, we can't be too late.

"It's six fifty," Flint groans as he rolls over, his phone clutched in his hand.

"Six fifty," I whisper. I'd checked sunrise before we left, and we still have time. "True sunrise is at eight twenty. We have an hour and a half."

I look at Jaxon and the others, all of whom continue to lie on the snow despite my announcement. None of whom seems to understand the sudden urgency we're facing. "We have ninety minutes!" I yell as I look around, trying to figure out exactly where on the Katmere grounds we are.

Macy pushes herself to her feet, and she looks as bad as I feel. Maybe worse. "Okay, okay, okay." She glances around, too, rubs a hand over her face. "The amphitheater is that way. We just need to get out of these trees."

"Come on," I say, pulling at Jaxon, who definitely isn't looking very good right now. Then again, I'm pretty sure the same can be said about me.

Flint rolls to his feet and helps me get Jaxon on his, but now that it's not as dark as at the gargoyle's cave, I can see just how bad his leg is. "You can't walk any farther on that," I tell him. "You have to stay here, and we'll send help."

"I'll stay with him," Eden says. "Him and Xavier."

But as soon as she says that, I look around for Xavier's body and realize he's not here. "We left him," I whisper in horror. "We left him there on the beach."

"No," Macy says. "No, we didn't."

"He's not here," Eden says, running for the closest trees. "Where is he? Oh my God, where is he?"

"He's light," Macy says, and her voice is thick with tears as she looks up at the ever-lightening sky. "We're still alive, so we could re-form back into our bodies. He wasn't, so my life-force magic couldn't work on him. He's gone." She starts to cry. "He's really gone."

I want to cry with her, want nothing more than to sit my weary, aching body down on this snow and sob like a child as guilt racks me. But I can't do that. *We* can't do that, not yet. Not when we have to be inside the arena in ninety minutes.

"I'm sorry, but we have to go," I tell Macy. "I can't do this on my own. I need you to come with me."

"I know. I'm sorry." She dashes her hands across her cheeks to dry her tears. "Let's go, let's go."

"I'm sorry, Macy." Jaxon's voice is low and hoarse with pain.

My cousin just nods. I mean, what else is there to actually say?

Eden and Flint wish us luck as we take off across the snow, stumbling a little under the weight of tiredness and injuries. But at least Macy's right. Once we break through the forest of trees we landed in, the arena looms huge over the landscape.

I glance at Jaxon's phone. We have eighty-five minutes to get inside. That doesn't leave much time for us to rest once we get settled by the field, but it's enough. That's all that matters.

"Go straight through there," Macy tells us, pointing to the closest entrance. "I'm going to find help, see if I can get Marise or someone to come out with me to try to help Flint. I'll also grab some blood for Jaxon and get to the arena as soon as I possibly can."

I don't have the energy to answer her, so I just nod as I continue to trudge across the snow, Jaxon's arm draped over my shoulders so I can support some of his weight. I'm tired, so tired, and every single bone in my body hurts.

I just want to sit down. I just want to go home. I just want to be anywhere but here.

"*Hey,*" Hudson says, and his voice is nearly as hoarse as Jaxon's and mine. Then again, he did do a lot of shouting there in the cave. *"You've got this. It's just a little farther, and then you can sit for a few minutes and just breathe, right? You and Jaxon can get your second winds."*

"Pretty sure you mean our fourth winds," I comment, but I take a deep breath and tell myself that he's right. That we can do this. It's only for a little while and then it's over. I can do anything for a little while. Even pretend that I'm not racked with guilt over Xavier's death.

But as we start down the final hill between the arena and us, Jaxon tells me, "We need to come up with a better plan for what we're going to do in there."

I glance his way. "I don't know that we can. Yes, we planned on using a lot of the portals, but you're probably not in good enough shape for it. The one I did during the game took a lot out of me."

He nods. "You know, I hadn't really talked to you about what I planned on doing in the Trial, but I was going to try to get it all the way down the field in one turn. Nuri held the comet for nearly five minutes. I figured I could do close to that, and then you wouldn't have to worry—"

"My pretty little head?" I ask as shock and outrage rip through me.

"What?" he asks, looking confused.

"You don't want me to have to worry my pretty little head about anything as strenuous as actually participating in the Trial that I called for?"

"Uh-oh," Hudson says faintly in the back of my head, but I'm not paying attention to him right now.

"That's not what I said." Jaxon eyes me warily.

"Maybe not, but it's what you meant, right? What did you think was going to happen in that arena, Jaxon? Did you think I was just going to sit back and let you do your thing while I just hung out and cheered? I mean, should I have brought pom-poms?"

"Hey! That's my line!" Hudson complains, but there's a little bit of glee in his voice when he says it.

"I didn't mean it the way you're taking it," Jaxon says, and he sounds pissed for the first time.

"Okay, that's fair." I stop hobbling forward and just wait. "How *did* you mean it?"

"Really?" he asks, and the wariness is more pronounced now.

"Absolutely," I tell him. "If I took it wrong, then I'm sorry. But I would like to know what you meant."

He sighs, runs a shaky hand through his hair. "All I meant was I'm trying to take care of you, Grace. I'm stronger than you and I can do more, so let me do more. There's nothing wrong with me taking care of my girlfriend."

"You mean your human girlfriend, don't you?" I ask, eyebrow raised.

"Maybe I did. What's wrong with that?" He throws his free hand up. "What's wrong with me wanting to take care of you?"

"Nothing," I answer. "Except with you it's a sickness. And I think it's a symptom of something a lot more problematic in our relationship."

"Problematic?" Now he looks more than just a little bit pissed. "What does that mean?"

"It means you think I'm weaker than you and that means you have to—"

"You *are* weaker than me!" he roars, cutting me off. "It's a fact."

"Oh, really?" I shrug his arm off, step away, and he almost falls flat on his ass. "Because right now it looks like you need me a lot more than I need you."

His eyes turn to pure, flat black. "Are you making fun of me for being exhausted after everything I just did in that cave?"

I take a deep breath and force myself not to yell at him even though I really, really want to right now. Because Jaxon just isn't getting it. For the first time, I'm a little afraid, because maybe he can't get it. Maybe he'll never get it. And then what will we do?

"No, I'm making fun of you because you don't seem to understand that we need to take care of each other," I tell him, backing up a few feet because I just can't be near him right now. "That sometimes I need help—"

"I know that—"

"Oh, I know you know that. You're super impressive at reminding me of all the things I can't do, of all the ways I'm weaker than you." I pause, my voice breaking. "Of all the ways my opinion doesn't matter to you."

"I've never said that." Jaxon staggers a little bit as he tries to close the distance between us. "You know I ask your opinion all the time."

"That's just it," I tell him. "You don't. You tell me what you think. I try to tell you what I think. And then you do what you want to do anyway. Maybe it doesn't happen that way all the time, but it happens that way at least eighty percent of the time.

"You don't tell me something because you're afraid it will worry or hurt me. You don't listen to me, because you don't think I'll understand. You always want to solve a problem for me, because the frail human can't survive having to do it herself."

"What's wrong with wanting to take care of my *girlfriend*?" he growls. "I lost you for four months. What's wrong with me trying to make sure nothing else happens to you—"

"Because you didn't lose me. *I* saved *you*, in case you've forgotten."

"By nearly dying," he shoots back, and he looks anguished, his face contorted, his hands clenched into fists. "Do you know what that felt like? To stand there in that hallway with you turned to stone, completely out of my reach, and to know it happened because I didn't protect you well enough? To know that you nearly died in the tunnels, because I was naïve enough to drink that damn tea from Lia? To know that you were stuck with my brother for three and a half months because I couldn't reach you, couldn't—"

"Save me?" I finish his thought for him. "That's the whole point. It's not your job to save me. Maybe it's our job to save each other. But you're never going to give me that chance. Because in your head, I'm still the frail little human who came to Katmere Academy back in November."

"You are human. You are—"

"No!" I tell him, and this time I get right up in his face to say it. "I'm not human. Or at least, I'm not only human. I'm a gargoyle, and I can do a lot of cool shit. Maybe I can't shake the earth like you can, but I can turn you to stone right now if I wanted to. I can fly as high as you. And I can take a hell of a beating and keep coming."

"I know that," Jaxon tells me.

"Do you?" I ask. "Do you really? Because you say you love me, and I believe you do. But I don't think you respect me. Not like an equal. Not like I need to be respected. If you did, you wouldn't have just ignored me when I told you I thought it was a bad idea to go after the Unkillable Beast."

"That's not fair, Grace. I still stand by my opinion that letting

Hudson into the world with his powers would be a disaster—"

"Xavier's dead, Jaxon. He's dead and it's our fault! How are we supposed to live with that? How am I ever supposed to forgive myself for not fighting you harder? For not demanding that you listen? For not getting through to you?"

"You learn to understand what the rest of us already do. That it is a goddamn tragedy—" His voice breaks, but he clears his throat, swallows a couple of times. "It is a tragedy that Xavier died. But he said it himself the other night. Some things are worth dying for. Because if Hudson gets free with his powers, then a lot more people are going to suffer, a lot more people are going to die than just Xavier. That's what you don't understand."

His words resonate. They do. Because I wasn't here eighteen months ago. I didn't see firsthand what Hudson did. I didn't see what led to Jaxon feeling like he had to kill his brother.

And that's when it hits me.

Maybe that's the problem. Maybe the reason he can't believe me is that if he does, he's going to have to acknowledge that he didn't have to kill his brother. He's going to have to acknowledge that maybe he made the worst mistake of his life.

But we can't keep doing this. We can't keep chasing after ways to keep the world safe from Hudson, not when those ways leave people dead or badly injured.

"You're going to have to trust me," I tell him. "You're going to have to believe me on this. Because if you don't, I don't see how we can get past it. You're my mate, and I love you. But I can't spend the rest of our lives together fighting for you to believe me. Fighting for you to believe *in* me."

Hudson has gotten very, very quiet inside me. And I can understand why. There's a part of me that can't believe I'm saying this, that can't believe I'm even thinking it. But I can't live like this. I won't live like this, where my partner isn't actually my partner. I deserve better than that...and so does Jaxon.

"What does that mean?" he asks, and for the first time ever, Jaxon looks panicked, out of control, desperate. "What are you saying?"

Part of me wants to admit the truth. To say that I don't know. I don't know what I'm saying. I don't know what I'm thinking. But that's a cop-out. Worse, it's weak. And if there's one thing I'm not going to be anymore, it's weak. Not for Jaxon. Not for anyone.

"I'm saying I need you to meet me halfway," I tell him. "I need you to try to treat me as an equal. I need you to listen to me, to trust me, even when it's the hardest thing in the world for you to do, because that's what I'm willing to do for you. But if you can't get there, if you can't even try, then I don't know where we're going to end up."

He doesn't say anything for a few seconds, doesn't espouse his undying love, doesn't promise me that he'll do anything I want. And actually, I'm grateful for that. I'm grateful for the time he spends thinking about it. Because that means it's real. That means he's really trying to listen.

Finally, when my nerves are stretched to the breaking point and the clock has ticked down as long as we can afford to let it, Jaxon says, "I'll try, Grace. Of course I'll try. But I've been like this a really long time, so you're going to have to cut me some slack. I'm going to mess up. I'm going to try to protect you even when you don't need to be protected, and some of the time you're going to have to let me. Because that's who I am. That's who I'll always be."

"I know," I answer, tears burning my exhausted eyes as I finally, finally lean in to him. "We'll both try, okay? And we'll see where that gets us."

He presses his forehead against mine. "Right now, I'm pretty sure where it's going to get us is into that stadium where we may very well get our asses kicked."

"Yeah," I tell him. "Probably. But at least we'll get them kicked together. That's something, I guess."

"Not something." He looks at me with eyes that burn like the blackest sun. "That's everything."

106

Stone Hearts Can
Be Broken

It takes a couple of minutes for us to hobble up to the back entrance of the arena, but just as we get to the ornately carved entranceway, Cole walks out from behind the closest tree and starts clapping as he puts himself directly in our path.

"What do you want, Cole?" Jaxon growls, but there's not a lot of strength behind it, and judging from the way Cole's eyes go wide, he knows it, too.

"I just wanted to see if you were actually going to show up, Vega. It looks like you did. I don't know if that means you're brave or just the cockiest bastard on the planet. I mean, look at you." He laughs. "I almost feel bad."

I know I shouldn't ask—he's too smug and I don't want to give him the satisfaction. But I'm tired and obviously easily bait-able, and the words come out before I know I'm going to say them. "For what?"

He looks me straight in the eye as he pulls a piece of paper, obviously ripped into pieces some time ago and now held together with tape, out of his pocket and says, "For this."

Jaxon's eyes go wide and he yells, "No!" as he makes a grab for Cole. But suddenly all of Cole's minions are there. Two wolves grab on to me, two of them grab Jaxon, and the last three position themselves between him and Cole.

"You're just *so* arrogant, aren't you, Jaxon? You didn't even hesitate to tear up something this powerful that could be used against you and throw it into the trash in front of everyone." His smile is pure malice and something more...jealousy. "What must it be like to be that confident everyone fears you, that no one would ever even dare to hurt you or your mate? Well just remember: you brought this on yourself."

And then Cole is reading a series of words that don't make much sense to my already addled brain—words that sound like a spell or a poem. I don't know. I'm so tired and it's so hard to follow... Except as he finishes, there's a giant wrenching inside me, a ripping in my soul that hurts like nothing has ever hurt before in my life.

I scream from the shock, from the pain, and my legs go out from under me. I hit the ground hard, my head bouncing off the packed snow as every single part of me shrieks in agony.

Make it stop, oh my God, make it stop! Whatever he did, please, please, please make it stop!

But it doesn't stop. It goes on and on and on until I can barely breathe. Barely think. Barely be. At one point, I try to push up to my hands and knees, but I'm too weak. It hurts too much.

I hear Jaxon shout, and I use the last ounce of strength I have to turn my head toward him. He's writhing on the ground, legs drawn up, body arched in pain.

"Jax—" I reach a hand out toward him, try to call his name, but I can't reach him. I've got nothing left. Darkness wells up inside me as I collapse back onto my stomach, and I do the only thing I can do to get to Jaxon.

I reach for the mating bond...and then scream all over again when I realize it isn't there.

I Never Asked for This Anyway

Time passes. I don't know how much, but it does.

Enough that Cole and his posse of sadistic wolves disappear.

Enough that dawn finishes creeping over the sky.

More than enough that the reality of my missing mating bond sinks in.

The pain is finally gone and, in another world, at another time, I guess that would be a good thing. But right here, right now, in this time, at this place, I miss the feeling of it more than I can ever say.

I miss the searing heat of it.

I miss the violent cold of it.

I miss the overwhelming omnipotence of it as it fills up every nook and cranny of my heart and soul.

Because without it, without the agony and the ache, all that's left is emptiness.

Yawning, gaping, everlasting emptiness.

I've never felt like this before. I never even had a clue I *could* feel like this. When my parents died, I was numb. I was angry. I was lost. I was sad.

But I was never empty. I was never destroyed.

Now I'm both, and I can't even summon up the will to care.

Time is ticking away, seconds fading into minutes that I don't have to spare.

I should be walking into the arena with Jaxon right now.

We should be taking our place on the field *right now*.

We should be fighting this atrocity, facing down Cyrus and the evil that's taken over the Circle like a cancer, eating away at anything good that might have once been there.

Instead, I can't even get off the ground.

I glance over at Jaxon, realize that he, too, is still on the ground. Unlike me, he's not lying flat, though. He's curled up in a ball, hands over his head like he's desperate to ward off the next blow.

But there are no more blows coming, because there are no more blows to be dealt. Cole, in his infinite hatred, struck the death blow, and I didn't even see it coming.

At least the worst is over. No matter what dungeon they throw me in, no matter what terrible things Cyrus has in store for me, at least none of them will ever feel like this.

At least I will never feel like this again.

I take a deep breath, then start to cough as I breathe snow into my nose and down my throat. I roll over out of the most basic form of self-preservation, then stay that way because there's no reason not to.

Sunrise is coming, turning the edges of the sky a myriad of colors— at least for a minute or two. And then lightning crackles across the sky. Thunder booms, and the darkest clouds I've ever seen move across the sky straight toward us.

"Grace." Jaxon calls my name in a voice made hoarse by too much pain, too much loss.

"Yeah."

"You can't go in there," he rasps.

"What?"

"The arena. You can't go in there without me."

"I know."

He rolls over to his side, reaches a hand out to me, and I think about taking it. I want to take it. But he's too far away, and it doesn't matter anyway. A touch of fingertips won't bring back what we lost.

"I mean it, Grace. They'll kill you if you go in there. Or worse, take you back to London and destroy you piece by piece."

Silly boy, can't he see that I'm already destroyed? Already broken into so many pieces that I can't even imagine what it would feel like to try to put them back together again.

My parents are dead.

My memory is gone.

My mating bond is gone.

Why on earth would I go in there to fight?

I've got nothing left to fight for.

The clouds creep ever closer, blocking out the last remnants of light as sleet begins to fall, the rain and ice stinging my skin, leaching the last little bit of warmth from inside me.

A heavy lassitude overtakes me. It has my eyes closing and my mind wandering and my breathing slowing to almost nothing. There's a voice deep in my head telling me that it's okay, that I can just stay right here. That I can rock shut as a seashell and let the stone take me.

I don't remember the last three months. Maybe if I stay stone long enough, I won't remember any of this, either.

I take one last breath and then let go.

108

Pom-Poms and Pompadours

"**G**race! Grace! Can you hear me?

"Damn it, Grace, can. You. Hear. Me?

"Don't do this. Don't you dare do this again. Don't you fucking dare.

"Get up! Damn it, Grace, I said get up!"

"Stop it." I don't even know who I'm talking to; I just know that there's a voice in my head, and it won't go away. It won't let me be. All I want to do is sleep, and it just keeps talking and talking and talking.

"Oh my God, there you are! Grace, please. Please come back. Please don't turn to stone.

"Grace? Grace? So help me God, Grace, if you don't wake up right now, I'm going to—"

"What?" I demand, cranky and pissed off and more than ready to bite the head off whoever it is who keeps bugging the hell out of me.

"Get up! I mean it. You need to get off this snow. You need to get into that arena. Now!"

I creak one eye open and see him staring back down at me with those ridiculous blue eyes of his. "Ugh, Hudson. I should have known it was you. Go away."

"I will not go away." His voice is all British again, dripping with perfect syllables and indignation. "I'm saving you."

"What if I don't want to be saved?"

"Since when has what you wanted even been of paramount importance to me?" he demands.

"You make a good point."

"I always make a good point," he snaps. "You're just usually too busy hating me to listen."

"I'm still too busy hating you to listen." But I push myself up into a sitting position.

"Good. Hate me all you want. But get your ass up and get into that arena before you forfeit everything."

"I don't have a mate anymore," I tell him.

He blows out a long breath. "I know the bond with Jaxon broke."

"If by broke you mean it was ripped apart by fucking Cole, then yes. It broke."

He looks down at me for long seconds, then sighs and settles on the snow next to me in his black Armani trousers and dark-red dress shirt.

"Why do you look so good?" I demand, feeling exceptionally annoyed by his ridiculously pretty face.

"Excuse me?" He lifts a brow.

I hold my hands up. "It's sleeting. Why aren't you wet? Why do you look like you just walked off a runway?"

"Because I'm not currently rolling around in the snow feeling sorry for myself?" he asks.

"You're a douche." I make a face at him. "You know that, right?"

"It's a gift."

"More like a curse," I tell him.

"All gifts are curses in one way or another, don't you think? Otherwise, why would we be here?" he answers.

I turn my head so I can get a good look at his face as I try to figure out what he means. But after a solid sixty seconds of staring at him, I still don't have a clue. I do, however, know that his blue eyes have a lot of green flecks in them.

"You're looking at me strangely," he says, tilting his head questioningly.

"I'm trying to figure out if you meant that existentially or if you meant it—"

"No, I didn't mean it existentially!" he barks at me. "I meant, why else would we be sitting out here in the bloody snow when your arse should be in that arena right now?"

"I already told you, I. Don't. Have. A. Mate."

"Who. Cares."

"What do you mean?" I demand. "I can't compete without a mate."

"Sure you can. There is no rule on the books that says you *have* to take your mate in there with you," he tells me.

"Yeah, but I can't hold the ball longer than thirty seconds, so what am I supposed to do if I don't have someone else to throw it to?"

"You're a smart girl," he answers. "You'll figure it out."

"If that isn't the most Hudson thing you've ever said, I don't know what is."

He sighs, then reaches over and straightens my jacket, flipping the collar over and smoothing out the sleeves. As he does, I keep waiting for him to say something, but he doesn't. Instead, he just sits there waiting, like he expects *me* to say something.

Usually, I can wait him out, but I'm cold and wet and empty and a whole lot of other things I'm not sure how to identify right now, and I don't want to play this game with him. Especially not when he's looking at me with that ridiculous pretty face.

"What am I supposed to do?" I finally explode. "Just go in there and throw the ball until Cole eviscerates me?"

"You're Grace Foster, the only gargoyle born in the last thousand years. I say, go in there and do whatever the fuck you want... as long as that includes kicking Cole's skinny wolf ass all over that arena."

"What should I do? Turn him to stone?" I ask sarcastically.

"Sure, why not?" he answers. "And then shatter him with a sledgehammer. I promise you the world will be better off."

"I can't do that."

"That's what I keep trying to tell you, Grace. You can do whatever you want to do. Who saved Jaxon from Lia? Who won the Ludares tournament for her team? Who figured out what was going on with the Unkillable Beast? Who channeled enough magic from the aurora borealis to light up New York and got all her friends home? That was you, Grace. That was all you.

"You don't have to be a dragon. You don't have to be a vampire. You sure as shit don't have to be a werewolf. You just have to get off your arse, go into that arena, and be the gargoyle girl we all know and love."

"But it's hard." I give myself permission to whine for one more second.

"Yeah," he agrees as he stands back up. "It is. But life's hard. So either get in there and do what you have to do or get the fuck off the ride."

"I tried to do that, if you remember correctly." I pull myself up to my feet. "You wouldn't let me."

"You're right, I wouldn't. Total waste of the sexiest gargoyle girl to walk this earth in a thousand years."

"I'm the *only* gargoyle girl to walk this earth in a thousand years."

He gives me an arch look. "Damn straight you are. Now what are you going to do about it?"

I sigh. "Go into that arena and get hurt a lot but then win in the end and shove a burning hot ball right down Cole's disgusting, ugly werewolf snout."

"Sounds like a plan," he tells me as we walk toward the arena.

"Thank you," I tell him, because if it wasn't for him, I'd still be lying on the snow willing myself to turn into a statue forever.

"You're welcome." He smiles slyly. "Gargoyle girl."

"Call me that one more time, and I'm going to eviscerate you."

"You'll have to catch me first," he tells me.

"You live in my head. How hard could that be?" I counter. "Besides, I'd catch you even if you didn't."

"Oh yeah?" Both brows go up this time. "Why's that?"

"Because I'm a gargoyle, bitch. And it may have been a thousand years since they've had to deal with one of my kind, but that ends now."

109

Where Do Broken Bonds Go?

I stoop down to check on Jaxon before I go. He doesn't look good, but then I'm pretty sure the same can be said for me right now.

But since there's no bossy Brit boy living in his head at the moment, he's still lying in the snow, curled up in a ball as if to ward off whatever blow fate decides to deliver next.

I know the feeling.

"Jaxon?" I call softly, but he doesn't answer me. More, he doesn't even open his eyes to *look* at me, which is so not like him that it worries me even more than the fact that he has yet to move. I'm sure he's exhausted—I am, and I haven't done half of what he has tonight, even after he was drained by Hudson.

Determined to make sure he's okay before I go anywhere or do anything else, I stroke my hand over his shoulder and call his name several times. Eventually, he opens his eyes, and I see the emptiness inside him—the same emptiness that I currently feel—staring back at me.

Still, he smiles at me as I take his hand in mine. "Are you all right?" I ask.

He doesn't say anything, so I ask again even as I slip a hand under his arms to help him sit up.

"Yeah. Are you?"

As soon as he repeats my question back to me, I understand his hesitation in answering. Because there is no real, true answer to that question that doesn't begin with, *I'm not sure I'll ever be okay again*.

And since we can't say that, at least not now when we still have so much left to do before we can rest, I do the same thing Jaxon did and answer, "Yeah."

His sad smile says he knows exactly what I'm doing as he grabs hold of my hand and squeezes it. "I'm sorry," he whispers. "I'm so sorry. This is all my fault."

"No," I tell him. "It's not."

"But, Grace, I threw the spell away and never thought about anyone finding it—"

"Still not your fault," I say, cutting him off. "If it's anyone's, it's Cole's. Or maybe it's your father's. I don't know, but assigning blame isn't going to solve anything right now, not when I have to—"

"Don't go in there," he tells me again, clutching at my arm. "You can't do the match by yourself. You'll lose."

"Probably," I agree. "But I have to go in there. There's no other choice."

"There is," he counters. "There's always a choice. You can forfeit—"

"And what? Go live as a prisoner in your parents' dungeon?"

"Better a prisoner than dead," he answers me. "I can't come find you if you're dead."

"You won't be able to come find me anyway. I'm pretty sure your parents will make sure of that." I lean forward, bring a hand up to rest on his cheek, then take my time stroking my fingers down the scar he used to hate so much, the scar he's finally come to grips with after more than a year.

"You don't know that." His voice reflects his desperation. "You don't know what the future could bring."

"Neither do you." This time it's my turn to smooth *his* hair out of *his* face. "Don't worry," I try to reassure him. "I've got this."

"Grace—" He tries to stand, but he's too weak. Between feeding

Hudson energy for so long, taking out the Circle guards, and then fighting the Unkillable Beast, he's got nothing left.

"It's okay," I tell him, propping him up against the stone wall that surrounds the arena, so that he can look out at the forest as he waits. "Rest now, Jaxon. Macy will be here soon with some blood for you. She just went for help for Flint and Eden. But she'll be here as soon as she can."

"I don't need Macy to take care of me," he argues and tries once again to push to his feet. Once again, he fails.

Which only pisses him off.

Jaxon curses in frustration, kicks out at the ground in frustration, and has the closest thing to a hissy fit I've ever seen my strong, proud boyfriend have. But in the end, he sinks back against the wall and closes his eyes for long seconds as pain and fatigue draw lines on his typically unmarred face.

When he finally opens his eyes again, it's obvious that he's blinking back tears, and just that easily my own emotions are back to burning in the back of my throat. "I wish I could go in there with you," he whispers.

"I know," I tell him, because I do. Mate or not, if there was any way Jaxon could fight by my side right now, I know he would do it.

But I also know that time is running out. Though he's trying to be respectful, I can feel Hudson's impatience pushing at me from the corners of my mind, urging me to hurry. Urging me to forget Jaxon and focus on the task ahead.

But I can't do that. I can't just leave him like this, not if this is the last time I'm ever going to see him. So I cup his face with my hands, tangle the tips of my fingers in the edges of his too-long hair like I've done so many times before. And then I press kisses against his eyes, along his scarred cheek, over his mouth, which is still tight with pain.

"I love you," I tell him, and out of habit I reach for him along the mating bond. But it's not there. Nothing is.

God, it hurts all over again.

"I love you, too," he says, and from the pained look on his face, I can tell he's feeling the absence, too. "Even without the mating bond."

He reaches out then, wraps his arms around me, and pulls me into a hug that is as painful as it is comforting. I bury my face in the spot where his shoulder meets his neck, and I breathe him in. Whatever happens with this Trial, however it may go, I want to remember this smell—and this moment—for an eternity.

Too soon, horns sound from inside—the seven-minute warning I remember from the tournament. "I have to go," I tell Jaxon. My Jaxon.

"I know." He lets me go slowly, painfully. "Be careful, Grace. Please, please be careful."

"I'll try," I tell him with a grin, because all this sadness is tearing me apart again. "But sometimes careful doesn't get the job done." I deliberately mimic the words he and Flint said during a study session not that long ago.

I push to my feet, swaying a little as I do. Jaxon tries to steady me, but I just give him a smile as I step out of reach. There's no part of this he can do for me. Now I have to do it on my own.

"I'll see you soon," I tell him.

"You better," he answers, fear plain on his face.

There's more to say—there's always more to say with Jaxon—but I really am out of time. So I just give him one last smile, and then I turn away.

110

Heeeeeeeeere's Hudson

I'm not that far from the arena door, but once I'm inside, there's a long walkway I have to go down to get to the field. Hudson hassles me about hurrying the entire time, even though I'm doing my best. It's not exactly easy when everything hurts when I run.

Or worse, everything hurts when I breathe.

Maybe that's why I don't remember until I'm halfway down the ramp. "Hold on a minute," I tell Hudson as I careen to a stop.

"There's no time to wait, Grace!" He shoots me an impatient look. "You've got to get on the field."

"Yeah, well, I don't think I can afford to *get* on the field without doing this, so they're all just going to have to wait a little bit longer, whether they want to or not."

I unzip the front pocket of my backpack and take out the small pouch I have hidden in the secret compartment at the back of it. I know it was a risk to bring these things with me to the cave of the Unkillable Beast, but I was afraid I might get injured while I was there—or worse. And if that happened, I wanted the others to have a way to get Hudson out of my head.

I didn't want him to have to die with me.

Turns out, I wasn't the one who died in that cave. And I will remember Xavier and regret his loss for the rest of my life—however long or short that might be. But I'm *not* about to go into another dangerous situation, one that can turn deadly at any moment, and not take care of everything—everyone—I can. Which means there is no other time. I have to do this now.

I open the pouch and slowly, carefully take out each of the four items inside it, one by one.

Hudson's eyes go huge as he realizes what I'm doing. "You can't do this right now," he tells me, backing away from me in such a hurry that he nearly trips over his own feet—and probably would have if he was actually in his own body. "There are other, more important things for you to—"

"I might die." Three little words, but they shut him right up, his mouth slamming closed fast and tight, even as his eyes implore me to stop talking. To not say what we both know I'm going to say.

But I can't give him that, not now when there's so very much on the line.

"Jokes about shoving the ball down Cole's snout notwithstanding," I continue, "we both know things could go really wrong in there today. Which means there might not be another time to do this. Ever. I know what I'm supposed to do—the Bloodletter told me—but can you help me? Make sure I don't mess it up?"

"This isn't what you need to be worrying about right now, Grace. You need to focus. Plus, if I'm still in your head, maybe I can help you. Maybe I can—"

"Die with me," I finish the sentence with a firm shake of my head. "I know you like to do things your way, but you don't get a vote on this. One way or the other, I'm getting you out of my head, so you can either help me or you can risk ending up haunting the hallways as Katmere Academy's very first ghost."

I throw my hands up in the air in a "what you going to do?" kind of shrug. "It's your choice."

"One, I wouldn't be the first ghost at Katmere Academy. And second, the ghost thing doesn't really work like that anyway."

"And you know this because?" I ask, brows arched.

"I was dead...?" He pauses. "Well, sort of."

"Sort of?" That's news to me. "What does that mean?"

"It means I'll tell you once you go in there and kick Cole's whiny little ass," he answers with his trademark smirk. "So don't screw it up."

"Not planning on it," I say, "but you know. Shit happens."

"It does," he agrees, face pensive and eyes sad.

I'm pretty sure this is Hudson's version of a sad puppy dog face— or as close as he gets to it—and I am not going to fall victim to it. There's too much on the line.

So instead of looking at him, I crouch down and place the four items the way the Bloodletter told me to: bloodstone in the north position, dragon bone in the south, werewolf eyetooth in the west, and witch athame in the east, all arranged in a circle large enough for two people to stand in.

Once he realizes I'm not going to change my mind, I can feel Hudson watching me with a somber face. But every time I glance up at him, the expression in his eyes is completely unreadable.

After I'm done laying the items out, I light the special candle Macy gave me for just this occasion and put it on the other side of the square, as instructed.

I'm not a witch. I don't have any of Macy's magic in me. But supposedly, that's what these four items are for. Their magic is so strong that I don't need any of my own to make this work.

I'm not sure I believe that, but I guess we'll find out one way or the other soon enough.

I close my eyes, take a deep breath, then step inside the circle— and right away, I know exactly what the Bloodletter was talking about. I can feel something start to happen. I have no idea what it is, but it's definitely something big.

There's a charge in the air, an electric shock that rides the air currents as they glide past me. As they do, every hair on my body stands straight up and my skin starts to tingle. My chest gets tight, my breathing labored, and it feels like I'm going to pass out.

"Get out!" Hudson yells at me, panic evident in his voice. "Get out of the circle!"

But it's too late. I'm not going anywhere—I *can't* go anywhere. The electric current that surrounds me is burning hotter, getting stronger, and the ground beneath my feet starts to vibrate.

There are loud gasps from the crowd, a few screams, and that's when I realize it's not just me who feels it. The ground beneath the whole arena is starting to shake.

I stumble back a little at the knowledge, nearly step outside the circle like Hudson begged me to, but the electric current catches me and refuses to let me escape. Instead, it zaps me and pushes me right back in.

Not going to lie—it scares me a little. I've never felt anything like this in my life, not even down in the tunnels with Lia when she called up that horrible black nastiness that nearly killed Jaxon and me.

But I don't have time to worry about that right now, not when it feels like the entire universe is about to lose its shit all over this place. My knees are turning liquid as the ground goes from trembling to full-on shaking, and I throw my arms out to help get my balance.

"Jaxon?" I call, but there's no answer. Still, I turn to look behind me, convinced he somehow managed to make it in here after all, because I don't know anyone else who can make the earth shake like this.

But the walkway behind me is empty.

There's no one here but me.

The five-minute-warning bell sounds, and I know that I don't have any more time to waste. It's now or never. I turn back around and look down at the circle—only to gasp, because the items are no longer on the ground. Instead, they're hovering about three feet in the air now. Not only that, but they're also glowing and vibrating so violently that I can feel it in the air all around me.

The ground shakes more violently, and I wait for something to happen, wait for Hudson to suddenly be standing in front of me. But I can still feel him in my mind, can hear him bitching at me even now, telling me to stop this madness before it's too late.

Obviously he hasn't gotten with the program, because I knew two minutes ago that it was already too late.

The Bloodletter told me I'd know what to do when the time was right, but I'm still waiting for the knowledge to hit me. All I know right now is that I better get some mystical, magical inspiration soon or this whole stadium is going to shake apart—and take Hudson and me with it.

The items are spinning around me now, circling me like some supernatural Hula-Hoop that needs no interference from me to stay aloft. Again, I rack my brain, trying to figure out what to do and again, I come up with nothing.

At least not until the spinning finally stops and the bloodstone ends up right in front of me, glowing more and more brightly with each second that passes. Ruby red light explodes off it in all directions, razor-sharp shards that slice the world around me into scarlet ribbons that are as beautiful as they are terrifying.

The stone is so close now that I can reach out and touch it, just wrap my hand around it and hold it tight. Keep it safe.

And just that easily, I realize the Bloodletter was right. I know exactly what it is I need to do.

Reaching out, I grab on to the stone, wrapping my hand completely around it. But it's so much sharper than it looks, and the second my fingers touch it, it slices a giant gash right down the center of my palm.

I cry out, pain and fear mingling inside me as I look at the blood dripping from my palm. I must have been wrong. I didn't have a clue what to do and now I've messed up everything. Too bad I have no idea how to fix it.

Figuring the best thing to do right now is to give the bloodstone back to its circle, I start to open my hand. But before I can drop it, the other three items begin to spin around me, whizzing by faster and faster until they blur together.

"Grace!" Hudson cries out, and he's reaching for me even though he's still inside my mind. "Hold on, Grace! Don't let go."

I try, I really do. but I have no idea what I'm supposed to hold on to in a world that's spun wildly out of control. The ground rolls beneath my feet, wind rips through my hair and tangles in my clothes while lightning sizzles along my every nerve ending.

I'm caught in a maelstrom of my own making, and I don't know what I'm supposed to do to make it stop.

And through it all, I hold the bloodstone in my hand, its strangely sharp edges digging into my palm. Drops of my own blood are streaming into the tumult now, and that might be the freakiest thing about this whole experience.

I want to let the stone go, need to let it go, but the voice deep inside me—the Unkillable Beast or something even older, I don't know—keeps telling me to hold on to the stone just a little bit longer. So I do, even as it feels like the world is going mad around me.

And then, just as suddenly as it started, the bloodstone cracks in half and everything stops. The wind, the quake, the electricity, and the spinning magical items, all gone in the blink of an eye.

I feel it then, another wrenching deep inside me. This one is different from what I felt with Jaxon, though. This one feels less like my entire soul is being ripped to shreds and more like something is finally sliding back into place.

I stand frozen for several seconds, unable to move or breathe or even think. But then I realize that it's over, that it's really over, and I close my eyes. Let the bloodstone fall to the ground at my feet. And breathe, just breathe.

Until it hits me that what I'm feeling is emptiness...because Hudson is gone.

111

Talk About a
Power Trip

There's no more sarcastic voice in my head, no watchful presence, nothing but my own thoughts and memories rattling around up there.

He's really gone.

I whirl around, shout, "Hudson—" Then freeze, because there he is, standing right in front of me.

Same Armani trousers and burgundy silk dress shirt.

Same Brit boy hair.

Same brilliant blue eyes.

Only the smile is different—his usual sardonic smirk replaced by a tiny, uncertain twist of his lips.

Oh, and his smell. His smell is new, too. But can I just say, holy hell? How could this guy have lived in my head for all those months and I not have a clue that he smells like this?

Like ginger and sandalwood and warm, inviting amber...and confidence. He smells like confidence.

"Hi, Grace." He gives me the little two-fingered wave he used to do all the time in my head that always exasperated me. Somehow, in person, it's just as bad.

"Hudson. You're..." I trail off, not sure what to say to him now that he's right in front of me.

Now that he's real.

"Listen to me, Grace. There's no more time." He glances behind him, toward the stadium, where the screams have finally died down. We can hear the king over the loudspeaker, trying to get everyone calm and settled. Telling them the Trial will start in two minutes…if Grace Foster bothers to show up.

"I have to go," I tell him, the urgency he'd had all along suddenly beating in my blood.

"I know," he answers. "That's why you need to listen to me. I left my powers inside you so that—"

"You left your powers inside me? Why? How do I get them out?"

"I'll accept them back from you eventually. I'm just loaning them to you for a while. You're a conduit, remember? You channel magic, and I've given you mine to channel for now."

"Loaning them to me?" I look at him like he's got two heads. "What does that even mean?"

The smirk is back, but it's coupled with a tenderness in his eyes that I can't begin to understand. "It means I'm mortal right now."

"What?" Horror explodes through me. "You said we couldn't do that to you. You said it would ruin everything. We decided—"

"Don't worry about what we decided. I know my parents. No way did they make this Trial something you can pass on your own. Remember, they were planning on you and Jaxon, so the Trial would have been close to impossible for the two of you. For you alone…" He shakes his head. "That's why you don't have a choice. You need to take my powers."

"Yeah, but that leaves you vulnerable, right? I mean, if you're mortal, doesn't that mean they can hurt you, too?"

He shrugs. "Don't worry about me. They've already done everything they can to me—especially my father."

He doesn't elaborate and I don't ask—there isn't time—but my heart dies a little bit with the acknowledgment of just how awful his life, and Jaxon's, have been.

"Take them back," I say, reaching for him. "If they find out you're here, and you don't have any powers—"

"They won't find out," he tells me, his British accept crisp with a combination of impatience and urgency. "Besides, you're in much worse peril. Without a mate in there fighting with you, you're going to need all the help you can get. Which is why I hid my powers deep inside you, so that the Council won't know they're there unless they search through all of your memories."

Maybe it's the whirlwind I just went through, but nothing he's saying is making any sense to me right now. "But how? You can't just drop things off in people's memories."

The look he gives me says that maybe I can't, but he certainly can. But all he says is, "When all that magic you just did put me back together, I chose to leave them behind for you, in my favorite memory of yours. It's the one when you were little and your parents were teaching you how to ride a bike. Remember? You fell off and skinned your knee, and your dad told you that it was okay. That you would try again tomorrow."

I nod, because I do remember that memory. It's one of my favorites, too, and I think about it every time I have something hard to do...and every time I miss my parents.

"My mom told him I could do it. She told us both I could do it."

"Yeah, she did. And then she smiled at you and it was so full of love and so full of confidence—"

"That I picked up my bike, dusted the gravel off my knees, and rode all the way home by myself."

"Yes, you did. And she ran along beside you the whole way, just in case." His eyes are soft as he continues. "But you only needed her once."

"Yeah, when I hit a rut in the sidewalk and started to wobble. She grabbed on to the back of my seat and held me steady for a few seconds until I could get control again."

"That's why I hid my powers in her smile. So you'd know that I believe in you, too. That I know you can do this. And while I can't be on that field to catch you if you fall, that doesn't mean I don't have your back."

I don't know what I'm supposed to say to that, what I'm supposed to say to *him*. This is the most selfless thing anyone has ever done for me, and I don't know how to feel about it. "Hudson—"

"Not now," he tells me. "You have to go. But remember, they're there if you need them. Just be careful, because you don't heal like I do, and you don't have the same kind of physical strength to withstand the pressure of them. So you can only use them once or they'll drain you completely. You'll know when you need them. Only once, though." He gives me a searching look. "Got it?"

Not even a little bit. I'm so mixed up inside right now that my brain feels like a box of confetti—lots of individual pieces in a confined space but nothing actually working together. I can't say that, though, so instead I just nod. "Yeah. Got it."

"Good. Now, get out there and show my father exactly what one gargoyle can do."

112

It's High Noon and Justice Doesn't Serve Itself

I reach deep inside myself and start to separate the colored strings as I walk the final steps to the field with my heart in my throat. When the others were in the arena with me, it was no big deal to shift out in the open. But now that I'm alone and everyone is staring at me, it feels uncomfortable.

Still, there's nothing to do but suck it up. So I do, and I shift right out in the open—in front of anyone who wants to look.

Which, it turns out, is *everyone*. I mean, who doesn't want to gawk at the new magical creature?

It's just one more indignity in a long line of indignities I've suffered at the hands of paranormals over the last five months, and I refuse to let it faze me. Especially since people watching me become a gargoyle like they have a right to see it is the least of my problems right now. The biggest? Figuring out how to do this without Jaxon next to me or Hudson in my head.

As I walk up to the gate that leads to the field, I can feel everyone staring at me. Discomfort crawls through me, and I realize how much I've come to depend on Jaxon—and Hudson—in the time I've been at Katmere.

Jaxon acted like he owned the place, so it was easy to just accept people's stares as par for the course. Hudson, on the other hand, basically had a kiss-my-ass attitude that made it a lot harder to care if other people were watching me, just like it made it nearly impossible for me to care what they thought.

But now I'm on my own. No Jaxon to hold my hand, no Hudson to say irreverent things that make me laugh and gasp at the same time. It's just me and a field full of people who all want to see me fail.

Too bad I'm not about to give them that satisfaction.

Closing my eyes, I take a deep breath and pretend for a moment—just a moment—that everything is going to be okay. That somehow I'll step off this field safe and in one piece. It's a good picture, so I put it out into the universe.

Then I square my shoulders and walk straight out to the center of the field, where the king is standing and Cole's team is lined up on one of the now-bloodred lines. Trust the king to change a detail like that...along with a few other ones that have my heart pounding and the dome closing in on me.

The other day, it was bright and cheerful in here, with pennants waving and people cheering and delicious snacks being sold. This morning, it's pretty much the exact opposite. The weather outside has turned everything dark and ominous...or maybe that's just the king's malicious presence. Whatever it is, it's absolutely terrifying to see dark shadows encroaching from every side. Which, I'm pretty sure, is exactly what Cyrus wants.

Chills slide down my spine, and the cold wind whipping through the whole arena with the dome open has fear settling in my stomach like a fifty-pound weight. It drags me down, makes me realize just how impossible a task I've set for myself. Just how impossibly tired I already am.

I want to turn around, want to run away, want to be anywhere but here, doing anything but this.

The feeling is so overwhelming that it all but smothers me as I try desperately to get it under control. But it just grows and grows and grows until I can barely breathe, barely think. As I finally find the strength to start the formidable job of fighting it back, I can't help wondering if the grayness is coming from inside me or if Cyrus has done something to the arena to make me feel like this.

Just the idea that he—or some member of the Circle—is messing with my emotions pisses me off beyond words. And makes me even more determined not to cave to these people. They think they can do whatever they want, that they can run over anyone in their path.

But they aren't running over me. Not anymore.

Besides, they may be pulling this with me now, but if it works, I won't be the only one. If I don't take a stand, if I don't make a point of showing them that they can't do whatever they want to whomever they want, then what's to say they won't do this again? I can't be the only person they're threatened by, can't be the only paranormal the king hates just because of who I am. If I don't stop this, *now*, he'll lock up a lot more people in that dungeon of his before he's through.

So I don't turn around. I don't run away. I don't even falter in my steps as I stride to the center of the field. Instead, I keep walking as I ignore the ominous feelings pressing in on me from all sides. I might very well die in this ridiculous quest today, but if I do, I'm going to die fighting. For now, that's all I can promise myself.

But it's enough. It carries me right up to the king.

Right up to the Circle, who are standing behind Cyrus in a semicircle of support as he whips the crowd into a frenzy.

Right up to the bloodred line that I have to stand on all alone.

I'm not going to lie. It's scary as fuck.

Then again, nearly everything has been scary as fuck since I got to this school, so why not just embrace it?

"Nice of you to join us, Grace," Cyrus says in a voice so barbed, it feels like he's flaying my flesh from my bones. "We were just about ready to give up on you."

"Sorry, I was unavoidably detained," I tell him as I look straight across the field to Cole, who is lined up directly across from me.

Our gazes meet, and the malevolent glee in his makes me
want to scream. But it also gives me the strength I need to not
look away. Because no way am I giving that jerk the satisfaction
of letting him know just how deeply he's hurt me. Just how much
he's torn me apart.

Cyrus looks me over, fake concern on his face as he plays for the
crowd. "Are you all right, Grace? You look like you've had a very
rough start to the day."

"I'm fine."

My answer is dismissive, and for a breath, something flashes in
his eyes: Surprise? Rage? Annoyance? I don't know and, honestly, I
don't care. This is going to go how it's going to go, and everything
else is just window dressing that I don't have the energy to analyze...
or participate in right now.

"Welcome, students and faculty of Katmere Academy, to the
rarest of occurrences—one of *your own* challenging for inclusion on
the Circle. And not just any student, mind you, but the first gargoyle
student Katmere Academy has ever had. It is a truly thrilling and
auspicious day."

Everyone cheers in response, but there's a malicious edge to it that
I wasn't expecting, considering these are the people who cheered for
me and the rest of my team a few short days ago. Then again, maybe
I'm just imagining it—seeing something that isn't there because I'm
so freaked out.

It's lonely out here by myself, lonely in this stadium, when the
last time I was here I had all the support in the world. But right now,
it feels like there's no one in the entire place who is rooting for me.
The lone gargoyle.

Jaxon, Flint, and Eden are injured and awaiting help.

Macy is trying to bring that help.

Mekhi and Gwen are in the infirmary.

Even my uncle Finn was powerless to do much more than clap

for me as I entered the arena.

And Hudson is probably outside, trying to keep a low profile now that he's mortal. Not that I blame him. I have my powers *and* his, and I still wish I was outside...or anywhere else but on this field.

Still, the last thing I want is to spend the rest of my life locked in a dungeon, praying Cyrus won't kill me. There's no one else to do this right now, no one else to challenge Cyrus and Delilah's power. No one else to do what has to be done.

So what I want doesn't matter. Only winning matters, because winning is the sole way I'll be able to stop this mess from unfolding.

Cyrus turns back to the crowd, arms open wide like a carnival barker as he begins to weave them a tale in his very proper British accent.

"The eight of us here"—he turns to look at the members of the Circle behind him—"are very excited to see if she measures up, has what it takes to serve on your ruling body. And I know some of you are probably wondering how this happened, how a girl new to your school and new to our world could possibly be afforded an opportunity like this. Where does Grace Foster get the audacity to believe she deserves to rule?"

The stadium fills with an uneasy silence—and a dark one—as the students and faculty turn to look my way. Again, I can't help feeling like something isn't right. Like there's something more at work here than these people suddenly thrilled at the idea of seeing me taken down.

I mean, I know Jaxon's not my mate anymore. Ostensibly, so does the Circle and all of Cole's team. After all, Cyrus hasn't yet asked me where my partner is for this Trial. But I doubt they announced it to the entire stadium in the time it took me to get in here.

So why do they suddenly hate me so much? What's happened to turn everything so dark? To make it seem like every person in the arena is suddenly against me? And how does Cyrus know to play on it unless he's causing it?

"It's okay," Cyrus continues as the crowd whispers awkwardly among itself. "It's okay to ask yourself these questions. Every member of the Circle certainly has."

He gives his best attempt at a sincere laugh, but it just comes across as creepy. Then again, nearly everything about the man comes across as creepy. I swear, how he managed to father two of the most heroic guys I've ever met, I'll never know.

"But whether it seems strange or not, rules are rules. Challenges are challenges, and we here at the Circle strive to always do the right thing. The rules of inclusion state that anyone who is from a faction with an unfilled seat on the Circle may challenge for inclusion. So we are, on this dark and gloomy day, waiting for the—very late—Grace to prove she is worthy." He laughs again.

"But no matter, no matter. Outsiders can't be expected to know all the rules, can they? Normally, members of the Circle themselves would fight, or choose champions from their armies, but your headmaster Finn Foster has rightly pointed out that we're on school grounds and must abide by the covenant of the school. Therefore, instead of bringing in generals, or sadly watch Grace fall quickly were one of the Circle to enter the Trial, we have agreed to choose our champions from the student body." Cheers go up in the arena as my opponents wave at the stands.

"And since these are but mere students, the magical safeguards against mortal injury have also been instituted—for everyone except Grace, of course." His smile stretches wide and reminds me of an alligator as he delivers this bit of good news.

He thinks by not being able to kill an opponent he's made me weaker—because that's how someone like him *would* think. But actually, he's done me a huge favor. Now that I don't have to worry about killing anyone, I can come full force with every ounce of power I have and not worry about doing something horrible. I offer him a smile even slyer than his own, not even trying to hide the satisfaction crinkling my eyes as Cyrus falters at my reaction.

But he quickly recovers and continues. "In the interest of being as fair as possible"—I give a snort-laugh that would make Hudson proud—"and to ensure that there is no outside interference on either side, Imogen and Linden have shielded the arena.

"The players inside will be able to hear you cheering for them, but none of your powers can get through to them, which guarantees this is a totally fair Trial—for both sides. Rest assured, no one will be allowed to cheat their way onto the Circle."

He pauses and lets that sink in, holding my gaze for a reaction. But again, he thinks he's limiting my chances when he's only further emboldened me now that I don't need to worry his team will cheat. Uncle Finn is the only person left here to cheer for me, and he's certainly not about to help me cheat, so this is no handicap.

I give him, and the whole stadium, a wide smile that has his gaze narrowing and his jaw clenching. But the show must go on, so he forces a condescending smile as he adds, "And no one on the opposing team will be able to get extra help to defeat our little gargoyle, either."

As I stand here, listening to him go on about how magnanimous he is to organize today—like it's not a part of the Circle's fucking charter—I realize for the first time why Hudson originally wanted me to challenge them. Not because he doesn't believe in me. But because he knows there's no way his father is going to give me, or anyone else, a fair chance—all his words to the contrary.

My heart beats wildly at the thought. I mean, I knew walking in here that I might not walk out again. But recognizing just how stacked against me this damn Trial is infuriates me. And only makes me more determined to survive. I just hope I have enough cunning and physical strength left to back up that determination.

"And finally," Cyrus says, the words drawing my attention because it sounds like he is finally tired of hearing his own voice, "to prove the Circle's impartiality regarding the outcome of this test, Grace will start with the ball, giving her a powerful advantage here at the beginning of the Trial."

He waits for Nuri to hold up the ball—which she does with an approving wink to me that seems both sweet and completely out of place in this ever-darkening arena—then turns back to the crowd.

Cyrus lifts his arms in a wide arc that sweeps through the air as he orders, "Let the Trial begin!"

113

A Match Played in Hell

I wasn't expecting to have the ball first—I didn't think Cyrus would give me anything that even resembles an advantage—and as Nuri walks to the center square with it, I start to panic a little because I'm not sure what to do. Jaxon and I would have just continually passed it back and forth (well, unless he'd managed to fade all the way to the end and win immediately like he'd apparently planned), but now that it's just me, that strategy is worthless.

Plus, I figured with two of them jumping for the ball at tip-off, I wouldn't have a chance. So I'd been hoping to let them do some of the initial work as I got to see what a few of the portals might do this time.

Now, though...now I have about fifteen seconds before that ball is in my hands and thirty seconds after that to get rid of it before I start losing pieces of my stone to its out-of-control vibration. Which, now that I think about it, might be exactly what Cyrus had planned—no advantage here after all.

As the fifteen seconds tick by between one long breath and the next, a dozen strategies enter my mind, and I discard them all. I briefly consider using Hudson's gift of persuasion right away—just end this Trial early and walk the ball in. But sadly, the other team is too spread out. I'm not sure how much time I'll have once I tap into his power, but surely not long enough to chase them all down and persuade each to take a nap instead of trying to kill me. I can't even bring myself to consider turning everyone to dust—even if I know the magic of mortal injury will save them. Plus, Hudson's worked so hard to keep that particular gift a secret, convince Cyrus it's dormant, and it's not my right to expose it now.

Other strategies come and go as well. All equally bad. And then it's too late, because the whistle is blowing, and Nuri is throwing the comet straight at me.

I catch it and start to run—there's not much else for me to do at the moment—then realize, not for the first time, that while my gargoyle form does a whole lot for me, one thing it doesn't do is give me speed and maneuverability. So I switch to human on the fly, and just as Cole and Marc close in on me, teeth bared in their werewolf forms, I dive into a portal.

I'm prepared for the stretching feeling, tell myself to just breathe through it. But this portal doesn't feel like that at all. Instead of stretching me out, it feels like I'm being poked with hundreds of thousands of pins all over my body at the same time. Each individual pin doesn't hurt much, but when put altogether, it's excruciating.

Even worse, the ball is getting warmer and warmer in my hands and this portal seems to be taking forever.

I tell myself it's not any longer than the other ones, that I won't go over the thirty seconds, which is the longest I've ever been able to hold the comet, but it's hard to think through the pain of being jabbed a million different times.

Then again, the pain is nothing compared to losing Jaxon and losing my parents, nothing compared to the guilt I feel over Xavier's death or not believing Hudson sooner about his father.

It's nothing, I remind myself, even as every inch of my skin stings. Nothing that matters and nothing that I can't handle. I just need to hold on and breathe.

Finally—*finally*—I start to experience the weird surfacing-through-water feeling that comes with the beginning and end of a portal, and I brace myself to be emptied onto the field.

I manage to land on my feet this time, but I'm still disoriented, because in the small amount of time I was in the portal, the arena has gone dark. Like really, really dark.

The stands are so dark, I can barely see the audience, which makes their shouts and cheers and gasps feel completely disembodied. Even the lights on either end of the field seem to be darker than they were just a few minutes ago.

I tell myself I'm imagining things, but when I look around, I can no longer see all of the field. I can only see the portion around me—at least in my human form—which can only mean Cyrus did this on purpose.

Of course he did.

It's a huge advantage for my opponents, because the wolves, dragons, and vampires can see perfectly in the dark, while I'm stuck squinting and trying to figure out which way I'm supposed to go.

The portal let me out about twenty yards from my goal line, so now I've got one hundred thirty left to go to get across theirs. The stone is burning red-hot in my hands, though, so I do the only thing I can do—I throw the ball as high into the air as I can, then shift on the run and launch myself into the air after it.

The wolves and witches can't get me up here, and the dragons are all the way down the field, blocking their goal line, so it works. I snatch the ball out of the air and start to fly as fast as I can toward the goal, thankful that my gargoyle eyes work slightly better than my human ones do.

I know I'll have to go low eventually—the dragons are racing straight at me as fast as they can, and while their magic doesn't work on me, they can still knock me right out of the sky. They're massive, and the fall is a lot from up here—I'll end up shattered, in human or gargoyle form, for sure.

But as they get closer, I realize one is going low—they obviously learned from the trick I pulled during the Ludares tournament—and the avenue of escape I had planned is cut off from me. The clock on the side of the field says I've got fifteen more seconds before the ball starts to become untouchable again, which means I have to figure this out *now*.

I think about voluntarily turning the ball over to one of them—desperate times and all that—but I can't bring myself to do it. So at the last minute, just when they start a pincher movement to squeeze me in, I shoot straight up, up, up into the air.

The dragons come chasing after me and I let them, bringing them in closer and closer the higher we get. I'm counting on the fact that Joaquin and Delphina have much bigger wings than I do—and are much heavier than I am—which means I should be able to turn around faster than they can. Or, here's hoping, anyway...

Which is why, just as they're about to get me—and just as the ball starts to turn superhot and vibrate—I drop it.

And then, as the crowd gasps and murmurs in surprise, I roll straight into a half somersault and go full-on diving after the ball.

The dragons bellow in rage, and blasts of fire and ice come shooting down after me. But I'm in my gargoyle form, so I barely notice as I race for the ball.

On the ground below me, one of the witches, Violet, tries to cast down the ball, but I get there before she manages to pull it to her. I swoop through her spell, causing her to shout—whether in rage or pain, I don't know—and I scoop the ball up right out of the air again. Then I'm racing, racing, racing for the goal line with the dragons coming up fast behind me.

They're closing in really fast, and though I'm immune to their powers, that doesn't mean I can't feel the brush of warmth as Joaquin's fire sweeps past my leg. Much closer and they won't have to use magic. They'll be able to grab on to one of my feet and send me careening across the sky.

I'm not about to let that happen—not the grabbing on to me and definitely not the "sending me flying" thing. But a superfast glance over my shoulder shows me that pretty soon, I'm not going to have a choice. So I do the only thing I can think of—dart into one of the few midair portals.

As I do, I pray it's not like the last one I entered. A girl can only take so many things going to shit around her at any given time, and I pretty much feel like I'm at my quota right now. Just saying.

Turns out it's not at all like the last one I entered—it's so much worse that I kind of want to cry.

I don't even know what to think about this one, except to say that whoever thought it up was pure evil. Brilliant, yes, but also completely evil.

Something about the gravity is all messed up, and I end up freefalling through the portal while also spinning head over heels. With each spin, the top of my head and the back of my heels scrape against the walls of the portal and I get an electric shock every single time. It's really, really not fun.

Even worse, from the scream I hear not too far behind me, at least one of the dragons chose to follow me into the portal and whoever it is is pissed. Then again, they're so big, they must be scraping against the sides of the portal the whole time. I'm having trouble feeling sorry for them, but I wouldn't wish that kind of shock/electrocution on anyone.

I try to take a guess at where we're going to come out—and how I'm going to gain control enough to keep flying when we do—all while holding on to a ball that's starting to vibrate hard again. And can I just say, it's beginning to feel like overkill... Bad enough that I've got eight homicidal paranormals on my ass. I need to also have a ball that's sole purpose seems to be to break me apart? I know Flint and Jaxon love Ludares, but I'm pretty sure it might be the worst. Game. Ever.

The portal finally ends, throwing me out into the near pitch black... and, I realize with horror, on *top* of someone.

What the hell? Afraid I landed on one of the werewolves, I start to push away, but then I realize I'm hearing human screams. And not one or two but several of them…all up close and personal.

Which means… I look around desperately, trying to get my bearings and find the goal at the same time, only to realize that I'm *not even on the field anymore.* This freaking defective portal dropped me off directly in the middle of the audience. Which means… Oh shit.

We're about to get squashed.

"You need to move!" I shout. "Move now!"

Then I take off, flying right over my classmates' heads even as I hope that they listen, that they manage to get out before… All kinds of screams ensue as Joaquin slides out of the portal and right into—and on top of—the crowd.

A glance behind me shows that Delphina follows right after him, belching ice, and the two of them manage to take out a whole section of arena seats—and the people sitting in them. Cyrus yells for order, and several teachers and Circle members race for the area, hoping to sort out the melee.

I make sure no one is seriously injured then take advantage of the ensuing chaos to toss the ball high enough in the air to reset it, then catch it again as I race back down toward the field. I'm in my gargoyle form, so despite the darkness, I can see well enough to figure out that I'm not that far from their goal line. I lay on the speed, heading toward that damn red line with every ounce of energy I can muster. I've got thirty seconds to get close to my goal and maybe, just maybe, figure out one more way to reset the ball without chancing losing it when I'm this close to the end. Now if everyone else on the field would also cooperate, I would really appreciate it.

But the upper balcony seats jut out over the field in this section, so I have to fly low in order to clear them. I do my best, dipping down and bringing my wings in low and close to my body as I make a beeline for the end. As long as the dragons remain tangled up with the spectators, I have a real chance.

I end up hitting the field about twenty feet from the goal line with the most intense tunnel vision of my life. I know things are going on behind me and around me, but I don't care right now. If they were seriously injured, or about to be, the magic of the game would pull them out anyway. All I care about is getting to that damn goal line before the dragons—or anything else—catches me.

And if I could do it before my hands literally shake off my body from the ball vibrating so intensely, that would be great, too. But I'm low to the ground now, too low, so I start to climb up again as fast as possible.

I don't make it. Quinn comes out of nowhere, in werewolf form, slamming into me so hard that he sends me careering into the ground.

It doesn't hurt—the stone keeps me from feeling too much—but the lack of pain doesn't change the fact that I'm on the ground with a wolf standing directly above me, snarling like I'm about to be his next meal.

He wants the ball—I know he wants the ball—but I'm not planning on giving it to him. At least not if I can help it. Instead, I grab on to the comet with one hand, then pull back my other hand and punch him in the nose as hard as I can with my stone fist.

He screams and rears back, blood spurting out of his nose, and I take the opportunity to roll over and start army crawling away, but the ball is vibrating so badly that it's almost impossible to hold on to it like this.

I manage it, though, and stumble to my feet at as close to a run as I can manage. I shift on the fly, going back to my human form so I can run faster. I'm so close, the goal line is only twenty feet in front of me, and I'm almost there, almost there. Back in human form, the burn from the comet is moving quickly from painful to agonizing, but if I can just hold on another few seconds—

Out of what feels like nowhere, Cam (Macy's right, he *is* a fucking traitor) hits me with some kind of earth spell, and vines shoot up from the field and wrap themselves around my ankles and legs. I go down hard and take the ball with me.

It's burning hot now, and when I fall on top of it, I can feel it branding me through my shirt. Can feel painful blisters starting to form. The pain is too much, and I gasp, roll off the ball, and just that easily, Macy's soon-to-be-ex-friend Simone swoops in.

She picks up the ball and takes off running full tilt for the goal.

114

Fake It Till You Break It

I jump to my feet, shifting into my gargoyle form as I do, so that the vines are ripped apart by my larger stone size. But I'm way behind Simone, and I'm terrified I won't be able to catch her before she tosses the comet to a teammate and I never catch up.

I launch myself into the air, and briefly I think about tapping into Hudson's powers. But he said I can do it only once, and to make sure that when I do, it's to win, because it will totally wipe me out.

I'm not there yet—I'm currently about as far from winning as I was at the beginning of the game, maybe even further—but if I don't catch Simone right now, it won't matter if I save Hudson's power for later because I will have already lost.

Desperate not to let that happen, I fly faster, determined to use the power if I really, really have to. One of the dragons—Joaquin, I'm pretty sure—passes Simone going in the opposite direction and heads straight for me, fire blazing and talons out.

I don't have time for him or his shit right now. Too bad he doesn't feel the same way about me.

He's heading straight for me like I'm personally responsible for whatever pain and humiliation he suffered coming out of the portal earlier, and he's looking for payback.

Also something I don't have time for at the moment.

But this is the path Simone is running, so this is the one I have to stay on—which means I can't afford to duck or change course or do anything at all but what I'm doing.

So I do exactly that, even though it means flying straight at Joaquin.

You know, if anyone had told me six months ago that I'd be playing a supernatural game of chicken with a dragon, I would have suggested they stop smoking whatever it was they were smoking. But six months makes a huge difference in this world—hell, at Katmere Academy, six *minutes* makes a huge difference—and I can't afford to blink. Not now. Not this time.

So I stay the course, no matter how scared I am.

No matter how fast my heart is pounding.

No matter how loudly my brain is screaming for me to stop, to go back, to turn around because there's no way I can win in a collision with a two-thousand-pound dragon.

But I *have* to win—this collision and this game. Which means there's no way I'm backing down now.

A quick glance at the field shows me that Simone has passed the ball off to Cam, who is now running for the goal even faster, with the wolves quickly approaching to flank him on either side. I have no idea where the other dragon is—and I try not to let that fear distract me—because I've almost caught up with Cam, and I need to get this giant freaking other dragon the hell out of my way.

So I'm just going to have to count on beating the warlock to the goal line and keeping the ball in play.

How I'm going to do that is another matter altogether, though. Especially since there's only one way I can think of to do that while we're both thirty feet off the ground—and it's pretty goddamn awful.

I know everyone on the ground thinks I'm out of my mind. I know they're convinced I'm about to die right here in midair, and maybe they're right. But times don't get much more desperate than this, so I aim for the dragon and brace myself for impact.

I let myself wonder briefly about not surviving the upcoming crush. And if I'm really willing to take that chance.

But the truth is, if I don't take that chance—if I don't fight this fight and win—I won't survive anyway. Besides, I'd rather die fighting for what I believe in than live as the victim of somebody else's whims—especially if that person is as evil as Cyrus.

There's no way I want to spend the rest of my very long life being Cyrus's prisoner or personal gargoyle-for-hire.

That being said, I don't actually *want* to die. And so I lay on the speed, using every ounce of strength and energy I have to go faster, faster, faster. Joaquin is still coming at me, but I can tell from the way he's flying that he's convinced I'm going to chicken out at the last minute. Convinced that there's no way I'm going to actually let myself get into a giant collision with a *dragon*.

But he's wrong, way wrong. And his mistaken conviction means I have an advantage. Right now, it's a small advantage, but I'm willing to take anything I can get. Which is why, as the dragon bears down on me, wings spread wide and flames shooting out of his mouth, I do the only thing I can do.

I veer just a couple of inches to the right and clench both my hands into fists as I straighten my arms out directly in front of me and tuck in my own wings…and then I punch a giant hole in the center of his wing and fly right through it.

Joaquin screams in agony and starts spinning out as he plummets to the ground, unable to do anything but fall with his broken, torn-up wing. I feel bad—of course I do—but an injured wing is totally fixable, especially with Marise in charge of the infirmary.

A gargoyle's lifetime chained up in a dungeon? Not so much.

Leaving half the Circle to run wild, power hungry and unchecked, throughout the paranormal world? Double not so much.

I vaguely notice Joaquin magically disappears from the sky just before he hits the ground, likely teleported to the infirmary. Either way, they're down a player, and that can only be good news for me.

The crowd is shouting now—at me or for me, I don't know or particularly care—but I don't take so much as a second to glance over at them.

Instead, I do a backward corkscrew and deep dive toward the ground as Cam closes in on the goal. No way is Macy's scummy ex getting that ball over the line. No freaking way.

Except Cole is there, too, waiting to take me out if I get too close to Cam—or if he can think of another reason to do it. But I haven't come this far to lose to some mangy dog with a God complex, even if he is in human form, so instead of moving in front of Cam to stop him, I take him from behind—with a well-placed kick to the back of his knee.

He cries out and starts to fall, bobbling the ball in the process—which is exactly what I've been waiting for. I snatch the ball out of midair and somersault backward, planning to take to the air a second time. With one of the dragons down, my odds just got a whole lot better in the sky.

But before I can get more than a couple of feet off the ground, Cole leaps at me. I'm not fast enough to get away, and he manages to twist his arms around my waist as he tries to wrestle me to the ground.

I fight him the whole way—the gargoyle's stone way more effective than my human body would be in this situation—but before I can land one really good punch, we're falling straight into another goddamn portal.

This portal is narrow and fast—so narrow that my wings are scraping hard against the sides of it and so fast that it's actually crumbling the edges of them. Terrified I won't be able to fly if I lose too much of my wings right now—the info from the library said gargoyles can regenerate certain things but it doesn't happen instantly—I do the only thing I can think of to do. I shift back to my human form.

But that's no better, because I'm still in this portal with Cole and the ball, and while I'm trying desperately to get my hands on the comet, Cole is trying desperately to get his hands on me. I start crawling away from him, using his own body as my ground, arms stretched in front of me as I try to grasp the ball that's spinning along in front of us. But Cole has a different idea, and he grabs on to the back of my pants and pulls me straight back toward him, even as I claw at the icy portal in front of me.

He finally manages to get me turned over and then wraps his hands around my neck and starts to squeeze.

115

He Totally
Deserved That

Panic fills me—wild, overwhelming, desperate—as I realize this isn't about the ball. It isn't about the game or even about the Circle itself. This is about Cole and how much he despises me. More proof—if there was any doubt—that Cole has never given a damn about the Trial. He only cares about hurting me.

Which makes him a million times more dangerous.

Get up! the voice deep inside me says. *Get him off. He'll kill you.*

I want to shoot back, *Thanks, Captain Obvious*, but the beast doesn't deserve my snark. He's just trying to help.

My hands are on top of Cole's now, my nails scoring his skin as I try to pry his fingers from around my throat. But he's a werewolf, with werewolf strength, and I can't get him off me no matter what I do.

And I do a lot.

I twist and buck and kick and claw and try to roll over, anything to make him let go, anything to dislodge his grip for even a second, but he doesn't budge.

Suddenly, I sense the weird feeling again, the one that says we're about to exit the portal, and I brace myself for my one chance to run, to get away.

But even as the portal empties us onto the field, shooting us out, Cole's fingers don't dislodge.

We hit the ground fast and hard, and Cole grunts in pain. I take that one split second of inattention and try to run with it, body bucking wildly even as I reach for the platinum string inside me.

If I can change back to my gargoyle form, I can end this right now—he can't strangle stone, after all—but no matter how hard I try, I can't do it. Keeping Cole from tightening his fingers and crushing my windpipe is taking every ounce of energy and focus I have. Grabbing on to the platinum string takes concentration and precision, and I've got neither going on right now.

Suddenly, the ball flies out of the portal, too, smacking Cole in the side of the face. He doesn't so much as flinch. To be honest, I'm not even sure he knows it hit him—once again reinforcing the idea that this Trial doesn't mean shit to him.

Get up now! the Unkillable Beast orders me again.

I'm trying, I really am. But I can't catch my breath, and I can barely think. Everything is going gray and cloudy inside my head.

There's a part of me that knows Cam just ran by and scooped up the ball, so I have a fleeting thought that I've already lost this game.

And then another fleeting thought about how fucked-up everything is if that's what I'm worried about right now, when death seems a much more imminent concern.

Desperate, I try to reach for Hudson's power—pretty sure now's the time to use it—but I can't unlock it, can't focus without oxygen to sift through the memories enough to find the one where he left—

"Grace!" Hudson's shout echoes across the field. "Get up! Get away from him, now!"

I want to, I really want to, but I can't. The darkness is coming over me, swallowing me whole, and I'm fading, fading, fad—

But before I do, I turn my head just a little to get a glimpse of Hudson, and that's when I see them—Macy and Jaxon and Hudson on the sidelines of an arena gone silent with shaken spectators.

Macy is standing by the fence that separates the field from the stands, screaming at the Circle.

Jaxon still looks half dead, but he's got murder in his eyes as he rests both hands on the magical wall. He's sending quakes of energy to unseat Cole, but the witch's magic is holding and he's only shaking the spectators instead.

And Hudson… Hudson is laser focused on me. His eyes are pinned to my face with an intensity that makes it impossible not to feel him and imagine him still in my head.

"Get that bloody wanker off you, Grace!" he orders me.

I don't know if it's the Britishism or the intensity of his voice, but suddenly it feels like he's inside my head again instead of all the way across the stadium. Snarking at me to stand on my own two feet, telling me I'm a badass, that I'm stronger than I think. Pushing me to try again, to reach inside me for my platinum string. And this time, even though I know it's too far, that I don't have the strength to grab it, I strain my fingers just enough to brush against its soft glow.

And with my last ounce of breath, I shift my knee into solid stone—and shove it straight into Cole's balls.

He yelps like a kicked puppy, and I'm not going to lie, a part of me is disappointed he doesn't disappear instantly from a mortal injury. I'll just have to comfort myself with the image of him limping for a bit, and regardless, his hands are no longer around my throat as he falls over to cup his injured flesh, and I can finally, finally breathe.

I roll onto my hands and knees, coughing my head off as I suck air into my oxygen-deprived lungs. I tell myself I need to get up, I need to keep moving, but there's a part of me that knows it's already too late.

Cam picked up the ball what seems like a lifetime ago. He's won.

116

Death By Ice Cube Is No Way to Start an Obituary

But as I look around, my gaze slowly coming into focus, I realize not only has Cam not run down the field to the goal—their entire team is standing still. And staring at me.

If I'd hazard a guess, I'd think they were enjoying watching Cole choke me to death. Bastards. But now they're staring openmouthed as Cole writhes around on the ground holding his hopefully busted junk, not sure what to do next.

Luckily, I have no such issues.

With every ounce of energy I can muster, I jump forward and shift, flying straight at Cam, my stone foot swinging under my body to connect with his to knock the comet free. But I needn't have bothered, because as my foot draws near, he drops the ball and covers his privates. I was aiming for his chin, but whatever.

I swoop down and snag the ball before anyone else.

I've been playing defense since I got the ball at the very first second of the game, trying to figure out how to stay away from all the people I'm playing against instead of trying to figure out how to beat them.

But that stops right now.

Because there is no way in hell I'm putting myself in another position like the one I was just in. No way Cole is ever going to get his supernaturally strong werewolf fingers around any part of my anatomy *ever* again.

It's time to even the playing field, and I'm just the gargoyle to do it.

My throat is still killing me, though, which makes it a lot harder to breathe than it should. Especially with a giant blue dragon on my ass, as Delphina was quick to recover from my snatch-and-grab and is already in the air, hot on my tail.

Delphina is faster than I am, and now she's shooting solid chunks of ice my way—and while I may be immune to magic, I am not immune to a ten-pound block of ice slamming into my legs at incredible speeds. Gargoyles still shatter, after all.

And I like my legs exactly where they are...

Which means I have to do a whole lot of zigzagging and even more bobbing and weaving as I fly down the field. With this ridiculous ball vibrating more and more in my hands every second.

No freaking problem.

But there's nothing like a near-death experience to keep a girl on her toes, so I just channel my inner snowboarder and try a whole lot of tricks I've never done before. Most of them turn out okay—I mean, it's definitely function over form here, but the crowd doesn't seem to mind, finally sounding like they're on my side.

Especially when a giant piece of ice goes whizzing right by my head. Thank God. Death by ice cube is no heading for an obituary.

And not going to lie, Jaxon, Hudson, and Macy being here helps a lot. I didn't know quite how alone I felt until I saw them standing there, trying to save me. Outraged on my behalf and cheering me on. Even if they couldn't reach me, their wanting to made all the difference. It gave me the third wind I didn't even know I was looking for.

I glance behind me as I race, race, race toward my goal. I know I'm not going to make it, though—it's still too far away—which means I need another plan. I just wish I knew what it was.

My normal throwing the ball or dropping the ball isn't going to work here, not with Delphina on my ass, just waiting so she can scoop it up and get back down the field with it. So instead of just letting it go, I grit my teeth and do a deep vertical dive down, down, down until I'm right next to Violet and Simone.

Then I drop the ball right into Violet's hands.

She shrieks with surprise and takes off running, just like I anticipated. Simone, on the other hand, turns on me with an air spell, whipping the wind into a frenzy and sending it straight at me like a heat-seeking tornado that chases me right back down the field.

It's moving fast—faster than I am, in fact—and it overtakes me a couple of times. Being caught in it feels like being stuck in a vortex, one that sucks away all the oxygen. And since I've already done the not-breathing thing tonight, I'm pretty much over it.

Still, I think I can use it if I play my cards right, so I don't put too much effort into losing the tornado. Instead, I hold it close as I keep time with Violet, waiting for her to make the handoff to one of her teammates. It's going to be Cam or Quinn—they're the only ones really close to her—and I'd be lying if I said I was broken up at the idea of going head-to-head with either of those jerks.

As her time runs down, I slow just enough to lull her into a false sense of security, but to do that means letting Simone's tornado catch up to me. So I do, taking a deep breath right before it overtakes me and holding it and holding it and holding it, even as the vortex spins around me.

Sure enough, Violet makes the handoff to Quinn, and I dive straight toward him. I'm going to get that ball back, and I'm going to shove this tornado down one of their throats while I'm at it.

Quinn is totally unprepared for the ambush—for me or for the tornado—and he bobbles the ball at the first gust of wind. And that's when I snatch it away from him and fly right out of the wind and into the nearest portal—leaving the rest of them behind to deal with the tornado.

I take my first deep breath in what feels like hours but is probably only about fifteen seconds. And then swear under my breath when

I realize I've wandered into the stretchy portal—the one from the very first game.

It's a million times better than being stuck with pins over and over again, but holding on to the ball is a big challenge. So is landing on my feet when I finally get dumped back on the field.

Still, I don't have time to waste—Cole will be out for blood now. So with him and Delphina on my ass, I'm really going to have to be on my game.

Unless I'm lucky, of course, and I finally picked a portal that empties me out near my own goal line. Then again, nothing about today has felt particularly lucky to me, so I'm not counting on it.

Besides, I totally wouldn't put it past Cyrus to make sure that all the portals emptied as far from my goal line as they could get—for no other reason than to make this as difficult for me as possible.

The weird vacuum feeling finally hits me, and I brace myself for hitting the field. Which I do, shoulder-first.

It jolts me but doesn't hurt—stone for the win—and I jump up as fast as I can.

But it's still not fast enough, because Marc is only a couple of steps away in his werewolf form, and one look at his eyes tells me he's here to avenge his alpha.

Maybe that's why I get so angry when he compounds that first assault by chomping down on my ball-carrying arm as hard as he can. It doesn't hurt—again, stone—but hearing his teeth scrape against me riles me an irrational amount.

So when he starts trying to drag me down the field again, I decide I've had enough of this shit. And I whirl around, punching him in his ugly wolf snout with my other fist. He whimpers but doesn't let go, his jaws turning into a vise on my arm.

Which only pisses me off more, so this time when I hit him I don't pull my punches. I use every ounce of strength I can muster as I lash out with my stone fist and hit him on the side of his head as hard as I can. And then I hit him again.

Third time's the charm as he finally, finally lets go, and I roll away from him. But a quick look back shows me that while he's shaking his head, he's planning on coming after me again. And I just can't have that.

I'm beyond exhausted, and there's no way I'm going to be able to keep going like this—having one after another after another steal back any progress that I've gained. This game is rough when you're playing eight on eight. When you're playing one on eight—or even one on seven—it's absolutely brutal.

Plus, each shift I make—gargoyle to human and back again—takes a little more out of me. As does being strangled by a superstrong were-jackass for nearly a minute...

All of which means I'm going to have to start taking out more of the competition if I have any hope at all of getting across that goal line. And I have more than hope. I have resolve. I've decided there is no way I am losing to that asshole Cole. No fucking way.

So the second that Marc lunges a little drunkenly my way, I decide it's time to even the odds. I protect the ball with one side of my body and then use the other to slam into him with a full-on roundhouse kick to the side of the face—thank you very much, miserable kickboxing class that Heather made me take with her sophomore year.

He yelps but still keeps coming—turns out wolves have very hard heads—so I hit him with another, even harder one, and then swing around to deliver another kick...but this time he doesn't just go down, he magically disappears. I swallow back the nausea as I realize if my next kick had connected, it could have been a mortal blow.

But now I've got even bigger problems. The ten seconds I spent taking Marc out of the game caused two new issues.

One, the ball is vibrating so much that it's about to take me apart.

And two, Cole is headed straight for me, and I gave him the time to catch up.

117

Raining Cats
and Dragons

Part of me is tempted to stay right here and let him take his best shot at me, but I've got more urgent things to do right now— namely, reset the ball.

So that's what I do, tossing it as high into the air as I can manage and then shooting up after it, about two seconds before Cole gets to where I'm standing. He makes a huge leap for me and his fingers brush against the bottom of my feet, but I'm already flying higher and he can't grab on.

Too bad the same thing can't be said for Delphina, who looks about as done playing as I am.

I'm almost to the ball, but she gets there a second before I do and uses her powerful tail to knock it all the way down the field—back toward the goal line I need to protect. Of course.

I zip off after it, already knowing I'm going to be too late and I'll have to wrestle it away from someone else. But I'm back to dodging giant blocks of ice, so for the moment, I've got other things on my mind—mainly how not to be the prize in my very own midair shooting gallery.

I do a pretty good job of it, mostly by doing more of the death-defying flips and turns I didn't even know I had in me before half an hour ago. But Delphina's getting better at shooting on the fly, and she catches me with a huge block of ice to the hip, which sends me spinning out of control as pain explodes along that side of my body.

I plummet downward in a flat-out spin. My brain is screaming at me to pull up, to get moving, to go, go, go, but gravity, aerodynamics, and exhaustion make a deadly combination. So in the end, I do what my driving instructor taught me to do when skidding out in a car. Instead of fighting to pull out of the spin, I turn into it.

Apparently, it's the right move, because it changes everything. I get control in a couple of seconds, and then I'm flying down the field, straight at Cam, who has cotton in his nose, blood on his shirt, and the ball clutched in his ham-fisted hands.

My hip is killing me, but that doesn't matter at this point. Nothing does but stopping Cam before he hands the ball off to Cole—because I know Cole is going to want to be the one to bring it across the goal line—and end the game.

Except either Cam is getting smarter or one of the witches is, because as I barrel down the field toward him, none of them tries to use a spell on me. Instead, they use a spell on *him*...and he effing disappears halfway down the field.

What the hell am I supposed to do with that?

I've got no time—*no* time—but the only thing I've got going for me is he doesn't have that much time, either. In fifteen seconds or so, he's going to have to toss that ball to someone else—invisible or not.

But I don't want to wait that long. Every second he runs is an extra several feet he gets toward the goal line. And that is not something I can let happen.

Glancing around, I'm desperate for an idea when one suddenly hits me. It's nothing I've ever done before. But then again, I've never before done 95 percent of the things I've done in the last twenty-four hours.

Is it a long shot? Yeah. Does that matter? At this point, not even a little bit.

I want to land, but I know better than to put myself down where

Cole might be able to get me. So I stay in the air and start looking for the ice Delphina's been shooting since we got into this hell-arena. There are hundreds of chunks scattered around the field, and I'm going to use them all.

Or at least, that's the plan.

Most of the books Amka laid out for me in the library really didn't shed much light on what gargoyles can do, but there's one thing they all mentioned... Gargoyles are naturally adept at channeling water—supposedly it's why, for centuries, so many buildings used decorative sculptures of us as water spouts. I don't know if any of that's true or not—and neither did Jaxon or Hudson, since I'm the first gargoyle they've ever met—but I'm going to operate on the idea that it's true.

And probably lose this game if it's not.

But I'm not going to think about that right now. I'm not going to think about anything but getting that ice to work for me. And so I start to focus on pulling the water to me. Just like I channeled magic into Jaxon through the mating bond or Hudson's magic to light candles, I let the energy build in me. Feel its purpose as it courses through my body, drawing it into my hand.

Once I can feel the ball of energy burning brightly in my palm, I clench my fist on it, draw it back in. And then I pull, pull, pull, pull the ice toward me, melting it into water even as it flies through the air. And it *does* fly. All of it. And no one is more amazed than I am.

It's an amazing thing to see, these giant blocks of ice flying at me from all over the field and melting into funnels of water in midair. But the one thing I didn't account for—the one thing that makes this even cooler *and* more terrifying—is the fact that there is a *lot* of water in the air.

And I am pulling it *all* toward me.

Suddenly my funnels become one giant wall of water moving down the field, and I've never seen anything like it. Judging from the way the audience is reacting—screaming and stomping their feet—neither have they.

I want to look for my people—for Hudson and Jaxon and Macy—and see what they think of what's going on. But I'm terrified of breaking my concentration, of what will happen if I drop my focus for even half a second.

I also don't have the time. I need to find Cam before it's too late.

Not going to lie, I'm freaking out a little bit, but I figure it's now or never. So I take a deep breath, gather all the water into my hold, and then throw it straight down the field at where I think Cam is.

Sure enough, as it falls, it falls around him, not through him, and that's enough to show me where he is—only about forty yards from the goal line.

I take off after him, flying at absolutely top speed, and still I don't know if I'll get to him in time. So I pool the water back together and create a giant wave of water...and bring it crashing down on him, Violet, and Quinn—all of whom are on that part of the field. And as the wave starts to dissipate, I pull the water back and, with a spin of my wrist, turn it into a whirlpool to trap them all.

Cam turns visible again somewhere in the middle of my whole water attack, but he no longer has the ball. None of them does, and I strain my eyes, trying to find it before someone else can.

I finally spy it resting near the bottom of the whirlpool. I was planning on letting them go after a few seconds, but I can't do that now. Not when they're so close to the ball and the goal line.

A quick glance around shows me that Cole and Simone have spotted the ball and are racing for it—even as Delphina is diving to intercept me. Keeping the whirlpool going is taking a lot of my energy, and I'm running out of ideas.

I have no choice but to try to get to the ball first.

Luckily, I grab it right before Cole, which gives me the lovely side benefit of being able to kick him in the stomach as I launch myself back into the air.

I've got to say, for someone who's always prided herself on being nonviolent, these last few punches and kicks have made me entirely too happy. Then again, payback's a bitch, and I've had just about enough of being poor, weak little Grace.

It's time everyone on this field—everyone in this paranormal world—figured out that I'm not fair game anymore. And that I don't need to hide behind Jaxon, either.

My gaze narrows on the finish line as I race toward my goal. Excitement burns in my chest as I realize I'm going to make it. I'm flying with every last ounce of energy I can muster, and as my goal gets closer and closer, I can't help the elation bubbling in my chest. I'm actually going to make it.

I've barely got anything left in me now, so I have to drop the whirlpool keeping Violet, Quinn, and Cam out of my hair.

But it doesn't matter. I'm only twenty feet from my goal, and they're all too far behind to catch me. As long as Cole hasn't suddenly learned to fly, I've done it. I've actually done it.

I've mentally celebrated no more than five seconds, though, before I realize I've made a giant strategic error.

I lost track of Delphina.

And she's a lot closer than I thought, blindsiding me just as I stretch out for my flight to the goal line.

She hits me full-on in the side with all her strength and velocity, and it knocks me out of the air. Even worse, I hear—and feel—the stone of my wing crack.

118

Stop Dragon my Wings Around

I manage to hold on to the comet for no other reason than I'm in such agony, every muscle in my body is contracting in an effort to protect the rest of me from further pain.

And this time when I plummet to the ground, I can't do anything about it but scream.

My right wing is obviously cracked—I haven't seen it yet, but the trauma has me almost blacking out—and I can't fly straight, no matter how hard I try. I can't fly at all, to be honest, and my only hope of not shattering when I hit the ground is gliding my way down on air currents. Quickly.

It's not easy and it's not pretty but it works, and that's all that matters. But thirty seconds have passed by the time I'm on the ground, and I have to get rid of the ball or the vibrations will nearly destroy me. Again.

I think back to Nuri holding the comet for five minutes before Ludares kicked off, and I'm in awe of her. Thirty seconds for me, and I would sell my soul to set it down right now.

I throw it up in the air and pray—just this once—for a small break. I can't fly anymore, so if Delphina gets it, I'm totally screwed. Then again, I'm probably screwed anyway, considering I'm now stuck on the ground with Cole, who's barreling toward me like the hounds of hell are after him.

Delphina doesn't get it, which is surprising. Then again, the way she's flying around in wavering circles at the moment hints at the idea that that last hit was as hard on her brain as it was on the rest of me. On a different day, with a different Trial, that might make me sad. Right now, I'm just glad it means she's out of commission for a few seconds.

Cole's racing straight at me—and the ball—in werewolf form, and I'm closer and know if I run, I might just beat him to it. So I change to my human form on the fly and race for the ball.

I manage to snatch it right out of Cole's open jaws. I hit the ground running, but a quick look behind me shows that not only is Cole hot on my heels, so is everyone else...except Delphina, who is still doing her best impression of a cuckoo clock.

But Quinn, Violet, and Cam have finally managed to find their way out of the whirlpool I left them in and are now chasing me like their entire reputation depends on bringing me down.

That may be true, but my entire *life* depends on me not letting them, so I put everything I've got on the line. I grit my teeth as I pass thirty seconds with the comet. The ball is so hot that it feels like I'm burning the skin right off my hands. But I can't get rid of it, can't give it away any more, either. My energy is flagging, I'm bruised, battered, broken, and I don't have much more fight in me.

This is it—I know it is. I can feel it in my bones, can feel it in every part of me. This is my shot to win, and if I don't take it now, then it's probably never going to come around again.

Which means I'm not giving up this ball, no matter how much it hurts. No matter how much I have to sacrifice to hold on to it.

And I run.

When I'm about ten yards from the goal line, I glance behind me—not the least bit surprised to see six pissed-off paranormals barreling down the field after me. Lucky me, it looks like the birdies have finally stopped circling Delphina's head because she is back in the game as well.

Which means, winning this thing just got much, much harder.

I'm so close.

But so is Cole.

I need to shift back into a gargoyle so the sadistic fuck doesn't kill me with his sharp teeth or claws. But what if my wing is so damaged, the pain causes me to falter? Even a second's delay is all Cole needs to have me in his powerful grasp.

I'd read in one book that shifting can cause some shifters to heal or partially heal as the magic transforms their body, not physiology. So there's a chance, a very, very small chance, that shifting could actually give me an advantage against Cole, too—I could get my flight back.

And so I decide to risk it. I shift.

I almost pass out with relief as I realize my wing has healed itself, and I launch into the air. It's not the best liftoff, as the comet is now so painful, tears are leaking down the sides of my stone face. But I'm only five yards from the finish line and flying.

119

Gargoyle Girls Do It with Grace

I barely make it a few feet before I feel something score my back, and the pain is excruciating.

Sharp talons wrap all the way around my arm, then sling me toward the ground with such force that it's impossible for me to right myself.

The ground rises up to meet me as my stone body slams into the earth, the comet trapped beneath one of my arms. My head is turned toward my goal, and I almost weep when I realize I'm only a few yards away. So close.

Even if I could move, which I most definitely can't, Violet sends vines from the ground to wrap around my arms and legs, pressing me farther into the earth—and the comet that's now vibrating so fast and hot, it's a constant mind-numbing pain.

I can vaguely hear the stadium erupt in noise, but I have no idea if they want to call a halt to the Trial or see me punished by death for daring to question the sanctity of their beloved Circle.

Simone snarls at me, goes to try to pry the ball from under my body, but Cole just laughs. "Don't worry about taking it," he tells her as he nods to the clock at the side of the field. "She's going on forty-five seconds now. She'll forfeit when it kills her."

He turns to me, the malevolent glint in his eyes growing more evil with every second that passes. "It has to be excruciating, right, Grace? Why don't you just let the ball go? Everything will be easier if you just give up."

"Fuck you," I tell him. "I wouldn't give you the satisfaction."

He grins. "I was hoping you'd say that." And then he punches me full in the face.

The rest of them take the punch to mean it's open season, and they leap on me. Quinn—now in human form—grabs on to my free arm and starts to yank it back, back, back until it feels like it's going to snap right off.

Delphina slams her tail into my face, and blood gushes down the back of my throat, choking me. I didn't even know I could bleed in gargoyle form, so thanks for that lesson.

Cam kicks me in the side and yells, "Payback's a bitch."

And Cole, Cole walks over to one of the straight, heavy rods the game uses as goalposts and uses his wolf strength to yank it right out of the ground.

I try to find a way to protect myself from a blow that can actually shatter me. I think about changing back to human form, but if I do that, a hit from Cole wielding that goalpost will kill human me.

I'm trapped, blows raining down on me, and I try to find the memory of my mother's smile, try to find Hudson's power, but I can't. I can't focus on anything except the next punishing blow to my body, the ball ripping me apart atom by atom now.

I can feel my eyesight grow dim, and I know I'm going to die.

And this time no one can save me, not even myself.

And still I don't regret coming to Katmere. I could never regret anything that brought Jaxon into my life. And Hudson. And Macy and Flint and Eden and Mekhi and Gwen and Uncle Finn and even poor, poor Xavier. My friends. My family.

My only regret is that my parents didn't live to see the life I've made for myself here. They would have loved my people as much as I do. My father would have loved Jaxon's protectiveness and Flint's ridiculous sense of humor. My mother would have loved Macy's sassiness and how often Hudson pushes me to stand up for myself.

It's as I remember my mother, my laughing, smiling mother, that an image shimmers before me, so clear that I can almost reach out and touch it.

My knees. My knees hurt so much. Scraped so badly by the concrete that a few trickles of blood are running down my leg and seeping into my pretty pink socks. Tears are falling down my cheeks now as I ask my dad why he didn't catch me before I fell. And I can see his heart break that he wasn't there for me. He should have been. But he wasn't. He leans forward and pushes a strand of hair behind my ear and tells me he's sorry, that we can try again later. He'll catch me tomorrow. And then he's reaching down to grab my hand, to walk me and my bike home. And I am so sad.

I didn't learn to ride my bike today. Instead, I fell down. I wasn't strong enough. I couldn't do it. My knees ache, but that feeling that I've failed my parents, that I've failed myself, hurts more than any scrape ever could. I look up to see if my mom is ashamed of me, too, but she's smiling down. Her eyes twinkling with unconditional love.

"You've got this, honey." She takes my hand and squeezes, then darts a quick look to my dad to encourage him to step back and give me room. "Now, get up. Get up, Grace."

And she smiles at me. A smile so filled with love, so filled with confidence and hope and warmth, that I feel it explode inside me, envelop me in its strength and power. So much power, sizzling just below the surface. Waiting for me to touch it. To take it.

To use it.

And that's when I know. When I recognize what this is.

This power lighting up every cell in my body isn't just mine.

It's Hudson's.

And it is ungodly.

120

Fee, Fi, Fo, F*ck

I don't know how Hudson knew I would need that memory at this point, right now, more than I've ever needed anything in my life. Not just his power but my mother's confidence in me, too. Maybe because he understood just how battered and broken and weary I would be coming into the end of this Trial. Or maybe because, after all this time trapped in my head, he just understands me.

I feel the ground rumble beneath my cheek, and I know Jaxon is doing everything he can to break down the barrier and get inside to save me. I hear Macy shouting spells, each one hitting the barrier like ringing the gong of a bell. And I know if Flint were here, he'd use every ounce of strength he had to burn the magic of the protective spell away.

But I don't need them to save me, not this time. Thanks to Hudson, I've got this. Even if no one on this field knows it yet. Because Hudson is the only one who gave me the strength to pick *myself* back up again.

Even if it meant giving up the very essence of who he was. For me. A girl who spent the last two weeks hating him. Who was at one point willing to take from him that which he willingly gave.

I take a deep breath, let the power flow through me. And realize that he didn't just give me some of his power. He gave it *all* to me.

And can I just say—holy hell! I knew Hudson was powerful, but

I'm used to powerful. I was mated to Jaxon, after all, and in the world I come from, it doesn't get much more powerful than that...or so I thought.

But the kind of power Hudson has? The kind of power that's coursing through my body right now? It's like nothing I ever could have imagined. Like nothing anyone I know could possibly imagine... even Jaxon.

I'm barely skating along the edges of it, and it feels like more than I can ever possibly hope to wield or contain. What would it feel like to have all that inside you? To know you could do whatever you wanted, whenever you wanted?

For a second—just a second—all the bits and pieces of what Hudson has told me over the last couple of weeks during our myriad conversations come together in my head.

Jaxon definitely got it wrong. Because if Hudson had really wanted to commit genocide, hell, if he really wanted to kill *everyone*, he wouldn't have wasted his time with only using his gift of persuasion. I see it now, what he's really capable of. With a mere thought, his enemies would have been turned to dust. Not just one. Or ten. Or even a thousand. *All of them*.

And now I can't help wondering if the only reason Jaxon defeated Hudson is because Hudson let him win. Because I know, without a doubt, all I need to do is think of something and it will, quite simply, cease to be.

But I don't have time to ponder this as Cole snickers and crouches down next to me, the goalpost still clutched in his hands like a child's security blanket—more proof of just how weak he is.

As if I need more proof. I can't believe this guy is alpha. He's pathetic—I just never knew how pathetic until right now.

"I can't wait until I'm done with you." He sneers. "You don't belong here. You've never belonged here. Foster's just too chickenshit to admit that. But I'm not. I'm going to do everyone a favor and take care of you once and for all."

Then he leans down to whisper in my ear. "And then I'm going to take care of Jaxon and Hudson. This is the time—can you feel it? Neither of them is looking quite like their old selves, are they? I have to admit, I was surprised to see Hudson was back. But hey, gives me a chance to kill him myself for the mess he made of my plans last year."

He nods to the others to get out of the way. And then he lifts the goalpost, preparing to deliver the blow that will guarantee an end to the game and likely an end to me.

In the background, Nuri's whistle is blowing loud and sharp, but Cole isn't paying any attention to it. And neither is anyone else. Which is fine with me. Because now that Hudson's power has spread all the way through me, now that I can feel it in every single part of me, I know exactly what to do. Because no way is Cole going to touch a hair on Jaxon's or Hudson's heads.

Not after everything they've done for me.

Not after everything they've been to me.

"They could destroy you with nothing but a thought," I hiss at him. "But by the time I'm done, they won't have to."

And so I dissolve the vines holding me to the ground with nothing more than the whisper of an idea in my head. I plant one hand on the ground and stagger to my feet, the agonizingly painful ball still clutched in my hand and Hudson's power flowing through my veins. It mixes with my gargoyle, grows even more powerful…then touches on something else deep inside me. Something I can feel but don't yet have a name for.

It all mixes together as I finally stand tall, ignoring the bruises and the small, broken pieces of me that litter the ground around us.

Cole's smug smile falters as he looks at me, but I don't know why. Probably because he's not used to anyone standing up to him, least of all the little human girl he's been messing with since the day she got here.

The little human girl who has turned out to be so much more than any of us ever expected.

Something akin to fear flashes across his face. But then the witches rush to his aid, wands raised as the three of them hit me with spell after spell.

But I'm in my gargoyle form—imbued with a vampire's power—and every spell they throw at me just rolls right off. Delphina hits me with an icy blast so powerful that it should chip a few more parts of me away—or at least rock me back on my heels. But it does neither, and as I take a step forward, I realize that the foot I'm looking down at doesn't belong to me. Or at least not normal-size me.

Because with every single spell they send my way, I'm growing larger.

With every chunk of ice Delphina spits at me, I'm becoming taller and stronger, my stone becoming more and more impenetrable.

This is Hudson's power? I wonder as I take a second step forward. This is what he can do?

But something inside me—my gargoyle or Hudson's power or some weird amalgamation of both—whispers *no*. Whispers that what's happening right now is something else entirely. Something no one has ever seen before—but it doesn't give me a clue about what it is.

Delphina hits me with one more blast of ice, right before Violet and Cam and Simone stand together, faces frightened and wands raised. I don't know what they have planned, and I don't care. All I want is to get to the goal and end this game once and for all.

But together they cast a spell that has long red ribbons flying through the air at me, wrapping themselves around me, binding my free arm to my side and the arm cradling the ball to my chest.

I don't know how they could possibly imagine for one second that these flimsy bindings would hold me, magical or not. I rip them away with barely a thought and keep walking, as the ribbons disintegrate into a million pieces of confetti that flutter and float around me.

And that's when it happens, when Cole and Quinn launch themselves at me. They are back in their werewolf forms, growling and snarling and clawing as they try to grab on to any part of me that might actually hurt. Any part of me that they imagine might bring me down.

But I don't have time for them. I don't have time for any of this pettiness anymore, and I wave a hand to shoo them away. They fall to the ground, whimpering and nearly formless, and I realize that simple wave of my hand has broken nearly every bone in their bodies to slivers.

They're crying when they change back to human form to help mend their bones, but I don't pay any more attention to them. As long as they don't bother me, I won't bother them.

I turn to the others, prepared to cut off another attack if necessary, but they're not coming near me. They're just watching me in horrified astonishment...which works for me.

But Delphina makes one last pass at me, diving out of the sky as fast as she can, talons aimed straight for my heart. With nothing more than a thought, with a wave of my hand, she disappears.

And the crowd roars even louder. Not because I've killed her, although I easily could have. But because she's re-formed in the infirmary tent on the sidelines. So strange to imagine I could have dealt a mortal blow with a mere thought.

I'm only a few steps away from the goal now, and with each step I take, I shrink a little more, until I'm back down to my normal size.

I pause before I cross, though, and hold the ball up to the audience, in the same way Nuri did. I challenge each and every one of them to hold it as long as I have—which by now must be at least ten minutes, including the time it was trapped, incendiary and vibrating, under my broken body.

Then I shift back to my human form, so that as I step across the bloodred goal line, it's Grace—just Grace—who is walking the ball across it.

Grace, just Grace, who has somehow managed to beat Cole, beat the Circle, beat the king, *and* beat the odds.

It's a good feeling.

As I cross the goal, the arena erupts in cheers and stomping, and I can't help taunting the king. I offer him the comet. I didn't think the noise could become more deafening, but it does. Somehow it does. Nuri dips her head in respect, and I wink at her. Then drop the comet onto the ground.

But that last blast of Hudson's power has decimated me, and the moment the words ring out across the stadium that I'm the winner, I stop. I just stop.

And then fall to my knees as wave after wave of exhaustion rolls right over me.

121

And the Crowd Goes Wild

It's over. It's finally over. That's all I can think as the world around me goes wild.

I want to get back up, want to check on Jaxon and Hudson and Macy and Flint and Eden and Mekhi and Gwen—all casualties in the battles that have gotten me here, to this moment—but I'm too tired to so much as turn my head. Too tired to do anything but lie here and try to absorb everything that's just happened.

The crowd is screaming and stomping so loudly that it feels like the arena itself is going to crack wide open. Students are cheering, faculty are clapping, and even most of the Circle are looking at me like they *might* have underestimated me.

It's a little strange considering how, less than an hour ago, it felt like everyone in this place was against me. Suspicious, angry, convinced that I didn't belong here...and now they're cheering for me like I'm actually one of their own.

And the only thing that's changed is I actually won the Circle's little Trial.

I'm still me, still Grace. Half-human, half-gargoyle girl. Only now they seem to think I belong.

Interesting, considering I've never wanted to belong less. Never wanted anything more than to simply walk away from this stadium and never look back.

There are only eight people in this entire place who I actually care about—everyone else can go straight to hell.

Ironic? Yes. Something I need to deal with right now? Not even close.

So I drop what I sincerely hope is my last entry into the "Shit I Don't Have Time For Today" file, then rest my head on the ground and breathe. Just breathe.

I'm going to get up—*I am*—just as soon as I'm certain that my legs can support me. Turns out doing the entire test on my own and *then* following it up with some kind of mega power explosion takes a lot out of a girl…especially with the night I had.

But before I can so much as figure out what hurts—or more accurately, what *doesn't* hurt, since that's a *much* smaller list—Cyrus has lowered the magical force field protecting the playing area just enough to let himself in and is now moving quickly across the grass.

I don't want to get up, but no way am I meeting this man facedown on the ground. Much less on my knees. So I dig into whatever last reserve of strength I have, and I push myself up and stand. I'm wobbly, but I'm on my feet.

As our gazes connect, I can't help but pick up on a disturbing amount of rage in his eyes, so much so that I expect him to start screaming and running full tilt at me any second.

But he's got too much restraint for that.

Instead, he walks slowly, deliberately up to me in his three-piece Tom Ford suit and tie, and he doesn't stop until he's only a couple of inches away.

The closer he gets, the more unsettling it becomes to be this close to him. Partly because he looks like a thirty-year-old version of Jaxon and Hudson—a little more scruff and a lot more sophistication, with an attitude that commands obedience—and partly because, when our gazes meet, there's something in the depths of his that gives me the creeps on a whole new level.

I start to take a step back—several steps, actually—but that's exactly what he's going for. So I force myself to stand my ground, lift my chin, and keep my gaze locked on his despite my misgivings.

I expect my small rebellion to set him off, but instead it brings an ever-so-slight smile to his face as he looks me over. He never says a word, never makes a move toward me, and still I feel all kinds of gross by the time his gaze travels from my muddy shoes back up to my face.

Maybe I should have taken that step back after all—onto the next mountain, if possible. But it's too late now. Any move on my part will look like retreat, and I'm not about to give him the satisfaction...or the power.

All of a sudden, the entire arena begins to shake, the ground rolling and jerking beneath my feet for a few seconds before settling back down again.

"So. You did it," he says, eyebrow arched and index finger running along his lower lip in that way some men do when they think they've found a snack.

As if.

"I did," I answer, lip curled in contempt even as every instinct I have is screaming at me to run, that a deadly predator has me in his sights. "And now I'm going to leave."

I go to move past him, and he reaches out, grabs my elbow.

The arena starts to shake again, and I glance over at my friends, see Jaxon's and Hudson's frantic faces, and know instinctively that Jaxon is the cause of this. He's fighting his father's protection dome, trying desperately to break through it.

The ground shifts again, and Cyrus adjusts his stance—and his grip—on my arm. I brace myself for pain, for punishment, for *something*, but his touch remains light even as he leans down to whisper in my ear.

"You don't really think I'm going to let you leave, do you?"

"I think you don't have a choice," I answer. "I played your little game and I won. And now I'm walking away. From you. From this arena. From everything."

I start to pull my elbow from his grip, and that's when his fingers tighten, pinning me in place. And there's nothing I can do. I'm fighting a fatigue so powerful, my entire body is shaking with the effort to stay on my feet. "You think I don't know you cheated?"

"Do you think I care what you know?" I shoot back.

"I designed this Trial. There's no way you beat it on your own." His fingers dig into my elbow a little more with each word that he hisses.

I don't flinch or pull away, even though the pain is getting worse by the second. Instead, I return his smile and answer, "I find it interesting that you felt the need to put together the hardest Trial ever for a half-human girl who's only had her powers about two weeks. Overkill much?"

"Are you saying you didn't cheat?" he asks.

"Are you saying *you* didn't?" I counter.

Because I suppose, technically, I did cheat a little—I used Hudson's power when only mates can help each other.

But that's nothing compared to what they did to ensure that I failed. They deliberately broke my mating bond minutes before I walked into the arena.

They deprived me of a mate, not just for this ridiculous game but for the rest of my life as well.

They *broke* me...*and* Jaxon.

And Cyrus thinks he's going to come down here and complain that I cheated? Sorry, *so* not sorry.

"Do you think this means you're actually going to get a seat on the Circle, little girl?" It's said with a snarl, though his face never changes—and neither does the pressure of his fingers on my elbow. "No gargoyle will *ever* sit on it again. Not while I'm king. Not after what they did."

I don't know what he means, and I don't care. Not now, maybe not ever.

Which is why I snarl back, "I don't give a shit about your Circle. I never have." I'm fed up with this conversation, fed up with him, fed up with this whole damn world and its arbitrary rules and out-of-control power grabs. "So why don't you and your little group of playmates pack up your stuff and go home? Nobody wants you here."

"You don't get to tell me to go home." He starts to circle around behind me, and I know something is coming, can feel it in my bones.

But I'm still not backing down from this man. I can't. More, I won't. Instead, I reach for my gargoyle. For the shiny platinum thread that has kept me safe for days now.

"You don't get to tell me anything," he continues.

I turn my head so I can track his movements. Just because I refuse to back down to him doesn't mean I'd ever let him out of my sight—especially when he's this close. "I feel exactly the same way, *Cyrus.*" I deliberately use his name just to piss him off.

It works, his voice turning to ice as he says, "You know we can't both win, right, Grace?"

I would congratulate myself for getting under his skin, but there's something in his tone that tells me I pissed him off too much. Something that puts me on high alert and has me pulling on the platinum thread. I start to shift even though I'm exhausted and I know it will cost me. But I'm too worn out; my gargoyle is sluggish.

And that's when Cyrus strikes, fangs flashing a millisecond before he sinks them into my neck, right over my carotid artery.

122

You're So Jelly

I scream as the world goes completely out of control, the ground shaking so hard that I swear it's going to tear itself apart. And then I scream again.

I can't help it. The pain is overwhelming, so different than when Jaxon bites me that I can barely comprehend what's happening.

"Stop!" I scream, shoving Cyrus off as I desperately try to complete my shift.

But I can't transform, my body already moving beyond my control as the pain starts shooting down my arms, turning my legs weak and my blood to fire.

Oh God, it hurts. *It hurts.*

Tears bloom in my eyes, but I blink them back as I push at Cyrus, desperate to get him off me. But he's already off, already pulling away. I don't understand how that's possible when the agony inside me is only getting worse.

And that's when it hits me. He's not drinking my blood like Jaxon did. All Cyrus did was bite me, and it's that bite that burns like the surface of the sun.

Venom.

Cyrus turns to the crowd, his arms wide, and announces in a bellowing voice that carries in the silence like a lone bell, "Our little gargoyle has admitted she cheated. We all saw it. And the penalty for cheating the Trials is death, is it not?" He holds the arena in the palm of his hand. "How dare she try to subvert our traditions, our rules. She is not one of us and never will be."

And on that final note, he turns back to me just as a loud tearing noise rends the air. Suddenly the crowd sounds much louder, even though the ground has finally stopped shaking. Which is good, I register, as everything starts to shut down inside me, because my legs are giving way.

I start to crumple, brace myself for the impact of the ground and whatever else will come from Cyrus when I'm finally lying there defenseless.

But I never hit the ground, because just as suddenly as Cyrus struck, Hudson is here, beside me. Catching me.

Like I was yesterday's trash, Cyrus has already turned and walked away. I stare at his tall form stalking across the field, and I wonder if anyone will ever challenge this brutal vampire. How much longer until the entire world is on its knees before him? How naïve was I to think I could temper his reign? Me. A tiny half-human gargoyle.

Hudson scoops me up into his arms, his face ravaged with a fear and rage like I've never seen from him before. "Grace!" he shouts hoarsely. "Grace, hang on."

There's nothing removed about him now. Nothing sardonic or defensive or even snarky at all. And I suddenly realize, even through the pain, that I might be looking at the real Hudson for the very first time.

I like what I see. Except...the sudden tears in his blue eyes only make them look deeper.

I reach a hand up and brush them away. "Hey, it's okay," I tell him even though I know it's not. "Don't do that."

I know this is bad, even without Hudson's tears. It's not like it's exactly a surprise as pain and burning continue to spread through every part of my body. It doesn't mean I'm not sad, though. I was looking forward to getting to know him when he wasn't in my head.

I was looking forward to a lot of things.

I glance over to where Jaxon and Macy are trying to get to me. They're halfway across the field, but Jaxon is struggling—I can't imagine what it must have taken for him to rip that magical dome apart, especially as depleted as he already was.

I wish I could go to him, wish I could hold him one more time.

But I'm already cold, the rain and sleet able to reach the stadium with the magical wall gone, and I can already feel everywhere Cyrus's venom touches as it works its way deeper and deeper into my system.

"Grace, look at me," Hudson says with an urgency I've never heard from him before. "I need you to look at me."

I slowly turn my head back to him, even as I wonder how much longer it's going to take the venom to kill me. Everything hurts so much, I can barely breathe, barely think.

"You have to hang on," Hudson whispers. "We can fix this—I know we can. I just need you to stay with me a little longer."

"Eternal bite," I whisper to him. A reminder that I know what's happening here. Just like I know that he's lying. Because no one ever recovers from Cyrus's eternal bite—not even gargoyles. History has proven that.

"Fuck the eternal bite," he answers. "You're not dying on my watch, Grace."

I laugh—just a little—because the pain makes it hurt too much. "I don't think even you can stop this."

"You have no idea what I can do."

Speaking of which… "I think I have something that belongs to you," I whisper.

Another wave of pain racks my body so hard, I almost pass out. I vaguely register Hudson's shouting at me, pleading with me, though I'm not sure why. He doesn't want me to do something…probably not die. Yeah, I don't want that, either. But if I'm going to die, I'm going to at least give him a fighting chance at living again.

As the pain finally recedes, I reach my hand up, lay it on his cheek. Then reach inside me to find the brilliant blue thread that's never been there before—it's right on top, laid over all the others like it's just been waiting for this moment.

Then again, maybe it has. I'm sure Hudson knows what to do with his powers much better than I ever will.

With the last remaining strength I can muster, I wrap my hand around the string and channel Hudson's power back into him.

There's a lot of it, more than I've ever imagined was possible for one person to hold, let alone wield. I've seen Jaxon's power, felt it through the mating bond, and it's immense. But this...this feels limitless.

The exchange goes on and on, Hudson's eyes glowing a little brighter with every second that passes, his lips moving, but I can't make out the words he's saying over the sound of his power rushing in my ears as it leaves me. Until finally, finally I'm empty. Finally, the last remnant of Hudson is gone, and I am well and truly alone.

Which seems fair, actually. I guess when it all comes down to it, everybody dies alone.

"I'm sorry," I tell him, tears blooming in my eyes once more and mingling with the soft rain on my face. "I should have—"

"You," Cyrus says, his fury barely contained as he stares down at the son he so recently lost. "How are *you* here?"

Someone must have told him Hudson was beside me, and he came back to see for himself. I wish he would leave. I can tell I only have a few more minutes left, and I want to spend them with Hudson.

"Does it matter?" Hudson responds. "You were always going to pay for this, whether I was here or not."

"She cheated. The rules are very clear—only a mate can help you pass the test, and she has no mate. Cole made sure—"

My heart stutters in my chest, rage and regret burning inside me at what Cyrus just revealed. He *did* know what Cole had planned—had maybe even put him up to it.

I want to say something to Cyrus, want to call him on the atrocity—or atrocities—he committed today, but I don't have the strength to fight anymore. It's taking every inch of strength I have left to try to follow what's going on. Arguing is impossible. And it wouldn't matter anyway—what's done is done, and it's not like getting him to admit his complicity changes anything. I just want him to leave me to die in peace.

Hudson doesn't argue, either. He just stares his father down, face blank and eyes blazing, until it's obvious that Cyrus starts to get uncomfortable, his face growing pale as he shifts back and forth. But still he blusters. Still he pits his arrogance against Hudson's strength.

"You know the rules," he says. "She cheated."

"She did *not* cheat," Hudson tells him. And neither says a word for a second, maybe more. "And I *will* find a way to heal her. She *will* rule the Circle one day."

Cyrus turns pale and panicked at Hudson's words, his eyes darting back and forth between us. "No gargoyle will ever rule the Circle again," he tells us. "Just suggesting it is to invite genocide against your own species, Hudson."

"No, that's your trick. That's what you brought to your people," Hudson snaps back. "And to too many others. Besides, pretty soon you'll be too busy healing to worry about who sits on the Circle and who doesn't."

"Healing from what? I'm—"

Hudson cuts him off with a wave of his hand.

And just like that, Cyrus screams in agony...as he seems to melt before my very eyes.

123

It All Comes Crashing Down

"What was that?" I whisper, torn between trying to watch what happens to Cyrus and closing my eyes and resting my head against Hudson's chest.

The closed eyes win, mostly because I'm so tired and everything hurts so much. But also because the little bit I just saw—Cyrus's body literally caving in on itself like he imploded from the inside—might be the most terrifying thing I've ever witnessed.

"Nothing for you to worry about. The bastard's bones will regrow... eventually," Hudson answers softly and smooths the hair around my face. But when I lay my head on his chest and try to block out the stomach-churning pain, he tells me firmly, "Don't go to sleep, Grace."

"I don't think vampire bites work the same way as concussions." I drag each word from my screaming lungs, trying to make a joke so I can see Hudson smile one last time.

"Yeah, because that's what I'm worried about," he jokes back as he scoops me up into his arms and carries me across the field. "You having a concussion."

Jaxon and Macy finally get to us, and Jaxon demands, "Let me have her," but Hudson barely glances his way. He just keeps moving. He's not fading, but he is striding out of the arena like a man on a mission.

The only thing he bothers to say is, "Push everyone back, make them leave this arena."

I don't know if Jaxon follows Hudson's directions, but I no longer hear voices coming closer. Everything seems to be receding. Then again, that could be the poison working its way through my system.

"Grace, just hold on a little longer," Macy tells me, her voice thick with tears. "We'll figure this out. I swear, there has to be a spell, something. My dad is talking to all the witches and vampires on staff right now. They're trying to find a way—"

She breaks off, unwilling to say what all of us are thinking, which is that it will take a lot more than a spell to save me now. Cyrus is too powerful, his bite too irrevocable. They can look all they want, but if what Hudson told me about his father the other night was true, they won't find anything.

And much as I don't want it to be true, the pain coursing through me right now says otherwise.

Still, I hate to see Macy like this. She's devastated, her face crumpled and wet with tears she doesn't even bother to try to stem. "It's okay," I soothe, because someone needs to. "You're going to be okay." I rub my hand against her arm, which is the only part of her I can reach.

"Where are you going?" Jaxon demands as Hudson continues to stride through the arena. "Where are you taking her?"

"I've got an idea," he grinds out from between clenched teeth, his arms tightening around me. "It's a long shot, but it's better than sitting here waiting for her to die."

The others wince, but I'm glad someone finally said it out loud. I'm going to die.

"What is it?" Macy whispers.

But Hudson isn't listening anymore. Instead, he's locked into the fury inside him, his wrath so great that it's threatening to rise up and swallow us whole. I don't know if the others can tell—his face is completely impassive—but I can feel it in the way he's holding me. See ignored

it in his clenched jaw. Hear it in his ragged breathing and the too-fast pounding of his heart.

"It's okay," I try to tell him, but a stronger, deeper wave of pain chooses that exact moment to hit me, and I can't stop myself from arching in his arms. From squeezing my eyes and fists and mouth shut as tightly as I can in an effort to stop the scream that wells in my throat.

"It's not okay," he growls as we finally step through the stadium doors into the snow and sleet.

The moment we do, there's a wrenching sound behind us.

Macy gasps, her face going as white as the snow-capped mountains all around us. And a few seconds after that, the entire building starts collapsing in on itself. I watch over Hudson's shoulder as wood and glass and stone and metal come tumbling down, the arena literally tearing itself apart piece by piece.

"What's happening?" Macy squeaks out. "Jaxon, what are you doing?"

But Jaxon looks as ashen as she does as he shakes his head. "That's not me."

You don't know what real power is.

Hudson's words come back to me now, as does that moment when I was returning his powers to him—the moment when I realized just how infinite they really are.

Infinite enough to reduce his father's bones to dust with the wave of a hand.

Infinite enough to tear down an entire stadium with barely a thought.

Infinite enough to do whatever he wants, whenever he wants.

And if Jaxon's gasp is anything to go by, he knows it, too. Which means he also knows that Hudson has been telling me the truth all along. Because if he had been dead set on the murder and mayhem and genocide that Jaxon had believed was his plan two years ago, then it would have already happened. It would have been done with a flick of his fingers—a wave of his hand—and there would have been nothing anyone could have done to stop it. Jaxon would only have found out about it after it was a fait accompli.

Because *that*'s the kind of power Hudson wields.

And now his brother knows.

People start running out of the arena screaming, and still the structure continues to fall, huge pieces of it exploding into dust before they even hit the ground. Seats from the top of the stadium, chunks of the roof, fragments of stone from the outside wall. All crumbling away. All imploding into the smallest particles of dust, harmlessly floating to the ground.

I know what Hudson is doing. I can feel the fury coming off him in waves. He wants to tear down the arena where people sat back and watched Cole try to kill me. Watched Cyrus actually kill me. And they did nothing. But he's not hurting them. I don't even have to look to know he's not. But he certainly is putting the fear of God into them, and honestly, I wouldn't be lying if I said they might deserve it just a little.

The amount of power it takes to tear the arena down and hurt no one. The amount of *control*. I smile. The one thing his father tried to deny him, control of his abilities, he found a way on his own terms. And Cyrus would have seen it, too, if he'd only ever bothered to pay attention to his son. That day in the memory... Hudson destroyed everything in the room except his father.

It makes me wonder what else Hudson can do.

I was dead. Sort of.

Sort of? What does that mean?

It means a lot of what I've believed for the last weeks, months, has been a lie.

It means a lot of what I blamed Hudson for wasn't his fault—or maybe didn't even happen at all. That he tried to tell me several times only makes me feel worse.

"Why didn't you tell me?" I ask as he strides away from the arena and back toward the forest we came through less than two hours ago.

And God, it feels surreal to be here. To see how much everything has changed. And also how nothing has. The pain is now so great, it's reached some level that my body can't even register anymore. A quiet calm settles over me as the pain recedes in soft waves, and all I see is Hudson. This moment. The last words we'll ever share. And I want him to know. I want him to know that I see everything now. I see *him*.

"Tell you what?" he asks. "Not to go anywhere near my father? I'm pretty sure we covered that several times."

"No," I respond after swallowing the lump in my throat. "Why didn't you tell me what a good person you are?"

Startled blue eyes find mine and our gazes lock, hold.

For a second, Hudson slows down so much that he nearly trips over his own feet while Macy and Jaxon demand to know what's going on.

He doesn't answer them. In fact, he doesn't say anything at all—and neither do I. We just stare at each other as a strange understanding passes between us.

"We'll talk about this later," he tells me as he starts walking again.

"There isn't going to be a later," I answer quietly, "and you know it."

He starts to say something, then breaks off. Swallows. Starts to speak again, then breaks off again.

As he struggles, explosions start going off around us. I drag my eyes away from his tortured blue ones in time to see a centuries-old tree turned to sawdust in the blink of an eye.

"Hudson—" I reach for his hand where it's clutching my thighs, his arm beneath my knees, and cup my hand over his. "What are you doing?"

He shakes his head, doesn't answer. More trees explode with every step he takes, the timberland around us turning to nothing, bark and roots and leaves just disappearing with each long stride. He's destroying an entire forest in the blink of an eye, in an absolute and perfect rage.

"Hudson," I whisper. "Please don't be like this. There's nothing you can do."

Dozens more trees explode around us at that, and then finally, finally, he comes to a stop in the middle of a clearing he just made, a hundred trees—maybe more—gone with just a thought.

One corner of his mouth ticks up in a teasing grin. "Jeez, Grace, your belief in me is overwhelming as always." But the humor never reaches his normally bright blue eyes, now turned nearly gray with the riotous storm of his emotions.

"It's not about believing in you. It's about the fact that I can feel your father's venom moving through me. You can't fix that."

He squares his jaw. "You don't have a clue what I can do." He doesn't say it to be mean. I know him now. He's trying to convince himself.

"Maybe not. But I know—" I break off as another fresh wave of pain surges through me and I gasp. I must have been in the eye of the tempest earlier, and now the pain is buffeting against me in growing agony. I'm out of time.

"You don't know anything," he answers harshly, his storm-tossed eyes wet with more emotions than I can keep track of. "But you're about to."

124

Long Time, No Sea

"**G**ive her to me," Jaxon demands for the third or fourth time since Hudson picked me up, but it's obvious Hudson couldn't care less what Jaxon wants.

He keeps his eyes on mine for several beats, his gaze searching my face as I fight against the pain. I can tell he wants to ask me if I want to go. To Jaxon.

And he would hand me over. One word from me, and he would step aside. But I don't even know what he'd be stepping aside from. We've barely tolerated each other for two weeks. And I was mated to Jaxon until two hours ago. So obviously I want to go to Jaxon.

But I don't say anything. I can't. Right now, I don't know what I want.

Another wave of pain rolls through my body, and this time, I can't swallow my scream.

"Don't fight it," he tells me in little more than a whisper. "Let the pain roll over you. Absorb it instead of fighting against it. It'll make the next few minutes easier."

I don't argue with him—the pain is too overwhelming for that now—but I want to ask how he thinks I can just surrender to it when it feels like every nerve ending in my body is being dipped in lava... at the same time.

Before I can think of a way to explain that, Hudson leans over and deposits me gently—so, so gently—into Jaxon's waiting arms.

It feels like coming home.

Despite how worn out he is, Jaxon takes me with ease, holding me steadily against his chest for long seconds before carrying me a little away from Hudson and Macy. Then he sinks down onto the snow and cradles me in his lap.

"It's okay," he whispers as he strokes my still unruly curls back from my face. "You're going to be okay." But I can see in his eyes that he knows the truth. Unlike Hudson, Jaxon understands that I'm already gone.

He doesn't like it, but he gets it.

Next to Hudson, the ground makes a sound like it's screaming, and we all turn to watch him turn the snow to vapor as he splinters the rocky ground in front of him wide open.

"What are you doing?" Macy demands. "I thought you were going to help Grace. I thought—"

Hudson holds a hand up and she freezes, which is ridiculous because he won't hurt her and yet totally understandable, considering she just watched him vaporize a stadium and a shit ton of trees all in the space of ten minutes.

As we watch, the dirt that was frozen beneath the snow explodes up and out. But Hudson barely pays it any attention as he digs deeper, deeper, deeper. The sounds get worse, the ground grinding against itself as he literally carves through granite with a thought.

"What's he doing?" Macy whispers.

"I have no idea," Jaxon answers, still watching his brother with bewildered eyes.

I don't know, either, but I know that whatever it is, it's his long-shot idea. And because I can't stand the thought of hoping, of thinking that Hudson might somehow find a way to save me only to have my hopes dashed at the last possible second, I turn to Jaxon, who looks as exhausted and traumatized as I feel.

I hate it—hate it for him, and I hate it for us. Maybe that's why I give him the closest thing to a smile that I can manage and softly ask, "Tell me the pirate joke?"

"What pirate joke?" he asks at first, still distracted by what his brother is doing right over our shoulders.

"You know exactly what pirate joke I'm talking about." I groan as another wave of pain rolls through me.

"The pirate joke from the hallway?" Jaxon says in disbelief. "You want to hear that *now*?"

"I've always wanted to know the punch line. And I'm probably not going to have another chance, so—"

His dark eyes fill with tears as he stares down at me. "Don't say that. Don't you fucking say that to me, Grace."

"Tell me the joke," I urge him again, because I can't stand to see the pain in his eyes. I'd take it if I could, take it all into me and away from this broken boy who's already suffered so much. "Please."

"Fuck, no," he says with a scowl that almost—almost—battles back the tears. "You want to hear the punch line of that joke? You don't die, okay? You stick around and I'll tell you next week. I promise."

Another wave of pain hits me, and this one is accompanied by a cold that chills every part of me. Together, they overwhelm me, nearly take me under. I struggle against it, not forever but for now. For a few more minutes to spend looking into Jaxon's beloved face.

"I'd really like that," I tell him after a second. "But I don't think it's possible."

I raise a hand to his cheek, run my thumb back and forth over the scar he's spent so much time despising and trying to hide. "You know that you're going to be okay, right?" I tell him.

"Don't say that. Damn it, Grace, you don't get to talk about dying as easily as brushing your teeth in the morning and then say that everything is going to be okay!"

"I love you," I tell him softly, wiping away one of the tears that fall in an endless streak down his cheeks. And I mean it. Maybe not in the same way I did when I first came to Katmere, but in a new way. Maybe even a better one.

"Please don't leave me." It's a whisper from the deepest, most broken part of him—from the little boy who's already lost so much—and it nearly shatters me.

I shake my head a little, because I won't promise him that. I won't be just one more person who treats him like he's somehow more than a god and less than a person at the same time.

So I do the only thing I can in this situation, the only thing we still have time for. I smile at him and ask, "What did the beach say to the tide when it came in?"

He just stares at me, seconds ticking by as silence stretches hopelessly between us. In fact, he waits so long to answer that I've almost decided that he's not *going* to. But then he takes a breath and blows it out slowly, so, so slowly. And says, "I have no idea."

Of course he doesn't. He's terrible at these, but he indulges me anyway. Which is why I'm grinning as widely as I can manage when I answer. "Long time no sea."

Jaxon laughs, but in the middle, it turns into a sob and he buries his face against my neck. "I'm sorry, Grace," he whispers to me as hot tears slide against my skin. "I'm so sorry."

"I'm not." I comb my fingers through the silky coolness of his hair. "I'll never be sorry for having found you, Jaxon, even if I didn't get to keep you as long as I would have liked." I pull his mouth down to mine, press my lips to his. And nearly sob myself when he whispers, "I love you," against my mouth.

Behind us, Hudson finally stops doing whatever it is he's doing to the land and takes a step toward me.

"It's time," Macy says, and there are tears streaming down her face, too, as she reaches for my hand.

"It's going to be okay," she tells me. "You're going to be okay."

I don't know how, but as Hudson bends down and slides me from Jaxon's arms back into his own, I get my first real look at what he's been doing while I talked to Jaxon.

And horror seizes my chest. For all this time, Hudson has been carving a *grave* for me out of the frozen earth and the granite that lies below.

My breath catches as I whisper, "Why?"

125

Between a Rock and a Hard Place

"No," I beg, confusion muddling my already pain-soaked brain. "Hudson, please. Please don't do it. Don't make me—"

"What are you doing?" Jaxon demands, shoving to his feet and moving toward us. "Dude, don't touch her—"

Without ever taking his gaze from mine, Hudson reaches out and explodes a wide fissure in the ground, leaving Jaxon and Macy on one side and he and I on the other.

"Do you trust me?" he asks.

"Of course, but—"

"Do. You. Trust. Me?" he asks again, and in the space between the words—the space between us—are all the things we've never said.

"Don't!" Jaxon shouts to me. "Don't believe anything he says. You know he can't be trusted, Grace. You know—"

"Yes," I whisper, even as my entire body recoils from the hole in the ground he's made for me.

"Yes?" he asks, his blue eyes a little disbelieving and a lot determined.

"Yes, Hudson. I trust you." It may be the most ridiculous decision of my rapidly draining life, but I do trust him. I do, more than I ever would have believed possible even a couple of short days ago.

"Do you remember that night we went to the library?"

"Which one?"

He rolls his eyes. "The night Jaxy-Waxy got you those street tacos."

I laugh just a little at how disgruntled he looks, then wish I hadn't when another wave of pain slides through me at the disjointed motion. "Oh, right. The night you behaved like a total ass. I remember that really well, actually."

"I think you're confused," he tells me with a heavy sigh. "But, considering the morning you've had, I suppose that's to be expected. I won't hold it against you."

"You sure about that?" I ask. "Because I've got to say, burying me alive seems like one hell of a revenge plot."

"Forget about the bloody ground for a second, will you, please?" he snaps.

"Easy for you to say, all things considered," I snap back. Then spend several seconds having a coughing fit for my trouble.

"I read something in the library; then when we met the Unkillable Beast—" He stops as the coughing fit overtakes me and I gasp for air, tears sliding unchecked out of the corners of my eyes. "We don't have time for explanations."

"Yeah." Another coughing fit comes on, this one harder and more painful than the one before.

"It's getting worse," he says, all traces of humor gone.

Now it feels like there's a weight pressing down on my chest, but I finally manage to choke out, "No...shit...Sherlock..."

We both know what I'm doing—making it easy for Hudson to bury me in the ground.

He doesn't want to put me there any more than I want to *be* there, but we're out of options.

And so Hudson bends down and lays me gently inside the grave he so desperately carved out for me.

It's terrifying—the most terrifying thing that's ever happened to me, even after everything I've faced in the last few months—and I tell myself to close my eyes. To pretend it isn't happening. To just breathe and wait it out.

But I can't, not when Hudson waves Jaxon and Macy over, and everyone is standing over my grave, watching me.

"Bury her—" Hudson begins.

"I won't," Jaxon insists. "No way am I burying her before she's dead."

But Hudson isn't in the mood to put up with anything from him right now. "Bury her," he commands. "Right now. Or you won't like what happens next. That much I can promise you."

Macy's eyes widen in fear, and I want to tell her he doesn't mean it. But both she and Jaxon must take him at his word, because Jaxon is using his telekinesis to slowly, methodically cover me with small stones and pebbles.

He starts at my feet, dropping more and more of the tiny rocks on top of me, then slowly, carefully works his way up until my legs are covered, then my hips, then my rib cage and arms.

I'm cold, so cold, but I struggle to hold on just a little longer. If this is the last time I'm going to see these people—my family—then I'm going to hold on until the very last second. I'm going to stay with them until I no longer have a choice in the matter.

Macy is full-on ugly crying now. Jaxon's eyes are locked sadly on mine. And Hudson, Hudson is crouched down at the head of the grave, his fingers gently, gently, gently stroking my hair.

I watch the three of them until the end. Until the stones reach past my neck and there is no more time left. Then, and only then, do I close my eyes and let the earth and the stone take me.

Amazing Grace

—Hudson—

I'm terrified.

It's not something I like to admit, even to myself—and something I'd deny if anyone ever asked—but I am bloody terrified watching Grace sink into the earth.

Watching the rocks cover her even as the cold rain and sleet pour down on us.

Watching her fade away a little more with each labored breath she takes.

This isn't how this was supposed to happen—it isn't how any of this was supposed to go. When we first made the plan to come back, together, I thought we'd covered every contingency, had thought of anything that might possibly go wrong. I knew it wouldn't be easy, but I never, *never* thought it would end up like this.

If I'd had a clue, I would have found another way. Any other way, even if it meant staying encased in stone, locked up with Grace, forever.

I run a hand through my hair, glancing around at the sheer destruction I'd leveled on this forest. I should come out and plant saplings in the spring. Grace would want that.

"If this doesn't work, I'll destroy you," Jaxon snarls at me as the last rock covers her. He's obviously spoiling for a fight.

But I'm not biting. I'm not going to be drawn into an argument when he wants to act like a child. So I swallow the eight thousand things I could say in response and settle for the pure, unvarnished truth. "If this doesn't work, you won't have to."

Because what the fuck am I supposed to do if Grace doesn't make it out of that grave? How the fuck am I supposed to live with myself... or just live, for that matter, without her?

"I can't believe this is happening," her cousin says, tears still pouring down her face.

Jaxon glares at me. "It shouldn't be happening."

I return the look with interest. "Maybe it wouldn't be if you'd killed that bloody wolf the first time you had a shot at him."

Okay, so maybe I am biting a little after all.

I can put up with a bloody buggering lot from my younger brother—and I have—but I'm not taking responsibility for something he should have taken care of to begin with.

"You really think my killing Cole would have prevented this?" he demands.

I don't know. Maybe *nothing* would have prevented this, short of wrapping Grace in cotton and keeping her as far away from our father as we could. Then again, he would have found her eventually. Whether any of them know it or not, Cyrus has been gunning for her from the moment he first found out she was a gargoyle. Probably before.

"So what do we do now?" Macy asks, her voice echoing in the tense, angry silence that weighs between us. Her tears have finally stopped, but she sounds almost as empty as I feel as she stares down at the stone-covered grave.

"Now we wait," Jaxon tells her. "What else is there to do?"

Nothing. If I thought there was something, anything else I could do to help Grace, I would be doing it.

"How long should it take?" Macy shifts her weight back and forth, like she's too nervous to stand still.

"I don't know." And I don't care. I'll stand here as long as I have to if it means Grace comes out of that ground healed.

"Is there anything you *do* know?" Jaxon demands, and there's a distrust in his eyes that slays me even as it makes me want to punch the shit out of him. "Why the fuck did you have to come back anyway? Things were fine before you got here—"

"By *fine*, you mean everyone thought I was dead, and you were wallowing in your own despair, throwing your life away like a total wanker? Because if that's your definition of fine, then yes. Things were great."

"Throwing my life away? I was trying to get my shit back together after everything *you* did and then what Mom…" He drifts off, but his scar stands out in stark relief against his cheek despite the weather.

And maybe I should feel bad about what our mother did to him, but fuck that. He has no idea how easy he's had it.

"Oh, did Mummy not love you enough?" I make a fake-concerned face. "Poor little Jaxy-Waxy. It's so hard to be you."

"I should have done a better job of killing you when I had the chance." He glares at me like he's measuring me for a body bag… again. Big surprise.

"You really should have," I agree with a deliberately bland expression. "Apparently you have a real history of screwing things up and then feeling bad for yourself. And of expecting everyone else to feel bad for you, too."

"You know what? Fuck you! I don't need anyone to feel bad for me."

"Umm, guys—" Macy tries to interrupt, but this is a fight that's way too long overdue and there's no way a sixteen-year-old girl—witch or not—is going to be able to stop it.

"Sure you do," I taunt, because I can't stop myself now that I finally have the chance to say just a little bit of what's been burning in my brain for weeks now. "When we were together, Grace went on and on about how *sorry* she felt for you. I kept telling her there was no reason to, but you know how softhearted our girl is."

"*My* girl," Jaxon corrects me. "*My* mate—bond or not."

His words hit with an accuracy that makes them feel like body blows. The last two and a half weeks have been a living hell for me, and now he's acting like he's got all the cards when he's the one who let this happen to Grace to begin with. It's shite, absolute and total shite, and I'm sick of listening to him whine about it.

"Your mate? Oh, right. That must be why you protected her so well that there's not even a bond anymore."

His hands clench into fists. "You're a real bastard, you know that, right?"

"And you're a pathetic child who can't protect himself, let alone anyone else."

"You're really going to come at me with that?" he demands incredulously. "Can we discuss—just for a minute—who the fuck I was trying to protect Grace from last semester? Oh, right. Your homicidal ex-girlfriend who wanted to *sacrifice* her to bring *you* back."

Guilt slams through me all over again, because he's right. This is all my fault. Not because I planned it, but because I couldn't stop it.

So here we are. Lia's dead, Grace is in the ground, and Jaxon—

"You guys!" This time Macy's voice is more forceful when she tries to get our attention. "Look."

The sleet is letting up, and Jaxon and I turn as one, just in time to see Grace's body finish absorbing one of the stones my brother laid on her chest.

"What's happening?" Jaxon asks, eyes wide and voice just a little awed.

"I'm not sure," Macy answers. "But that's the third one she's absorbed in the last two minutes."

"Really?" I watch as another stone starts to quiver and then gradually sinks into her flesh.

Our fight forgotten, Jaxon and I stand with Macy for long minutes while Grace slowly, slowly, slowly absorbs every stone, every rock, every *pebble* that Jaxon laid over her—hundreds of small shards sinking into every inch of her flesh, one by one by one.

When it's over, when every single speck of granite has been

absorbed into her body, we stand over her, waiting…for a sign, for a breath, for something that proves she's alive.

Something that proves that this last-ditch desperation on my part actually worked.

Several nerve-racking seconds pass where nothing happens. And then, just when Jaxon starts cursing and I'm about to give up, Grace's eyelids flicker open. It's all I can do not to put my head down and sob in relief.

"Oh my God!" Macy's hand flies up to cover her mouth as shock rockets through us all. "Grace! Grace, are you okay?"

Grace doesn't answer, but as Jaxon races to sit beside her head, she smiles up at him.

"You're okay?" he asks, and I've never heard such joy in my younger brother's voice in our lives.

"I—" Her voice cracks and she coughs, licks her lips.

"Here!" Macy reaches into her ubiquitous backpack and pulls out a bottle of water that she hands to Jaxon.

He opens it, then helps Grace sit up in her bed of granite so that she can take a sip.

"How are you feeling?" I ask, slowly walking to the other side and crouching down beside her.

"Okay, I think." She coughs a little more, then pauses like she's taking inventory of herself. "Pretty good, actually. I think I'm…okay."

This time when she takes a deep breath, she doesn't cough.

"Do you remember what happened?" Macy asks, excitement and concern warring on her face.

Grace thinks and then says, "I do, yeah."

And just like that, my hands are shaking, when they never shake. I can't figure out what to do with them, so I shove them in my pockets. And wait.

"I won the game and Cyrus bit me. You guys brought me here and—" She turns to me. "Hudson, thank you. Thank you so much."

Disappointment racks me, but I ignore it. I'm certainly used to it by now, and—on the positive side—at least my hands aren't trembling anymore. So what if she remembers the facts of what happened today and nothing else. Certainly nothing that came before. It's probably better that way.

"Don't thank me," I tell her, even as she reaches for me, her hand clutching at my arm as she smiles up at me in a way I haven't seen from her in quite a while. Now my whole body is trembling…and I don't have a bloody clue what to do about it.

Especially when Grace is full-on grinning at me despite the fact that her grip isn't quite as strong or as firm yet as it would normally be. "And why is that exactly?"

A half a dozen answers come to mind, but in the end, I don't say any of them.

"That's what I thought." She rolls her eyes. "Just admit you saved me, Hudson. I promise, it won't make you any less of a jerk in the long run."

"I think you're confused." I shake my head again, more determined than ever to make it stick this time. The last thing I want from Grace is gratitude. It's the last thing I've ever wanted from her. "I was just—"

"I don't want to argue with you," she says. "Especially over something so ridiculous."

"So don't," I answer. "I'm sure you've got better things to do right now." Besides, you know, ripping my heart out of my chest again.

Things like returning to Katmere and taking her rightful place in the Circle.

Both necessary.

Both important.

And both extremely dangerous.

Because Grace may have survived my father's bite, but that only makes her more of a target, not less. He will heal eventually, and when he does, he'll be angrier, and more afraid, than he ever was before.

Which means it's already too late.

The war I've worked so hard to prevent—the war my brother

and others have tried to blame me for inciting—will come whether we want it or not.

Whether we're ready for it or not.

And now that we know what side the wolves will fall on... It took an army of gargoyles to defeat them the last time the vampires and wolves fought together. Who knows what it will take today, especially when all we have is one gargoyle and a few rogue vampires to join the witches and the dragons.

Not great odds.

But thinking about the war will wait...at least a few more days. Because as Jaxon reaches down to help Grace from the hole I created for her, he wraps his arms around her and presses her body to his. And I begin to see red, even before he leans down to kiss her, and every ounce of chill—and emotional self-preservation—I have goes out the fucking window.

My hands curl into fists, my fangs explode in my mouth, and though there were a million other ways I was hoping to break my newfound knowledge to Grace, the words come out before I can even think about stopping them.

"Jaxon, if you wouldn't mind, take your fucking hands off my mate."

END OF BOOK TWO

But wait—there's more!

Read on for an exclusive
look at two chapters from
Hudson's point of view.

Everything is about to change...

Didn't Want to Wake Up Like This

—Hudson—

Something's not right.

I'm not sure what it is yet, but something definitely isn't right.

"Grace?" I ask, waiting for her to give me that smile she reserves just for me—half amused, half exasperated, all sweet.

But it doesn't come.

Nothing does except blankness, and that scares the bloody hell out of me.

What if something went wrong?

"Grace?" I try again, making my voice slightly louder this time and my presence a little more known.

I never had to do that with her before, but that's when it was just the two of us existing on a separate plane—there was no background noise to compete with, no snowstorm fluttering by, no inane high school students chattering to themselves about God knows what, no chimes playing an old Rolling Stones song because the headmaster has delusions of cool.

It was just us, and while I was all for Grace's plan to come back—because when she's around, I am nothing if not a bright-eyed optimist (said no one about me ever, except Grace)—I have to admit, I didn't expect it to start out like this.

She still isn't answering me. Instead, she's walking down the stairs of Katmere Academy like it's been sixteen minutes instead of sixteen weeks since she's been here.

I don't get it.

"Grace!" This time, I burrow into the path in her brain that makes it impossible for her to ignore me (and vice versa), the path that was our very first clue we were locked together all those weeks ago.

She falters, her foot coming down wrong on the stair, and nearly falls. I grab on to her, taking control of her body for just a second so that I can help steady her. I know we agreed that I would only take control of her if I really thought it was necessary, but keeping her from falling down the flight of circular stairs seems necessary to me.

Once she's steady, she pauses and looks around like she's trying to find someone…or looking for whoever called her name.

Excitement thrums through me at the idea that she finally hears me, so I do it again. "Grace! Grace, can you hear me?"

She startles again, and again she looks around. But it's barely eight in the morning, and none of the students out here are paying any attention to her at all as they rush to class. "Grace, I'm right here."

She gives the landing up above her one last glance, then shakes her head a little and mutters, "Get a grip, Grace," before hustling down the last couple of steps and turning onto the main hallway.

Damn it. Something definitely went wrong. She honestly doesn't have a clue I'm here. I'm not sure how that's possible after all our plans. I also don't get why she isn't at least trying to figure out what went wrong. She may not hear me, but isn't she at least wondering where I've gone?

It's that thought more than any other that has me combing through her thoughts, trying to figure out what's happening. But it's not until she steps into the melee of the crowded hallway without so much as a pause that the truth finally hits me in the face. It's not just that she can't hear me anymore. It's that she doesn't remember me.

What. The. Everlasting. Fuck?

I tell myself that I'm wrong, that I'm freaking out over nothing.

That there's no way Grace has just forgotten me. No way that she's just forgotten *us*.

But then a vampire with long locks—a friend of my brother's if I remember correctly—stops her in the hall. "Grace?" he asks, and he looks like he's seen a damn ghost. Then again, he probably thinks he has.

There's a part of me that still expects Grace to reassure him. To tell him that she's okay, even after being gone for so long. But when she just smiles at him and says, "Hey, there you are. I thought I was going to have to read *Hamlet* all by myself today," I realize just how fucked everything's become.

Because not only has she forgotten *me*, she's forgotten *everything*.

For the first time, I start to worry there's really something wrong with her. That shifting back to her human form—and bringing me with her—has done something to harm her. Just the thought has me ready to climb the walls—that and realizing there's no way for me to communicate with her or anyone else. No way for me to tell them what might have happened to her.

"*Hamlet*?" the vampire asks, looking as worried as he does confused.

"Yeah, *Hamlet*. The play we've been reading for Brit Lit since I got here?" Grace starts to shuffle her feet, and I can feel her sudden nervousness. "We're performing a scene today, remember?"

I'm beginning to think that maybe she *should* be nervous—maybe we both should. Still, I hate seeing her like that, so I do my best to calm her down through the mental path we share, but I have no idea if anything I'm doing is actually getting through. Also, it's hard to help keep her calm when I'm one very small step from freaking the fuck out myself.

"We're not rea—" The vampire breaks off as he starts to text someone. Too bad, I have a feeling I know exactly who he's texting.

"Are you okay?" Grace asks, stepping closer to him. "You don't look so good."

"*I* don't look so good?" He laughs, but it sounds about as humorous as I feel. "Grace, you're—"

"Miss Foster?" One of the teachers comes straight up to Grace, cutting off the vampire. "Are you all right?" he asks.

"I'm fine," she answers, taking a startled step back.

But it's obvious that she's far from fine. Her thoughts have gone from calm to a jumbled mess, and I can feel her emotions pressing in on her. Fear, confusion, annoyance, worry—they're closing in from every side, and the beginnings of one of the damn panic attacks she hates so much are starting to tighten up her chest.

She takes a deep breath, then seems to calm down just a little as she explains, "I'm just trying to get to class before the bell rings."

I stroke a hand down her back, whisper, "You're okay. Everything is okay."

I know she doesn't hear me—doesn't even have a clue that I'm here—but she must feel me, at least a little, because her breathing smooths out and her entire body loosens up some.

"We need to find your uncle," the teacher—a wolf—tells her as he starts to almost push her down the hallway.

The vampire practically falls on his ass trying to get out of their way, which doesn't make me think much of him. But I don't have time to worry about that, because the farther Grace gets down this hall, the more nervous she grows.

I can feel it in the way her heart is beating wildly.

Taste it in the metallic aftertaste on her tongue.

Hear it in the ragged breathing she's trying so hard to keep under control.

"I'm here," I try to tell her, using the path from earlier—the path I'm sure she's heard me on twice now. "I've got you."

This time, though, all it does is freak her out more. "Can you please tell me what's going on?" she asks, her voice about an octave too high as the crowd parts right in front of her.

I get a glimpse of how much she hates when they do that—as well as a passing reference to how it comes with the territory of dating my brother. Present tense.

And fuck. Just fuck. I don't even know what I'm supposed to do with that.

"You don't know?" the teacher demands, and he sounds a lot like I feel. Worried and stressed with a side of pissed off.

"Grace!" one of the dragons calls out, bounding out of the classroom so he can walk alongside the two of them. "Oh my God, Grace! You're back!"

A closer look at him through Grace's eyes has me registering who it is. Flint Montgomery. Bloody hell. The hits just keep on coming today.

He looks like his brother. So much so that it feels like a fist to my fucking gut just being in the same hallway with him. It's been almost two years since Branton died—*nineteen months*—and the pain of his betrayal, the betrayal of my best friend, my only friend, still cuts like the edge of a very dull blade.

"Not now, Mr. Montgomery," the teacher snaps, his teeth clicking together sharply with each word.

I never thought I'd be grateful to a wolf in my life, but when the teacher—Mr. Badar, Grace calls him—rushes us past Flint, I'm definitely thankful. Dealing with this disaster with Grace is nearly impossible as it is. Dealing with it and having to face the broken pieces of my past, too...

"Wait, Grace—" Flint reaches for her, but the wolf blocks his hand from connecting.

"I said not now, Flint! Go to class!" the teacher snarls, teeth bared.

Flint looks pissed, plus like he wants to argue—dragons are like vamps, in that none of them wants to take orders from a wolf, even at the best of times—his own teeth suddenly gleaming sharply in the soft chandelier lighting of the hallway.

He must decide it's not worth it—despite clearly spoiling for a fight—because in the end, he kind of stops in his tracks and watches

Grace and the wolf walk by...just like everyone else in the hallway.

Several people start to say something to her, but the teacher gives a low, warning growl that keeps everyone at bay. I, for one, am glad this guy's bite must be as bad as his growl. Because Grace is getting tenser and tenser, more and more panicked, and the last thing she needs is to deal with more people.

Especially since nothing I do seems to be able to calm her down.

This isn't the first time she's been like this. It happened several times when we were trapped together. At first, she would only do things on her own, but as time went on and she started to trust me, she began to let me help her.

Not with my power, since that doesn't work on her anyway, but with my presence. With my voice. With my touch, or a close facsimile of it anyway. I've grown so used to reaching out to her—so used to feeling her reach out to me—that going without it now, when she's so upset, is bloody well killing me.

"Hold on, Grace. We're almost there," the teacher says.

"Almost where?" she asks, and her voice is high-pitched, tight.

Her mind is racing as she tries to figure out what's going on, what she's missing, and I'm worried about what she's going to do when she finds out.

I'm also worried that the truth will only make her ground herself more firmly in this world, which, in turn, will make it a lot harder for me to reach her.

I can't fucking believe all our careful planning went so bloody wrong—especially right out of the gate like this.

We turn the corner onto a narrow hallway, and Grace reaches into her pocket for her phone. As she does, all she can think about is Jaxon.

Jaxon, not me.

I don't understand.

I know that the mating bond is supposed to be unbreakable, but hers and Jaxon's had faded into nothingness the first month we were trapped together—before we could stand each other. Long before we developed feelings for each other. I had looked, at least once a week since then, and I couldn't see it at all.

We both thought it must be because we were trapped together forever. Mating bonds break when people die. Was this really so different?

But once we discovered a way to come back, we both knew we had to take it. We owed Jaxon at least that much.

Now that she's back at Katmere and we're no longer trapped on some other plane, though, their mating bond is impossible to miss. It's right there, front and center, functioning like it's always been there.

Flashes of him—of them together—come through as she thinks of Jaxon. Smiles. Touches. Kisses. She loses herself in one of the memories, and it tears me wide open. Makes me feel pretty fucking worthless.

I expect the anger that hits me, the rage that the girl I love—the girl who has told me almost every intimate detail about herself and who knows nearly every single one of mine—is standing right here, mooning over another guy. And not just any guy: Jaxon.

But the pain comes out of nowhere.

It crashes into me like a tsunami, drags me down, pulls me under.

Shreds what's left of my soul into pieces so small, I can't imagine ever fitting them back together again.

If I had a body right now, I'd be on my knees. As it is, there's nothing for me to do but stay right here and feel—no, endure—the love and excitement building inside her at the idea of seeing Jaxon again.

But it's not all excitement in Grace's head. There's confusion and apprehension and more than a little bit of anger on her side as she finally asks the question I've been both waiting for and dreading at the same time.

"What the hell is going on?"

The teacher answers. "I'm pretty sure Foster was hoping you could fill him in on that."

It's not the answer she's looking for, and her uneasiness moves into panic. I hate it. No matter how angry I am—no matter how much I'm hurting—I can't stand to know that she's hurting, too. And so I reach out along the pathway that goes right to the center of her mind and her soul, and I send her everything I have left inside me to give.

It's not much right now, and nothing compared to what I'd like to give her, but after a minute, I can feel it steady her. Feel it calm her, even before the assistant behind the desk says, "I'll be right with you. I just need one—"

The woman glances up at Grace over the top of her computer screen and her purple half-moon glasses, then stops mid-sentence as she realizes who she's looking at. As soon as it registers, she jumps up from behind her desk and starts yelling for Foster like she's just seen an entire contingent of ghosts.

"Finn, come quick!" The older lady circles out from behind her desk and throws her arms around Grace in a way I can only dream of doing. "Grace, it's so good to see you! I'm so glad you're here!"

Grace hugs the woman back, but the fact that she really doesn't have any idea what's going on is just another slap in the face to me. Just another reminder that everything I thought was between us doesn't mean anything anymore.

"It's good to see you, too," Grace finally responds.

"Finn!" the woman shouts again. She's right next to Grace's ear now, so her voice jars both of us—not just Grace. My own ears are ringing even before she starts yelling some more. "Finn! It's—"

The door to the headmaster's inner office flies open. "Gladys, we *have* an intercom—" Foster, too, breaks off mid-sentence, his eyes going wide as he registers that Grace is standing in front of him.

"Hey, Uncle Finn." Grace's mind is a seething mass of confusion when Foster's assistant finally lets her go. She waves at him, but it's obvious she doesn't know what's going on.

I've never missed being fully alive more—right now, I want nothing more than to put myself between her and the others so that she can have a minute to just think. Just breathe.

But that's not to be, as her uncle continues to stare at her in shock.

Grace stares back before finally shrugging awkwardly and saying, "I'm sorry to bother you."

If she's so far gone that she doesn't even register that there's been a lapse of time between what she remembers and now, then I've already lost her...before I ever had the chance to really have her.

As I watch all our careful plans go up in smoke in front of me, everything inside me burns to ash. And I can't help wondering how Shakespeare got it so fucking wrong. Because it turns out all that "better to have loved and lost" stuff really is just a bunch of bullshit.

They Can All Kiss My Ass
—Hudson—

Two years ago

What does a guy have to do to get his ass kicked around here anyway?

A fist comes flying at my face, and on a normal day, I'd lean back a little, let it go right by without even using my powers, but this isn't a usual day. Not by a long shot. So instead of leaning back, I fight the urge to roll my eyes as I lean forward, straight into the punch. And let it hit me squarely in the jaw.

I'd like to say I see stars or at least feel the explosion of blood in my mouth, but the truth is, my mother hits harder than this. A lot harder.

But I'm trying to make a point here, so I do what I can to make the hit look worse than it is. Of course, I have to bite my tongue to do it, but desperate times call for desperate measures. I even stagger a little to make it look good, then deliberately turn *into* the uppercut coming from my left.

That one actually stings a little, and it even opens a cut on my jaw—courtesy of the bloodstone ring on my assailant's finger. The guy laughs and then raises his fist to deliver another blow.

It's the laugh that gets me, and I can't help thinking about wiping the smug look off his face. It grates—not because he's better than me but because he isn't. I'm literally fighting with both my powers tied behind my back here, and he's still acting like he's actually doing something. Still acting like he's the badass in this equation when the truth is, it's all I can do not to yawn.

But yawning doesn't get the job done, and neither does kicking this guy's ass the way it so richly deserves to be kicked. I've waited too long for this opportunity to let a little pride—or, you know, basic athletic prowess—stand in my way. So I pretend I don't see the second guy's foot coming at me and let it hit me right in my solar plexus. Then I drop to my knees and take several more blows to my shoulder, neck, and chin.

Out of the corner of my eye, I see my father leaning up against the wall, arms crossed over his chest and disgusted sneer on his face. Next to him is some werewolf creep who looks even more disgusted— and amused—than my father does. Then again, his son is one of the assholes currently kicking the shit out of me...Cole, I think the douchebag's name is.

Another kick—this one to the side of my head—has the werewolf kid laughing...and me contemplating murder. But I decide to hell with it and go down anyway. The sooner this is done, the sooner I'll be able to move on to the next part of my plan. Besides, much as it's necessary, I dislike giving this much enjoyment to assholes like these.

I fall forward and hit my already-split-open chin on the ground, hard. This time, blood flows a lot more freely than it did the first time... Head wounds really are a bitch.

My father steps forward, the signal that he's seen enough, and I expect him to stop the beating now that he knows for sure just how worthless I really am. But he doesn't stop it. Instead, he gives a little nod to all three of my assailants, and they start wailing away on me in earnest. Fists and feet, elbows and knees, coming at me from all directions.

And still I don't fight back. Still I let them do whatever it is they feel the need to do to impress my father. Because it's not about what they do to me…it's about what I *let* them do to me. Right now, the means justify the ends, and I've been working toward this particular end for a very long time. Way too long to let my father's sadism derail me.

On and on it goes, until my head really does start to ring. Everything hurts now, a dull throbbing that I know is going to be a lot worse later. But things are winding down. I can hear it in my assailants' heavy breathing, feel it in the way the blows are coming slower and slower, see it in the way my father doesn't even look disgusted anymore. He just looks done, which is what I've been going for all along.

Finally, the old man waves a careless hand to call them off. The blows stop as abruptly as they started, but as they walk away, one of them—the werewolf kid, I think—deliberately steps on my hand hard enough that I can hear, and feel, my bones crunch beneath his boot.

It's the first injury I've gotten today that I care about. Definitely the first one that pisses me off.

My father barely spares me a glance before leaving the room, the werewolf alpha and his entourage trailing behind him. And as the door closes, I realize that it's finally happened. I've finally gotten what I've been aiming for for so long.

I lay on the ground a few more minutes to make a good show of it just in case they come back…and also, maybe, a little bit because my head is now throbbing like the drums in an Aerosmith song. Eventually, though, it's obvious the king won't be coming back to check on me.

I knew the moment he waved that careless hand that he was done with me, that he'd *finally* written me off, but one can never be too cautious when dealing with Cyrus. He may not be the sharpest tool in the shed, but he's got one hell of a survival instinct. That, combined with the fact that he's willing to do whatever it takes to get his message across, makes him very, very dangerous.

Eventually, I peel myself off the floor, doing a quick catalog of my injuries. Judging by the way my head hurts, I've definitely got a concussion. My jaw's not broken, but it's bruised, and my shoulder is dislocated. A few ribs are cracked, and the rest of me—even the parts that aren't broken—feels like it's had the crap kicked out of it.

Truth in advertising for the win.

The worst part of the whole thing—besides having to swallow my pride enough to let it happen—is my hand getting broken all to hell. That damn werewolf doesn't weigh much, but apparently his boot packs one hell of a wallop.

A glance at my watch shows me it was broken in the "fight." A glance at my phone tells me the same thing, which pisses me off more than the actual beating did. After all, I've been expecting it for weeks. Hell, I've been courting it. But I really needed this damn phone.

Walking is a bit of a challenge, but I'm more worried about getting my hand and shoulder back in place before my body starts to heal this way. A quick slam of my shoulder into the nearest wall forces it back where it belongs, and an excruciating couple of minutes working on my hand does the same thing. I wrap the hand—for a few hours at least—and then head back to my rooms. I have an appointment I can't miss.

Waters is already there when I arrive, and though he doesn't criticize my tardiness, a scornful sniff and eyebrow arch do the job for him.

At least until I tell him, "This will be our last session."

The scorn turns to something else entirely. Caution? Regret? Hope? I don't know, and right now I can't afford to care. I've got too much else to worry about.

"Are you okay?" Waters asks as he sets out a block of wood for me on the shelf near the window.

I don't bother to hide my disdain as I walk to the workstation he's set out for me. It's the only answer he's going to get, and judging by his sigh, he knows it.

"I'm proud of you," he tells me.

It's the first time in my life someone has said that to me, and for a second, I can't talk for the desert that's taken up residence in my mouth. "You don't have to be," I finally manage to answer.

"That's not how pride works." He very precisely lays out the tools next to the block of wood.

"I wouldn't know."

I reach for the coping saw first, but as soon as my fingers close around its handle, my hand screams in agony. I grit my teeth and hold on anyway, but it only takes a couple of tries for me to figure out this isn't going to work.

Anger swells up inside me. Irrational, I know, to be angry about this after the beating I just deliberately took, but that doesn't make my rage any less. I don't care about the punches or the kicks, don't care about the concussion or the blown-out shoulder. But the hand, and more importantly, this last lesson…missing out on it hurts more than I will ever admit to anyone.

"I don't think we'll be able to carve today," Waters says, and there's no trace of regret in his crisp, precise syllables.

"I can do it," I tell him through my clenched and aching jaw. "I just need a different tool."

But no matter what I reach for—the carving knife, the gouge, even the chisel—I can't get any of them to do what I want them to do.

Finally, I give up in frustration, slamming the gouge down on the shelf and turning to look out the window. "You can go," I tell Waters dismissively. He is only my tutor, after all.

A long silence follows my words, and then a sigh that sounds like it comes from his very bones. "You're going to be all right, my boy."

"I can take care of myself, present evidence to the contrary."

"I never doubted it for a moment." He lays a hand on my shoulder, and I can't help thinking that it is the first time he's touched me in all the decades he's been teaching me. "In case I don't get another chance to tell you this, it has been my great privilege and honor to serve as your tutor for the last several years. I—"

"You don't need to say that," I tell him as my heart starts to beat double-time.

"I don't need to say anything," he snaps back, his syllables even crisper than normal. "That, however, does not make what I *choose* to say any less true."

He pauses, takes a deep breath, then lets it out slowly. "My boy, watching you grow up in this…home filled me with fear for the kind of man you would become."

"Yeah, I know. I'm no good."

"That's not what I was going to say."

"You don't have to say it," I answer him, ignoring the fact that his words make me hurt in a way a thousand blows never could. "I know what I am."

"Do you?" he asks, and there is more sarcasm in those two words than I have ever heard from Waters. "Do you really?"

I wave a hand toward the sofa in the center of the room—and it disintegrates in an instant. "I am…an abomination. A mistake."

"You are what you choose to be," he answers.

"If only that were true." I pick the wood up in my uninjured hand, turn it around and around. "I know what I am. I know who I came from."

"But that's the rub, dear boy. Who you come from is only the smallest part of who you are." He looks me over from head to toe. "This horror you've just endured proves that."

"It was nothing," I tell him.

"It was everything," he snaps back. "Don't dishonor yourself—or me—by trying to pretend otherwise."

He looks down at the wood still spinning in my hands. "Where you come from, what you endure, are only a fraction of who you are and what you can become. The true test is what's inside you…and what you do with it."

"I showed you what was inside me." I glance back at where the sofa used to be.

"No, you showed me what you can do. It's not the same thing at all." He takes the wood from me and puts it back on the workstation. "That gift you have can do more than just destroy."

"That's not true."

"It is." He nods to the wood. "Go ahead and try."

"My hand—"

"Don't use your hand this time."

At first, I don't understand, and when I do, my first instinct is to laugh. To tell him no. But the truth is, I want him to be right. I want there to be more inside me than just the ability to destroy things... even though that's the ability I'm going to need if I have any chance of stopping my father. It's why I had to prove to him that I was useless this afternoon. Because if he thought there was a chance, even a chance, that he could use me as a weapon, he would never let me go to Katmere.

Never let me be free for even a second.

Never give me the chance to stop the horror he has planned.

"I can't do it," I tell him, even as I focus on the wood. Of course, nothing happens.

"Your problem is you associate your gift with death. You see only the destruction it can bring. But it can also create the space for something beautiful to emerge."

I swallow the tightness in my throat. "You don't know what you're talking about."

I expect his eyes to narrow at the insult, but they soften instead. "What do we do when we carve a block of wood but remove the negative space? Something beautiful already lives within the material; it just needs the right person to set it free."

My hands start to shake a little, but I don't reach for the wood. I can't. Maybe because I want his words to be true too much.

"Don't be afraid of destroying it, son. Picture what the wood *could be* and then let go."

"If I let go, I'll destroy *everything*."

"If you let go," he answers, "you will find what you need."

I don't believe him. I can't afford to believe him. But the look in his faded green eyes tells me that I'm not going to get out of this. That the only way to avoid the piece of wood in front of me is to tear this entire place down brick by brick.

And that will defeat everything I've already worked for. I can't afford to let that happen. Jax, and the world, can't afford for me to let that happen.

So I do the only thing I can do in this situation. I picture in my mind what I want the final product to look like. And then I let loose a tiny stream of power, knowing the whole time that it won't work.

Except…it does. Well, almost.

Every part of the wood I don't want disintegrates, turns to the finest sawdust imaginable. And what's left…what's left is a carbon copy of the horse I made for my brother all those years ago. Upon closer inspection, there are a few flaws, a few places where I didn't get it quite right. But my heart is pounding in my chest now. What if I *am* capable of more than just destruction?

"Very good," Waters tells me as he starts to pack up his satchel. "Very good indeed."

"But what—" I break off, swallowing the lump in my throat. I never would have imagined that damn horse if I'd thought there was a chance in hell of Waters's idea working. "What do I do now?"

"Whatever you want," he answers, putting his own block of wood back in his bag.

"Whatever you can," he continues as he snaps the bag's buckle into place.

"Whatever you have to," he concludes with one final pat of my arm. "It's all on your shoulders now."

And so I practice. For hours. Until I can duplicate the horse down to the last swoosh on its tail to perfection, not a single particle removed except what I want.

We both stand back and look at my final piece. I've always known what I needed to do. But now I know *why*.

I'm not going to Katmere to destroy my father's evil plan. I'm going to Katmere to remove everything ugly and wrong so the real beauty of what that school can be is revealed.

Acknowledgments

Writing a book this big and complicated takes more than just one person, so I have to start by thanking the two women who even made it possible: Liz Pelletier and Emily Sylvan Kim.

Liz, I feel like we've been through a war, or three, and I can only say thank you, thank you, thank you. Thank you for pushing me and this book past my comfort zone, thank you for your unflagging determination to tell this story, and thank you for the Herculean effort you put in to make sure that we got it done (in a ridiculous amount of time). We make a great team and I adore you more than I can say.

Emily, what do I even say? You've been with me through every twist and turn of the last sixty-four books and I am so incredibly grateful. Thank you for your enthusiasm, your support, your friendship, and all the late-night solidarity sessions. You are, sincerely, the best agent and friend in the whole world.

Stacy Cantor Abrams, while I was working on this book, the anniversary of my first YA novel passed, and I realized that we've been working together for ten years. I'm so, so lucky that you bought *Tempest* all those years ago. I've learned more from you than I can ever say and am thrilled to count you as a great friend as well as a great editor.

To everyone else at Entangled and Macmillan who has played a part in the success of the Crave series, thank you, thank you, thank you. Bree Archer and Elizabeth Turner Stokes for making me *all* the beautiful covers *all* the time, Jessica Turner for the amazing marketing and publicity, Meredith Johnson for all your help with this book in all the different capacities, Toni Kerr for your flexibility and the incredible care you took with my baby, Curtis Svehlak for making miracles happen on the production side and for putting up with me being late on everything, Katie Clapsadl for answering a million questions with such grace, Riki Cleveland for being so fabulous always, Heather Riccio for all your enthusiasm and help with a million different things, Jaime Bode for being such a devout advocate for this series, and Nancy Cantor, Greta Gunselman, and Jessica Meigs for taking such care with every page of this story.

Eden Kim, for being a fabulous beta reader and the inspiration for one of my favorite characters ever.

Sherry Thomas, for all these years of friendship and for your daily messages that, I swear, were the only thing that kept me going when things got hard. I am so, so lucky to have you for a best friend.

Megan Beatie, for all your help and enthusiasm with launching *Crave*. You're the best!

Stephanie Marquez, for everything. For all the help, support, love, encouragement, enthusiasm, and excitement that I could ever ask for. Thanks for keeping the peace, for taking care of my mom and my boys on the days I couldn't take my fingers off the keyboard, for taking care of me always, and for putting up with the no-sleep grumpy days with such grace, kindness, and love.

For my three boys, who I love with my whole heart and soul. Thank you for understanding all the evenings I had to shut myself up in my room and work instead of hanging out, for pitching in when I needed you most, for sticking with me through all the difficult years, and for being the best kids I could ever ask for.

And finally, for fans of Jaxon, Grace, and the whole crew. Thank you, thank you, thank you for your unflagging support and enthusiasm for the Crave series. I can't tell you how much your emails and DMs and posts mean to me. Thanks for choosing to take this journey with me, and I hope you enjoyed *Crush* as much as I enjoyed writing it. I love and am grateful for every single one of you. xoxoxoxo

Grace's story continues in

Crown